P9-CFA-085

GEORGE MILLS

GEORGE MILLS

A NOVEL

STANLEY ELKIN

E. P. DUTTON, INC. | NEW YORK

Parts of this novel have appeared in *Playboy, Triquarterly, Anteus* and *Perspective*
· Copyright © 1982 by Stanley Elkin · All rights reserved. Printed in the
U.S.A. · No part of this publication may be reproduced or transmitted in any form
or by any means, electronic or mechanical, including photocopy, recording or any
information storage and retrieval system now known or to be invented, without permission in writing from the publisher, except by a reviewer who wishes to quote brief
passages in connection with a review written for inclusion in a magazine, newspaper
or broadcast. · Published in the United States by E. P. Dutton, Inc., · 2 Park
Avenue, New York, N.Y. 10016 · Library of Congress Cataloging in Publication
Data · Elkin, Stanley · George Mills : [novel] · I. Title · PS3555.L47G4
1983 813'.54 82-2494 · AACR2 · ISBN: 0-525-24141-8 Published simultaneously in Canada by Clarke, Irwin & Company · Limited, Toronto and Vancouver
· Designed by Nicola Mazzella · 10 9 8 7 6 5 4 3 2 1 · First Edition

To Joan

GEORGE MILLS

PART ONE

1

Because he knew nothing about horses. Not even—though he made wagers—how to what would not then have been called handicap them. Betting the knight, his money on the armor, the intricate chain mail like wire net or metal scrim, being's effulgent Maginot line, *his* stake on the weighted mace and plate mittens, on the hinged couters and poleyns, on vambrace and cuisse and greave, banging the breast-plate and all the jewelry of battle for timbre and pitch like a jerk slamming doors and kicking tires in a used car lot. Not even betting the knight finally so much as his glazed essence, his taut aura. (And in winter something stirring and extra in the smoke pouring through the fellow's ventails, as if breath were a sign of rage or what would not then have been called steam a signal of spirit.) But nothing about horses. Under their fortressed heads and jousting pads, their lumpish disfiguring raiment, perhaps not even what they looked like, in his head a distorted image of frailty, an extrapolation from their pointy hocks and slender shanks and still more slender pasterns of something more scaffold than beast.

A sissy sir far far down the primogenitive pecking order, a younger son way, way below the salt. (This to become a great joke between them later in Wieliczka.)

It just so happening that he was all the lord, his father, could spaie at the time. Anyway, who even knew what they were talking about? *Franks?* ("Crusade" not even coined yet.) Still, how did one answer Godfrey of Bouillon? Well, as his father himself said, G. of B. —they were cousins—could be answered, but an emissary? An *envoy?* An envoy was very heady and impressive stuff. You didn't muck about with envoys, you didn't make waves with what would not then have been called the Geneva Conventions. An envoy was worth *curteis* and that was that. Frankly, he thought his dad was a little jealous. Having spies and envoys and proconsuls was a little like being in two places at once. Class. A surrogacy his pop, the lord, for all his staff and retinue, could not even imagine until the man appeared, sailing up the Humber into Northumbria in the swan-necked, jib-lashed, cursive-prowed ship the very week the river had become navigable again. Listening patiently, even curiously, to the fellow's strange pitch. To come along. To go with them the thousands of miles to Jerusalem with all the men he could muster in their Sunday-go-to-battle best. And for what? What for? (The reasons not much clearer really in the emissary's note.) The fuzzy spiritual politics of Christianity? Oh? And would have turned him down flat, sent him packing in his boat, but then he glimpsed the emissary's retainers carousing in the minor hall with his knights and he understood how good it must feel, how grand to command such surrogacy, to live the remote, levered, long-distance life!

He would send Guillalume, the one who knew nothing about horses. (Godfrey's emissary spoke of barons, earls, dukes and princes, of counts and marquis, of all the king's men, of all graduated picture card aristocracy and rulerhood, of all blue-ribbon force. No Irish need apply.) Guillalume. Send Guillalume. Gill could go. Him. His out-of-the-picture card, below-the-salt son. A great joke on Godfrey and his envoy, or fun with the Franks.

(This all by oral tradition of course, the hand-me-down history of a millennium of Mills raconteurs, impossible to check, particularly the motives of the lord, his pop. But what else could it have been? What else could it be? Although as Millses, almost a thousand years of enlisted men and their NCO'd vision behind them, they understood well enough, had often enough heard, had had drummed into them, had even themselves—the NCO's proper—often enough said that some assholes *never* get the message. So much of it could have been bullshit, horseshit, scuttlebutt, crap, the dreary speculation of barracks lawyers. Particularly the motives part. But finally, a thousand years later, George didn't see it that way. What George thought now was that Mills must have had it from Guillalume himself. Hadn't his own Harvard second lieutenant come across man to man, GI to GI, in Inchon that time, the two of them on patrol, the woods full of gooks and the Harvard guy actually spelling him at the wheel of the Jeep? So George thought that great great great great great to the umpteenth power Grandfather Mills got the lowdown from Guillalume somewhere between a rock and a hard place in old Wieliczka.)

If Guillalume even knew. If he had been let in on the joke. If anything, even a wink, had passed between them on the occasion of the summons: "Guillalume." "My lord?" "You're to travel a journey with this man." "With this man, sire?" And the emissary, "Oh no, my lord, not with *me.* I've arrangements to make in Mercia and Saxony, business in Scotia and Friesland. He'll have to cross the Channel with his men and horses and join Godfrey's forces at the Meuse at the Waal channel of the lower Rhine." And Gill: "The Meuse? The Waal channel of the lower Rhine?"

"He'll be there, sir."

"Good, my lord."

But he knew nothing about geography either.

And Greatest Grandfather Mills probably even less. Pairing the two of them, Greatest Grandfather hand-picked most likely by Guillalume's lord, the Dad, probably arbitrarily, spied at the stables, say, where the man had been accustomed to see him—though not notice him, not *conscious* of him—always there, always around, for that was where the horseshit was, always there and always reeking of horse so that Guillalume's father somehow associated the smell of the man with a knowledge of the beast. Hence the promotion—— the irony being that he had never made yeoman, only yardman, and this, the stink of horse his credentials, making him the first Mills in history to be enlisted and promoted at the same time, their yardman-yardbird Founder.

And the father playing it *that* straight at least, or what would be the point of the joke? It never even occurring to him to wonder what if they got lost. Because what value a surrogacy if they could not even find the spot where the surrogacy was to begin?

And that was that. The two of them, who had none, left to their own devices. The one who knew nothing about horses or geography and the other with no notion of geography and only a stableboy's notions about manure.

Though somehow they managed not only to find the Channel but to cross it. Tracing, very likely, the Humber as it flowed to the sea

3

and crossing in a good-sized oarboat—water plow, sea shoe, whatever their awed poetic term for it must have been—which would accommodate the horses. Then, in Europe, Guillalume throwing himself completely on Mills's mercy, though it wouldn't have appeared that way to Mills, who, though in the lead, took for granted that it was Guillalume's job to get them to wherever the hell it was that the Waal channel of the Meuse met the lower Rhine, who assumed he went first to blunt danger's brunt and who did not once question Guillalume's failure to give a single command. Guillalume's error like his *père's*— — total reliance upon Mills's equine stench. Though the stableboy actually had a theory about horses. It was this: That *they* knew what they were doing. And this an empirical judgment. Hadn't he seen them returning riderless to the stable again and again? Mountless mounts? And watched their thrown or fallen riders lagging two or three hours behind reeling like drunks? Thinking: Leave it to the 'orses. Great snooty brutes. Droppin' their dirt where they please. Leave it to the bleedin' 'orses. Knowin' their 'unger—though they didn't have this dialect in those days—an' tossin' off even fine gentlemen, be dey ever so well turned out, like dey 'ad no more weight than toys. Cor blimey, leave it to the fuckin' 'orses. The stableboy's theory of horses being an exact paradigm of his theory of great men—— Guillalume included.

So each leaving it to the other in mutual unconditional surrender and deputation. Guillalume leaving it to Mills and Mills to Guillalume and the horses. Even Guillalume's horse, as much a stranger to Europe as either of the men, involved in the delegation of responsibility, it devolving at last upon the lead horse—Mills's—to get them to that fabled cusp where the Waal channel of the Meuse met the lower Rhine.

Thus missing their turn-off entirely. Failing to hang a right in the Netherlands, sticking to the flat country, the topography of least resistance, a good green graze across northern Europe, Mills's horse out for a pleasant month-of-Sundays stroll—it was high summer now —and taking the rest along with him. And pleasant enough for Guillalume and Mills, too. So many new sights to see, so many strange new fruits and raw vegetables to eat and queer tongues to hear. And that year—it was 1097—the weather absolutely beautiful, a mild winter, a fresh and pleasant spring, a cool and perfect summer, the delightful climate prelapsarian and Nature never more generous. As though the biblical seven fat years had been squeezed into one delicious obese season. Bumper crops all over Europe that time, so lush the barbarous

4

landowners and peasants thought the gods Wodin, Odin, Thor and Christ had been placated forever, and flashing their hospitality like fathers of brides, shining it on whomever they saw, our friends, the strangers, now so irrevocably lost that Guillalume himself, by-passing Mills, had begun to leave it to the horses.

They spoke of it. Why *not* leave it to the horses? Look how well they had served them so far. Taking them from the rough, chunky dissolution of the Northumbrian winter through the evolving spring and developing summer of western Europe fifteen miles a day closer to whatever pitch-perfect paradise lay at the end of their journey. As if they possessed some tropism for grace which sifted them through danger and past all pitfall's parlous, aleatory, dicey circumstance, a daily accretion of joy, incremental as snow rolled downhill. Horse-sensing the continent's gravitational pull and advancing along the ebb tides of earth so that—though they were actually climbing longitudes and latitudes and grazing a very orbit of the tonsured globe—they seemed to be proceeding in that rich alluvial trough between beach and sea, skirting not only danger but even ordinary difficult country.

There was no sea of course, only the flat and fertile plains, pastures, arbors, and orchards—a green garden of agriculture in which the peasants and farmers seemed engaged in some perpetual in-gathering, a harvest like a parable, as astonishing to themselves as to Guillalume and Mills who, in what was not then even England, had, in that wet and misty bronchial climate, seen bumper crops merely of grass, measly grains, skinny fruit. Here it was the actual skins and juices of fruit staining the farmers' flesh and beards, all their up-shirtsleeved bucolic condition, their breechclouts puddle-muddied at the knees with a liquid loam of opulent fermentation, a liquor of citrics, a sour mash of rotting—because there was too *much* to in-gather, vegetables discarded half eaten—potato and cabbage, squashed squash, cucumber and carrot, a visible strata of vegetable artifact, a landscape of the overripe like a squishy gravel of flora. The horses leading them through all this, grazing at sweet-toothed will, chewing in surfeited content from the broad green groaning board of earth. And so satiated finally that they—the horses—seemed to bloom beneath them—Guillalume reminded of his father's quilted cavalry— the former nags filling to Clydesdale dimension (Guillalume and Mills, too, heavier now), and gradually reducing their pace, the fifteen miles a day diminishing to thirteen, to a dozen, to nine, to a sluggish seven, so that they seemed at last barely to progress at all, managing, even as they moved, merely to keep abreast of the countryside, to pace the farmers and landlords and peasants on foot, appearing to convoy them, cordon them off in some National Guard relation to their fields, creating—they (all of them: the horses, Guillalume, Mills, the ingatherers) wouldn't know this—the illusion of some governmental sanction to strikebreakers, say. So slow and easy that it would have been embarrassing to all of them had conversation not been struck up. Guillalume leaving this to Mills, too. (It wasn't the old confidence—Gill reeked of horse too now and knew better—but laze, all avuncular, subruminative, long Christmas dinner sloth.)

"Ask after them, Mills."

"I haven't their language, m'lud."

"Smile. Offer fruit."

"They've fruit enough, sire. It's a nation of flatulence here. Did not the breezes quicken the air as soon as it's fouled we should die of the farting sickness, sir."

"Well do *some*thing, man. It's too nuisance-making to ride beside them on this cushion of silence."

So he asked directions. Speaking in the universal tongue of petition, greenhorning himself and his master. "Moose?" he said. "Wall channel of the lower Rhine? Moose? Godfrey of Boolone? Wall?" The words making no more sense to him—they were in Friesland, they were in Angria, in the Duchy of Billungs, in Pomerainz—than they did to them, but the sound of distress clear enough. Even if Mills knew that the distress was feigned, who had begun to suspect—though not yet acknowledge aloud to Guillalume—that the horses were no Christians, that the horses had betrayed them, gotten them lost, and that long since, and who asked for directions—might even have asked for them even if Guillalume had not instructed him to speak—merely to be polite, to demonstrate with each rise in the pitch of his voice that he and his companion were foreigners, that they came as friends to kill the Islamic hordes for them. (Having absorbed at least this much of their mission from Guillalume.) "Moose? Wall? Killee killee smash balls son bitchee pagan mothers? Killee killee bang chop for Jeezy? Which way Moslem bastards?"

And everyone smiling, offering food, sharing lunches from wicker baskets spread out on white cloths in the open fields——*picnics.* (It was Mills who introduced the concept of picnics to England, bringing this foreign way of dining back to Blighty like Marco Polo fetching spaghetti from China.) Slaps on the back all round and the wine passed. And always during those idyllic seven fat months well met, hospitalitied as candidates and, when they had run out of toasts—always before they ran out of wine: the bumper crops, the vintage year—they were returned the mile or couple of kilometers or verst and a third to where they'd met, where Mills had first spoken his gibberish of good intention, always careful, though they did not travel in armor, to lean down from their mounts to shake hands in the trendy new symbol of emptyhandedness and unarmedness that they'd picked up on their travels. Or, though they wore no visor, to try out the rather rakish novelty salute which was just then coming in among the better class of knights. Although more and more of late some did not seem to know *what* to make of their toney salutes, but smiled anyway, enjoying the sight of grown men banging themselves on the forehead with the flats of their hands.

And then, often as not, the salutes were unreturned and the proffered hand ignored. And after a while it was taken again, but turned over, examined as carefully as if it were about to be read, and later as gingerly as if it were a rope or a chain, and once or twice it was actually bitten.

"Bleedin' wogs," Mills would say, turning in his saddle to wink at Guillalume.

Which was how they ultimately discovered that they were lost.

"Mi-ills," Guillalume said one evening when they had tucked in in one of the barns where the farmers permitted them to stay.

"M'lud, m'lord?"

"I was just thinking . . . Have you noticed how no one will shake hands with us anymore or return our salutes?"

"No class, guv. They're a bolshy lot."

"Well perhaps, Mills, but it occurs to me that they haven't the *cus*tom."

"Just what I was sayin', your lordship."

"Well, but don't you *see,* Mills? If they haven't the *cus*tom, then it's very likely no one's *shown* it to them."

"I 'ave."

"Yes, certainly, but if *real* knights had been by, cam*paign*ers— — well, it's just that one would have thought they'd have seen it by now. They're not a *stu*pid people. Look at the stores in this barn, think of the delicious produce we've seen them grow, the delightful cuts of meat they've shared with us, all the fine stews."

"Yar?"

"Butter. And, what do they call it, *cheese?* Yes, cheese. I've kept my eyes open, Mills. That butter and cheese are made from ordinary cow's milk. *We* don't do butter, *we* don't do cheese. This is an advanced technological civilization we've come upon here. And *wine*. They do that out of fruit.

"They never."

"Oh they do, Mills, yes. Out of fruit."

"Bleedin' Jesus."

"But they haven't the handshake, they haven't the salute."

"No manners."

"Quite right. One suspects one is off the beaten track, rather. I don't think *our* fellows have been by. I think we're lost."

But what could they do? If they were lost and had left it to the horses—as both now openly confessed—and the horses had taken them deeper and deeper into ever more amicable country, what could they do but leave it *entirely* to the horses? Mills articulating that if horses knew anything—hadn't he seen them return to the stables riderless?—it was the main chance, their own steedly interests. They had done pretty well by them thus far. Why shouldn't they do even better? Take them into even finer country? Guillalume's fright seemed tuned by the moonlight.

"What?" asked Mills.

"They'll take us to Horseland."

"To Horseland, sir?"

"Someplace where there are *no* riders, where the hay grows wild as meadowgrass. Carrying us through the better weather as if we ambled along the Gulf Stream or the tradewinds of earth."

And a few days later—still high summer—someone twisted Mills's fingers when he extended his hand.

"Here you!" Mills shouted at him, pulling his hand back. "Fuckin' barbarian!"

They had come—or Mills thought they had—to the Duchy of Barbaria. Guillalume, once the sense of Mills's word forcibly struck him, could not conceive of where they now were as a place given over to any sort of organization at all. He intuited, and spoke of this in whispers to Mills, that there would be no kings, no barons or dukes here, no knights allegiant, no sheriffs, no treasury to exact taxes or a yield of the crop, no astrologer or priest and, if there were armies, no officers to lead them.

"No law," Guillalume said, "only custom. No rule, only exception. No consanguinity, only self. No agriculture, only Nature; no industry, only repair; no landmark; no——"

"Shh," Mills cautioned, and pointed fearfully toward the man who had pulled his fingers. The barbarian had turned and, making

8

some shrill signal, whistled his horse from the dark forest where it had been foraging. It was eighteen hands at the very least and its upper lip had been torn from it violently, leaving a visible picket of filed, pointed teeth. Its flanks were scored with a crust of wounds, a black coping of punishment, its entire body studded, random as stars, with war wart, bruise. The man placed his shoe deep in a ledge of whittled horseflesh and pulled himself up on its back where he sat in a bare saddle of calloused lesion and looked down on Mills and Guillalume, shook his finger at them and laughed, baring teeth which perfectly matched the horse's own. He lashed viciously and wheeled.

"We'll double back," Guillalume said.

"How?"

They had in fact left the last roads behind them weeks before and since then had traveled cross country through fields, along stubbly verge, vague property. They had come to rivers—not for the first time; they had been coming to rivers since crossing the Channel; always, so north were they, the current had been gentle, little more than oblique pull, the minor tug and Kentucky windage of a just now bending inertia—shallow enough—leave it to the horses—to wade across. But it was not even Europe now, not even the world. They were no place cultivated, months away from the frontier, beyond all obedient landscape, behind the lines, surrounded by a leaning, forbidding stockade of trees, so stripped of direction they quibbled left and worried right and troubled up from down. Bereft of stance, they indiscriminately mounted each other's horses and hot-potato'd the simplest decisions.

"Shall we try the blue fruit?"

"The blue? I should have thought the silver."

"Maybe the primrose." But there was little sweetness in any of them, or in the flesh of fish or hares. There was a saline quality in everything they ate now, an essence not so much of condiment or seasoning as of additive, long-haul provision, the taste of protected stores, the oils that preserved and kept machinery supple, the soils and salts that extended meat. They were always thirsty.

Then one morning Mills refused to mount, refused to advance further. "They've betrayed us," he said. He meant the horses. And he laughed bitterly. "So this is Horseland!"

"There *is* no Horseland!" his superior said. "Get on your beast, Mills."

"Why should I? You said yourself there's no law here, no kings or treasury. We ride each other's horses, share and share alike. We

9

discuss lunch, decide dinner, choose the blue fruit or the primrose. Why should I? You said yourself—— "

"Exactly! *I* said. *I* did. Listen to me, my Mills. I'm your superior, just as that barbarian we saw was mine. Learn this, Mills. There are distinctions between men, humanity is dealt out like cards. There is natural suzereignty like the face value on coins. Men have their place. Even here, where we are now, at large, outside of place, beyond it, out of bounds and offside, loosened from the territorial limits, they do. It's no accident that Guillalume is the youngest son for all it appears so, no more accident than that you are the Horseshit Man. It isn't luck of the draw but the brick walls of some secret, sovereign Architecture that makes us so. It's as simple as the scorn in my voice when I talk to you like this, as natural as the italics my kind use and your kind don't. Now do as I tell you, get on your horse. No, wait."

"Sir?"

"Have I hurt your feelings? Have I saddened you? Because I didn't mean—— There *can* be respect, you know; there can be affection, *noblesse oblige.* So come on, Mills, bear up, *carry* on. We'll get back on our horses and—— What is it?"

"You've doomed me," Mills said. "You've cursed my race."

It was so. Mills apologized silently to the sons he was yet to have —if they ever got out of this mess—for the heritage he was yet to give them, grieved for the Millsness he was doomed to pass on, for the frayed, flawed genes—he thought blood—of the second-rate, back-seat, low-down life, foreseeing—if he ever got out of this mess—a continuum of the less than average, of the small-time, poached Horseshit Man life, prophesying right there in what Guillalume himself had told him could not have been Horseland all the consequences to others in the burdened bestiality of his blackballed loins.

"Come on, let's go then," Guillalume said.

"I'm staying," Mills said.

"What? *Here?*"

"I don't wish on no one the injury of my life."

"What are you talking about?"

Mills explained, sulking, and Guillalume laughed. "Well, that's a good one all right," he said, "but it comes a little late after what you told me on the journey. Unless you were lying of course—— or boasting."

"What I told you?"

"In the ripe times, when we cruised geography, when we lay in our sweet, wine-stained straw and listened to the music and watched the girls dance. Not one as pretty as your own, you said. The damage is done. Your son will have been born by now. The generations are unleashed. Get back on your horse."

But he didn't. He simply walked off deeper into the forest. He could hear Guillalume call. "Mills? Mills! I'm still your master."

"I don't think you've jurisdiction in Horseland," he shouted back.

"Mills? Mills? I have something to tell you. Mills? We're not lost!" The stableboy turned around. All he could see was the green armor of the woods. And then Guillalume appeared in a green archway he'd made by pushing back two thin saplings. "We're not lost," he said again.

"I am."

"Oh, I don't know where we are, I don't claim that, but we're not lost. Being lost is the inability to find the place you want to be. I'm going to tell you something. I knew the turn-off."

"What?"

"I knew the turn-off. You were in the lead. I didn't signal. I *let* you miss it."

"But why?"

"You must promise never to tell anyone."

"Who would I tell?"

"Promise."

"There's no one to tell. There's only barbarians around and I don't speak Asshole." Guillalume looked at him. "All right. I promise."

"They sent us to fight in a holy war. We would both probably have been killed. That's why I let you go on when we came to the turn-off. Let's *be* barbarians, Mills. *They* don't have younger sons. Perhaps they don't even have stableboys."

This was ten centuries ago. Greatest Grandfather Mills wasn't born yesterday. His master may well not have had jurisdiction in the —to them—lawless land not to which they'd come but to which they'd been translated by the footloose, fancy-free horses. There were no typewriters then, no room at which an infinite number of monkeys at an infinite number of keyboards in infinite time might have knocked out *Hamlet,* but, in a way, the just two horses in the just seven months had done just that—— not *Hamlet,* of course, but Adventure, Adventure itself, bringing them through the random, compassless, ever swerving obliquity of tenuously joined place and across the stumbled, almost drunken vaulting of nameless—to them nameless—duchies and borders and diminishing jurisdictions to this—— the at last rag-ged, corey chaos of alien earth. What else was Adventure if it was not only not knowing where one was but where one *could* be, not only not knowing where one's next meal was coming from but even what color it was likely to be?

Mills understood this, as he'd understood, was way ahead of, Guillalume's heartbreaking explanation of fixed men, of the mysteri-ously gravid and landlocked quality in them that forbade all yeasty rise and usurpation and that put even self-improvement perhaps and the transmigration of privilege certainly—he was not convinced so much that Guillalume was his master as that *someone* was—out of the question. It was only this—that someone was—that kept him from slicing Guillalume's throat. Let him rave in his precious italics. (Let's *be* barbarians, Mills! Oh *do* let's!) He had Guillalume's younger son number. And even understood what was behind the let's-be-barbari-ans crap: the principle of bought time—— the sly, unspoken notion that at any moment death could elevate him, like the man who wins the pools, the death of brothers, Guillalume's long-shot hope. Whereas for him, for his lot, death would merely hammer him—them —more deeply into place, delivering as it would mere heirloom, his father's—got from *his* father who got them from his—nasty tools of the Horseshit trade.

Of course he would go with him. It was only for a bit of a sulk that he'd wandered off into the woods within woods where Guillalume had found him.

So he knew his life and, dimly, the lives of his progeny, knew that all men are the founders of their lines, was reconciled, however un-easily, to what seemed to him his excellent educated guess about his fate—— to be first among little guys, little men: God's blue collar worker. To serve, to travel for others; to see much of the world without in the least knowing what stood behind whatever had been left outside, up front, there for all his furlough'd, shore-leave'd fellows —the waterfront bars and strange hoosegows and chief points of interest, all its—the world's—Tours Eiffel and Empire State Build-ings, all its Chinatowns and interesting cathedrals, the capital sights of the capital cities, the velvet ropes around rooms open to the public in palaces, congresses, parliaments in session, a subliminal taste of the foreign for Mills and his kind who would, as Mills had just missed doing, be sent off to fight in foreign lands, serve overseas, living for years at a time perhaps in the trenches and foxholes of French or Indo-Chinese or Korean earth itself, or cooped up in Japanese and

German and Holy Roman Empire and Hanseatic prison camps, internment a certainty, and some even to be buried there or, missing in action, never found, but never, no matter the duration, to learn the language or the customs—— not even a gawker race of unwelcome men, history's not even peeping Toms.

But Guillalume had blown it, finessed an entire crusade simply because he wanted to be alive if a brother should die. And of course he would go with him, play the fellow, be for him Guillalume's very own my Mills, obeying all the reasonable orders, and if there was to be affection why it would probably be Mills himself who would mete it out, serving it up as he might Guillalume's dinner. No harm done. It was adventure he was after—he'd only just learned this—and Guillalume was the key, holding as he did all the credentials, for Guillalume was the founder of his race, too, though, unlike Mills, he didn't know that yet. And what a race it would be! Generation after generation of subalterns, of second lieutenants, ROTC boys whose gleaming bars and Brasso'd buttons and shining boots would make them, for all they knew the languages, superior targets. Guillalume's rod and his staff, they comforted him. Better, they shielded him. For Mills instinctively understood the percentages, blood's and politics' unfavorable odds, advantage to the house. He pitied his master and followed the damn fool out of the woods, even taking the saplings from him and pushing them still further apart, allowing the younger son —he could have been Mills's younger son—to pass through first.

He stepped through himself and the saplings sprang back into place, the woods immediately disappearing behind them. But the horses were gone. They could just make out the tail of Guillalume's horse closing like a curtain over its own asshole exactly as the Chinese fan of forest closed behind the horses themselves.

This was almost a thousand years ago. Horses did not have names. Guillalume and Mills brayed fatuously after them into the brackish air.

"Guillalume's horse," Mills shouted.

"Mills's steed," cried Guillalume. "Guillalume's and Mills's animals!"

But they were gone. Mills and Guillalume ran toward the hole in the forest into which the horses had disappeared. "You, horses! Come back!" Guillalume commanded. "Return to your riders!"

"I've seen this happen a hundred times back at your father's," Mills said. "They don't like the work, 'orses. They'll go out for a morning's canter with a knight errant and they're always so anxious to get back to the stables where it's warm and they can laze about chewing their hay or muck around with their sweethearts, they just pick up and come back riderless. They do that."

"My father's stables, Mills, are half a million miles, versts, hectares and rods from here. They're nothing but dastardly traitors and deserters. Afraid of a little holy war, that's all." Then he giggled. Then he stopped. "Mills," he said thoughtfully, "do you suppose they sense the *proximity* of stables? They haven't had hay or proper water in weeks. Do you think—— ?"

"And they ain't 'ad no quiff neither they 'aven't." He looked at Guillalume.

"We'll give chase, follow their spoor. We'll run them to earth. Pick up our gear and come. We'll harry and tally-ho them."

"We'll assist the police in their inquiries," Mills muttered and stepped in their spoor—— a loose, damp signature of ropey horseshit. And it was then that they discovered what they should have noticed a week before—— that the animals' crap (as well as their own) was finely studded with a sort of silverish jewelry, a crystalline dust that didn't so much refract light as expel it.

"El Dorado!" Guillalume exclaimed.

"Wieliczka," said a voice.

The Englishmen—it wasn't England then; Guillalume hadn't said El Dorado but some other fabled name—looked up. They glanced all around. There was no one. Had a bird spoken? Guillalume actually asked the question.

"Some bird," Mills said softly. "Sounded more like Asshole to me."

"Barbarians, you mean?"

Both remembered the enormous man they had seen and fell silent. Turning in a tight circle where they stood they looked about cautiously. Everywhere there was the immense expanse of forest. They had entered a medium of wood, as the ocean was a medium of water. The thick, ancient trunks black as charred flesh, the low branches with their strange burden of woolly leaves that all but hid the sky. Though they had been awake less than an hour it might have been late afternoon, though they were dry it might have been raining. It was autumn now, the queer leaves had begun to turn, and even in the dim light they could perceive that their colors were like nothing they had ever seen. And at their feet the sparkling dung of their faithless horses.

"An enchanted forest?" Guillalume said tentatively.

"Wieliczka," said the voice.

"Who's there?" Mills's master demanded, his hand grasping the sharp snickersnee at his side. "Who? Barbarian? Infidel? Muslim? Jew?"

"Merchant," said the voice, and a man less tall than themselves materialized from within the feathery camouflage of forest. Mills stared first at the stranger, then at Guillalume. It was as if his master's questions had invoked a sort of ecumenical man, some magical creature of compromise. The fellow was adorned with all sorts of symbolic jewelry—— the crescents of Islam like tiny portions of honeydew, an alphabet of assorted crosses, from the lower case *t* of the Latin cross to the *x* of St. Andrew. There were patriarchal crosses like telegraph poles and papal crosses like railroad ties. There was the Cross of Lorraine like a stumpy ladder and a Maltese cross like Baltic decoration. There was a Celtic cross with its double nimbus and the puffed sleeves and booties of the botonee. There were the petaled uprights and transverses of the Moline cross.

He wore a skullcap and a Mogen David, Solomon's Seal and something which looked like the pyramid and radiant eye on the back of what was to become the dollar bill. These—though neither Mills nor Guillalume recognized them, as they failed to distinguish between the odd Christian clefs of the crosses—along with diminutive cabalistic awls, trammels and calipers, were the symbols and signs of what perhaps even the man himself did not know were the heraldic tonics and staves of Freemasonry. There was Thoth's beaked being. There were the rounded, interlocking palettes of Yin and Yang, and even, carried in a pouch at his waist, the fierce horned helmet of the Viking, the brutal mace, like an unlit torch, of the Vandal. He looked—they could not know this, though the man, understanding at least something of the semaphoric implications of his semiological, talismanic chevronicals and tokens, must have had some sense of their powers —like the doors and sides of a transcontinental rig studded with license plate, certificate, seal, registration.

"Merchant," he said again, and smiled and threw them a highball and extended his hand for them to shake.

"English?" Mills said, accepting his hand and returning the salute.

"English sure. Merchant sure," said the badged being, and fumbling among his various necklaces and pins selected a vaguely British device, a sort of arrowhead which the two recognized as a hallmark stamped upon the equipment of archers and yeomen back home.

"You speak English?" Guillalume said. "You know who we are? You know the way back?"

"Come sure," said the panoplied person. Mills hefted his and Guillalume's gear and together they followed the strangely burdened man who jingled as he walked like an immense keyring.

It was a sort of underground cavern.

[Though Mills and Guillalume didn't know this either. They had followed the merchant, an oddly surefooted man as seemingly certain of direction in the closed and mazey woods as a compass. Tracing no, to them, visible trail, he walked past several trees, turned right, proceeded some yards, cut a defiant leftward perpendicular, proceeded further, tacking, zagging, zigging, making casual doglegs, then an abrupt circumscription, as sharply defined as close-order drill, around what did not even seem to Mills or Guillalume a particular grouping of trees, and then as suddenly as they had been plunged into woods they were out of them again. Seeing mountains in the distance. And not knowing what these strange growths were either, since they'd never seen mountains before, thinking the hulls and loaves and peaks individual, gigantic trees, awed, wondering at the massive rains which must have grown them, Noah weather, tidal waves from the sky, and dreading the intense sunlight which must have shined on them, actual fire perhaps—yes, Mills at least, thinking themselves closer to the sky, the sun, observing the empirical evidence of the upward slope of the land like an actual ramp between themselves and the distant what they did not know were mountains, and looked upon their guide with a new fear and respect, suddenly inferring the meaning of the various crucifixes and holy medals he wore: why, he's a messenger from Heaven! from *all* the Heavens! the godly, factioned principalities of death—a country—Guillalume thinking—of intermittent flood and drought, understanding, he suddenly felt, the queer saline quality of everything they had drunk and eaten recently: heat did that, sacrificially lifting the sugary remnant in substance just as certainly as fire burned upward and smoke rose, sucking sweetness in columns of riven temperature and tilting the delicate alchemical balance that moderated the warring atoms of taste (who had bitten into the dry salted sticks of bleached driftwood exposed on the summer beaches of his homeland), and leapt to a different conclusion than Mills, fearing the stranger as much even as he respected him less, thinking their curiously bedight leader a parched and salt-maddened man. "Beasts be there. Come," said the merchant, pointing toward the mountains rising from the gently elevating plain. And *both* thought: Yes! Beasts *would* be there where single trees—they counted at least a dozen—could grow so high. They looked at each other and both had suddenly the same memory, the same awful thought. Guillalume shuddered and Mills nodded gravely. When the messenger spoke, Mills thought, when the man from the skies spoke who had not uttered a sound during the entire time he had been guiding them through the undifferentiated scaffolding of the forest, not one word said during all the—to them—arbitrary shifts and turns and mute drill-sergeant rights and forwards and lefts and obliques of their close-order, parade-ground negotiations; when the sandy, dehydrated madman spoke, Guillalume thought, when the thirsty shipwrecked man spoke and raised his arm to point out the now dozen arid, wrung-out, flame-cured, behemoth gorbelly trees, when the salt-addled lunatic spoke who had not made a sound during all his crazy follow-the-leader hairpin squiggle tactics in the wildwood, Guillalume suddenly remembered, and saw from his expression that Mills did too, the gross, huge, almost leather-headed, spike-skinned, scale-nailed barbarian they had seen previously. And knew his—their—mistake. Why, he had not been a barbarian at all, simply—simply?—one of the beasts their crazed companion had referred to. Probably his clan was somewhere bivouacked in the copse of immense trees. He was certain he was right. Not a barbarian at all, but a baby beast indigenous to the place, wandered off probably from his parents and as lost as themselves—himself and Mills—in the normal-scale world. That's why he'd laughed. It was at the—to him—teensy saplings and weeny toy grass and at Mills and himself too. So not only not a barbarian but not even a beast yet, only a child of beasts and giants, his great steed only a beast kid's pony! And he halted where he stood, catching Mills up with a warning glance. The merchant, no longer hearing them behind him, turned. "Come," he said. "Come." And there was no question in either of their minds but that they'd have to, Guillalume fearing what the madman, small as he was, might yet do to them with his Vandal's weapons if they balked, and Mills understanding that you did not wrestle with angels. They started walking again, Guillalume thinking, and thinking Mills thought: If we could only find the beast child and bring him—though perhaps she was a girl beastess not yet started in her monthlies—with us, that might placate the distraught parents, show our—mine, Mills's—good will. But on the vacant plain the child was nowhere to be seen and Guillalume walked closer to Mills. "Are you thinking what I'm thinking?" he asked in a low voice. "I think so," Mills whispered. "I have a plan," Guillalume said. "We need one." "When we get there—— " "Yes?" "Be quiet." "Sir?" "I mean no talking. Coo. Smile and dribble. Wet your breeches. Shit them." "Smile and dribble? Wet my breeches? Shit them? Coo? This is your plan?" "Don't you see?" "I'm only a stable-hand, I 'aven't 'ad your advantages, sire." "They'll think what that oaf brat thought when he laughed at you. That we're babies from a different tribe!"

[So they followed the merchant to the mountains. Which they realized as they came closer were not twelve trees at all but hundreds —thousands—and oddly tiered, amphitheater'd, on huge swollen bulges of earth, stranger to them in a way than even the idea of only twelve individual trees grown to the stupendous proportions they had imagined, for what they knew of earth was that it was dirt, clay, malleable as pitch. You could take a tool and make a hole in it. You could cultivate it, plant seeds and grow food on it. Clods of it could be held in your hand and broken into smaller clods, into smaller still, into smallest, ultimate grains and nubs until you got down to what they thought of as seed earth, earth seed itself. But who could have cultivated such earth as this? Altitudes of earth! They thought of such wizards and their magical oxen and were more fearful than ever.

[And fearful, too, of having to scale the fabulous, vertical piles, knowing they'd certainly fall, that no man could stand on the sides of such ramparts and parapets, that they would have to cling to the very trees if their bodies were not to be crushed and broken by the awful fall.

[But they didn't have to. The merchant showed them passes in the mountains invisible to themselves, plunging between hedgerows of trees as he'd marched them through the forest. So they went up into the mountains, unaware, so gentle was the grade, that they were even climbing. "He's good," Guillalume said softly, "he's very good, he knows just how the gardeners landscaped it." And Mills thought but did not say, Why of course he's good, you ninny, he's an angel.

[And camped for the night. It was very cold, but the merchant built a great fire for them and that, along with the gear Guillalume had had Mills bring with them, was enough to keep them warm.]

It was late the next day that they saw the apparently makeshift and deserted town with its stark wooden cabins. "Boom town," the merchant said as he hurried them through its single long and empty street to the lip of the shaft which they did not know was a shaft and started them down into the underground cavern which they did not

18

know was a cavern. All they knew was that they were entering earth and they started to scream. (Independently they thought of all awful Chance which had brought them there, of Fate and annihilate alternatives. A thousand years later George Mills would, with disgust that he knew no languages and did not play an instrument, whistle the aleatoric music of license plates, thinking even when he caught a melody: the breaks, the breaks, my clumsy dribbleglass life—— mourning in retrospect all missed chances everywhere, crying over spilled or refused choices. Thus, inventing a form of negative inspiration, the two Britons, who did not even know that that was what they were, abandoned philosophy and went to fear.) They keened, they whined, they wailed.

"Wieliczka sure," said the merchant and urged them after him, holding out a lantern he had produced from his pouch and stepping into the dark, downsloping passageway. Mills and Guillalume shied but were coaxed back between the traces of harness earth by their guide. "Yes. Good, good. Yes. Be men. Good. Come. Come good," he said, and Mills, who had really wanted adventure thought that now that he was about to get it it would be in Hell. They were inside earth. As they proceeded they could feel the proximity of the earthen floor beneath their feet, the cool, close, smooth, slightly damp earthen walls on either side of them, the marl roof as high above their heads as tree limbs over a man on horseback. (Once George Mills had helped dig a grave for Guillalume's father's favorite horse. There had been sky, sunlight. He had stood at the bottom of the planet. He had not dreaded then—and to a certain extent did not, as he became used to it, dread now—the idea of such a grave. He had stuck his finger into one side of the horses' clay tomb and gouged out some damp earth, licking it from his finger as a child licks chocolate frosting from a pot. "I should like," he'd said, "to eat a peck of dirt before I die." He had been observed and overheard and his remark repeated. Unconsciously he had invented the original version of a phrase—in those days, as in these, everyone invented *something*—which was to become a part of folklore, and, also without knowing it, given a name to a pathological urge—pica—which many of his descendants would share.)

And so they came to the underground cavern which they did not know was a cavern and which only the merchant knew was a mine. Not even the Polish miners who worked it knew it was a mine. They thought themselves farmers, agriculturists, as the merchant trader and the merchant trader's father and the merchant trader's father's father who had discovered Wieliczka and recruited them from all round the Carpathians had told them, that they were salt farmers, convincing them that no cash crop would grow where salt had poisoned the soil, convincing them, too—this an argument begun three generations earlier—that they must forget about the bitter fruits and saline potatoes which they had managed to raise and on which they had subsisted and still subsisted years after the old man had gone down the natural shaft and discovered the natural payload of rare condiment beneath the earth there.

"What lucky men!" he'd said. "What fortunate beings! Blessed is the farmer who does not have to wait on rains, who can turn his back on the sun, who has merely to harvest, as a boy casually pulls milkweed to chew, what is and what's always been already there, planted at the beginning by God Himself."

The recruits objected that they would be working in the dark. He showed them how to make torches of dried grass. They complained of the effort it took to dig. He told them of the great plows ordinary aboveground farmers had to attach by heavy biting straps to the shoulders of their wives and children, of the hideous pain involved in turning and guiding furrows in the frozen winter earth. They objected to the smoke from the torches which got into their lungs and made them cough. He pointed out the constancy of temperature in their underground farm. They begrudged the heavy lifting they had to do. He showed them how to rig pulleys that would fetch great buckets of salt out of the earth. They cursed the cave-ins that killed them. He showed them how to shore up the farm with scaffolding and told them that everybody dies.

So it was a working mine that Mills and Guillalume had come to. In the ninety or so years of its operation—it still exists—the Polish salt farmers had learned to operate it with great efficiency and had come to scorn aboveground farmers, and to take pride in the rare spice —it was the merchant who had told them that salt was found only in Wieliczka—they brought up out of the ground and which the merchant or one of his partners—brothers, a son—came to collect every three or four months, bartering for it the stock—milk cows, rats, chickens, a sheep, alley cats, a dog—animals, to them, even more exotic than the caravan of camels on whose backs he took away the salt. The salt. The farmed food. For far-off kings, he said, for giants and emperors. (He drew an elaborate and fanciful map of the world for them, sketching in mythical kingdoms, weird and awesome topographies, showing them in realistic detail the thirty-five-mile radius of forbidding Carpathians around Wieliczka itself, the, to them, immediately identifiable landmarks around the salt farm, the latest channels and newest shafts. Then, beyond the actual thirty-five-mile ring around the real Wieliczka, charting hideous, frightening, impossible country—high Himalayan walls of sheer ice cliffs geometric as a flight of stairs and leading to lands that were constantly ablaze, these next to high seas luridly logjammed on his map with crocodiles, dragons, fierce seaborne lions and apes. "It keeps them down in the farm," he would explain later to Mills and Guillalume. "It would me," Mills said.)

"This stuff?" one of the miners said, holding out a palmful of salt. "Those emperors really like this? All it does is make me thirsty."

"They've different digestive systems," the merchant explained. "Water makes them thirsty. Keep digging."

"We're lucky, I guess," one permanently stooped salt farmer said. "We're bent down over a gold mine here."

"Look," said Guillalume, "isn't that—— It's so dark I can't tell really, but it looks rather like—— "

"It is," Mills said excitedly, "it's Mills's horse. Good old Mills's horse," he said, rushing up to pet it, "but where's Guillalume's horse, huh boy? And what have they done to you, fella?" He had to jog along beside the horse as he petted it and said these things, for it had been hooked up to a sort of subterranean merry-go-round, four horses forming a crude equine flywheel.

The merchant took them on a tour of the mine, proudly explaining the operation. The horses they'd seen dragged heavy spokes which were attached to a thick central post, one end of which was planted in the floor of the mine in a wooden pot. At the ceiling, hanging from supporting wooden struts was a similar pot. The horses had been linked to these devices by complicated harnesses, great leather hames, hame tugs, traces run through bellybands, hip straps, breeching. The spokes ended in great shovel-like blades which rubbed along the sides of the mine, scraping flinders of salt from the walls. Adjusting the length of the spokes made it possible to make deeper and deeper incisions into the salt walls. A pit boss watching over the shower of salt judged when it was about to become critical and gave the order to clear the chamber. Then the scaffolding and struts were removed and the horses and men retreated into a heavily reinforced area. There they stood by while wreckers rushed in with mallets and pitchforks to bring down the chamber they had been working just moments before. A priest made a short prayer over the heavy drifts of salt, and the pit boss called in new gangs to harvest it. Meanwhile, in other parts of the mine, the farmers would be shaping new chambers and setting up new scaffolding. Then the horses were reintroduced and the process began all over again. It took about five weeks for a cycle to complete itself. There were, the merchant explained, approximately four complete shifts of men—chamber shapers, carpenters, wreckers, harvesters, salt carriers, pit bosses and horse talkers—on duty throughout the vast complex of the mine.

The merchant showed them—the mine employed a full-time cartographer—one of his maps. What they saw was astonishing—a nexus of honeycombs, larger, more elaborate than the greatest castle, salted cones and salted tunnels, salted chambers, salted halls, moats, amphitheaters, salted playgrounds, salted shafts. And, in black on the map, the great salt ruins where the delicate, saline architecture had collapsed, myocardial infarcts of salt.

"Best place to dig," the merchant said.

"But wouldn't there be—— "

"Oh yes sure. Good yields. Many bushels. Bumper crops. Salt ruins best place to dig."

"But where it's collapsed, the salt, under all that—— "

"Down there under? Oh sure yeah. The farmer boys. Tch-tch. But preserved. Looking good like new."

2

Mills was a horse talker. So was Guillalume. (The barbarian they had seen was actually a pit boss. It had been he who'd discovered and stolen their horses. The merchant, hearing the pit boss's description of the horses and the markings on their saddles, had determined that the men would have to be stolen as well. "Need," he'd said, "people who can talk to them.")

Mills was always thirsty now. Talking to his horse, coaxing him along the orbit of the salt carousel, his tongue flecked with salt dust, his throat burned raw with the dry pebbles, gagging and talking baby talk, horse talk, nonsense, philosophy. He did not know what the other horse talkers told their beasts—the merchant was disinterested; it made him drowsy, he said, to listen; he did not like, he said, to stay long in the farm—because they spoke in what Mills did not even know was Polish, and in addition to his constant thirst, to the annoyance caused him by his great raw burning and wounded mouth, to his stinging eyes and smarting, salt-oiled skin like the sticky, greasy glaze of ocean bathers, there was the problem of finding things to say to it, of *saying* them, getting them out through the hair-trigger emetic atmosphere of his throat and mouth. And in the mitigated light, watery, milky as the hour before sunrise save where the torches, igniting salt, exploded into a showerwork of sparkler ferocity, white as temperature. But mostly the talk, what to say.

"Well, Mills's horse, here we go again. Round and round, hey, old fellow? No, no, can't balk, lad. We're in this together. Got to pull your weight. It's all teamwork here. Can't let them other fellows' horses catch us shirking. That's it, that's the way.

"It's hard times, Mills's horse, I'll give you that, but we've seen better, what? Oh, but wasn't it lovely getting here though, doing them countries, eating the fruits and choice cuts, the good cheeses and grand breads and everything shipshape in the posh weather! But all good things come to an end, they say, and it's hard to keep the splendid up. So perhaps we're for it now.

"What I think, my view of it, is they'll keep us only as long as you pull your weight. These salt farmers don't seem very good Christians to me, Mills's horse, old fella, old boy. Awful bloody blokes they be. And their women—— whoo. Can't get near 'em. Smell as bad as the wreckers. Saucy strumpets though, I think. Ah, the wenches, Mills's horse, oh the crumpet, ah the birds!

"But they've no manners hereabouts, nor a bit of breeding. I showed them my handshakes, displayed my salutes. Water off a duck's back, Mills's courser.—No no, dray it, dray it, old shaft horse, pull it, old pony. That pit boss has eyes like a peacock's tail. That's it, that's it.—Not like with Nancy, not like with Joan. They appreciated a bit of culture now and again. It wasn't all dicky in the furry. There was respect, foreplay, handshakes and salutes.

"I'll tell you a thing about females, old cob. Hey! *Hey!* Keep moving, old goer. Raft it, old jade. Trant it, punch, trant it! Caddy and fetch it, old four-foot and nag-pad, keep on, old cinchfarm, or they'll turn you to tack. (Good Lord, Mills's horse, you're carrying me more than ever you did when I was only your rider.) What was I on about then? Oh—— the women.

"All that gynecic crowd. Oh, the splendor and Orient glory—— the fine, fair furniture of flesh. Prone, how like the Persian's couch—— the flufféd pillows of their breasts, the long, soft bolster of their thighs, their pink hips curving like the tiding sea. And their hair— oh, their hair, Mills's horse—sable, gold, bay and wine like all the point-blank brights of heraldry, more potent than the ensigns, guidons, jacks and pennons of inspirate loyalty! Seated, how like the fabric'd thrones of kings and potentates, ease coiled in their laps like springs! The odalisque miracle of those candied cabinets, the smoked,

24

spiked licorice of the cunts and the chewy charming sweetmeat of the ass.—Keep going, keep going, old sleigh-pull!—Their fuméd groins like a perfect delta in geography, the salty hollows of their underarms and the perfect upholstery of their frictioned genitals. Oh, *oh*. (Hold up, hold *up* old grasschew!) How fashioned to function, how molded to use. Perfect and practiced as a ball. They say He made them from a rib. 'Tis proof of alchemy then and there's juice in stones and soup in straw.

"Have I told you of their faces? I've eyes, nose, mouth and lips, the same consanguineous skin stretched cross the same kinned, reciprocate bones and appendage, the same androgynous flaps and trenches, planes and ovals, and yet I am without beauty, am not beautiful. What differentiates us then? It's not hue or texture. It isn't the cant of the bones or the slow, lifelong settle of the skin and skull. It isn't the smile—men smile—or the postures of shyness over their akimbo bearing. There is, I think, some meter in the faces of women, the iambs, anapests and dactyls of arrangement that female their expressions and lend them the look of children even when they're old, that takes, I mean, the fierceness out and moderates the anger and toys the grief. Yes, it must be that, something like that, beauty that seditions their emotions and turns even fright to ornament and pain to grace. Keep moving, keep moving."

And on like that. Sometimes telling him not only the story of his life but the story of their lives together since they left what neither of them knew was England. Or making up stories, singing him songs, telling him jokes. He recited special horse prayers and even tried to imitate the harshly consonanted jabber of the horse talker behind him or the horse talker in front. There came a time when he could think of nothing more to say. Then he remembered his mother's recipes and relayed them to the horse. He counted—Guillalume had taught him to count to 127—for the beast. And sometimes even described what the horse was doing.

"You're taking a shit. You're peeing on top of the other horse's shit."

Or he'd groan, imitate belches, farts, pretend to moan, laugh, whinny.

And then he went blank and fell silent. Mills's horse refused to move. The furious pit boss raged at Mills. Mills called for the merchant to translate his reply.

"Says lose tongue," Mills had the merchant explain.

The pit boss, unimpressed, had the merchant warn Mills that

he'd better say something to get the horse moving again. Mills, insulted, attempted to justify himself to the merchant.

"Ask him how *he'd* like to have nothing but a fucking horse to talk to all day? Tell him that this particular fucking horse wasn't too fucking bright to begin with or we wouldn't fucking be here in the fucking first place, would we? Tell him how I give the nag my best stuff, and all he fucking does by way of polite conversation is shit and piss on the fucking salt!"

That night he spoke to Guillalume about it in the long wooden barracks they shared with the other horse talkers.

"What do you talk about?"

"Talk about?"

"With Guillalume's horse. To get him to move. To keep his spirits up while he goes round and round in circles pulling the two-ton goddamn tree trunk."

"His spirits?"

"What do you tell him?"

"Nothing."

"Nothing?"

"Nothing at all. He knows what he has to do and he does it. I think he likes it rather."

That night he had a dream and next morning, not knowing—as he had not known about horses or picnics or what a crusade was or the language he had been hearing for two months now without understanding a word—that he had just invented psychiatry, he began to tell Mills's horse about it, speaking easily, effortlessly. "You weren't there, Mills's horse," he said, "you never saw this—this was my dream and what happened, too—but once, when I was a small boy, there was a rider hurt. And he must have been an important man—from the castle—because the others, the knights, their squires, were very concerned, frightened. Because by ordinary they were a bung and lively lot, always laughing and passing off jokes when a fellow had fallen, even when he'd been hurt more than this one was, this fellow who'd only had the wind knocked out and was a bit silly, not even bad limping, mind, but light-headed and reeling about like someone mixed up." Mills looked across at the animal, which seemed to like, be actually interested in, what he was saying, so easily did he move in his harness, almost too easily. Mills had to increase his pace to keep up with him. "Well then," he said breathlessly, "like I was saying, they were very alarmed like and called in the men from the stable to pull off his armor for him and other men to support him back to the

26

castle. And I was there and this great knight saw me and says, 'You, boy, fetch Sir Guy's lance and come along,' and we all went up to the castle together. And you know, Mills's horse, that was the first time and the last time too that I'd ever been there, though I could see it sometimes from the stables in winter when the leaves were down.

"And my heart was pounding then, I tell you, though I never thought they'd take me inside, imagining that they'd leave me behind this side the drawbridge. And when we got to the moat I must actually have stopped, balked, because one of the sirs turned and said, 'Hurry, boy, hurry. You're Sir Guy's spear carrier now. You must keep up.' Oh, Mills's horse, I was dreadful ashamed, stinking as I did of stable —no offense, old plop dropper—and we went in through the great crosshatched gates with their dark iron spikes at the top like aces of spades, and in the courtyard there was pages and heralds no older than myself but dressed like face cards, and retinues all milling about, and maids and ladies-in-waiting, counselors and even an astrologer in a cone hat. It was lovely lively, Mills's horse. Like Fair Day it was. There was jugglers with balls and acrobats four men high—— ever so cunning, ever so deft. There was musicians and peacocks and archers with arrows. All this in the courtyard, all this in the air.

"Then seeing Sir Guy, a jester come limping, mocking his manner, joking his pain. A knight kicked his arse and another set his bells ringing, punching his head. And we went on together, up to the castle, leaving the life.

"And all I could think was: If it's this way outside what order of prosper must go on indoors?

"It was like the inside of a well—this is still the dream and still what happened, too—the scut-wake contrariety of the world. Not gay but murk, not glister but the subfusc verso of the year. Oh, they had good pieces about—mahogany, oak—all the thick woods bloody as meat and marbled with grain. There was musical instrument on the muniment floors like a luggage, and a hearth so wide and deep they could have burned villages in it. I was a boy then—understand this —I was a boy then as I'd never been a boy before, I think, growing as I had with the ordinary and nothing to pitch my wonder at I mean. There was a quartered arms above that great fireplace and all I could do, no matter they nudged me, was stare at the escutcheon, the bright shield mysterious to me as the position of the stars, one who only having heard of honor suddenly confronted with it—oh, the knights used to jabber of it enough, but it was just chatter, just shoptalk— staring up at Honor's manifest lares and penates glowing like primary color on the very shape of Honor. It was illegible to me of course, the chiefs and bases, the dexters and sinisters, fess points and nombrils, no more meaningful to me than the symbols on the wizard's cone or the precedence of picture cards. But I knew what it was. I *knew*. Document, credential, pedigree, warrant. The curriculum vitae of Honor—its probative ordinates and abscissas, scaled and calibrate as weights and measures. All aristocracy's home movies. An eye-opener to the kid from shit. The history of my master's master's family stamped like a veronica on the blazoned crest. (And oh, Mills's horse, the dyes, the dyes! No such colors in Nature or life. No sky so blue nor blood so red nor grass so green; the lineage repudiate to Nature, candescent even in the measly taper'd dark, the fuels they burned the oils of unicorns or the sweet fierce heroic burning breath of the gilded rampant animals themselves perhaps!)

"All this I saw last night in my dream, saw it as I'd seen it then and, as then, heard the scolding of the knights: 'You, boy! Woolgatherer, what are you staring at?' 'Come away, come away!' 'Kid, kid, bring the spear, you'll eat your heart out.'

"But I wasn't, you see. Not angry or jealous, no covet or revolution in my heart. Not even reform there. Only wonder at the curious assortment of life, its dicey essence and laddered station.

"We went upstairs. Through the cold scarpéd halls, the parapeted, circumvallated keep and fastness, through miles it must have been of that fortress house. And that's where I saw it. Along one immense stairwell. A hanging, they told me, a tapestry. Woven in Germany, I think, or France, or some such far-off place. Whatever name they used as meaningless to me as the sandpaper syllables of animals.

" 'Please, sir, may I look for a bit?'

"And one of the men raised his hand as if to strike me, but Sir Guy himself stayed the blow. '*Noblesse oblige,* asshole. Let him. What? The ink not yet dry on the Magna Carta and you'd strike a stableboy for looking at a tapestry? Give Elvin my lance, lad. Thank you for carrying it this far. Take my coin. When you've done, go out quietly.'

"It was like a flag, Mills's horse—— only larger than any real flag. And the colors not as bright as they'd been on the escutcheon, for those were the consolidate, idealized, concentrate colors of claims and qualities, the paints of boast and fabled beasts. This was a picture. Not a picture like a picture in a church. No saints with halos like golden quoits above their heads, no nimbuses on edge like valued coins, not our Lord, or Mother Mary, or allegory at all, but only the ordinary pastels of quotidian life. A representation, Horse, in tawns and rusts, in the bleached greens and drought yellows of high summer, in dusty blacks and whites gone off, in blues like distant foliage. Everything the shade of clumsy weather. There were gypsies in it and beggars. There were honest men—— hewers of wood and haulers of water. Legging'd and standing behind their full pouches of scrotum like small pregnancies. There were women in wimples. Ned and Nancy. Pete and Peg. It was how they saw us—— see us. Shepherds and farmers. Millers, bakers, smithies. Mechanics with wooden tools, leather. Pastoral, safe, settled in the tapestry condition of their lives, woven into it as the images themselves.

"Only I knew *I* wasn't like that—— though I wouldn't have objected if I was. Maybe the Germans, maybe the French, but not me, not anyone I knew. We are a dour, luteless people, cheerless, something sour in our blue collar blood."

He fell silent. Yet the horse continued to turn in its orbit and he in his, the two of them reflective now, ruminative, Mills and the horse too, not even taking for granted the respite and thoughtless free ride earned for them by Mills's calm oratory. Indeed, when Mills looked up he saw that he had been talking to a different horse entirely, that he walked beside another horse talker. "Oh," he said, " 'scuse me," and caught up to Mills's horse. "I got lost," he explained to the beast. "I got caught up in what I was saying. I lost my place," he apologized.

"Where was I?" he asked of it, who first picked up its shit and then had to sweet-talk it, playing up to the very horse he'd serviced before ever he'd serviced Guillalume. Humiliated, his life proscribed and red-lined from the beginning, and angry now, heavily caused as an underdeveloped nation or a leftist history of legitimate beef, no longer soft-soaped by life, and suddenly frightened too, frightened beyond immediate threat, frightened to the bone, scared right down to hope itself.

He knew he had to escape. Not because he thought things would be different elsewhere—he knew they wouldn't—but because he needed comfort and even his own old turf would do. (Nor did he care about Guillalume now, whose people had perpetrated the tapestry against him, nor about his—Mills's—horse, or Guillalume's. There was nothing personal. There was everything personal.)

He would need the merchant.

After his shift he returned in the dark to his hut, the communal long house where he and the other salt farmers stayed. He did not

even begrudge the horse talkers and the other farmers their wives—
— square, blockish women who ministered to their men with their
soft songs and heavy bodies. Partitions blocked his view like stalled,
angled space in public toilets. There were no proper walls, only
hanging rafts of nailed baffles, so that what he saw from his cot were
bare feet, legs, the dropped clothes of lovers. He had a sense of
timeless peep show, of infinite availability, of his own discretionary
participation. If he so much as stooped to undo a clog he knew he
would see animal vistas of coupled flesh, himself protected by the
blind abandon of the others' concentration. He might have crawled
unchallenged and unassailed the entire length of the long house,
tunneled beneath their lovemaking, bellying like some fuck farmer
just beneath the lovers' groans and clipped cries. There were more
than thirty cots, and their orgasms seemed peremptory and staggered as farts or coughs, a continual hubbub of what he could not
even bring himself to believe was ecstasy, only some long, ongoing
conjugal Las Vegas of copulation, ceaseless as card game, not even
heeded. Not even heeded by the occasional laughter and applause
which was the collective, mechanical acknowledgment of these performances. But he did not stoop, did not undo his clogs (though he
held in reserve his right to do so). Nor, after a while, did he even
stop to think: *Beasts. Animals.* Semen and the smoky smell of female parts were simply the prevailing weather of the place, change-
less as California. Mills was without lust. Unsmitten, bored by concupiscence in a foreign language. Though he'd had his chances.
Knew there was great curiosity among the women, and even the
men, about his foreign parts.

"I get you girls," the merchant told him.

"No."

"No trouble. Easy. I tell them you got square balls. I tell them
you got pecker that don't go down except when you're sleeping. I tell
them your ass got two ruts like road. Or one up and one over like
crossroad. What you want me to tell them?"

"Nothing."

"Too late to tell them nothing. They ask me."

And so, apparently, they had. The merchant brought them to his
doorless cubicle where they stood watching him, chattering. There
were one or two men among them.

"Better show stuff," the merchant said.

"Show stuff, show stuff," they took up the cry, understanding
well enough what they asked.

Guillalume smirked. "Go ahead, Mills," he said, at ease on his pallet, "better not keep them waiting."

"As to that," the irritated Mills shot back, pointing at Guillalume, "he's more foreign than I am, being an aristocrat and all. You've only got to look at his fine cheekbones and delicate features. Look at his fair skin, why don't you? He's like that all over. I'm his valet. I dress him. I know. Fair down there he is as flour with a foreskin you can see through and testicles so clear you can spy their milk. Make him show you his nipples, white as shirt buttons. Make him show you his forked cock, one for piss and one for love."

The merchant translated what Mills had said and the others stepped back involuntarily, peeping out between the fingers of their laced hands over their shielded eyes.

"That was insubordinate, Mills. You're for the rack and strappado when we get back."

"In that case I've nothing to worry, have I?" Mills said, raising his voice. "When we get back! We're the other side of hell, we are. We might as well be where the Meuse River meets the Waal channel of the lower Rhine. Ha! High and dry on the bloody floating islands off the bloody drifting shores of the bleeding loose lands! When we get back!"

"No more today," the merchant told the women. "All over now. Good night. Good night."

When they were alone it was Guillalume who apologized. "Sorry," he murmured, "didn't mean to wake the dander. It's just our adventure has gone boring and uncomfortable. Father's fault. Adventure should never take place more than a day's journey from the castle." Mills stared at the rough wooden ceiling. "Forgive me? Give us a smile?" Mills smiled dutifully in the darkened long house. Mills heard the rattle of the shucks as Guillalume turned on his pallet. When he spoke again his voice was still conciliatory. "What are you thinking, Mills? What are you thinking, George?"

"I'm wondering what I'm going to tell the horse tomorrow."

"You take that part too seriously."

"If it stops they'll kill me."

"You think too much in terms of punishments," said the man who had just threatened him.

It was true. Once Mills knew that they—he still thought "they" —would need the merchant he wondered what they would do to him —he thought "him"—if he was caught. They could stone him, flay him, hang him, cut away his features as you'd peel a potato. There were hundreds of punishments on the books, for the other end of the tapestry condition was the conditional condition, the notion that he held his life by sufferance, the moody good will of his unpastoral superiors. (The chain of command was unclear: there could be women in the long house who had authority over him. He did not even know if he was a slave, if Guillalume was.) Men of his station lived ringed by deterrent and each time he thought of a way to use the merchant to make good their escape—he thought "their"; Guillalume, though his master, was his charge, too; and there were also the horses—he thought of the terrible retribution which would come with capture, and constantly modified each violent plan with a gloss of extenuation. (He had invented a sort of Mexican bandit, a fellow who joked with a hostage, who plied him with drink and cigarettes and sent out for hamburgers, who offered him extra blankets, and shared jokes, all the while sleeping with pulled pin grenades and a cover-story smile on his lips. It may even be that he invented the Robin Hood legend itself, bringing hospitality and class and a light heart to violence, all the forced, hypocritical courtesies and jolly rogering that come with bright ends and hardened means.) It made no difference. A month later he was still tampering with his plans, ballasting action with all that was incompatible with it.

Then one day Guillalume appeared in the salt chamber where Mills, on duty and alone during a rest period, was entertaining Mills's horse with supposition.

"Say this: say we bring him the months' journey back with us, letting him ride while I walk, *stumble,* my feet bloody and my body bruised. And say we set him on the lee side of the clearing at our evening debouch with yourself and Guillalume's horse and me to keep the wind off. Say we do all the hunting and fishing while he dozes, and cook the meat the way *he* likes, never mind that I favor mine rare and can't chew gray food. Say I strip myself to put additional cloth on his body and always let him have the last of the fresh water. Say I do all his heavy lifting and learn his favorite songs and call him by honorifics, upping the ante of his natural caste, so as to say, 'Yes, Merchant Minister,' or 'Indeed, Money Grower,' 'Aye, 'tis so reported, Your Mercantileship.' Suppose I did all this and said all this and only begged of him—always deferentially, always with respect—the right turn from the wrong, petitioning him not even for information but just for hints, as children look to the Master of the Revels for clues in games. 'Cold, *cold,*' he could say, or hearten us by a cheerful 'Warm and warmer.' And let's say that there's ransom on Guillalume and that it goes to the merchant with an income on a portion of Guillalume's lands for he and his heirs in perpetuity? Would not all this mitigate the original offense and cause him to soften his denunciation? Suppose we—— "

"Cut inches from his throat and scatter his nostrils, slice his kneecaps and knot his veins," Guillalume said. "Come, old son, when you unhitch tonight bring Mills's horse up through last week's channel. We're going to scarper. I've got the old bastard. He'll see us home or I'll feed him his bones for breakfast."

Mills grimaced. "He's in pain?"

"Like a horsetalker's throat."

"You threatened him?"

"Like a widow in arrears."

"You've got him tied up?"

"Like his catalogued salt sacks."

And since Mills had spent more time in his salty underground confessional talking to his horse than he had in the long house with his mates and master, he turned now almost involuntarily to the beast.

"Oh now, *now* we're for it, old fourfoot. *Now* we're outlaws in this outlandish land where the customs of the country are more vicious than the circumstances, more obdurate than the very earth the men perforce work beneath." All the strange rules and punishments he had heard of in the months he'd been there came to mind—taboos against using unproductive tones to one's horse; prohibitions against using more than one's small salt allowance; all the salt ordeals: the stuff forced up nostrils and down throats and into cuts carefully barbered into one's flesh like the shapely sound holes in violins. Law proscribed his life like those, to him, mysterious rules of curteisie— — the knight's complex code, the squire's. One had almost to be a very musician of citizenship. It was safest to sleep (though one could not oversleep), safest to take one's meals silently in the mess, safest to crap (though one's bowels were subject to salt inspections), to pee (encouraged as an evidence that one was not pilfering salt), safest finally to be about the merely physical business of one's person, all else, save actual work, the careless free time of dangerous carouse.

"I learned my body here," he told Mills's horse, "and it learned me, accommodate to the inflexible laws of my necessity as the fixed stars. It could not dance on Sundays or during office hours if it tried."

Guillalume stepped in front of him and did a jig.

"They'll soon be back," Mills warned, "they'll see."

"Don't be cowardly. You're still my father's subject, you know. Mine, too, for that matter."

"I'm *everybody's* subject," Mills groaned. "I have more law than a company of solicitors."

It was true. If before he had felt slandered by their notion of him —the tapestry condition—now he knew himself crushed and circumscribed by the jurisdictional one: state, sultanate, realm, duchy, palatinate, empire, dominion, kingdom, and bog—all suzerainty's pie slice say-so.

"Through last week's channel," Guillalume said, a finger to his lips. "And don't tell the nag, for God's sake. I've been teaching the farmers pieces of our language. They might overhear."

Guillalume left.

"Taught them our language," Mills said admiringly to the horse. "Our fortunes are mete in this world, coarse Mills's coarse courser. We're graduate as staircase. Only see what power's in the blood. Mine all red and sticky gunk, his a potion. Well-a-day. Hey nonny nonny."

The merchant had been stashed in a salt pile, buried to his neck, and Guillalume was digging him out.

"Grab a shovel," Guillalume told Mills, "take a spade."

"Give us a drink then, luv," the man pleaded when they had extricated him. Salt clung everywhere, in the folds of his clothes, inside his boots, all along the fine filigree of his hundred ornaments. There was salt in the lashes of his eyes, in the ledges of his lined face. It was a capital offense of salt hoarding. "I've got to have water. Please!"

"It's all right," Guillalume said, "slake him. Use the bucket."

Mills obeyed, watering the man as he would a horse.

"He doesn't know what we want yet. He thinks it's some mutiny of my own."

"It is," Mills said. He turned to the merchant. "It *is,*" he said. "I never knew, your honor."

Guillalume frowned. "Do you know Northumbria?" he demanded suddenly of the merchant. "Could you take us there?"

"Northumbria?"

"Aye."

The man squinted. "Scept'red isle," he asked after a few moments, "other Eden, demi-paradise?"

"That's it," Guillalume said.

"Fortress built by Nature for herself? Happy breed of men? Precious stone set in the silver sea?"

"Aye. Aye."

"Earth of majesty, seat of Mars, blessed plot? That the place?"

"Aye! You've struck her off!"

"Rains almost daily? Cold scuzzy climate? Bleak economic outlook, nothing worth trading. You boys better off in Wieliczka."

"Take us to Northumbria!" Guillalume commanded.

(Oh yes, *commanded*. Certainty in the tone of his voice, according to Greatest Grandfather Mills, like a flourish of syntax. High rage on him like the shakes, the easygoing youngest son suddenly recalled to himself and his heritage as if aristocratic mood were transudate and collateral with entirely personal states of emergency. All leaves were canceled according to Greatest Grandfather Mills, all priorities magically shifted, and authority itself suddenly transubstantiate with the worn, work-tattered, salt-torn rags Guillalume wore for clothing. There was no mistaking Guillalume's purpose, the determined, dangerous set of his jawline that seemed to grow at the bottom of his face like a beard. Mills had never seen him like this, had never seen *anyone* like this, and for the first time in his life he envied purpose, lusted for will. Then there were suddenly knives in Guillalume's hands, hangers, dirks, claymores, a blinding, whirling brace of the sharp. He drew the merchant's blood at a dozen points, the wounds spectacular but superficial as paper cuts. He buttered them with salt with the flats of his arsenal. The merchant howled. Guillalume howled louder. *"Compass! Card! Binnacle! Plumb bob!* Fix thy course for Northumbria!" "But the crops," the merchant whined, "the harvest—— " *"Geography!"* Guillalume hissed. "For Northumbria, *Map!"* "But the caravan," the merchant pleaded, "the camels—— " "We don't need the salt." "We do. For barter. We do. We'd never get past the tribes, we'd never—— " "The tribes?" "The tribes, Your Majesty, the clans. The bands and companies. All affined agnate generation." "All affined agnate—— " *"Men,"* the merchant said, "knots of the kindred between here and there, cousin clusters 'twixt hither and yon. Who guard the passes and bar the borders. Frontiers of *men,* sir, horizons of *flesh.* The landscape is toll'd, m'lud. This is no civil world, Master. It's filled with patriots to place. There are holy hectares, restricted rivers. Even the wilderness is posted. They kill trespassers." "Maybe there's some other way of going," Mills suggested. *"Liar,"* Guillalume boomed, "I've *seen* the maps you show.

35

Firelands, Giantlands, Dragonlands! Continents of monster, terra terror! How do *you* make your journeys? You bring no salt with you. How do you make *your* journeys?")

The merchant watched him, then answered coolly. "I'm impunity," he said, "vaccinate 'gainst xenophobia. The token interloper I am, the consanguinitic vagrant totem. I come from the far. From distance itself I come." He shook himself, shedding even the damp salt which clung to his clothes and flesh, showing them the refractive shine of his person, the odd insignia they had seen in the forest almost blinding in the open sunlight and making, as the merchant shook himself, a mysterious preen of jewelry. His pins and pendants made a sensible bell-like music.

"He's God," Mills muttered. "He's God," Mills told Guillalume.

"He never is," Guillalume said uncertainly.

"No, no," the man said, "not God, only a traveler, a man of mileage just, a courier along the vault and arch of landscape is all." He paused and looked at them. " 'Follow me,' He said." "But I go further, outdistancing atlas."

Four days later they left. He needed the extra time to organize his foremen—the caravan expected in two months, bills of lading to be signed, vouchers, arrangements of usance, details worked out about the consignment of the salt—but by now the merchant had seemed to come round to the idea of the journey. "We shall have to travel light," he told them, "only the odd sack or so. Oh, and put by your weapons. They won't do any good where we're going."

"We take our weapons," Guillalume said.

The merchant glanced at them. "As you wish," he said.

"Maybe he knows something," Mills suggested softly.

"Only what I tell him," Guillalume said, and then to the merchant: "We'll follow, but if you lead us into a trap I'll kill you."

The man shrugged and mounted.

For a week they rode, traveling along the spines of high mountains, Mills and Guillalume breathless in the thin air, their speech irregular, a low, broken, breathless panting. Then winds came, snow, the two Northumbrian horses first listless, then actually balking, while the merchant's trotted on as nimbly as before, finally disappearing in the snow-obscured distance.

"Now— now— we're for it," Mills complained. "We were better — better off— in— in the farm." His horse moved in front of Guillalume's.

"What— what— do you mean? Are you blaming— blaming— *me*— for this? You wanted to— to— get back home as much— as I did," Guillalume said, and the horses were abreast of each other again.

"It's— a— tr— *trap.*" Mills's horse edged forward.

"What— *what* is?" They were neck and neck.

"Th— this." He indicated the altitude, the four or five inches of snow through which they plodded. "It's— it's a— trap and now— you'll— you'll have— to kill him.— Like you, you said." Mills's horse took the lead. "Have to— to— to— kill— kill him." Mills started to laugh. He laughed giddily in the high air, unable to stop. "Only— hee hee— where— where— *is*— hee hee— he?" He looked around. Guillalume had disappeared behind him in the white heights, in the heavily falling snow.

"Where— air— where— air— are yooo?—Where are you, Mill — Mill— *Mills?*"

Mills was helpless to answer. He turned and saw Guillalume's horse emerge from a cloudbank. It's the talking, he realized. That's what engines them, fuels them.

"Damn— *damn* you, Mills—— Wait *up.*" (Though Greatest Grandfather said Guillalume had no breath for italics, that it was not class now or affectation which punched up his words so much as the actual explosions of his pressured lungs.)

So they had a horserace. Talking to each other while the horses overheard, seeming actual interested parties, cantering eavesdroppers. And this was when Mills got to say things to his master, and his master to Mills, which otherwise neither would have said to the other.

"The reason," Guillalume said, his breath easier now, "some men command and others obey, has nothing to do with fitness, nor law, nor even custom. God does not sanction nor Nature compel fatality." They believed—the snow had stopped falling and the mountains glistened like great bright boulders—that they rode in the sky, that their horses brisked along a ledge of cloud. The broad valleys beneath them seemed domesticate, lulled, standing pat as potted earth, quiescent as houseplant. "Only man needs men. I require a valet because I cannot dress myself, an upstairs maid because I can't make beds. My doorman knows better than I the ins and outs of my house. You should be flattered, Mills. The drudge, the erk, the groom and porter—— the help, Mills. The char and babysitter, the footman, lackey, cook and page. The turnspit and amah, the housecarl and equerry. Seneschals and cellarers. All my menial men, Mills, fixed more by skills than bayonets, talent than circumstance. You brood too much on blood, boy."

"I lug your bathwater," Mills called after him. "It's my finger scalds to test the temperature. There's no talent there, only patience and torpor. You got the guns. Your lot does. Where you got them or who gave them I don't know. The devil, I think, because only the devil wouldn't know better or wouldn't care than to trust somebody with a gun who can't make a bed."

Guillalume's long list had put him in the lead but Mills's shouting had narrowed the gap and they were almost abreast of each other again, Mills a length or so behind. They had been descending and were now in the valley they had seen from the sky. The trail had ended, beaching them in abrupt wilderness. Mills looked round from where his mount had just nosed out Guillalume's and recognized with some surprise that it was fall. It was the first time he'd been conscious of season since coming to Wieliczka. The mines had been landlocked in time, and his shift, from just before daybreak till the sun had gone down, and his exhaustion, had kept him thoughtless of the calendar. Neither of them had any idea where they were. They were lost and did not even know in what country they were lost, or even if it were a country, if it was still the planet, still earth. All they could see were, behind them, the mountains, and everywhere else, save the small apron of clearing on which they stood, the high, blond grasses of a giant, endless steppe.

"Where'd he go?" Mills said.

"He gave us the slip," said Guillalume.

"We couldn't have passed him."

"In the snowstorm. We might have missed him in the snowstorm."

"That trail was too narrow."

"He isn't out there."

"He give us the slip."

Then they heard a noise coming toward them through the tall, brittle grass. The next moment the merchant materialized before them as the grasses parted and a hundred wild horsemen followed after.

("These were the Cossacks," Greatest Grandfather Mills would explain afterward, "and all they wanted was the Word. It was all any of them wanted.")

"The word?" Mills said.

"Messages," the merchant said, having taken the two of them

38

aside. "What the entrails said, what the Tablets. Afflatus, avatar, vatic talebearing, godgossip, gospel."

"They're infidels," Mills said, eyeing their weapons, their pikes ready to their hands as their reins, the whips which lay like embroidered quoit over their saddlehorns.

"No one is infidel," the merchant said. "Show them death and they whistle hymns. Speak to them."

"Me?"

"They watched you come down the mountain. They saw you bring up the rear, they watched you pass."

"I don't—— "

"They saw your sacking, Guillalume's linen."

"I don't—— "

"They know their textiles. 'The last shall be first.' Strangers rare here. No concept of travel. Someone just passing through beyond them. They think you come to tell them things."

"Me?"

"You speak now."

"What will I say?"

"Make it good."

"I don't even talk their language."

"I translate." The merchant yanked his horse about, turned away from him. "Make it good," he warned again, his back to him. He joined the warriors.

The merchant said something to them and the wild men looked at Mills as if through a single pair of eyes. Guillalume separated himself from Mills and went toward the merchant while the warriors waited for Mills to begin. "Make it good," he mouthed before riding off.

"I have come," Mills said, "I have come—— " The merchant translated and the warriors watched Mills closely. Mills cleared his throat. "I have come," he began again. They watched him impatiently and one drew a pike from where it rested in its sheath. "I've come, I say," said Mills and looked helplessly at the merchant. The merchant translated. One of the warriors clutched his whip. The man drew his arm back slowly. "No, wait," Mills shouted, clambering down from his horse. The merchant translated. "I've come to tell you," Mills said nervously, "that—— that—— " The Cossack with the whip gently rolled the hard, thin, braided leather within inches of Mills's feet. Mills looked down gloomily at the dangerous plaited rawhide. "*Not,*" he exclaimed forcefully, "to hit. Not to hit. I have come to tell you not to hit!"

39

"He's come to tell you not to hit," the merchant translated. The wild Cossacks looked at Mills questioningly.

"Right," Mills said. "Hitting's bad," he said hopelessly as the merchant translated. "God hates hitters," he said. "He thinks they stink." Tentatively the Cossack withdrew his whip. "Oh yes," the encouraged Mills went on, warming to his subject, "hitting isn't good. Yes, Lord. Thank you, Jesus. He told me to tell you you mustn't hit. If you have to hit you mustn't hit hard. And killing. Killing isn't nice. Neither shouldst thou maim. Maiming's a sin. It's bad to hurt. It's wicked to make bleed. God can't stand the sight of blood. It makes Him sick to His stomach. Thank you, oh *thank* you, Jesus!" Mills said. He had spoken these last few sentences with his eyes shut tight and now, cautiously, he opened first one eye, then the other. The pike was back in its sheathing, the whip wound tightly round the saddlehorn. The warriors were gazing at him transfixed, wilder somehow in their concentrate attention than they had been in their hostility just moments before. They seemed to have broken or at least relaxed their formal formation, listening now as a crowd might rather than a trained phalanx. "This lot's easy," Mills remarked offhandedly to the merchant. "I needn't tell you not to translate." He advanced toward them, wanting to work them closer up, but they pulled back on their reins and opened up additional space between themselves and the speaker.

"Oh yes," Mills continued, feeling his immense power and beginning to enjoy himself. "Here's more stuff God told me. He wants you to lay down your pikestaffs." Mills stepped back out of range as first one wild man then another lobbed his weapon into the clearing. "Throw them down, throw them down," he said, and was astonished to see a rain of wood gentle as pop flies come floating down with an impotent clatter not two dozen feet from where they sat on their horses. "Now the bullwhips. Yes, Lord. Thank you, Jesus." The merchant translated and the bullwhips made a harmless leather pile next to the staffs, intricately interlocked now as collapsed fence.

"It's how they make war," the merchant whispered.

"Ain't gonna *study* war no more," Mills said.

"They need their weapons to hunt," the merchant said.

Mills shrugged. "God wants them to eat berries," he said. "Tell them." The merchant looked at Mills with interest. "Go on," Mills said, "tell them." The merchant translated. "That's right," Mills said. "He wants you to eat nuts and boil your grasses for soup. Soup is holy. Fruit and nuts are a blessing to the Lord, praise His Holy Name."

40

He stared at his auditors but they looked away from him, fearfully avoiding his gaze. So this is what it was like to be Guillalume, Mills thought, or no, Guillalume's eldest brother, even Guillalume's father himself. He sized them up, their rough, thick clothing, their sharp teeth and solid bodies, their tough skin the color of hide, the sinister vision which slanted from their peculiar eyes. A rough bunch. He could do some real good here. "God wants you," he told them earnestly, "to take the stableboys who shovel your horseshit for you and make them princes. Just after not hitting that's what He wants most."

"Oh, Mills," the merchant said.

"Tell them," Mills commanded. He folded his arms across his chest.

And that's when he saw it.

"Jesus!" he said.

"Jesus!" the merchant translated.

"No," Greatest Grandfather said fearfully. "Have them dismount. Tell them good-by." Not taking his eyes off them—they wouldn't have seen anyway, they weren't looking, they were watching Mills's horse—he backed slowly away. "Stand still, Mills's horse"— because he knew nothing about horses, not even enough to say "Whoa"—"stop while I mount you." But the horse continued to go round him, turning circles which were identical in circumference to the circles he had turned in the mine. Mills ceased talking and Mills's horse stopped in its orbit and Mills got on. "Let's go," he said. "Straight lines only, Mills's horse. Follow the merchant, fellow. Follow Guillalume's horse." And guided him with the reins, pulling the bit roughly whenever the animal started into one of its turns. To keep him moving Mills chatted amiably, mindlessly. "Well, that's it, folks," he said, "bye-bye. God's instrument tells you 'so long.' God's instrument's instrument—tell them, merchant—asks you to abide here and pray a while. Pray and fast four days. Amen and thank you, Jesus."

"You mean you didn't *know?*" Guillalume asked him later.

"I didn't," Mills said, "I didn't truly. Bloody goddamn horse worshippers. And that one says there's no infidels."

So he gave them the Word. (And, indirectly, ultimately, invented dressage too who knew nothing about horses, inventing *haute école* for them and the principle of the pony ride.) The Word changing as they worked their way backward across not only geography but culture as well. Telling them not only and not even always out of self-defense, but for hospitality, three squares and a kip for himself and

41

his companions, spouting Jesus for their entertainment as he might, if he'd had a good voice, sung them songs. In Russia he told them, in Romania, in Bulgaria. In Greece and in Turkey. And doing them miracles out of their small store of salt. Changing fresh water to sea water in jugs which he permitted them to dip into their own sweet lakes and running rivers, elsewhere pressing the salt onto their very tongues, a mumbo-jumbo of condimental transubstantiation.

Saying "I shall make you the salt of the earth." Or demonstrating its emetic properties, swallowing any poison they wished to give him and coming back to life before their eyes. Telling sailors along the Aegean and on the Ionian and Adriatic and Mediterranean and ports of call up and down the Atlantic.

And *that* was the First Crusade.

And then they were in England again, and then in Northumbria, and the other crusade was over too now, ended, the one Guillalume's brothers, who had gone to Palestine after all, had gone on, to be killed by the infidels the merchant did not believe in, and now Guillalume was the eldest brother and, in another year, would be the lord of the manor himself, and Mills was back in the stables because it would not do for one so high placed to have as a retainer a man who knew nothing of horses.

PART TWO

1

Louise lay beside him, her flannel nightshirt bunched beneath her chin. The nightshirt was baby blue with tiny clusters of gray flowers and smelled of caked Vicks and cold steam from the dehumidifier. Her fingers probed her breasts, stroking, handling boluses of flesh, sifting tit like a cancer miner or a broad in pornography.

"All clear?" George asked as she lowered the nightshirt, yanking it down under her backside and consecutively rolled hips.

"When you bite me," she asked, "do you ever feel anything hard?"

"When I bite?"

"When you take them in your mouth. Do you feel anything hard?"

"I spit it out."

"Someday I'm going to find something."

"Well," he said, "you'll be catching it early."

"I spotted again. It wasn't much. A little pink on the toilet paper."

Louise got out of bed and put on her house slippers. She smiled and raised the nightshirt. She pulled it over her head. She drew the shades and turned on all the lights, even the one in the closet.

"I have to tell you something," George Mills said.

Television had taught him. Edward R. Murrow had shown him their living rooms and studies, the long, set-tabled dining rooms of the famous. Commercials had given him an idea of the all-electric kitchens of the median-incomed, the tile-floor-and-microwave-oven-blessed, their digital-fired radios waking them to music. He knew the lawns of the middle class, their power mowers leaning like sporting goods against their cyclone fences, their chemical logs like delivered newspapers, their upright mailboxes like tin bread.

"I used to want," he'd told Laglichio's driver, "to live in a tract house and hear airplanes over my head. I wanted hammocks between my trees and a pool you assemble like a toy."

They had four hundred dollars in savings.

"I'm poor," he'd said. "In a couple of years I'll have my silver wedding anniversary. I'm white as a president and poor as a stone."

"They give to the niggers."

"Nah," he'd said, "the niggers got less than I got. I'm just poor. You're a kid, you're still young, you'll be in the teamsters one day. You know what it means to be poor in this country? I take it personally. I've been poor all my life. I've always been poor and so have my people—Millses go back to the First Crusade—and I don't understand being poor. We've always been respectable and always been poor. Like some disease only Jews get, or women in mountainous country."

"You got a car. You got a house."

"A '63 Buick Special. A bungalow."

He worked for Laglichio, carrying the furniture and possessions of the evicted.

Usually they had no place to go. Laglichio had a warehouse. The furniture was taken there. Laglichio charged eight dollars a day for storage. Anything not called for in sixty days was Laglichio's to dispose of. It turned up in resale shops, was sold off for junk or in lots at "estate" sales. The newer stuff, appliances, stereos, the TV's, went into hock. Laglichio had a contract with the city. He got a hundred and fifty dollars for each move, half of which was paid by a municipal agency, half by the evicted tenant. Laglichio demanded payment up front. It was rare that a tenant had the cash, and Laglichio refused to put anything into his truck until the owner signed a release assigning his property to Laglichio should he be unable to repay all of Laglichio's claims against him—the seventy-five dollars he owed for the move, the eight-dollar-a-day storage fee—after the sixty-day grace period. He worked with sheriff's deputies. He had the protection of the police at each eviction. He paid Mills one hundred and eighty dollars a week.

"You're free to make a new start now," Mills might explain to one of these dispossessed folks. "Look at it that way." Sometimes he would be sitting outlandishly on the very sofa he had just carried down into the street when he said this.

"New start? To do which? Sleep in the street?"

"Nah," he'd say. "Without all this—— this hardware." He indicated the intermingled rooms of furniture exposed on the pavement, a kitchen range beside a bed, a recliner in front of an open refrigerator, tall standing lamps next to nightstands or potted in washtubs.

"Shit."

"I mean it. Footloose. Fancy-free. Not tied down by possessions." He *did* mean it. He hated his own things, their chintz and walnut weight. But of course he understood their tears and arguments and nodded amiably when they disagreed. "I'm Laglichio's nice guy," he'd confide. "I understand. I'm poor myself. I'm Laglichio's public relations."

"Get your ass out my sofa."

"But legally, you see, it isn't your sofa. It's Laglichio's sofa till you pay him for moving it for you out into the street. But it's okay. I'll get up. Don't get sore."

"Is there some trouble here?"

"No, deputy. Don't bother yourself. The lady's a little upset's all there's to it." And he might wink, sometimes at the cop, sometimes at the woman.

"How this happen?" the woman cried. "How this come to be?"

"Poor folks," Mills said philosophically.

"What you talkin' poor folks, white folks?"

"Oh no," he'd say courteously, interested as always in the mystery, the special oddness of his life. "You must understand. It's difficult to fail in America."

"Yeah? *I* never had no trouble. None *my* people ever found it so tough. Look at Rodney. He be young. He be my youngest. All this exciting to him. He think he gonna live and play outside here on the pavement an' I never have to call him. Why, this be sweet to Rodney. Ignorant. Ignorant and dreamful. But soon's he get his size it don't be no hardship to fail."

"My people do awful things to your people, but even so it's hard, it's hard to fail. Simple animal patience will take you immense dis-

45

tances. Bag in the National, horse the carts in the parking lot. Make stock boy. In a couple of years you'll trim lettuce, in a couple more you'll be doing the produce like flower arrangements. No no, lady. Success is downhill all the way. You put in your time, you wait your turn. Not me, not any Mills ever. A thousand years of stall and standstill passed on like a baton."

"How this cost me money?"

"No no. Nothing I say costs people money."

Laglichio appeared in the doorway and signaled Mills toward him.

"Did she sign?"

"No."

"Then what were you shooting the shit about? Here, give me the papers." Laglichio returned with the executed forms. "I told her the papers proved it was her furniture. That's all you got to say. How many times do I have to tell you?"

"Sure," Mills said.

"You know something, George?" Laglichio said. "You ain't strong. You don't lift high. You're what now? Fifty? Fifty something? You ain't got the muscle for this. What am I going to do with you, George? You ain't got the beef for this business. And any white man who can't get a nigger to sign a binding legal paper probably ain't got the brains for it neither. Put the shit in the truck and let's get out of here."

He wasn't strong. At best he was a student of leverage, knowledgeable about angles, overhangs, the sharp switchbacks in stairways. He was very efficient, scholarly as a geologist about floor plans, layouts, seeing them in his head, someone with an actual gift for anticipating and defying tight squeezes, lubricant as a harbor pilot. Not mechanically inclined but centrifugally, centripetally, careful as a cripple. And the furniture of the poor was light, something inflated and cut corner about it that reduced weight and turned it to size. He wore the quilted protective pads of long-distance furniture removers and affected their wide leather belts and heavy work shoes and gave the impression, his body robed in its gray green upholstery, of someone dressed in mats, drop cloth. He thought he looked rather like a horse.

Laglichio would not fire him. Mills was not union. Often laid off but rarely fired, he was a worker in trades that jerked to the whims of the economy, a stumbling Dow-Jones of a man. It was this that had brought him to Laglichio in the first place. He worked in unemployment-related industries.

Mills and Lewis, the driver, had started to load the truck. The child was crying while his mother painted a bleak picture of homelessness and bedlessness, table and chairlessness, an empty landscape of helpless exile.

"Where we sleep, Mama?"

"Ask that white man where we sleep."

"Where we eat?"

"You ask them white men."

"Where we go to the toilet?"

"We just have to hold it in."

Rodney clutched his teddy bear, its nap so worn it seemed hairless, a denuded embryo, and howled.

Laglichio nudged Mills. George sighed and picked up a carton of broken toys he'd packed. He hesitated for a moment and tried to hand the carton off to Lewis. Laglichio shook his head and, using only his jaw, indicated Mills's elaborate route, past the couch, by the lamps, through the randomly placed chairs.

"What's that you're carrying, George?" Laglichio called in a loud voice.

"Toys," Mills mumbled.

"Toys?" Laglichio called out. "*Toys* you say?"

"I'm fixing to load them on the truck," he recited.

"Toys? Boys' toys?"

"They're toys," Mills said. "That's all I know."

Laglichio came up to where Mills was standing amid a small crowd of neighbors who had begun to gather. "Are those your toys, sonny?" Laglichio asked the boy. "Show him," he commanded George. Mills put the carton down and undid the cardboard crosshatching. "Are those them?" Laglichio asked the kid kindly. The child nodded. "You give him back his playthings," he demanded. "You give this boy back his bunnies and switchblades." The little boy looked at Mills suspiciously. "What's your name, kiddo?" Laglichio asked. "What's his name?" he asked the woman.

"It's Rodney," Mills said. Laglichio glared at the furniture mover.

"Go ahead, angelbabes," Laglichio said, "take them back."

Rodney looked away from the dead balls, broken cars and ruined, incomplete board games to his mother. The woman nodded her head wearily and the boy took the box.

"All right," Laglichio said, "my men got their work to do." He glanced at the deputy, a black man who shifted uncomfortably from foot to foot.

"Folks in trouble want their privacy," he said softly. "Don't shame her," he said, working the crowd until there wasn't a soul left to witness.

"Hotshot," Laglichio said to Mills in the truck. "Big guy hotshot. 'Rodney.' You almost blew it for the kid, you know that? I had a mind to keep that shit for spare parts. Donate them to Goodwill Industries and take the tax write-off. Don't you understand yet," Laglichio lectured him, though he was fifteen years Mills's junior, "what I do? It's orchestrated. It's a fucking dance what I do. On eggshells. You're always bitching to me and Lewis here about how poor you are. This is because you don't think. The subtleties escape you. You don't have a clue what goes on."

"I have a clue," Mills muttered.

"Yeah? Do you? Yeah? There were *riots* before I took over. *Riots.* You think a lousy deputy could do diddly with that kind of shit coming down? They had them. Blacker than the boys I use. The city gives me seventy-five bucks. You think that's a rip-off? It's no rip-off. I save the taxpayer a dozen times that much just in the blood that ain't spilled, that don't have to be replaced by transfusions."

He understood. He loved the shoptalk of the go-getters, loved to hear wealth's side of things. And Laglichio enjoyed giving his tips, took pleasure not only in the boasts but in sharing his secrets, outrageously touting them, daring Mills with proposition, low down, the goods, his insider's inside jobs and word in the ear.

Once, Mills's car wouldn't start, the battery dead, and Laglichio had to come with Lewis to pick him up in the truck. Mills was waiting when they drove up but he'd forgotten his lunch and had to go back into the house to get it. Laglichio couldn't have been waiting for him more than two minutes.

"I noted this morning," Laglichio told him later, "seventeen seven got a For Sale sign up." Seventeen seven was the bungalow next to Mills's. It seemed, if only because it was unoccupied—the owner, a woman in her eighties, had died a few months earlier—even shabbier than his own. "You buy that house, George."

"Buy it? I already got one just like it."

"Buy it as an investment. I called the realtor. They're asking twenty-three thousand. Offer fifteen five. They'll counteroffer nineteen two. How long is it been vacant?"

48

"An old lady owned it. She died three or four months ago."

"Sure," he said, "I figured. The realtor told me about the old lady but tried to make out she just died. I figured four months. The yard's too run down. Old people, they could be on their last legs, they could have cancer in one lung and ringworm in the other, but if it's theirs and it's paid for they're still out there patching and scratching. Sure. It's been on the market four months. Counter their counteroffer. You could nail it down for the address, seventeen seven. Sure," he said, "ain't nobody in the market for a house going to buy *that* house. It's crying out for a captive audience. Buy it and list it with Welfare. They'll give ninety-five a month toward the rent. We're tapped into every homeless son of a bitch in St. Louis here. You could get a hundred fifty a month for it. Depending on your down payment you could clear fifty to seventy-five a month."

"What down payment? Where would I get it?"

"Take out a second mortgage. Borrow on your equity."

"We rent."

"What do you pay down there? A hundred fifty? Am I in the ballpark?"

"A hundred and fifty," Mills said.

"Sure," Laglichio said, "I hit a fucking home run. Want me to guess your age and weight?"

Laglichio bought the house himself and asked George to collect his rents for him and to serve as his agent, calling the glaziers whenever a window was smashed. The neighbors were fiercely white, almost hillbilly—the Germans and Catholics and older residents called the newcomers hoosiers—but Laglichio rented only to blacks with small children. The neighbors terrorized them and they moved out quickly, sacrificing not only the month's rent they had paid in advance but their security money as well. Laglichio realized fifteen to seventeen months' rent in a normal year.

The hoosiers who lived on Mills's block had dogged his life for years. They were a strange and ruthless lot, and George Mills feared them, people who had come north not merely or even necessarily from the South so much as from America. From the Illinois and Pennsylvania coal mines and the oilfields of Oklahoma and Texas, the mineral quarries of western Colorado and the timberlands of Minnesota and the Northwest, from the dirt farms of Arkansas and Georgia and the dairy farms of Wisconsin they had come north. There were shrimpers from Louisiana and men who'd raked the clam beds of Carolina's outer banks. Farmers or fishermen, miners or loggers or drillers for

49

oil, he thought of them as diggers, men of leverage like himself, who worked the planet as you'd worry knots in shoelace, string, prying gifts like tomb robbers, gloved men dislodging stone by stone all the scabs and seals of earth.

They had this in common—— that their oceans and forests and hillsides and wells had played out, dried up, gone off. And this, that though they did not read much they believed it all, and believed, too, all they heard, as long as what they read and what they heard was what they already believed. They were not gullible, only devout, high priests of what they knew. Mills knew nothing.

They were armed, almost militial. They owned rifles but few handguns, hunting knives but few switchblades. There were tire irons in the family generations but when they murdered each other they killed like hunters.

Mills's wife was one of them. Louise had come to St. Louis with her family in 1946 when her father had simply walked away from his farm in Tennessee after three successive years of devastating spring and summer floods. He had hired on with a barge company. "Any experience on the river?" the man who hired him had wanted to know.

"Shit," his future father-in-law said, "ain't I navigated my own farm these past three years? Sailed up and down them four hundred acres on every vessel from mule to chicken coop? Man, I been experiencing your river before it ever got to *be* your river. Since it was only just my own four-hundred-acre sea I been experiencing it." The old farmer—he was fifty then, though he must have looked younger —signed on with Transamerica Barge Lines as a deckhand from just above St. Louis at Alton, Illinois, to Gretna, Louisiana, six hundred miles south. The round trip took three and a half weeks and he seemed to enjoy his new work. Only when he floated past Tennessee on the return trip did his real feelings come out. "We're riding my corn now," he'd tell his mates, indicating the Tennessee portion of the river. "We're over my soybeans like a sunken treasure. We're under way in my pasture. The fish down there are some of the best-fed fish in any river in the world."

At his pilot's urging he took the test for his seaman's papers when he was almost sixty. It was as a favor to the pilot—— he never studied for it. It was the first test he had taken since the spelling and arithmetic and name-the-state-capitals tests of his childhood and he failed because he did only those questions he didn't know the answers to, leaving contemptuously blank all those to which he did, his notion being that if you knew a thing you knew it and it was only a sort of chickenshit prying to ask a man to identify pictures of knots he could tie in the dark and identify constellations whose whereabouts he could point to in broad daylight. He worked patiently—his was the last paper in—on the three or four questions which he had no knowledge of, hoping, or thinking it useful rather, to arrive at truth by pondering it. He received the lowest score ever given a man of his experience on the river and he asked if he could have the paper back. The chief— the tests were administered by the Coast Guard then—shrugged and thinking the old man wanted the paper expunged from his records, let him keep it. "Say," the chief said, "you were the only one to get the part on navigable semicircles. And you did the best job on Maritime Law." He put the exam in a tin box with his marriage license and Louise's birth certificate and the now voided mortgage of what he still thought of as his underwater farm. He remained on the river another ten years, serving as cook for the last five of them, though his wife, Margaret—cooks were allowed to travel with their wives— helped with a lot of it.

"It was grand," Mills's mother-in-law told him once, "like being on one of those cruises rich people take. Only ours is longer, of course. Why, you'd have to be a queen or at least an heiress to have done all the voyaging we done." When she drowned north of Memphis her husband asked to be put ashore. He never went back on the river. He refused, he said, to sail those nine or ten upriver trips a year which would take him over his wife's grave. He dreamed of her in the flooded, overwhelmed corn, her bones and hair indistinguishable from the now shredded, colorless shucks and muddy fibers of his dissolved crops.

Mills himself had not been back to Cassadaga since he was twelve years old.

He wore the same high, cake-shaped baseball caps farmers wear, with their seed or fertilizer insignia like the country of origin of astronauts. His said "Lō-sex 52," and he often wondered what that was. All the men in his neighborhood, landless as himself, wore such caps, the mysterious patches suggesting sponsored softball teams, leaguely weekends in the city parks. Louise purchased T-shirts for him in discount department stores—she bought all his clothes in such places—beer and soft drink logos blazoned across their front. He could have been a boy outfitted for school. The caps and T-shirts— he had a brass buckle stamped "John Deere"—and khaki trousers were like bits and pieces of mismatched uniform, so that he sometimes

51

looked looterlike, a scavenger in summery battlefields. He still wore a mood ring.

But nursed the mystery of the caps, bringing it up only once, in a tavern where he sometimes went to watch NFL games on an immense television screen.

"You eat a lot of that Bladex, Frank?" he asked an old barber on the stool next to his. "What's that stuff?"

"It's chemicals. It's some chemical shit."

Mills had had three or four beers. He was not a good drinker. He did not get mean or aggressive. Alcohol did not loosen his tongue or alter his mood. Rather it pitched him deeper into himself, consolidating his temper, intensifying it, pledging it for hours afterward to the mood in which he had started and which persisted to the point of actual drunkenness. He had entered the tavern feeling a bit silly.

"Look there," he told Frank, "Al Amstrod's wearing Simplot Feeds. I've seen Dekalb Corn and International Harvester and Pioneer Hybrids and Cygon 2-E. Seeds and pesticides, weed killer and all the rolling stock of Agriculture. It's America's breadbasket in here. What'd the Russkies give for your wheat?"

"Now you're talking," Frank the barber said.

"I am," George Mills said. He took off his cap and studied it. "Lōsex 52," he said. "You suppose that's what makes the bacon lean? You think it has half-life?"

"Half-life?"

"That it cancers the breakfast, outrages the toast?"

"Now you're talking."

"Where do we get these caps? Where do they come from? I don't see them in stores."

"George," the bartender said, "could you hold it down a little? The boys can't hear the game."

"Tell the boys we're the reds, they're the greens."

[Because he was too old to fight, too old to be fought. Because he did not work beside them in their plants, because he earned less than they did, because he didn't moonlight or ump slow pitch. Because he was not a regular there, only George, a fellow from the neighborhood. Because there was something askew about his life, something impaired, that didn't add up. He had his immunity. This an advantage to him, something on the house. He called women in their thirties and early forties "young lady," "miss," men almost his own age "young man." Not flattering them, not even courteous, simply acknowledging his seniority, a reflexive formality that floated like weather from his kempt fragility, his own unvictorious heart's special pleading like a white flag waved from a stick. He felt he could have crossed against the lights during rush hours or asked directions and been taken where he wanted to go. He felt he could have defied picket lines, hitched rides, butted into line or copped feels. People he hadn't met would make allowances for him as if he lived within an aura of handicap like someone sightless or a man with a cane. "I'm a Golden Ager," he had told ticket sellers in the wickets of movie theaters, "I forgot my card." And they called him "sir" and gave him the discount.

Louise was horrified. "Why do you do that? *I'm* no Golden Ager. I'm barely in my forties."

"It's all right," he said, "you're with me." He could not have explained what he meant.]

"About our caps," he said, addressing the men in the bar.

"Give that guy a beer," a man said and laid down a dollar.

"Here," another said, laying a dollar beside the dollar the first man had put down, "give him a pitcher."

George raised his glass to his hosts. Who's that, Sinmazine? Thanks, Sinmazine." He drank off two glasses quickly, stood and walked the length of the bar. "Dacthal," he chanted. " Dīpel."

"George got caps on the brain," Frank said.

"Lōsex 52 to Treflan 624," George said. "Come in Treflan 624." Some of the men examined their caps.

"Breaker, breaker, good buddy," Treflan 624 said amiably.

Mills winked at him. "Take off your patch you could pass for a golfer." He took in the men sitting around the bar. "I see," he said, "tennis stars, fishermen, long-ball hitters, pros." He stared at his reflection in the mirror behind the bar. "I look," he said, "like an old caddy."

"Aw, George," said one of the two or three men who knew his name.

"Does anyone know where he lives?"

"Over on Wyoming, I think. A couple blocks."

"It's halftime. Come on, I'll give you a hand."

The two men stood on either side of him and carefully arranged his arms about their shoulders.

All the way home Mills asked himself, "You see? You see what I mean?"

They were hoosiers, men he feared. Though he was no stranger to violence. Having lived in its zodiacal houses and along its cusps,

53

having done his time—a stint in Korea, his job with Laglichio, other jobs—beneath its sullen influence, the loony yaws of vicious free fall, all the per second per second demonics of love and rage. (Not hate. He hated nothing, no one.) His wife had walked out on him once for another man. And had a feel for the soap opera condition—where he got his notions of dream houses, interior decoration—and imagination for the off-post trailer court one, all gothic, vulnerable, propinquitous nesting. Something disastrous and screwy-roofed about his character which drew the lightning and beckoned the tornado. It was as if he lived near the sites of drive-ins or along the gulfs and coasts, all the high-wind districts of being.

But now these dangerous men who humored him home were protecting him, shielding him. He believed they would do so forever, that it was over, that what had happened to him was done with and that now he could coast to his cancer or whatever else that would finally get him. He believed, that is, that he was free to die. A year or so past fifty, he was as prepared for death as someone with his will drawn up or all his plans carried out. Everything that was melodrama in his life was behind him. The rest he could handle.

And just about then, a few days before or behind the day the two hoosiers helped him home, somewhere in there, he was born again, saved.

He didn't know what hit him. He didn't go to church. He didn't listen to evangelists on the radio. Nothing was healed in him. His back still hurt like hell from the time he had picked up a television funny. He didn't proselytize or counsel his neighbors. He talked as he always had. He behaved no differently. Not to his wife, not to the dispossessed whose furniture he helped Laglichio legally steal. Finally, he did not believe in God.

Louise was naked on the floor of their bedroom. She opened her legs. She looked like a pair of sexual pliers. George watched neutrally as she performed—it was a performance—holding herself, plumping her breasts like pillows, licking her finger and touching it to her vagina like someone testing the pornographic weather, roughly tousling her pubic hair, arching toward him, hands along her thighs, just her head, shoulders and feet touching the rug, her open crotch like dropped stitches. She was moaning in some whiskey register and calling his name, though it could have been mankind she summoned.

"I'm wet, George," she told him huskily, "I'm just so wet."

"Get to bed, Louise," Mills said.

"I changed the sheets today," she said.

"You also vacuumed. Get to bed."

She rolled over on her belly and worked the muscles in her ass. Her cheek against the floor, she pouted directions at him. "Come in from behind, I'll give you a ride." On her side she rotated her body for him. George sat at the foot of the bed and watched her. She could have been a late-model automobile on a revolving platform in an airport. "Do you love me, George? Do you like my body?" He did. Louise was a jogger. An exercise of the middle classes, Mills thought she ran above her station but in middle age she still had a grand body. She lay on her back again and raised her arms. Mills saw the thick black tufts of her underarms. He got down beside her and patiently masturbated his wife till she screamed. Individual hairs stuck to her forehead and cheeks. He brushed them back into place with his fingers.

"You didn't do anything," Louise said.

"No."

"It's psychological."

"No," he said, "I don't think so."

"You don't think I'm attractive."

"You're very attractive."

"Then why didn't you get hard?"

"I tried to tell you."

"What, that you're religious? I'm religious."

"I'm saved," Mills said quietly.

He was saved, lifted from life. In a state of grace. Mills in weightlessness, desire, will and soul idling like a car at a stoplight. George Mills, yeomanized a thousand years, Blue Collar George like a priest at a time clock, Odd Job George, Lunchpail Mills, the grassroots kid, was saved.

2

The Reverend Raymond Coule was minister of the Virginia Avenue Baptist Church. He was a large, heavy man in his early forties who wore leisure suits, double knits, checkered sports coats, Sansabelt trousers. Bright ties flared against his dark rayon shirts. Carnations twinkled in his lapels. There were big rings on his hands.

For many years he had had a nationally syndicated television ministry in Ohio and been famous as a healer. He specialized in children with hearing problems, women with nervous disorders, men with bad hearts. Then something happened. He lost his tax exemption, but that wasn't it. He had become involved in a malpractice suit. On national television he had pronounced a woman cured of her cancer. This was rather a reversal of normal procedure. Always before, the people he had healed, preening their miracles, volunteered their own testimony. All Coule had to do when the ushers had preselected members of the audience—congregation—to appear with him on that portion of the program—service—given over to their witness, was to ask them questions. He rarely remembered the men and women he had touched, was as curious and surprised as his viewers to hear them, months and even years after a campaign in Roanoke or Macon or Wheeling, remind him of what God had done. God, not Coule. Coule was simply Christ's instrument. Coule stressed the point, seeming modest, almost shy as he made his disclaimers. He interrupted harshly and became severe whenever someone who'd been healed momentarily forgot the facts and attributed the miracle to Coule himself. He would scold the offender and fly into a rage, a rage that seemed incongruent with his floorwalker presence, this fact alone seeming to lift his anger out of the range of rage and turn it into something like actual wrath.

"*I*" he might shriek, "*I* healed you? I couldn't cure ham! Jesus healed you, brother, and don't you forget it! Unless you remember that and make your thank-you's out to *Him* you'd better get out your bathrobes and bedclothes all over again because you might just be headed into a relapse! Didn't no Raymond Coule ever heal you, didn't no Reverend Raymond Coule put your spine well! That bill goes to Jesus! And you better remit, friend, cause old Jesus He don't dun, He just forecloses!"

And for all that Reverend Coule felt genuine anger at these moments, the offending party was as joyous as the congregation, flushing not with embarrassment but with what Coule himself took to be health, a shine like a smug fitness. Then the born-again sick man might deliver himself of a jumpy, gleeful litany, a before-and-after catalogue of deadly symptom, marred X-rays, the peculiar Rorschach shapes of his particular defilement, a tumor like a tiny trowel, a hairline crack along the bone like an ancient river in Texas or bad handwriting in a Slavic tongue. Blood chemistries invoked in real and absolute numbers, the names of drugs flushed down the toilet. The circumstances of their attendance, what they had said, what Coule had said, the doctors amazed, the new X-rays bland and undisturbed by disease as a landscape painting.

But once, during the healing, that portion of the show when Coule touched the supplicants on camera, a woman was helped forward by her husband. The woman, a girl really, years younger than her husband, who was about Coule's age, stood mutely before the minister. "What is it?" Coule asked. The husband could not control himself. His grief was almost shameful, a sort of shame, that is. He blubbered incoherently. His nose ran. Coule was embarrassed. He was embarrassed by the man's love for the woman, which he somehow knew had never been reciprocated, just as he also knew that the husband was unaware of this. He turned to the woman. "What is it?" he asked her. She shrugged helplessly. "What is it, dear?" Still she wouldn't answer, and though the man tried to speak for her he was tongue-tied by grief and love. Somehow he managed to mutter that his wife was going to die. "What do you mean she's going to die?" Coule said, and then, just for a moment, it was as if he was scolding one of the carelessly faithful who had rendered unto Coule what was properly God's. He began to scold. "Don't you know that there's no death?" he shouted, not at the woman but at the man. "Don't you know Christ did away with death? Don't you know—— "

"I have a tumor," the woman said. "They took my biopsy. It's bad cancer."

"Where?" Coule demanded.

"Here," she said. She pointed to her stomach.

He had a feeling about this woman.

"There? You mean there?" He clutched the woman's arm and drew her to him and pressed his palm hard against her belly. "There?" he shouted. "*There?*" The woman screamed in pain. "What are you shouting for? It's not malignant. It never was. They made a mistake. Stop your shrieking. You're healthy. You don't have any more cancer than I do. Hush. Hush, I tell you. Praise Jesus and honor this man who was so worried about you."

The woman looked at him. She was frightened, but for the first time she seemed to realize what he was saying. "I'm healed?" she said. "I'm not dying?"

"Don't Christ work on the Sabbath even though it's His day?"

"I'm not going to die?"

"Not of any cancer," Coule said.

The fright hadn't left her eyes but Coule saw that it had changed. It was the fear of God. The real thing. It was the first time Coule had ever seen it but he recognized it at once. It was terror, dread, God panic. "Take her home, Mister," he told the husband. "You go along with him, Mrs."

The woman was dead within three months. She had believed him, had refused to return to her doctors even when the pain became worse. Her husband had tried to reason with her but it was the Lord she feared now, not death. The doctors claimed that the cancer had been caught in time, that it had been operable, that with the operation and a course of chemotherapy the chances of saving her were better than seventy-two percent.

The husband wanted to sue Coule's mission and threatened to sue all the television stations that carried his program.

The case never came to trial. Coule's lawyers had persuaded the husband's lawyers that faith itself would be on trial, that they could never win, that the dead woman's religious belief, regardless of who had originally inspired it and however naive the actions it prompted her to take, were forever beyond the jurisdiction of any court in the land. Obtaining a judgment would be tantamount to convicting God. The man was poor, the case extraordinarily complicated. They would be working on a contingency fee. They talked the husband into dropping the case.

Coule gave up the mission. The television stations refused to carry his programs, but he'd made his decision before he learned this. When he left Ohio the only thing he took with him was his flamboyant wardrobe. He gave the campaign's immense profits to charities and for a period of years gave up preaching entirely. He had known better. What he'd said he'd said for the husband, not because of his grief but because of all that unrequited love.

Nor was it the fear of lawsuits that caused him to give up his mission. He knew better there, too. It was her eyes, the holy panic, the fear of the Lord he saw in them, a fear more contagious than any disease at which he'd ever made passes with his ring-fingered hands.

It was Coule Louise went to when Mills told her he was saved.

They were nominally Baptist, or Louise was. They belonged to the church which promised the greatest return on their emotional dollar. The Baptists had the hymns and water ceremonies and revivals, though not the latter, not since Coule's time, and the Virginia Avenue Baptist Church was a large, almost theaterlike building which had been a Catholic church until its chiefly German congregation had moved to more affluent areas of South St. Louis. One or two of the old families, with no place else to go, continued to come not to attend services—the church had been deconsecrated by the Cardinal himself —but to pray in its familiar pews, crossing themselves timidly, rather like people adjusting their clothing with rapid, feathery movements. These people, mostly women, were like folks caught short in the streets. They felt that way themselves, and Coule thought Louise one of them when he saw her sitting by herself in a pew in the dark, empty church. He was turning to go when Louise saw him and waved. He still didn't recognize her. He might not have recognized her even if she had been one of his regulars. It was the old business—though his congregation was smaller now, numbering about two hundred or so where once it had been in the thousands—of not remembering the faces of the people he served.

"I don't come often, Minister," she said. "We're Baptists here, but we don't come often. Well George doesn't come at all. He does sometimes, you know, at Christmas, like that. He's not much of a church-goer." She told him about George, about his salvation, then wondered why she'd come at all. Salvation would be a run-of-the-mill event for a minister. Here she was, she said, going on about nothing. She had seen him on television, she said. She giggled.

"What?"

"I was almost going to ask for your autograph. You're the only famous person I know." Then she did something she hadn't done since she was a child. She vaguely curtsied. Embarrassed, she made the same exiguous gestures the scant handful of Catholics did who still came by from time to time. She touched her hands to her hair as if she were wearing a hat. Everything she did suggested imaginary items of clothing to Coule—— pushing up on the fingers of one hand with the fingers of the other as if she wore gloves, lightly brushing her throat as if a scarf were there. He walked outside with her through the big church doors.

"I'm sorry," she said, "I don't guess being saved's such a big deal to a man in your line."

"Of course it is. I just don't know what you want me to do."

"I wish you would see him."

"Certainly," Coule said. "Have him call my office, we'll make an appointment."

"Oh, he wouldn't come here," she said.

"But if he's saved—— "

"He says he's saved. That he's in a state of grace and doesn't have to do anything."

"Tell me," he said, "did I save him?"

"Nobody saved him."

Coule waited for Mills's call, though Louise had told him not to. He looked for them on Sunday morning. They weren't there. They weren't there the following Sunday. He was bothered by the woman, by her face, which recalled to him the face of the husband and had about it that same sense of wounded reciprocity. Marriage is terrible, he thought.

What bothered him most was his question. "Did I save him?" he'd asked. He, Coule, famous from coast to coast for what had seemed like wrath—he'd edited his shows himself, purposely building them around his furious disclaimers—had not let her leave until he'd asked it. And imagined the look on his face, the coast-to-coast wrath crestfallen, declined to disappointment, acknowledging, if only to himself, what the husband and Mills's wife had never acknowledged —though what did he know about hearts?—the nonreciprocity of desire, its utter pointlessness.

There was currently a campaign on to bring people into the church. It was the membership's doing, Coule pretty much staying out of it for he had rather renounced proselytizing when he left Ohio. When the chairman of the committee reported to him he could not help himself. "Has anyone contacted the Millses?"

"The Millses?"

"They live over on Wyoming Avenue. Mr. and Mrs. George Mills?"

The man referred to his list.

"It's all right," Coule said, "I'll call them."

He called that night. George answered the phone.

"This is Reverend Coule, Mr. Mills. Virginia Avenue Baptist?"

"Yes?"

"We're having a membership drive. I wonder, could I come over and call on you sometime?"

"You want to speak to Louise," Mills said.

"Well, frankly, I was hoping I could speak to you."

Mills didn't answer at once. When he did Coule was surprised by what he said. "I'm busy," George told him. "I do heavy work. Nights I'm tired. I watch television. I got all my programs picked out for the week. I don't like to miss them. I know what you're going to say."

Then his wife had told him of their meeting. "Oh," Coule said. "I'm sorry I bothered you."

"You're going to say I could always catch the reruns. But they don't repeat all the shows. Only the best. What *they* think is the best. I have no way of knowing which show's going to be repeated. You see my position."

This man was saved? This was the delivered, salvationed, redeemed, and ransomed fellow for whom Christ had died?

And then he knew. Of course he was.

"I do," Coule said. "I see your position. You know," he said, "*I* used to be on television."

"Louise told me. I never watch any of that stuff. I never watch those shows."

"Because you're already saved," Coule said quickly.

"Louise tell you that?"

"Yes."

"Well I never told her it was a secret."

"Look," Coule said, "I really think we should talk. Perhaps I could drop by where you work."

"I work the nigger neighborhoods. I carry their furniture down the stairs. They got black ice in their ice cube trays. Their furniture slips through my fingers from their greasy ways. There's come stains on the drapes. Their rent money goes for Saturday night specials. Welfare buys them knives."

"You're saying you won't see me," Coule said.

"Sure," Mills said, "I'll see you. Don't get in my way. If I drop a couch you could break your legs."

"Who was that on the phone?" Louise asked.

"Coule," Mills said. "He says you told him all about me." Like Greatest Grandfather Mills, he was bilingual. He talked in tongues. The neutral patois of the foolish ordinary and a sort of shirty runic. He had used both on Coule but the minister had not been put off. "I could have said no," he told his wife, "but I would have gotten you in Dutch."

"I'm already in Dutch."

"No," Mills said.

"I live with one of the elect. I'll never catch up. Will I go to hell, George?"

"Gee," Mills said, "I don't know, Louise."

They met in an almost empty apartment in the projects. There were still some cartons to take down, a broken chair.

"I'm Ray Coule," the minister said.

"Will you look at that?" Mills said. "We're on the seventh floor here and the windows are all covered with wire mesh. They got to do that. That's government specification. *Steal?* They take from the sandbox!" There was a framed picture of Martin Luther King on the living room wall. "This go, Uncle?" George asked an old man in a wooden wheelchair. Mills winked at his visitor.

The old man whimpered.

"Stop that whining," George said, "we ain't going to leave you. Me and my partner here"—Mills indicated Coule—"going to set you down like a pie on the kitchen table in the truck. The man's a minister. Like the jig in the picture. Come to bless the eviction."

Laglichio was in the doorway. "What's holding it up? Let's move it, Mills. Who's this?"

"Reverend Coule," Mills said.

"Listen, Father," Laglichio said, "you got a beef, take it up with the city. We got sheriff's orders to move these people. There's a deputy downstairs with seals and documents, with notarized instruments like a file cabinet in City Hall."

"I'm here to see Mr. Mills," Coule said.

Laglichio shook his head. "George has work to do. It ain't right he conducts his spiritual business on the taxpayer's time. Let's get with it, George. They already signed the papers."

"I could use some help with these boxes," Mills said.

Laglichio looked at him. "Just finish up, will you? I'll be downstairs."

"My boss is on my ass," Mills said.

"I'll help." Coule lifted a carton of dishes.

"No," Mills said, "you don't have to. How's your lap, Uncle? Think you could handle a few of these if we held them down steady?" He picked up a carton and placed it in the old man's lap. Another box went on top of the first. A third was stacked on the second. The old man's head had disappeared behind the cartons, muffling his whimper. "I'll just peek in the other rooms for a minute, see if I missed anything." Coule was left with the old man.

"Is this too heavy? Are you uncomfortable?"

"He's feeling grand," Mills said and stepped behind the wheelchair. "You know what a forklift is, Uncle?" The old man whimpered. "That's it," Mills said, "you got it. Why don't you step out in the hall, Reverend, see if we're going to clear that front door?"

Coule, walking backward, steading the load as Mills pushed. They went toward the elevator as half a dozen blacks watched the strange procession. "Punch 'Down,' " Mills instructed one of the blacks cheerfully. Two black men got into the elevator with them. "Sure," Mills said, "come on, we'll give you a ride. Whoo," he said when the doors had closed, "stinks of piss, don't it? You brothers got no patience. Stinks of piss, shit, barf and blood. I never been in no jungle, and likely you folks ain't neither, but I'll tell you something, I'd vouch you got the smell down. I reckon this is just how it stinks near some big kill. What was you wanting to talk to me about, Reverend?"

Coule glared at him. "I'm no whiskey priest," he said, his voice at once strained and repressed, tight as a ventriloquist's. "I'm no one defrocked. I'm clean-shaved. I don't court the devil like some kid playing with fire. I am not tormented," he said, his voice on the edge

63

of rage. "My heart's at the softball game. Someone brings potato salad. Someone brings chicken."

"Sure," Mills said. The old man whimpered. Mills hacked a ball of dark phlegm into a corner of the elevator. The blacks stared at him.

"You're saved?" Coule demanded.

"Who you talking to, Reverend? You talking to me? The Uncle? These spades? We having a revival here in the elevator?"

"You know who I'm talking to. You're saved?"

"Like money in the bank," Mills said mildly.

The black men laughed. When the elevator opened on the ground floor there was a crowd in the lobby. Mills stood behind the wheelchair. He turned to one of the men. "Hold that door, will you, Kingfish? Ready, Uncle? Here we go." He shoved the chair through the milling blacks and out the door toward the waiting truck.

He handed the last of the cartons up to Lewis and started to get into the truck on the passenger side. Coule touched his arm. Laglichio, who was already seated, leaned toward the minister. "We're running late, Father. I need my man. Can you finish it up?"

"Something come up at church that Reverend Coule needed to tell me about. He's about done."

"At church," Laglichio said. "I never knew he was so devout."

"My boss," Mills said when they'd stepped a few paces away from the truck, "gives two-week paid vacations but me and Louise usually don't go nowhere. Louise's dad still lives in the city. We drop over once in a while, take the old fellow out for a little drive. I got this '63 Buick Special but wouldn't trust it on no long—— "

"How?"

"Pardon?"

"How were you saved?"

"That's between me and the Lord," George Mills said mildly.

"Don't talk to me like that. *How?*"

"In my sleep," Mills said. "Sure. In my sleep I think. What are you looking at? It's the truth. In my sleep."

"When?"

"I don't remember when."

"Are you baptized?"

"I don't think so. Not that I recall."

"Do you pray?"

"You mean on my knees? Like that?"

"Do you *pray?*"

"Of course not."

"Have you renounced the devil?"

Mills laughed. "Jesus, Reverend, don't talk like a fool. If there was a devil and he could work all that shit, would *you* renounce him?"

"Do you accept Christ?"

"Christ ain't none of my business."

"You don't believe, do you? You don't even believe in God."

"No," Mills said.

"Why did you say that to your wife? Why did you agree to see me? You're not baptized, you don't pray, church means nothing to you, you never accepted Christ, and don't believe in God. You're thick with sin. *Saved!*"

"Who says I ain't?" Mills asked furiously. "You were there with me on that elevator. You saw me. You heard me. Who says I ain't? I parted them niggers like the Red Sea. They never touched me. You know how they do people in these projects? They didn't do *me*. They never will. Who *says* I ain't saved?"

Coule had seen his eyes. They were nothing like the dead woman's. There was no God panic in them. They weren't bloodshot with love as her husband's had been. They glittered with certainty. Coule would ask him if he would preach a sermon.

Louise bought a douche bag, stringent douches. She bought shaving soap, a lady's discrete razor. She proceeded to cut the devil's hair, shaving down there till she was bald as a baby.

3

The griefs were leaking. Everyone was watching the telethon and the griefs were leaking. Everyone was giving to the telethon and sympathy was pouring. There was lump in the throat like heavy hail. Everyone was watching and giving to the telethon and the griefs were big business. The Helbrose toteboard could barely keep up. The griefs were pandemic. There was a perspiration of griefs, tears like a sad grease. He watched the telethon from his bed and was catching the griefs, coming down with the griefs, contaged, indisposed with sentiment.

Cornell Messenger watched the telethon almost every year. He had been with Jerry for seven or eight telethons now. He knew when Lewis would take off his bowtie, he knew when he would cry. I know when *I* will, Messenger thought.

It was astonishing how much money was being raised. He was positive all the other channels were dark. It was Labor Day weekend, but he was certain that even those off on picnics had seen some of it, that almost everyone had been touched, that this year's campaign would beat all the others. He expected Frank Sinatra to bring Dean Martin on the show any minute now. He expected everyone to forgive his enemies, that there would be no enemies left. We are in armistice, Messenger thought. Truce is legion, all hearts reconciled in the warm bathwater of the griefs.

During the cutaway to the local station he watched the children swarm in the shopping center. They told their names to the Weather Lady and emptied their jars and oatmeal boxes and coffee cans of cash into great plastic fishbowls.

The sums were staggering. Two grand from the firemen in Red Bud, Illinois. Who challenged the firefighters of Mascoutah and Belleville and Alton and Edwardsville. This local challenged that local, waitresses and cab drivers challenged other waitresses and cab drivers to turn over their tips. He suspected that whores were turning tricks for muscular dystrophy.

He saw what was happening in the bi-state area and multiplied that by what must be going on in the rest of the country. They would probably make it—the twenty-five million Ed McMahon had predicted the telethon would take in. But there were only a few hours left. Would MD be licked in the poster kid's lifetime?

Messenger didn't know what he thought of Jerry Lewis. He suspected he was pretty thin-skinned, that he took seriously his critics' charges that he'd made his fortune mimicking crippled children, that for him the telethon was only a sort of furious penance. It was as if —watch this now, this is tricky, he thought—the Juggler of Our Lady, miming the prelapsarian absence of ordinary gravity, had come true, as everything was always coming true, the most current event incipient in the ancient, sleazy biologic sprawl. Something like that.

I guess he's okay, Messenger thought. If only he would stop referring to them as *his* kids. He doesn't have to do that. Maybe he doesn't know.

Jerry sweats griefs. His mood swings are terrific. He *toomels* and scolds, goes from the most calculated sincerity to the most abandoned woe. A guy who says he's the head of the Las Vegas sanitation workers presents him with a check for twenty-seven thousand bucks and he thanks him, crying. Then, sober again, he *davvens* his own introduction. The lights go down and when the spotlight finds him he's on a stool, singing "Seeing My Kids." It's a wonderful song, powerful and sad. The music's better than the lyrics but that's all right. The griefs are in it. The griefs are stunning, wonderful, thrilling. I'm sold, Messenger thought, and called for a kid to fetch his wallet from downstairs.

He'll phone in his pledge in front of the kid who brings his wallet up first, reading the numbers off his Master Card. He is setting an example. The example is that no one must ever be turned down.

He is surprised. He's been watching the telethon for almost nine hours now, and in all that time the St. Louis number has been super-imposed on the bottom of the screen, alternating with the numbers of other communities in the bi-state area, but he still doesn't know it and has to wait until the roster of towns completes itself and the St. Louis number comes back on. He cannot read the number on the screen and calls from across the room to ask the kid to do it, first telling the thirteen-year-old boy what to look for.

"S?" Harve says uncertainly, "T? L?"

"No, Harve, the number. You're spelling St. Louis. The number's what we want here. Jeanne, help him."

His kid sister whispers the number to him and Harve brokenly begins to relay it back to Messenger, checking the numbers she gives him against those he can find on the screen. Then the number goes off and Harve calls out numbers indiscriminately. He gives Messenger an Illinois exchange.

"Damn it, Jeanne, *you* give me the number."

The delay has cost muscular dystrophy ten bucks. Grief leaks through Messenger's inconvenience. A cure for this scourge will forever be ten dollars behind itself.

The announcer is complaining that less than half the phones are ringing, that Kansas City, with less population, has already pledged forty thousand dollars more than St. Louis. Not that it's a contest, he says, the important thing is to get the job done, but he won't put his jacket on until we go over the top. It doesn't make any difference what happens nationally, we don't meet our goal he won't wear his jacket. He's referring to a spectacularly loud jacket he wears only during MD campaigns. Messenger, who's been with the telethon years, wants to see him put it on. It's a dumb ploy. Messenger knows this. So unprofessional that just by itself it explains why he's in St. Louis and Ed McMahon is out there in Vegas with Jerry and Frank and Dean, but no form of Show Business is alien to him and Messenger hopes he gets to see the announcer put on his sports coat.

His grown son picks up an extension. "Get off," Messenger says, "I'm making a call."

"This will take a minute."

"So will this. Get off."

"Jesus."

Why don't they answer? He carries the phone as far as it will reach and sits down on the bed. It's true. Most of the volunteers have nothing to do. They know the camera is on them, and those who aren't actually speaking to callers try to look busy. They stare at the phones, make notes on pieces of paper. His son picks up the phone again, replaces it fiercely.

"Do you want to break the damn thing?" Messenger shouts. "What's wrong with you?"

There are three banks of telephones, eight volunteers in each bank. Though he's never seen one, they remind him of a grand jury. The phone has rung perhaps twenty times.

"Jeanne, did you give me the right number?"

"727-2700."

It's on the screen. Messenger hangs up and dials again. This time someone answers on the third ring.

"The bitch gave you the wrong number," Harve says.

"I did *not,*" Jeanne says.

"That's baloney-o. That's shit," Harve says.

"Please," Messenger says.

He says his name to the volunteer and gives his address. Speaking slowly and clearly, he reads the dozen or so numbers off his charge card. He volunteers its expiration date, his voice low with dignity and reserve, the voice of a man with eleven months to go on his Master Card.

"Are you going to give them three million dollars, Daddy?" Harve asks. Messenger frowns at him.

"What do you want to pledge, sir?"

"Twenty dollars," he says, splitting the difference between anger and conscience.

"Challenge your friends," his daughter says. "Challenge the English department. Challenge everyone left-handed. Make her wave, Daddy."

What the hell, he asks if she will wave to his daughter and, remarkably, from the very center of the volunteers, a hand actually shoots up.

"Ooh," Jeanne says, "she's pretty."

"Dumbshit thinks she can see us," Harve says. "Can she, Daddy?"

"Are you almost through?" his other son asks on the extension. "Mike wants me to find out when the movie starts."

"Goddamn it," Messenger roars into the phone.

"Will the little boys walk now?" Harve asks. "Will they run and read?"

"Tell your brother I'm off the phone."

Harve hangs back. "What if there's a fire? How would the crippled children excape from a fire?"

"*Es*cape, Harve," Messenger says.

"*Ex*cape," Harve says.

"There's not going to be any fire. Stop thinking about fire." The griefs were all about. The griefs were leaking. Harve's third-degree-burned by them.

"They should take all the money and get the cripples fire stingishers."

"Cut it out. Stop with the fucking fire shit."

"They should."

"Do what I tell you!"

His son leaves the bedroom, his fine blond hair suddenly incendiary as it catches the light from the window.

The horror, the horror, he thinks absently.

Once he's phoned in his pledge he loses interest. It's what always happens, but he takes a last look at the telethon before he dresses. The entertainers sweated griefs and plugged records. It was all right. Messenger forgave them. This was only the world.

Of course they'd reach their goal, Messenger thought. Everybody was watching the telethon. Besides, the fix was in. Eleventh-hour operetta was ready to put them over the top. Soft drink, ballpoint pen, timepiece, fast food, twenty-four-hour Mom and Pop shops, roller skating and dancing school cartels were already in the wings. An afflicted airlines executive and a backyard carnival representative stood by. Why, his own kids had dropped three or four bucks at a neighbor kid's carnival two months before. Then what was the telethon for anyway? TV time that Messenger's twenty bucks and the fifty or sixty the kids had raised and the perhaps half-dozen million or so of other private grievers all across the country might not even cover, make up? What *was* it for?

Why, the griefs, the griefs, of course—— remotest mourning's thrill-a-minute patriotics, its brazen, spectacular top hat, high-strutting, rim shot sympathies.

Cornell was high. For three years now it was the only way he would see people. His friends knew he smoked grass, as they thought they knew—as even his acquaintances and some of his students did —almost everything about him. He was contemptuous of whatever quality it was, not sincerity, not candor, not even truthfulness finally, that compelled his arias and put his words in his mouth. It was as if he had felt obliged to take the stand from the time he had first learned to talk, there to sing, turn state's evidence, endlessly offer testimony, information, confession, proofs, an eyewitness to his own life who badgered his juries not only with the facts but with the hearsay too.

"Anybody see the telethon?" he asked the group around the pool. "I pledged twenty dollars. I was going to give twenty-five but at the last minute I welched because I got sore at my kids."

They were his closest friends. One—Audrey—was having a nervous breakdown and cringed like a monkey in the shade of a big sun umbrella that bloomed from a hole in Losey's summer furniture. Losey was the proprietor of this big house with its flourish of rose and sculpture gardens, tennis court, swimming pool, potting sheds, patio, and large paved area outside the garage like the parking lot at an Italian restaurant. There was even a dish antenna on the grounds like a giant mushroom. Losey was having an affair and had hinted he might even be in love. Nora Pat, Losey's wife, was a second-year architecture student in the university and was probably going to flunk out. Thirty-one years old and the wife of a successful surgeon, she was on academic probation. Messenger's wife, Paula, had her own sensible troubles. Victor Binder, Audrey's husband, did. What the hell, they all did, some of them with griefs so bad they had had to stay home.

There was a blight on their lives even (speaking for himself, as he would, did) unto the next generation. He preferred not to think about it. He preferred to be high. He preferred television, movies, music. (He had bought quad, which had never caught on—the griefs, the griefs—and albums were piled high on each of his four speakers. They could have been mistaken for the collection of a teenager.) What he really preferred was watching the news high, welcoming public crisis, absorbed by all the terrorism and confrontations, obsessed as a president by interest rates, inflation, unemployment, living from one "Washington Week in Review" and "Meet the Press" and "Face the Nation" to the next, from one "Issues and Answers" to its sequel; "NBC Nightly News" the best half-hour of his day, "Sixty Minutes" the best hour of his week. He was burned out, at forty-five reconciled to death.

Though only Judith was actually dying.

Judith Glazer had pancreatic cancer. She was the only person Messenger had ever known with six months to live, the only one who had ever had to listen to such a pronouncement. He had known others with cancer, fated as Judith Glazer, but their cases, though terminal, had been open-ended. Some lived years, some were still alive. Only Judith's life was timed. That this should be so struck Messenger as extraordinary. "There is," he'd said, "a cancer on her cancer," and he did what ordinarily he would not have done when a friend was ill. He paid a call, the high seriousness and formality of the occasion so strange to him that he did not go high, visiting as callers must have done in old times, with the sense that he went gloved, hatted, walking-stick'd. As one might go to a salon, or visit a duchess. Bearing no gift save his presence, offering the sober ceremony of his conversation and hoping he was up to it, that Judith would feel them both under some superior obligation and not fuck around with him. Not acting, behaving certainly but not in the least acting, he on his part stripping himself, for all that he felt himself diplomatically dressed, prime ministerially encumbered, of all airs.

Paula went with him. Even without a strategy worked out between them beforehand, they had both chosen their garments—it was September, the woman would be dead by the end of February—with great care, as if they were going to an afternoon wedding, flown to some city three or four hundred miles distant, come not from their home but from a good motel near the airport, say, all dressed up after their morning poolside, their breakfast things still on the ground-level patio outside their room. It might have been a wedding, it might have been an anniversary luncheon. It could have been a funeral.

They had not been good friends. Judith had always been too testy for Messenger, something vestigially about her not so much mad—she'd been institutionalized for years before Cornell had ever met her—as angry, the anger a sort of prerogative clung to, even cherished, Messenger supposed, from the days when she'd been wacky, and he still didn't understand her flash points, the vagrant, moving lesions of her multitudinous grudges. To disagree with her, even about a movie, was to risk the challenge of her wrath or, what was worse, to hurt her feelings. He had never outright told her that she was a pain in the ass, and that was how they got along. That was how even her husband, Sam, got along with her, humoring her fidget convictions.

So, though Messenger genuinely liked her, he had never been comfortable with her, had never adjusted to her own impatience with herself, her modest, willful withdrawals inside her muu-muus when she felt herself too fat, all her tense temperance. My God, he'd thought on more than one occasion, I treat her exactly the way Sam does, and, indeed, it *was* as if they were married. He'd imagined himself married to the woman, a fantasy never indulged with friends' wives—and there were many, or used to be, till they got too old—who actually turned him on.

Now, near the start of her precious six months, she surprised them all. (He hadn't yet seen her. She'd returned only recently from her devastating tests at the hospital.) Report had it she had become gracious, solicitous, a hostess of last resort. Having taken herself seriously all her life, she would, he supposed, treat her last months on earth with all the composure—whatever lingered of her madness was a sort of composure, a kind of sky-high deportment grander than Messenger's in his Sunday best—of which she or any other terminal human being was capable. It was—Cornell knew he was wrong to feel this way—Sam who had most of his sympathy, and not only because his wife was dying. He had it because in Sam's place Messenger would have felt put upon, outraged even, the duties of nursing become a sort of horrible, ultimate housekeeping he could not have held up under. Bedclothes, laundry, picking up children, taking them to lessons, preparing meals, even paying bills—— these were things Messenger would not or could not do. He did not condone his sloth. Detail crippled him. Errand raised him to rage, then reduced him to tears. He was overwhelmed by such things, a man content only with contentment, truly happy only when others, too, were at leisure, made nervous even as a guest if his host was not as comfortably seated as himself. He was a summer soldier, a sunshine patriot, a good time Charlie.

So they had called and been given a time for their audience. (Visits as such were forbidden. Always formal, punctilious about their hospitality, mixing their guests with the scruples of pharmacists, Judith and Sam had in misfortune become tyrants of timing.) They parked their car and walked up to "The Cottage." (The Glazers' home seemed exactly what it was called on the sign above its small screened porch at the side, the only house in this neighborhood of $100,000 to $125,000 homes—their inflated values—to have a name. There was something vaguely European about it, or British—— its brown wood-work, the flowered wallpaper in its living and dining rooms.) Though it was no smaller than the homes surrounding it, it seemed so. There were pebbles beside the walk leading to the front door, bushes growing in the center of the lawn, great cement urns beside the steps which dwarfed the tiny flowers they contained, making them look, for all their color, like so many cigarette butts or discarded gum wrappers. Inside, the rooms were ugly, the sofa and chairs protected from their two elderly dogs by thin blankets. The Oriental rugs were threadbare, the stuffed chairs deflated. One wouldn't have guessed Judith an heiress, her husband the head of his department.

Messenger rang the doorbell, annoyed as always by the "Operation Ident" decal on the window of the front door. Thieves were warned that all objects of value had been "etched for ready identification purposes by the appropriate law enforcement agencies." That meant the stereo and Sam's expensive camera equipment, purchased at discount in duty-free shops in the Middle East when the Glazers had spent a year abroad. (They had gone around the world and their house was tricked out like the gift shops of selected international airports.)

Sam opened the door, looking, as always, confused by visitors. "Oh," he said, "hi. Judith's on the phone. All right, come in." He seemed feverish to Messenger, the eyes in his youthful face—he was seven years older than Cornell but looked ten years younger—lustrous with mucus. "The phone company put in a special phone with hold buttons. Judith gets so many calls we really need it. Now if someone calls while she's talking, she gets a signal that there's a second call on the line. All she has to do is excuse herself, put the first person on hold and take the message from the new caller. It works just like the phone in my office."

"Who shines your eyes, Sam?"

"What? Oh, yeah. I haven't been getting much sleep. Judy? Honey? Here are the Messengers come to see you."

The woman waved at them to sit. Messenger waited while Sam chased the dogs from the chairs. Judith Glazer chatted amiably on the telephone, her skin as jaundiced as her blond hair. Sam had disappeared.

Messenger had the impression she was performing for them, dragging the call out till someone else rang up so she might demonstrate the complexities of the new phone. She prattled about third parties, alluding to people Messenger had never heard of, would never meet. Her speech was for Sam too, he thought, off and busy somewhere in the house, her voice raised theatrically, its octaves just beyond her vision. She spoke with all the authority of her doom, arranging with only a minimum of consultation all the car pools of ordinary life. She spoke not as if she were not going to die before the winter was out, but as if she was never going to die.

Sam returned with the glass cylinder from a blender. It was filled with some sort of pinkish malted. He poured out the thick pink liquid for his wife and set the cylinder down on a community newspaper.

Messenger noticed that the yellow hold button was lighted. "If we're interrupting—— " he said.

Judith shook her head, her strawberry mustache like a third lip. "Sit still," she said. "Talk to Sam. Comfort Sam."

Sam smiled. "People have been wonderful," he said. "Judy's lining up next week's dinners."

"Next week's dinners?" Paula said.

"They bring casseroles, roasts, full-course meals. Bunny Fletcher's coming over later to barbecue steaks for us."

"What a way to go," Messenger said comfortingly.

"It's a picnic," Sam said.

"We heard about it when we were still in Vermont," Paula said. "Bill Richards told us."

"What else did the provost say?"

Paula shook her hands helplessly, lowered her voice. "He told us about the prognosis. I'm sorry, Sam."

Sam shrugged. "Bill's been super. He stayed with me in Judy's room during the exploratory. Adrian was there, too." He looked down at his fingernails. "When the surgeon told me what they'd found, Adrian held my hand. How do you like that? He just took my hand and held it. When we got to the restaurant the chancellor was already there, waiting for us. Bill must have phoned him, or Adrian. Anyway, there he was, waiting for us. He still had jet lag. He and Bunny had just flown in from London that day."

"Who picked up the check," Messenger asked deliberately, "dean, provost, or chancellor?"

Sam laughed. "Life goes on," he said.

"What's going on?" Judith said, her phone call ended. "Why am I missing all the fun?"

"'Cause you've got cancer," Messenger said, stripped of diplomatic status and settling for bad taste in this house of bad taste where *Consumer Reports* lay on the surfaces of the furniture like coffeetable books. Sam's meanness was famous. Even Judith, who came from money, an heiress who would never now collect her birthright, whose great expectations had been shut down by the doctors and who, though her wealthy, highborn, Episcopal parent be struck dead that afternoon or catch the lightning in his hair, would never live through probate, joined in this joke on Sam. Who brooked no criticism of him, whose trigger-happy anger was always at his disposal, always in his defense, as much a species of big brother to him as wife, permitting no slight to her slight Jew and going along not so much dutifully as obediently with all Sam's bargains and schemes, all his duty-free, marked-down, consumer-reported *tchatchkies* and appliances, his Sam Goody records and bulk film, his examination copies and suits by Seconds—and Sam a clotheshorse—and international flights by mysterious charter clubs and groceries from a co-op some assistant professors and grad students had founded, his order actually smuggled into their kitchen by some eligible TA. Why she even *enjoyed* his fabled economies, the fabled part anyway, encouraging them, Messenger supposed, as a harmless outlet for an anti-Semitism she had been unwilling entirely to surrender, writing them off as a cute trait of her clever Yid, much, he hoped—*oh,* how he hoped, his sense of propriety in the balance now—as she accepted the hold buttons on her telephone and the command performance dinners and her jaundiced skin the color of Valium, and her cancer.

"I never," she said, "objected to your bad taste, Cornell. It only matters that you love me." And she waited for his declaration.

"Of course I love you," Messenger said, the heat on.

"All right," Judith said, swallowing malted, refilling her glass from the cylinder, extending the glass. "Drink," she said, "it's delicious. There's no medicine in it. It's only a strawberry malt. I take it to fatten me up for when I start my chemotherapy on Thursday. Will you drink from my glass?"

"I'm already fattened up," Messenger said.

"Maybe the Messengers would like to hear our news," Sam said, suggested.

"They may hear our news when they have broken malted with us. They may hear our news when they have sipped from the glass touched by my pancreatically cancered lips."

"Sure, Judith. Gimme," Messenger said.

"Here," she said.

He downed all the malted. "Gee, Judy," he said, "there's nothing left for you."

"The news, of course, is that I'm dying. Well, that's *my* news. People are so embarrassed by other people's deaths that I've drawn up a sort of list—— 'Everything You Always Wanted to Know About Judith Glazer's Death But Were Afraid to Ask.'

"First. The girls know. I told them as soon as I learned the results of the operation. Milly doesn't accept it yet, I think. I mean she doesn't believe it will happen. That's unusual, because of the two she's the more mature, though she's younger than Mary. We told the two of them together. Mary's the one who cried. Now she wets the bed and goes around stinking of urine. Well, I understand rage. It's always been one of my subjects. But she's twelve years old and almost six feet tall and she won't change her underwear and goes about soiled and —— "

"Look," Messenger said.

"Oh, you're just like Milly, aren't you? Isn't he just like Milly, Sam? He doesn't want to know. He doesn't accept things."

"I accept things."

"No," Judith Glazer said, "if you don't want to know you can't accept things. Oh. You're embarrassed. For all your tough talk, you're embarrassed, gun-shy. There's hope for you. Shyness is a kind of love, too. Like chugalugging from the cancer cup."

"Come on, Judith," Messenger said, "cut it out."

"Standing up to me is. It's all right. If I bring you these messages from the deathbed it's not because I want to rub your nose in things you aren't up to, but because I love you, too, Cornell. I never loved Paula. Paula, I'm sorry but it's true. Perhaps I will now, I can't be sure. I shall certainly have to try. You, for your part, Paula, you shall have to try, too."

"I'll try," Paula said.

"Do. Please do," the woman said, and went on. "Have I told you about the girls? My medication's wearing off, my pain confuses me. Where was I? Oh, yes, the girls."

"If you're tired, sweetheart," Sam said.

"I have cancer, not fatigue. Try not, please, to be humiliated by me. You never were before. All those years I was crazy. Stand by me now. These are the facts, pet, this is the way I wet *my* bed. Humor your horrible wife." She had been lying on the sofa. Now she sat up, her housecoat parted and her nightgown hiked. Messenger saw her bald, prepped groin and looked away. "I shall make a family man of him yet. I've barely more than five months, but we're well begun. Oh, yes, we make furious love."

"Sweetheart, I don't think the Messengers . . ."

"Of course they are," she said, "but even if they aren't . . . As long as I have strength to speak and warn I shall use that strength to speak and warn. There's grime in even the purest death, things the clearest-headed among us wouldn't expect. Well, the children are an example, aren't they? Oafish Mary and tender Milly. Their grandfather and uncle try to turn their heads, to bribe their attentions away from truth. The fact is they're quite successful. They are. My girls will remember their mother's passing as a shower of gold. Tennis and swimming and private lessons. Golf and horseback riding and dinners at the club—— all lovely summer's fine rare prizes. They're going to the academy this year. Daddy's paying their tuition. I don't mind. It's hard for kids. Milly doesn't believe me and Mary pees her bed.

"But I haven't told you yet how we do it. The stitches and pain and my cancer shining through my skin like sunlight. How does he get it up, do you think?"

Sam got it up and left the room. He went through the small dining room into the kitchen.

"Poor Sam," his wife said. "I won't talk behind his back, only out of his line of sight. He hears me now. You hear me now, don't you, Sam? You're listening to all this, aren't you?"

"Yes," Sam said, his voice fainted by the intervening rooms.

She lowered her own voice. "How does he get a hard-on? He *wills* it. It's his decision. Why, it's no more trouble to him than acquiring a tan or arranging his hair. It's biofeedback, Sammy's sex. Decisive grooming, like the way his pants hold a crease or the fact that his hands don't get dirty. And there's no weight. Our skins barely touch. Platonic fucking. Orgasms like something shuttled back and forth in a game. Because he never comes until I do." She was speaking normally again. "You don't come till I do, do you, Sam?"

"I'm a gent," Sam said in the kitchen. "I'm something in armor, something in tails." He was crying.

"Baby, don't cry," Judith said. "Hush, courtly lover." And he hushed. "Bring me a pill, Sam." They heard the faucet in the kitchen. Sam appeared with a pill and a glass of water. "See?" Judith said. "Thanks, darling." She turned to the Messengers. "See? My last few months like a sort of pregnancy. See? Judith lying-in with doom and whim and old Sam hard by all hand and foot to fetch all the pickles of the grotesque, we never close.

"Sam, Sam, you Jew, you Jewish husband. Shall we tell them our news?"

"We've told them everything else."

"No," she said, "no we haven't." She turned to Paula. "Once, maybe two or three years ago, we gave a party. Cornell brought the ice, do you remember? Sam had called at the last minute to ask one of those gee-it-must-have-slipped-my-mind favors of his. Though we know better, don't we, know that nothing ever *slips* Sam's mind, that his mind goes around in galoshes and snow tires, radials, chains, and Cornell was high, stoned, and I'd been talking about TM, and your husband asked me to tell him my mantra. Do you remember that? Do you, Cornell?"

"I think so," Messenger said. "Yes."

"Yes," Judith Glazer said. "And I wouldn't tell you. Well I'll tell you now. Lean toward me, I'll whisper it."

"I was kidding, Judith. I don't have to know."

"Suppose what I tell you were my last words? Not have to know what may be a poor dying woman's dying wish?"

Messenger looked helplessly at his wife. She was already packed, checked out of the motel, all gone. He looked at Sam, similarly fled, browsing inside info on cordless telephones in *Consumer Reports*.

Messenger got out of his chair and went toward the poor dying woman. He knelt at her side and she blew softly in his ear as if testing a microphone. Then she whispered four senseless syllables into it which he would never forget. He felt himself blush.

"An obscenity?" Paula suggested.

"My mantra," Judith Glazer said. "There. I feel better. Only Cornell and my guru know. I can give it away because I don't need it anymore. You, Sam. I just gave away my three-thousand-dollar mantra to Cornell." She smiled and Cornell felt something like affection for the nutty lady. "I'm dying," she said jovially, "and going to Heaven where I can look down on Sam. Only I may look down on Sam, you know. I earned the privilege by living with him, earned it at discount, the odor of his odd-lot, uncut, 35mm film on my breasts when he came to me from the darkroom where he cut and rolled it onto used cartridges, the cutting and winding done at midnight in closets so that we didn't have the expense of even that single low-watt dim red bulb. I'm going to Heaven where I can look down on Sam, on his thick soft bundles of hair, Sam's plateaus of head like actual geography, and let him know if he's fucking up as dean. That's *our* news. Sam's to be appointed dean when Adrian steps down at the end of the semester."

"Under the circumstances," Paula said, "I'm not certain congratulations are entirely in order."

"Oh yes," Judith said, "of course they are. I'm going to Heaven and Sam's going to the Administration Building."

She seemed actually gay, her jaundice a kind of radiance. She *was* gay, even her crazy close-order drill less irritating than it could have been. There was a sort of warmth and comradeship in their edgy intimacy. There was a kind of truth in truth, Cornell thought. "How do you know you're going to Heaven?" he asked.

"My rector thinks so, all the church ladies do. Besides," she said, "the Bible tells me so." She grinned. "Well," she said, "if you can't put your friends through it, what good are they anyway? I've put you people through it this afternoon. You're good sports. Once in a while you weren't even humoring me. You deserve a reward."

"I couldn't touch another malted," Messenger said.

"No," she said, "no more malteds. You know," she said, "these are still the good times. No one's ever paid this much attention to me. Not even when I was mad. But now, in the springtime of my death, when the pain is still manageable and discomfort's only the mildest death duty, easily paid, easily confused with convalescence even; now, when my weight is down and I look as I used to as a girl, better really, for I was crazed then and had on me the stretch marks of my terror, now it's all easy and there are hold buttons on my telephones and people bring us their covered chafing dishes and best recipes all made up and ready to go like take-out or room service and there's nothing to do but visit with my girls when they come in all tan from the club, scrubbed as princesses, and I've time and inclination to answer all their questions, posing others that they dare not ask, stuffing them like French geese with hope and love, it's not so bad.

"I've no recriminations, none at all.

"But dying's like the marathon, I think. There's no way to go the distance till you've gone it. And sooner or later you hit the wall and whimper if you cannot scream. I seem a saint and so far think I am one.

"Listen, everyone. I make this pledge to you. There will be no trips to Mexico for Laetrile, and I'll never call out for any other of those fast-food fixes of the hopeful doomed. Neither will I be wired to any of those medical busy-boxes to extend for one damned minute what only a fool would call my life. If Jesus wants me He can have me. To tell you the truth, He can probably use me.

"Now, Cornell, I want a favor."

"Of course, Judith," Messenger said, "if there's anything I can do."

"I want you to take over my Meals-on-Wheels route."

4

Because he knew Coule's type. Recognized retrospectively the solid, bulldog centers of gravity of his kind, his big-bodied, full-bellied, hard-handed, heavy-hammed, iron-armed, thick-throated, barrel-chested lineman likenesses and congeners. Not overgrown, like giants, say, such men did not, or so it seemed to Mills, even *possess* glands, lacking not a pituitary so much as the space for one, mass not a function of secretions, of body-buried wells of the cellular juices splashed and splattered indiscriminately throughout the skeletal sluices of their frames, nothing endocrinic, hormonal, for there could have been no more room for these, or for organs either, than there was for glands, their insides pure prime meat, human steak all the way through, gristled perhaps and marbled possibly and certainly scaffolded with bone, but nothing liquid to account for size, and even their blood only for coloring, flesh tones, flush; their pee and excrement, too, merely variants of their blood's limited palette, affected by the air perhaps, the light, like exposed film. So nothing leviathan in their genes—he'd seen their parents, their brothers and sisters like the law of averages—their physical displacement a kind of decision, the ukase of their boom town wills, their realtor reality. And many *were* realtors, or at least landlords. It would have been difficult not to be in the Florida of the thirties, even though this wasn't Miami or even Tampa or Jacksonville, even though it wasn't anywhere oceaned, beached, or even, particularly, mild.

It was Cassadaga, and except for the fact that George knew they had come south, that he and his mother and father had changed their lives and been translated to a state called Florida—he had no memory of how they'd gotten there, probably some of the way by bus, some by hitchhiking—where his father meant to pick oranges, become a migrant worker, it could have been not Milwaukee, since Milwaukee was a city of some size and Cassadaga was barely a town, but some residential neighborhood in Milwaukee. Stucco might never have been invented or Florida so new it had not yet become indigenous there, its properties undiscovered, it no more occurring to the other Easterners and Midwesterners to mix cement and sand and hydrated lime to make their homes than to build them out of thatch. So the houses were wooden as the trees, the ordinary oaks and elms and maples of any Iowa or Wisconsin yard or street. And perhaps that's why he had no memory of how they'd gotten there (he'd seen no sea, no gulls or beach), because the landscape was the same he'd lived in all his nontropical, Tropic of Cancer life, along the bland, unrainy seasoned peel of earth with its gray and temperate gifts of the to-scale regular.

He did not even know where the oranges would be, could be. There were no groves near Cassadaga, nothing citrus in the odor of the wind. He'd seen more fruit in Milwaukee. And no palm trees except for the one by the bench in the town's small square, its tall stem and leaves like an immense shredded umbrella.

"That's a tree?" he'd asked.

"Hell," his father said, "I don't know if it's even wood."

He pointed to its sky-high shells, shaggy, brown as bowel, clustered as cannonball or the cabbages in produce bins. "Are the oranges inside those things?"

"If they are you don't pick oranges, you climb them."

Because this is where they'd been dropped, the young men who'd given them the ride—it was their journey he couldn't recall, not their arrival—driving on toward Daytona Beach. "Looks nice and homey," one of them said. "You should be able to get a room here. Tomorrow you can walk the few yards to where the groves begin."

They had no luggage to speak of, only the single suitcase between them which contained not all their clothes but all the clothes which they still had, which they had not sold along with their furniture and dishes and odds and ends in order to get a nest egg together, a stake, to make the trip. Anyway, they had all the clothes which they believed they would need in the hot new climate to which they believed they had come—— socks, the three changes of boys' and men's and women's underwear, the two sets of overalls and denim workshirts, the two cotton dresses. They had not even brought handkerchiefs because they thought they had come to a place where no one caught cold. They had not brought anything dressy for Sundays. They were not religious and so wouldn't need anything for church. For Sundays and holidays there were the three brand new bathing suits in the brand new valise. The only other things in the grip were a change of sheets and pillowslips and a large box of laundry powder. They were ready to make their new life, traveling light as any three people could who had excised not only fall and winter from their lives but the very idea of temperature.

And so if Cassadaga looked homey—and it did—they looked, save for the single clue of the single suitcase, already at home.

"Look here," his father said. He was standing by an immense glass-enclosed hoarding at the entrance to the square. "It's the church directory. Just look at them all. Did you ever see so many? Maybe it ain't even Florida. Maybe we hitchhiked all the way to Rome."

"I don't *see* any churches," his mother told his father. "Seems in a town as tiny and churchy as this one you'd be able to spot at least one spire. Wouldn't you think so, George?"

"Maybe there's an ordinance against them. Maybe they only run the crosses up on Sundays, like flags on the Fourth of July."

"Oh, George," his mother said.

"Well," his father said, "we didn't come all this way to sightsee. And tomorrow we got to look for work. I think our best bet is to find somewhere we can get a place to sleep. You tired, George?"

"Yes, sir," George said.

They walked through the little town. Mills remembered it yet. It was a paradigm of neighborhood, not a town but a constituency, not a place but a vicinity, homogeneous as graveyard or forest or a field of wheat. There were no stores or gas stations, no public buildings, neither school nor library nor jailhouse—— whatever of municipality or commonwealth, canton, arrondissement, deme or nome, whatever of government itself centripetalized in the bench in the small square. There were no churches.

"I think it must be one of those suburbs," his father said.

"What of?" said his mother.

"I don't know," his father said. "Maybe the highway."

They passed several blocks of neat frame houses, not identical but all lawned, porched and porch-swing'd. Many had gardens, some narrow driveways that led to tiny garages that looked like scaled-down versions of the houses themselves.

They walked up a side street, turned south at the corner, went down that street and entered another side street. They turned at another corner. It was the same everywhere they walked. (He was carrying the suitcase now. It was that light.)

They came out of the town and were in open country.

"I think those houses must be the main crop around here."

"Oh, George," his mother said.

"Look there," his father said. He pointed to the open country. "They must already have harvested that part."

"Oh, George," his mother said. "You tired, honey?" she asked Mills.

"A little I guess," he said.

"Here. Give me that." She took the suitcase from him. "We better turn back, George. The kid's falling off his feet."

"Suits me," his father said, "but I didn't see signs for lodging, no folks either, if it comes to that."

"We'll just knock and ask if they have a room. Some of these houses must be where the ministers live."

(George had seen the owners' shingles nailed to their front doors like addresses or planted in their yards like For Sale signs, the saw-toothed, varnished boards suggestive of resorts, fishing lodges, summer camps, things Indian, rustic, though the names on them were almost defiantly white.)

"That's what I was thinking," his father said. "Give me the case. We'll just go back into town and ask if we can be put up for the night in some spare room of the parsonage. I don't expect they'd charge travelers and strangers too much if they at least looked like Christians."

"I don't remember how to say grace," his mother said.

"You can remember how to say amen," his father said. "Just fold your hands and try to look like you don't deserve what they feed you."

His father was not a bitter man. Like all the George Millses before him, he had known subsistence but rarely hardship, treading subsistence like deep water but never really frightened, comfortable enough in his own dubious element as steeplejacks or foretopmen in theirs. So the Depression was no real setback for him. Indeed, it had presented possibilities to him, an opening of options. He had all the skills of the unskilled, chopping, digging, fetching, a hewer and drawer of a man, not strong so much as knowledgeable about weight, knowing weight's hidden handholds the way a diamond cutter might know the directions and cleavage points of a gem merely by glancing at it. So it would not have been correct to say that the Depression had changed their lives or even that they had come south to seek their fortune. It would never have occurred to Mills that fortune could actually be sought. Fortune, if it had been his birthright ever to have more than he could use, would have sought him, it, She, Fortune, in his father's view, being a sort of custom tailor of the goddesses, like talent perhaps, who did all the really hard work. "I promise you we'll never starve," his father had told him once, "we'll never even go hungry. We won't freeze for want of shelter or die for lack of medicine. We're only low. We ain't down." So if they came to Florida to find employment it was because his father understood that there were chores in Florida too, that the menial was pretty much evenly distributed throughout the world, that Florida had its weight as well as Milwaukee—he'd shoveled coal there, been a janitor, collected garbage—its tasks and chores, odd jobs, stints, and shifts. "Our kind," he assured his son, "could find nigger work in Paradise. What, you think it isn't dirty here just because the sun is shining?"

So it was only a change of scene he'd wanted. And hadn't gotten yet. "Maybe we aren't close enough yet, maybe we're still too high up the slope of the world. Maybe we have to be where all you have to do is just nudge a stone with your shoe and it rolls all the way downhill to the equator. But whatever, I don't see no parrots in this neighborhood. I ain't spotted any alligators." (Because they'd been in Florida better than a day now, crossing from Dothan, Alabama, into Marianna, Florida, passing Tallahassee and Gainesville and Ocala and De Land, all of which could have been Northern towns except for the souvenirs in the gas stations and grocery stores—the toy 'gators and candies in the shape of oranges and grapefruits, the rubber tomahawks and Seminole jewelry, drinking glasses with scenes of St. Petersburg, Miami, Florida's keys, fishing tackle with deep-sea, heavy-duty line—where they bought his father's cigarettes and his mother the makings, the dry cereals and packaged breads and luncheon meats and quarts of milk, for their meals. There were suntan lotions on the drugstore shelves, cheap sunglasses on pasteboard cards. This is where his mother had bought their three new swimsuits. "It stands to reason," she'd said before they'd ever left Wisconsin, "bathing trunks have to be cheaper down there." And picked out the swimsuits in the first town they came to after they crossed the state line. "Sure," his father had said, still good-humored, "maybe we should never have got George that cloth alligator when we were still up North. I think we made a mistake there. That stands to reason too. A cloth souvenir toy doll lizard should cost a lot less money in some grocery store near the swamps where there ain't no call for pretend alligators because there's the real thing snapping at your toes no further off than the distance of your own height.") But still good mooded, the absence of physical evidence that they were there still within the acceptable limits of credulity. It was only late summer. They would have to wait months yet before they would get the benefit of the hot winter weather, before they would have any reason to wonder where the snow was, where the ice. His father's mild complaint about the where-abouts of the strange birds and animals only the teasing echo of his own kid questions and alerted suspicions. He was obviously enjoying himself, the twelve-hundred-mile journey they had already come itself a vacation. He was having a good time, his temper was sweet, he was feeling fine, even the queer, beachless, ungoverned and, for all they knew, spare-roomless town a pleasant curiosity. His father, all of them, were happy.

Then they saw the chain gang.

It was policing the small square where the bench and palm tree were.

Two guards with rifles slouched along on either side of the line of convicts as they moved across the square picking up cigarette butts, Coca-Cola bottles, the feeble litter of the lightly trafficked park. A third guard sat on the bench watching the prisoners as one might casually watch a ball game played by children, his arms embracing the back of the bench, his rifle balanced against his crotch.

The convicts were actually chained at the legs, the chains drawn so close the men were almost shoulder to shoulder like men on parade. They took small steps like Chinese house servants or young girls in heels. With their backs to them, the thick white and black horizontals of their uniforms seemed a single broad fabric like a wide flag flapping. They looked like staves on sheet music.

George and his mother followed his father to the guard on the bench.

"How do you do?" his father said.

"Are there real bullets in that?" George Mills asked.

"They're shells, son. Bullets is in handguns."

"My boy never saw a chain gang," his father said. "We're from up North."

"Up North they lock folks up," the guard said. "Here they get to go outdoors."

"What did these men do?" his father said.

"All different things," the guard said. "Murders and armed robberies. Rapes. Different things."

"Murders," his son said. "Gee, they're not even very big."

"Size got nothing to do with it, son. Big men can get what they want without killing people."

"See what can happen, George?" Mills said. "See what they do to you if you grow up wild? Officer, would you mind if we had a word with these men?" His father winked at the guard.

The guard looked at George and returned his father's wink. His mother said nothing.

"These shells is real, son," he said, and tapped the chamber of his rifle. "They call 'em shells 'cause they're so big. They're bigger than bullets. You get hit with a shell you never get better. You go along with your dad. You listen to what these cons tell you." The man stood up and blew two shrill blasts on a whistle that hung from his neck. The convicts stopped where they were and came to a sort of attention. "Gary and Henry," he called out to the other two guards, "these folks is from up North and got a little boy with them who don't always mind." He accompanied Mills and his son to the rank of convicts.

"Tell the kid how old you was when you come to us, Frizzer," the man said.

Before Frizzer could answer, George's father did an astonishing thing. He took his hat from his head and held it in his hands in exactly the attitude of supplication George had seen hobos employ when they came to his mother's door in Milwaukee. Status seemed instantly altered, perspective did, his father exchanging actual inches and pounds with the prisoner. There was something religious, even pious about the gesture. It startled George, it startled them all, the prisoners literally moved, forced back, their chains scraping in a sharp, brief, metallic skirl.

"It's true what your captain says. We're Northerners. Hard times forced us south. There's no work up there no more. We come for the sunshine. To catch fish from the water. My boy ain't had no nourishment in two days. His ma is pregnant. If you got some candy, the sugar in gum . . . If you could let them drink off the last sweetness in those soda bottles you picked up from the ground. If you could—— "

"Wait a minute, hey," the guard said who had told them about the shells.

"If you saved something from your lunch—— "

"Hold on there. What—— "

"My boy ain't had nothing in his mouth these two days, my wife's been hungry three. Flowers we eat, the crusts from peanut butter and jelly sandwiches from other folks' picnics in the public parks."

"Now just a golden goddamn min—— "

"I guess I don't need this fruit," the convict Frizzer said, and produced an orange from where it had been stored in his blouse.

"Me neither," said another con and handed over a second orange, placing it beside Frizzer's in his father's upturned hat.

"I ain't hungry," said a third man, handing his orange to the boy.

"What the *hell!*" the guard shouted.

"Thank you," his father said. "God bless you. God bless you, men. God bless you," his father said, still like the hobo, dispensing love's holy wampum, and hurried his wife and son from the square. They disappeared up a street.

"But we all had sandwiches and milk two hours ago," George said.

"Son of a bitch," his father said. "*Son of a bitch!*" He was furious, his size restored, not magnified, compact as a middleweight, coiled, latent with force and uppercut, like the clever laborer he was who took weight's measure, gravity's marksman.

"What is it? What's wrong?" his mother said.

"Working conditions!" his father roared. "The competition!" He turned and, as hard as he could, threw the two oranges he still carried back in the direction of the square. "The way they organize the labor around here! Evidently they got to arrest and chain you before they let you work in their parks or pick their oranges. Apparently you first got to kill a man, then arm-rob and rape him before they let you into their union! We might as well stay and get a good night's rest before we start back home in the morning."

It was getting on toward dusk. There were cars parked in the street now, two and sometimes three cars in each of the driveways, giving the town or neighborhood or whatever it was a vaguely prosperous look.

"Look at them," his father said, pointing to the houses, which

88

had now turned on their porch lights, "they're blind pigs. Or cat-houses. This must be where they apprentice their farmhands. What's that piano music?"

"Organ," his wife said.

When he was calmer he jabbed the doorbell of the first carless, unlighted house they came to.

"Reverend?" his father said to the large, powerfully built man who opened the door for them, the hearty, glandless and even organ-less type George would remember all his life (though he didn't know this yet and saw only a big old man who looked even bigger in the dark, loose flowing robe he wore like a dress, only not like a dress any woman would wear, and suddenly recalled the prisoners' strange garb, thinking, So it isn't the land or trees or animals or even the houses that's weird down here, it's the clothes; thinking, There ain't nothing in Mama's suitcase like anything they wear in Florida, Mama packed all wrong). "Reverend," his father said again. "Joe sent me, Reverend. My wife figures you have a spare room, but I figure it's more like a back room, so you can bring me and her a couple of beers and the boy a Coca-Cola."

"Why don't you set your case down?" the big man said. George had never heard a voice like it. Vocal cords could not have produced such clear, resonant sound, only hard, unflexed, lenient muscle. "Your boy's tired. He's falling asleep on his feet."

"We're all tired, Reverend," his father said. "Or maybe I should call you Foreman."

"Foreman?"

"Well, it's just that I've seen your work detail or day shift or whatever you call those chained, shotgun-trained fellows down by the square. I figured the bosses would have to have somewhere to sleep nights, too. Where they could rest their bodies and put down their rifles and jackboots. It would be pretty uncomfortable, fitting all them gun-toting foremen and overseers on just that one bitty bench. Ain't this the hotel?"

The man seemed bewildered. He turned to George. "Where have you come from?"

"Milwaukee," George said.

"Was it your brother or sister you lost?"

George looked to his father for help.

"Hey, you, watch it," his father said angrily.

"Which was it, Mother," the big man asked, "your son or your daughter?"

"I miscarried some years ago," his mother said. "A little girl." Her eyes were red.

"Had you named her yet? They're easier to locate if they had a name."

"She was born dead," his mother said.

"Of course," the man said, "but often a name's been picked out. Even if there were only one or two you were merely favoring. Were you going to call the child after a relative? Were you thinking of giving her your name?"

"Come on, Nancy," George Mills said. "We've made a mistake."

"Nancy," the man said sweetly. "She'd have been Nancy."

"Let's go." He picked up the suitcase and turned to leave.

"I preferred Janet," his mother said softly.

"Yes," he said. "Janet's a fine name."

"Let's go," Mills said, "let's just *go.*" But his wife was weeping now, his son had begun to sob. "Ah, for Christ's sake," his father said, setting the suitcase down again.

He was not crying for the stillborn sister whom he had seen only briefly in a blur of swaddling and whose name he had just heard for the first time, and not for his mother whose grief seemed to trigger his own, nor even for his suddenly confused, uncomfortable father. He wept as children in fairy tales did. It wasn't even grief. It was fear. How could he ever have supposed that there was no difference between where they were and where they'd come from? They were lost, all of them. They were missing persons.

He had little moral imagination. His sense of evil was circumscribed by his ideas about the wicked, what they could do to you, the harm in villains. Only the monstrous and disfigured. Not murderers and holdup men but murderers and holdup men hobbled and joined at the ankles—— some chain reaction of the irrational. Even their uniforms—the guards' as well as the convicts'—suggesting action in multiples, armies of bad men, familied, for all he knew actually related, blooded. (This would have been in the days of the Dillingers and Babyface Nelsons and Capones and others, gangs, clans, tribes, confederated in wickedness and villainy like the red savages he read about in books.) The town, the community itself, presented just such a face to him, its east-west axes like its north-south ones, the configuration of each block like that of its neighbor. All the churches—he knew they were churches now—advertised on the glass-encased hoarding and reverends—he knew there were reverends, men and maybe even women, too, like the dark-robed fellow who spoke of his dead sister, the two-year-buried little girl—in all the rectories, vicar-ages, and parsonages like the one they stood in.

"I said let's go," his father said. "I said let's get out of here."

"Before I've shown you your daughter?" the big man said. "Be-fore I've brought her back to speak to you?"

His father was holding the door open. "George?" he said. "Nancy?"

"Can't we just see her first, George?" his wife said.

"Can we?" his son asked. He had an idea she was somewhere in the house, the old man keeping her for them like shoes brought in for repair.

"Go on," the man told them gently. "I'm sorry," he said to his father. "It's near dark. If you leave now you can walk back to the highway while there's still some light left."

"How do you know one of those cars parked outside isn't mine?"

"You have no automobile."

"Sure we do. It's parked a few houses down."

"You have no machine," the old man said.

"You hear that, Nancy?" his father said shrewdly. "That's the man you'd let show you the child we lost. An old woman who ain't got nothing better to do than hide out behind his curtains and spy on folks."

"If you had an auto you'd have locked that suitcase in it."

"All right, Reverend," his father relented, "I guess you got me there. There's no car. But here's where I got you. We ain't got any money for your medicine show. We've put a little by for milk and bread and a buck or so for a clean kip once in a while till we get settled, but we failed to set anything aside for apparitions or haunt house card tricks, so unless you work free like those orange picker murderers, you might just as well lift the charm or spell off Nancy and the kid and let us all get going."

"A dollar?" the man said.

"Sure," his father said, "if you start acting like a proper landlord and just keep the tables from rapping so we can get some sleep. If the ouija boards are all put away and the sheets are fresh. I'll give you a dollar. What do you say, old Merlin?"

"Stay the night. I won't charge you."

"Here's your buck," his father said.

"I won't charge you."

"You ain't my uncle," his father said, pressing money into the man's hand.

"I invited you," he said.

"And I'm obliged to you," his father said, "but near as I can tell you're just some working stiff like me and George too will be someday if we can only just get him the proper sleep every so often. Don't worry about the money. You'd have taken that, and more too, I guess, if only we'd agreed to look into that crystal ball of yours."

"You think I'm a fake," the big man said, slipping the dollar his father had given him into a pocket in his robe.

"Well," his father said mildly, "at least a rotten businessman. I see lots more cars parked in front of them other congregations."

The big man made their bed up for them in what they did not know yet was the master bedroom. Then he went downstairs to his dimly lighted parlor, waiting, they supposed, for someone else to come to his door. Later, George Mills heard his heavy step on the stairs when he came up again to make up his cot and lie down in the small spare bedroom down the hall.

In fact, the loose dark robe was a sort of dressing gown, not Wickland's working clothes at all. These, like those of most of the psychics, parapsychologists, clairvoyants, and occultists in Cassadaga, were ordinary business suits, the customary browns and grays and faintly baggy wool garments of traveling salesmen or reporters, say—— vested, fobbed, long and thickly flied. He was given to brightly colored sleeve garters. Otherwise his clothing was sober, the color of fedoras or suits in snapshots. Nor was there much in the way of paraphernalia about the house, little of the gear George or his parents might have expected. Though they were to see this stuff too, plenty of it, during their long sojourn in the queer town, George, before Wickland found other uses for him, a sort of errand boy, as the only kid in town a community asset, his services on call, available to everyone, all of them, like the Fire Department they did not have or the doctor they did not need.

Meanwhile his father found work, underbidding the prison officials for the contract on the town's small square and streets. He did other things too of course, driving one or another of the spiritualists' cars the fifteen miles into De Land each day—where the circus had its winter quarters—to pick up their mail at the PO boxes they rented there, mailing the parcels and pamphlets they sent out, the letters and phonograph records with their special messages from the dead, to almost all of the forty-eight states. And working in the darkrooms, taught to develop the blurred photographs he was told were auras,

92

bringing out the burning images of spirit photography in sharp detail so that he became almost a technician, driving with their copy all the way to the Orlando printers and, after a while, choosing the stock, selecting the font, sometimes even suggesting the layouts, the color of the boards, a sort of agent ombudsman who dickered with the printers about the proper discount when mistakes were made, the proofreading off or the bundles mismanaged. And a kind of constable too, without the powers of arrest of course, but a sort of agent for the town here too, like a volunteer in a tourist booth, actually wearing a badge with a four-digit number on it, like a code stamped on a tin can, and from time to time getting actually physical, servicing the town the way a bouncer might vigilante a bar or roadhouse, though these occasions were rare, the grief-stricken and mentally ill being by and large a docile lot, wonderful folks to do business with.

In less than three months the spiritualists, though to use the term was to paint with too broad a brush, there being as much difference between a clairvoyant and clairaudient as there was between a holy roller and a bishop, wondered how they had ever gotten along without him. Bill J. Pierce, a Spirit Photographer who'd been photographing auras for over fifty years, said Mills had been sent to them.

He made enough to pay Wickland for their room and board. He made more in fact than he'd ever made in his life and was actually able to bank a part of his earnings. He forgot all about orange picking as soon as he returned to the hoarding at the entrance to the small square, studying the board, reading the rubrics he had at first only glanced at, assuming it to be the town's directory of churches, knowing only now where he was, what the fine-sounding titles, the "Doctors" and "Reverends" and "Professors" with their long tail of high-toned initials, really meant.

It was not no-man's-land but one of those places like Hollywood or Broadway, or Reno, say, or somewhere offshore, beyond what was still the twelve-mile limit, where gambling ships dropped anchor and the high rollers had to take into account not just ordinary house odds but the pitch and yaw of the salon, too. It was a district, as Covent Garden was a district, as the Reeperbahn was, given over to a single-minded commerce not with no real reason for it to be, but with no real reason for it to be there, or none that anyone understood, not even Pierce, the aura photographer of fifty years. It was evidently famous —Mills checked off the license plates; more were from out of state than from Florida—as something is famous only after you discover you have a need for it, as when you take up tennis or golf and find out that there are magazines that advertise not only racquets and clubs, but devices for restringing racquets, bulk catgut-like balls of twine, tees specially designed to stand straight in sandy earth. (Or if you need an abortionist, his father thought, and discover all the abortionists are within a two block area a quarter mile from the Milwaukee Zoo.)

So Cassadaga was famous. At least twenty pages of *Hartmann's Directory of Psychic Science and Spiritualism* were given over to its closely printed ads. It was famous for its occult hardware, the arcane merchandise which Mills toted into the De Land post office—— tiny heart-shaped planchettes and ouija boards like odd altars or artists' palettes, pocket breath controllers, aura charts, the rich colors painted on linen and attached to rollers like window shades, Aurospecs, seance trumpets, gazing crystals, spirit restraints, prisms, joss sticks, tarot cards, exorcism salts, sheet music, lullabies for the infant dead, marches for soldiers fallen in battle, witch waltzes. There were dictionaries of magic words, Seals of Solomon, mock-ups of left- and right-handed palms, telekinetic dice, outdoor seance furniture, occult recipes, three-dimensional models of the human soul, wands and charms, bells, books, candles—— all Sorcery's fee faw fum, all Belief's hocus pocus dominocus.

And this just a sideline, though he didn't know that yet, though his son found out first and even tried to tell him about it, to warn the father not to be taken in when he sometimes boasted that for the first time in a thousand years the Millses had risen above their station and gotten into crime, escaping if only briefly and if only through the odd historical accident of the Depression, that old curse on all fallen men that they must labor by the sweat of their brow and the clench of their muscles locked as fists just to eke out a measly subsistence which had to be pledged daily, renewed daily, like prayer or exercise.

"What do you mean a thousand years?" George asked.

"A thousand years. It's a figure of speech."

"We've been poor a thousand years?"

"Did I say that? We're with the crooks now, that's all. This is the age of busted law, sonny boy. We're on the side of the corrupt for once. Watch our smoke."

"But we're not. They're not."

"Not much."

"They believe in it."

"Tell it to the Marines. Ain't I got bills of lading for all the spook

94

house swag the Cassadaga College of Cardinals sends to suckers all over this God-fearing country? And that's just in one pocket. Ain't I got promissory notes from the COD, and postal and international money orders and stamps and even cash in the others? We should have tied in with the criminal element long ago. We missed the boat there, George. It's the land of opportunity down here. A few years ago they were running rum, all the boozes, not fifty miles from where we're standing. We missed the boat. We missed the boat they run it in on."

Because his son was the only kid in town. Because he was more than just an errand boy. Because, if the truth be known, it was his dad who was the errand boy, who they paid, and well enough, too, but didn't bother to impress. So he knew it was a sideline, little more than a service to their clients, a nuisance, like free delivery. As a cab driver might write down flat rates to distant cities or a hooker have in her wardrobe, along with her regulation lace panties and see-through bras and garter belts, the odd cat-o'-nine-tails and cruel boots or nun's habit, holding them in readiness not because she was often asked to use this stuff but because they were part of the repertoire, even though she knew that all that was really expected of her was the ordinary push-pull of standardized lust.

This was the way with almost the entire army of Cassadaga spiritualists.

"Many of the faithful have no faith," Professor G. D. Ashmore had told him. "They want the atmospherics of the visible and invisible planes of existence. They know that Death is a misnomer but can't break their Halloween habits, their skull and crossbones prejudices."

It was so. He was errand boy enough to know that much. He had often enough been sent off to borrow a pinch of ghost spice or jar of phantom powder as another child might be sent to neighbors for sugar or milk.

"The Spirit Kingdom is real as Canada," L. R. F. Grunbine— initials preceded their names like train whistles—liked to remind him, "but association drives their wills. They want mortuary silts, floral arrangements, candles, incense, all the hearse perfumes and cemetery aromatics. They believe with their noses, love stuck in their olfactories like grime. They want soul thrills but shop like savages, the cheap built into their psyches like bad breath. They gypsy our science and Coney Island our cause. Superstition is the enemy of the occult, George." And W. A. Oaten Ernest had the same complaint. M. R. R. Keller did. (Mills no longer referred to them as Dr., Professor, Reverend, or Madam, dropping their honorifics before his father ever did, though it was his dad who continued to think of them as crooks and charlatans, addressing them for all that as they listed themselves on what he now called the billboard.)

Only Wickland was still Reverend.

Of all the mystics, psychics, theosophists, astrologers, telepaths, palm readers, metapsychologists, diviners, fortune tellers, alchemists, necrophysicists, crystal gazers, and figure flingers in Cassadaga, only Wickland was Reverend. Nor did George believe any more in Wickland's bona fides than he did in the spiritual and scientific ordainments of Cassadaga's other metaphysicians. It was a simple matter of distancing.

The town's only child—nephew and grandson to all—he was in on their secrets, the tricks of their trade. Lessoned as a novitiate, closely drilled as an apprentice, often permitted to help with their proofreading, the pamphlets and handbooks they were endlessly writing, the psychic newsletters they were always getting out, he was their confidant, too. He read their mail to them, petitions of the mortally ill—the divines of Cassadaga were a forum of last resort: requests for clues to stave off death, appeals from widows, widowers—he learned that couples in their fifties and sixties and seventies still made love, ardent as teenagers; he learned, if not of the sanctity of marriage, at least of its addictive power, that love was always the last habit broken —to contact their dead.

There were letters of inquiry:

"Dear Professor M. R. R. Keller,

"I am eighty-two years old and very infirm. I do not expect to live out the year. Indeed, I feel so bad now and everything is so hard for me that I don't much want to. I am not a religious person, but I read your book about contact with the invisible world and I have followed your experiments and truly believe I have benefited from my experiences with discarnated Intelligences.

"I am writing for information. My problem is this. Nowhere in your book are any rules set down on how to behave when I am dead. Is there an etiquette in such things? Will I still be desirable to Lionel? He was only fifty-six when he passed. Is it permissible for a woman my age to make the first move?

"I suppose I shall find out soon enough, but if you could suggest what is expected in these matters it might help to avoid awkward and unnecessary embarrassment."

Keller's answer was straightforward as the letter which prompted it.

"Dear Mrs. Line,

"I regret to say that my researches have not extended to the delicate areas in which you seek information. Might I suggest, however, that you consult some dear and trusted discarnated Intelligence directly and ask her?"

The Cassadagans never put a price on these exchanges, though a few dollars almost always accompanied a letter of inquiry. When it didn't the letter was answered anyway. George judged that most psychics were good for between twenty to thirty dollars a week from such correspondence, and though they made more by filling orders for the merchandise his father took into De Land, the merchandise remained the sideline, their psychic services the real business of their lives.

He was permitted to handle the gazing crystals, the clear, flawless globes like temperate, neutral ice, so transparent he felt he held invisible weight. He looked through prisms, altering light as one might pull the strings on marionettes. And tried the Aurospecs, seeing other people as if they were on fire, their green and red and orange radiance exploding off them like gasses from the surface of a sun, their jeweled and kindled selves seething about their persons like rainbows boiling. And pressed his ear to the seance trumpet and heard the muted sharps and flats of invisible performance.

But it was the letters which interested him most.

"Dear Dr. N. M. M. Kinsley,

"I have been a practitioner of the Kinsley Astral Projection Method for the past five years and have had dozens of successful expeditions. I have visited the homes of several relatives at distances in excess of two thousand miles, although I am still unable to get past the Rocky Mountains.

"Always before, as your method proclaims, I have been most successful where need is greatest, when subliminal, subconscious Soul cries out to sensitized psychic Soul. These, as you well know, have not always been 'pleasant' experiences, the comfort I have been able to impart to a grieving cousin who has lost her young husband or a father temporarily separated from his son by the wall of death, being a fleeting, cold sort of comfort at best. I have tried, as you suggest in your superb tract, to bring them good will and the good news of immortality, but in their grief states I have noticed that they are not always, or even often, responsive. Indeed, since I am unable to take

97

with me the departed's actual astral imprint, I have sometimes come away feeling of no more real use to the family than the ordinary well-intentioned condolence caller from church with her cakes and casseroles. However helpless I may feel psychologically when even under the best of circumstances I am able to leave only my well-meaning spiritual calling cards, a gesture which, in terms of lasting benefits, I dismiss in the very act of writing the word 'gesture,' I find that I return to my bed after such dubious house calls, enervated, depleted, exhausted, and profoundly unhappy.

"Here is the burden of my complaint. I am not by nature a Diabolist, no more than yourself. I have never subscribed to the old Manichean principle of the Good/Evil, Light/Dark, Heaven/Hell contrarieties. But now, well, I'm not so sure. It's not that my belief has been shaken, but really rather the opposite—— that my belief has undergone an enhancement. Now I believe *everything*. There are more things, Dr. Kinsley, than are dreamt of in your philosophy. And 'dream,' I think, is the operative word. Those *I* am privy to through my nocturnal visitations have been, are, depraved. My own grand-mother, a religious and even naive woman who has never harmed anyone in all her ninety-one years, has dreams which may not even begin to be described by the word 'randy.' They are filth, Doctor, pornographic in the most debased sense of that term. Genitalia are undisguised, not Freudian obelisks or large bodies of water, not tele-phone poles or dark tunnels, but swollen cocks and moistened cunts, baby dolls with curling pubic hair about their slits—I am not being 'frank;' if anything I am glossing out of decency—erections severed from their groins and glistening in their dewy juices. My relatives' dreams, my cousins' and in-laws', are the very models of lust. Sodo-mies are become exponential, perpetrated on dead house pets, onan-ism and fellatio commonplace as scratching one's back or getting a haircut. I shan't recount the awful details. You can't imagine them, and I won't describe them, but if this is what is meant by 'Negative Life Forces with their capacity to deflect the subject's concentration from his loss,' then I suggest that further studies be done, that your treatise be updated. If these were simply my own observations I would be willing to discredit them, dismiss them on the grounds of anomaly and insufficient evidence rather than question fundamental scientific principles established over a lifetime of good and careful work, but the experience of other adepts confirms my own. Practitioners here in Michigan have told me at our monthly meetings of salacities which I dare not write down lest I come into conflict with the rules governing the postal service. They dream, the grieving do, of excesses and improprieties unknown even in the lowest days of the Roman Empire, unknown to history's heathens and pagans and barbarians, unknown, I daresay, even to the great perverts, the rippers and sexual surgeons, innocents all in depravity when compared to these lechers of the hearth.

"I have an Uncle Joe in Vermont, a blacksmith by trade and, or so I would have thought, temperament, one of those red and black wool-shirted men who wear the checkerboard, who dress, I mean, like a game. A crony of a man, long underweared and gallused and wide leather belted too, one of the dark pantsed and wood stoved of earth who has the names and faces of his townsmen like a postmaster. A fisherman of a fellow, honest as a hunter, more loyal to the local woods and streams than to any nation, who has all the intricate weathers like a second language. A whittler of course, and volunteer fireman, a loresman of stone and all the materials of Nature, beech and maple, elm and ash, and all the secret, invisible grains of the human heart. Whose word is his bond—— and he has many words, as comforting as honest. For children, for men with troubles and for sad ladies, for lame dogs and lamer ducks. You know the type, or if you're lucky do, an unofficial mayor of a man, powerful of course, muscled I mean, with strength that comes as much from virtue and good will as from hammer or heat. His power great but never guarded, not held like a secret or watched like his fire, no caution catching it up or checking it in, not anything fearful. My uncle's great strength, innocent as talent, like a good singing voice, or the gift of speed.

"And no bachelor. Uncle Joe a family man, that organic guy. The sort of man—this didn't happen—who might have married the sister-in-law when the sister died, who found the fit of love, I mean to say, who'd find it anywhere and count it as a wonder that his loved ones, all the folks he wanted most to be with in the world, his wife and children, nephews, sisters, nieces, brothers, should live so close to home, not even in the next valley but right there in the very town, beside him in the very section of the very church he prayed in, the very lake he swam in, the store he bought his staples.

"He married Aunt Elizabeth when both were twenty-eight. They had four children, my cousins Redford and Oliver and Susan and Ben, and raised them, he and Elizabeth—I don't mean strictly, I don't mean by any theory, I don't even mean good-naturedly—as naturally as Aunt Elizabeth might put up strawberries, following nothing more than the natural laws and time-honored processes of canning, first this, then that.

"Elizabeth died when the youngest, Oliver, was still in his teens.

"Fine young men, a lovely woman, whose only quarrel that I can now recall was who would get to stay with Joe. The smith profession is, of course, a languishing one, and while it was never a matter of who would make his way in the world, who would get to go off to the state university at Burlington—none would, none wanted to—but rather which would have to hire out, which would have to work the timber or the nearby farms or go to the factories where the money was, and which would remain—they wouldn't have thought of it as behind—with the benevolent, godlike father they loved as much for his kindness and wisdom as for his paternity.

" 'Mother's dead,' Susan told him. 'You have no woman, Father, no one to cook your meals or mend and wash or sing for you. The trade is falling on hard times. You're only fifty-two. You don't yet even need our young strength to help you at the forge. Send them away, dear. Let me stay.'

"Redford said, 'I'm the oldest, Father. It's the privilege of the oldest son—I don't say "duty," I say "privilege," I could say "right" —to follow in his father's footsteps, to help him in his profession. I don't want to take it over, sir. For this I care nothing, though should you desire it I would stay at the forge till after the last horse in Vermont had died, and after that as well. I would repair tools, fit new disks, harrows, shape new heads to nails, fashioning your iron as you taught me, building the fire to 1,535 degrees Centigrade, puddling and shingling, adding your water like transfusion. Allow me to remain, Father. I ask in the name of primogeniture.'

" 'I'm the youngest, Pa,' said Oliver. 'My boyhood isn't finished yet. I lost a mother. I'm not ready, Daddy. Don't send me off.'

"And Ben reminded him he was neither oldest son nor youngest, not special at all, not even female like his sister, that nothing about his birth gave him the special prerogatives or claims the three others had lived with all their lives. It was only justice and fair play, qualities whose names he might not even know had he not learned about them, a mute listener, an undistinguished son and brother, in his father's shop all his unexceptional life. It was only retroactive equity and redress he was seeking in asking to be allowed to stay with his father. It was only the presentation of a twenty-odd-year-old bill and quit-claim.

" 'You can't ask me,' Joe told them—they had come separately to make their cases but he answered them together—'to choose among my children. Your sexes and ages are of no importance. Years make no precedence in love. Biology has no claims on it. You shall have to decide among yourselves.'

"It was only the next valley over, Dr. Kinsley, not the next state or county or even village. None was to be exiled, banished. It was understood that they could take their dinners together, not weekly, mind, but daily if they chose. Joe had built rooms onto his house as they were needed, had carpentered the beds and other furniture for each of his children, so that their living arrangements were not only adequate but actually lavish, the house as trim and ordered and ample to the needs of their bodies and imaginations as a child's tree house. It was their sense of seemliness and honor that guided them, their knowledge that if they continued to live together as a family now that all but one of them was grown, it would be as a family that had somehow gone off, spoiled in some acute, vinegarish way.

"That was when they quarreled. They did it where their father could not hear them, could not know of it. They had been told that they had to decide by themselves. Logic was useless. These were the claims of need and love. They soon saw that right had nothing to do with it, that each of their arguments was checked and canceled by the equally legitimate arguments of the others.

" 'We'll never convince each other,' Ben said. 'We'll have to fight it out.'

"Even Susan understood that Ben meant physically, that they would have to wrestle and punch for the right to stay with the wonderful old man. They were a blacksmith's children, had the blacksmith bone and blacksmith muscle. Each had grown up by the forge, each taken his or her turn with the hammer at the anvil. Susan had played with iron as another child might play with sand. They had never quarreled, never fought. They had no idea who was strongest. They didn't want to hurt each other and, at least in the beginning, each held back, withdrew not as an actual miser might actual money but like some old chivalrous soldier from the hoard of his strength and wile that measured, calibrated advantage he perceived as waste, brutality, overkill, unfair edge. Merely pushing and shoving at first, merely milling about in the baled field of their combat, not so much testing the power of his or her foes as on guard to arrest and counter any sudden thrust. They might have been confronting each other tentatively as so many strikers and scabs, police and demonstrators, so that Redford must have thought of Ben, 'Why, he's delicate,' and Ben of

Oliver with whatever of regret his nervousness permitted, 'Poor frail Ollie, so attenuated finally in those work clothes. He *should* hire out, the outdoors will do him good,' and Susan of herself, remembering the anvil she had once actually lifted off the ground just to see if she could do it, 'Perhaps women are stronger than men, perhaps it's virginity which gives us the advantage, perhaps all force is moral force.'

"They feinted with each other for half an hour until it must have seemed even to themselves like some badly managed charade, even to country people who had never seen an actual prize fight in an actual ring, whose work was with the seasons, who levered Nature and Nature's crops, more a shy and nebulous routine of courtship, or the obscure, oblique forms preparatory to hard bargaining and doing business, than anything they were really there for.

" 'I've been fooling with you,' Susan admitted suddenly, and knocked Redford down with what she did not even know was an uppercut. Ben jumped on her back and tried to ride her to the ground but Oliver grabbed him from behind and pulled him off.

"The sister and brothers were startled by what had happened, amazed and ashamed by the sudden change that had come over them. Mutual protectors, they were mutual protectors still, but furious now, each rushing to the defense of the other, calculating punishment, doing the meticulous equations of violence and charging against the perpetrator the exact measure of the blow that had been struck. Susan, who had knocked Redford down with an uppercut, was knocked down by an uppercut by Ben. Oliver, who had pulled Ben's head back while Susan carried him across the field, was himself grabbed about the neck by Redford and thrown to the ground. Susan leaped at Redford to avenge Oliver. They struggled this way for perhaps a quarter of an hour.

" 'What we got here ain't no fight,' Ben managed breathlessly. 'What we got here is some antifight.' It was so. All could see it was so.

" 'We got to go all out, I guess,' Oliver said, 'or we'll never fix who gets to stay with Pa.'

"Possibly it was Oliver's logic. More likely it was the invocation of their dear father that brought them round. In either event, there was a battle royal, a free-for-all which bore about as much relation to the first fifteen minutes of their conflict as the last quarter of a football game does to the pregame ceremonies—— the marching bands and prancing mascots and flash cards and all the simple pictographs of loyalty.

"In another twenty minutes it was over. Susan almost won. Their father had said that biology made no difference. To him, of course, it didn't, but her daughter's—you could have said woman's—status and distancing had loaned her a strength and fierceness that was unavailable to the boys. They were fighting for the right to stay with their father. She was fighting for the right to remain with her father and also—if this isn't misunderstood—with a man. But it wasn't enough. She beat two of the brothers but lost out to the third.

"Redford won the fight, though they still didn't know who was the strongest. That was beside the point. Their father had said that years made no precedent in love and for that love-rounded man they didn't, wouldn't, but Redford was the oldest, had known him the longest, had one or two years more tenure in love, that much more priority and seniority and simple brutal rank with which and for which to fight.

"So it seemed that logic and right had decided it after all, that strength flowed to the one who had the most to lose. Redford won, Susan placed, Oliver, whose boyhood wasn't finished, showed, and Ben, undistinguished by placement or sex, came in dead last.

"They went to the old man to tell them what had been decided. 'Redford gets to stay, Father,' Susan said.

"Joe looked at her, at his three sons, and nodded.

" 'It's your decision,' the blacksmith said, 'but that's just about how I'd have handicapped it.'

"Redford took his place at the smithy beside his father and the others, who did not move out after all but went out each day to follow their new pursuits—Ben at timbering, Oliver at farming, Susan in the chain factory—and returned each night for their meals and lodging and to listen to their father's wonderful afterhours conversation and watch his grand game of checkers by the ancient anvil he used as a table in the snug smithy by the cooling but still warm forge.

"A strange thing happened. At least unusual, at least unexpected. It was as if the addition of Redford to the small business, instead of halving the work, somehow compounded it. Perhaps it was the sense that people had of dealing with the beginning of a dynasty, a House, or perhaps it was simply the practical Vermonter's suspicion that Joe, by taking on additional help, was getting ready to expand, introduce intricate new refinements to the blacksmith trade. In any event, Doctor, they now came with their horses and broken equipment as never before. They came not only from all over the county but from the next county as well, and some from as far away as the

Northeast Kingdom. To the old-timers, and to his new custom, too, Joe was as convivial as ever, as wise as ever, as reasonable, as much the, well, *American,* as he had ever been, the man most likely to break up a lynching, if you know what I mean.

"Only Redford had the feeling that his father was unhappy with the new arrangement. They never spoke of it, Redford never mentioned it to his brothers or sister—I have it from an astral projection to one of his dreams—yet as time passed Redford was more and more convinced that his dad found fault with his presence. He queried himself constantly, went over and over his behavior and performance to see how he had given offense. He could find nothing. He was tormented. Perhaps he would have preferred Oliver, he thought, perhaps Susan or Ben. He was tormented and his work suffered.

"A blacksmith must concentrate. His work is as dangerous as a surgeon's. There must be steady-state attention, attention as focused as acetylene, as managed as meditation.

"He was stirring pig iron in the puddling furnace and did not read the gauges properly, mistaking the first 3 in 1,335 centigrade degrees for a 5. He was still 200 degrees below the melting point of iron but did not know this and could not understand the strange and sudden obdurance of the metal. He put on his almost opaque smoked glasses and long asbestos gloves and opened the door to the furnace to investigate. Behind smoked glasses iron ingots look like peeled, pale bananas, less bright than new rope. The brilliant red bed of heat in which they rest is dimmed the color of roofing tile.

"He was a blacksmith, used to heat, as at ease in Celsius as in spring, cozy in Fahrenheit, cold-blooded as fish or bird. Of *course* he didn't feel the heat who testing himself as a child had plucked live cinders from the shingled iron with his fingers, moving the hot dross about under his hands like chessmen or checkers in a game. And he was distracted by his good-man-against-the-lynch-mob dad, that serene, knowing, grandfatherly man whom he of all the elder sons on earth was (not as a grandparent and not in fly-fisher affiliation or woods guide relation or even priest counselor one, and all this even if not in actual dotage—Redford himself would already be twenty-four years old on his next birthday—from a fellow getting on, an old-timer, part of whose virtue must have come from things got past, put by, some *nolo contendere* deal with greed and lust, but as a still in-there, live-and-kicking actual viable Pop) not done with yet, and who for as far ahead as Redford could see would never be done with him, who still had plenty to teach to someone who still had plenty to learn. And if his father's new queer distance from his eldest boy had any cause at all, it had to lie with Redford, some mysterious, unmanly infraction yet to be decoded. No insubordination or defection or noncompliance, no sedition, putsch or blackleg treason—— a breach, blemish, some piddling moral caesura visible only to his pa's Indian vision.

"So he was distracted, he did not feel the heat. Behind the dark glasses the iron pigs, 200 degrees centigrade below the boil, looked dark as stones on a dull night. He reached forward into the furnace and lifted one out, the size and shape of a small book, bringing it close to his face to examine. His hands ignited like kindling. His head caught fire.

"Joe built the coffin himself. He dug the grave next to Elizabeth's on the flank of Kingdom Mountain and eloquently spoke the psalms he did not even have to read. He delivered the eulogy.

"Susan took her brother's place beside her father at the blacksmith shop. She worked as effortlessly as Redford but with better concentration. She was dead within the month. Tearing her hymen in the rough-and-tumble with her brothers, she had somehow ruptured something important in her womb. The hemorrhage had been slow, almost undetectable, the bleached red smear she saw on her toilet paper of no more significance than the trivial spotting after a period. The hemorrhage had been slow, something that happened almost without her, like air deflating from a football in a closet in the off-season. The bruises, green as olives on her belly, she put down to the punches she had traded with her brothers. Oliver's would be darker, she thought, Ben's would. It was not the heavy lifting which exacerbated the bleeding; it was the work which she did with the sledge at the anvil, shaking her blood down through the sluices and flumes of her body with each powerful blow of her arm. Finally it was as if she had too vigorously shaken ketchup from its bottle. 'Perhaps,' she mused again, when she saw the immense sticky bolus of blood at her feet, felt it in her shoes, between her toes, just before she died, 'it's virginity gives us the advantage. Perhaps all force is moral force.'

"Her father buried her as he had Redford, on the same green mountain, in a coffin exactly the dimensions of her eldest brother's, reciting the same psalms and, word for word, the identical eulogy.

"Oliver came forward.

" 'No,' the father said. 'I know the sequence. Didn't I handicap your decisions? Didn't I have the morning line on it? Your boyhood ain't finished, you said. Why should you do up the end of your life before you've done up its beginning? Ben will work with me.'

"So the unadvantaged (not *dis*advantaged, just only undistinguished by age or sex) Ben put by his axes and saws and cleared his cuffs and cleats and clothes of the wooden flammable chips, shavings and twigs, the residual timber that clung to him like dew, and reported to his father at the forge.

" 'Well, one thing,' his father said, 'now you've got your priority, too.'

" 'Sure,' Ben said.

" 'Work the bellows while I start this fire.'

" 'Sure,' Ben said.

" 'Just remember what I told you. Squeeze it like you would an accordion. Easy. Easy. Try to imagine you're playing a waltz. It ain't no march, it ain't any square dance.'

" 'Sure.'

" 'Still too fast,' the father said. 'What we want is to give this fire a shove in the right direction. We ain't looking to blow it out the other end of the forge.'

" 'Sure,' Ben said.

" 'Ayuh. That's it. That's it. See how the color is evenly distributed? Just like leaves turning up on Kingdom Mountain.'

" 'Sure,' Ben said. 'Father?'

" 'You can put that down now. Why don't you just lay out my tools? I'll be needing my peen and maul. You can hand me the tamp and my small stemmer.'

" 'Sure. Father?'

" 'Fetch my spalling hammer too, why don't you? That special one with the claw head. What?'

" 'It's about my eulogy.'

" 'I fashioned the claw on this myself. Don't know why someone didn't think to do it earlier. Seems a simple enough adaptation. Stand back for a minute. I need some elbow room to swing this thing. What about it?'

" 'I don't mind about the psalms. Anyone would be pleased with those psalms. They're good psalms.'

" 'They're stately psalms.'

" 'Sure,' Ben said. 'It's the eulogy. Seeing as how I was neither eldest son nor youngest, nor even a daughter like Susan, seeing as how I was always sort of lost in there—I ain't saying misplaced, I ain't saying forgotten or even mislaid, though mislaid gives some of my sense of it—seeing as how I was just kind of ganged up on by accidental circumstance, I was wondering if you couldn't sort of distinguish me a little in the eulogy. All you'd really have to do is mention what I just said.'

"His father didn't answer him. They got through the day, Joe doing the close work, Ben relegated to helper, but a helper, he knew, of little more urgency and use to the blacksmith than the merest customer who might, the smith's mouth full of nails and his hands busy with tongs and sledge, almost casually tie up the back of his leather apron if it came undone. Joe referred to what his son had said only once. It was after they had finished for the day. He was banking the fires. 'Don't think about your eulogy,' he said.

" 'You don't believe anything's going to happen?' Ben asked.

" 'Don't think about your eulogy,' Joe said. 'It's a towering sin for a man to second-guess what folks are going to say about him when he's gone. Don't think about your eulogy.'

"But it was *all* he could think about, all his father gave him the *chance* to think about. Coddled as he was in the dangerous shop, protected by his dad from any work which could result in a fatal mistake, buffered even from the friendly banter of the customers and idle men who came to watch the blacksmith at his interesting work or hear him talk—'Stand well back, Ben,' the smithy warned, 'these fools are knee slappers and it's close quarters here. Just a sudden gesture of comradely affection or approval could send something irrevocable flying or shy the horses and bring us down'—he could think of nothing else.

"He was not distracted. Kept at a safe distance from the furnace so that he never had a chance to become acclimated to it, he could feel the heat. Having no reason ever to put on the dark smoked glasses, he saw everything clearly in its natural light.

"He believed what his father said, what the best man he had ever known had told him. He knew it was a towering sin always to be thinking about what the man would say of him in his eulogy. He knew he was wrong, deeply wrong, wrong to the bone, that at last he had the justice and fair play he had begged for when he'd asked his father to allow him to stay and to send his brothers and sister off. He knew he'd always had it and he was ashamed of himself.

"So he was not distracted. He felt the heat. He saw everything in the shop in fine detail.

"He remembered the precise degree of temperature when iron smelted. He could estimate almost as precisely the heat in the shop twenty feet from the fired forge, fifteen feet, ten, five, a few inches. When he opened its door that night after his father and Oliver had gone to bed and put his head inside it, he could make out for an instant the exact color values of the fulgurant ingots and could detect, flaring down from true against the corona of the iron soup the just darker flecks of slag and carbon like the specks of some stone seasoning.

"Uncle Joe buried Ben alongside Elizabeth, Redford and Susan, his coffin, though Ben was a few inches taller than the others, the same size theirs had been. He spoke the same stately psalms and offered a eulogy which, though richly delivered, did not vary from the earlier ones by so much as a comma.

" 'You don't have to if you don't want to,' he told Oliver.

" 'Hell,' said Oliver, 'we got a tradition. We're on a roll. You don't just walk away from a tradition like you'd move out of the kitchen once the dishes are done.'

" 'Don't say hell,' his father said.

" 'And I'm twenty now,' Oliver said. 'I got ten months till I'm twenty-one. I figure I got at least that much time to get so expert in the trade that by the time I reach my majority and circumstances swarm me I might even be of some use to you.'

"He was wrong though. Not about his ability to learn, though he was in fact already expert and of great use to his father. He was the one who had hired out, who had driven the disk harrows and tractors and balers, who had handled the plows and cultivators, who was as familiar with the machinery and wagons of agriculture as any cowboy with his mount or musician with the pegs and valves of his instruments. He knew their tensions and faults, could guess from a funny sound in the field just which part had busted off, and was so familiar with their shapes and resistances that he could estimate to within a foot the direction and angle of their roll. What he brought to the business was a knowledge of broken pieces, shard, some synecdochic, jigsaw sense of the whole. 'Here,' he'd say, 'let me do that,' when some farmer helplessly held out the ruined rude pinnings and copulas, the pegs, dowels, brads, and hasps of his sad, collapsed one-horse-shay equipment.

" 'He's like a jeweler,' they said. It was true.

"Oliver halved the time that would ordinarily have been given over to fashioning new pieces from scratch, and the business, always steady, began suddenly to flourish.

" 'Are you pleased?' he asked his father one day.

" 'I'll work with the animals and run off the big shapes I'm familiar with,' Joe said. 'You do the Swiss watches.'

"He set up a corner of the shop for his son and now the boy was screened from his father and all the activity by the large anvil as ever Ben had been. Few cared to watch him work and, when sometimes people did drift over, they could see very little of what he was doing —his work was too meticulous, it did not lend itself to raillery—and soon moved back to where the grander, more dramatic activity was going on at Joe's end.

"Oliver listened with his back to them while he worked, much as he had heard the sudden pings and small crashes of the brittle machinery in the fields, hearing everything only after it was already behind him but making his adjustments for deflection and pitch and yaw by the sound of the voice, guessing not only the speaker but the one addressed and listening, too, for the rhythmic, sedative slaps of his father's hammer on the steel anvil.

"What happened was this:

"Their voices were suddenly lowered. He was fusing a hitch, one he had never seen before but like a delicate ampersand or the treble clef on sheet music.

" '. . . got what he wanted,' he heard. '. . . did take . . . their deaths.'

" 'Hush,' he heard, and a low laugh. And his father's hammer, the loud crack of steel on steel undiminished, if anything quickened, lending a kind of fillip of assent like a rim shot under a joke.

"He grabbed the sharp, short-handled cooper's adz he had just set down on his workbench next to his blacksmith's chisel and rushed from his place to the burly farmer who stood beside his father at the anvil. 'You son of a bitch!' he screamed, and raised the tool high above his head.

" 'Don't say son of a bitch,' his father said without turning.

"The astonished farmer barely had time to step aside. Oliver was already into his downstroke when he stumbled, the momentum of his tremendous blow pulling him forward and causing his head to fall upon the center of the anvil just as his calm, phlegmatic father, that masterful pipe smoker of a man who did not join their gossip but only counseled and advised, was delivering the last packed smash that would put the arch of the horseshoe exactly right.

"They hadn't even been talking about him. It was a joke about a necrophile. Farmers always lowered their voices when they told smoking car stories, even when women weren't around. His father supposed it was the way decent men cheated on their wives.

"The burly farmer, who had stepped aside instinctively, tried to apologize, his eyes still wet with laughter from the good story he'd told, but Joe already understood.

" 'He wasn't quite twenty-one yet,' he said. 'Ayuh. Kids go off half-cocked sometimes.'

"Over the last casket he would ever have to build, the blacksmith said the psalms one last time. He didn't change the eulogy because it was a father's duty to treat his children equally, but he added a final statement for the cronies and customers who had turned out to hear him.

" 'Being a pa's a terrible burden,' he said. 'Now maybe I can get some peace. I've learned from all this. Maybe I ain't so good a blacksmith as I thought I was. I couldn't do the delicate work good as my boy, though no one's better with livestock than I am, I think. A man should stick to what he does best. If it's small motor control, as it was with my Oliver, then he should stick a jeweler's loupe in his eye, keep it there, and leave the heavy lifting to others. My son would be alive today if he hadn't gone for the fences with that last big bulldozer cavalry charge.

" 'I'll continue to honor your custom and do the best I can with your horses and tack, though after what's happened I think I'd prefer to work by myself for a bit.'

"It was better than an ad. Indeed, it *was* an ad, almost a decree, nothing barker or ballyhoo about it or undifferentiated as the handbill stuck under your windshield wiper or circular shoved through the letter slot with your mail, but touching, sort of, and tremendously official and solemn and even final, like banns or the little notice of bankruptcy in the public press that the bankrupt has to pay for himself, something understated, even unspoken, but there anyway, like those sad little admissions of guilt and responsibility in the classifieds when there's a divorce and the husband publicly disavows liability for his wife's debts. You know the lawyer made him put it there, that it wouldn't have occurred to him otherwise.

"So Joe's announcement that he was best with livestock was no boast, the reverse rather, a kind of confession that he was good with little else, the Swiss movements of agricultural machinery or children either.

"Whatever, it had its effect, even if it was an effect my uncle could not have anticipated.

"Have you ever seen a barn raising or any of those episodes of country charity where the feelings of the participants are not those of obligation or even duty so much as the sheer amplitude of the heart, its cheerful, generous, almost maritime displacements buoying cause and mission like stalled shipping? Or have you ever been to a surprise party, Dr. Kinsley? Or anniversary, or testimonial dinner? Have you risen to your feet with the others in the hall to give someone who doesn't expect it a standing ovation? Then you will recognize the inclusive, almost religious good will of such moments. There's something in it for you, too, though it may not be what you think. It isn't the sense of a paid-up debt or the satisfaction that is said to come from good behavior. It isn't anything peripheral or serendipitous or spin-off or sidebar or fallout at all. That barn you helped raise is forever after your barn too, just as the surprise is your surprise—'Were you really surprised? Did you suspect anything? What did you think when you saw all those cars in the driveway? We'd have parked on the street but all the spots were taken'—and the ovation not just a declaration of your gratitude and love but an affirmation of your taste.

"What Uncle Joe said was repeated all over the state, given motion and impetus by word-of-mouth, some relayed, passed baton or aloft torch quality of marathon unimpedance. And not just Vermont but New Hampshire too, parts of Massachusetts and Maine and New York State and corners of Connecticut.

"It was how I heard—I don't recall who told me, some friend of a friend who'd been traveling in New England that summer—all that far away in Michigan. It wasn't astral projection. Joe hadn't written. His last letter had been when Elizabeth died. She was my mother's sister, my aunt. I suppose he believed that as a nephew I had a stake in that loss. But he never wrote about Susan or his sons. Perhaps he felt cousins aren't relatives at all, only friends. Or maybe there's just something too sour in the death of children. Tragedy, but tragedy spoiled, gone off like meat. It wasn't anything one would want to write letters about.

"Anyway, the response of the farmers and sportsmen was incredible. It was as if no one in Vermont could mend tack or shoe a horse except my uncle. They brought him their hobbled animals as if they were making a pilgrimage, some long, lame march to a Green Mountain Lourdes. They went out of their way to come to him and, since my uncle had expressed the wish to work alone and no longer be for them that cracker-barrel or wood or potbelly stove or general store philosopher that had gotten him into trouble in the first place, they simply turned their beasts over to him, disengaging the animals from the wagons they pulled as if they not only had come to a sort of hospital but were brought there in a sort of ambulance which they, the lame horses, had had to pull themselves, and then went off to drink or actually register for the night at the local inn. So it cost them money and time too, though possibly they didn't see it that way, still riding the wave of that conjoined magnanimity and effluent participatory chivalry which is not only the inspiration for surprise parties but the only reason you can get people to come to them in the first place.

"They had to knock now. Then my uncle would come out to them, take their animals and damaged tack, give them a receipt (which they did not always want later to surrender, the slip of paper being the stub, the souvenir of their attendance), and lead their property back into the blacksmith shop.

"I wrote Joe when I heard what had happened and, when he didn't answer, I wrote again. I wrote a third time, a stolid, solemn letter of patient unput-out condolence. I asked if he wanted to come to Michigan for a while. He didn't answer.

"I would have gone to him in Vermont. In my last letter I had suggested as much, proposing it as an alternative should he not wish to make the trip to Michigan. So you see, Dr. Kinsley, there was no astral trigger finger, no metempsychotic quick-draw pyrotechnics. I have, as I've said, been an adept for more than five years. But I gave up joy-riding long ago. The occult airs are too chill, its weathers too tempestuous. I was forced, you see. I loved my uncle, my dead cousins. To have lost almost all of them at once, as I had casually learned I had, was simply too much. Uncle Joe wouldn't answer his mail. Perhaps he was holed up in his grief. Perhaps he needed me. Perhaps I needed him.

"I tried to enter his dreams. He had no dreams. He slept like someone napping. I don't mean fitfully; I don't mean lightly; maybe I don't even mean uncomfortably, but with just that hibernant, abeyant doze one sees on the faces of sleepers in railway carriages or in the awry angled heads of passed-out drunks. My uncle could have been an uncle in parlors after family feasts, or paralyzed, all his features—eyes, mouth, nose, forehead, cheeks, chin—in some leaden, unresisting mandragoran acedia, even his bones in coma, not piled so much as stashed unarchitecturally as firewood. Quite simply there was no one home, and his face had about it some lifeless, awful quality of nonuse, like clothes, say, in the closets of the dead.

"I entered his head through his nostrils, thinking my rubbery passage there might act like some chemical reagent, but I know dreamless sleep when I see it. He was as nerveless there as toenail, his body lulled as hair.

"I became bolder, even naughty. I entered his head through his anus, his ears, the littorals of his sex—— all the watched passes and zebra-gated, checkpoint vulnerables of his ticklish borders. I would have done as well to have entered his head through his hat.

"Once inside I moved about as freely as a man in his own rooms, but with as little sense of voyage, journey. I probed his brain like a caver, but the cave was featureless, dead, the bland limestones and indigenous geologies ordinary as cellar. There was neither grief nor joy, his unconscious recessive as his hunger.

"I slipped outside again with the intention of reconnoitering his room, more cop than nephew, more scientist than mourner. I looked for—— what? A Bible perhaps, open at some telling passage of consolation or bleak denunciation, or perhaps at one of those two psalms in my uncle's repertoire that might indicate the words meant more to him than just a formula for the disposition of bodies.

"There was no Bible.

"I looked for framed photographs of my cousins, posed, frozen, idealized Sunday bested, their young lives solemnized and potentiated by their severe clothes and managed expressions, neither openly smiling nor hardened in some scam seriousness but posed nevertheless, genuinely *posed,* to give off their own real considered sense of who they were, all they intended to be. Or loose snapshots, deceptive candids, my cousins tricked out in life as they worked by the forge or were snapped in repose, horseplay, seated at table or dancing the jig.

"There were no framed photographs, there were no loose candids.

"I looked for memento. Not locks of hair or the stuffed toys of their childhood—I knew there wouldn't be any—but their heights sketched with a pencil mark on the doorways and walls, or a window hairline cracked by one of them in roughhouse. For diary, journal, a note passed at school. For their lucky coins and stamp collections. For anything beside the way which had once engaged them and which now, in death, might be allowed to stand for the obscure talismanics of their father's engagement.

"There was nothing.

"Ah, thought the astral detective, then doesn't the persistent absence of such stuff suggest their willful repudiation? Wouldn't Joe have gone the other way altogether, sweep away, get rid of, jettison forever all trace, spoor, vestige and relic of his all-gone family, doing the conscientious spring cleaning of death?

"No evidence warranted the assumption. In their rooms, their furniture and lives, if not just as they had left them, seemed to have been put in a more logical order, arranged, even enhanced. I had last visited three years earlier. Aunt Elizabeth was still alive. I remember Susan had remarked that she had no place to store her things. There was a chiffonier in Redford's room. Redford himself volunteered to let Susan have the piece. Elizabeth seconded, adding that she had always thought the bureau too feminine for her eldest son anyway. Joe, however, had objected to its removal, pointing out that the blond finish matched the color of the bed he had built. Susan's furniture was dark. He said that when he had time he would build her a chest of drawers of her own, one that would go with what she already had. She didn't want to wait, she said, and, since Redford didn't mind giving up the chiffonier, her father soon agreed. It was a heavy piece to move and I recall being drafted to help in the rearrangement of the furniture.

"Now the big chest of drawers was back in Redford's room again, no new piece having replaced it in Susan's.

"Such arrangements seemed universal throughout. Spreads and curtains which had been distributed with no thought to decor now complemented the beds they lay across, were assimilate with the windows from which they hung. This was not the grieved archeologist's loving reconstruction nor even the sensitive curator's historical placements. This—— this was show business!

"But nothing in the house gave any clue to my uncle's state of mind. Nothing about his look in sleep did. (I was with him until just before dawn. He didn't even turn over.) Even his body—which lay on top of the sheets—seemed neutral, gently in idle like a good car at a stoplight. He could have been his own easy effigy lying on his bed like a dead pope on a sarcophagus.

"And what *was* his sleeping body like? What secret language did it speak? None. It was mute. (He didn't snore, his breath was regular, even, neither shallow nor deep.) He looked like a man floating in heavily salted water. And, undressed—he was a blacksmith, a man who may even have conducted heat—naked, oddly unfit, powerful of course but with the power off plumb, like a klansman's or bear's or vaudeville deputy's. His body saddened me—even his beard did, its poor dumb brush cut, the misguided bristles of rectitude and economy like primary growth on some elemental sea thing—but told me nothing.

"In a week I returned. Nothing had changed. If he hadn't been wearing pajamas I wouldn't have known he'd ever awakened. He was dreamless as ever. I made three more visitations. He was always dreamless, his sleep undramatic as a doll's.

"Because it was love which brought me back, some recidivist exercise of honor and homage to an uncle blacksmith whose two women and three boys had once represented a kind of full house, anyway luck, anyway moral force, the view from the rocker, the view from the hearth, some sung song of engagement and dignity and pride, my opinion of the man not unlike my cousins', not unlike those country peers and cronies whose spit sizzled like some tempering principle on all his blacksmith's machinery of heat. Because only love could have made me do it, my appetite for the parlor tricks of magic and sorcery having long since been brought down, leveled and flattened, of no more interest to me, now that I could do them, than the charms of money, say, to a tired sheik. (Because I don't know how God does it, don't understand what's in it for Him, why his limitless power and the limitless demands on it don't bore Him to death.) And if you're not God it drains you, really takes it out of you, runs down your health, grinds your teeth, there really being such a thing as beginner's luck, those lively gushers of commencement like the hefty, undepleted reserves of sperm in a fifteen-year-old boy. I had no such energy, and each trip, each paranormal, theurgic transport told heavily on my—well, what have you?—blood, bone, skin, bowel, urine and saliva. I would return each time after my nocturnal sojourns to a body whose blood seemed to have thickened and cooled. I cut my hand, bled. Fat bubbled in globules there like oil slicks in soup. My bones burned. My skin rashed. My bowels loosened. My urine hardened, painfully scraped the walls of my urethra. My saliva congealed. I had to pick it from between my teeth with floss. What if I caught a draft? Exposed, sloped as a flier gone down on a glacier, my lungs would have shipped the pneumonic poisons like locks filling. (I shut the windows before I went to sleep, pulled the shades—this was high summer—closed the doors, arranged myself between quilts and comforters.) What if I became overheated? I would have expired of all the miasmas and malarials of Michigan concentrated in the bedroom. (And without even delirium to comfort me, my mind fled with my spirit.)

"And it has never been easy for me. Maybe I haven't the stomach for it. Even in the beginning, when I was younger, stronger, it wasn't easy, all that steep, uphill, roller coaster and ferris wheel verticality, all that roil and flux and vertigo, spiral roll, reel, twirl and turn giving me the staggers, shakes, totters and spastics, giving me the flutters, flops, snaps and palpitations.

"Also, frankly, it bored me. I mean the astral projection itself, if one can even think of boredom in connection with an enterprise filled with such dread and such terror, immaculate as the edge of a knife. I am afraid I am afraid of the dark.

"The trip from Michigan to Vermont is almost a thousand miles and is accomplished in time. No dimension is finessed, and even if my body is incorporeal, the Great Lakes are wet and deep, the cold night air piled with isobar, pressure, front, moisture and electrical charge. There are birds that could snap up my soul in one peck. There is gravity and the hard, wide black landscape beneath it like a net. There are rough trees and treacherous limbs and sharp-edged leaves like a dangerous vegetable cutlery. There are small animals in the grasses with their honed, predatory temperaments. There are vicious puddles of oil on the highways, noxious, cloying as quicksand. There are tile and slate roofs like strips of sulfur below my astral friction. There is the air mail. There is everywhere beneath me and all along the route of my medium impediment like land-mined space or badly laid track. There are the poisoned, awful molecules of the supernatural, and the blinded atoms of the dark.

"And once, streaming through space, I felt the presence of some *ignus fatuus* and could just make it out, a phosphorescent, not point, *grease* of light that maneuvered with me, kept pace with me, swerving to the left when I did, soaring when I soared, swooping when I swooped. I thought it might be a bird but no bird could fly at such speeds. I tried to evade it, losing my course but not my companion. I did barrel rolls, loop-the-loops, plunges, spins, stalls, slips and slides, all the dives and glides of Chagall acrobacy, but it kept up with me, I couldn't shake it. Terrified, I climbed—I could have made it over the Rockies then—higher than I had ever climbed and, at the apogee of my endurance, suddenly leveled off, thinking to outrun it. I could still hear it, its pierce through space, but behind me now and not so loud as before.

"At the last it called out. 'Please. Please,' it called, 'I'm lost. Please. Let me come with you! Please,' it cried. 'Something's wrong. I can't get back. Won't you help me? Please,' it wailed, *'please!'*

"It was another astral projectionist. If it hadn't been exhausted, if it hadn't been on its return trip, it would have caught me. It would have followed me back. It would have burrowed into the vacant body on my bed like a worm hiding in fruit.

"So of *course* it was love which took me there, not curiosity. If I needed to know what my uncle was feeling it was so I could console him. But he would not dream, he was dreamless. I would have to make the trip in daylight.

"Forget that I would have to face in light the thousand terrors I had merely glossed in dark, that each stone would now not only be palpable but visible, and all rough terrain writ large, the confused blur of geography, the rooftops, kids, dogs and all sharp spikes of the world present to me as temperature. Or maybe it was that height, height itself (and distance too) would become a landmark, a physical, ponderable corporeity solid as the calculable per second per second acceleration of falling bodies. Forget *all* my misgivings. There was still left the physics of the thing, the fixed givens of technique like the constitutional stipulations governing a presidency. The spirit may separate itself from the material plane only when the physical body is sleeping. There is that same guard-prisoner relationship one runs across in melodrama—— jealousy, suspicion and the followed heart.

"I am not one of those fortunates who can nod off anywhere. I haven't the gift of napping. Sleep is a ceremony with me. There must be weariness, yes, but also beds, night, pajamas and turned-down blankets. The clocks must be wound, the house locked and the cat put out. There must be bedtime. Even when I'm ill, I've noticed, I find it hard to doze in the daytime. Healthy, the task is almost impossible.

"But I made the effort. I undressed as I would at night, carefully folding my shirt, still fresh—I'd put it on that morning—and hanging my suit neatly in the closet. I lined up my shoes, the toes just sticking out from beneath the bed but hiding the part where the laces begin. I put my bathrobe on over my pajamas and brought my socks, handkerchief and underwear to the laundry hamper. I emptied my bladder and brushed my teeth. I got into bed. I sighed and yawned, attempting to trick myself with the noises of ease. I was quite wakeful of course. I knew I would be. I decided to read for a bit, selecting for my reading matter not only the dullest book I could find but one I had already read. I turned on the reading lamp beside the bed, though there was light enough to read even with the shades drawn and the curtains pulled tight across the window. Wakeful as ever, it seemed to me that I was becoming hungry. I nibbled fruit, drank warm milk, grazed cold chicken. At three that afternoon I dressed, went to my office and put in three hours' work before starting home. I repeated my efforts the next day and the next after that, and though I slept soundly at night, my insomnia disappearing at my normal hour for retiring, I was unable to sleep at all during the day.

"On the fourth day it occurred to me to try to lull myself with the habits of my childhood. I had no toys now of course, but I brought the cat into the room and encouraged it to stay beside me on the bed, a privilege it is at all other times refused. The cat was terrified and I let it go. I said my prayers. I prayed for sleep. I counted sheep. What *didn't* I do? I even obtained a rather powerful sleeping draught from a pharmacist friend and took it late one morning with a cup of warm honey. The potion worked and I was soon asleep, but I had not realized that inside my drugged physical body my astral one would be narcotized too. We are a curious mix of curious psychology, Doctor, a patchwork of whim and fixed idea. I don't know if you will understand this, or if the boy you show this letter to will, but I was more bitter about the seven wasted hours of drug-induced sleep than I was about all thirty of the wakeful, working, tossing and turning ones I had put in trying to lose consciousness.

"The solution to the problem when it came in the middle of the second week—the seventh week after I had first learned of my uncle's difficulties—was absurdly simple. Or perhaps not simple, merely correct, merely honorable. It was never just family feeling that had drawn me on those night flights to Vermont. It was never, though it should have been, that avalanche loss of prized cousins, that cumulative, rolled-snow cataract of exacerbate, bumped-up death. It wasn't even my sense of my uncle's awful losses, the terrible casualties he was taking that year. It was my uncle himself, his being, legend, whatever it was in the man that had captured first the imaginations of Susan and Oliver, Redford and Ben, and then their souls, whatever it was that had made them do actual physical violence to each other, even delayed murder, just for the right not to live with him since they already had that right but to stay in the same room with him while he worked, even, for appearances, decorum, taking on that work themselves, the watchmaker, the woodsman, the young man with tenure in love, the young woman who lifted anvils not just to see if a girl who weighed perhaps one hundred thirty pounds could raise and hold off the ground an object two and a half times her own weight but just to be ready to do so if the time ever came when she might be required to. It was Joe, it was my uncle, whatever he had been—was, is—that had caused his children to repudiate whatever potential they may have had for individual distinction—none even *wished* to attend the state university at Burlington—and collectively subsume all future, even after the pattern was established and they saw it was certain to be a doomed one, under his. Not apprenticed to the blacksmith, apostled.

"So it was simply a matter of putting things into perspective. If my cousins could lay down their lives for my uncle, surely I could lay down and sleep for a few hours.

"I rose on a Thursday morning in the second week of my efforts to sleep during the day. I showered, dressed, made my bed, breakfasted and returned to my bedroom, where I undressed, got into the pajamas I had taken off less than an hour earlier, removed the spread from the bed I had just made, got into bed and was asleep almost as soon as my head touched the pillow.

"Separation came quickly, my astral integument peeling off from my body like rind. The trip to Vermont was uneventful.

"I am, perhaps, too sentimental, but it was a place I'd summered when I was a child, where I'd spent all those sharp, bright weeks of un-Michigan youth, where I was a visitor, privileged, glamorous even to myself, cargo'd by all that distant geography of the Midwest, the kid who'd seen Chicago, who'd lived for a time in Detroit, where the automobiles came from, where dozens of factories employed thousands of men simply to tighten a bolt, or just to patrol, take down the names of men talking, where there were machines, assembly lines longer than the main street of my cousins' New England town, where somehow—I knew it, my aunt did, my cousins—the scale was different, not just the buildings that were bigger and taller, but the people, too, who would have had to be if only to manage those immense planes and perpendicularities. (They asked if there were mountains in Michigan. I told them no. Of course, they said. Meaning, I think, that there wouldn't have been room for them, that something would have to give way in the fierce moil of all that activity and that of course it would be Nature.) So, welcome as I was, I was looked on by my cousins with something like awe, and if they took me on trails in their mountains or patiently taught me to fish in their streams, or side-stepped with me, hugging the loose timbers for handhold, along the outside ledges of their covered bridges or sneaked me into their granges and meeting halls where we hid in the back or crouched beneath the stage while the grownups argued, or invited me to church on Sunday mornings or quickly hustled me inside their one-room schoolhouse after they had picked the lock or read aloud the strange motto—'Live Free or Die'—on the New Hampshire license plates on the occasional car parked near the green, or Vergil'd me through the small, ancient graveyard, waiting while I read each tombstone, the dates and names and epitaphs, it was not so much to show off as to brief me, actually lobbying I think, pressing me with information, facts, their identities subsumed even then, if only I'd known it, their decisions already made, goners to the twentieth century and asking only that their mottos, names and epitaphs be taken back with me to what even they thought of as the real world.

"So if I hesitated outside my uncle's smithy it was not grief, though it may sound like it, not a moment of silent prayer, though it may sound like that too. It was not even tribute. It was nostalgia. Not for my cousins, for myself. For those good old days when they had imbued me with the mystery of distance. (Who had it now, who could hopscotch space like a token on a Monopoly board, negotiate the round trip of half a continent in a piece of a night or day—— the astral leapfrogger, the astral miler.) I did not re-attend those old haunts, the greens and streams and trails and halls, graves and grange, schoolhouse and covered bridge, merely taking them in at a glance, no more, the lovely street of the lovely town—it was daylight, not yet noon—and guessing at the weather like a sailor—in repose the astral essence, the astral gist is insensate as coin—gauging the temperature of the late August Vermont morning by the hard edges of the shining clouds against the high sky, blue and crisp as a fresh workshirt, putting it in the mid-sixties, say, from the legible, razor-sharp shadows of the leaves. It could have been twenty years earlier, I could have been that proud, privileged visitor who'd seen Chicago, who'd lived for a time in Detroit. I tell you all this to prepare you.

"The street outside my uncle's shop was practically deserted. No farmers with wagons were lined up outside waiting. There was nowhere to be seen those cronies I'd heard about or seen myself when I'd made my visits as a child. A single wagon stood unhitched and pulled up against the great, shut, almost barnlike doors at the side of the shop. I could see smoke rising from one of my uncle's special chimneys but in no great quantity and with no special force. I couldn't hear anything, neither the ringing slam of the blacksmith's hammer nor the great low huff of his fire. I went inside. I shan't set the scene.

"My uncle was alone in the locked shop. Perhaps I had misread the weather signs, I thought, or maybe heat was cumulative, like sweets or starches, and if you stayed around it long enough you began at last to store it, like a fever thermometer that has not been shaken down. Except for his leather blacksmith's apron he was naked.

"There was a mare with him, a Morgan, I think, a little darker than most Morgans, but maybe less full in the flank and croup. I'm not really expert in these matters, only what I picked up—overheard —from my uncle when I was a kid, but *some*thing off about her proportions. Her front, from chest to withers and elbow to shoulder, was full as a gelding's but she tapered at mid-rib to an attenuated hind quarters and she gave one the sense—listen to this, I refer to the astral pith as 'one;' you get used to anything—of prow, some foreshortened, figurehead horse.

"Pay attention, listen to me. What do *I* know about a horse's proportions? Perhaps something *was* a little off, but I dance around like this because I don't know how to say it. I've come this far, those two weeks of insomniac days, those four deaths, those five round trips from Michigan to Vermont, and I don't know how to tell it.

"My uncle was directing the horse like a ringmaster. I don't mean that the horse moved around him in circles but that my uncle constantly repositioned himself within her arcs and windings, ducked inside her torsions—— more sheepdog, really, than ringmaster.

" 'How's that shoe?' he asked in a low voice. 'Go ahead, put your weight on it.'

"Then he spoke to it more gently still, his open palms moving in and away from his body, doing the passes of perspective and appraisal, his low voice choked with implication. 'Sets the hoof off nice.'

"The words were strange. He spoke of her walls and white lines, of her bars and buttresses and frogs. 'Your elastic was almost thread-bare,' he said. 'I could feel horn. In places it showed through the pulp like new tooth. Well, your frog's so big. I never seen such frogs on a mare. I had to hold it with both hands. I had to hold it with both hands, didn't I? No, no,' he said soothingly, 'you got the bulbs for it, sister. It ain't as if you didn't have the bulbs for it. Bet you could kick a man to Kingdom Mountain with those bulbs.'

"He might have been a shoe salesman, with all such a salesman's oblique, evasive flattery. He was almost flirting with the animal, talking in tongues of the equivocal, the shy acrostics of obsession, his words almost matching the shifting position of his hands.

"He never touched it. All he did was look, encouraging its aimless parade around his smithy and constantly adjusting his own relation to it like a man changing seats in a movie.

" 'Well,' my uncle said finally, 'your owner will be calling for you. What do you say we get into our tack?'

"He turned to some harness hanging from pegs on the wall of the shop, pacing back and forth beside the gear before choosing.

" 'Let's get a look at you in the bellyband,' he said, and took down the thick girth, angling it from just behind her withers and along the forward line of her belly. He buckled it slowly, stepping back when he'd finished, drawing deep breaths. 'Don't *you* look provocative?' he said. 'Too tight?' he said. 'You don't want it loose and it'd take more than *I've* got to do a wench like you a bruise. Nice you're so dark. I like a dark mare. It brings out the power. I'm a bit of a dark horse myself. Well,' he said, 'a girl has to breathe. I'll take that off for a bit.' He unbuckled the bellyband, let it lie where it dropped, fallen as garter on the floor of the shop. Then he selected a bridle, setting the headstall loosely, the thin, unfastened straps vaguely wreathing her face like the struts of some extraordinary veil. He attached the bit and curb and added a set of blinders which he took from the pouch of his leather apron. 'Eye shadow,' he said, then removed one of the blinders. 'Don't *you* look haughty. Like some old, one-eyed whore. Let's take that off, missy.'

"The bridle's reins and checkreins he allowed to hang loose, then, studying them, proceeded to wind them like sandal straps about the horse's chest and belly and flanks. He watched silently as the mare, reaching behind her with her long head, began to undo the great, loose package of itself that my uncle had made. 'Oh,' he said, 'aren't we shameless, aren't we bold?' He scooped off the bridle and reins and, opening her jaws, pulled the bit from her mouth, transferring it, before I realized what was happening, into his own mouth, impossibly, greedily shoving all of it inside his distended cheeks. He started to gag. He stood over the looping reins of his retching. 'No, no,' he said breathlessly, 'it ain't you. Your breath's just as fresh, as fresh—— ' He vomited again, hitting the side of her muzzle. Stooping quickly, he raised a corner of his apron and wiped his mouth on the leather. The startled horse shied obliquely, prancing back and sideways away from my uncle. I thought she was going to back into the forge. So, apparently, did my uncle, who, recovering immediately, sprang forward while she was still off balance and, shoving against her haunch, managed to knock her over.

"You'd think he'd have stopped. He was a Vermonter, a canny New Englander. The owner might already be on his way back. He was still naked, the mare was too. You'd think he'd have stopped. He cradled her head for a moment in his great arms, then allowed her to rise, studying her now from underneath. You'd think he'd have stopped.

122

"Then maybe he did. He stood and put the bellyband on again. Working quickly, he attached the breast collar to it, tightening it across the mare's shoulders and holding it in place with the straps that went over her back. He stepped back.

" 'Lewd jade,' he said. 'Hussy horsy, minxy mare. Piece, baggage, chippy, drab! Floozie, doxy, harlot, tart! *Racy, ain't we, in our horse brassieres?'*

"He set the breeching between her loins and croup and around her buttocks. He looped a thong through both brass breeching links and tied it off tightly under her belly. Her rump suddenly jumped into place, set off like something mounted. My uncle walked around behind her.

"He's going to cover her! My God, I thought, he's going to cover her!

"He raised his apron. He was wearing her crupper, my uncle's penis in the leather loop. He'd been wearing it all along, big enough all along *to* wear it. 'The smith,' he said huskily, 'a mighty man is he,' and loosened the loop, rolling it down the length of his cock. Then, raising the mare's tail, he passed the loop quickly under it, buckling it to the harness so that the tail, arched now, perked in some counterfeit of swank and hauteur and pride, the beast, arranged in leather, seeming as abandoned and wanton and vainglorious as anything my uncle had yet called it, its own leathery being made for harness, for all the dressings, gauzes, slings and splints, all the bandages, swabs and tourniquets, all that Sam Browne belt kink of girdled loin, and the intricate sexual square knots of leverage, actually prosthetic perhaps, the bandoleer and bunting arrangements, the flashy, fleshy piping of possibility.

"He's going to cover her. He's not even going to remove his apron. He's going to cover her.

"But he didn't. All he did was squat behind her on his bare feet, his long testicles grazing the floor. All he did was watch.

"Then, suddenly, the mare stiffened, locked her legs and shit a steaming mound of manure bright as tobacco. And so did my uncle.

"Yes. I wondered about that part, too. It had been a good projection, I mean an easy one. The trip to Vermont was uneventful. I wasn't even winded. What had happened to the astral telegraph? Where was the soul semaphore, the point-to-point red alert of the heart? At first I was going to 'speak.' I had meant to. I had my objections and chastisements and pleas all ready. I had meant to speak out.

"First I didn't. Then I couldn't.

"The smith, a mighty man is he. Who denied the claims of biology and brooked no precedence in love. Who would not vary a psalm or alter an iota of eulogy and who built his coffins not to custom but to paradigm. He didn't want his children to die, he couldn't have known that they would. I can only presume that he knew the preferences of his glands, that he had identified them from the beginning, from the time he first went into blacksmithing—he could as easily have tapped the maple trees or farmed cider or made a crop of hay —before, perhaps, perhaps from the moment he had first seen a horse saddled. Not only permitting the old-timers and cronies but actually hosting them, wearing the scratchy checkered shirts (who wanted hide next to his skin or nothing) out of some native patience and politeness, some I'll-come-as-you-are deference and courtesy, like a man who manages to get down some food he can't stand simply because his hostess has taken the trouble to prepare it for him. And then permitting the children as he had permitted the cronies, not a host this time but a father, and evidently a good one, possibly a great one. Not forbidding their attendance on him even after their mother had died, only—love makes no precedence, no distinction—asking of them that they settle the pecking order themselves. The glands in abeyance, their rampage not tamed but checked, whip-and-chair'd up onto the heavy platforms of decorum, and his back never once turned.

"As I say, astral projection can take you so far and no further. As I say, it can't even get me past the Rockies. As I say, it is often a cold comfort, well intentioned but of as much real use as the casserole of a condolence caller. It can clear the air though. Sometimes. A little, a little it can. That blazing sprint of the soul can clear the air, and perhaps may even explain the good weather, the briskness of the day, its sharp shadows, focused as ink on a bright page.

"Faithfully,

Lewis Press Ringlinger"

Kinsley was across the room watching him read, knowing, the boy believed, just where George was in the letter at any given time, not only which page but which paragraph, which sentence.

"Well?" the man said as George looked at the signature. "What do you think?"

"What did he mean 'the boy you show this letter to'?"

"Ah," the big man said.

"What did he mean?"

Kinsley smiled. "Perhaps only that we're being watched."

"Watched," George said.

"It's the West he can't get to, not Florida." George looked in the corners of the room, on the lookout for the telltale point of greasy light Ringlinger had spoken of. "I'll tell you what *I* think," Kinsley said. "I think it's the pornography business we're in. Death and the supernatural are merely the covers it takes. I think we're in the pornography business, that the religion we practice, the hoodoo consolation we give away, is sexual. I'd like you to work the seances with me. I want you to be my contact, my messenger boy from Death. You're not twelve yet. I want you to work nude. No pasties, no Indian loincloth or oversized dressing gown with its planets and crescents and five-points-to-the-star astronomy. Naked. Nude. No one would touch you. You won't have to touch anyone. It will be dark. No one will even be able to make out your face.

"It's a good idea, you know. We'd make a lot of money. There's so much lust. The stitching of sex everywhere, common as knot, pandemic as signature. More lust and combination than the ingredients in recipes. Ask your parents. It's a gimcrack idea.

"You know," Kinsley said, "it's a shame finally. It's all real, you know. The supernatural plane is real as a breadboard. Astral projection is real. All of it is. I'm certain of my facts. (I get *past* the Rockies.) Last night I visited my dead. It's just you can't always reproduce it for them. It's just you have to be alone. Isn't that right, Mr. Ringlinger? Isn't that right, sir? Am I lying to this boy?"

George held his breath. It seemed to him that just for a moment, and out of the corner of his eye, he saw the dark stain where greased, oiled heads had rested against the back of a wing chair glisten and flare.

"So," Kinsley said, "what do you think?"

What he thought was that it wasn't the first time. It seemed that someone he knew of was always talking to horses. Perhaps only what they said was different. Or maybe not. Maybe they said the same things finally, choosing language good as any to talk to horses in, trying to get through, past, like Ringlinger, like Kinsley, like all the others in Cassadaga, telling them in words even people would have trouble with what they wanted, who they were.

He had known the secrets of seances for almost a year, had attended, diligent as someone learning a card trick, as almost every spiritualist in Cassadaga had explained his particular techniques, un-burdening, trusting him with their mysteries, dragging him into their conspiracies. It was not the way grownups normally behaved with children. Even his parents had said "when you're older," putting him off with their "not yets" and "not nows" (filling him in only on this: family history), but the Cassadagans had fixed on him as if he were some kid confidant, inundating him with some need they had to provide the plausible, satisfy logic, purge belief, lapse faith.

If he was taken in by some particularly striking effect, they could become almost shrill in their contempt.

"My God! Didn't you even *feel* it?" Reverend Bone demanded.

"My left arm moved."

"Not *that!* Didn't you feel it when we shook hands and I planted the fishhook in your shirtsleeve?"

"You were talking about the spirits being angry. Something touched my sleeve. My arm flew up."

"Christ, kiddo, it's a good thing you're too small and I had to throw you back. Otherwise I'd fry you for lunch. Something touched your sleeve! Yeah, right. My nickel fishhook and my ten-pound line! You were rigged as a puppet, Pinnoch! You were struck as a pom-pano."

"There's nothing there."

"Jesus! You don't know beans about good manners, do you? When people shake hands hello they usually shake hands good-by."

"That's when you took it out."

Bone rolled his eyes and raised his hands in the air. "Curses, foiled again," he said mildly.

It was always their mildness which was feigned. All they de-manded of him was pure doubt, unrelenting skepticism. It was as if by exposing the five-cent fishhooks and ten-pound lines that were nearly always the simple solutions—they shunned the elaborate, were unreconciled to the complicated; if a seance couldn't be conducted by a spiritualist and one assistant it was not a clean operation—to what were only tricks, hammering at him with explanation, clarification, cracked code and truth, they were free to contemplate mystery, the wonderful, all the elegant hush-hush of the riddle world.

They were childless of course, or their children were grown, gone, and that may have had something to do with their attitude toward him, but even George, grateful as he was for their attention, understood that at bottom their feelings were neutral, they did not care for him—— not in that way. He was no surrogate.

"No," Professor G. D. Ashmore told him, "you're no surrogate. You're it, the real thing. You know why we beat at you with our greenroom shoptalk and regale you with our wholesale-to-the-trade secrets?"

"Because you trust me?"

"Trust you? Why would we want to trust you? You're a kid. What are you, eleven, eleven and a half? You're a kid. You walk on the grass. You fish out of season. You're a kid, you're nasty to cats. You break a window you say it was an accident. You're a kid, you play hooky, you mock the deformed. Why would anyone trust a kid?"

"Then why?"

"You're going to be twelve soon. You're going to have to make up your mind, George. You're going to have to choose."

"Choose what?"

"Leave me alone, don't bother me. I don't talk turkey with kids."

This was before he'd seen his sister.

His instruction continued.

"In street clothes, I seem ordinary as a fourth for bridge. Pour yourself some lemonade, dear," Madam Grace Treasury called from behind the dark, heavy curtain that served as a partition between her seance room and her parlor. "Pour some for me.

"I could be someone shopping, who does dishes, make beds. In elevators, crowded buses, in all the rush hours, men, women too, find my bearing undistinguished, so like their own that we are almost interchangeable. They can scarcely see me, make me out. It is not prurience or avidity or passion which knocks men against women, which grinds their backs into our busts or makes them lean, close as ballroom dancers, along the cant of our thighs and hips. It is that reflexive indifference to flesh, feature, organ, skin, which sprawls mankind, which, beyond a certain age but implicit at any age, potbellies posture and un-sealegs gait. It is, I think, gravity which opens our mouths like the imbecile's and mutualizes our bodies and sexes in those elevators and buses, permitting touch touch, skin skin, body body, the coalescing rhomboids and circles of our let-be geometrics like some backward parthenogenesis.

"I have no person, I mean. Few people do. Otherwise we should arrange ourselves, even in buses, even in rush hour, like chessmen on boards before play begins. Otherwise—were I beautiful, were I hideous—I should, even in the most crowded elevator, be given that same jagged fringe of elbow room and breathing space, like a nimbus of limelight, that is granted to drunks and royalty and people felled by their bodies collapsed in the street."

She came into the room. She was dressed in a sort of robe, dense and massy as a habit, larger than he'd ever seen her, taller, her face, even her hands fuller.

George saw her strange make-up, her blue face powder, her black lipstick, her face blocked off in queer colors, like the hues of a wound or hidden organs suddenly visible. She seemed immense in her turban, her big seance dress.

"Thank you for pouring the lemonade, dear. My," she said, taking a window seat in the bright parlor, "it's just so *hot*. Sometimes I think it isn't any special favor to us to have all this Florida sunshine. Oh, I know they envy us up North and it *is* a comfort in the winter, but, gracious, it does get hot, and we don't get the cooling breezes that folks can at least hope for in other parts of the country. That's one of the reasons I bought such a large Frigidaire. So I'd always have plenty of ice cubes for my lemonade. When it's hot like this, I like it cold enough to hurt my teeth.

"Will you listen to me nattering on about lemonade and there you've gone and poured me a glass I haven't even made a move to taste. The ice is probably all melted now. Well, no matter, I like the taste almost as much as I do the chill."

She crossed the room, moving behind the small coffee table on which the pitcher and lemonade glasses had been set down and lowered herself beside him on the sofa. He felt the cushions and springs compress as if air and all tension had been squeezed from them, himself suddenly angled toward her, his stiffened body bracing, like some cartoon animal unsuccessfully resisting momentum.

"May I have my glass of lemonade?" she asked.

She seemed less than inches off, her body glowing with its presence and weight and power.

"Give me the lemonade," she said. "I've already asked you once."

He picked the drink up from the table and held it out to her. She made no move to take it from him.

"The lemonade," she repeated. He pushed his hand closer, but felt reined, checked, doing some strange balancing act of the level ground, some odd, squeezed constraint like a resisted fart.

"Set it down," she commanded. "Do I look like a woman who drinks lemonade? Stop that whimpering." She handed him a tissue.

"What is it?" he asked.

"Rush hour," she said. "My askew totemics."

"It's the black lipstick, your blue face powder."

She didn't answer.

"It's the dress," he said, "it's the turban."

She said nothing.

"It's my good posture," she said softly. "It's my sealegs. It's my specific gravity and unsprawled essence."

"You scared me," George said.

"Ah," said Madam Grace Treasury.

He was a bit scared of all of them.

Even of Professor John Sunshine, psychic historian and Cassadaga buff, who lectured him on the subjects of Cassadaga, midgets, freaks, and what Sunshine called "the marked race of Romany."

"The development of Cassadaga and the establishment of the circus's winter quarters in De Land were almost attendant," he said. "You could have had the other without the one but not the one without the other. It's almost as if the town were founded on some debased bedrock of declined, vitiate genes, as if blemish and the sapped heart were to the origins of Cassadaga what a fresh water supply and the proximity of a railroad were to the development of Chicago, say.

"We don't know either the significance of the name or how the area came to have it in the first place, but in all probability it goes back to that marked race of Romany, that same hampered, degraded, clipped-wing brood which was the town's reason for being. Perhaps a curse or threat, some gypsy-hissed snarl or deterrent. Perhaps even an ultimatum, some sinister dun, the soul's dark invoice. So even if I don't have the literal translation—this would be slang, you see, idiom, some word or words fugitive *(Cassadaga. Cas* sa *daga! Cassa! da Ga!)* even to that touring company of the fugitive, double-talk to the ensemble, the swarthy old-timers and pierce-lobed regulars, slang, patter, argot, cant—I have the metaphorical one: some busted negotiation between buyer and seller. Maybe not even language finally, maybe only furious extemporized sound, the clicks and spirants, dentals and velars of Romany rage. Cassadaga! Ca *ssad* a ga! Cock-a-doodle-doo!

"Nor do we understand why, if the founding of Cassadaga and the founding of the circus's winter quarters in De Land were practically collaborate, Cassadaga would be fifteen miles from De Land. We may speculate, of course.

"The mark of the marked race of Romany is to a large extent

self-inflicted. They are an aloof, self-exiled, stand-offish people, wanderers who carry their ghetto with them, who move through the world like refugees, as if whatever they may have left in any direction in which they are not immediately traveling is either already burning or contagious. Cassadaga wouldn't have been Cassadaga then. Whatever it was that happened between the gypsy girl and the *gadge* wouldn't have happened yet. It would have been a clearing, a place to put the caravan down, at once far enough off from De Land and close enough in, situated nearby the *gadge* money and opportunity which would have been the marked race of Romany's equivalent of fresh water and the proximate railroad.

"Of *course* they fraternized with the stiffs and roustabouts. It wouldn't even have been fraternization in the strict sense of the term, the stiffs and roustabouts—my God, even the tumblers, acrobats and flyers; even the clowns, wire walkers and animal trainers themselves —barely a step up the evolutionary ladder from the marked race of Romany."

He looked at George with his intense eyes, examining him as he spoke. He didn't miss a beat. He didn't miss anything, and the boy felt Sunshine's hot scrutiny and wondered if perhaps something shameful weren't happening on the surface of his skin. Sunshine might have been a G-man, George suspect currency.

"Have you seen them? When you go into De Land with your father or to school, do you take a good look at them? Not just giving them the once-over for ringlets or swarthy skin, for holes in their ears or a garlic in their mouth—hair can be combed straight or hidden under a cap, skin can bleach out in winter quarters; holes fall in on themselves and a clove can be covered by a tongue, though most of them don't bother—but really *looked* at them, at their foreigners' cheekbones like subcutaneous wales or some dead giveaway marked Romany spoor of indefinite half-life, at their scars and tattoos like marked trees or a vulgar postage? Have you looked in their eyes or smelled the smoke on their skin? (It gets into their pores. They can never get rid of it.) Have you seen their bunkhouses? The floors have great wooden wheels under them and the wheels are buried in the ground. You didn't look at them, you look at them next time."

All the while looking at George—who hadn't seen his sister yet but had recently had from his father a bit of the story of the first George Mills—examining him as he'd advised George to examine the roustabouts and circus performers. (And when, George wondered, will I be brave enough to look at another human being the way this strange man is looking at me?)

"Of *course* they fraternized. Hell, maybe it wasn't even fraternization, maybe it was just family reunion. But remember what they were there for, too. Marked race of Romany or no, cousins or no, these roustabouts and artistes were just so much *gadge* gold to the gypsies. (And maybe that's why you don't find rings in a roustabout's ear. Because the gypsies stole them!) They sold them their daughters' virginity, or its appearance, its raw chicken skin prosthetic equivalency, its family secret recipe cosmetic blood, or sold them to the roustabouts anyway, the artistes having daughters of their own, their own merchandise, and gambled with them, the artistes, too, and told their fortunes and worked spells against their enemies for money, and something which was even of more importance and real value to them, to the artistes, not the roustabouts, than anything else. They sold them magic.

"The marked race of Romany sold the circus people their talent. They sold them magic balance. Before the gypsies came in from Cassadaga, the wire walkers were merely skilled, trained, vaguely equilibriumally inclined, say. Afterward, they were surefooted as mules, as cats and mountain goats, with a gift for recovery and balance like a bubble in a level. There was inner ear in the soles of their feet. They could walk up a tree as casually as you climb stairs.

"They sold strength to the acrobats, infusing their legs and arms with the force of bombs, selling them flexibility, endurance, the tractables of great apes, a lung capacity that was operatic. The pyramids they did now were Cheopsic, Pharaonic. They could hang by a pinkie or stand on their hair.

"And height to the flyers, loft and lift, the tucks, spins and gainers of birds, the timing of salmon.

"And sold to the animal trainers, the lion tamers and bears and elephant handlers, the equerry and equestriennes, a Doolittle knowledge of the beastly heart, some Braille brute feel for fauna that was not so much mastery as plain hard bargaining, actual clausal, contractual negotiation, some stipulate Done! Shake! binding agreement, and the locked cage like a union shop! Selling them not magic courage, because you can't buy courage, but a gift for magic enterprise, magic haggle—the bull market, the bear—faerie quid pro quo, the tiger's leap through a fiery hoop knocked down for red meat, the bears and horses humbled for a sweet, extra straw. Selling them not courage but courage's opposite—— risklessness: that watered cement and shortcut materiel of the soul which permitted the purchaser never even ever to need courage again, so that each time he walked into the cage or raised the now entirely ornamental whip in the center ring as the panthers fled past in lively lockstep dressage, it was with the knowledge—his *and* the animals'—that the fix was in. (Maybe *that's* what 'Cassadaga' means. Perhaps it's only Gypsy for 'Do this trick and I'll leave you alone.')

"And even something for the clowns. The marked race of Romany sold the clowns mark, the putty projections, high relief like Nepal on a map, some magic dispensation for the malleable, lending their faces and heads a talent for perspective—— for protuberance, salience, jut and cavity, some easy canvas character in the skin itself which permitted their faces to shine like chameleon, to glow in primary colors like a waved flag.

"(Selling all of them the same thing finally, even the earthbound, giftless roustabouts on whom they turned loose their supposititious virgins, dealing in the one legitimate, renewable resource they had going for them, their heritage you could say. I mean their sticky-ringlet swarth and smoked-game stink, their forest-scarred skin and bad breath. Their animality I mean.)"

Why's he telling me all this? George wondered. How does this show me the tricks of the trade or help prepare me to choose whatever it is I'm supposed to choose?

"Because we're no better," Professor Sunshine said. "If we think we are we're only kidding our—— " He broke off. He reached over and grabbed the boy's hand and pulled it toward his face. George thought he was going to kiss it, but the man only gathered it in and held it there. His nostrils flared and relaxed. He's sniffing me, George thought, and wanted to cry. "You're not from around here," Sunshine said. He released George's hand. "Where do you come from? I forget."

"I came from Milwaukee with my parents."

"Gypsies have parents," he said. "There are gypsies in Wisconsin," he said slyly.

"We're English," the boy said, and thought: We're English. Father says Millses go back to before the Norman Conquest. Then he remembered what his father had lately been hinting was their doom: never to rise, never to break free of their class, marked as Cain—my God! he thought, marked!—forever to toil, wander, luckless as roustabout.

Professor Sunshine smiled, no longer looking at George. Some of the edge had come out of his voice. He spoke, George thought, as his teacher sometimes did when she was telling them about some place in the world that neither she nor anyone else in the class would ever see. "The psychics came only after the gypsies had already cleared off, but, like the marked race of Romany itself, settled in Cassadaga. They showed little interest in the roustabouts or circus performers and, except for the occasional seance or consultation, had almost nothing to do with them. From the first their attention and interest, to the extent that they were drawn to the circus at all, was focused on the personnel from the side show.

"Not the fire eaters or sword swallowers, not the geeks—they had geeks then—or any of the rest of those who had trained their appetites or reamed passages in their throats and bellies to bank their snacks. They were just more athletes. Not even the fat ladies or giants. Bulk couldn't be feigned but it could be cultivated. You could grow a fat lady as you grow a rose. And height, though unintentional, was merely excessive, the stockpiling of what otherwise was not only a normal but even an attractive quality.

"No, the brotherhood was attracted to monsters. It sought out bogy, ogre, eyesore, sport—— all those unfortunates whose busted bodies were the evidence that they came directly from the pinched hand of God Himself. It wanted the alligator woman and the dogfaced boy, the pinhead and the Cyclops, the Siamese twins and the herma-phrodite. It wanted people with extra thumbs, too many toes. Too many? There could never *be* enough!

"They were from up North. I don't know how the paranormals found out about Cassadaga. Perhaps they read the trades. They'd have done that. They do it today. What we do, our gifts, has never been that far removed from show business. My colleagues would not only have kept up with the trends but followed the gates too—— of vaudeville, mud show, circus, nightclub and novelty acts. They'd have read all about it when the circus came to De Land to set up permanent winter quarters. Or maybe it wasn't the trades. Maybe they just used their talents for divination, telepathy, second sight, all their occult, mystic jungle telegraph.

"There was a sort of gold rush. Cassadaga became a kind of boom town, some Sutter's Mill of the extraordinary. I have some of their early correspondence with the freaks, though most didn't bother to write; they just came. It's very strange stuff. Even the envelopes are strange. Well, they would be, wouldn't they? They had no addresses for them. Christ, they didn't even have their names!

133

" '*To the young fourteen-year-old girl,*' they would write on the front of the envelope above the De Land destination, '*with the gray hair and withered body of an old woman.*' '*For the man,*' they'd write, '*born with sores.*' '*The lady with green blood.*' '*Personal!*' they'd write.

"The letters themselves were always elaborate concoctions of sympathy, buttressed with the writer's credentials and followed by a request for an interview with a view to the misfit's throwing his lot in with the writer's. They couldn't expect to be paid much of course, at least at first, but if the spiritualist was correct in his assumptions about the unfortunate *lusus naturae*—spiritualists were wonderfully euphemistic with these freaks and death's heads—then perhaps they could get to the bottom of things together, and settle once and for all the nagging, age-old question 'Why me?' "

Why me? George Mills thought.

"You'd be wrong if you assumed my paranormal friends sought the freaks out just to juice up their failing acts, that they were in it simply for the money. Well, you'd be partly wrong.

"Because they really *did* believe that the body's disgrace, that cleft blood and blighted flesh and faulted bones brittle as toothpick —there was one fellow, the Glass-Boned Man, who would permit children to shatter his fingers for a dollar; you could hear the snap as his bone fragmented; there wasn't much to it; the bones in his arms and hands were fragile as Saltines; the sound was real, but it was an ever depleting resource; the bones became smaller and smaller chips; after a while all you could hear was the muffled grinding of sand— were the outward, visible signs of inner psychic energies. These were your real McCoy Cains, your truly marked. Marked and marked down, too—— discounted, slashed from the human race itself, whom chipped genes and bombed biology had doomed. Such things count. There's compensation. Surely that centered eye of the Cyclops wore a honed vision, and the ping-pong ball brain of the pinhead felt what it couldn't know.

"Superstition? Medieval? Just one more way of rubbing luck like paint off a hunchback? All right. Maybe. Even probably. But they put them through it, our forefathers did, and went through it themselves, too. It was almost as if they had to test them out, to prove to themselves that the dogfaced boys and the pinheads, that the alligator girls and glass-boned guys hadn't any more real psychic powers than a dollar's worth of loose change before they ever dared to use them in the act or teach them the scam.

"Because there really is such a thing as hypnotism and these

134

folks, the paranormals in all their infinite varieties, were past masters of the art. They had *some* sessions, believe me.

" 'Where do you come from?'

" 'Hartford.'

" 'No, before that. I'm going to take you back to the time of the womb. What do you see?'

" 'Pussy.'

" 'You're no longer in the womb. This is before conception now. I've set you down on the astral plane among the primary emanations. Describe what it's like.'

" '_____'

" 'I command you to describe the dematerialized world.'

" 'Ain't no worsteds, ain't no wools. Ain't no cotton, ain't no silk.'

" 'At the count of three you'll wake up refreshed.'

"Sure they were disappointed. So were the dwarfs. (There were dwarfs now, they'd gone over to dwarfs, had graduated downward in birth defect, some unevolutionary, pulled-horns substitute that covered over the scabs and open sores and inside-out arrangements of ordinary physiological disfigurement.) You'd have been disappointed yourself. The desire and pursuit of the mysterious is a lifelong life. The occult is a hard taskmaster. Like mathematics or physics or astronomy or any other science. Like painting or music or sculpture or any other art.

"So of course they were disappointed. But a little relieved, too, not to have ready to hand a key to the astonishing secret of life, its nagging riddle: 'Why me?' Because people, God bless them, are terrified of the strange. It may be that you've seen a man in a bear suit. On the street, say, or at a game between halves. You know that the man is a man, the costume a costume. But when he comes to *you* to dance, you pull back, you shy. You're pulling back now. Has such a thing happened?"

He thought of Madam Grace Treasury's bruised cosmetics.

"How much more effective when the costume is shriveled skin, limbs that don't size, a dubious sex? Power is only amok scale, the gauges off true and the needle in red. Send in the dwarf."

George looked up but there was only Professor Sunshine, talking to himself.

" 'How far can you expect to go in circus on your little legs?'

" 'Go ahead, I heard it all. Go ahead, I'll help you out. I sleep in a crib, I eat in a high chair. I got a dong the size of a safety pin

135

and I bite my wrists when the Campfire Girls come to town. Go ahead, I heard it already. I have a tiny appetite. If the thermometer reads 98.6 I'm running a fever. If I work hard, someday I can make it in the small time. I'm a little late for an appointment.'

" 'Isn't it humil—'

" '—iating for me when some broad picks me up and puts me on her lap? Nah, I got high hopes. Go ahead.'

" 'You can read my mind. Evidently you have second sight.'

" 'Nah, I'm shortsighted.'

"Because they were runt realistic. All wrong, you'd suppose, for our founders' purposes. But think about it. Who would have been better? My God, *some*body had to be in control. Somebody had to hold in check those airy fairy elements of our fathers' style. Who'd be better with their sideshow hearts and their eye for a mark than those little rationalists?

"And wasn't it just good sound show business after all to make it appear that the dummy was in control and not the ventriloquist? Wasn't that as much a part of the program as an intermission? You don't horse around with what works. So all that was left was to teach him the fundamentals, show him what had already been shown to the phony red Indian, that marked man whose time had gone, and the nigger slave and gypsy before *him,* and let the midget take it from there. (They were midgets now, dwarfs being still too deformed for the public taste, something too bandy and buckled in their being, their botched, bitched bodies; you don't want to scare the customers half to death, you know, and a midget was just a little scaled-down man; a midget was almost cute, but still tight enough to the terror, close enough, enough nicked by it to leave its mark.)

" 'I can give you fifteen weeks back to back between Thanksgiving and the middle of March. Circus goes out again in April, but I got to have some time off before rehearsals start up that last week in March. Oh yeah, I don't know if you're Christian or not, Reverend, but Christmas week's mine.'

" 'Christmas week?'

" 'I take the Mrs and the kids to their grandma's in Memphis Christmas week.'

" 'The Mrs? Their grandma's?'

" 'The Mrs, yeah. The little woman. The little ones, sure. Their grandma in Memphis. Right, the little old lady.'

" 'You're married?'

" 'Fourteen years next June. Oh, and listen, I ain't never worked double before. I always worked single or with the ensemble but.'

" 'The ensemble?'

" 'The ensemble, the troupe. Yeah. In the Grand Parade. *The Big Finish!*'

"That's the upshot. That's how the midgets came to work with us for a time. Only a few winters, really. *They* called it off. Anyway, a midget always sounded a little like a record speeded up on a gramophone.

"But mostly, mostly they didn't like coming all the way out here to work. To this joined caravan of a town. To us. To Cassadaga."

And C. L. Gregor Imolatty was an authority on ectoplasm. He had converted his spare bedroom into an ectoplasm museum, the only one, he said, in central Florida.

"I couldn't have done it," he told George as they stood just outside the museum's black door, "if it hadn't been for my wife's cooperation. Sylvia's support has been invaluable. I tell all my visitors that. It gets them involved. Here's what we'll do. When we go inside I'll give you the same talk I give my clients. I'll deliver it just as I always do. I won't change a word, but you have to stop me whenever you hear me say something you think might be fake. You got that? If you think I'm lying, stop me. Just go ahead and interrupt. Isn't that a good idea, Sylvia? Isn't that a wonderful way for the boy to learn?"

"We tried that with the Mortons," Mrs. Imolatty said.

"You know you're right?" Imolatty said. "I forgot about the Mortons, but the Mortons were afraid to interrupt me. I think they thought they'd hurt my feelings. You mustn't be afraid you'll hurt my feelings, George. You're here to learn. You chime in now if you think I'm making believe. Just call out 'Lie!' or 'Fake!' or 'Cheat!' Cry 'Stop!' or anything else that occurs to you. All right. Here we go then. Oh. Usually I pause for a moment outside the museum.

" 'Ladies and gentlemen,' I say, 'we're going inside now. You'll notice that the door is painted black. In the museum itself the door, walls, ceiling and floor are all painted black. There's a reason for that. Light is a stimulus, a reagent. It excites ectoplasm and, if sufficiently bright, could cause seepage. So we like to keep it a little on the dark side. You'll be able to see the exhibits perfectly well, but if any of you is carrying a flash camera I must ask you please not to use it.' "

"Stop," George said.

Imolatty gave him a puzzled look. "Why did you stop me?" he

said. "It *is* dark inside. It *is* painted black. I *don't* permit flash cameras."

"Not that," George Mills said, "the stuff about bright light making ex—— exto—— "

"Ectoplasm."

"Ectoplasm seep out."

"Excellent!" Imolatty exclaimed. "He's very smart, isn't he, Sylvia?" He turned to George. "You're absolutely right. We keep it dark for other reasons. Light has nothing to do with it. What would happen to ectoplasm in the daytime if it did? What would happen when the sun rises, or even at night during an electrical storm? Let's go in then."

It was very hot in the dim room. "Thank you, Sylvia," Imolatty said when the woman had flicked on the wall switch. He looked toward George again. "I couldn't have done it if it hadn't been for my wife's cooperation. Sylvia's support has been invaluable," he said.

"It's long been acknowledged," he went on, "that the ancients sought the so-called philosopher's stone in order to transmute base metals into gold. What is perhaps less well known is that the alchemists' researches drew them down *other* paths of the physical sciences and metaphysical arts. On this table, ladies and gentlemen, you may see some of the results of their experiments with crude, or secondary, ectoplasm. Naturally, I don't pretend that these masses you see before you are the original work of those early experimenters. It would be remarkable indeed if such flimsy stuff endured over long centuries while whole cities have faded from the face of the earth, but—— Did you say something, George?"

"No."

"You didn't? All right then. —— but their writings *have* been preserved and are available to anyone who will simply take the trouble to look for them in our great public libraries. Working then from their original formulas, Sylvia and me have been able to duplicate their results in our lab. The three piles in front of me are various forms of crude, or secondary ectopl——"

"Stop."

"George?"

"They're not."

"Not what?"

"Ectoplasm."

"What are they?"

"I don't know. They're not crude ectoplasm."

"Cobwebs! They're cobwebs, George! Ordinary cobwebs! All scrunched and rolled like a fine, thin dough. Do you remember, Sylvia, how we collected this stuff?"

"Oh, those filthy rooms!" Mrs. Imolatty said.

"They *were* dirty."

"The rubbish was all over my dress, in my hair, everywhere."

"It was a mess all right," Imolatty admitted. He turned back to George. "Good for *you,* George!" he congratulated him. "You're not letting me get away with a thing. You're a clever boy. The alchemists *never* experimented with ectoplasm. No, they were too greedy. I doubt if they gave a thought to ectoplasm.

"That low box on your right, the object rather like a foot bath at a public swimming pool, is a sort of 'planter' for ectoplasm. The woolly, grayish substance you see there—just a minute, George—is not itself ectoplasm, but is latent with a dormant *form* of ectoplasm which may sometimes be released through the process of agitation or 'bruising'. Watch the planter. Look closely now."

Imolatty stepped into the box and began a silent shuffle in place.

"Stop." George said.

"Are you watching closely?" Imolatty said. "Can you see what's happening?" he asked breathlessly.

A silverish froth had begun to bubble up in the ectoplasm planter, a queer chalk brew.

"Stop!" George cried. *"Stop!"*

"There," Imolatty said. "You may try it yourselves, ladies and gentlemen."

"I told you to stop," George said.

"So you did. Why?"

"Because it's not true."

"What's not true, George?"

"Everything. It's not true that stuff's ectoplasm."

"Brillo pads, George! Soaped Brillo pads! I wear crepe soles moistened beforehand. That's very good, George. The folks on the tour never catch on."

"What if they touch it?" George Mills asked angrily. "Supposing they touch it?"

"Isn't he smart, Sylvia? He's smart as a whip. 'Better let it calm down, folks,' I say. 'Agitated ectoplasm's dangerous, too hot to handle.' "

"Stop!" George said.

"Caught out again, by golly!" Imolatty said. "Right you are,

George. It *isn't* too hot. All right, ladies and gentlemen, suppose we turn our attention to some of the museum's major acquisitions."

He led George and the woman through the black, hot room, not a guide now, a curator, with the curator's furious pride, his curious, almost fanlike, supportive stake, his enthusiasm intimate reciprocity between speaker and topic, scholar and subject. He revealed background, rattled off commentary, footnote, marginalia, joyous gloss—— all enthusiasm's inside information, George Mills all the while muttering then practically shouting, "Stop, Stop! *Stop!*"

"Yes? Was there a question, George?"

"That glass case is empty. There's nothing in it."

"Yes?" Imolatty said.

"You said it's pure ectoplasm."

"Pure *primary* ectoplasm. Yes?"

"It's empty."

"No, George. I'm afraid you shouldn't have stopped me that time. I get that one."

"There's nothing there."

"Nothing but pure primary ectoplasm, no."

"I can't see it."

"That's right. Because it's pure. It doesn't have that faint yellowish cast primary ectoplasm sometimes gets. Do you remember, Sylvia, that batch we had once?" He turned back to George. "We'd gone after some stuff—incidentally, 'stuff' isn't slang in this instance but a perfectly acceptable, even scientific, term for primary ectoplasm—to bring back to the museum. This was in the early days and we didn't always understand what we were doing. We set out before breakfast and had gathered the ectoplasm before noon—"

"Oh, Clement," the woman said, "you're not going to tell *that* story, are you? The boy will think we're fools. I declare, whenever Clement wants to embarrass me he trots this story out."

"We were *kids,* Sylvia. What did *we* know? Besides, I was as much the goat as you were. Anyway, to make a long story short, we'd collected all that we needed—"

"More than we needed."

"All right." Imolatty said. "More than we needed. As it turned out more than we needed. Our mistake, you see, was to gather the stuff while it was still light. You can't see the yellow cast of impure primary during the day. It just looks like more sunlight."

"Stop," George said lamely.

"It's true," Imolatty said. "It just bleeds into the sunshine. It's like trying to show movies outdoors on a bright afternoon."

"Stop," he said mechanically.

"I'll never forget it," Mrs. Imolatty said.

"Stop," George told the woman.

"Sylvia trying to drain off that yellow cast," Imolatty said, "running it through her sifter like it was a cup of flour."

"My hands cramped," she said.

" 'You think it's any paler now, Clement?' " Imolatty mocked his wife.

"Well, you were the one thought that maybe if we washed it," Mrs. Imolatty said. She looked at George. "You know what Mr. Imolatty did?" she said. "Just went and carried all five bushels and dumped them into the tub one at a time and filled it to the top with piping hot water every time he emptied a bushel, that's all."

"Stop."

"Well, not piping hot *every* time he filled the tub. After the first two times the water was tepid. The fourth and fifth times it was outright cool."

"I thought if I let it soak a spell. We were kids," Imolatty said.

"What do kids know?" Mrs. Imolatty said.

"Stop," George said. "Stop. Stop. *Stop.*"

"Not at all," Imolatty said. "I'm telling you about ectoplasm. That's what you want to know about, isn't it? Because it isn't all brick in the world, it isn't all mortar or bulk or whatever it is that's material reality's equivalent of fundament, firmament. The heart has its atoms, too. Its monads and molecules, its units and particles. Soul has its nutshell grain of integer morsel. Instinct does, will. And ectoplasm is only the lovely ounce and pennyweight of God.

"You're not as smart as I thought, George," Imolatty said. "You should have called me more often. My wife's name is Sonia, not Sylvia. The Mortons constantly interrupted."

Imolatty turned away, moved to another part of the room to stand beside a neat mound of earth like a stack of cordwood. "This, ladies and gentlemen, is pure unprocessed primary. Me and Sonia thought you'd like to see what first-quality ectoplasm looks like before it's been treated. This high-grade ore comes directly from ectoplasm mines in extreme northern Florida. You're welcome to take a handful with you as a souvenir of your visit to the ectoplasm museum. We're sorry that we have no bags for you to put it in, but you'll find that it keeps just as well in your pocket or purse. This concludes our tour, folks. Sonia and me thank you very much. Sonia?"

She flicked off the wall switch.

"Stop!" George shouted. *"Lie!"* he screamed. *"Cheat! Fake!"* he called in the dark.

He hadn't seen his sister yet. Reverend Wickland hadn't yet shown her to him, but at this time his relationship with their landlord was the most important thing in his life. Only Wickland (and his mother of course, though his mother's silence the boy took for granted; she had, he supposed, nothing to say) did not bother to instruct him, all the others coming at him like coaches with a pupil of genius, one talented at piano, say, or blessed with a great, undeclared voice—George's had only recently begun to change—their attitude—the coaches', the mentors'—not only feigned but even the limits of their sternness fixed, established by custom and principle and the laws of cliché. Even George knew this, wondering at the seemingly boundless gift adults had for the servile vicarious and fawning reflexive. Without understanding such investment and at the same time peeved that his docile, silent mother hadn't seemed to make it. Taking his case to Wickland.

"They keep bothering me."

"Bothering you?"

"Telling me stuff."

"They have a lot to say."

"They tell me about their powers. They like to talk about the stuff they have to fake."

"I see," Wickland said.

"In Milwaukee one time my dad took me to see wrestling. There was a wrestler who was crazy. He was big, a real mean ugly guy. The guy he wrestled was big too, but normal, you know? The mean guy wouldn't fight fair. Everybody booed him. I booed him too. Sometimes the crazy guy would poke his fingers in the regular guy's eyes or pull his hair or choke him. The referee didn't always see this and that's when we booed. My father said it was fake, that they rehearsed all this junk, that probably they were even friends. He said the crazy guy sent the normal guy birthday presents. One guy was supposed to act mean and the other decent, my father said. He said it's all fixed, that they already know who's going to win. He said the good guy would do something terrific just when it looked like he was in his worst trouble. Only he didn't. The bad guy licked the good guy. My father said that that was fixed, too, that they did that to make it more exciting. The bad guy could have beat the good guy anyway. He was so much bigger than the normal guy even though the normal guy was big too. He could have licked him anyway. He didn't have to pull hair or bite or choke or do any of that stuff."

"That's right."

"It didn't have to be fixed."

"No," Wickland said.

"He could do the job. You could see he could do the job."

"Yes."

"I asked my father why they'd go to all that trouble. They had to rehearse. I mean why would the normal guy have to rehearse losing if he had to lose anyway? If just being shorter and fifty pounds lighter and, you know, normal, was all he ever needed to lose? Why did it have to be fixed?"

"You should listen to your father."

"He said they did it to make it more exciting."

"You should listen to your father."

"He said it's all fixed. That even the championship is fixed."

"I don't follow wrestling," Wickland said. "I'm certain he's right. You should listen to your father."

"They believe in it and fix it, too," George said.

"You should listen to your father," Wickland said.

He did listen to him. To the long story of Greatest Grandfather Mills and his adventures in Europe, to the stories of subsequent Millses in the male, unbroken, centuries-long Mills line—the women shadowy figures, like his mother, like the woman he would one day marry—wondering why his father never spoke of his own life, if anything had ever happened to him worthy of even being related. He did listen to him. He listened to all of them—— to Kinsley and Sunshine and Madam Grace Treasury and all of them, making a fourth at their seances, a silent partner at their consultations.

He listened to all of them and watched Bennett Prettyman.

He was the largest of Cassadaga's large men, that meaty fraternity of flesh Mills would all his life associate with what seemed most rival to it. "I don't know why," Kinsley had once told him, "spirit runs so much to size and bulk. It would seem that the bigger someone is—the more space he takes up—the more room his soul would have. It could afford to stay home you'd think, and not go flying off to look for trouble somewheres else." Wickland, too, had mentioned it. "Perhaps," he'd said, "the radical nubbin requires something solid by way of atmosphere. Would man be man if he didn't have a whole universe to rattle around in?"

George Mills could not vouch for his soul or what Wickland called "the radical nubbin," but he was prepared to swear that Bennett Prettyman did not rattle. Indeed, he made no noise at all, was quiet as photograph, silent as sky.

"I'm a lullaby," he said in that low, soft, almost timbreless, cooing, asibilant voice like that of a baby given vocabulary. "I don't know how I do it. Shut your eyes. Listen. Here I come." George was seated in Prettyman's office, a large, square, lean-to like room with a concrete floor like the floor of a garage. Prettyman was in his swivel chair at a roll top desk across the room from him. "Go on," he said, "shut them. It heightens the effect." The boy shut his eyes. "Are they shut?" he heard Prettyman ask.

"Yes, sir," George said.

"Well open them," the man said. "How do you expect to see me in the dark?"

Prettyman was standing inside George's spread knees. "You ain't no Indian boy," Prettyman said. "Indian boys' hearing is honed by the dark. You never heard me come up. I was already standing here when I asked if your eyes were shut. Well, sure," he said, "you figure there must be rubber casters on my chair. Go look for yourself if that's what you think."

"That's not what I think," George said.

"Go on, satisfy yourself. Sit right down in it. There ain't any trick, but a doubting Tom always got to test for himself if the knots is loose or the handcuffs is real."

George got up and crossed the room, conscious of the hooflike claps his shoes made on the cement. He pulled the chair out from the desk. Its wooden legs scraped the hard flooring. He sat and the chair creaked.

"Haw!" Prettyman exploded gruffly. He was standing behind the startled boy's left shoulder.

"I didn't hear you," George said.

"I was with you every step of the way," Bennett Prettyman said. "And don't think I walked tippy toe or under cover of your footsteps either, or that I'm wearing crepe soles or maybe sponge or velvet. That's an idea lots of them get. Lay it to rest, lay it to rest." He tugged at his pants pleats and exposed dark, hard bluchers. "See?" he said. "Heavy-duty work shoes. Course, *that* don't prove nothing. I could still be standing on top of powder puffs. You think? You think so?" He raised his shoes, exposing the soles for George's inspection. They were cleated. "Haw!" he barked. "I suppose you want to touch them to feel if they're metal. Here, I'll save you the trouble." He stamped his left foot on the ground heavily and pulled it shrilly across the cement floor. When Prettyman stepped back, George could see the ten-inch slash the big man had made in the concrete. "Haw," he laughed, and leaned toward the boy, his face red and his huge shoulders shaking, silently breathless. "But something important as conversion is worth more than a few flashy card tricks, ain't it? You don't give your heart just cause the fella fooled you with the green pea and the walnut shell. Open that top drawer."

George pulled at the drawer. "It's locked," he said.

"It ain't locked. I don't lock it."

He tried again but couldn't budge it. "It's stuck," he said.

"Here, let me," Prettyman said. George watched as he came noiselessly from where he'd been standing. Though Prettyman walked as other men did, it was as if he moved on air. When the man was almost beside him he suddenly stumbled and fell. He made no sound when he hit the floor. "I'm that tree in that forest when no one is by," he said. "Help me up," he said. "I'm too big for these pratfalls."

"You're bleeding," George said.

"Yeah? Am I?" he said, and raised a finger to his lips. "Hush. Hush then and listen."

George could just make out a faint sloshing sound, like soda splashing into a glass.

"I ain't got you yet, do I?" Prettyman said. "You're some tough customer. I thought I asked you to help me up." The boy took hold of the big man's suit coat and helped him stand. "That's seersucker. My clothes don't crinkle. That drawer still stuck?" He pulled on it with all his heavy force. The boy knew how he operated now, not how he did it, but the pattern, something of his magician's preemptive sequences. He knew there would be no sound as the drawer came suddenly unstuck. He even anticipated the noiseless crash Prettyman would make as he was thrown off balance against the wall, the drawer still in his hands.

"Haw," Prettyman said, watching him narrowly. "Haw?" It was a question. It was like the cocked, sidelong glance of an animal who has just fetched or performed unbidden some difficult trick. The boy had the power now. The coached and lectured, instructed, explanationed boy did. He looked blankly as he could at Bennett Prettyman, still off balance and clumsied uncomfortably against the wall by his hunched shoulders. Prettyman held the drawer out to him. It was filled with nails, wax paper, gravel, marbles, broken glass, sandpaper, cellophane and a small brass bell.

"Haw," Prettyman said softly, "haw."

George Mills started to cry.

"You ain't crying 'cause you're scared," Prettyman said. "You're crying 'cause you think I tricked you."

"I don't," George said.

"You don't?" Prettyman said. "Then you ought to," he said softly. He was being scolded, shouted at in that strange, unamplified, timbreless, infant's voice. "What is it if it ain't tricks? Look at me. *Look* at me. You can't hear me, look at me."

"I hear you."

"Don't sass me. Don't you be fresh.

"Because I don't know how them other folks do it, the ones that claim to fly and the ones that have the dead over to supper like they was cousins from out of town. Prophets better than the newspapers or wire services who fix where the spring earthquake in China will be and know which movie stars will come to grief and what will happen to the presidents. I don't *know* how they do it. I don't know how they touch her handkerchief and know where the little girl's body is buried, or tip off the cops where the kidnapper is. (There's men on that chain gang that your daddy laid off—did you know this?—there's men on that chain gang who'd still be at home if it wasn't for clues that a crystal ball give.) I don't *know* how they do it, the ones that know the future from arithmetic or give you your character from the salt in the sea. Hell, I don't even know how the fella at the fair does it, how he can tell you your weight before you step on the scale.

"So you better *start* thinking is it a trick, and wondering what it means if it ain't. We're in big trouble if it ain't, kid, cause the universe won't be through with us even after we're quits with it. Forget God. God ain't in it. Forget God and Satan, too. We got enough to worry about just from the folks in Cassadaga. Between them and our widows we stand to be horsed around the afterworld from now till the cows come home. So you better hope it *is* a trick, cause if it ain't, if it ain't, ain't no one ever lived who'll know a minute's peace or get a good night's sleep!

"And I'm telling you all this for nothing. I can afford to 'cause I do a single. I can't use you, I don't need you. Them others are after your ass. They got some idea that one kid is worth two red Indians or nigger slaves. They—— "

"That's why?" George said.

"Pardon?"

"That's why they tell me this stuff?"

"Sure that's why. Didn't Kinsley already make you an offer? Sure it's why. Didn't you already know that? Didn't they tell you? Then the joke's on them, ain't it? You got even less extrasensories than them phony injuns and old Pullman porters they work with now. But you think about it. Because if they ain't fakes then maybe you got a calling, vocation, a proper apostolate. Death is the only legitimate work for a man if there isn't any. It stands to reason. Death is just good business if there ain't no death."

Prettyman stopped talking, closed his eyes. George rose to go. "So I don't know," the big man said. George sat back. "I don't know how they do it. I don't even know how I do it. Gift or trick?

"How did I come by my mute body or ever get to be this soft-shoe dance of a man? Because the voice is put on, trained. I do the voice like bel canto. A lot of the rest of it's real.

"I've always been big. I've always been graceful. My pop thought I was stealthy, a kid like a cat burglar. And one time he slapped me and it didn't make noise. Or if it did, then the noise was in his fingers, in his palm. I hadn't learned to control it then. (So some of it's trick. What ain't gift is trick.) I wasn't this athlete of silence then. I hadn't learned all there was about balance, even keel, equilibrium. I couldn't deadlock the marbles or stalemate the stones. I hadn't learned to walk on eggshells. I do that. I walk on eggshells at my sessions. (They aren't seances, I don't draw the curtains or turn out the lights. The eggshell stunt kills them, stops the show cold. Come by sometime, you'll see. Well, you have to give them *some*thing, after all. You have to give them *some*thing you don't show them their dead or put their voices in your mouth like fruit. Come by. Come by sometimes. Bring your lovely mother if you can tear her away from the others. But don't build up her expectations. Tell her it's just a show.) I hadn't discovered how to control it, maneuver my muscles like so many lead toy soldiers or send my weight through my body as if it was blood. Lift my pinkie."

He removed a marble from the drawer and placed it on top of the desk. He put his little finger on the marble. "Go on," he said. "Try to lift it."

"My mother?"

147

Prettyman folded his hands. "Never mind," he said, "you wouldn't be able to anyway. I transfer all my weight to the first joint of my little finger."

"My mother?"

"She goes to the seances. To see your sister. She even came to me once. She's quite a beautiful woman, isn't she? She would have given me money. A very sweet woman, *very* beautiful. You're quite the lucky young man. I told her I couldn't."

He stood abruptly and walked over to a pail that had been set down in a corner of the room. He scattered sand from the pail onto the cement floor. "Hey, d'ya ever see this one?" he asked him. "I got to give them something. Hell, the dead don't talk to *me.*"

He had begun to dance on the coarse sand which lay on the cement like one of those portable floors used by roller skating acts in close quarters. He tapped on it soundlessly in his big cleated bluchers. He closed his eyes, speaking as he danced in that soft, frictionless voice which was like that of a baby.

"If Mom asks you," he said, "tell her that that death is only pieces of life. Why *shouldn't* I come and go there so long as I make no noise?"

He stopped. "Slide up that roll top, will you, George? It ain't locked. It ain't even stuck. There's a gun inside, but don't touch it, it's loaded."

But he didn't, wouldn't. He thanked Mr. Prettyman and said he had to be going. He didn't want not to hear the report when the gun went off.

They were at dinner table—— he, Wickland, his mother and his father.

"No Mills," his father, tipsy, was saying, "ever pushed his kid into a career, or stood in his way once his mind was made up. He wants to go into songwriting or the pictures, I say let him. I give him a dad's honest blessing and step out of his way."

George was trying to remove the bones from his fish. His father, who had been observing the boy's efforts for some minutes, was inspired to proceed. "Or a career in the surgery profession," he said. "Or banking, or law. Politics, anything. How about it, George? You thinking of replacing Mr. Roosevelt? You don't have to be coy. We're family. I have the honor to include you, Reverend."

"Thank you," Wickland said. "Who'd like more iced tea? You, George? Your glass is empty."

148

"Yes," the boy said, "if there's extra."

"Certainly. How about you, Mrs. Mills?"

"I'm fine, thanks."

"The pitcher's cooling in the fridge, George. Why don't you bring it out for all of us?"

"Of course," his father said before George could get up, "of course he might always join his pop in the fallen candy wrapper trade, the chewing-gum-under-the-bench profession, the lawn upkeep calling."

It had been like this for a week, since Prettyman had told him why the mediums were so interested in him. Though no one had spoken to him directly since the funeral, several had approached his father. There was even something courtly about it, his father had said, as if they were asking for his hand in marriage.

"He might even choose the ministry," his father said, looking directly at Wickland. "His mother might like that. She might like that very much. Course he might have to move out, live with, you know, his order, but you'd always see him at church."

"Please, George," his mother said.

"Now Nancy, you know how proud you'd be. Our loss would be the haunts' gain."

For all his sarcasm, his father wanted him to do it. Chiefly it was the extra money, but the boy understood, too, that in a crazy way it had something to do with the honor. He'd winked at him when the boy had relayed Kinsley's offer. "Lord," he'd said, "not only have I risen above my station by janitoring and fetching for crooks, but I got one in the family myself now. We're coming up in the world, George."

It was a sort of joy his father felt, and though the boy couldn't identify its source—he hadn't been around long enough, his father had said, had still to understand the terms of his life, its service elevator condition—he recognized exaltation when he saw it. He'd seen it often enough on the faces of his instructors in the past year or so. As always, it terrified him.

"I've seen my sister," he said suddenly.

But he hadn't. Not then, not yet. Immediately he regretted what he'd said. He had meant to warn his father. He'd tried to warn him for days, to knock him awake with his knowledge. But the man was too exhilarated, as tone deaf to implication as he was, evidently, to actual sound.

"George," he said, "they're crooks. They're crooks, George. They don't do real harm or they'd have to shut down. They're crooks but white collar. Like salesmen, like priests, like anybody alive in the business of making people feel good. Because don't kid yourself, kid, comfort is an industry. It always was. The king's wizards and jesters, and the king himself. And all the rest of us too most likely, all us hired hands, on the job, on duty, on call, dishing out concern and comfort and busting our butts to remind the next fellow that it could be worse, that he could be us!

"I won't lie to you, George. I won't tell you that plenty of honorable folks before you have done such things, though plenty have. But here, in Cassadaga, on the front lines of grief, you'd be with the rascals, you'd be with the knaves and villains. I say it makes no difference. Knaves and villains never did anything to anybody but take their money. What's that? We hung on a thousand years without any." His father looked at him. "Oh, I heard you," he said. "That's only Wickland. And I know what bothers you," he said. "You're scared of the sincerity, what stands behind it, or could. You're scared these guys are who they say they are, you think they might be able to deliver."

"Yes," George said.

"You got so much faith, you give doubt so much benefit, take this on faith: there ain't no one, there ain't no one ever, been able to deliver the goods. And I don't care," his father said, "—didn't I say I heard you?—*who* Wickland shows you!

"Relax," he said, "let's think about the practicals of this thing. We got to decide which one of these figure flingers and ghost brokers to go with. Bone says he'll give you three dollars a night. That's about the same bid we got from Ashmore and Sunshine and that woman, Grace Treasury, too. In my judgment it'd be a mistake to go with any of those. Kinsley offered a dime less, but they're all within pennies of each other. There must be a blue book value, or fixed rates, like meters in taxis."

"What do you think?"

"I'd have to say Kinsley," his father said.

"He wants me to work naked."

His father shrugged.

"I don't understand," George said.

"Kinsley's the one your mother goes back to. She's been to them all but goes back to Kinsley. The man must have something. If she keeps going back then Kinsley's the best."

"I couldn't do it," George said. "Supposing I had to be my own sister? Supposing Mother came in and I had to be Janet?"

So his father instructed him, too.

"Supposing you did? It's Kinsley she goes back to, not his control. You think she doesn't know, that those other customers don't know, that whoever it is comes through those curtains or crawls out from underneath that table isn't just some haunt house stooge? You think she could ever believe in anyone who calls himself Dr. N. M. M. Kinsley?

"It's the faculty, the power, of which Kinsley is only some petty instrumentality, like the wall outlet or light socket are the petty instrumentalities of the generators, dynamos, dams and racing waters. It's the *power,* and if they use controls it's because they're not fools, or anyway not fools enough—you were the one who was supposed to take his clothes off, not Kinsley—to go into that room naked without any insulation or just plain honest grounding between themselves and the customers.

"Which is another reason for Cassadaga incidentally. Because all the mediums and their controls are just so much interference and insulation between the madness of grief and loss, and the comfortable luxury of talking out loud to the dead."

He went with Kinsley. (He'd had his twelfth birthday months ago.) Not only did he not work naked—Kinsley himself had had other ideas about it now—but was required to wear clothing which, in that hot climate, was not even stocked in the stores. He was dressed as a schoolboy. He wore corduroy knickers and a bright argyle pullover over his plaid wool shirt. He wore a peaked tweed cap like a golfer's and carried his books in a strap.

He was already seated when the others arrived. Kinsley didn't bother to explain the presence of the boy. He simply introduced him as George Mills, pronouncing the name solemnly, even gravely. Then he proceeded with the seance, warming them up in the early stages with an account of the physical and supernatural planes, their synchronous and contiguous attributes. When Kinsley asked if there were any disembodied spirits among them, George raised his hand, and Kinsley called on him.

Soon everyone at the table was calling out the names of dead relatives as if they were favorite tunes they wanted played on the piano. They asked him questions which the boy would answer in the vaguest and most general way. Kinsley didn't even allow him to alter his voice. Though he was a young man one moment and an old woman the next, everything was delivered within the familiar, given octaves of his normal speaking voice. It was astonishing to him how effective he seemed to be.

They had nothing to say. The physical and supernatural planes might be synchronous and contiguous, but the dead, by dying, had created a breach which could not be mended, only smoothed over there in the semidark, glossed by politeness and the trivial courtesies. They were like people lined up to talk to each other over the long-distance telephone on the occasion of national feast days or the junctures and set pieces of private commemorative.

"How are you, son?"

"Fine. I'm fine."

"We miss you."

"I miss you, too."

"Mother couldn't come with me."

"How is Mother?"

"Not real well. She still can't get over that you were taken from us. She sorrows so."

"Tell Mother not to sorrow."

He didn't even need the coaching and background information Kinsley had supplied him with, passing the time of day with these people as he had with dozens of strangers. Indeed, the aloofness and love which dovetailed nicely on their synchronous and contiguous planes seemed precisely the tone to take by survivor and ghost alike.

Sometimes—this happened less frequently than he would have thought—a client was dissatisfied with his generalities and tried to get him to be more specific, even to trap him.

"Bob, is that you?"

"Yes," George said.

"What was the name of that cat you found?"

"I don't recall."

"You don't recall? You paid more attention to that cat than you did to your brothers and sisters."

"I don't remember any cat. It was too long ago."

"Too long ago? It was only last year."

"It was when I was alive. I don't remember any cat."

Then they both cried.

It was the same even when his mother called on him. He gave her no more than he had given the others. Evidently it was enough. Only for George it was not enough. One night he volunteered information, then asked his question.

"I met someone you know. Bennett Prettyman?"

"It was very sad about Bennett."

"He thinks you're lovely. He says you're very beautiful. He wanted you to stop by with George and see his show. I think he was sweet on you, Mother."

"Poor Bennett," his mother said.

"Were you sweet on him, too?" George asked.

"Of course not, Janet," his mother said.

"Sometimes," George said, "I don't know how I think up what to say."

"It's because you're inspired," Kinsley told him. "You're a true vehicle, George. It's no fake. You have real powers. The spirits guide you. They wouldn't let you misrepresent them."

He told Reverend Wickland what Kinsley had said. (He was still seeing Wickland, spilling the beans.)

"He thinks it's real," George told him, "that I'm not even faking when I say I'm their wife or daughter or fiancee killed in the war."

"Let's have a seance," Wickland said.

"I'm working tonight."

"Not tonight, now."

"It's not even dark in here."

"Not here, outside. In the air. On the bench. I'm going to show you your sister."

They went to the small square where George had stood with his parents over two years earlier. The palm might have been a statue of itself, a memorial like a doughboy or Civil War cannon. No longer strange nor quite yet familiar, George suspected it had the ability to proclaim the seasons, something shifted in the configuration of its pods or missing from its leaves, its long bark wrappings, its careful shadow legible as a sun dial. He regretted that he had not observed it more closely.

Wickland was seated on the little bench.

"You don't play here much," he said.

"No," George said, his back to the reverend. He was browsing the hoarding.

"No. Who would there be to play with?"

The boy wheeled about swiftly. "Is my—— ?" Wickland was alone on the bench. "Oh."

"No, not yet," he said. "By and by. There's got to be a build-up.

153

Didn't those other swamis tease you a bit before the main event? Let's just chat."

"We've already chatted," George said.

"Anyone would think you'd been close to your sister," Wickland said.

"I just want to see if you can do it."

Wickland shrugged. "Jack Sunshine may be a little miffed you didn't throw in with him when you turned professional. He puts it out you're a midget."

George laughed. "He thinks about midgets a lot."

"His father was one."

"Really?" George said. "No kidding."

"Jack was born in Cassadaga," Wickland said.

"He did what *I* do!" George said suddenly.

"Jack? I don't think so. For a while, I suppose, he may have assisted, but—"

"No," George said impatiently, "not him, not Jack, the father. He was a control. He did what *I* do!"

"Larry?"

"Right. Larry. He was a control. He was with the circus. Then he came here to Cassadaga. He met the mother here. I don't know how he managed the courting. He did what *I* do. I mean I guess it would be pretty tough if you're supposed to be this disembodied control and then you fall in love with one of your customers and you have to explain that the next time she sees you you'll be just like everyone else, only shorter. But he must have figured out *some*thing to tell her, because they were married and had Jack!"

"You see it very clearly," Wickland said.

Yes, he thought. He'd told Wickland what he'd told Kinsley, that he didn't know how he thought up what to say. Calling him Jack like that. The other stuff. Kinsley said he was inspired, that spirits guided him, that he was a true vehicle, that he had powers. Yes, he thought. Yes.

"I do," he said, "yes. Once you told me his father was a midget then that explained why—"

"Why?"

"It explains why he's so sour on—— Wait. I did see it clearly. Only I didn't see all of it. What *could* he say? I mean if she was here to get comforted by visiting some dead person, then it would be pretty hard to take that the fellow who was tricking you one minute was in love with you the next. So she couldn't have known he was a control.

154

She didn't do business with him. She just thought he was—— She thought he was just——

"Maybe he'd seen her around town, maybe sitting right here on this bench, and he told her that that was why he was here himself, that he'd lost someone very dear to him too, and still wasn't over it, but almost was, nearly was, and just wanted to get in contact one last time to say good-by because the departed may have died suddenly or gone out of town and there'd been no real chance to say farewell by the book, which is what Kinsley says is all a lot of them really want. Sure," George said, "and I know from other stuff he's told me that there used to be more repeat trade than there is today. Probably the roads weren't as good, the distance to De Land would have been greater back then, so they had to have somewhere to stay, to put up." He indicated the little neighborhood of a town. "Wait. I know. Some of these places must have been boarding houses before they ever got to be haunted houses, and he knew, Jack's father did, that she'd be around for a while and they started seeing each other, but only during the daylight hours because he couldn't let her know that he was in the business. Not after what he'd told her he couldn't. So then maybe he told her he'd seen whoever it was that he'd come to see because she still couldn't tell *him.* Not if she liked him she couldn't, because then she wouldn't have any excuse to stay on, and if he told *her* first that was the equal of saying he liked her without really saying it. Because he was, you know, shy, being so little and all, and would naturally be afraid of saying it straight out. So that was the way they courted, asking each other if they'd seen the spook yet, and Larry, Jack's father, gradually working up his nerve to tell her well, yes, as a matter of fact he had, needing the nerve because he was afraid she'd say 'Well, aren't you the lucky little man?' or something even meaner.

"But one day he just did. He said it. And she said 'I did too, Larry,' and that was that."

"Was it?" Wickland said.

"Well sure," George said. "Oh, you mean what would he do now? I mean about telling her he was in the business. He'd still have to tell her. You're right, she'd have to know. He had to come up with something fast because he had to go to work that night. He didn't have the excuse anymore that he was just going around the corner to the seance, and she'd be free, too, of course, so whatever he told her he'd have to tell her right off. Yes, I see. But he couldn't. He'd just told her he'd said good-by to the specter. There wasn't anything he could say that could put all those lies he'd told her in a good light. I mean he was so *small.* He was already at all the disadvantage he could afford. There was nothing he could say. Unless . . ." Yes, he thought again. I *do* have powers. It's all these psychics. Maybe they're carriers. "Unless she already knew. Sure," George said, "she knew. But not that he was a control. These were the olden days. Controls were lowered on ropes from the ceilings or rose from the cellars like organs in theaters. That was the old style. They didn't have sound effects or trick lighting. They didn't sit up on chairs like I do. So she already knew. But he *wasn't* a control. He was the medium. And she wasn't a customer. You don't fall in love with the customers. Most of the time you don't even respect them. You certainly don't let them know you're human!"

Even to himself he didn't sound like any kid who'd ever lived. He'd picked up their lingo, the conversational Urgent they spoke. He used to be the only kid in Cassadaga. Now there were none.

"Why couldn't they already have been married?" Wickland asked.

"That's so," George said angrily, "they could." He kicked at one of the fallen palm pods. *"Damn,"* he said, "they could." And he wondered what he was going to say next, then he was saying it, his voice raised in that High Urgent that had no proper names in it, the trees and people and animals pronoun'd and anonymated into the clairvoyant's confrontational style. "No," he said, "no they couldn't. You said he was born here. She was pregnant. You don't make a big move like that until after the baby is born. They weren't married when they came. When they came they—— *They?* There wasn't any they to it. *They* didn't come. *He* did, the midget. Because he *was* a midget. A midget and a medium both. Where else could he go? *He* came! She was already here! Or in De Land!

"He said he had letters. She must have saved them. Of course. She *would* have had letters and some would even have been marked *Personal,* because people who are upset want to make sure that their mail gets through and probably they figure that if they've put down *Personal* and drawn a line under it they've warned the authorities and the busybodies at the circus that they mean business. Maybe they even think there's something official about it, that it's an actual aid in sorting the mail and seeing that it goes where it's directed, like sticking on the extra postage that buys special handling. So that wasn't why she saved it. If all she wanted was letters that said *Personal* on the envelope she could have had a hope chest full of them. Haven't I read enough mail down here in Cassadaga to know that people will say anything if they've pencil and paper and a few cents for stamps? That they address letters to the dead or particular saints or even to God Himself because they've heard and even believe that we're this clearing house for the extraordinary? It wasn't the *Personal* that made her keep this one out of all the crazy correspondence that had come her way. It was what was inside. Not the expression of sympathy, because every last letter she ever got would have started with that. That would have been as regulation as the salutation. Even the mad-men who wished her an even worse life than the one which had already been visited upon her would first have showered her with their declarations of pity, waiting until all that was out of the way before ever taking up the matter of reproach, blasting her with what would not even occur to them was ill-nature and ill will and citing her 'condition' as evidence that a retributive Lord not only existed but was at all times on His toes, no procrastinative, Second Coming Lord who put off till tomorrow what could just as easily be done today, but an eager beaver early bird God who didn't care to wait till even today, who did His stuff retroactively, smiting you if He had a mind to in the cradle, in the womb. So it wasn't the sympathy. Maybe she even skipped that part. Probably she wasn't interested until she came to the stuff about the writer's credentials, and maybe she was relieved when she saw that it wasn't a doctor this time because she'd heard from the doctors before, so interested in her 'case,' so sure a particular pill or course of some special serum or amazing, recently discovered diet was just the thing to fix her up. Doctors were quacks, and reverends were worse, because when all was said and done the reverends were usually on the same side as the madmen and believed that the Lord had made her what she was, and that rather than flaunt it she would do better either to hide it away or send it on tour as a warning to others. Proceeds to charity."

"Yes," Wickland said. "Proceeds to charity is a good touch."

"But a *professor,*" George said, "a professor was different. She had never even *seen* a professor. She knew about them though. They were the ones who followed truth as if it was a river in New Guinea, who looked for it to come out only where the river itself comes out." He's making me say these things, Mills thought. He puts these words in my mouth. "And this one was going to get to the bottom of things. Or no, if all he had promised was just to get to the bottom of things, she'd probably have disposed of this letter as she'd disposed of the others. What he really said was that *together* they would get to the bottom of things. He needed her help. Which already was not only twice as much as what the others had asked for but something she could actually give.

"But I don't think that even then she would have taken it upon herself to write back 'Sure, come on down.' She would have wanted certain things cleared up first, certain nagging doubts put to rest that this time had nothing whatever to do with the age-old question 'Why me?' For one thing, she'd have wanted to know what a *lusus naturae* was before they went any further.

" 'My dear lady, *lusus naturae* is Latin for freak. I myself am a *lusus naturae.*'

"So," George said, "not only a professor but a fellow *lusus naturae* as well! And one, furthermore—though she'd noted this before it still touched her—who signed his name to his mail and provided a return address. What could she *do* but write back?

" 'What sort of *lusus naturae?*'

" 'I am a tiny fellow, dear lady, a midget.'

"So not only a professor and fellow *lusus naturae* but a *lusus naturae* who for all his smallness stood at the upper levels and very heights of *lusus naturae* respectability.

"Until the letters—sure he has letters, of course he has letters—made quite a tidy correspondence, thick as a book perhaps, or a packet of love letters. Which is what they were. Probably she never even got the chance to write the one that said 'Sure, come on down.' Or their letters crossed in the mail, his, the one that said he was on his way, the one in which he proposed.They might even have been married by the time hers had been returned to sender.

"I don't know if she ever worked with him as a control or not. All I know is that *'the young fourteen-year-old girl with the gray hair and withered body of an old woman'* must have been the one who gave Jack Sunshine his height!"

"Is that what you see?" Wickland asked.

"Boy oh boy," George said. "I do. I really enjoyed our chat."

He was pleased with himself. He had raised the dead, momentarily held them aloft on the energy of concentration, argument and the polar shifts of alternative. He was convinced and wondered if he had convinced Wickland. But Wickland *knew* what had happened and was beyond his arguments. And suddenly, simply by knowing something George didn't, the reverend seemed smug, and George began to understand something about the nature of the place he had lived in for over two years now. Nowhere he would ever live would be so *theoretical.* Cassadaga was a sort of stump, a kind of congress. It was somewhere one could orate, a neighborhood of debate. (Perhaps that was why there were no stores or restaurants, no schools or hotels, only this little square of the civic.) All, all longed to be heroes of life, even Wickland, even himself. Now the reverend would show him his sister. She would go up like fireworks and now he'd be wowed. It was simple, really. One lived by sequence, by a sort of *Roberts' Rules of Order.* Cassadaga was only a kind of conversation.

"Your mother," Wickland began, "is very nice."

"Yes."

"I wonder why she's so quiet though."

"She talks."

"She's most polite."

"What's wrong with that?"

"She is not *wild,* George."

"I don't want a wild mother."

"Isn't it interesting that she is not interesting?"

"Sunshine's mother was interesting," George said. "My mother is good."

"I gather from what you've told me that all the women in your family have been good."

"I never told you about all the women in my family. I hope they've been good."

"Otherwise we should have heard," Wickland said slyly. "Don't be defensive, George. I'm not going to insult your mother. I'm not going to call you a son of a bitch."

"Hey," George said.

"That bristle you feel is not pride," Wickland said. "It's breeding. Ten hundred years of doggy antagonism and the biological bitters of instinct."

"Here we go," George said.

"Indeed," Wickland said, "for isn't it curious that you Millses, servants and dog soldiers of the domestic, think Honor only on the occasion of its aspersion and only when the distaff takes the slur?

"You were not bankers or lawyers or politicians or even merchants. A millennium of benchwork. That's your tradition, George. A thousand years. And your women the same."

"Hey!"

"A thousand years in the typing pool."

"Hey."

"Have you never wondered how you've managed to last so long, how there could be this unbroken thousand-year streak of George Millses? It's your women, George, your nice, quiet, polite, unwild women."

"You keep my mother out of—— "

"Look at you. *Look* at you! I see your gums and balled fists, your hard-on hackles. Don't worry, you won't. You won't have to. This is the seance now. I'm only explaining. You won't have to.

"Not bitch, not bitch anyway. Hen. Sow. Cow. Not bitch, not even filly. Mare! Not wench, not even lady. Virgin, maiden! Certainly not dame or broad or bimbo. Mother, parent, housewife, spouse—— all the feminized, maidenly matronics of passive womaninity."

"What's wrong with that?"

"Nothing. It's what kept you alive. It's what killed your sister."

"Hey!"

"Because you don't last a thousand years in this dispensation unless you've got something special going for you. Luck couldn't account for it. It wouldn't.

"A thousand years of benchwork, ten centuries of day labor. Not even clerks, though you'd an eye for the clerical, the file folder heart, the women who would prove in motherhood what they'd already testified to by the filing cabinet, their gift for organization, their prim loyalties like a lesson to passion. They'd spend a lifetime as mothers and would die old maids.

"No wonder they bore male children only! It was only more deference, birth a sort of muscle control like the swift bows, nods and courtesies of a maître d'. (Alphonse and Gaston must have been women, too.) They had minds like Miss America. (Don't tell me 'Hey!' I'm being kind.) We're talking marriage like motherhood in guitar songs, we're talking self-denial, devotion. (No wonder you guys bristle. It isn't your women you're defending, it's your moms.) And maybe when your sister died it was just intuition. Maybe stillbirth is just the female Mills's way of saying 'No thanks, I gave at the office!'

"You know why she goes to the crystal gazers and tarot dealers? Because we don't read breakfast cereal, because we don't read laundry. Because women like her don't *have* daughters!

"I tell you, George, these women were wonders. The cookbooks of obligation, the flannel of duty, the curlers of love!

"But why are they so dowdy, eh?

"Because dowdy is what you choose them for. Because dowdy is part of the package, part of their heritage, like the cheekbones of Scandinavians or the dark skin of belly dancers. Have you ever seen them dolled up? They look, in their make-up, as if they've been crying, in their white shoes and cheap dresses like hicks at matinees. Do you see your sister?"

"No."

"Because your mother is different," Wickland said. "Nancy is different." And it was true what Wickland had been saying. He *did* want to hit him. He *did* bristle, enmity crawling his skin like a contact rash and his saliva a rich soup in his jaw. He felt actual aversion, fear, the cornered, grating grudge of opponents in nature. This man is my rival, he thought. I've been reckless, he thought. I've told him too much.

"Your father knew beans about plumbing," Wickland said. "He could use a plunger and work the shutoff valve with his wrench, but the scaffolding of pivots, shafts and pipes and the improbable ball that floated at the top of the tank like a lesson in leverage were about as meaningful to him as airplane engines. Also, he was squeamish. The black rubber plug at the bottom was something he didn't have to hold to feel. His greatest grandfather had shoveled manure for a living and your father suspected that was where his antipathy came from, not custom and acclimation catching in his genes but the original shock and revulsion themselves.

"Which was why he hoped to God it was a big job when Mindian sent for him, something they would have to tear the walls out to get to. Mindian had authorized him to call in a plumber for the big jobs. He climbed the back stairs and pressed the buzzer by the back door. The pretty cleaning girl opened the door.

" 'I'm the janitor,' he said. 'I hear you got big trouble with your WC.'

"There are three things you should know about your father. I've already told you he was squeamish, and perhaps you already know that at this time, at the time he met your mother, he lived in a basement, in a room in the cellar of one of the buildings he serviced. The third thing is that he was thoroughly versed in the family history.

"The room in which he lived was not a real room at all. It was a wooden-slatted storage locker, one of several that had been set aside for the tenants, where they could put odd bits of furniture, old mattresses, castoff stoves, the children's bicycles, busted lamps, cartons of outgrown clothes, derelict chairs and beds, whatever was remnant in their households, whatever they could find no use for yet could not bring themselves to throw away, whatever they had forgotten they still owned. Not for safekeeping—the locks that went through the flimsy hinges were ceremonial rather than effective; often they were not even fastened; any burglar who cared to take the trouble could have come into the basement and browsed the equivocal possessions there like a window shopper; the dark, six-by-ten-foot cells were slatted, the thin boards not carpentered so much as slapped together like so many kids' tree or clubhouses—perhaps not for keeping—except possibly for the bicycles—at all. A place where possession was not so much protected as simply resolved, defined, where one family's cargo left off and the next one's took up.

"Your father's cubicle had walls of oilcloth nailed to the slats for privacy and it was furnished with what the tenants let him have. He had a youth bed, a lamp which was plugged into an extension cord that went into an outlet near the zinc washtubs, a broken card table chair, and two cartons, one for his clothes and personal possessions, one for his dirty laundry. Heat was provided by what slipped off the coal furnace your father stoked, and he used the spigots by the gray tubs for his water and the lidless toilet behind the furnace for his needs. Yes?"

"How do you know this?"

"He was almost twenty. He had no family in Milwaukee, no friends even among the other janitors in the neighborhood, immigrants whose Polish and Lithuanian and Sicilian had not yet lapsed into even broken American speech. He was old enough. Certainly he was lonely enough. You'd think he would have seen that she was weeping.

" 'I'm sorry,' she said. 'What did you say?'

" 'I'm the janitor. I've come to fix the WC.'

"That was how they met. She was the maid. He was the man who came to fix the toilet. She was as ignorant as he was. Afterward, because she was in from the country less than a month—this was her first job; she'd been hired when the new tenants moved in—and had heard Mrs. Simon make the same offer to the painters and moving men and delivery people who carried the new Frigidaire up the three flights of stairs, she asked him if he cared for a shot. She took a whiskey bottle from the liquor cabinet in the living room and poured a jigger of rye into a water glass which she left for him on the kitchen table.

" 'Your drink is in the kitchen,' she said and your father nodded. He sat by himself in the kitchen and looked absently at all the food, the canned goods and condiments and boxes of cereal in the pantry. He barely tasted the whiskey, which he drank down in one swallow.

Though he didn't see Nancy she must have been watching him, because as quickly as he was done she came back into the kitchen and began actually to scour the glass from which he had just drunk.

" 'Why don't you just break it and throw it away?' he said.

"He didn't drink; he may not even have been sober. Certainly Nancy didn't think he was. When she had offered him what she had heard Mrs. Simon call a shot he believed she was going to join him, at least sit down with him. She didn't know what to say when he asked his question about the glass. She had merely been following what she thought were the forms, embarrassed about offering the drink but offering it anyway because she thought he expected it. She began to cry and he believed she was afraid of him.

"Squeamishness lives neither in the gut nor in the head but in the entire organism. It's a sort of constriction of the self, a physical pulling back, as if the hand has been offered fire or the soul affront. They were both squeamish, both embarrassed, both hurt. It was only your father, however, who had somewhere to go, so he was the one who left.

"This was a Thursday. So tenuous is life, so random, it needs all the help it can get, and enters into conspiracy with everything, with all that's trivial and all that isn't. If that toilet hadn't broken down on a Thursday you wouldn't exist. This was a Thursday. Everywhere in middle class life Thursday afternoon is the maid's day off, like some extra, fractional Sabbath.

"She sought him out in the basement of the building where he lived, going up to the oilcloth-rigged room where he was chewing the bread and raw, whole vegetables, the carrots and tomatoes and green beans and lettuce which he bought as he needed them and kept in their original paper bags.

" 'Are you in there?' she asked.

" 'Who is it? Who's there?'

" 'It's Nancy. From Mrs. Simon's.'

" 'Wait a minute.'

"He drew back the bolt on the inside of the storage locker. It was all that made it a room. Not the spurious oilcloth walls nailed to the random, jerry-built joists, not the ruined, odd-lot furniture. The oilcloth was only a kind of screen, and the very nature of the furniture seemed to signify the little area's storage function, as exposed bedsprings or wheel rims or empty oil drums signify a dump. Only the thin, four-inch bit of metal lifted it into the margins of architecture at all.

" 'Yes?' he said.

"She did not say, 'You're eating. It's your lunchtime. I'll come back.' Not because she didn't understand that she was intruding but because she still didn't believe that this was where he lived, where he dressed and slept and ate and spent the time when he wasn't working. She would not even say, 'Is this really where you live?' She was squeamish, too, recall, and she knew that if it *was* where he lived it didn't have to be, and that by asking outright she would be demanding reasons of him that she wouldn't want to know.

"But she had hurt his feelings, and she had never hurt anyone before. And, too, something happened that morning that made her anxious for her honesty.

"She said she was sorry if she'd done anything to make him uncomfortable but that she had found something of Mrs. Simon's that had been missing since just after she had come to work for her and that—she didn't want to ask him about himself so she couldn't stop herself from telling him about everything that had led up to the insult —she had become too excited and had suddenly gotten the urge.

" 'The urge?'

" 'I had to go to the bathroom,' she said.

"He didn't really follow.

" 'That's her bathroom,' she said, 'Mrs. Simon's. I'm not supposed to use it. I have my own I'm supposed to use. But I'd just found Mrs. Simon's wrist watch. She never accused me of stealing it, but of course she thinks I did. She took me without references, you see. It's my first job. I'm seventeen. I didn't have references. But she said she'd give me a chance if I would let her read a letter I was sending to my folks.

" 'When I found her watch this morning I knew it would look more than ever like I was the one who'd taken it. I thought I'd leave it somewhere she could find it herself, you see. Then I realized she'd know I'd put it there or I'd have found it when I was cleaning. That's when I was caught short, when I had to go to the washroom, and'— she was blushing but it was too dark for your father to see—'as luck would have it, that's when it busted. She'd told me not to use hers. So, what with the wrist watch and the broken washroom and all, I didn't know what to do. I was only trying to do everything right when I offered you the shot.'

"Your father understood. She couldn't have said anything that would have made him more certain that he'd just found someone so like himself that they might already have been related. He believed in relations. No one living set more stock in them than he. He'd come to Milwaukee when he had heard the history of his family, the same long history you've been hearing. He heard the story and exiled himself to that basement, that strange room.

"Because Nancy was right. No one had to live that way. It wasn't Mindian's, the landlord's, idea, it was his own, and he was not so much living as sulking there, feasting on his role as outcast, protecting his heritage in that stick fortress as if it had been a reign, some government in exile, signaling God knows who that, well, what could you expect, he was a Mills. Millses lived in the ground, a whole story below other people's lives.

"And Nancy had heard of him. Everyone in the neighborhood had heard of him—— and not just the people in his buildings either, the two hundred or so men, women and children in the forty-eight units, in the eight apartment houses, on the two blocks, but all the people along Prospect and Kenwood Avenues. And not just the tenants who spoke his language, but the janitors who didn't. He was famous, as the hermit is famous, as the savage who moves to town is, as anyone distinguished by mythology or distanced by dream.

"He was famous. Nancy had heard of him. Only she was surprised that he was so young, so beardless, so cute. Tales had gone round. People who knew better told them, the tenants who had actually seen him, whose garbage cans he had carried down the back stairs to the alley, whose busted locks he had replaced, whose paint-fastened windows he had opened, whose sprung doors he had planed. And the housemaids in the building where he actually lived, who used the laundry room that was, in effect, his patio, his front yard. The children brave enough to ask his help in pulling their bicycles out of the storage lockers and carry them up the stairs to the street.

" 'It was the way,' she said, 'I'd seen Mrs. Simon wash out those glasses. It wasn't because I heard you live down here all by yourself like some old bear.'

" 'You heard that?' He was genuinely surprised. He truly did not know of his fame. His act had been for his own entertainment; he didn't realize others had been enjoying it as well. 'What else did you hear?' Nancy blushed again, this time so deeply that even in the dimness he saw it, even felt its heat perhaps. 'No, go on,' he said, 'what do they say?' She's stalling, he thought. He could just imagine what people told one another. That he'd been cut off, that he'd cut himself off without a penny, the monk of modern times. People's imaginations! 'What?'

" 'That you're not right.'

165

"He exploded. 'Of *course* I'm right! I didn't come down here without thinking about it. What do *they* know! It was a carefully thought-out decision. I weighed the pros and cons. Not even my fath—— '

" 'That you're not right in the head.'

" 'That I'm crazy?'

" 'That you're not smart enough to be crazy. That you're slow.'

" 'Hey!'

"Because already they were talking about *him!* Not five minutes into the courtship and already they were talking about *him!* The slight to his pride in the kitchen explained, Nancy forbidden access to certain toilets forgotten if it had ever registered in the first place, the wrist watch back-burnered. Maybe he *wasn't* right in the head, not crazy but slow. Here he had just found out that he had what he didn't even know he wanted—fame, notoriety—and all he could think to do was quibble with its nature. He set Nancy straight, you bet!

" 'You just go back to those biddies and tell them to mind their business. If they have nothing better to do than talk about people, the least they can do is get the facts right.'

"Which was really the official beginning of the courtship, your father laying out his reasons and justifications for the bewildered girl as if they were stunning chess moves or winning hands in poker, reeling off his history like debater's points or telling arguments in a letter to the editor. And indeed it had just that quality of pent righteousness such letters have, that same burst, off-the-chest violence of nourished grudge.

"She had never met anyone with anything so fancy as a fate before. She couldn't even follow him.

" 'No,' he said, summing up, 'I won't kill myself. That's not the scheme. It's to hide out for the fifty or so years I have left to live, go about my business and accomplish by myself in a single lifetime what all my family haven't been able to pull off in a thousand years—— the extinction of my long, bland, lumpish line.'

" 'What are you going to do?'

" 'I just told you. Nothing.'

" 'Oh,' she said, 'it sounded as if you were going to do something crazy.'

" 'Not crazy, slow. So slow it will amount to nothing. I'm going to remain a bachelor.'

" 'You're never going to get married?'

" 'I'm never going to have children. I'm never even going to go near a woman.'

"Which was absurd. He lived in proximity not only to the six housemaids in that very apartment building, but every day except Thursday afternoons and Sundays had to walk the same saucy, laundered, hung-to-dry gauntlet of damp female apparatus, brassieres, corsets, panties and garter belts—— all the luscious, silken, sexual bunting of all the mothers, housewives, sisters, maids and daughters in all those eight apartment houses he serviced. It brushed his face like climate, it pierced his skin like itch, and, because it was empty, it could have been filled with anybody, anyone.

"Fate really *is* a lame way of doing business. It's a wonder that history ever happens. Your dad said he would never marry, never have anything to do with women. She had no reason not to believe him, so if it had ever crossed her mind that he was an eligible young man, he disabused her of the notion within minutes of her having formed it. What I said about Thursdays notwithstanding, the odds against your ever being born were overwhelming. No, Mrs. Simon was your real fate.

"But a word about your father. It's one thing to hide out, it's another to be misrepresented. No sooner did he learn from your mother not only that people thought of him but *what* they thought of him, and no sooner did he understand that Nancy was the very one to set them straight—he was overreacting of course; they knew about him but he was hardly the only thing on their minds—no sooner, that is, did he realize that he had need of Nancy—and we're talking, too, of how she looked in that little make-believe doorway of his little make-believe room—than he repudiated her."

It felt good to sit there, George thought, knowing the end of the story, that whatever its complications, it would turn out well, that his father would turn out to be his father, that his mother would turn out to be his mother, and that he himself would eventually be brought to life.

"You see," Wickland said, "everyone is something of an occasion. Even the kings, even the officials and presidents, those, I mean, whom history has need of. But you're even more of an occasion than most. You were proscribed. Think about it. Your father said he would never go near women. Your mother believed him.

"So it was up to Esther Simon. She was the deciding factor in your existence.

" 'Doll,' she called when Nancy returned that evening from her afternoon off. 'Can you come into the master bedroom a sec, doll?'

"I don't think it ever occurred to Nancy that her employer, the woman who presumed to read her mail in lieu of references, who suspected her of being a thief, who called her doll because she couldn't always remember her name, who ordered her about, could almost have been a spoiled, slightly older sister. Esther Simon was only twenty-two years old. She had known her husband, Barry, a distant cousin, all her life, since they had been children in adjacent Hyde Park mansions in Chicago. It did not even occur to her as odd that when Mrs. Greene came to visit her daughter and son-in-law in Milwaukee, the Simons were 'the kids,' Nancy 'the woman.'

" 'Yes ma'am,' your seventeen-year-old mother said to her twenty-two-year-old boss.

" 'Your sweetie must have dropped this,' she said. 'You better not wait till next Thursday to return it.'

" 'What?'

" 'What indeed? It's a wrench. I found it in the master bathroom.'

" 'That's not mine,' Nancy said.

" 'Well of course it's not. It's *his*. He must have dropped it when he presumed to use my toilet.'

" 'Please, Mrs. Simon, you're making—'

" 'A mistake? Of course, doll. It's probably Mr. Simon's monkey whoosis, only Mr. Simon's out of town and it wasn't there when I left this morning.'

" 'It's the janitor's.'

" 'Yes,' Mrs. Simon said, 'I suppose that strange young man has unusual bathroom arrangements and from time to time is compelled to move his bowels above his station, but not in *my* house. Is that clear, doll? Look, your Thursday afternoons are your own affair, but you are not to make appointments in what is after all my home. I shall certainly speak to Mindian about this. Change my sheets.'

" 'I changed the sheets—'

" 'I know. Yesterday. Unless, of course, you were about to say afterward.'

" 'We didn't do anything, Mrs. Simon.'

" 'It's enough if you so much as sat with him on the side of the bed. Change my sheets.'

" 'Look—'

" 'Oh no, doll. *You* look. You're seventeen years old. This is your first employment. You don't have references. You're not used to living away from home. Certainly you're unused to living with your employers. Mr. Simon and I, however, have lived with servants all our lives.

" 'Do you know why it's necessary that you girls have references? Do you know what's actually *in* those characters we write? Our phone numbers and addresses, doll. So we may telephone each other. So we may visit. So we may say to each other what it would not always be wise to put down on paper.

" 'Some girls are sickly, some nasty, some dishonest.'

" 'I'm not any of those things,' your mother said.

" 'Oh?' Mrs. Simon said. 'But as soon as my back is turned you invite a janitor into my home to use a bathroom you were specifically told was out of bounds. Mr. Mindian will definitely have to be informed.'

" 'He didn't use your toilet. I did.'

" 'You let him watch? Oh,' she said, *'loathsome!'*

" 'No,' your mother said. 'Oh my God, you don't understand. Here.' And chose just that moment to return Mrs. Simon's wrist watch, which she took out of her purse, having put it there because she had not yet decided how to tell her she had found it.

"It was almost a formal exchange, trade. Wrist watch for wrench, the two objects changing hands, not returned so much as simultaneously surrendered, restored, like spoils appropriated in a war.

" 'I want you out of my house,' Mrs. Simon said.

" 'But where could I go?'

" 'Why, to your janitor,' she said. 'What, will he want a reference? Very well. You may tell him that you are a lying, quarrelsome young girl who steals watches and permits men to observe her while she sits on toilets. I will vouch for it. Get your things.'

"She kept house for him in the storage locker.

"It was more like a kid's clubhouse than ever, that tucked snug sense of coze and warm comfy, all of luxury they would ever know, the two of them, the brooding, self-conscious young man and the farmer's daughter returned to a kind of sybaritic nest condition, some quilted idyll of semiconscious life.

"It wasn't even sex. It was more like bathing, some long, painless, post-op ease.

"They knew she was there, the maids and tenants and children. Even Mindian knew she was there. No one complained. Why would they? They were fearful of driving off for nothing in return the one absolutely special and spectacular thing that had ever happened to them. It was like having peacocks in your backyard, tamed bears, docile deer. Just knowing they were there lent a sort of glory and luck to the neighborhood. They didn't even discuss it among themselves —— as his catcher and teammates will say nothing even in the seventh and eighth and ninth innings of the pitcher's no-hit game for fear of jinxing they can barely say what—— love *in vitro,* domestic science in the cellar. The freak your father and the freak your mother belonged to all of them, and if they happened to make their queer nest in one of Mindian's buildings rather than in another, why that was merely the way Nature arranges these things. It was understood, accepted, the way Catholics understand and accept that the Pope must reside in Rome, or a Normandy Frenchman that Paris is his capital. If George, living alone in that storeroom, had been famous, the two of them down there were twice as famous, more. (Yet everyone, even those who were not Mindian's tenants, understood that they were not to be disturbed—— that is to say, stared at; that is to say bothered.)

"So they knew they were there. The housemaids even agreed, it may even have been without conferral, upon a suitable genealogy for the pair. They had it that your mother and father were the daughter and son of Polish and Italian janitors in the neighborhood, that not only could they not speak English, even though they had heard them speak it, but could not even speak to each other, even though they had heard them.

"The neighborhood, still without conferral, knew it had a problem. (They really didn't want anything to change.) It knew it was not enough not to rock the boat or simply to maintain silence. If they ignored the principals to their faces, wouldn't this be taken as a sign of disapproval? The lovers—though God knows that whatever they were it wasn't lovers, highly developed animals, perhaps, of two entirely different species, each the last of its kind, who took their comfort from each other only because there was no one else in the world they could get it from; lovers? they were too far gone in despair, too lonely to love; lovers? they were the King and Queen of cuddle is all—needed reassurance they thought.

"The maids and housewives sometimes took Nancy with them when they went shopping. In the stores they would hold up ripe tomatoes, crisp stalks of green celery, fruits of the season, *candy,* for God's sake, whatever was accommodate to that heatless, iceless larder in which they lived, whatever could be consumed raw. (Or left treats for them on the cellar steps, fresh-baked cookies, hard-boiled eggs, leftover meats which even your doggy daddy and puss mom understood were scraps.) Using Nancy's (George's) money of course, but giving it to the grocer themselves, the lovers' middlemen and agents, and counting the change, too—though who who had ever heard of them would have ever shortchanged them?—before handing it over. As if Nancy were a child perhaps, or handicapped. And who knows, maybe they did need help. How many pounds of tomatoes and grapes do you need when you're shopping for two and tomatoes and grapes are all that you're buying? But the food was the single overture they made. They never attempted to add anything to, or alter anything in, the room itself. As if your parents really were animals and it was understood that animals knew best how to furnish their lairs and nests and dens. (If your father's light bulb had burned out, I don't think anyone would have thought to offer the loan of a spare for so much as a night.)

"George had his chores, his work. He rose at 5:00 A.M. to climb the twenty-four flights of back stairs in Mindian's eight buildings to take down the forty-eight garbage cans. He had his furnaces to tend, the small repair jobs, the sleds that he carried up from the basement for the smaller children, the three or four emergencies a day that he could absolutely count on. (People locked themselves out of their apartments, they ran out of fuses, they let their bathtubs spill over.) I say count on because he counted on them for tips. (They tipped him now. All the world loves a lover.)

"When he got out of their narrow bed in the fifty-degree room (the temperature of a cave) he told her to stay where she was and she did. While he dressed in the dark. She could just make him out, his naked body. And wondered: What is happening to me? What has already happened? Wondering not who this stranger was who had taken her virginity and with whom she had committed acts that had been reserved in her head not for some future when she was safely married but for other people altogether. Not questioning, as you might think, her own, or even George's, character so much as marveling at her luck. She loved it. She even loved the little room, their unicorn position in other people's imaginations. She too believed they brought luck to the neighborhood. She believed that she and George were a blessing to all of Milwaukee, a feather in the cap of the United States of America.

"And your father had barely got going. Having given her an

overview of George Mills history, he had not yet unburdened himself of more than two hundred years of particulars. She loved it. History had been one of her favorite subjects in high school. Your father did not know he was wooing her and she didn't know she was being wooed. And *that's* what was happening to her.

"She loved it. Whether the lovemaking—"

"Hey," George Mills said.

"—was an adjunct to the history lessons, or the history lessons a subscript to the lovemaking was a matter of indifference to her, as was, as you already know, the tininess of the room, which could have been, and in effect was, like a kind of carrel in a library. Even the narrowness of the diminutive youth bed—it was a time when as many undergraduates as could squeezed themselves into flivvers, phone booths, changing rooms at beaches—had an air of the makeshift collegiate. Your mother and father matriculated on that little, cotlike bed."

"Hey," George Mills said, "hey."

"Maybe she even expected to. It was the sort of virginal, celibate, nunnish, monkish bed she had slept in all her life. If she was at all romantic, the serf prince who was to free her would have come and ultimately joined her there. She would not have anticipated that it could have been otherwise. She may even have thought that that was part of the lovemaking, part of the act itself, that that crimped, cramped, rush-hour press of person, that closely close-quartered, neck-and-neck propinquity was concomitant with the conditions and moods of penetration. She may even have thought that that stall-like storage room in the basement of that apartment building was an out-and-out bower. And perhaps that was why she had been so offended the first time she had seen your father's living arrangements, not because she knew that no one had to live that way but because she knew that *no one was entitled to occupy a bower by himself!* Perhaps she even moved in with him out of a sense of decorum and decency, out of some innate knowledge of how architecture was intended to be filled up and used.

"Mindian came.

" 'Be right with you, sir,' your father said. 'Just give us a moment, sir, if you would.'

"He slid the bolt back and opened the door, exposing the bright, flower-print oilcloth walls. Nancy was behind him. 'Yes sir?' your father said.

" 'It looks like a kitchen table exploded in here,' he said. 'Step out from behind George for a moment please, Nancy. I want to look at you.'

"She did as she was told. Mindian regarded her as he had regarded the interior of the room. 'So it's true,' he said.

" 'True?' George said.

" 'This woman is pregnant,' Mindian said. 'How far along are you? Four months? Five?'

" 'Not five I don't think, Mr. Mindian.'

" 'The maids told me. My tenants did.'

" 'A lot of busybodies,' your father said.

" 'Yes,' Mindian said. 'The same busybodies who've been protecting you for half a year now. Who not only countenanced your dalliance but actively supported it. We'd become fans, you see—I do not except myself—boosters and rooters. You kids were love's home team. Even the polack, dago and wog janitors were for you. You were everybody's darlings, apples of eyes, teacher's pets, America's sweethearts. I'm your landlord. I've come to marry you.'

"You will believe that your mother must certainly have thought about marriage. I tell you she did not. It's not even certain that she loved George Mills.

"And your father. Have we not already seen how he repudiated women? And do we not know from his actions that it wasn't women he meant but only the entailments pursuant to liaison, nervous not about his responsibilities to a real wife and a material son but to a hypothetical posterity which was even then fifty to sixty years off? Your father was an intellectual. He believed, that is, in the palpable reality of any idea or event which had not yet come to pass in his own lifetime. That's why, squeamish as he was, he hid out in basements and cheerfully shouldered other people's garbage—— to subdue allure and retract hope. He was a victim of myth and handled himself as other myth victims have, finding his solutions in amateur and immediate expediency, rarely reading between the lines, which is where fate always has its way with you. Told, say, that he would murder his father and marry his mother, he would quit Corinth; or that no man born of woman could harm him, he would confidently chum even his enemies.

" 'I'm your landlord. Marry or leave.'

" 'We can stay if we get married?' your mother asked.

" 'Hey,' your father said.

" 'Not down here,' Mindian said. 'The Board of Health would condemn my basements.'

" 'I can't marry,' your father said.

" 'Then I shall have to fire you,' Mindian said. And then, more passionately, with a concern that was the measure of how your parents had touched the life of this landlord, he asked your father if he really meant to abandon the girl.

" 'It's the kid I'm abandoning, not Nancy.'

" 'You needn't worry,' Mindian told your mother. 'You and the child will be taken care of. There's a vacant apartment in one of my buildings. It's one of the apartments reserved for the janitors. You may have it. The tenants and I will see that you and the baby are provided for.'

" 'Hey, wait a minute,' your father said. 'You mean they'll be all right anyway? Nancy and the kid, too?'

" 'Certainly,' Mindian said. 'Until they're on their feet. Certainly.'

"Your father groaned."

"Hey, wait a minute," George Mills said. "What did he think—— "

"He'd spilled the beans by this time," Wickland said. "Nancy knew as much of the family history now as he did. Even he knew how interested she'd been. He figured she'd tell the child the story anyway, out of spite if nothing else. But he knew how good a scholar she was, that she wouldn't even have needed spite, that she would have told it out of the simple love of truth, out of innocent deference to the fact that history had been one of her favorite subjects."

"No," George said, "I mean about the baby."

"You were the baby."

"Then about me. What about me? I would have been in the picture anyway. Whether they got married or not. Whether Mindian took care of Mother and me or not. Or did he want Mother to have —— "

"I don't think he even thought about it," Wickland said. "I think he simply trusted his bad luck. That he believed his bad luck had gotten her pregnant. You see he loved her now. He believed his bad luck would kill her."

"But that doesn't—— "

"It does if you believe you're a myth victim. If you believe a thousand years have been up to nothing but shaping the fate of a single man. Expediency. Flee Corinth, kill a man, fall in love, marry. Tell yourself your hands are tied.

"They were married in the basement on a Thursday afternoon in front of the maids and janitors and other tenants.

"Even Mrs. Simon was there. 'Well,' she said, 'you're married now. Is there anything you particularly want for a wedding present, doll?'

" 'Could I have a reference?' your mother asked.

"But I believe the community would have preferred it if your father *had* abandoned your mother. They wanted their darlings, you see, and if they couldn't have their passionate darlings whom pregnancy and the realities had taken away from them, then they would have been quite content to have their victim darlings, substituting without turning a hair a wronged girl and a baby for a hero and heroine of love. Married, and with a baby on the way, they were just like everybody else.

"They even lived like everybody else. In a first-floor apartment in one more of Mindian's buildings. They took the youth bed, but they were just another couple now, just more neighbors. That's not she."

"Who?" George said.

"Your sister."

"Where?"

"Never mind. It isn't she.

"Your father wanted a girl. He hoped for a girl. Though he knew that no Mills in a thousand years had put forth any but male children only, he even *expected* a girl. That was at the back of his mind all along, of course. That's why he'd agreed to marry her. If you'd been a girl he thought he would still have been able to dodge his fate. He still believed in his fate, you see, still saw himself in the myth victim's delicious position, squeezed dry of force to change his life, with, at the same time, his eye on all the eleventh-hour opportunities that could change it for him. Almost, as it were, on fate's side, confident he'd broken the code, taking the position that destiny has its fine print, oracle its double entendre, that whatever happens to people is a trick —— God's fast one. If she could find me all the way down there, he thought, in these conditions, living like someone on the lam, and if she not only stood still for what we did to each other but didn't even once get up on her high horse or stand on her rights or read me the riot act when I put a bun in her oven or call in the Marines to shotgun the wedding and Mindian himself practically saying no harm done even if I didn't marry her, well, it's been too easy for all concerned, I think, for me and the grand George Mills design, and for Nancy, too. There's a dozen ways I could have blocked it, stymied circumstance, and I'm still only twenty, I haven't known this crap but a year yet, I wasn't even trying, or shown them my stuff, or seen theirs. Hell, I practically didn't put up no fight at all, I'm hardly winded and nothing I seen yet, nothing they thrown at me and nothing I been forced to take, could have busted the will of a child. It's been too easy for all concerned so there's got to be a catch. We'll name the little tyke Nancy.

"But he named it George because it was a boy, because you were a boy. He named it George who wanted the character of a rebel without any of the expense.

"Because if he'd been really serious he could have stopped it right then, asked your mother to marry him like a proper gent and never used Mindian as a broker at all. If he'd really been serious he could have called you Bill or Steve or anything at all, or teased what he thought he had for nemesis with the very initial 'G,' calling you Gill or Giles or Greg or God knows what. The point is it was always in his power to break the chain, as it was in the power of any of his ancestors before him, back to and including the first George Mills. But he didn't. None of them did. (Because people are suckers for fate, for all the scars to which they think they're entitled.) The point is he never wanted to.

"Though by the time of the second pregnancy Nancy did. Look sharp. She's coming. She's almost here."

The boy looked up. It was an ordinary afternoon. He could not have told by looking if it were Thursday or Monday, March or November. He was only twelve years old. There were people who believed he carried messages from the dead, that when he spoke their loved ones used his voice, that he knew things they would have to die to find out, that he had power, dread gifts. It was an ordinary afternoon. He knew his place in history and was waiting to be shown an infant ghost whom he would not be able to question because she had no vocabulary. It was an ordinary afternoon in his life. In Cassadaga. Where ego did not exist. Where it merged with bereavement, where grief was the single industry. Where children grieved. And soon his sister would be there. To give him a message. Which he thought he had already guessed. That there were no ordinary afternoons. That not just houses but the world itself was haunted. That death was up the palm tree. On the hoarding. In the square. It was an ordinary afternoon.

"Quite simply, she was bored. Fed up. She was the myth victim's victim and, now she had heard the whole story and was actually a part

176

of it, wanted nothing more to do with a man who saw everything that happened to him as a decree, a doom, whose every action, no, *activity,* whose every activity was part of some ritual of resignation, who believed, and performed *because* he believed, that history was looking. Or not history, autobiography, diary, home movies and scrapbook and family album—— all self-absorbed church rolls and records, deeds and registers: 'Now I am taking out the garbage.' 'Now I am shoveling coal.' 'Now I am fixing a toilet.' 'Now my sweat stinks of the lower oils and grimes, all the menial silts.' 'Now my back's stiff and there's a cramp in my leg.' 'Now I'm thirsty, now I'm hungry.' 'Now I am fucking my wife whose people are country people, farm people, and who has no references.' He was not even serving God, only some image of his own abasement, his soul gone groveling beneath the thousand top-heavy lean years of his second-fiddle fate.

"While all she wanted was to be like Mrs. Simon. To learn bridge. Mah-jongg. The ladyfied games and graces. Gossip and shopping and haggling with tradesmen not over price but quality. Learning pot roast and studying chop, a fruit wisdom and a vegetable cunning. Now that she was no longer a lover she yearned to be a wife, Mrs. Simon's kind of wife, not George Mills's, to decide menu and judge drape, to fuss furniture and worry hors d'œuvre. To run her house like some Wisconsin geisha and know the neighbors. She even looked at those manuals—God knows where she got them—that explain what goes where and when, and set up the secret asiatic pleasures like a blueprint or a diagram for wiring houses, the simple line drawings, about as erotic as the illustrations in gymnastic texts. (Though she knew your father would never have permitted these refinements, declining them not on moral grounds but on aesthetic and class ones, as he would have refused to eat cold soups and high-faluting breads if she had prepared them.)

"To be like Mrs. Simon, who had become in even the short time Nancy worked for her a kind of heroine to the country girl. Not resenting for a moment that the master bath was off limits to her but, on the contrary, made a little weak in the knees in the presence of such contrived disdain, for, give her credit, she had it on the evidence of Mrs. Simon's underwear that the disdain and distancing were entirely willed. That's what *she* wanted. That complete, casually indifferent and solidly confident social hypocrisy. Not, you will see, to make herself over—that's too hard, it can't be done anyway—so much as to make others over, to get them to accept at least a little her judgment of them. That's what *she* wanted. You will see that it was the exact opposite of what your father wanted. Who *lived* by other people's judgment of him. Who refused to live otherwise.

"Above all, she wanted to write references. (If she wanted a maid it wasn't so someone else might do her work for her, it was so she could always have someone around who would feel the force of her judgments.) In the absence of a maid of her own she borrowed other people's, the girls she saw in the laundry room, or the ones who came to their apartment to report things that required the janitor's attention. She watched them in the park with their charges, the children of the other tenants, who would never quite be neighbors, when she wheeled you in your carriage, when she pushed you in your stroller —both, not gifts exactly, hand-me-downs from those strange storage lockers which had served first your father, then your mother, and now yourself, like some queer furniture and appliance mine (so that in a way you were already sister'd, brother'd, not just because older children had outgrown the baby and toddler implements which you yourself would outgrow and which would be held in a kind of brotherly escrow for the child your mother would bear dead, but because they came up out of those same dampnesses and darknesses where you yourself were conceived, the ground of your being in the ground)— and carefully noted how attentive or inattentive they were, whether they exceeded their authority by abusing children who did not mind, and observed them marketing, whether they watched the scales when meat was weighed, produce, whether they counted their change. Discovering what she could of their personal habits, whether they were clean, whether they flirted.

"But mostly she talked with them. (And they with her, her mystery and whatever of aura and cachet she possessed for them dissolved by the marriage they had so fiercely supported.) Asked leading questions and closely considered their answers, grading them, listening, the janitor's wife, to their grammar, discovering what interest they had in history, current events (though intelligence and knowledge were the least of what she looked for, only seeking to get by these methods some clue to their intentions, their loyalties and commitments).

" 'You said you have a fellow back in Menomonee Falls.'

" 'Oh yar. Pete. Pete's all right. He's real cute, but he's awrful shy.'

" 'Shy.'

" 'Well, he ain't like Roger, my other beau. Roger's a scamp. He

178

don't hardly give a girl time to say yar even if she's of a mind to. Roger just goes ahead and makes all the big decisions hisself.'

" 'Doesn't that bother you?'

" 'Why? Roger ain't never yet took me no place I didn't really want to be.'

"And Nancy, the handwriting flourished, almost sculptured, more elaborate than any she'd ever used, would make a note: *Molly. Molly is a cheerful, healthy girl of doubtful morals. She has at least two boyfriends, and has hinted at her willingness to go 'all the way' with both of them. While Molly's personal life is her own affair, she strikes me as sexually careless. She could become pregnant at any time, leaving her employers high and dry.*

" 'Mrs. Faber's dishes seemed very beautiful when I saw them that time.'

" 'I should say so! They're *ever* so expensive. Forty dollars a place setting and they have service for *twelve*. I don't know what they'd do if a plate were to break. They don't even make that pattern anymore.'

"Or: *Helen. Helen is a very serious young woman who knows the value of her employers' things and has a respect for them which is admirable. She displays concern for their safety which leads me to believe she would care for the goods of a household as if they were her own.*

"But something sad and pathetic about the characters she was always perfecting in her head. She never actually wrote them down, knowing that as long as she was married to your father she would never have the opportunity to give a genuine reference. She knew more. She knew that if she had a son nothing would change. Your father wouldn't change. She made a promise to herself."

"A promise?"

"That you were never to be told about the Millses. That the buck stopped there.

"But nothing changed. And your mother was forced into a position people seldom find themselves in. She was forced, that is, to make plans.

"It is an astonishing fact, George, but the truest thing I know. Our lives happen to us. We don't make them up. For every hero who means to cross an ocean on a raft, there are a hundred men fallen overboard, a thousand, who find themselves in the lifeboat by accident.

"Not Nancy. Nancy had plans. What she planned was a new life.

She meant to take you and the baby—she was pregnant again—and to leave your father, to get as far from the apartments and basements of Milwaukee as possible, not to divorce him, because she didn't want your father to know where you would be, and once she brought the law into it—separation agreements, court decrees, visitation formulas—there would be no hiding from him. She planned, you see, to disappear in America.

" 'Maybe it's a good thing that I have no references, that I'm one of those for whom there is no record. Look at my husband. He is all references. The trouble is he believes them. They are all he believes. I will have to write home less often. One day I shall have to stop altogether. They don't know yet I'm pregnant with Georgie's sister. It was a mistake to tell them about Georgie. I didn't know. Oh well. Live and learn. They won't find out about baby Janet. Leaving George I leave them all.

" 'And if I meet a man? On my travels? Wherever it is I'm going. New Jersey! I shall go to New Jersey! If I meet a man in New Jersey and he wants to marry me and give me maids, what does it matter if he thinks me a widow? How would he ever find me out? My kind is free.'

"She found out the coach fare to New Jersey and began to save for it by not spending all the money George gave her for food. She hid what she was able to put aside in their storage locker off the laundry room in the basement of the apartment where they now lived. She hid it under the thin mattress at the bottom of the stroller you had now outgrown and which was being kept for your sister.

"The handwriting in her head now:

"*Nancy. Nancy is a basically honest person. Forced by circumstance to deceive her husband by withholding money specifically budgeted for household expenses, she carefully saw to it that she and she alone did the stinting. This, incidentally, is evidence of her organizational abilities, her initiative and growing skill with detail. She planned nutritious, comprehensive menus, carefully subtracting from her own portions what would look to the casual observer like hearty enough breakfasts, quite appetizing lunches, full-course dinners. She knew down to the unpurchased potato and unsqueezed orange, she knew to the slice of toast, to the egg and very fraction of stew or knifeload of peanut butter, the exact cost of what she would not be eating that day. Her hunger was her bankbook, and if she carefully managed to set aside from seventy-five cents to a dollar or so a week toward the price of her railroad tickets, George her husband and George her son were*

*not only none the wiser but not a bit less comfortable for it. (Nor did
she, as some might, add to the nest egg by telling her husband that Len's
meat and produce were inferior and could she have a little more money
—fifty cents a week would do it—in order to shop at Hilton's.)*

"She was trying to save three lives—— hers, yours, your sister's.
By the sixth month she had socked away most of the cash for her
tickets—the baby, of course, would ride free—and had even selected
a place to go to, Paterson, a small industrial city in northeastern New
Jersey, about seventeen miles from New York. She had gone to the
library. She even knew what they did there—— textiles, cotton and
silk. (She had always sewn, she knew material; she didn't think the
big treadles and looms of Paterson, New Jersey, would be that much
more difficult to handle than the Singer she was already accustomed
to.) So it was all planned out, not only where she would go and what
she would do but—she got hold of the Paterson newspaper—where
she would live. All this from a woman who when she had been fired,
sent away a few years before, could think of nowhere farther off to
go than just downstairs.

"It wasn't just the money for your ticket, George, that gave her
second thoughts.

" 'George can almost read now. He'll be writing in a year. He
knows his address. Suppose he wants to get in touch with his daddy?
How could I stop him from writing a letter? If I can prevent that, how
do I keep him from running back in three or four years with *my*
address? And there's his ticket. I'll have put away only enough to pay
for our fares. They'll be nothing left to start over with when we get
to Paterson.' "

"She was going to leave me? She was going to *leave* me?"

*"Nancy. Nancy is devoted to her family. She is determined that
her children remain with her no matter what. I should add that this
is not a decision arrived at lightly, or reached on the basis of emotion
alone. (Though a naturally warm and loving person, the young woman
in question doesn't allow her heart to interfere with the facts. Nancy can
be depended upon to look at all sides of an issue and to take decisive
action only after her judgment has been thoroughly consulted.)*

"She counted the cost. She counted the cost as she had estimated
not only the price of the meat the others would consume in a week
but the value to the penny of the two and a half or three slices of red
beef she would not."

"She was going to leave me?"

"Forcing herself to post the debits and credits involved if she took you.

" 'Debit: He would have no father to play with or take him to ball games.

" 'Debit: He would want toys.

" 'Debit: These are hard times. With two extra children to provide for, a man would think twice before asking a woman to marry him.

" 'Debit: He's so much like his father.

" 'Debit: He'd have to be told some story about why we left Milwaukee, why I no longer ever even talk about taking him to visit his relations there. I couldn't tell him the truth. I'd have to lie. I'm basically an honest person. I'd probably tell bad lies.

" 'Debit: If I *do* meet someone George might blurt out that I'm still married to a man in Wisconsin.

" 'Credit: He's my son, after all.' "

"She's going to leave me."

"No," Wickland said. "The debits were chiefly contingency debits, things well into the future, things that might never happen. She might never meet anyone who would want a woman with even one child. She was a person who required maids for those references she had never stopped making up in her head. You could do things around the house, you could help with the baby. She wasn't going to leave you. She was going to take you."

"So she could watch me. So she could make up references for me."

"It was almost the eighth month now. This pregnancy hadn't been as easy as her first. She was frequently in pain. It was a first-floor apartment but she had difficulty with the stairs, feeling each step in her gut, a pregnancy like appendicitis. She couldn't do laundry. She couldn't cook or clean or make beds. She took to her bed.

"And now she *had* maids, all she could want. They were girls from the buildings, not just from the building they lived in now or from Mrs. Simon's building or even the building where they had first lived, the one with the famous storage locker (retired now, withdrawn forever from the category of lease, freehold and shelter, vacated, vacant, not exactly condemned nor quite yet memorialized as lovers' lane, bower, star-crossed grottic coze, but doing a brisk business in necking, heavy petting, nakedness, with the now almost adolescent kids whose bicycles and sleds your father had once pulled up the cellar steps, the flowered oilcloth walls still up, unfaded and still redolent of the mysterious janitor and the exiled maid), but from *all* Mindian's buildings, girls out on loan not just from the tenants who had lived there during the glory but from those who had come later, who had only heard about the glory and who wanted a piece of the consequences, the promissory moral catastrophic denouement. And not just on Thursday afternoons either, but every day, practically around the clock, making the apartment shine, eagerly doing your mother's bidding, anticipating that bidding, getting you ready for school, making breakfast, making lunch, making dinner, *doing the shopping!*

"All this in deference to what they had been, to the now slipshod memory of what they had been, not a willfully world-shy young janitor and a fired, forlorn, loose-ended country girl, but defiant lovers who took their love into the ground and closed the door after them, like people waiting for the end perhaps, or folks buried alive.

"In any event, Nancy and George did not want for help, nor Nancy for characters to define and read, as my co-spiritualists in Cassadaga read auras, handwriting, palms, gazing crystals, making of life, the future and past, a kind of immense, customized calendar of personality. Though to tell the truth, she wasn't quite up to her opportunities now. She was uncomfortable and all these helpers seemed to have been cut out of the same cloth. She knew distinctions were always to be made but she was tired; she couldn't make them.

"One size fits all. These girls are very willing but they are very trying. It isn't so much that I have to tell them what to do but that I have to entertain them. Evidently they want to be my friends, to be on personal terms with me. They want to know about our lives.

"It's all very well to have an amicable relationship with the help but something else entirely when they feel they can take liberties with you. It shows a want of respect and leads to a breakdown of the employer-servant relationship.

"But her heart wasn't in it. She rarely composed these characters now. She was too tired, too weak. All she could really think about was when the baby would be born, when she could move to New Jersey. She was constantly nauseous and couldn't even think about food, not even to plan the menus she had once taken such pride in, the carefully conceived shopping lists with their attention to taste and nutrition and that cunningly shaved economy the proceeds of which were to go toward the purchase of your half-fare ticket to Paterson, New Jersey."

"She's not going to take me," George Mills said, "she's not going to take me."

" 'There's never enough *change,* George. They spend every nickel you give them. There's food rotting in the pantry.'

" 'Just relax, darling,' her husband told her. 'Just lie here and try to get your appetite back. Don't worry about the food bills. Don't worry about a thing. The food isn't rotting. All the work they do around here, these girls are entitled to a little something to eat. Please don't worry, dear. Your friends are taking care of everything.'

"The baby wasn't even premature. One Tuesday while you were at school your father came in and heard her screaming. Or heard her screaming at Bernice, whose eleven-to-noon shift was just ending and who was waiting to be relieved by Louisa, whose lunch shift was about to begin.

" 'No, you foolish girl. I *cannot* get dressed. The doctor will have to come here. It is impossible that I get up.'

" 'But Mrs,' Bernice objected. (Which is how your mother preferred to be called. Not Mrs. Mills, and certainly not Nancy, but Mrs, as though the girls were incapable of learning her name, only her distance. That she got them to agree—she told them it was a pretty game—is a measure of the awe in which they still held her.)

" 'What is it? What's happening?' your father shouted.

" 'It's the baby, George. I think I'm having the baby.'

" 'She's in just horrible pain,' Bernice said.

" 'What does the doctor say?'

" 'The doctor is a fool.'

" 'She says the doctor must come to the apartment. I told him how it was with Mrs, but he says these things is best handled in the hospital.'

" 'Then we'll just take her to the hospital. Take it easy, dear. Take it easy, sweetheart.'

" 'I cannot get dressed.'

" 'That's all right. I'll wrap you in a blanket. I'll carry you.'

" 'Do you want me to have the baby in the hallway? Do you want me to have it in the street? Is that what you want?'

" 'Bernice? Bernice?' Louisa called. 'I'm here, Bernice. You can go now. I'll fix lunch and bring it in.' "

"Did this happen? I was at school. I remember those girls. There were a bunch of them there when I got home."

"Because nobody had *two* maids," Wickland said. "Because nobody had two maids, let alone five. She wouldn't let any of them leave. Not that they wanted to. Or maybe she did it for your father. Whom she had made a kind of squire, laird, gent, swell. Who suddenly found himself Duke of Milwaukee.

" 'Call that doctor again. Say that it is impossible that I get out of this bed. Say that he is the one who confined me to it. Ask how it may be that at the moment when we are most precarious we should quit it. No, George, you stay. Rosalie will call.'

"Perhaps it was the screaming, but they were coming all at once now and not waiting upon their designated times.

" 'Louisa,' your mother said, 'stand at the door. Admit no one but those girls who are trusted.'

" 'How will I know?'

" 'Pass in the names. We'll let you know.'

"He thought she was hysterical, that to move her by force would rupture not only the female mechanism which had caused her difficulties but his life, too. He couldn't lose her. He couldn't. He had already quit Corinth once and even gotten away with it. He didn't want to give fate a second chance to nail him.

" 'Look babe,' he pleaded, whispered in her ear. 'We're just like everyone else now. George don't know a thing. I'm these folks' janitor because that's the agreement, the bargain I made, but this is America here. There ain't any kings or princes sitting on his face. He could grow up and, I don't mean be president, it's only America, not fairyland, but go to work for some fellow, mind his P's and Q's, get raises, responsibilities, and one day maybe do all right for himself, the only Mills with enough guts ever to break the chain letter. Don't die, kid. Jesus, don't die. You'd make me out some kind of hero to these people. Christ, sweetie, I ain't but twenty-five. I'd be their haunted young widower, Georgie their orphan. They'd pull us to pieces. I'm weak, Nance, I'm weak, babe. We'd be a goddamn folk song in a month. Don't die, kid. Please don't. I love you, Nancy. Georgie has his chance now. You die and I'll blow it for him. I know I will.'

"*In my judgment Nancy was always rather a sensible girl. At the moment when more attention was being paid to her than she had ever received in her life, when Bernice, Louisa, Rosalie, Irene, and Vietta were waiting on her hand and foot, and Jane, Frances, Mattie, Joan, and I can't recall the names of all the girls turned away by Louisa, she never, sick as she was and feeling as bad as she did, for a moment believed that the attention they paid her came her way as a mark of respect either to her person or to her position. Rather, she recognized it for what it was—— base curiosity. These girls were, most of them, maiden, virgin. What they knew of sex and life they knew by report rather than experience. What they knew of Romance they had by legend. Nancy concluded, and concluded under stress and concluded correctly, that there was not a little animus in their affiliation. Without wishing her any personal harm, they were nevertheless pleased to have some physical confirmation of their own old wives' prejudice that you can't get away with it, you can't go off to a tree house and live for love without there being some heavy price to pay, you can't lord it over others and have them attend your every whim and make it understood that you can call them Bernice or Mattie or Joan or sometimes get their names mixed up altogether while they must call you Mrs, without your being dealt severe blows or taking heavy losses. Nancy is sensible. She manages to keep not just her own but other people's priorities straight.*

" 'Oh, I heard them. Even through my distraction and pain I heard them. George out of the room, gone to watch for the doctor. Oh, I heard them. Through the sedative the doctor phoned in that Rosalie fetched from the drugstore. As they lathered and shaved me. And scalded the water. And laid by the sheets—you'd have thought it was a laundry in there—and fluttered about, positively gay now, their tongues loosened in direct ratio to what they thought was my pain and semiconsciousness.'

" 'She did it in a stall. She wants straw, not sheets.'

" 'This is the youth bed where she surrendered her youth.'

" 'Never mind her youth. I'm shaving her youth back for her.'

" '*Ooh,* don't it *smell* awful!'

" 'Mrs' cooze is all stinky.'

" 'Ain't it though!'

" 'They say that's why Mrs. Simon didn't want her sitting on her toilet.'

" 'Haw! That's not why. She was afraid Mrs would steal it like she did her watch.'

" 'I heard them.'

"Such girls should never be entirely trusted. I would say this: Have them if you can afford them. But despise them always. Never forget how things stand.

" 'Dear God, help get me to New Jersey.'

" 'What's that, sweetheart?'

"To Whom It May Concern: I should like to add that while I understand that such considerations have no immediate bearing on the specifics of your needs, and muddy the waters without altering the circumstances and, in a way, smack of special pleading and may even

beg the question (a question which I daresay I have already answered:
she had been loose; she married a man she did not approve of; she made
plans, though the less kind but perhaps finally more accurate statement
would be that she plotted), it may nevertheless be of some use to you
to know something of Nancy's mind at this time. (Mind and attitude
are character, too.)

"*I should like to say, then, that she was always fully in control of*
the ironies. Even then, pampered as she certainly was, hurt as she
certainly was, no longer in any way in control of her circumstances,
having every reason to give over the ironies; indeed, having every reason
to let happen whatever was going to happen and to solace herself with
a warming hatred for those who hated her, she nevertheless continued
to command them, to command the ironies:

"*If I die I leave as estate the value of one one-way, full-fare coach*
ticket to Paterson, New Jersey, plus that portion of Georgie's fare which
I have already saved. If the baby dies, nothing is gained, since Janet
would have traveled on my ticket free.

"*If I don't die—and this, I rather think, must be the case—there*
would still be the remainder of Georgie's fare to get, but I don't think
I could do that now. I would not, I think, be too weak to continue to
save, put by money for an event that now seems pointless even to me,
but too dispirited. Yes, and too weak too, for if flight is pointless if
Janet dies, surely it is a pointlessness for which I have been the chief
agent. (My husband is wrong. There is no fate where there is no char-
acter. We are what happens to us.) As first my discomfort and now
my danger were caused by the very plans I had made to escape dis-
comfort and danger, too. I doomed myself by trying to save myself. I
muffed my pregnancy by starving myself. I was too honest to eat for
two. And too dishonest to eat for one. If I really wanted to get to New
Jersey, I should have given the Georges the smaller portions. If I had
had real appetite for my salvation, I should have stinted on theirs. It's
all ironic, all of it. If I had told the girls to hold back just thirty-five
or fifty cents from what George gave them to buy food, I could have
had both our tickets by now. Even if Janet dies there is nothing to do
but just go.

"The doctor was there now."

"I was there," George Mills said. "My father was there."

"Your father was drunk."

"He was crying. He was talking to me. He was trying to tell me
something."

"He wasn't talking to you, he was making a speech. Like the best man at a wedding. He had found his audience and pinned it to attention by its own captive courtesy and embarrassment.

" 'Why shouldn't I?' he demanded. 'Why *shouldn't* I drink? What do they give me all those bottles of scotch and bourbon for Christmas for if they don't expect me to get pie-eyed? Hell, it may even be part of the bargain. Maybe they actually *want* me pissed. It's not even bad booze. Only the best. Don't they tell me that themselves as if maybe I couldn't read the grand ads in the fine magazines that they save up for me and give me two and three months past their dates? Oh oh, my hand-me-down perks! Liquor twice as old as my son. Where *is* that rascal? Here, boy, you want a drink? Here. I think I've been remiss with you, behindhand in the instruction. Maybe even the doomed have to be trained up to their doom. So they can think about it, turn it over in their minds, connoisseur it like booze for the janitor so it won't be wasted on someone who can't appreciate it. Bottoms up, son. Here's mud—— Look out, stomach, here she comes! Drink, lad. Drink for the hair on your chest. Drink to low ways!'

" 'Come on, George. Hold it down. The doctor can hear you. Your wife can.'

" 'Sure, Irene. Sorry, Irene. It's just that I'm a little nervous. No Mills woman ever had any trouble before with anything low down and natural as just birth. They take their inspiration from the beasts in the field. Mills women don't just have babies. They litter, they foal. They farrow, they spat. They brood and spawn. They fucking fledge!'

" 'You all right, George?' Vietta said.

" 'Hey sure.'

" 'Easy there, George.'

" 'Right, Bernice.'

"That's when he took you into the bedroom with him.

"I think the blood reassured him. I think he was right in at least one respect. I think your squeamish father had some instinct for the placentary, for the treacly obstetrical a step up from mud, for caul haberdash like the bonnets of being. For all gynecology's greasy modes, for its fish bowls of amnion and its umbilicals like ropes down wells.

" 'What's that damned kid doing in here?'

" 'He's my son, Doc.'

" 'This man is drunk. Get him out of here. Come on, Nancy, push. I can't do a Caesarean here in your bedroom. Push. *Push.*'

" 'It hurts.'

" 'Of course it hurts. *Push!*'

"But the doctor knew Janet was already dead, your sister was already dead.

" '*I* knew she was dead. *I* knew. It just didn't feel right. Something dead weight to the pain, to the pain itself. It was nothing to do with me. Like a splinter, say, or a cinder in my eye. Like a bone caught in my throat or brambles stuck to my insides. Like decay in a tooth. Something dead weight, foreign matter about the pain. Something violating me. Like a body blow. Like a wound picked up in a war. And, oh God, my dead Janet like so many shards of busted girlbone. Help me, Janet. Help *meee!*'

"Perhaps the doctor didn't really care that a child was watching, that the father was, nor the curious young women, neither nurses nor midwives, not even related to the patient, in what the doctor, distracted as he was, busy as he was, may not even have noticed was not a hospital bed it looked so much like one.

" 'Something dead weight, out of place, your tiny daughter-corpse caught trespass in my thousand-year male preserve Mills belly like some spooked purdah.'

"Perhaps he even wanted them there. To watch him. To see what he was doing. To grasp a little of what he was up against some of the time. Not just a go-between between a mother and her infant but occasionally having to do the actual main-force dirty work itself. About as scientific as someone pulling teeth or tearing up the ground. Horsing death around in the dark and trying not to cut anything important. Maybe—had he dared—he would have asked one of them to spell him, like a lifeguard over someone drowned. And when he said, 'Come on, Nancy, push,' it was at least a little to get Nancy to spell him.

" 'Take him out,' Nancy said. 'Take George *out.*'

" 'Is that child still here? Go on, sonny. Wait outside.'

" 'When Georgie had gone. Then I pushed. Then I did. At last it came free. I had not known I could raise the dead.'

" 'What's wrong? What's wrong with my kid?'

" 'Give me one of those sheets,' the doctor said.

" 'Here,' Louisa said.

" 'Wrap it in this.' But Louisa just stood there. The doctor looked at each of the girls, then wrapped it himself. But he was a good doctor really, not finally used to infant mortality. When he swaddled the child he left a little open space for the head. He carried it through the living room on his way out."

"It was blue," George Mills said.

"Yes," Wickland said.

"Behind the blood. Under the blood it was blue."

"Yes."

"Like a black eye. I saw her. I—— "

" 'What?' your father said. *'What?'*

" 'Because if you leave history,' your mother said, 'you think you have nowhere to go. That's why you married me. That's why you said we had to name him George. That's why you teased my womb with little-girl bait. Yes, George, *teased* it, then set all your dependably overwhelming centuries of male Mills history against what was after all only my country-girl biology. That's why our daughter died.'

" 'Oh, Nancy,' your father said. 'Oh, Nancy, oh, Nancy.' He was crying.

" 'Rosalie and Vietta,' your mother said. 'Bernice, Louisa and Irene and all the others.'

" 'What?' your father said.

" 'We'll have to let them go, won't we?'

" 'Let them go?'

" 'I mean they can't do for us anymore. We can't keep them. There's only the three of us. Our apartment isn't that large. You're out most of the time. Georgie's in school all day.'

" 'They pitched in,' Mills said. "They pitched in, Nancy, when you weren't feeling well.'

"It isn't what you think," Wickland said. "It wasn't what it sounds like. She was mad, not crazy. She was still in control of the ironies. She didn't want you ever to find out about the Millses. She made him promise. Only then would she agree to stay with him.

"The girls wouldn't be coming once she was on her feet again. She would have no one to work her judgments on. She had already judged her husband. She had already judged you."

"Me?" George said. "What did she say about—— "

" 'This child must have no ancestors. I am on the child's side in this. If the child is to assign blame it will have to assign it to the near-at-hand, to its own propinquitous, soured operations, its own ordinary faults and weaknesses, errors in judgment, deficiencies of will, the watered cement of its inadequate aspirations and glass-jaw being. I will have done all I could. I will have set it free.' "

"She's going to leave me after all," George said.

"She's not even talking about you," Wickland said harshly.

"But—— "

190

"The girl," Wickland said. "She's talking about the girl, she's referring to Janet."

"But—— "

"*Janet starts school in September. I don't think she knows we're poor. She knows I have to work of course, and that our little family is dependent upon even what George brings in from working after school. She isn't a stupid child, but when she asked me that time about her daddy she seemed to accept my answer. She only questioned me that once. Perhaps she's really rather sensitive. Perhaps she understands more than she lets on. Maybe she speaks to Georgie about it at night in their room in the dark. Up to now, I don't think he's told her any more about it than I have, but I've noticed that he's restless and a little angry. Someday he'll tell her the truth, what he knows about it. Why kid myself? He's told her already. Of course he's told her. He's told her of a grand man, a strong, kind man waiting in Milwaukee, and that if things are ever terrible enough he'll take her there and then they won't be terrible anymore. And if he hasn't written yet, it's because things aren't terrible enough yet. He's afraid of course. It's his trump card and he's afraid to play it. Poor Georgie.*

"*But I hope she's sensitive. But who knows? She's so docile. She accepts everything. She's like everyone else finally. As Georgie is. As I am. As George is like a thousand years of Millses and has never dared not to be.*

"*We take what comes. Everybody does. Even a little girl. I am certain she has never said, 'Write him then. You showed me his address. Write him then.' We take what comes. And if nothing comes we take that. Everybody does. George was wrong. You can't quit Corinth. There isn't any Corinth to quit.*

"*You're wondering if I shall ever get to the point. But I already have, you see. Must I spell it out for you? Very well then.*

"*I shall do no more references. There's no need. In my judgment there isn't a dime's worth of difference between any of us. There's no such thing as character. It's as I said in Milwaukee. One size fits all.*

"Now look," Wickland said. "Can you see her?"

"Yes," George said, sobbing. "But I don't want to."

"It won't last," Wickland said. "Nothing lasts."

"But—— "

"Yes?" Wickland said. "Was there something else?"

George didn't know. That is, he didn't know what it was. He was certain there was something else and that Wickland would show it to him, and that it would be terrible, worse than anything yet. It had begun by his wanting to know if he had powers. Kinsley had said he had and, for a time, he thought he had. But only Wickland had powers. He was a reverend of reality and George believed that at that moment he could have shown him anything, everything. But he didn't know. He didn't know what was left to see or if he wanted to see it, but Wickland had powers and Wickland hadn't dismissed him yet.

They sat for perhaps an hour. The sun was beginning to set. There was a chill. He wanted to be released but the reverend was not ready to let him go. Or he wasn't ready.

Then George sighed.

"You said he didn't want me to find out about the Millses. You said she got him to promise that he wouldn't tell."

"Yes," Wickland said.

"But I *did* find out about them. He *has* told me."

"Yes. He still thinks there's a Corinth. He thinks it's Cassadaga."

"I don't—— "

"Because he's no rebel," Wickland said, "because there's nothing you can do to him to make him one. Because telling you was *his* trump card, and playing it was the only way he had to avenge what I did and to stand by history."

"What you did?"

"You told me you saw her, you said you could see her. She's going to have a baby."

He did not return to Kinsley's. It was already dark when he left Cassadaga. In the sky the stars must have looked like salt.

PART THREE

1

Messenger, running late, found the little street off Carondolet and parked. It was his second day on Judith Glazer's route. When he took Mrs. Carey's tray from the insulated box there were three left. He locked the door on the driver's side, found the house and opened the gate of the little low fence, low as a fence in storybooks.

He had called first, phoning from Albert Reece's apartment, the man's permission grudgingly granted.

"That wasn't long distance, was it?" Reece asked when Messenger had hung up. "If it was only across the river they'd charge me a toll."

"It was in the city," Messenger said.

"Could I see that paper?" Messenger showed him the number and Reece studied it for a moment. "All right then," he said. "Call it a dime." Cornell handed him the coin. "If this was Russia you could call for free. They got Socialized Telephone in Russia."

"Long distance too?"

"Kids," Reece said, "don't ever talk about you. You get a free ride with kids. Kids don't give a shit about your morals or your politics. I'm talking infants, toddlers, boys on tricycles. Kids just ain't shockable. If a little golden fairy was to tip his cap to a kid in the street, the kid would just look at the fairy and tell him good morning.

The only way to shock a kid is to hold his finger to the socket. The elderly is different. Old-timers love to correct you. They enjoy it that you're a traitor or that you live in sin. They love that you sit with your legs apart or are on the take. It warms their hearts the parks ain't safe and you're going to hell.

"Don't get me wrong, Professor. The old are just as hard to shock as any six year old. They not only seen it all, they done eighty-six percent of it. Christ, they're as crazy about bad news as you are. Why shouldn't things stink if you're going to die soon? It's just that we love to correct, show our disapproval like preserves we've put up. If we had the strength we'd throw stones. So just don't underestimate us. Don't be sly and don't be disrespectful. Don't ask an old-timer 'Long distance too?' when he's trying to explain Socialized Telephone in the USSR to you.

"All I want to know is this. How'd a son of a bitch like you get into this line of work?"

"What do you want from me?" Messenger asked. "Tomorrow we have chunks of braised beef served with noodles in a rich broth, buttered Texas toast, French-style green beans and glazed pineapple tidbits. Or you could have breaded beef cutlet, Wisconsin whole-grain corn and red beet slices. What do you want from me?"

"Wise guy," Reece said. "That's all right. We love it you're a wise guy. We think it's terrific you're a horse's ass."

Messenger, understanding that they didn't like him, was untroubled. He only found it a little unfair. He brought their dinners, he did for them, even helping to feed those one or two of his clients who could not manage for themselves. He spent perhaps fifteen minutes with each of them, twice as much as Judith told him would be necessary. At some other time of his life he would have been bothered perhaps by their hostility, but now it was a matter of indifference to him, as things were a matter of indifference to him to which he had never thought he would become accommodated.

Messenger had had what he thought of as a curious life. He had published a collection of stories and three novels, all of which were out of print, none of which had ever come out in paperback. And though he was still occasionally invited to read from his work on various campuses, the fees were always small and the invitations invariably came from friends who themselves hoped to be invited to his school in return. (It was a point of pride with him that he never returned the favor.) There were seldom more than thirty or forty people in his audiences, half of whom were there because they had been asked to the party in his honor afterward. He was forty-five years old and accepted these offers not for the money and certainly not for the opportunity they gave him to see his old friends but because on one such trip, shortly after the publication of his second novel, he had met a really beautiful young graduate student who had driven him back to his motel after the party and spent the night with him in his room. She said she was nuts about his work, but when he ordered breakfast for them the next morning it turned out she had read only one of his stories. It was the single story he had published in *The New Yorker,* the title story of a collection he was to publish a year later, and the only thing he'd ever written to be optioned for the movies. The amiable madman who had purchased the option, Amos Rope-blatt, a hopeful fellow who had once had something to do with an Orson Welles film made back in the fifties, renewed it annually for five hundred dollars.

Messenger felt he was clearly second string, a man who had been granted tenure by his university when he was still in his mid-thirties, on the basis, it seems, of that same *New Yorker* story that had gotten him laid a dozen or so years before, the memory of which incident kept him returning to those campuses neither for his token fees nor for those sparse audiences to whom he read from what even he could not seriously think of as his "work," and still less for his friends, but for those parties.

Then, at a time of his life when he no longer really needed it, he came into an inheritance, or an inheritance by default. An aunt, preceded in death by her maiden daughters, left him three hundred thousand dollars. On two occasions he had himself almost died, once from a heart attack and once from a bone stuck in his throat on which he had nearly choked. And he was troubled by his children.

And something else. He had grown tolerant of his own bad driving. Regularly he dinged cars in parking lots, gouging metal divots from his once smooth fenders and altering the face of his grille, the delicate crosshatching piecemeal collapsing as he sought to negoti-ate parking spaces at four and five and six miles an hour. There was one car, a black '76 Gremlin, that, parked by the curb in the narrow faculty lot behind his building, seemed always to be in his way, the dark molding about its left rear wheel an obstacle he seldom missed as he attempted to move into his slot in the single cramped row of cars. Each accident, each small engagement, brought a brief anger, then a queer, righteous, irrational fulfillment. The car was never *not* there, always, it seemed to Messenger, in a favored position among the automobiles lined up like race horses at a starting gate. Messenger cursed its owner's regularity, the long-suffering smugness of the scarred and battered Gremlin. He never left a note—when he left in the afternoon the car was still there—or sought to hide the evidence of his guilt, the injured auto's black paint smeared like spoor across his cream-colored Pontiac. On each occasion he made the same speech to himself. "My hand-eye coordination's going. Fuck him. Why should I worry about a little scratched paint?" But he knew he would neither die nor ever hurt anybody in an accident, that he would simply drive over curbs as he turned corners, skin cars parked along side streets, dent the odd fender here and there along life's highway.

He was forty-five years old, an old middle-aged man, and required marijuana whenever he left his home.

"Meals-on-Wheels," Messenger called as he pushed open the unlocked door.

"That's all right," a voice called thinly.

The house looked like the inside of a stringed instrument, the wood unpainted, gray as kindling. Even the furniture was unfinished. Messenger, looking at the warped woodwork and canted floors and walls, had the sense that the rooms needed to be tuned.

"Is it still hot?"

"Should be," Messenger said, raising his voice to the woman he had not yet seen. "I could warm it up on your stove if you like."

"Yeah," the woman said, "that'd be terrific. A hot free lunch would make all the difference in my life." She came out of her room. She was pushing an aluminum walker. "I'm Mrs. Carey," Mrs. Carey said.

"Cornell Messenger."

"Yeah," she said, "how do you do? I missed you yesterday. I was to the clinic for tests. I didn't know I'd be gone so long or I'd have left a note. Cigarette?"

"No thanks." He had already begun to reheat the chicken-fried steak and mashed potatoes.

"It was the first time I was out in over a month," she said. "It felt real good. They picked me up in one of those minibuses they send round for the handicapped. They got them equipped with special lifts for wheelchairs. Welfare gave me a wheelchair but I swear to you it's easier to get around with my walker. I ain't got the strength in my arms to roll it. A woman needs somebody to push her. I'll tell you something," Mrs. Carey said. "I think it looks common when a lady pushes her own wheelchair. That sound funny? That's the way of it.

I'm a heavy smoker but even when I was walking I never smoked in the street. That looks common, too. You think it's foolish a woman with a Welfare wheelchair and a free walker that travels the town in the handicap bus and waits on the warmed-over charity lunch should say such things and have such notions? You put me down for pride I sit in the kitchen in my nightgown and robe while some strange guy heats my meal?"

"No, of course not."

"Ain't you nice," she said. "I'm going to tell you something you're so nice. I qualify for benefits from seventeen agencies of the United Way. Last year it was only six. Next year, if I live and nothing happens, it could be thirty."

"You should look on the bright side," Cornell said.

"Yeah? You think so?"

"I certainly do."

"How about that? Say, let me ask you something. Are you important? You told me on the blower you're making Mrs. Glazer's deliveries, and she's married to a big shot over at the university. Maybe you're important too."

"No," Cornell said.

"Yeah, I'll bet. What's wrong with Mrs. Glazer anyway?"

"I guess she's sick."

"Mind my business, huh? Okay. Let me ask you something else. What did you do with that lunch you had left over yesterday?"

"I ate it."

"No kidding? Yeah? Maybe you ain't important."

"Important people eat a different lunch?"

"They eat omelets. They eat salads. They eat cold soups and thin fish. Let me ask you a question. I don't get out much anymore. Just to the clinic, just to the agencies. Mrs. Glazer used to tell me, but she ain't been by in weeks now."

"Mrs. Glazer has cancer," Messenger said.

"Oh shit," Mrs. Carey said.

"I'm sorry. I shouldn't have said anything," Cornell said.

"No no, that's all right. Can I call her up? Is she home?"

"Well she's home," Messenger said, "but she's very tired. It might be better if you waited."

"You know a lot about it."

"She's a friend of mine."

"Geez, I almost put my foot in it, didn't I? How about that?"

"What do you mean?"

"Hey, forget it," Mrs. Carey said. "I didn't know you was *that* Messenger."

"*That* Messenger? What do you mean? What were you going to ask me?"

An odd change seemed to have overtaken her. She became suddenly coy, teasing, returned quite mysteriously to a time when she had not been ill, the new quality somehow unseemly, as if she powered her own wheelchair perhaps, or smoked in the street. She wanted coaxing, Messenger saw, but he was annoyed. "Ha ha," she laughed, almost singing. "Ha ha ha." It was as if she remembered not flirtation exactly but flirtation's poses and noises. He hoped she wasn't going to hold her knees and sway in place. "Ha ha," she chirped again.

"I seem to have been a regular tonic for you," Cornell said. Was she rolling her eyes at him? Was she pursing her lips? What was this teenage pantomime all about?

"Are you holding? Have you got any mary jane on you?"

"What?"

"Are you high? Do you see visions? They jump the rates on your car insurance?"

"What are you talking about?"

"Ha ha."

"Look, lady, dinner is served."

"Maybe you ought to give me a puff. I hear it does wonders for chicken-fried steak."

"Yeah, well, I'm not an agency of the United Way."

"Ooh, you're angry." Cornell had started to leave the kitchen. "What *I'd* like to know is how you find the time to come down here when *there's so much to be done at home?*"

"Nice meeting you."

"I'm a goddamn shut-in, Mister. You think it's a disappointment to me they give a marathon in the park I can't run in it? It ain't the long distances that get to you, honey, it's the yards and inches. Time and tide took the world away. You think you can buy me off with TV, radio call-in shows, fucking Action Line? My good friend got cancer and you lay down the house rules? She's tired, it might be better if I waited? She ain't taking calls from the lower classes just now? She'll take mine though. Want to bet?"

"Hey, come on, what are you so excited about? Don't get so excited."

"How's whoosis, Audrey? Does she still bust out crying when she reads the paper?"

"Look."

"Can she get her own breakfast cereal yet? Or is she still too upset about the French Revolution? How's her husband? Is he still going to commit her if she don't shape up?"

"Judith had no right—— "

"Oh, rights," she said. "Rights ain't in it, just needs. Like your pal, the one that's in love. Losey. And what about his wife, the woman on whaddayoucallit, academic probation? How's your kid?"

"What about my kid?"

"Well, we don't know," she said. "We ain't sure."

It was an exquisite situation and Messenger had to admire his dying pal and her still lively genius for humiliation. It was the wackiness, her locked-up years, all that time getting well when, denied the world and everything that was not therapy, everything not grist for her health, from Mrs. Carey's omelets and cold soups—her digestion in those years (she'd been a long time loony, almost, she'd said, a lifer) a lesson in nutrition (he could imagine her sturdy, high-fibered boweling the consistency and color of Lincoln Logs)—to her family, the ordinary aunts and uncles (though by "ordinary" one did not mean anything bogtrot or rank-and-file: he had seen the men's distinguished hair, their pewter sideburns, the women like seeded tennis players with their flat behinds and bellies and their hard, suntanned skin) and good-natured cousins—he'd seen them, too, and could not remember whether they were men or women: he supposed that what they had in common with each other and with Judith was not their character or sense of humor but only a frame of reference, the names of headmistresses and masters and coaches and ministers and cooks and servants, their generation itself, he guessed—and the brother almost old enough to be her father. Denied the parents themselves, those daughter-scorned victims who might, if they'd only been ministers or cooks, have gotten off, been dismissed as merely two more names in the lexicon. (And he'd seen them too, and come away impressed, even charmed, by that Chairman of the Board and his meticulously courteous wife, now dead, amazed and astonished as he always was by a wealth that seemed to have no immediate source or, what was even more astonishing, product, that did not burn gas or coal, or supply widgets, or grow food, or win or even just fight wars, or get rolled up and tossed onto your lawn each morning—— that was simply, as far as Messenger could see, just pure wealth, pure money, withheld from the planet's effects entirely, like the invisible original resources of a king or government.) Denied everything that could not induce health,

199

hard news and strong books not permitted her, even, he'd heard, prime-time television, even make-up, even card or board games with the other patients in the common room. Allowed two things only: The first her psychiatrist (hers literally; they paid him seventy thousand dollars a year; he had no other patients), a stickler for every event of her mind who, if she had not already been mad, might have made her so with his endless inquiry—she was, it was said, his unpublished book—— *Judith: A Study of Causes*—into her responses and reactions. And the other her lover, Sammy, the future husband and dean a simple graduate student in those days who may or may not also have been on retainer.

So that her talent for creative abuse, for industrial-strength practical jokes, must have dated from those days. Indeed, she had once said as much at a dinner party.

"When I was being fattened up back there on the farm, when they were getting me ready for the world, I wasn't permitted drugs. I wasn't even permitted sleeping pills. Hell, I wasn't even permitted shock therapy. I can remember looking at the faces of some of the other patients on my wing when they came back from electric shock. They looked as if they had just been jabbed in the eyes with Novocaine. I envied them their dulled wits and hamstrung wills. A crazy is so helpless anyway. No one believes her. That's the ultimate outrage anyway—— that everyone's always considering the source. I tell you if I had smelled smoke and yelled 'Fire!' not a nurse or orderly would have looked up. You had to do grand opera to get a response from those people. I wouldn't do that. I became a sort of mad politician instead. I schemed constantly. We became pen pals."

"Pen pals?"

"I wrote them letters. I reminded them of everything I knew about them, all I could think of that had just been jarred loose by the electric company, everything their doctors and the public utilities wanted burned out of them. It was one public service against another. They turned on the juice, I turned on the heat."

"Did they ever answer?"

"You bet they did! Among all those get well cards and cheery letters from home, I venture to say mine was the only mail with any *real* news. They answered all right. They told me stuff about themselves their docs didn't know."

"Oh, Judy," Sam said.

"Oh, Sam. What's so terrible? We believed in trauma then, in dreams and childhood. In the raised voice at the vulnerable moment.

It was a sort of astrology. The houses of Jupiter, the cusps of Mars. We believed in everything but character. ——And I didn't do anything with their letters. I didn't use them for blackmail or flash them for gossip. I was interested in only one thing."

"Judy, please."

"Sam, please. ——I was interested in only one thing. I was a kind of alchemist. All I cared about was the transubstantiation of dross into mischief."

The cunt, Messenger thought, and knew something he hadn't known he'd known. She'd made Sam dean. He didn't know how, but he couldn't recall either which were girl cousins, which boy, or where the money came from or if it even *was* money at the bottom of the family fortune. It could have been anything. It could have been God's good will. Sam was Judy's man. Judy was Sam's friend downtown. He was *her* dean, *her* mischief.

And it was still an exquisite situation. Judy was dying, he couldn't lay a glove on her. Judy was dying, she held all the cards. She was a hell of a foe. She was a hell of a foe with her scorched-earth policies and land mines and booby traps and all the rest of her devastating paraphernalia and time bomb vengeance.

That she had planned this he had no doubt. That she had known who her victims would be was another question. (Excepting the immediate family of course—— Sam, the girls, possibly her father.) Was *he* meant to be a victim? Messenger thought so. "If there's anything I can do," he had said. It was what everyone said. Surely he had been saved for the Meals-on-Wheels route. But how could she have known his schedule that semester, that he was conveniently free just those two to two and a half hours she would need him? How could she have known Mrs. Carey would be so cooperative, blurt out the names and disgraces of his friends, accuse Cornell of his habit, and hint at inside information about his children? How, finally, could she have known she would get cancer?

But that was the point, wasn't it? She couldn't. Judith made mischief the way some people made money. Not to buy anything with it, just to have it ready to hand. If she was a vague irritant to them while she was alive, how much more of a pain in the ass would she be when she died and there was no stopping her? Who else in the city knew of the griefs in the west county? Messenger saw these now as Mrs. Carey must have seen them—— distanced by soap opera, attenuated in a medium of insulate otherness, flattened by the fact that they were not shared in any real way. Judith's achievement had been to trivialize what was most important to them, what kept them going and made them friends.

He would not eat the next leftover lunch. He would bring it to Judy.

2

No one has called him Captain in years. He's Mr. Mead now. He
would be Mr. Mead to anyone. To a president, to an enemy or friend,
to the public health nurses who have the most intimate knowledge of
what remains to Mr. Mead of Mr. Mead's body. To God Himself
perhaps. It seems strange to him, and a little impertinent—for great
age alters relation as well as vocabulary—that Louise should call him
Dad. He can be no one's dad.

Because you outlive everything if you live long enough.

What changes he has seen!

And has outlived change too, the years, even the epochs of his
own life, no longer discrete to him, or that things done one way were
now done—if they were done—another, of the least importance. He
is too old to be an old-timer, too old for that county courthouse ease
where soul takes tea with soul or cronies swap cronies not viewpoint,
opinion—they can't hold their bowels, how can they hold opinions?
—but simple, loquacious mood, up there, static, displayed as artifact,
veteran'd whether or no they have ever been to war, even the benches
on which they sit become a sort of reviewing stand. He is too old to
be a grandfather, too old to fish, whittle, lie, too old even to be marked
by a distinct disease. That those nurses know him so well, and know
so well what can be expected of him, has nothing to do with his being

Mr. Mead. (There is a chart at the foot of his bed even though he is home and not in a hospital. Nothing is written on it except his name —Mr. Mead—not his pulse or blood pressure reading or temperature, no note about diet or medications—— possibly his age.) They know him so well because he's a category, not a person. As an infant is a category. Finally, he is too old even to be Mr. Mead.

He tries to follow what his daughter and that fellow George, his son-in-law, are saying. It isn't really difficult if he concentrates. He recognizes the names even without the elaborate reference points and documentation his daughter insists on supplying each time her narrative turns a corner or comes to one. He has been a sailor. It isn't difficult to orient himself.

"You remember, Dad. He used to have that TV show on Sunday mornings where he healed people of their sicknesses. Well, he's minister at Virginia Avenue Baptist now. That big old church that used to be Catholic? You remember. It was just over from Crown's? You used to take us to Crown's and treat us to ice cream when you came back from a trip. That time George got his Buick we went there. You, Mom, George and me—— all of us. We had to park three blocks away because mass was still going on, and you told us about that river pilot who'd put into shore on Sunday mornings just to find a mass he could go to."

"Channel 11," Mr. Mead said.

"You hear that, George?" Louise said. "Dad still remembers all that river talk."

"That was the TV station he was on—— Channel 11."

"What's that, Dad? Oh. Well he's the one who wants George to give the sermon."

His son-in-law brings the young man into the bedroom with him. He has his dinner but doesn't quite know what to do with it. He has never seen visitors in the house before. Perhaps he thinks that Louise and George are from the City, that they have come to sweet-talk him into going into a Home. Perhaps Louise thinks the young man is an official, that the City of St. Louis caters her father's meals.

"Oh, look Dad, it's your dinner. What did they bring you today? Ooh," she says, "tuna noodle casserole. Hot Billy roll and butter. Peach slices served on romaine lettuce with creamy dressing." She used to work in a school cafeteria. She actually recognizes this stuff.

As the young man feeds him—his daughter makes no move to take the tray from him—Louise rambles on. "Mr. Laglichio—you remember, Mr. Laglichio, Dad; it was his truck George used when you got Mom that stove—has to hire a new driver. Lewis—you never met him, Dad; he came after you were already bedfast—won't go into those neighborhoods anymore. Mr. Laglichio told him half the people in the city go into those neighborhoods. Cops, the people who deliver their mail and read the meters and fix the phones. All the delivery people. Even cab drivers. Social workers." She looks in the young man's direction and blushes. "Anyway it might be a good opportunity for some young fellow. And George can't be expected to handle all the work himself. Maybe one of your mates knows someone looking for a job. I'll write Mr. Laglichio's number down and make a note what it's all about so you don't forget."

"Write it on my chart."

"What?"

"Nothing."

"Aren't you going to eat your nice peach slices? You should eat fruit, Dad. That's what makes BM's. You don't want the man to tell them at City Hall that you waste food." She winks at the young man. "Dad knows better. He used to be a cook on the river. You cooked on the river five years, didn't you, Dad?" This is not like her. She talks this way, Mr. Mead thinks, because she loves to fuss over him and he is so invalid she thinks he can no longer be embarrassed. She's right, he can't. "It's all a damn bother anyway," she says suddenly, feelingly. "You don't have to eat fruit, and the last thing you need to worry about is whether Laglichio gets a replacement for Lewis. Lewis doesn't have to be afraid of the jungle bunnies anyway. The cops could go down there without their guns and pull cats out of trees. The man who reads the meter could read it in the darkest cellar as if it were the best news in the paper. The delivery man is welcome as Santa Claus, and the postman safer than the guy who brings the Bumsteads' mail."

"Louise," George says.

"Louise," says Mr. Mead.

"Well it's so," Louise says. "Isn't it so, George? You're saved. I mean all you got to do is pray. All you got to do is pray for us. Just open your mouth and let her rip. 'Make things swell, Lord. Do all the other folks like you done me. Make things grand altogether.' Ain't that about the size of it, honey?"

"That's about the size of it," George says.

"I have another delivery," Messenger says.

"Hey, don't run off," Louise tells him. "Stick around while my husband changes the world through prayer."

Mr. Mead laughs. Then George and Louise do. Cornell Messenger also starts to laugh.

"What?" Mr. Mead asks. "What?"

"*I* hate to come into *this* neighborhood," Cornell manages.

"Happy birthday, Dad," his daughter says. "You thought we forgot, didn't you? Oh," she says, "I bet you forgot yourself. I'm ashamed of you, Dad. That means you forgot Mom's, too, because hers was yesterday. Did you forget that, Dad?"

"I did," Mr. Mead says.

"Is today your birthday?"

"She says so."

"Of course it is," Louise says. "I made pumpkin pecan pie. I'm going to fix you a piece too, Mister. I hope you don't mind using a napkin on your lap instead of a plate."

"I pray he don't mind," George says quietly.

"I forgot my own birthday," Mr. Mead says approvingly. "I was a sailor twenty years and lived by landmark and azimuth and time. I was a sailor twenty years, five of them cook. I was already old but even down there in the galley I always knew where I was, could tell which farms we'd passed from one seating to the next."

"Tell about the time the boat was stuck in the ice, Dad. When you and Mom and the rest of the crew had to walk across the river to the Arkansas side."

"No, no," Mr. Mead says. He wonders why he said that about being a sailor. He is too old to make overtures, too old to give assurances that he had once been young or known a world wider than the room in which he now lies. Evidently he has not always been so reticent, though he has no memory of decorating his life with anecdote. Perhaps she heard the story from her mother, though it's possible she had it from him. People had their own frequencies, were constantly sending messages of self, flashing bulletins of being, calling stop press, overriding, jamming the weaker signals of others.

George wonders about the Meals-on-Wheels man. He knows of course, as Louise must, despite what she's said to the old man, that he doesn't work for the city. He doesn't have the look of a civil servant. He would look out of place at the Hall, even paying a traffic fine or property taxes. He can't imagine him buying license plates or going to the clinic for a vaccination. He suddenly realizes that he's been denied access to an entire class of people. He has never been in their homes or done business with them. He watches Cornell pick at his pie as if it were somehow extraordinary, something ethnic.

"How about another slice?" George asks.

"Me? No thanks. It's really quite good."

"Sure. It's from a recipe."

"You remember, Dad. I got the recipe in trade school that time I thought I'd bake for the school lunch program. You thought it was delicious but told me all those ingredients would have tied up the galley." She turns to Cornell. "There wouldn't have been anywhere to store the pumpkins."

She is embarrassed that a stranger brings her father's lunch. It looks bad.

Messenger believes they don't know anything about him.

Mr. Mead, the old farmer, the old sailor and river cook, the ancient, if Louise is right, birthday boy—— Mr. Mead, on this ordinary afternoon in St. Louis, has a moment of special clarity, brighter and more exciting than the routine orientation and simple daily legibility of his life. His body, which these past—— How many years has he been an old man?

"Is it really my birthday?"

"Of course, Dad." The woman nods almost imperceptibly in Cornell's direction.

"Is it?" he asks the man who has brought his lunch.

What's going on? Cornell wonders. Are they having the old-timer on? Didn't he just have bakery in his mouth? How old he must be. Cornell raises his fork toward Mr. Mead. "Happy birthday," he says.

Louise is a little irritated with her father. They've never been separated—the trips on the river were business—but they were not really close. His fault. He was independent always. Even old he is independent. People in a family shouldn't have to woo each other. She's always sent him cards, brought gifts, kept track of his anniversaries and celebrations, kept score on his life. Now he asks a stranger if it's really his birthday. She's not sore because he doesn't trust her —he's old, it's easy for a person her father's age to become confused —but because *all* his confidence has not been blasted. Some remains. He appeals to strangers, outside authority.

He remembers now. Not because Harve's father has wished him happy birthday. He *remembers*.

He's going to die. It isn't a premonition. No Indian instinct commands him to cut himself from the herd. He is under no compulsion to be alone, to be anywhere but where he is. His knowledge of his death doesn't even come from outside himself. And now he pinpoints the exciting clarity, the special orientation. It's his body which has had the first inkling, his skin which cannot feel the bedclothes or register weight. His toenails which no longer slice back into his flesh, and his bones which no longer harbor pain, the gray blaze of years' duration which has served as a sort of measuring device. (I am as tall as my pain.) His teeth which no longer have dimension, their honed edges and the bump of gums and the false-scale depth he has plumbed with his tongue. His stubble which he no longer feels when he draws his lower lip into his mouth. He is neutral as hair. And though residual movement remains—he can draw his lower lip into his mouth, he can open his eyes, shut them—and at least the minimal synapses which permit him his speech, he can no longer feel it resonate along its dental and aspirate contacts and stops, his voice as alien to him as if it came from a radio. (How can it even be heard?) His nervous system is shutting down, fleeing its old painful coordinates as if a warning had been given, like the blinking of lights, say, that signal people to leave a public building. He is dying.

And now he can't speak either. Or close his eyes. And death has come to certain emotions. He means to be afraid, is certain he *is* afraid, yet he *feels* no fear, his mind and body not up to it, unable to accommodate it now that his resources are so depleted, as if on the occasion of final things, in emergency conditions, life entertained only that which was still essential to it, like a level-headed victim, like a clever refugee. Though he should be surprised, the nerves of astonishment have been cut.

Though he can no longer see or hear her—just now his ears have turned off—he knows that his daughter is beside him. Probably she is holding his hand. And he tries, helplessly, uselessly, to return the pressure. He could as easily fly. (Is he flying?) And now affection is deadened too, *all* the emotions tapped out as his skin. He knows what he *should* be feeling—and now italics leave him—as he had known seconds before that he should be afraid, that he wanted to be afraid, but it is all impossible. He may only—blinded, deafened, without italics—witness his death, less involved, finally, than the man, what's-hisname, the lunch guy's pal, who was going to have his wife committed if she didn't cheer up. He'd be grateful if gratitude were any more available to him than fear or sight or the weight of his bedclothes.

Now he is almost used up. Denied physiology, he regards his Cheshire decline with what? With nothing. What should have been of interest, the most personal moment in his life, is now merely consciousness, knowledge, the mind's disinterested attention. He is like someone neither participant nor fan who hears a ball score. Like a man in Nebraska told it's raining in Paris. He watches death with his knowledge and no money riding on it.

He is alone in the map room, cannot perceive the quadrants of his being as his sectors succumb and are obliterated and do not, for all their pale, attenuate traces, seem even poignantly to flare in the face of their extinguishment. Typography and symbols fail him, all the niceties. He cannot read the signs and illuminations, the channel buoys, all the white lines in the road, all the lodestars and mileposts, vanes and windsocks and load-line marks that could show him boundaries or indicate how low he rides in the water. (And now even the circuits that make analogies have been discontinued.) He is almost history, narrative, gossip.

He knows he cannot see. Has he eyes? He knows he cannot hear. Has he ears? He knows he cannot feel. Has he flesh? Is his sphincter open? Has he still a body? Is it turned to bruise? Does it run with pus?

All that is left to him finally—and he could use his astonishment now if he were able—is what he will become when he no longer knows it. Nothing sacred is happening here, nothing very solemn, nothing important. There is almost certainly no God. He would tell George Mills not to bother about his salvation if he could, but it doesn't make any difference that he can't. What could he use now if it were still available to him? His amazement? No. His fear? Certainly not. His old capacity to care for them? Useless. Any of his feelings? No. Useless, useless.

He remembers—peculiarly, memory still flickers, and a certain ability, probably reflex, to muse, to consider; all this would be something to share if he could, to tell them that memory is the last thing left in the blood when you check out, that you die piecemeal, in sections, departments, and it's memory goes down with the ship, though it might be different with different people; maybe it's important sometimes, maybe it's sacred once in a while, and God might come for some but not for others; Christ, he's dying like someone stabbed in *opera,* stumbling around with a mouthful of arias (Jesus, is there hope? Where did the images and italics come from? He isn't sure but certainly there is no hope. *He* does not hope.), and maybe that's why death was so long-winded, why disease took as long as it did—— to give the systems time to wind down, but that'd be different for different people too; maybe some went with a great flaming itch they couldn't get to—his first large woman.

Well, *woman.* She was fourteen years old and weighed one hundred and seventy-four pounds. Lord, she was big. It wasn't fat, circus lady fat, jinxed genes and a broken pituitary. What was merely chemical—he imagined cells in geometric replication, like a queer produce that laced some glandular broth—did not become human for him. It was never just weight which tickled his fancy, great boluses of flesh which draped their heavy arms and thighs like a sort of bunting. Great heavy asses so big their cracks seemed like surgical scars. Immense bolsters of breast that piled and rolled on their chests like tide. But some *idea* of heaviness, of mass and strength and density which sent out a kind of gravity.

It sure attracted *me,* he thinks, whose prick has just gone out, its nerve ends snuffed, doused as wick, and who recalls, with detachment, almost dead, too, not against his will but in dead will's leaden absence, all sexual nostalgia gone, all bias—— *that* stout girl. (Always one of the code words. Stately, plump, buxom, portly. Words whose meanings he knew but looked up in a dozen dictionaries just to see them written out.)

That stout girl. Her strapping, robust, sturdy sisters. Their heavy haunches, their meaty hams. Their thick hair and big hands. Their full busts and statuesque figures.

Because maybe we really *are* clay. Something in flesh which takes an imprint and strikes us off like medals, human change.

"You can't," she said, and hoped he could, that someone could.

"I don't know," he said. "I'd have to try."

"Maybe in water."

"Oh no. On land." (And that moment has before him all his fantastic, dumb ideal. The woman who can't be raised even in water, who drops on him like female anchor, sunk, unbuoyant treasure, against all the annulled, mediate influence of displacement, whelming him, his striving, kicking, bucking limbs. All I ever needed, he thinks, was to be drowned real good, and does not remember his actual wife who actually was.)

"You can try, but if I fall and hurt you it's not my fault."

She was not even teasing, he thinks now. Nor was I. I had such dialogues by heart. I put them through them like a cross-examiner with my ploys like so many idioms, leading them on, and my professed disbelief just one more idiom.

"No, that can't be so. Your bathroom scale is off."

"You think the doctor's scale is off?"

"Oh, the *doctor's* scale. You didn't say it was the *doctor's* scale."

"Yeah, well it was."

"Still, no scale's *always* reliable. Unless you're one of those people who looks lighter than she actually is. Let's see," he has said, "I know I can lift" and names a weight ten or fifteen pounds less than the one she has told him, fifteen or twenty more than he knows he can raise. "If I can't pick you up, the scale's probably right." And he can't, his knees already buckled in capitulate sexual deference to female mass, this body of body against whose volume he opposes his own, and not even *he* knows if he's really trying, though he thinks he is, hopes he is, even as he fumbles, slips, goes down.

And if his tears had not already died he would be weeping now, and if his ability to sorrow were not gone he would be wretched.

And sees one last time their outsized dresses, their hundred relaxed postures—— large women on benches, in bleachers, in stockinged feet along the slopes of shoe salesmen's stools, sidesaddle on horses or climbing out of cars or down steep hills, sprawling in parks, on picnics, on beaches, floating in water or soaking in tubs, clumsy in changing rooms, bulging the sheets on examining tables, sitting on toilets or putting on shoes, reaching for dishes or passing the soup, turning in sleep, their nightgowns hiked up, or fetching a slipper from under a bed, stretching or bending or praying to God, sweating in summer and fanning themselves, looking behind them in mirrors for bruises, doing an exercise, letting out seams. In all disarray arrayed. Mead's large ladies, Mead's fat forms, his sprawled, spilled women tumbling his head like the points of a pinwheel.

He is already dead when God comes to collect him, already dead before Mills or his daughter or Messenger notices that he has closed his eyes.

He has died with Louise's birthday pie in his mouth, with Cornell's plastic Meals-on-Wheels fork in his teeth.

"Tell us about," the brand new orphan demands of her parent, and asks for some event she herself has fleshed out into a story. "What is it, Dad? Are you asleep?"

The death is discovered and the irrational is suddenly loose in the room, all the gases of the unstable like heavy weather. The house is too small to contain its tricky, too fluid volumes. Even the dead man's stolid constancy seems willful, some petulant obstinacy. George Mills's mood ring flashes a bright yellow, cautionary as the back of a school bus. For all of them, mood is wayward, volatile, uncapped, at once murderously resolved and open as the tempers at gaming tables. They are not in shock but in shock's agitate, high-strung otherness, their reckless affections jumpy with rampage.

"Well this is it," Cornell says. "Who needs this? I don't need this. Under the circumstances I said a perfectly normal, natural thing. The woman's *dying*. All I said was is there anything I could do. Bam! She dumps her volunteer work on me! The horror, the horror! Now I see my mistake. I rushed things. In these situations you wait, you buy time and keep your own counsel. Afterward, if you want to be helpful, you say a word to the widower. You never ask the principal. Never. You ask the principal it's like some deathbed pledge, high oaths. God knows what they'll come up with. They could whisper the name of their killer in your ear. Then where are you? I'll tell you what I learned from this. If it's terminal you shake their hand if they're a man and kiss them on the lips if they're a woman."

Mills's wife says, "There wasn't a thing wrong. Nothing. He was old is all. That's no sickness. I won't say I never saw him looking better. That would be hogwash. Sure I've seen him look better. He wasn't *always* old. He used to be young. I've seen him when he could be downright playful. There was this great big gal the next farm over that whenever Dad saw her he'd say how she must have been dieting and that he knew he could lift her. And he'd try. Then and there. He'd try to pick her up. But she was so big, well of course he never could. Sure. I've seen him look better. But I've seen him look worse, too. He even laughed. He was laughing not ten minutes ago. You heard him, George. What? What are you making that face for?"

"I mean it never even occurred to me that it would be open-ended. Even after she told me I could take over her Meals-on-Wheels and I found out it fit my schedule, it never occurred to me it would turn into this ongoing thing. I don't know what I was thinking of. I must have been stoned. I wasn't, but I agreed. You'd have to be stoned or otherwise impaired to agree to such a nutty proposition. I'm needed at home, for God's sake. I got a teenage kid doesn't get the point of knock-knock jokes and one old enough to vote thinks he's a fucking prince. Works part time, minimum wage, to get cash to see ball games, calls the movies eleven times to check when the show starts. I mean look what time it is, for Christ's sake. When is lunch over? When some old fart dies? Oh."

"What is it, George?"

"His bowels. Phew! It's got to be his bowels."

"Do they do that? I heard they do that, but I've never been sure. It's like that thing you hear about hanged men, that they get, you know, a big one. Is that true, too? I shouldn't be the one to have to clean him up. He was my father. That's what I'd remember. That wouldn't be fair. It wouldn't. It isn't right to expect a daughter to wipe up her father's intimate dirt. What's that, a way of dealing with grief? I guess if you have something practical and nasty to do you don't feel so bad afterward because all you remember is how awful it was and you're only glad he doesn't have to die again. Oh, these arrangements. Everything supposed to come out even. What's even about it? What's so damned *even* about it? Dad and I didn't have such an easy time together. No thank you! If the city wants him cleaned up, let the city do it!"

"*Phew!* I'm going to open the windows. He'd have had to been poisoned to stink like that."

"He loved that pie," Louise says. "That was his favorite pie."

"How do I go to her? What am I supposed to say? 'You, Judith! What do you think you've saddled me for, the duration? You've got pancreatic cancer trouble. You're a goner, but you could last six months. Since when do saints subcontract? I never signed up for any war on poverty, *you* did. I'm clearing off for Canada.' "

"They've got to be smelling it in the streets. Like sewer smoke. He had to be poisoned. No *peaceful* gut stinks like that."

" 'You want something reasonable, just ask. You want magazines? You want someone to fetch your prescriptions or drive your visitors home? Sure, I can do that.' "

"Poisoned? You really think so? Those peach slices on lettuce with creamy dressing. Where are *you* going?"

"This is terrible," Cornell says. "I'm very sorry. I guess the only good thing about it is that he had his family with him. Look," he says, obedient to his civilized life, "if there's anything I can do—— "

"Clean him up."

"What?"

"You're an agency, aren't you?" Louise says. "Or if you ain't an agency you work with them. Clean him up. Clean my father up!"

"I can't."

"Why not?"

"I'm a food handler. I handle *food!*"

"Yes, and it was your food he was eating when he died!" Louise shouts.

"Like hell! He was eating that pie you made from the goddamn recipe!" snaps outraged Cornell.

"You had some *too!*" Louise yells at him. "*I* ate it, *I'm* all right!"

"I didn't actually mean he was poisoned," George says quietly. "There was nothing wrong with him."

213

"He was old," Cornell says. "He was a very old man."

"Sure, and that's all the reason your kind needs, ain't it? It isn't enough a person may have pain, or outlived his family, or he's got worries, or can't stretch his benefits. All that ain't enough. You fix it so he's got to sleep with one eye open and be on the lookout for someone with a needle from the government who's decided he ain't productive no more or's a drain on the taxpayer! When all that's wrong is he's some lonely old man who's only got left what might have happened to him when he was young. Then it's all 'Oh, the poor dear, let's put him out of his misery, let's stick the needle in his arm or give him a pill or slip something in his food.' Where are you going? Don't you *dare* leave! George, stop him."

"This is crazy," Cornell says.

"Don't call *me* names. I don't need any murderers calling *me* names. George? *George!*"

Except for the fact that he misses his father-in-law and wishes he were here to enjoy this, George Mills is having a grand time. His enjoyment is his share of the irrational.

"Why do you think he ain't in a Home? Why do you think the VA don't have him? He wanted to steer clear of people like you. *He* wanted to decide when enough was enough and not some bureaucrat mercy killer. Who made you God? You ain't God. When you came in, didn't you see that he had folks, that he had a daughter who still made him birthdays, a son-in-law who took an hour off from work to share them with him? Couldn't you have changed your mind? Would it have been too inconvenient to back out without giving him dinner? You had the tray with you. I know you can't just dump your poison in the street because if a dog died, or somebody's cat, and if there was an investigation the whole thing might just come apart. Or maybe whoever it is you work for already wrote him off and it would have taken too much explaining. Do you know what that makes you? Not *even* a mercy killer. You killed him for paperwork! Oh," Louise says softly, "oh, oh." And begins to cry, her lump of the insanity wearing off like a drug, pulling her passionate madness, which she will never be able to account for, no more than the others, when they are once again sane, will be able to account for theirs, George his glee, Cornell his blabbermouth anger.

"Oh," she says again, stunned, her orphan's grief not even in it, none of her precedent loyalties or bespoke associations with the corpse on the bed, knowing the deepest shame she has ever felt, humiliation so profound apology would be unseemly as its cause. If she could die herself she would do so, if she could will Messenger dead she would, or George—— anyone witness to her outburst. Only Mr. Mead is dead, and she turns pragmatically to him, not for forgiveness, for relief. He's the only one in the room who's neither seen nor overheard her lapse, and she's actually grateful to him because only he has nothing to forgive.

Carefully, she begins to clean her father.

But Cornell is not through yet, and because Cornell is still mad George still has someone to entertain him, so George is not through yet either.

"Jeez," he says slyly, "she sure had some things to say about you."

"They're lies," Cornell says, "they're crazy lies. I'm from Meals-on-Wheels. Not even from Meals-on-Wheels. I'm filling in. This ain't my corner. If you were on better terms with your neighbors you'd know that."

"My neighbors?"

"Your neighbors. The shut-ins. That take from Judy Glazer when she isn't dying from cancer and has more time for them. They know all about it. Judy keeps them posted from the deathbed."

"What does she tell them?" George asks.

"What are you smiling about? You enjoy it you know our secrets?"

Mills shrugs.

"Big deal. *Everybody* suffers. If you want to know the truth I didn't even know I *had* secrets until I found out that strangers knew them."

"Don't be ashamed," Mills says with cheerful compassion.

"Wait a minute. Is this about the Lord or something?"

"The Lord?" says the saved man.

"You know what I mean. If Audrey Binder cringes in the corner when there's a misprint in a book she's reading or the line is busy, it isn't because she guessed wrong about Jesus. Unhappiness is her dirty little secret. I can't keep up with it."

"No," says Mills, all understanding.

"I mean we live this Top Secret, Eyes Only life. I don't see the point of it. You know what I think? I think we make too much of things. We're the crybabies of the Western world! Boy oh boy, do we carry on! Pain, real pain, stuff wrong with your joints, that's something else altogether." Messenger lowers his voice and begins to bad-mouth his west end pals. "I mean who gives a shit Sam Glazer might not be able to handle the deanship?" he asks. George shakes his head, and Cornell fills him in on all the juicy gossip he can think of about his closest friends. He tells him about Victor Binder's troubles with the IRS, about Paul Losey's malpractice premiums and how Paul, smitten as a teenager, has evidently fallen hopelessly in love. "Nora Pat's guessed *some*thing's up, but she hasn't a clue really. She'd bust if she did. It's supposed to be someone right here in town."

George nods.

"Say," Messenger asks, "you're not a blackmailer, are you?"

"I evict poor people," Mills tells him expansively.

"Nora thinks all she has to do is fix an exciting bedroom, but I'll tell you something. Nora's got a mouth on her like the iron jaw lady. What difference does it make? She can lick and suck and blow on his balls till the cows come home. The guy's in love. What can she do? If some other chick gets him off, that marriage is curtains. That's why she's on academic probation. Architecture flies out the window when a *femme fatale* comes in at the door. Hell, what does it matter? As if problems could ever be solved. I mean, shit, that's why they're problems, right? I mean if anything's wrong it's wrong forever. You can only make things worse. That's where I screwed up with Harve. That's where I screwed up with my kids. They're bad kids, so I had to go and be a worse father. The horror, the horror, eh?"

But George is suddenly embarrassed. It's his sanity returning. Only Cornell still steams with madness. Waves of it seem to come off his head like distorted, illusory vapors in a road, like the transparent parts of flame. It is astonishing to Mills how all mood cancels itself, how satiety sours abandon and compromises everything. Is there anywhere an experience one can walk away from with a clear conscience? He understands practically nothing of Messenger's complaints and confessions, though he knows enough to be troubled by their intimacy. He does not want Cornell for a friend. He does not want friends. It's too late. He is the man to whom everything has happened that is going to happen. This is his grace.

"Could you help me turn him please, George?" Louise asks politely.

The old man is naked on the bed. The sheets and pillowslips, smeared with feces, are in a corner of the room with his soiled pajamas.

"Sure, Louise," Mills says.

"Wait, I'll help you," Messenger says, and handles the man as if he were changing a tire.

"My husband and I can manage," Louise says.

"What? Oh. Sure. I just thought I might be able to help. Say," Cornell says, "did anyone think to make a phone call?"

"A phone call?"

"Well when something, you know, like this happens the authorities have to be notified. It's just that they're supposed to know. And I guess arrangements have to be made."

"Oh. Right. Who do we call? You know who we call, Louise?"

"Dad was a member of the union, but I don't know the number. He might have written it down somewhere."

"I can look it up," Cornell volunteers.

"It was the Barge and Shippers' Union."

"I can handle that. I can make that call."

"It's just that I'm upset. I don't exactly feel like . . ."

"Well sure, of course not," Cornell says. "You can't be expected to. That's why I suggested I do it myself. Of course you're upset. Where does your father keep his phone book? Never mind, I see it."

"This is very considerate," Louise says.

"Hey," Messenger says, "that's why it's important to have a neutral party around at a time like this."

He dials. They wait silently as the phone rings at the other end.

"Hello? Hello, Judy? Cornell Messenger. Listen. That nice Mr. Mead died."

3

"Where's the deputy?" Laglichio asked in the inner city, in the ghetto, by the projects, in line of sight but out of earshot of twenty or so dangerous-looking blacks. "Did you call him?"

"Maybe he already went in to serve the papers."

"You see a patrol car, George?"

"Hand them over. I'll serve them myself."

"Make a citizen's arrest, will you, George? Going to serve Xeroxes on these people? Going to show them carbon copies, flat, smooth seals like a sketch of the sunrise? They don't read, George, just rub the paper to feel if it's embossed. They live by a Braille law in this neighborhood.

"I like my work," Laglichio said. They were leaning against the truck's front fender. Laglichio seemed a changed man this morning. Not, George thought, because of his high spirits or even his rusty patience. He seemed, Mills thought, interested, expansive. "Not all of us can be bombardiers," Laglichio said, "or sit by the machine gun on the penitentiary watchtower. We can't all be turnkeys, and the state main't juiced no one in donkey's years. I like my work. I do. It's only evicting folks, but it makes a difference. They remember you. Long after they've forgotten the landlord's name, they still remember the guy who put them out on the fucking street. Where's that deputy?"

218

"Let's go in without the papers," George Mills said. "Let's kick the door down and throw everybody out."

"Oh ho," Laglichio said. "Without the papers. That'd be something. That'd be smooth sailing, wouldn't it? Where's that mother? They're watching us. There must be a couple dozen dark-skinned people just watching our truck."

A man in a dashiki came over. He wore a dull brass necklace and a tiger skin beret.

"How you doing, Chief?" Mills asked serenely from his state of grace.

"What's this truck?" the man asked.

"This truck?" Mills said. "Supplies. You know—— bandages, serums, shots for the kids, Bibles, some pamphlets on family planning for the women in your village. Just about what you'd expect."

"I'm Bob," the man said cheerfully. "I guess you ain't feeling well. Healthy man don't be talking to no ugly customer like this, show respect, *know* some cat in a beret jus' *got* to be arm'. Well man feel in his bones a dude like me be holdin' a bomb in the dashiki, a razor in the boot. Man *got* to have a hunch the blood is po-*lit*-ical. You got three seconds to the revolution, fuck!"

"I can't lose," Mills said mildly.

"You dig this clown?" Bob said to Laglichio. "Hold on, clown. I want the brothers to meet you."

Mills showed him the eviction orders. "This man and I are establishment," he explained. "These are official instruments of the United States of America. You can't touch us." Bob scanned them, tore the papers to bits.

"Boy, are you in Dutch!" Mills said.

"He *that* Laglichio?" Bob asked. "Say on that paper I rip Laglichio. No shit, he *that* Laglichio? For real now, you fellas the Laglichio boys?" Quietly the other observers had come up from their positions against the playground fence. "'Cause it don't say nothin' on the truck here. 'Cause the truck don't say a word about what it do to the furnitures of my peoples." He opened its rear doors. "Oh oh," Bob moaned, "I look in here and I like to cry for the furnitures of my peoples. These drop cloths is filthy," he said, and tore them to shreds. "And look these scrawny, itty bitty pads. Fuckin' *Kleenex*. What kind of candy ass protection these give the furnitures of my peoples? Look all the sharp edges in here, man. It look like a open soup can."

"Hey," Laglichio said, "get down out of my truck."

219

Bob was jumping up and down heavily in the empty truck. "They try to tell me, but I didn' believe them. They say Mr. Laglichio's shocks is shot. They say all he do he drive over the white line in the road and *smash,* there go the dishes of my peoples! He take a outright pothole an' boom, my peoples's paper plates be bust."

"What's going on, guys?" Laglichio asked amiably, and Bob sat down on the tailgate to tell him.

"We putting you to pasture, nipple drippings," he said kindly. "The refugees got them a hot line now. Got them a Twenty-Four-Hour Self-Help Removal Service. Got a lovely Action Volunteer Cartage Platoon. Got a free, no rip-off, We-Hump-for-the-Brothers-and-Sisters Emergency Hauling Service. I'm official dispatcher for the revolution, and I'm tellin' you, dick sweat, no authorization papers you be holdin' now nor in future neither ain't never gonna be serve."

No one touched them. They dismantled Laglichio's truck like soldiers breaking down a rifle, roustabouts pulling down a tent. It was at least as deliberate and controlled as Laglichio's and Mills's own scorched-earth procedures.

"What'd we do?" Mills mused aloud. "All we ever tried to do was help. Supplies. Vaccines and bandages, birth control, Bibles. See where it gets you? Our work here is finished," he told Laglichio.

So it was that George Mills, in grace, out of harm's way, beyond life's reach, became unemployed.

He tried to reassure Louise.

"It's not even October," Mills said. "In a month or so we'll have our first big snowfall. The caterpillars are fat and fuzzy. Trappers want their fur. Accu-Weather says it's going to be the winter of the world. I can go on the plows. They can always use a guy like me on the salt trucks. When spring comes I can patch potholes. Don't be downcast, Louise. Don't be downcast, sweetheart. There's a fortune to be made from other people's bad weather."

Louise demanded that he not speak so, that he be like other men. "You're out of work," she said. "We've got bills. The gas. The phone. The electric. I don't have a nice dress. My coat's too thin. I don't think it will last the winter. What if one of us has to go into the hospital? What if we have to see dentists? What if there's car trouble, if we need a new battery or a tire gives out? How will we pay for prescriptions? Suppose we decide to take the paper? What do we do if the TV breaks, the hot water heater? What would happen if something came up?"

"Nothing will," Mills said.

"I can't hide my head in the sand," she said. "Things happen."

"Nothing happens," George said.

"It's no joke. You're over fifty."

"I am," Mills said.

"George, it's scary."

"Don't take on, Louise. Please don't."

"Don't take on? Don't take *on?*"

"Your disasters give me the creeps, doll."

"My disasters—— "

"They wear me out, Louise. They get me down, babe."

"They wear you out? They get you down?"

"Sure," Mills said, "if my banks don't fail, if no one's after my companies. If the young Turks and wise guys can't force me off the board of directors, or my country doesn't give a damn if I defect, sure. Sure they do. You're saying I'm a failure, Louise, that the worst thing that can happen is we can't take the paper, that something could break, that we'll wash in cold water and ride on the bus."

The telephone rang and Louise went to answer it.

It was a Judith Glazer, Louise said. She had known Louise's father and regretted she'd been unable to attend the funeral. She had called to offer her condolences. Mr. Mead had told her about them. She wanted George to come see her. She had a proposition for him.

4

From the address he'd expected a mansion, something grander than the ordinary brick home set back less than forty feet from the street where he'd parked his car, and at first—the houses beside it were larger—he thought Louise had gotten the directions wrong. It was the only house on the block without a garage. The only other car on the street, an old, pale green Chevrolet with modest tail fins and a partially deflated rear tire, was parked by the curb, obscuring the black street numbers that would have been painted there. The windows were up but George could see two people sitting inside. The woman in the back appeared to be napping. He could imagine precisely how it would feel and smell inside, almost tasting the car's close quarters, its stuffy, hundred-thousand-mile, yellowing newspaper'd, overflowing ashtray and worn seat-cover'd essence. And feel the oxidation of apples in the stale stilled air, the sky-high temperatures where cantaloupes combust. He rapped on the driver's window with his mood ring. The man looked at him but wouldn't roll the window down. George checked the address with him through the glass.

A big girl in yellow lounging pajamas opened the door for him.

"Do you work for my daddy?" she asked.

"No," George said.

She seemed disappointed but brightened at once. "Oh," she

said, "you're the man from the boat club. Or are you here to see Mom?"

"Is that Mrs. Glazer?"

"I'll see if she's awake. Oh," she said, recalling instructions, "you're not a tradesman, are you? There's tragedy in our house and we're turning tradesmen away. I'm sorry." She genuinely seemed so, and started to close the door when Mills told her his name and said that Mrs. Glazer had asked to see him. "Oh, then it's all right," she said. "I'm sorry Milly didn't get the door. Milly's my sister. I'm older but she's more mature."

"Who is it, Mary? Who's out there with you? What does he want?" a woman asked from the living room.

"I forgot your name," Mary said.

"Mills."

"Mills," Mary said. "I don't know what he wants."

As soon as he heard the woman's voice something happened to George. It would not be extravagant to say that he was thrilled. It was quite inexplicable. He could not have told you anything about her from its sound, not what she looked like, not her age. Nothing. Unless it was something of his sudden anticipatory sense of his place in her life. It didn't make sense. It was crazy. It was not love at first sight —he hadn't seen her yet—it was not love at all. But something. Loyalty perhaps, some deep-pledged human patriotism.

"You'll have to go in," Mary said. "Mother's not going to come out here." And already, though he knew nothing about the child, he was preparing concessions, making allowances, giving dispensation to her absent, younger, more mature sister. His regard was loose, and he took impressions like a pilgrim, like a man at a reunion. He had spent much of his working life in other people's rooms. He knew the handholds of sofas and box springs, all the secret toeholds of furniture, but knew them as increments of size and weight, without associations. Now he noticed the hallway's umbrella stand, two tightly furled black umbrellas, and had a profound sense of the Glazers' weather. He glimpsed their dining room out of the corner of his eye and guessed their appetite.

He walked into the living room.

The child preceded him and went to the head of her mother's bed —Mrs. Glazer sat on the side of a rented hospital bed that took up much of the room—and fished a cookie from the rumpled sheets. She slouched against her mother with a type of sullen possessiveness. He might have been sympathetic to the girl's fawning panic, but he'd already guessed the woman's irritation and felt his precarious allegiance sway.

"I'll be with you in a moment," she said, and turned to her daughter, stroking and chastising her. "Mary dear," she said, "it isn't convenient for you to hang on me. And if you've hidden any more cookies in my sheets I wish you'd dig them up. Why don't you go play with your sister?"

"I'm on the door."

"Mr. Mills can get the door while he's here. I'll call you when he leaves."

"Can I make a milk shake?"

"Didn't you already have one today?"

"So did Milly."

"But Milly hasn't asked for a second. And aren't you supposed to be going out on your uncle's boat this afternoon?"

"Has he called? *Has* he?"

"Oh, *make* the damn milk shake! Wait. I'm sorry, Mary. Of course you may have a milk shake. One scoop, remember. Perhaps Mills wants one too."

"No ma'am. Thank you."

When they heard the blender Mrs. Glazer finally greeted him.

"Thank you for coming," she said. "I'm sorry I wasn't able to attend Mr. Mead's funeral."

"Oh that's all right."

"It's not all right. He was a lovely man. We were good friends. I was about to say that I couldn't attend your father-in-law's funeral because I was arranging my own. My bishop, Mr. McKelvey, was here that morning with Mr. Crane, my funeral director. We were going over the music I've chosen. I also gave Roger the names of my pallbearers, and dictated the letters I had him send them. Most of these people are extremely busy men. There's no guarantee any two of them will even be in town when the time comes, so I've put them on notice. I picked my casket out from photographs, and selected the clothes and shoes I'm to be buried in. Two costumes really, two pair of shoes. My nice tweed if it's chilly, my linen if it's mild. Well, I can't be absolutely sure of the season, can I? I sent the garments with Mr. Crane to be dry-cleaned, and the shoes to the dago to be resoled.

"Well, I would have been unable to attend Mr. Mead's funeral in any event. A woman in the position of making preparations for her own funeral may be excused certain obligations—— though not, I trust, her sacred ones. You may tell Mrs. Mills that we prayed that

224

morning for the repose of Mr. Mead's soul. McKelvey is a splendid pray-er, even when he does not know the principal, as, I pride myself, I am. Crane didn't know what to make of it all, but I put in sufficient allusions to Mr. Mead's connections with water and shipping to make him think he had missed out on a handsome commission. God so loves a good joke, I think. The poor dear loves His laugh.

"Well," she said, "you must think it strange for someone to take on so about the protocols of her own death, or arrange her funeral as if it were her debut."

"No."

"No? Good for you then. But you must forgive my misdoubts. People not themselves under the Lord's protection frequently asperse the confidence of saints."

"I'm saved too."

"Well, maybe," Mrs. Glazer said, "but do you really think that because you've had your five or six seconds down by the riverside, or that your heart keeps time with the tambourine, you know the elegant dismay of God? Or perhaps Jesus spoke to you during a hangover or warned you of a speed trap. Please, Mills, God made the sky blue but He is not flamboyant. If I choose the music for my service it isn't because the Lord has a favorite tune but because *I* do. Anyway, organists play better when they know the dead are listening.

"Well. Let's climb down from this. For all my brave talk about obsequies it turns out that it's inconvenient for me to die just now. It isn't that I object to death. Indeed, I'm for it rather. But you saw yourself. There was a cookie in the deathbed. There will be crumbs in the winding sheet. Mary has accidents. She pees her bed and has nightmares. She weeps during recess and suddenly claims not to be able to see blackboards. She says she's forgotten the multiplication tables, and neither Sam nor I can get her to do her homework. Her periods started over a year ago but stopped when I became ill. In a girl her age her psychiatrist thinks it an hysterical pregnancy on a heroic scale. But there's nothing heroic about it. She's simply craven regarding the idea of my death. Nothing I or Sam or her relatives do to distract her distracts her. Several thousand dollars have already been spent on tutoring her pleasure, but how do you distract the distrait? Such grief would be flattering if it was not clearly so self-serving.

"But all that's beside the point. The point is that I may not die with Mary in such a state. It isn't that I'd have no peace or that my daughter's uneasiness would in the least mitigate Heaven's perfect terms, but that my death just now would destroy her. She could die herself. As she doesn't yet have the character for Heaven I can't let that happen.

"Do you see my situation? I need another year. It may even be that Mary is part of God's plan to fight my cancer. —— Did you say something?"

"Why *wouldn't* I be spared the ticket?" Mills grumbled.

"What?"

"On that highway, that speed trap. I'm elect as the next guy."

Mrs. Glazer looked at him a moment, then went on. "The doctors think I'm crazy," she said, "but as neither Paul nor the oncologist believes he can do anything for me and has given me up, I have their blessing. Sammy was more difficult. He secretly believes it beneath the dignity of a dean to have his doomed wife go lusting after miracle cures or traffic with quacks. When he heard what I was thinking of he urged me to take the money and go to Lourdes instead. He is a Jew and at least believes in the efficacy of psychology. I am Christian and an ex-madwoman, and don't give a fart for psychology. I *already* believe. How would it help to drag my piety to a shrine?

"It's probably hopeless, but I mean to go to Mexico for Laetrile treatments and need someone to accompany me, to assist me. It is impossible that Sam come with me. He will have to stay with the children. This is what I will give you."

She named a figure which George thought was probably fair, within pennies of what he supposed people in her circumstances paid people in his. Allowing for inflation, it was probably pretty close to what Guillalume had given the first George Mills. It was certainly fair. It may even have been generous, and he saw that grace was not without its opportunities. But he had misgivings. The woman wasn't easy. Compared to her, Laglichio, who knocked down esteem as easily as George broke down a bed, was a thoughtful, magnanimous person. Whatever Laglichio did, Mills knew, was in the service of angles, bucks. There was nothing personal. She would stand on a thousand ceremonies. But what the hell? It might work out. It might even be pleasant to be at last under the touchy guns of the fastidious. He was in his fifties, and though he was not a bad man—wasn't he saved? elect as the next guy?—he'd had practically nothing to do with morality. There was no call for it in his neighborhood, not much call for it generally. There were no lovely lives, Mills thought. The world was charming or it wasn't. He, everyone, paid lip service to righteousness, but only good order quaked their hearts. In Mills's experience no one shot first and asked questions afterward. First they asked questions.

And then he thought, get down, be low, be low.

"What's wrong with you?"

Mrs. Glazer looked at him, surprised. "I have cancer," she said. "I already told you."

"I figured it must be something like that. My wife's always examining herself for that stuff, but so far she come up emptyhanded."

Mrs. Glazer stared at him. "Are you a fool?"

"I'm different."

"Indeed."

"Look, lady, your proposition sounds like it could be a really sweet deal, but all you told me so far is about your high hopes and funeral arrangements."

"What are you talking about?"

"I'm trying to get an idea how sick you are. My kind can be pretty long on loyalty, but there's a foreign country involved here. That funeral you keep talking about is supposed to take place stateside, but what happens if you die down there? I don't speak Mexican. Maybe them other applicants do. They look foreign enough."

"Other applicants?"

"Parked outside. In that car." He pointed past the living room window and indicated the Chevrolet.

"Oh," she said, "Max and Ruth. They must have slept late. They're brother and sister. They live in their car. They're not applicants."

"For real? In their car? You let them park there?"

"Whoever is dean," Mrs. Glazer said. "They park in front of the dean's house. They're really quite harmless. They go to all the public lectures at the university. The concerts and poetry readings. They eat the cheese and crackers. They stuff cookies into their pockets and drink the wine. It's how they live."

Mills nodded. Squatters, he thought, poachers. The old planted immunities and small piecemeal favors. The poor's special charters and manumissions, their little license and acquittals, all law's exonerate laxity and stretched-point privilege. He had to make himself low.

"Yeah, well," he said, "they look like ordinary thieves to me, my way of thinking. I could run them off for you. No charge."

"You're very boorish, aren't you?"

"Nah," Mills said, "no. I'm pointing out possibilities. I'm looking for the fly in the ointment. That's how I operate. In a way I'm

227

protecting you. You'd want someone tough, am I right? In this situation you'd need a guy who could set aside his delicate feelings, not someone who starts bleeding at the sight of puke. Lady, I *eat* puke! And not at no concerts, not at no poetry readings."

"Yes," Mrs. Glazer said, considering.

"Sure," Mills said.

"Yes," she said.

"Sure," Mills said. "My God, Mrs, listen to the way I build your confidence. I think I'm your man." It was *exactly* what he thought. It was what he thought when he'd first heard her voice, when he'd listened to her prattle. He wanted this job, needed it. He had to make himself low, reserve and brutal syntax in his jaws like chewing gum.

"You just better not die," Mills warned.

"I don't intend to."

"I want to go too," Mary said from where she'd been listening in the hall.

"Mary!"

"I want to go too," she said, still concealed.

"Don't be silly. What about school?"

"Kids can get off if it's educational. There's going to be a unit on Mexico. I'd get extra credit. I want to go too."

"Mary, I'm going down there to get well. I'll be taking treatments. All the people will be sick there. As sick as Mommy."

"Let me talk to her, Mrs," George Mills said, and promised he would bring back a wonderful present for her.

"Oh, presents," she said disparagingly. "My grandfather buys me all the presents I want. My Uncle Harry does."

Mills barely glanced at the woman for permission. "Gee, kid," George Mills said, guarding his protector, "I meant your mommy."

5

To the poor most places are foreign, all soil not the neighborhood extraterritorial and queer. They cling to an idea of edge, a sense of margin. It's as if space, space itself, not climate or natural resources or the angle at which a town hangs from the meridian, dictates situation and size, even form, even vegetation. They believe, that is, in a horizon geography, a geology of scenic overlook, the visible locutions of surface like merchandise arranged in a store. For them, Nature, the customs she fosters, seem to exist within serially located parallel lines. Science and history are determined by latitude and longitude, little else. Savannas and rain forests, jungles, seashores, mountains and deserts—— those were the real nations.

The people were not strange to him, only their white shirts. Only their artifacts, their basketstraw heritage and adobe being. So much silver—it gleamed everywhere, so accessory he suspected that even the policemen's badges were made of it—made his soul reel. So much marquetry—even the benches in the public squares and gardens seemed a sort of crocheted wood—gave him a sense of an entire country artisan'd into existence. The sun seemed a feature of the landscape, and he was enough conscious of the tremor-settled streets to suspect the delicate arrangements of the earth he walked upon, and to sense it sensed his steps.

It was all as mysterious and significant as the skinned rabbits and shaved chickens that hung upside down from hooks in the butchers' shop windows, red and naked as political example.

They had been in Mexico almost four days and Mrs. Glazer had still to receive her first treatment. They had rented a car in El Paso and crossed the Rio Grande to Juarez, Mrs. Glazer insisting they stop for the hitchhikers standing on the Mexican side of the bridge. George handled the money, the blue, red and yellow tissues of currency, soft as old clothes. He signed the insurance forms and answered the border guards' questions. She gave him her tourist card to carry. He signed the register at their motel while she remained in the air-conditioned car. He settled her in her room and turned down her bed. She had him call Sam before he went to his own room. Standing, he relayed both ends of the conversation to and from the easy chair in which she sat. They had arrived safely, he said. He and the children already missed her, he said. The girls had to do all their homework before they went out. Mary couldn't have a milk shake till after dinner. Milly wasn't to make any arrangements for Wednesday afternoon. That's when auditions for *Nutcracker* were scheduled, he said. The trip had tired her, he said, and she thought she'd put off her first visit to the clinic till morning.

A boy rose from a camp chair in which he'd been sitting, handed something to an old woman, and came up while George was still parking the car in the lot.

"Joo here for treatments?"

"Do you speak English?"

"Ain't that English? Joo here for treatments?"

"Information."

"What informations joo want? *Si.* Sure. It work. Cure up jore cancers. Fix joo up fine."

Mills started past the boy.

"Hey," called the boy. "Joo, Misters. Joo got to take number. I give joo."

But Mills ignored him.

Two receptionists in nurse's uniforms sat at registration desks at the back of the crowded room. George went outside to get a number.

"Joo need me to watch jore cars? I watch jore cars," the boy

230

called after George as he started back toward the clinic. "That ways nothing awfuls happen. Nobody break jore window or puncture jore tires or tear off jore antenna or pour sugars in jore gas tanks."

George turned around.

"How much?"

The boy grinned at him. "Joo got a Joo.S. dollars on you?" George handed him a dollar.

"Crowded in there? Many peoples?" The boy wiped imaginary sweat from his forehead, pulled at his shirt, pretended to fan himself. "Joo want to rent my chair for a quarter? Sick peoples need to sit down."

"What's your number?" a very old man asked him, smiling, when he was again inside. He wore an old-fashioned taxi driver's cap with a button that said "Official Guide" where the badge number would have been.

"Ninety-five," Mills said.

The old man's smile disappeared and his eyes filled with tears. "Ninety-five," he said feelingly. "You come all this way, all this far from *el Estados Unidos,* and they give you ninety-five. Tch-tch."

"It's all right," Mills said.

"No, *señor! No* all right! I jam shame for my people. I jam shame for those two whore daughters of whores who call themselves typists. So slow. Tch-tch. They call themselves train typists? They are train pussies! Customers have to spell out for them all everything. Ninety-five." The old man spit on the floor. "You be here all week. I get you thirty-seven. Five pesos."

"No thanks."

"Five pesos. That isn't even a quarter."

"I'll wait."

"Sure," the old man said, "wait. You in good shape. I can seen it for myself. Your tumor ain't bad. You got all the time in the world."

"I'm not sick," Mills said, "it isn't for me. I'm making arrangements for the lady I work for."

"*Verdad?*" the old man said. He seemed relieved. "I'm happy for you, *señor.* I am happy but puzzle. If it isn't for you, then why you waste your time in such a place? Plane to El Paso, *verdad?* Rented a car? First time in ol' Mayheeho, *si?* Sure. Is beautiful day, *si?* Gift me seven pesos, I get the cunts to call out ninety-five, we go for a ride."

Mills looked at the young women. Twenty-eight had been the last number called.

"Could you do that?" he asked.

231

"Caramba, señor," the old man said, "thees girls is my sisters!"

"No," Mills said. "I don't think so."

"Seven pesos. That's thirty cents."

"It's thirty-five cents," Mills said.

"Where do you change your money?"

"At the motel."

The old man groaned. "No, *señor,*" he said patiently, "never change money at the motel. Always go to the Midas Muffler. Change it there."

"Jesus, leave me be, will you?" Mills said. "Everybody has his hand out. I had to pay the kid in the parking lot to watch the car."

The old man was horrified. "The kid? Not the old woman? The *kid?* How much you give him?"

"A buck."

"Sure," the old man muttered, "he'll go to the Midas Muffler and get twenty-three point eight pesos for it. Here," he said, *"take* thirty-seven. I jam shame for my people." He put the number into George's hand.

"What about the car? You think he'd do anything to the car?"

"No no," the old man reassured him, "the machine will be fine. You bribed him good."

Mills made Judith Glazer's arrangements with the receptionist and returned to the car. The old man was with him, watching him as he unlocked the automobile. "I already gave you your five pesos," George said. "What do you want now?"

The old fellow shook his head. "You could have done all this over the phone," he said tragically.

"Is that what you do? Give advice?"

"I am a tout," he said proudly. "I saved you two hours. It cost you less than a quarter."

"Yeah, well, when I come back with the lady I work for don't expect any more."

"Don't come back," he said earnestly, touching George's arm.

"What?"

"Don't come back. This is not a good place. For rich *gringos.*"

Mills, who was only a delegated *gringo,* and for whom wealth and international travel and the perks of life, sleeping in motels and eating out, were merely assignments, was not so much offended as surprised by the old tout's warning.

"You listen to him, Misters," the boy said who had watched his car. "Father Merchant is the wisest tout in all Mexico."

232

"He didn't have such terrific things to say about joo," George said.

"Father Merchant knowing my heart," the boy said sadly.

Mills opened the car door. "Uhn uh, uhn uh," Father Merchant said. "Always is it too hot. Crack the window of the side of the passenger three inches, and the window of the side of the driver two, to force the circulation of the air. Carry the towel with you to protect yourself when you touch metal surfaces." Mills looked at the wisest tout in all Mexico. "*Es verdad,*" he said. Mills started the engine and began to back out of the space. The old man walked beside the car, trying to hand a card to him through the open window. Mills stepped on the brake and put the car in neutral.

"Please," he said.

"Nightspot," said Father Merchant, and gave George the card. "*Instituto de Cancer* too sad. No cover, no minimum. Very refine. Intimate. No clip joint. Sophisticate. Tell them who sent you, they let you sit ringside, close enough to stick your finger up the pony's asshole. Go, *señor.* Take the *señora.* All work and no play make Jack a dull boy." Mills started to back out again. "Father Ixtlan Xalpa Teocaltiche hears confessions in English. Thursdays before 6:00 A.M. mass. He's been to Chicago. Church of the Conquistador Martyrs." Mills was out of the space and pulled hard on the wheel to turn into the street. The old man called to him through cupped hands. "On Sundays, at the bullfights? *Sol y sombre?* Shady side is not always the best choice. You could freeze your nuts off if it's a cool day." Mills could see him now in the rear mirror. "*Don't drink the water!*" the old tout shouted.

They sat by the small pool in deep lounges, idly watching children play Marco Polo. The kids had driven most of the grownups out of the water, making it impossible for anyone to swim with their excited thrashing and sudden, abandoned lunges that obliterated the pool's invisible lanes whenever the child who was *it* moved away from the coping and plunged, eyes shut tight, toward the voices that answered "Polo" in response to his honor-blind "Marco."

Mrs. Glazer seemed rested, looked better. Mills remarked on this. "It's my sunburn," she said. "It covers the jaundice. Oh, Mills," she said, "I've been to the lobby. It's more hospital here than motel. The guests bring their nurses. Some arrive in ambulances. I saw one with New Jersey plates. Have you looked at the room service menu? The salads and entrees have been approved by the clinic's nutritionist.

Monks openly solicit money to pray for the remission of your cancer. Urchins show you the candles they'll light if you'll give them some dinner.

"And everyone's so hopeful, Mills! As if the decision to come here, break with their doctors, defy science and throw themselves into all the desperate optimisms of last resort were measures in the cure. I myself have not been unaffected. Why, we've not been here two days yet and already I'm feeling better than I have in weeks. A little, a little I am. Oh, Mills," she said, "how are we to know what is so and what is just psychology?"

"From the blood tests," Mills said, and his charge glanced at him.

"Yes," she said. "Well, what do we do now?"

"Maybe you should rest."

"No. No, I'm not tired."

"Do you want to eat something?"

"I'm not hungry. I'm raring to go. What?"

"Nothing."

"No, what? What is it?"

"A Mex at the clinic gave me a card."

"A card?"

"The address of some nightclub."

"A nightclub? Oh, I don't think I'm up for a nightclub. Oh," she said, "a *night*club, a border town nightclub. Exhibitions, you mean. Burros and girls. Fetishists. Consenting adults. I don't think so, but I'm feeling well enough to spare you. You go, Mills. Take the car."

"No," he said, ashamed he had spoken. "I don't want to go."

"It's all right," she said. "The motel has a caretaker service. All I have to do is notify the desk. Someone checks the room every fifteen minutes. Go on, go ahead. I don't expect you to be always on duty. Go, you've the urge."

"No. Honest," Mills said, "I don't have any urge. It was a joke. When you said you were raring to go. It was a joke."

"Because I won't think less well of you, you know. People are curious about what they think of as depravity. The act means nothing. The curiosity's at least as depraved as anything the girl will do with the beast."

"I never put it in any animal," Mills said, hurt. "I ain't never licked instep or spanked ass or sniffed panty. I never gave pain or asked for it. It never came up."

234

"Well I have," Mrs. Glazer said. "Nearly all those things. What difference does it make?"

"You have?"

"I was a madwoman eleven years."

Which was when it came up. Welcome to Mexico, he thought. *Bienvenidos* to the border towns!

They drove, at the woman's discretion, through Ciudad Juarez, Mrs. Glazer in the wide back seat murmuring the turns, calling their routes, demanding the sights. She pronounced herself dissatisfied with Twelfth of August Avenue, the long main street, all appliance stores and tire shops, and asked that Mills show her the clinic. Somehow he found his way back to the low stucco buildings of that morning, and drove into the parking lot. A watchman stopped them. "All close," he said, "*finito.*"

"Should you give him a tip?"

The man poked his flashlight through the open window into the back of the car.

"Hey," Mills said, "turn that off. You're shining it in the lady's eyes."

"It's all right," she said. "It's his job, Mills."

George turned to look, following the tight white beam that lay across his shoulder like a rifle. Judith Glazer sat prim as a confirmation girl, her hands folded in her lap, her eyes lowered. She looked like someone in a tumbril. Inexplicably, the guard crossed himself.

"Give him money," Mrs. Glazer said. "He may be an old lover."

"What for? Why'd he do that?"

"He saw my condition," she said.

"Are you tired?" Mills asked. "Do you want me to take you back?"

"Not at all."

They passed the church where the priest who had been to Chicago heard confessions in English. And stopped for a light on the corner where the nightclub was situated. It was on a narrow street with much traffic. A boy came up to the driver's window and offered to watch their car.

"No," Mills said. "We're not parking."

"No," the boy said, "till the light changes."

"Maybe we ought to start back," Mills said when they were driving again. "It's pretty late."

235

"No," she said, "I'm enjoying my joy ride."

"You had a long trip yesterday. All the way from a different country."

"If you're tired I'll drive."

"No," Mills said. "That's all right."

"Let me. I feel like driving."

"You'd better not."

"Pull over. If you're afraid you can go back in a cab."

"Please, Mrs."

"I want to," Mrs. Glazer said. "My pill is wearing off and I'm beginning to feel uncomfortable. It would distract me." She was kneading her thighs and legs with her hands, taking her flesh and squeezing as if she would wring water from it. "If only I could get the knots out," she said.

"I'm turning back," Mills said.

"I told you no," Mrs. Glazer said. "I don't want to. If you insist on driving you may, but I won't go back. I was crazy more than a decade, shut up when I could have been traveling. What's the good of being rich anyway? I never got anything for my money but the best care. In the end I simply grew out of my madness anyway. Now I'm dying. That watchman saw it with a flashlight. I don't want the best care. That's why I came to this place. That's why I chose you to bring me. Perhaps it will be like the last time. Perhaps I'll grow out of my cancer too. Don't you *dare* turn back."

"You're the doctor," Mills said gloomily.

"I am," she said, "yes. Don't sulk, Mills. Look at the countryside." They had left the city and entered the desert.

"It's the idea of the pain," Mills said when they had driven perhaps five more miles.

"Did you say something?"

"It's the idea that somebody only three feet away has pain. It fills up the space. It's all you can think about so it's all I can think about too. I can't stand it if I know my wife has a headache. I get mad at her for telling me."

"I'll take my pill," she said.

"You took one before we left the motel. It isn't four hours."

"What do you think will happen? Do you think I'll become addicted? Turn around," she said. "There's nothing here."

In the city, children were sleeping on the sidewalks. They lay solitary, curled as dogs on the pavement. A small girl lay on her back,

her arms thrown out behind her head. She looked like someone floating in a pool toy.

"God is good," Mrs. Glazer said.

"Sure."

"He really is. He's a genius. He creates the poor and homeless
and gives them a warm climate to sleep it off in. Shall we wake them?
Shall we give them money?"

"They're street kids. They'd have their knives in me as soon as
I shook their shoulder."

"I want you to go back," she said. "Give them twenty pesos
each."

Mills left the motor running. He woke the children and put
money in their hands while Mrs. Glazer sat in the back seat and
looked on through the rolled and dusty windows.

It was how they spent their first days in Mexico. Mills gave Mrs.
Glazer's money away. Considerable sums. As much, he estimated, as
the rental car would cost, or his motel room. Often as much as a
hundred pesos to an individual beggar. They crossed themselves before their benefactress's deputy with beggars' gratitude, conferring the
lavish, sinister blessings of the down-and-out. It was not his money.
It was not their benediction. And he had a sense of proxy encounter,
a delegate notion of agented exchange. At first he followed their
responses in a dictionary, nervously had them repeat themselves when
he did not understand, and scrupulously relayed their thanks in English equivalencies, rendering the tone and degree of already hyper-
bolized requital, hoping to suggest to the woman that the poor and
homeless were on to her.

"The starving woman thanks you on behalf of her five starving
children, and wishes you to know that every bite of their first meal
in four days will be dedicated to the honor of your gracious self."

"Hmph," Judith Glazer said.

"The legless cripple is profoundly moved by your generosity, and
says that he will direct the nephews who carry him to his post every
morning and pick him up again in the evening to take him up the steps
and into the church so that he may light candles for your continued
health and good fortune."

"Tell him," Mrs. Glazer said evenly, "don't try to thank me."

"The impaired wino sends his and his Saviour's compliments,
and resolves to pledge himself to a new life in partial repayment for
the three dollars."

She had him take her into poorer and poorer sections of the city, abandoning the busy street corners and entrances to the fashionable shops and restaurants, the hotels and museums where beggars congregated to groan their appeals against the chipper discourse of the rich, driving with her into the narrow barrios, the blighted box board and charred, tar paper slums, places where the beggars had only each other to importune, raising the ante of their already stretched humility to outright, outraged fantasy.

And now she had him lower the car windows. And now she had him open the doors.

They looked on the big, late-model American car with as much astonishment and fear as if it had been a tank. Children backed against the jagged, chicken wire frames they used as doorways and called their adults to witness the strange new avatar, the queer incarnation, sudden in the roadless, streetless jumble of singed, mismatched shacks as a visitation of angels or government.

Seeing it was only a lone man, a lone woman, they lost their alarm and began to push forward.

"This is crazy," Mills said. "Let's get out of here."

"Sound the horn," Mrs. Glazer said. "Let them know we're here."

"They already know we're here."

Mrs. Glazer raised herself from where she was slumped in the back seat and leaned forward. She reached over Mills's shoulder and pressed the horn.

"Oh boy," Mills said.

"Don't get out. They can come forward and you can hand the money out to them."

When Mills didn't move she reached for her purse and undid the clasp. Hands and arms like the feelers of sea creatures groped toward her through the car's opened doors. Mills, frightened, pulled out his pesos and started to cram them into the first hand he saw. "No," she said, "just one note. Just *one!* Here," she said, "give me." She pulled the notes out of his fist and, selecting the smallest denomination, pushed it into one of the outstretched hands. Then, inspired, she smiled, dropped the rest of the money into her lap, and took some loose change from her purse. She held out a handful of coins to them, ten-centavo pieces, twenty. "For all of you," she said. *"Para todos. Para todos de usted."* She sat back in her seat, lightly tapping the thick pile of bills in her lap, her gold and diamond rings loosely spinning on her thin fingers. She looked on serenely while the Mexicans talked to each other in whispers. Then, with great effort, she moved out of the car toward them, holding out the last of her change, perhaps six or seven cents.

He thought they would both be killed, but the Mexicans only drew further away from the car, their mood nervous and apprehensive and lined with a sort of amusement. A woman indicated the two Americans and shook her head. Then they all did, making the high signs and hand signals of aloof contempt, the shrugs and semaphores of all touch-temple allowance. "Help me back into the car," she said, disappointed.

Mills was determined that they wouldn't try *that* again.

Meanwhile she continued to avoid the treatments.

George drove her to the clinic each morning and called for her again at noon. It was she who sent him away. "There aren't enough chairs," she'd explain. "These people are waiting to see the doctors. You'd only be taking up the seat of someone terminally ill." But when he returned he would find her sitting where he'd left her, or rummaging through a table of Mexican magazines. "Oh, Mills," she said, "waiting rooms are the same all over the world. Only the names of the film stars in the periodicals are different, or the wall hangings in the legislative chambers. These hemlines are shorter, but I believe I saw this salad in the Sunday pictures section of the *Post-Dispatch.*"

"What did the doctor say?"

"Oh, I haven't seen the doctor yet. I was about to but this little girl—she couldn't have been more than six—arrived with her parents. I gave them my place."

She'd had her tests, the blood profiles and X-rays and urine analyses she had first had done in St. Louis, as well as a cancer immunological test which was not performed in the United States. It was patented, the Mexicans told her.

"Of course, I don't really *buy* any of it," she told him in the car. "But I believe that dreams come true."

She suggested they go out again that night on another alms spree.

"You're tired," Mills said.

"Yes," she admitted, "I'm very weak."

"Look," he said, "if it's all that important to you I'll go myself."

"No," she said.

"Don't you trust me? You think I'd keep the money?"

"I trust you dandy. It wouldn't mean much unless I went. All right," she said, "we won't plan anything. We'll wait and see how I feel this evening."

She felt terrible that evening. She couldn't even get out of bed. Mills knew she'd made a mistake to bring him. He had no touch with pain. He had fears and misgivings about everything he did for her. At the height of her pain and nausea he thought she should try to eat something, that food might confuse the beast in her gut. He wasn't sure but he thought it was probably a good idea. He wanted to phone the clinic but officially she hadn't been assigned a doctor yet. He couldn't remake her bed properly, and thought he should call Housekeeping to have them send someone while he carried her to the room's other bed, but she objected to having anyone else in the room.

He spoke to her, but it took so much effort for her to talk he cringed when she answered. He said nothing, and she thought he'd left her. The pain had affected her vision. "I'm here," he said, "I haven't gone anywhere. You mustn't talk," he said. "You've got to save your strength." He watched her thrash in the bed, the sheets and covers and pillows in such disarray he could not straighten them without causing her pain. He moved her back into the other bed. He wondered if he should call St. Louis. It was after two in the morning. They'd be alarmed. He knew they'd blame him for everything that happened. He was no nurse. He recalled how peacefully Mr. Mead had died, the old sailor slipping beneath his death as casually as one enters tepid water. He decided she should be in a hospital and said so. Groaning, she shook her head. "They're equipped for this stuff," he said.

"No good," she managed. She'd already explained why. She was afraid they wouldn't give her her pain pills when she wanted them, that they'd withhold them. She wanted Mills to give her a double dose now, two large, oddly shaped blocks of morphine like tiny bricks. It would have been the strongest dose she'd had yet. He broke a tablet in two and fed the halves past her impaired vision. He called the front desk and got on their caretaker service, although the caretaker had already left on his 2:00 A.M. rounds.

"You have only one?"

"The guests are either sleeping or already in the hospital this time of night."

"Get in touch with him. Send him by."

Suddenly she was worried about the expense. There was an extra charge for this amenity. It was middle of the night, they had you over a barrel. "Shh," George said. She wanted him to cancel the order, she became quite hysterical about it. He hadn't, he told her, made one.

"I heard you."

They lost each other in explanations.

"I'm hungry," she said, and he told her that was a good sign, but he didn't think he should give her anything too heavy. "Feed a cold and starve a cancer," she said lucidly.

The morphine was beginning to ease her. She dozed off. The caretaker waked her when he knocked on the door. It was the kid from the parking lot, the one he'd given a dollar to watch the car.

The boy glanced at Mrs. Glazer. "She fine, man." he said. "See joo in fifteen minuteses."

Strangely, the boy seemed to have reassured her. "Ask him," she said, "if he thinks I should have something to eat."

"Him?"

"He's the caretaker. He sees dozens of patients. Ask."

The boy was standing beside a door three rooms down. "Good," George said, "I thought I'd missed you."

"No, man. There's this Mercedes SL 100 I watching out for on this side. Joo see it?"

"No."

The boy shrugged. "Maybe they checked out."

"He says room service is closed," he told her.

"It's just as well," she said. "Everything is so expensive." She questioned him closely about their expenses, recalling each traveler's check she'd given him to cash, and demanding an account of how it had been spent.

"We don't get a good rate of exchange," she mourned.

They lived in waves, something peristaltic to their moods, reality pushing them to the wall one moment and surrendering not to joy so much as to a sort of deranged confidence the next. He understood that their burlesque hope had its source in her pain's by now ludicrous remissions. In an odd way he had become dependent on Mrs. Glazer's morphine, remotely hooked on the woman's transitory well-being. He telephoned St. Louis only when she was without pain.

Also, he was still unaccustomed to himself in a foreign country. This was more difficult to figure, but it had to do with his horizon vision, his sense of a life lived within parallel lines. Ciudad Juarez was situated in the open end of a three-sided valley, a trough of drying world set down within the clipped, broken waves of the surrounding hills and mountains. These became landmarks and mileposts. More. They were the spectacle mien and proclamation of his distance, exotic and outrageous as a milliary column in a woods. Snakes oozed in the hills. Queer lizards turned their heads in strobic thrusts. He was where the mountains were who had lived on plains beneath unpunctuated skies. He came from there. He was here. He was here and not there. And lived with a notion of having doubled himself. It was not unlike what he had felt in Cassadaga when he was a boy.

She had started her treatments. After her terrible night there were no more delays. The curious dalliance was over. "It won't work anyway," she'd said the next morning. "Let's get going."

They wanted to keep her in the clinic annex for two days to administer calcium in an IV solution. The nurse touched Mrs. Glazer's hair lightly. "It will help keep your hair that pretty yellow color."

"My pretty yellow hair fell out. This is a wig."

George went with her to a sort of orientation seminar in the clinic's cafeteria. They sat with other patients in the Eleventh of May Cafeteria. Father Merchant, at a rear table, was picking from a cylinder of popcorn. A tall man in hospital whites leaned against a stack of trays and greeted them.

"*Buen dia.* I'm Dr. Jesus Gomeza. So," he said, "I will answer all your questions about *el grande* C.

"You know, not so long ago, people like you would hear cancer and think, Oh boy, sure death. Certain curtains. Even now. I know. I know what happens. I interned in your country. These white duds are from a Sears Roebuck in Omaha. So I know what happens.

"The tests come back. The doctor breaks the news to a wife, or to some take-charge guy in from Portland with a good vocabulary. The patient is the last to know. Listen, I've been there. It's this hush-hush, very top secret disease. The family cocks around with each other for weeks. Then this one tells that one, somebody else overhears someone on a telephone, but no one's ever sure who knows what. Am I right? They're not even sure if Pop knows what's what, and he's the poor bastard losing important pieces of himself on the operating table. They're getting ready to bury him and the whispering campaign still ain't over. 'Did he know what he had? Does he know that he's dead?'

"But you know, don't you? You folks know what you have, so we don't have to worry about that part. You've got cancer. Say it. Say 'Cancer, I've got *cancer!*'

"I don't hear you. Good golly, am I wrong? Have I made a mistake? Aren't these the cancer people? Father Merchant, you rascal, have you played one of your tricks on me? Did you bring one of your tour buses by? Are you folks healthy? You don't *look* healthy. Hell no, you look like you've got cancer. Why, I can see the tumors from over here. I can hear the brain tumors rolling around in your skulls like marbles. I see extra lumps in the bras. I can almost make out some of the more difficult stuff, the crapola tucked away in your organs like contraband. Hey, Mister, the guy in the green shirt——don't turn around, you're the one I'm talking to. What's wrong with you?"

"I've got a cancer," a man said shyly.

"Sure you do," Dr. Gomeza said cheerfully. "And the lady at the long table holding the flower, what have you got?"

"Cancer."

"I want," he said, "to see the hands of everyone who believes that the national medical associations have conspired to suppress our so-called unproven treatments, that vested establishment interests are afraid to risk a head-on confrontation with the proponents of Laetrile research. Let's see those hands.

"So many? Tch-tch. The cancer's spread that far, has it? It's bitten that deep? No no, put your hands down. You're too sick to be waving them about like that. Your disease has metastasized. It's into your beliefs by now, it's knocked the stuffing out of incredulity. Your gullibility glands are amok. Tch-tch.

"So that's why you've come. Not to be cured but to stand up and be counted on the deathbed. What, you think this is a protest rally? You hate your doctors? You begrudge your oncologist because he made you nauseous? There's no conspiracy. They're good men. My *God,* folks, nine out of twelve of you came down here with their permission, with their *blessing* even. I'm going to tell you something. American doctors are the best diagnosticians in the world. Those guys *know* what's wrong with you. And I'll tell you something else. If it were in their power they'd even *cure* you!

"Say it," he commanded. "Say *'Cancer! I've got cancer!'* "

"Cancer!" they called out cheerfully, *"I've got cancer!"*

"I've got something to tell you," Dr. Gomeza said.

He told them about Laetrile, how it was found in the pits of peaches, apricots and bitter almonds, and gave them a chemistry lesson, explaining amygdalin and how hydrocyanic acid worked against the betaglucosidase in tumors, and even listed for them the drug's pleasant side effects. He went over with them just what they must do, describing the regimen to them, a book of hours for their three daily injections, their course of special enzymes, the ritual of their vitamins, their diet.

"Look," he said, "we're going to lose some of you. People still die of appendicitis, too. And sometimes even a paper cut has been known to derange the system and the victim dies. So maybe you're out of luck. It could even be you're stuck with some fluke cancer which doesn't respond to fruit. It's possible. This is the world. Unexpected things happen. Go ask Sloan-Kettering. How many of *their* guys go down?"

He wished them luck.

And when he finished they applauded. Even Mrs. Glazer. Even George.

Father Merchant finished his popcorn and left.

Now he was her visitor as well as her employee. She sat in one chair by the side of her bed, and he in the other. Since coming back from the clinic she had somehow created the illusion for him, for them both, that when he arranged a pillow behind her head or poured her a drink of the clinic's bottled water or brought her the El Paso newspaper or turned the channels on the TV set until they found a program acceptable to them both, it was as a guest, some loyal companion who might almost have been female, a bridge partner, say, someone who had served with her on committees.

"What are you having for dinner?" she might ask.

"I thought I'd go to that Mexican place again."

"Oh, don't say it. I'm fond of Mexican food, too, but my husband won't touch it. We almost never go."

"It's time for your injection."

"Could *you* do it? The nurse the clinic sends bruises me so. I've never really been a delicate woman. It's cancer which softened my skin and made me petite. Just look at these legs and thighs. You'd never suspect that at one time I had the limbs of a six-day bicycle racer."

At four in the afternoon they would watch a program on Mexican television, "Maria, Maria," a soap opera set in the nineteenth century, about an illegitimate servant girl lusted after and badly treated by all the men in the benighted town in the obscure province in which she was indentured. It was the most popular program in Mexico, one of those shows that stops a country's business for an hour or so and encourages people to believe that they are participants in an event of carefully resolved attention, their own lives temporarily

244

forgotten in careless, throwaway sympathy. Mills and Mrs. Glazer had been watching for a week, and though neither understood the Spanish they knew the characters, and by reading the El Paso paper, which followed the plot with a daily summary like the synopsis in an opera program, they were able to understand the story.

"The president is watching this now in the capital," Mrs. Glazer said. "He is suspicious of Maria's new friend while the Minister of Internal Affairs plots against him with his most trusted generals."

"The Minister of Internal Affairs? His generals?"

"Oh, Mills, they are no fans of that poor, troubled girl."

One day when she was dejected she speculated that she might die before learning the fate of the characters. Mills tried to reassure her. "Then before I've lost interest," she said. "I could die while I'm still curious about that new one. What is his name?"

"Arturo?"

"Arturo. I may not be around while I still have questions about Arturo."

"Don't talk like that. You're feeling better every day."

"Am I? I believe," she said, "in life everlasting. I believe in Heaven, yet there are no dramatics there. God would not permit His angels to be troubled."

Mills was not at all certain he was correct in his assessment of her treatments. It was certain that she had not again had the kind of night that had so frightened them both, but her energies were low, and she was no longer up to the car rides she had at first been so intent on. He suggested that if she was still concerned about expenses he could return their rental car and take taxis whenever they went to the clinic. She told him she thought they should hold on to the car a bit longer. "I may feel stronger. We would need it to get around when I am well enough to give alms again."

Now he was giving her all her injections, feeding juices from the pits of apricots into her bloodstream, daubing alcohol across her once maddened flanks and stirred despite himself at the sight of her yellow, degraded hips. He knew he must be hurting her but she was unwilling to let anyone else do it. He didn't know why.

And now he was bathing her too, carrying her naked to the tub and lowering her into it like an offering in pageant. Her eyes were closed all the time he washed her, and she was the very type of humiliation, stoical, never wincing, patient degradation on her like a scar.

"I was nuts eleven years," she said. "In a private hospital with a small staff for the elegance of the thing. They couldn't watch you all the time. We did frightful things to each other. Soap my crotch please, Mills." And as he lowered the cloth she opened her eyes and forced herself to stare at her oppressor.

Because she believed in martyrdom. She hadn't told him this but it was the only thing that explained her actions. Because she believed in martyrdom. Saint Judith Glazer of Cancer. Because she needed holy bruises, some painful black-and-blue theology of confrontation. And that was when he realized she was dangerous.

"Those people we picked up on the bridge and gave rides to," she said one evening.

"Yes?"

"They were wetbacks."

"They were coming into the country, not leaving it."

"They were illegals. They go over for the day to work. The maid who cleans the room told me."

"I don't follow."

"I could drive to El Paso. I could dose up on morphine and take someone with me. He could use your tourist card."

Mills excused himself and returned to his room.

Where he hid, where he tried to figure out what to do. He remembered the times they had driven through the city seeking out beggars, showing their funds, flashing their pesos like scalpers. And recalled the visit to the barrio, her lap filled with cash. She would be a saint and throw herself into all the trenches of virtue, poised as a zealot for the last-ditch stand with her ducks-in-a-barrel innocences and vulnerabilities. He was only beginning to understand the Turk role she had assigned him, the barbarian and Vandal and red Indian possibilities. Stuffing money in his pockets, putting needles and syringes in his hands, her jaundiced cunt, bald as a babe's, making him privy to her weakness, her body's worst-kept secrets, a seductress with nothing left but the final, awful charms of earth and the terrible with which to provoke him. Leading him right up to the distant cusps of extradition and dismay, the very borders of flight and exile.

"I want," she said, "all the traveler's checks cashed."

"It's entrapment, Judith."

"I want them cashed," she said. "I'll need it in pesos."

"Sure," he told her, and brought the money to her, the heaps of paper with their spurious glaze of value, like stock certificates, like Eagle stamps, like lottery tickets and the come-on bonanzas brought in the mails. He didn't even tell her to count it. "That's twenty-five hundred dollars," he said.

"Yes," she said. "I've called the desk. They've agreed to take a personal check. They called my bank. They sent someone to their bank. The money will be waiting for you at the cashier's office. You'll have to sign for it."

"Sure," he said. She made out a check for fifteen hundred dollars. He fetched her money. "That's only four thousand dollars," he said when he'd placed it beside the money from the traveler's checks. "Do you really think I'd murder you for four thousand dollars?"

"Oh no," she said, "there's my rings and pearl necklace. There are things in my jewelry case."

"Sure," he said.

"There are my infuriating ways."

"Get the maid to do it. Call room service. Ask the caretaker kid. Sit parked in the car. Everyone in town recognizes it by now."

Because it was no secret anymore. And when she told him again she'd been crazy eleven years, he corrected her. "Twelve," he said. "It used to be eleven."

"No," she said. "I know you won't do it. You misjudged *me*, not I you. What's so disruptive to your imagination," she asked him, "about the idea of getting something for one's death? Cancer gives you little enough return on your money. Not like bludgeoning. Not like street crime or poor Maria's trusting betrayals. This is a Catholic country. No one here will harm me for my faith. Oh, Mills, they're *all* Catholic countries now. They pray openly behind the Iron Curtain. My options are closed off. There are no more frontiers. When I die there will be no arrows in my breast. I won't be torched like St. Joan or crucified on the bias like St. Francis. Beasts will never chew me. So where's the harm in flaunting my pesos or flashing my jewelry? It's only a farfetched possibility anyway, too oblique a contingency that I might ever be killed doing good deeds. It passes the time. And perhaps some bad man will take the bait, and God never notice that it was entrapment."

"*I* noticed," Mills said.

"We'll leave the money lying around just in case."

She did. When he came into the room now it was always there, at the foot of the bed or on the sink in the bathroom in the way of the housemaids or the man who came in to fix the air conditioning. Only Mills took money from the strewn cash. For expenses. For the serums renewed and paid for daily and kept in a refrigerator in the motel's restaurant. For the El Paso newspaper, for Father Merchant, who had become a sort of dragoman, the sidekick's sidekick.

It was Merchant who brought the medical supplies from the clinic, Merchant who sat with him sometimes while Mrs. Glazer dozed.

"Apricot pits," he scoffed. "How could an extract of apricot pits cure a cancer?"

"Don't talk so loud," Mills said.

"She knows she's dying. The *señora* is a realist. But *apricot* pits? Where is the realism in apricot pits?"

"I know," Mills said. "You're going to say it should have been peach pits."

"Chemotherapy," Father Merchant said. "Surgery. Maybe a nice hospice. But she should never have smoked. She should have watched her diet from the beginning."

Mrs. Glazer opened her eyes.

"You shouldn't leave your money lying around, *señora.* "

"Oh," she said listlessly, "he knows about the money. He knows about my jewelry. Now I shall be murdered in my bed."

But no one wanted her life, and their life together—for now he lived with the woman more intimately than ever he had with his wife —had become relentless.

He knew the shape of her appetite, the shade of her stools. It was extraordinary. He knew her past—as she knew his; he told her about the first George Mills, he described Cassadaga for her and the Mills who had intrigued with courts and empires, filling her in on how the family had bogged down in history, how it remained untouched by the waves of rising expectations that had signaled the rest of Western civilization out of its listlessness, giving her the gray details of a survival that was neither hardy nor valorous—but with her own governing, emergent lassitude, she had broken off her once ordered narrative. There were odd lacunae. She was nuts in one frame and securing a large dance band for her elder daughter's confirmation party in the next. He learned about the struggle for Sam's deanship, Milly's progress in piano. But what had happened to Judith, any coherent feel for all that had predated their introduction to each other on the strange occasion of his going to collect her condolence call, all, that is, that was beyond his immediate observation, or not pertinent to either her needs or her demands, remained privileged information.

He was interested of course. She was all he had to fill up his time. And, as she herself had insisted, she had no secrets. If she had stopped talking, if she had stopped listening, it was because all she had to fill up her time was herself. She was simply too busy now feeling her way along the murky routes and badly graded switchbacks of her decline and separation from the world to have much time for him.

Meanwhile, though he did everything, there was not much he could do for her. Occasionally, in the cool mornings, Mills still carried her outdoors and bundled her in one of the lounges where she could watch the children playing in the water, holding their breaths, racing, playing Marco Polo. But soon she lost interest in even this passive diversion and asked to be taken back to her room.

He fetched and carried from moment to moment and caught real glimpses of her only during the brief respite between the chores he performed in the name of her body. Which had gone into crisis, some emergency alert lived, or at least felt, at the pitch, the up-front prerogatives of her thirst or her weariness or even of the foul taste exploding in her mouth like the bomb of a terrorist.

Handling her nausea was a two-person affair, one to describe it, the other to chip the light dusting of salt from her soda crackers and feed them to her in pieces. She had lost impassivity only where her body was not concerned and guided him now through his massages, telling him where the flaccid muscles in her foot still pinched, warning him of a cramp developing in her neck, detailing discomfort as well as suffering, totally involved in getting off every last one of her body's messages, in translating from further and further away the foreign language that was all around them, all the sense of her senses. He was an expert, reeling off for them, the nurses and doctors at the clinic, Judith's infinite symptoms and impressions with an impressive and devastatingly authentic Siamese collaterality. ("This woman I live with . . ." he'd said to the pharmacist, scraping away the last conjugal implications of the phrase. He meant *lived with*.)

"I have," she said, "a thickish wet in my groin."

"I'll get Kotex," he said, for he somehow understood that she was describing not some new trial but the onset of her period, which, oddly, had not yet stopped.

Then, suddenly, she stopped even that crimped sharing. She lay in waiting, somewhere between the terror of calling it off and going back home and the terror of continuing in Mexico.

On the one hand she knew the Laetrile had failed, on the other that in Mexico she was out of the hands of the doctors, that in St.

Louis they would start the chemotherapy again, baking and stewing her with their lasers, their cobalt, turning all the peaceful uses of atomic energy against her.

"I've been a fool, Mills. I could have died a martyr to cancer by letting them treat me. Tell about today's episode."

She was no longer well enough to watch "Maria, Maria," and kept up by having Mills read her the synoptic squib in the El Paso paper.

Father Merchant came in one Friday evening but Mills gave him the key to his room and waved him off. He waited there until George called him. It was past nine.

"She's had her bath," George said softly. "She's almost comfortable. The *señora* can hear you. Go ahead, please."

"Madam," said the old man, "this week Maria's father is released from the jail and finds the *patrone* to who he have saled his daughter. Of course he does not recognize her because it has been nine years and she has flowered. The girl was hardly barely inside her puberty when he has sell her. He have a beard now and white hairs."

"Mills has read me all that," Mrs. Glazer said. "The courtship scene, please, Father. The dialogue and fine points."

"Buen dia, señorita. *No, no, please don't get up,* por favor. *Well well, I have not see such a lovely creature as yourself since, since . . . My my, it is the truth, there are none such pretty ladies in the country from which I have came.*"

"*What is that country,* señor?"

"*Its name is loneliness.*"

"Señor!"

"*The thousand pardons,* señorita. *The hand of my arm is a rough beast. The filthy scoundrel is forgot its manners.*"

"Por favor, señor!"

"*If you would but permit it to touch the face of your head.*"

"*But—— *"

"*It is just that it cannot believe such a haunch is real.*"

"*Oh.* Ooh!"

"*Ai ai! It is the miracle.*"

"Por—— *ai* ooh *ooh* ai!—— favor, señor! *This thing that you do is glorious but shameful. I must ask that you stop.*"

"*But* señorita—— "

"I must ask that you stop," Mrs. Glazer said. "Get my morphine, please, Mills."

"She has pain? She wants her medication?" Merchant said. He

250

examined the vial into which Mills had just plunged a hypodermic syringe. "Twelve milligrams of morphine? *Twelve?* Not fifteen? What have you done, *señor?* What have you allowed them to sell you?"

"You'd better leave now," Mills said. "Her stomach hurts badly. Your voice grates her ears. There's this indescribable itch in her left shoulder blade, and when she tries to ease it by rubbing it against the sheet a horrible pain shoots through her calves and jaw."

And he knew, too, when the narcotic caught hold, when the nerves relaxed, aligned themselves and fit once more into their sockets. He did not feel these things himself but knew she felt them. And knew, at one that morning, the immanence and alarm she'd felt in her sleep—it was not a dream, no vision or prophecy, neither Shekinah nor rapture, but information, disclosure, some red message of the blood—that her body was done with its phases, that death was by.

He called St. Louis but at the last moment withheld his news. "Who's this—— Mary? Hi, Mary. I didn't mean to wake you. I'm still mixed up about the time difference. It's me, Mills. Is your daddy there? May I speak with him, please?" Rushing the words because all the time he was watching Mrs. Glazer. Who seemed momentarily to have quieted. "Who's this? Isn't this Mr. Glazer? Who?—— Cornell Messenger?—— What about your son? I don't know your son. Where's Mr. Glazer? Never mind. Listen, she's waking up, I've got to go."

"Marco," she said.

He rushed to her side. She was feverish, so covered with sweat she seemed to lie under a thin layer of magnification. Her yellow wig had slipped off her head and her skull gleamed. The thin scuzz of gray fringe about her temples had turned dark with moisture. George bailed at the perspiration with towels that said Juarez Palace Motel. She was so thin she gave an impression of incredible flexibility.

"I've called the doctor," he said, and watched the pains arc and register along all the fronts of her body as if pain were almost some repressed geological flaw, and her skin, joints, bones and orifices the weathered, levered, earthen flash points and levees of prepped vulnerability.

"Marco," she whispered.

"I'm going to give you some morphine. An injection would hurt too much right now. You'll have to take these by mouth."

"Marco?"

He took her jaw in his fingers and pried it open. He tried to roll the morphine capsules they used now down her throat. Her mouth, for all the moisture on the surface of her body, was dry as fire. Some of the gelatin casing stuck to the inside of her cheek, and he had to tear it free, like cigarette paper caught on the surface of a lip.

"Marco," she said.

He pulled the two halves of the capsule apart and powdered her mouth with morphine. Her pain was so great it had doused her sense of taste. The stuff lay in her mouth neutral as teeth.

"You've got to swallow," Mills said. "Please swallow. I'm going to wet your mouth." He dipped a teaspoon with some congealed dessert still on it into a water glass and tamped the water into the corners of her mouth, sprinkling it there as if he were ministering to a bird. The drug turned to paste. He took up the glass of water and began to pour it into her mouth a little at a time until some vestigial reflex took over and she gulped.

"Marco," she said, her eyes wide, terrorized, the irises fleeing inside her head. *"Marco!"* she screamed. *"Marco! Marco!"*

"Polo," Mills answered.

"Marco," she called, lowering her lids.

"Polo."

"Marco."

"Polo."

They called the challenge and response from the old game and it seemed to soothe her heart that, blind and maddened as she was, she was not alone in the water.

6

I told her, *I* don't know the matter with me. I suppose I love the neighborhood. I'm no native son, I didn't even grow up there, but I —most folks—recognize home when I see it. Something old shoe in the blood and bones, at ease with the brands of lunch meat in the freezers and white bread on the shelves. At one with the barber shops, the TV and appliance repair. The movie houses in my precincts still do double features. Those that don't do evangelists, I mean, those that don't sell discount shoes or ain't political headquarters or furniture stores by now, the little marquees fanned out over the front of the buildings like a bill on a cap. We still have bakeries, and there are mechanics in the gas stations who can break down your engine in the dark. I root for our neighborhood banks, the local savings and loans, you know?

Stable, we're a stable neighborhood. How many areas are there left in the city—the city? Missouri? the country? the world?—that still have a ballroom and live dance bands that play there three nights a week? And even the discos bleed an old romantic box step, the generations still doing the stable dances under the revolving crystal. We have a saying in South St. Louis—— "We're born out of Incarnate Word and buried out of Kriegshauser." The stable comings and goings of hundreds of thousands of people.

They cross the river from Illinois and come from far away as west county to eat the immutable old ice creams and natural syrups at Crown's, less flavor, finally, than the cold and viscid residuals of produce and sweetness themselves. A kind of Europe we are.

I knew all this back in '47 when I first saw this section of town, recognizing at first glance that what the cop was walking was a beat, the grooved stations of vocation carved like erosion into the pavement, the big dusty shop windows with their brides and grooms and graduating seniors in their dark marzipan robes balanced on the topmost layer of the cake as if they were going to stand there forever. Something already nostalgic in the framed portraits in the photographic studio window, in the crush of the sun on the low two- and three-story commercial buildings up and down Gravois and Chippewa Avenues, something daguerreotype, a thousand years old, mint and lovely as a scene on money. I was nineteen but the Millses were a millennium. Here was somewhere I could hang my hat, here was a place I could bring our history.

I found three rooms in one of the blood brick apartment buildings on Utah, and there I began my life as a free man.

Where do we go wrong? How does joy decline? What rockets us from mood to mood like a commuter? So that, years later, in Mexico, that stable neighborhood of restlessness and revolution, I perfectly understood Mrs. Glazer's valedictory. She could have been speaking for all of us.

She was in the hospital by then. Dr. Gomeza had withdrawn from the case. And she was no longer a patient, not in the sense that what she had was treatable, not in the sense that what she had had ever been treatable.

"I don't live here anymore. I feel like something in a warehouse. Oh, Mills," she said, "it's not so bad to die.

"Weather. I've never liked weather. Too cold in the winter, in the summer too hot. Wood too damp to build a fire and the picnics rained out.

"The bad hands and heavy losses and clothes off the rack that never quite fit. Shoes pinch and the hairdo sags and the roast's overdone. The news is bad in the paper and one's children fail. I'm disappointed when the show isn't good I've heard so much about, and hats never looked right on me.

"My cats are run over. Moving men chip my furniture and the help steals. You can never get four people to agree on a restaurant.

"Wrong numbers, mismanaged mail and wasted time. Car pools and jury duty. Pain, fallen expectations and the fear of death.

"Who would fardels bear, Mills? The proud man's contumely?

"Mary is jealous of Milly's skill at piano, Sam's salary was too low years. No one loved me enough, and I never had all the shrimp I could eat."

Mostly all I could do was sit on the side of the bed and hold her. Like people in a waiting room we looked, Mrs. Glazer swaddled as a sick kid. Worn out, embraced as infant, loomed over, dipped in a dark dance.

Because I was twenty-seven years old before I ever entered the Delgado Ballroom, my shirt size determined years, my waistline fixed and what length pants I wore. No youth but callow still, the city hick, a sort of pleasantry. (You will understand that I played softball with what I still called "the men" on Sunday mornings in the schoolyards and parks, everyone, me too, in a yellow T-shirt and baggy baseball trousers, beer on the sidelines and packages of cigarettes and the equipment in someone's old army duffel.) We bloom late into our mildness, or some do, our character only a deference, a small courtesy to the world.

We played softball—— slow pitch, the high and lazy arc of the big ball so casual the game seemed to go on over our heads. Softball is a pitcher's medium, slow pitch especially. I thought the pitchers rich, or anyway leaders, privileged, gracious. They gave us our turn, permitted us to stand beneath the big, deceptive, graceful ball, shaking into our stance like dogs throwing off water, seeking purchase, hunching our shoulders, planting our feet, hovering in gravity as the softball hovered in air. Neutral gents, those pitchers neither smiled when they struck us out nor frowned when we connected. Good sports acknowledging nothing, neither the hoots of their opponents nor the pepper encouragements of their mates. Captains of cool benevolence, trimmer than the beefy Polacks and Krauts, all those swollen, sideburned others who were always talking.

In that league if you weren't married you were engaged. Engagements seemed to generate themselves almost spontaneously. There wasn't, except for myself, a fellow who wasn't already, or who wouldn't within the year become, a fiancé. Every girl on the bus wore a ring. Rings, or at least high school graduation pins, were an article of clothing, a piece of style, as much a part of ordinary human flourish as a cross on a chain. They were serious people, with their scouts' eyes peeled for the sexual or domestic talent. It was a world of starter sets, registered taste, the future like a lay-away plan.

Those pitchers, I'm thinking of those pitchers, the men chosen to get the blessings. Maybe because I didn't grow up there, maybe because when I came they were already doing their lives. Maybe it's having to come from behind (who came from behind history itself; oh, Greatest Grandfather, why didn't you rise up and smite Guillalume and the merchant? why didn't you kill Mills's horse when you had the chance?) which blights possibility and poisons will.

What I wanted to tell her about was the Delgado Ballroom——soft romance's dark platform, that marble clearing, that courtyard of the imagination, that dance hall of love. No playground or rec room, no nightclub or fun house. Consecrate as confessional, the priests came there, marriages were performed, girls confirmed, classes graduated.

I saw it first in the daytime when it had that odd, off-season calm of deserted amusement parks, unoccupied classrooms, restaurants with the chairs bottom up on the tables, all the wound-down feel of an energy absent or gone off to catch different trains. Maybe I was moving a piano. (This was what I knew of the high life, my stage door connection to the extraordinary, who brought cargoes of sand to the carpeted shores of the country clubs and filled the deep ashtrays there. George Mills, high placed as a head waiter, situate as a man in an honor guard. George Mills, the Velvet Rope Kid.) Or buffing the dance floor. Or installing the Coke machine. It was darker in the morning than it would have been at night, the windowless room cool as a palace. The manager gave me two passes. "Here," he said. "Bring your girl."

I went the following Saturday, who not only had no girl but who had never danced, whose music—the tuner on my little Philco was busted, the dial stuck just off key of a station that broadcast the Browns games, so that the play-by-play seemed to occur in a shrill wind, the star-of-the-game interview overseas—was mostly whatever people happened to be whistling, the pop tunes reaching me downwind, degraded, in a sort of translation, the melodies flattened, the high notes clipped. But I was twenty-seven years old, my Sunday mornings squandered in playgrounds with "the men," those imaginary big brothers of my heart. I didn't even own a suit. (And what *did* I own? Not my furniture, not my knives and dishes, not my sheets and pillowslips. I think I had bought—let's see—a shovel, a hammer, a tape measure and hand saw, my fielder's mitt of course, my baggy baseball pants and spiked shoes, my cap and my T-shirt, a Louisville Slugger, a sixteen-inch softball. Even the Philco was furnished. I honestly can't think of anything else. Yeah, the mismatched clothes in my drawers and closets.)

I went to Famous and Barr to be outfitted for my free passes, and when the salesman in Men's Furnishings asked if he could help me I think I told him just that, that it was for the free passes I'd come, to be outfitted, done up like the box steppers in the Delgado Ballroom. I didn't even understand about alterations, you see, and thought the trousers and jackets he had me try on cut for bigger, taller men. "I can't buy this," I told him, glancing at myself in the three-paneled mirror (and the first time, too, I had seen myself in profile, in holograph, maybe the first time I understood I had sides, a back). "I already told you it was for dancing. I'd trip on the whaddayacall'em, the cuffs."

The tailor told me I could pick the suit up Thursday. (And that was something, I tell you, the dapper Italian with pins in his mouth, chalking my crotch. "Stand still," he demanded. And the century's squirming, woebegone hick replied, "I can't, I can't.") "But I need it tonight. Tonight is the dance."

"Tonight? Tonight is impossible. On Special Rush maybe late Wednesday morning. Wear something else."

And I had to tell him I had nothing else, only my work clothes, only my work boots, only my softball gear, only my cleats. Only not entirely the hick. The hick is without my margin of peremptory foreboding, my self-serving ingenuousness. He does not throw himself so easily on the mercy of the court.

"It's for tonight, you see. The dance at the Delgado. The manager invited me. He said to bring a girl. I could meet one. I don't own the right clothes."

"Hey, Albert," the tailor said.

"Yeah, Sal?" said the salesman.

"Thirty-two years in the business and Cinderella here thinks I look like a fairy godmother."

"You going to fix him up, Sal?"

"What the hell, Albert, I'm going to put it on Super Special Crash Rush and see to the alterations personally."

"That's wonderful, Sal. I know my customer appreciates that."

"Thank you," I said. "I want to thank you."

I sat on the little bench in the tiny dressing room two hours, my curtain open to the weather of the other customers, men with wardrobes, with three and four and five suits in their closets, with dressy slacks and sports coats, with—I didn't know this then—tropical-weight worsteds for the warm seasons, heavy tweeds for the cold, who examined themselves imperially in the glass and spoke without looking at them to the salesmen at parade rest behind their backs, scrutinizing the mirror close as shavers or people examining blemishes in a good light. They talked knowledgeably about buttons, the slant of a pocket, the cut of lapels, and I, alien as a savage, listened greedily. I couldn't have been more interested if they had been women.

"Hey," Sal said, when he came down to check a customer's measurements, "it's going to be a while yet. You don't have to hang around here. Walk around the store."

"I'm all right. This is fine."

"Buy your shoes," Sal said. "Buy your shirt, buy your tie."

"That's right," I said. "I forgot." I stood up.

"Tell the shoe man a brown oxford."

"A brown oxford. Yes."

"Maybe a tan shirt with a thin stripe. A dark, solid-color tie, no pattern. If there's a pattern it should be delicate, no heavier than the stripe on your shirt."

"Thank you," I said.

"You got a decent leather belt? Something the color of new shoe soles, I think, but stay away from oxblood."

"All right," I said, "thank you."

"Stockings," he called after me. "Black. Knee length."

It is perhaps the first time he has ever really examined himself in the glass. Looking for blemish, sorting rash, feature, the inventory of surface, the lay of the skull. He sees with wonder the topography of his hair, the evidence of his arms beneath his suit coat, the hinged and heavy wrists. He leans forward and splays his lips, stares at the long teeth, touches them. Before, if he has looked in the mirror, it has been with the shy, cursory glance of a customer into a barber's glass, that automatic, that mechanical.

I was no *virgin,* you understand.

His sexual encounters had been in bars, low dives, his conquests drunk, mostly older, fumbling his cock in the alley, blowing him in cars, deeply, deeply, smothering his foreskin on their sore throats, scratching it on dentures. Hoarsely they had moaned, called out

258

someone else's name. Or come to them always in *their* beds, in cold rooms, in badly furnished apartments above beauty parlors. So that he believed, vaguely, that females had regulated intervals of abstinence, cycles of seasonal rut, their need encoded, driven by the calendar, the tides, the moon, by floundering glands, secret biological constants. (He stayed away from whores not because he believed their need was shammed but because he believed they had no need, that their natures had been torn from them, that their cunts were quite literally holes, hair and flesh covering nothing, like houses built on the edges of cliffs. He thought of them as amputees. He did not go with whores.)

[I did not *go* with anyone. When I wanted a woman I knew where to find her. Those bars. Maybe once a month I'd leave my neighborhood and take the bus north or south, get off somewhere in the city I had never been and find a tavern, and usually it was the only place with the lights still on, settled among the frame houses and dark apartment buildings—bowling alleys too, the lounges there, those Eleventh Frames, Lovers' Lanes, Spare Rooms and Gutter Bowls near the pinball arcades and shoe rentals—so that I always had the impression I had come to the country. I didn't waste time. I ordered my beer, showed them my money—I didn't have a wallet; in those days I carried my cash in my pay envelope—and looked around, smiling not broadly so much as inconclusively. If I saw a woman put money in the jukebox I listened to hear what songs she'd picked and I played them too, leaning backward or forward when the music came on, waiting to catch her eye, raising my glass to her, toasting our taste. Almost always she smiled. I took my beer and moved down the bar toward her. If the stool next to hers was empty I sat down. I'd read the label on her beer and signal the bartender to bring us another round, talking all the time, not lying, you understand, but this wasn't conversation either, telling my name and where I worked, the position I played, other things about me, all I could think of who didn't know what my hair looked like or what were my strong points or the condition of my teeth, and never asked anything about her unless it was what she was drinking if it wasn't beer or something I recognized, the difficulty being finding things to say after I'd told her my name, what I did for a living, where I was from, conversationed no better than a candidate, some pol at a gate when the shifts change, but talking anyway, having to, the distracting spiel of a magician, say, the cardsharp's chatter, friendly, open, frank for a man in work shirts, boots, but steering clear, too, of questions and promptings and preemptive reference, not rude or aggrandizing but shy for *her,* modest for the lady, in charge only through consideration, a ricochet restraint, the billiard relationships and carom closures and retreats tricky as dance steps. Because I figured we both knew what was what, who, one of us at least, knew nothing. And assumed she assumed I would not mention it, her presence a matter of course, the body's will, some compulsion of the skin, shame's innings and lust's licks, as if, were I to permit her the edgewise word that word would be a groan, a speech from heat, not conversation either, as if the both of us were mutes, but the driven diction of desire, I more than hinting she had gotten there as I had, on a bus, come in a car from some distant neighborhood, as much the stranger in those parts as myself. And where, I wonder, did those gestures come from, that silent toast, that almost knowledgeable little bow of deference and tribute, that polite, bar-length greeting, romantic, so close to civilized? How would I have learned these signs who had learned nothing? Not my profile, not my air. But deferential, always deferential, as deferential to her hormones as a gent to disfigurement or some grand-mannered guy to handicap, deferentially drilling her with my attentive small talk, clocking the parameters of her drunkenness all the way to its critical mass. Like a scientist, like a coach, like a doc at the ringside, gauging, appraising and contemplative, only then stepping in, cool as a cop: "That's enough, don't you think so? Look, you're beginning to cry. Listen how shrill you've become. You don't want to throw up, do you? You don't want to pass out. Where are your car keys, where is your purse? Is that your coat? Did you come with a hat? Splash water on your face, go relieve yourself first. Beer, pee and estrogen. That's a tricky combination. The beer's in the pee. The pee floods the estrogen. Go on, go ahead, I'll wait." And damned if she didn't. Do as I say. And grateful as well. As if I'd actually helped her. So that by the time I had her skirt up, her brassiere down, lowered her corset, raised her slip, sucked the garters, kissed the hose, and had the cups of her bra loose on her belly or awry at her side, she was actually watching, amazed as myself at her condition, convinced by her gamy, ribald chemistries, struck by what was neither rape nor love but only my simple, driven confidence, a kind of carnal transfusion, sexual first aid and the terrible blunt liberties of emergency, averting her eyes not even when she came, her moans and cries and whines and whimpers and skirls of orgasm a sort of breathless yodel, Baby Shameless beneath this fellow like some heavy lifter or love's day laborer who did all the work and insinuated knees, fingers, hands, lips, mouth, tongue, teeth and cock too at last, not as weapons—as little seduction as rape—and not even as parts, members, but as tools, the paramedical instrumentality of the available—as if I lived off the land, made do like a commando—so that only when *I* came did she avert her eyes, blink, as if only then I had exceeded my warrants, behaved less than professionally. But reassured the next moment by my withdrawal, suddenly thoughtful, charmed and sad. "Oh, say," she'd say, "where'd you learn to do a girl like that? That was really something. *Really* something. You know I never . . . I didn't frighten you, did I? When I made those sounds? Did I? Tell the truth, were you embarrassed? Honest, I never . . . It was like someone else's voice. I swear it. It was like someone's voice I've never heard. I never *have* heard it. I didn't know I even knew those noises, words." I all skeptical reassurance, muzzling my doubts as till the last minute I had muzzled my lust, as accomplished a dresser in the dark back seats of cars or on the damp sheets of those strange beds as undresser, saying: "Oh, hey, listen, that's okay. That was only nature. You mustn't mind what Mother Nature says. You're not to blame—here's your stocking—you couldn't help it. Don't you think I know that much? Sure. Anyway, it was your glands talking, only your guts' opinions, just some tripe from the marrow. You think I pay *that* any mind? That I listen to endocrines? Women *do* that stuff when they get excited. They're not in control. I know *that* much. It was just Nature and your ducts' low notions. *Hey* now, cheer up. Do I look like the kind of guy who sets store in a fart? Here's your earring. It must have slipped out when you were thrashing around like that."]

As he believed, again vaguely, in virgins. Not—he was no prude —in their moral superiority. Not in some special quality they possessed which their fallen sisters—not even, particularly, in the fall of those sisters—lacked. Not in their fitness as brides or suitability as girl friends, not in their congenial apposition to grace and tone or in their conformity to a grand convention. Not, in fact, in anything petite or chaste or delicate, prudent, pure, virtuous, discreet or even modest. In virginity, in virginity itself, in its simple mechanical cause. He believed, that is, in the hymen. In the membrane, that, he took it, air- and watertight occlusive seal like cellophane on a pack of cigarettes or the metal cap on a soda bottle that somehow shored for as long as it was still in place all the juices of need, all the sexual solutions, that endocrinous drip drip and concupiscent leak which he so expertly stanched in cars and plugged in those furnished rooms.

And just as he shied away from the whores, he shied away from the virgins, and for much the same reason—— that they had no needs. They were too much trouble. They would take seduction, courtship, the long, difficult ploy of friendship.

[What was the point? How could I deal with someone who did not mean to be dealt with? Did I have beer money and bus fare to burn on women and girls who had an existence aloof and outside the terms of my desires? If I did not think of them as incorruptible then I thought of them as indifferent, people outside my sphere of influence. I might as well have had conversations with ladies whose language was French, who could not understand my English, who may not even have heard it.]

Which explains why, at twenty-seven, George Mills, who'd had his ashes hauled as often as he'd felt the urgency, who'd been blown, whose flesh and buttocks had been chewed and clutched, whose back and backside raked in wanton, dissipate zest, why George Mills, bruised by delight and all the hijinks of high feeling, had never so much as kissed a maiden. It was that membrane, that cherry like some mythic grail or fortified fastness, which kept him off, not so much at bay as at home, like some frail, stiff, awkward peasant mowing in a field who sees the battlement, the walled, high, thick and ancient parapet and, behind the casement, the oppressor himself, say, taking the sun on the bulwark's broad and open deck, defenseless, alone, who looks once, shrugs, and embraces the hay, the infested, heavy bales, to shove them about with his last declining energies.

[It was the two free passes.]

He wasn't shy around these women, any more than one is shy around furniture—— tables, chairs. He wasn't overly modest or unassuming. (He had his assumptions.) It was that in their presence—the presence of virgins—he had some genuine gift for the revoked self, a redskin caution, an anonymity reasonable as a good alibi. It was only afterward that a teammate ever remembered that he had failed to introduce George to his girl's friend, her roommate, a cousin in town on a visit. The roommate or cousin would not even have noted this much. On a streetcar or bus, in a private automobile going back to the neighborhood after a game in the park, he could sit thigh to thigh beside the strange girl without contact, his skin as nerveless as his clothing.

[I figured why bother, and made myself as indifferent as I supposed her to be. I looked out the window. I watched for my stop.]

He might have gone on this way forever.

[It was the two free passes, at two bucks apiece the sixteen bottles of beer they represented, which, if you figure the woman in that tavern was already on her second bottle by the time I put my coin in the jukebox to play her song, and when you remember that I nursed mine —someone had to drive, someone had to stay sober enough to take responsibility for my erection—often drinking only one to her three or, if I ordered a pitcher, maybe glass and a half to her four, and if you add to the equation the fact that she rarely drank more than seven bottles, two of which she'd paid for herself, and usually not more than five or six, three or four of them on me, then the two passes stood for two to three women successfully courted, successfully wooed. I'm not mean. Money doesn't move me. I'm talking about effort, all that waiting at bus stops, listening to songs played over and again again that I hadn't liked the first time, all those strained and jumpy monologues, the patient stints at their bodies, watched as boilers, supervised as machinery. So it was the two and a half months I was thinking of —I'm a working man, I punch time clocks, I'm paid by the hour— when I made the connection between the two free passes and the trio of women. It wasn't the money. A fifth of my working year. It wasn't the money. Didn't I spring for new clothes? Didn't I pop for accessories? And it wasn't any investment I was seeking to protect when I bought them. The poor aren't cheap, there'd been no investment. "Bring your girl," the manager said and gave me free passes. So it wasn't the money and I had no girl. Hell, maybe it was the manager's investment I was protecting. Though I still think it was the effort, that I suddenly saw all the man-hours and elbow grease that just those beers and bus rides entailed.]

Stan David was the orchestra leader at the Delgado Ballroom. David's was a regional band, almost a municipal one. They played at proms and weddings and, during the week, at the Delgado. They cut no records but had been often on the air. Theirs was the studio band for the local Mutual radio station, and they had been heard behind the victory celebrations in the ballrooms of many downtown hotels a few hours after the polls closed on election days.

David was a small man, prematurely gray and responsible-looking. He looked more like the orchestra's business manager than its conductor and, when he sat down at the piano to lead his band, he somehow seemed someone from the audience, the father of the bride, say, or the high school's principal being a good sport. Indeed, he'd joked with the man who'd hired him for the Delgado and who'd commented on the fact that Stan wasn't dressed like the other players. "I know this town. It's a conservative town. I'm as much a master of ceremonies as a musician. These people will take more from a gray-headed guy in a business suit than they would from some boob in a yellow show biz tux."

On the Saturday night of George Mills's free passes it was not yet an orchestra when Mills walked in. Unaugmented by strings or woodwinds, it was barely a band. They were still setting up.

George glanced at the small group, at their odd displacement on the commodious bandstand, at the gap, greater, Mills judged, than the distance between home plate and pitcher's mound, between the trumpet and the drummer. He looked at the arrangement of the vacant, freestanding, streamlined music stands like big phonograph speakers, at the sequin flourish of their initials.

Gradually the band fleshed itself out, but the dance floor seemed as unoccupied as the bandstand had, the handful of couples dancing there as reluctant to move next to each other as the musicians. They swayed skittishly to the temperate brass, the long, queer beat of the piano.

George is aware of his new clothes, the creamy fabrics like an aura of haberdash, a particular pocket like a badge of fashion, the vaguely heraldic suggestion of his collar, his lapels like laurels, his cuffs like luck. He strolls across the dance floor and, absorbed in all the flying colors of his style, already it is like dancing. He moves in the paintbox atmospherics of the big glowing room, the polished cosmetics of light.

Chiefly he is aware of his shoes, his elegant socks, his smooth, lubricate soles like the texture of playing cards. Always before the earth has resisted, stymied his feet, and he has walked in gravity as in so much mud. There has always been this layer of friction, of grit. Now he moves across glass, ice, the hard, flawless surface of the dance floor packed as snow. He feels swell.

Stan David, his voice augmented by saxophones and clarinets, by drums and bass, calls the room to attention. He is neither seductive nor peremptory but matter-of-fact as someone returned from an errand. He breaks into their mood seamlessly. "The boys and I are awful glad to be playing for you folks tonight. It's an inportant date for us because it's the first time Mr. Lodt has asked us to do a Saturday night at the Delgado, so first off we want to thank those old friends who've so loyally supported our week-night appearances and who Mr. Lodt tells us have been requesting our engagement for the big one."

Most of the people applaud Stan David's announcement. George, on the strength of his good mood, applauds too.

"Well, thank you," Stan David says, "thank you much. God bless you all." He turns momentarily to the band and brings the song they've been playing to a conclusion. It is, George guesses, their theme song, though he does not recognize the melody. Immediately they begin another, softer, slower, as unfamiliar. "While we were jamming," Stan says turning back to them, "I noticed a few unfamiliar faces in the room, a few new friends, I hope, I hope." There is additional, louder applause for David's familiar tag line.

"You know, it's funny, the lads and I have been doing gigs in this town since almost just after the war and, you have my word, I never forget a dancer. If a couple comes by the bandstand and I happen to spot them I have their style forever. I can recall all the different partners they dance with and know even the kinds of songs they sit out. That's what our music's all about, you see—— dancing. That's our bread and butter, that's what pays the rent. If just listening to music is what you prefer, better get yourself a high hat and a box at the opera. Buy records, a radio, tickets to concerts. Go with the highbrows when the symphony plays. That goes for the chaperones, that goes for the shy. Mr. Lodt thinks so too. He doesn't want any wallflowers blocking his fire exits. We don't get paid for our fancy solos and hotsy-totsy musicianship. It ain't Juilliard here, it's a dance hall. Now it's a big floor . . . What's that Mr. Lodt? Right. Square foot for square foot the biggest in the Midwest. So there's no need to bump into anyone. We want you to enjoy yourselves but expect you to behave at all times according to the international rules of ballroom etiquette. If you've come to show off or act like a rowdy you might just as well leave right now, I hope, I hope.

"Okay? Okay. Now, you gals who are here for the first time, who came with your girl friends to see what it's like, it's a scientific fact, it takes forty-eight muscles to frown and only half a dozen to smile.

You guys remember that, too. But *everybody* pay attention—— we might just be playing your song when you fall in love!"

George has seen the bar, more like a soda fountain than a bar, more—though he has no firsthand experience of this—like the sinks and Coke cupboards in rec rooms, finished basements. He has a forlorn sense of other people's families, of uncles and dads in sports shirts, of daughters who babysit one and two years after they have graduated high school, a notion of these girls in baby doll pajamas, rollers, furry slippers, of brothers called out for swim practice, track, even during vacation. They run punishment laps.

But it is the girls who choke his spirit, the peerless globes of their behinds full as geometry, their breasts scentless as health. He imagines their lingerie, the white cotton average as laundry. He knows there are virgins about, feels the concentrated weight of their incurious apathy, their inert, deadpan, ho-hum hearts. And is oppressed by obstacle, the insurmountability of things.

Yet he knows that it is only through some such girl—he hasn't seen her yet, has merely glimpsed her type gossiping over a soft drink, or dancing with a young man or another girl, not heedless so much as inattentive, not wanton, even when her partner tentatively divides her thighs with his leg, so much as absolved, locked into a higher modesty—that he may begin his life, be freed from the peculiar celibacy that has marked it, his periodic, furious bachelor passions like seizures. But he has seen the beerless, liquorless bar who till now has only wooed with chemicals the chemically primed. There is no jukebox. How may he cope? He is ready to leave. And is actually walking toward the exit and past the gilt chairs that line the margins of the dance floor when Stan David speaks.

"Girls ask the boys to dance. Girls ask the boys to dance. Step up to some fellow, girls, and invite him to dance."

"You want to dance?" Louise asks him.

"Me?"

"Stan says."

"Sure. I guess. I'm not much of a dancer."

"It's a box step."

"Oh, a box step."

"You can do a box step, can't you?"

"Is this a box step?"

"That's right. You've got it."

"Like this?"

"You've got it."

266

"I'm dancing," George says.

"Louise Mead," Louise says.

"George Mills."

"Mrs. Louise Mills. Mrs. George Mills. George and Louise Mills."

"What?"

"Oh," she laughs, "you're not from around here. When a girl tells a boy her name and the boy tells his, the girl gets to say what her name would be if the girl and the boy were married."

"I'm not really a boy."

"What a thing to say!"

"I mean I'm twenty-seven years old."

"An older man," Louise says. "You're an older man."

"That depends," he says, pleased with his response.

"I'm nineteen," she says, and he has a sense that things are going well. He's following the conversation and doing the box step. The song —Stan David and his orchestra are playing "Getting To Know You" —has been going on for almost seven minutes.

"Did you come with someone, George?"

"No. Did you?"

"That's for me to know and you to find out."

"Oh."

"Do you think I did?"

"I don't know."

"That's not very flattering. It's Saturday night. I'm nineteen years old. Do you think I'd come to a place like this by myself?"

"I guess not," George says.

"It's still the same song," Stan David says. "It's still girls ask the boys, and it's still the same song."

"I love your togs," Louise says.

"My togs?"

"Your clothes, silly."

"They're brand new. They're brand new togs."

"The boys and I just might play this song right to the end of the set. We might play it all evening. Does this tell you something about the human heart? Anybody can fall in love with anybody if they stand close enough long enough."

"He always says that."

"Did you know about this? Did you know there'd be girls ask the boys?"

"What if I did?"

267

"I don't know."

"Do you want to sit down, George?"

"If you do."

"I'm by myself," she says, and lays her head on his shoulder. "I came with my folks."

The cat has his tongue. In a bowling alley, in a bar, she would have had the story of his life by now, the comfort of his theories, but like this, in the dim room, a virgin in his arms, their bodies' curves and hollows adjusted by the dance, customized by music as by tailoring, he has no words, is adrift in a soup of contrary sensations. He is that self-conscious. He wants to kiss her. But knows that if he does —she is with her folks; where are they?—it would be a declaration helpless and humiliating as the raw need of those chemical-flooded ladies to whom he's ministered, revealing as a stump. He feels his erection, which he manages to keep out of her way, and glances furtively at the pants of the other male dancers to see if he's out of line. He is astonished. There are erections everywhere. It's a logjam of hard-ons.

"Why'd you ask if I knew Mr. David was going to make the girls ask the boys?"

"I don't know."

"Was it because you thought I'd been watching you? Is that the reason, Mr. Stuck-Up?"

"No."

The lights in the room are turned up and George can hear laughter, whistles, catcalls, bursts of applause. It's the people on the golden chairs. They are appraising the swollen crotches of the men. The ballroom has exploded with laughter. The drummer peppers the hall with rim shots, great percussive booms. "All right, all right," Stan David says, "let's have some order here," and the music sweetens, the lights dim. "Hey," he says when the dancers have reestablished themselves with the dance music, "you like this, don't you? Sure. We do all the work, background your courting like music in a movie, and you get the glory. Bet you'd like us around always. Be there in the trunk of the car playing your song. Hanging just out of sight, crouched behind bushes while you're kissing good night. Or strung out on rooftops lining your way when you walk your girl home. Some nerve. Some nerve I say. Change partners! Go on, change partners or we quit playing. ——All right. I warned you. You can't say I didn't warn you. Lads?"

The music seems snagged, caught on the baton David jabs into the midst of the orchestra. A clarinet breaks off, a saxophone. The drummer quits in mid-phrase. Stan David snaps his baton in two like a pencil. The bass man leans his instrument against the proscenium, takes a folded newspaper out of his back pocket and sits in a chair to read it. Piecemeal, they wind down, the music thins, is gone.

"Come on, will you!" a voice calls from the dance floor. "Strike up the band!"

The bandleader shuts the piano lid. He turns on his bench and folds his arms.

A few of the dancers begin to hoot. It's as if the film has gone out of synch in a movie house and they are whistling the attention of the projectionist.

"Nope," Stan David says, "nope."

"Come on, Stan. Play, for chrissake."

They start to clap.

Lodt has climbed up on the stage to confer with Stan David. The bandleader shakes his head. Lodt turns to the crowd and shrugs.

George grins at Louise. "It's part of the show. Is it part of the show?" George asks the nineteen-year-old girl.

"He's really angry," Lodt tells the crowd.

"Make him play or give us our money back."

"I asked him," Lodt says. "You all saw me."

"Make him play."

"He's the bandleader," Lodt says. "He's like the captain of a ship. He's in charge. He could marry you legal."

Louise squeezes George's hand. She is the one who has taken it. As soon as the music stopped George had let go, had taken his arm from about her waist.

"Come on," someone shouts, "what do you think this is? Don't jerk us around. We're veterans here."

"You're veterans?" Stan David calls back. "Veterans? Oh, if you're *veterans,*" he says in mock conciliation, and produces a new baton and gives a downbeat. The band strikes up a march tune and the veterans groan.

"I think it's part of the show," George Mills says.

The march is concluded. The trumpet sounds retreat. Stan David plays the national anthem on the piano.

Many of the dancers have lost their partners, couples walk off the dance floor together, a few wallflowers drift off by themselves. George Mills tags along beside Louise. It's as if he had come with her. She introduces him to her friends, to a girl named Carol, to another named

269

Sue. He meets Bernadette and her husband Ray. He meets the Olivers, Charles and Ruth. Ellen Rose and Herb, her fiancé. And this is something new to him from ordinary life. He can't recall when he's met so many people at one time. Or himself been formally introduced. When he was a child perhaps. Vaguely he remembers comments about his growth or the similarities of certain of his features to those of his father. He half expects these people to offer a remark about his eyes or smile, and though he realizes he is no longer tall for his age he would be more comfortable if they took note of his height or remarked upon some other aspect of his physical appearance. It is something to which he could respond, as he must have done in the past, smiling shyly or agreeably nodding. As it is he has no repertoire, is actually uncertain how to reply when someone says "Pleased to meet you, George." He answers "Pleased to meet you, too," but it sounds flat to him, foolish. He is uneasy among all these virgins—Louise, her girl friends—uneasy with her pals, the young marrieds. With Ruth Oliver, visibly pregnant, with Bernadette, who does not yet show in her fourth month.

"Yes," Charles Oliver tells him when they shake hands, "I saw you dancing with Lulu," and George feels himself blush.

Meanwhile Stan David has begun to play for them again. From time to time George thinks he recognizes a song he has played on the jukeboxes in the bars, and again he feels himself blush. He's mildly afraid Louise will notice his embarrassment but knows she could never guess its source. The men would understand of course, Charles and Herb and Ray, and though they are four and five years younger than he, there could have been times before they'd ever met their wives when they too had been at the mercy of glands, their willful and whimsical insides, their rude juices.

"My friends like you," Louise whispers in his ear when they are on the dance floor again.

He wishes she wouldn't do this. He wishes to be in control of his body. Breath in his ear does things to him. He knows how reckless he has become, his polite analyses forgotten, his calm science, when even slatterns in bars have brushed his ear with their lips.

"Change partners," Stan David says ominously. The band-leader's words are a kind of fatality, a soft force as threatening to mood as an announcement of war or a train conductor's no-nonsense "All aboard."

"Damn," George says, and Louise smiles. Somehow she takes the measure of the music, absorbs its implications and impulses, the secret energies of the song, and takes them into her body, changing not partners but patterns, by some subtle shift of weight signaling George to follow, to come with her, and it's as if they're hiding in the melody, dancing counterclockwise, their gait disguised, their bodies subsumed within some more anonymous shape. Their form throws off detail, thickens to silhouette, and George feels invisible.

"You just won't listen, will you?" Stan David says sadly.

But Mills would be content if the dancing were done with altogether. They have been with each other almost an hour. For almost half that time she's been in his arms. They have spoken perhaps two dozen sentences to each other, and if she is friendly he knows it is just the good will of her optimism, the unmarked chemicals of innocence pure as fruit juice in her virgin's blood. She cannot know that a smile is the leading edge of seduction, that the warmth of her body cannot be stored, that contact with a man releases it as energy, that the energy fragments and beads like moisture when it touches the surface of his skin, that the beads penetrate the follicles where the hairs grow on the backs of his hands and along his arms and the nape of his neck, and sink to the nerve endings to travel the synapses to his genitals and suffuse his body with what in other men is the patient will of courtship but which, in him, is degraded, only low lust. It is this lust which thickens his speech, which turns him clumsy during introductions and blunts the strategies of wooing—are his togs too tight? do his arms thrust from his sleeves?—and bewilders his bones and staggers his box step.

"Because you're too young," Stan David says while the band plays on. "Because you think you know it all, and you don't know anything. My God," he says, "just look at the slave bracelets and school rings and fraternity pins twinkling in here. You'd think it was the midsummer night's sky, another solar system. Those are the fairy lights of crush and puppy love. You think you know what it leads to. You don't. You're in the dark about this stuff. Is it vine-covered cottage in your guts? It's the projects. Is it moon and June? It's a high of thirty, a low of twelve. It's all glum drizzle and the engine won't turn over in the street and the kid's spitting up and there's maybe two eggs in the house and a heel of stale bread. The zip's gone out of the three ounces of open Coke standing in the fridge and your nose is running and your throat is sore.

"Sometimes I think maybe me and the guys are in the wrong business. We're ruining lives here, confusing you with bad signals.

Excuse me, Mr. L., but I've got to say what's on my mind. It would trouble my conscience as a musician if I didn't.

"Most bandleaders—Mr. Lodt can correct me if I'm wide of the mark—most bandleaders tell you you're playing for keeps. Heck, it's what the songs themselves say. That every love's true, till the end of time guaranteed. You can keep track of it on the 18-karat gold watch, the 17-jewel movement. But figure it out. Stop to consider. How could it be? This is stuff you should have learned in the home. It ain't something you should have to hear from a bandleader. You're young. Get some experience under your belt. Don't be so serious, play the field, there's other fish in the sea. Have some fun, please.

"*Change partners!*

"—The theme from *Moulin Rouge,* ladies and gentlemen."

George is the first to let go. He pushes off from Louise as if it were a maneuver in water. Louise reaches out for him. "It's part of the show," she says.

"No," George says.

"If you cut in on anyone right now you'd be laughed right out of the Delgado. Or get punched if the fellow isn't in on the joke. It's part of the show, I tell you. He does that to instigate. *It's part of the show!*"

"You don't know, Louise."

"Sure I know," she says. "Sure I do."

"I mean you don't know what's up. You don't know what's what."

"He's got his eye on you. Can't you see that? He's smirking at you, just waiting to see if you're going to cut in on somebody."

"I'm not going to cut in on anyone. I haven't got the patience for this stuff, Louise. You're a nice person but I haven't got the patience for this stuff." Suddenly he is trying to tell her why. They are dancing again. She has brought this about by falling forward on him. She is leaning on him with all her weight and he staggers into a kind of tango. He is trying to tell her why.

"*Haven't you ever been in a nightclub?*" she asks forcefully. "Weren't you ever in a nightclub and the comedian sees someone who has to go to the washroom and then he singles that person out and him and all the guys in the band and even the people in the audience sing 'We know where you're going, We know where you're going'? *Haven't you ever been in a nightclub?*"

"No," George says, "never. I was never in a nightclub."

"It's part of the show. It's all part of the show."

Everything is part of the show, George thinks.

[Maybe everything was part of the show, I thought.]

["Maybe we ought to sit down," Louise says.]

[I was this musical comedy lout, an oaf of vaudeville, the hick from history. But was Louise any better? Virgins were a sort of lout, too, I thought. Oafs of the ovulate, hicks of hemorrhage. I should have told her, "No, sweetheart, I've never been to a nightclub, but I've been in a bar." I should have told her, "No, lady, never in a nightclub. In the back seats of cars. I ain't talking lovers' lanes, some place the cops stake out with their flashlights and warnings. I'm not talking drive-ins or all the clubby, sanctioned green belts of love, fairways and parks and a view of the falls. I'm not talking cozy, I'm not talking snug. Where voices don't carry, the moans muffled. Alleys, vacant lots, rooms the bed ain't made days." I should have told her, "No, sister, but I been where nothing's part of the show, where the calls and rasps, the yelps and barks, the bleats and brays and blatter and whines and grunts, the neighs and howls and cackles and hisses ain't even noise, they're just vocabulary. How ladies talk when they're in a hurry and trying to slip two or three of their fingers, and for all I know maybe the whole damn hand itself, in there with my tool!" I should have asked her outright. "Are you cherry, Louise?"]

Mills tries to explain again how he hasn't the patience or craft, but somehow it seems he is saying how formidable she is. She interrupts him.
"Say, are you married?"
"No. Of course not."
"I'm not Catholic or anything, but are you divorced?"
"No."
Her friends join them. Ellen Rose and Herb think they should all go out afterward for pizza and want to know how the rest of them feel about it.
"I'm trying to watch my figure," Louise says, glancing at Mills.
"Aw, come on, Louise," Herb says, "George'll watch it."
The Olivers want ice cream. Ruth has a yen for a dish of maraschino cherries and whipped cream.
Ray knows the manager of this White Castle who's on duty tonight. "You met him, Bern. Pete McGee."

"Oh, yeah," Bernadette says, narrowing her eyes, remembering. "That guy with the tattoo. He'd be kind of cute if it wasn't for the tattoo. I don't know why guys disfigure themselves like that. Oh. Me and my big mouth. I beg your pardon, sir," she tells George. "You may be tattooed yourself."

"I'm not tattooed."

"Is he Lulu?" Charles Oliver asks, winking.

"I'm sure I wouldn't know." Now Louise is blushing. "No one's asked George what he feels like. What do you feel like, George? Pizza or hamburgers or ice cream?"

"I don't care."

"He's very polite," Ruth Oliver says.

George listens as they make the arrangements. It is the committee work of friends and very complicated. He understands that Herb is to phone ahead and arrange the pizza which he and Ellen Rose will pick up. Ray and Bernadette will see Ray's friend, Pete McGee, about the White Castles, and Ray will try to talk him into taking a break for an hour or so and joining them all at Crown's Ice Cream Kitchen, but Sue will have to talk Carol into coming along as Pete's date.

"What's going to happen to Sue?" George asks, genuinely interested.

"Sue has her car," Ellen Rose explains.

"Sue's a good sport," Louise says.

"Oh God, yes," Ray and Bernadette agree.

"Would you and Louise go down to Crown's and reserve a table for eleven?" Ruth Oliver asks George.

"I don't have a car," George says.

"Twenty-five minutes," Herb says. "I ordered one large plain and one large peperoni with mushroom. And one medium anchovy. I figured that way everyone would be happy. Did I do wrong?"

Ellen Rose tells him he did exactly right.

"I figured everybody'd be happy. This way, people who don't like spicy can have plain. Is George getting us a table for eleven?"

"George doesn't have a car," Ray says gloomily. Two or three of the others look stymied, and it seems to Mills that everything is about to collapse because he has no car.

"How far is this place? Maybe I could walk," he says.

"The pizza is going to be ready in twenty-five minutes," Bernadette says, and though George doesn't understand how this is an objection he knows that it is.

"I don't think I better," Carol says quietly. "Go without me."

"I ordered all that pizza," Herb says.

"You mean you gave them your real name?" Charles Oliver says.

"Hey, I thought it was all set," Herb says defensively.

"Oh Carol, he's the *manager* of the place for gosh sakes," says Sue.

"Sure," Carol says, "the *night* manager."

"It's when they do most of their business, Carol," Charles Oliver tells her. "Isn't that right, Ray?"

"What? Oh. Yeah, absolutely."

"How can he get off then?" Carol asks. "If it's when they do most of their business, how come he can get off for an hour?"

"Well he's the *manager.* I already told you."

"Gee," Carol says, "I don't know. Don't tattoos itch?"

"Do they, George?" Charles asks.

"I'm not tattooed," George Mills says.

"It's just too creepy," Carol says. "Go without me."

"If you're not going *I'm* not going," Sue says resolutely.

"Herb's ordered the pizza," Ellen Rose says. "Two large and a medium in his own name."

"A Sweetheart Dance," Stan David announces. "I'm calling a Sweetheart Dance."

Two thirds of the couples walk off the dance floor.

"It's the Sweetheart Dance, Herb," Ellen Rose says. "We've got twenty minutes to get there."

"We'll dance two minutes and leave in the middle."

"I'll phone for a taxi," George says.

"What for?" asks Ray.

"To take us to Crown's to reserve a table for eleven." He's pleased to have thought of the idea of the cab and wants to make additional arrangements now that he begins to understand not the mechanics, and perhaps not even all the principles, but the theory itself who had entered this community cold, who for the seven years it took him to get from Cassadaga to St. Louis had entered *all* communities cold, like a beggar at the back door, presenting himself at foundling homes, orphanages, and, during the war years, sometimes actually passing himself off as a refugee, who had been born, it may be, with no ear for complication, with no gift for the baroque, but who has begun to see that youth—he himself is already twenty-seven—will try anything, say anything, in order to salvage its plans, which are never plans of course, never goals and their concomitant procedures, but the blatant articulation of whims, the accommodation of which involves the overriding and placation, if that was the order, of other, contrary whims. It is a kind of power, and he has never before felt its urgency, never before wheeled and dealed in the arbitrary.

"You been to Crown's?" Ray asks.

"No."

"It's booths. It's booths and stools at the soda fountain. They got a loose booth they let you move if nobody's in it and you're a party of ten. Pete McGee won't come without Carol, and Sue won't come unless Carol does."

"But Sue's a good sport," George says petulantly.

"Carol said I should go without her. A good sport doesn't do that."

"Your folks!" George says. He is still planning, tuning solution. "Your folks, Louise. That would give us ten."

"I told him I came with my folks," Louise says.

"He's not from around here," Bernadette says.

"Until a girl knows what a fellow's like, George, she tells him she's with her folks," Louise says.

"Louise's folks," Ruth Oliver says, and giggles.

"What's so funny?" her husband asks. "They have a car."

George Mills doesn't understand any of this. He doesn't understand why it's necessary to get the roving booth at Crown's, or why Pete McGee should join them, or why Carol thinks tattoos itch, or what makes Sue such a good sport. All he knows is that the pizzas are burning and that Ellen Rose and Herb, who have returned from the Sweetheart Dance, have made no move to leave. "The pizzas," George says.

"Is everything settled then?" Herb asks.

"Nothing's settled," Ruth Oliver says bitterly. "Not a damn thing."

"The pizzas?" George says again.

"Screw the pizzas," Herb says. "You don't think I gave them my real name, do you? A medium and two *large?* What's the matter with you? You lost? Ain't you from around here?"

"I don't *know* if I'm from around here," George Mills says miserably.

"Herb's the only one with a car," Louise tells him.

George looks up. "What about the Olivers?"

"In the shop," Charles Oliver says.

"Ray?"

"Bernadette's folks went out tonight," Ray says.

He is beginning to understand. "Pete McGee has a car," he says. Ray nods, Bernadette does.

"Pete McGee has a car but he doesn't like to lend it."

"Pete's okay. It isn't broken in yet."

"And he certainly wouldn't let *me* drive it. A total stranger."

"Probably not."

"So I was going to drive Sue's car?"

"Not exactly."

"No," George says, "that's right. Not exactly." It's like being a little drunk, he thinks. There's just that edge. Or no. It's like having the one bottle to their three advantage, the glass-and-a-half to four ratio that accounted for his inspiration in the bars while he was pumping change into the jukebox and his science into their heads and all the while listening to what the song was saying about their lives. "Because you thought all along that I'd have one, a twenty-seven-year-old guy like me. But it was all right even when I didn't. Because the more the merrier. There'd be six in one car and five in the other. That's when I was going to drive Sue's car. We were going to make the switch at Crown's, and Sue would drive Pete McGee's like a good sport. Crown's was just the staging area. The only thing I don't really understand is Sue. No. Wait. Sure I do. Sue's spoken for, right? I mean she's here tonight but she's spoken for. The guy's in the army or off somewhere making his fortune until he can send for her, and they've exchanged pledges, oaths."

"He's in Texas," Sue says. "He's stationed in Texas."

"But just because you're promised and can't have a good time yourself, that doesn't mean you can't hang around those who can. It might even be good for you."

"He's with *his* buddies," Sue says.

"Sure," George Mills says, "sure he is. It was the cars," he says. "It was the cars, it was the cramped quarters. It was the necking in the cars." He stops and looks at them. "But you're married," he says helplessly. "Ruth's pregnant. Louise tells me Bernadette's in her fourth month. Herb is Ellen Rose's fiancé. What do you need this stuff? School's out for you people. You graduated high school. Your diploma hangs on the wall with the prom bids, or's shoved in the drawer with your underwear."

The men look shamefaced. They stare at the buffed tops of their dancing shoes. Ellen Rose picks absently at her corsage. Bernadette and Ruth seem suddenly tired. Only Louise and Carol's energies seem unimpaired, Sue the grass widow's.

"Bernadette's folks are out tonight. Oh," George Mills says, "oh."

Because only now, years after he's moved into it, does he comprehend the stability of the neighborhood. He perceives with horror and the communicated shame of the wives and husbands what he's gotten into here, the force fields of wired intimacy he has somehow penetrated. Discovering, he feels discovered. Like a child rolling Easter eggs on trespassed pitch. He's not from around here, but it's as if he's never lived anywhere else. If he intuits their customs it is done joylessly, with no pride in his cleverness. He has the solution now, of course. To invite them home with him, to open his apartment to their terrible honed occasion, to fetch them pizzas, White Castles, imperial gallons of Crown's ice cream, the syrups and sweet, auxiliary garnish of their ceremonial cravings.

He was right. He was always right. His logic is a Jacob's ladder of successive vista, a nexus of predicative data. The foot bone's connected to the shin bone, the shin bone's connected to the thigh bone, and so on up through all the bones and glands of need and time and loneliness.

Bernadette's folks are out, they've taken the car. But their house has aunts in it, uncles, the busted survivors of their youth.

Because they're only alone with their kind, he thinks. Charles' and Ruth's baby was conceived in an automobile, Bernadette's and Ray's was. I'm sure of it, he thinks. He thinks I'm positive. Sue was driving, he thinks, a godmother and good sport fiddling with her radio dial and hearing their tongues in each other's heads in the back seat and thinking of Texas.

I *haven't* the patience he thinks. It isn't just time. It isn't just effort. There are too many virgins to deal with.

But Louise is smiling at him. They damned near all are.

[Because I was twenty-seven years old before I ever entered the Delgado Ballroom.]

Stan David calls for a Relative Dance with cut-in privileges for anyone of any generation so long as he is blood or connected by marriage. Only George and Louise and a handful of others sit this one out, and soon the room is rocking as parents, sons, wives, sisters, cousins, husbands, in-laws, daughters and brothers seek each other out on the dark, crowded dance floor of the Delgado Ballroom.

He is twenty-seven years old, an age when many scientists have

278

already done their best work. He doesn't understand what he's seeing, he can't give it a name, but, in the spiraling life on the packed floor, George Mills has a vision, and can just make out the shape of a perfect DNA molecule.

7

One morning when George Mills entered Mrs. Glazer's room in the small, private hospital in Juarez to which she had been admitted, the tout, Father Merchant, was already there.

Mrs. Glazer was asleep or unconscious in the hospital bed, her breathing so light it seemed a stage of rest different in kind from anything he had yet witnessed. It was so deep a state of relaxation that it appeared to Mills as if she had just received good news of the highest order. She might just have closed her eyes for a minute. She might have been meditating, or in a trance, or drowned.

George placed his package on the nightstand and sat down.

It was not really her apparent contentment that had caught George up, or the presence of the tout, or even the extraordinarily tidy, shipshape condition of her room. (Which he noticed. Mrs. Glazer had not been a particularly fastidious patient. She wadded Kleenex and dropped it on her bed, the carpet. Though she did not smoke, her ashtrays were always full—— with pins, with sputum, with bits of string. And though she had not gotten dressed in a week, underwear caught in the chest of drawers, stockings lay over chairs, dresses were askew on hangers or visible in the open closet. Sections of the El Paso newspaper, though she barely glanced at it, were everywhere, under the bed, beside the toilet, on top of the television set. There were the peels of tangerines and oranges, fragments of lunch and—he had no idea where these came from—husks of dry chewing gum. The telephone cord was unaccountably tangled, the tuning knob on the radio twisted above or below the frequencies printed on the dial. The faucets dripped. Motel soap lay in the bottom of the basin or wrapped in damp washcloths on the surface of the writing desk or even in the peels of the fruit. It often took Mills the better part of an hour merely to straighten the mess and, by the time he was done, Mrs. Glazer, practically immobile in her wide double bed, had somehow begun the room's piecemeal derangement. It was the same sloven story in the back seat of their rental car.) Today her hospital room seemed immaculate, almost alphabetically arranged.

But it wasn't the condition of the room, or Father Merchant, or Mrs. Glazer's strangely exalted sleep which had startled Mills. It was the current magazines, the box of candy, the potted plant and mint bestsellers on her nightstand.

"What's happened?" Mills asked Father Merchant.

The tout shrugged.

"There's something you don't know?" Mills said. "There's still some circumstance in this world of which you're ignorant?"

"There's nothin' I don' know."

"Where'd she get that candy? What's that stuff?"

"Gif's," the tout said. "Everywhere the ill are made offerin's, Meals. Throughout the worl' presents een sick rooms are an *el grande* part of the gross national produc'. Even disease ees good for business."

"Do you know who brought them?"

"There's nothin' I don' know."

"Has her husband come?"

"Sam's in San Louis," Father Merchant said, "an' won' arrive till later. He have an meetin' *muy importante.* The chairman of the philosophy departments have receive *el* offer *fantastico* from the Universidad de Alabama. Eef Walter leavin' they don' no good logician have. Blauer can't thin' straight. They are approach Gutstein een Hawaii. *Mucho dinero tambien.* Personal I feel he don' come. *Es verdad,* cos' of livin' chipper in Midwes' than the islan's. *Todos* he do to sale his *casa* in Waikiki an replace eet on the mainland two as *grande* he ahead. *Pero* money's no *el problemo.* Eet's Grace. She have art'ritis. I don' thin' she lookin' forward to no bad winter. *There is nothing I do not know!*"

"Hold it down, will you!" George hissed. "You'll wake her. She needs the sleep."

"She's going to die," Father Merchant replied. "She needs all the wakefulness she can get. You should go home, George. You should go back to your wife. Laglichio has work for you. You have been too much with this woman."

"Oh," Mrs. Glazer said, "it's you, Mills. Did Father Merchant tell you? Mary's come with my brother."

"Mary?"

"I thought it would be best," Father Merchant said.

"*You* did? *You* did?" George Mills said.

"Please, Mills," Mrs. Glazer said, "they'll be back soon. We don't want a scene."

And, before he could make one, a girl he recognized and a man he didn't, appeared in the doorway. Mary was even larger than the big girl who had reluctantly admitted him to the house just over a month before. The man was in his mid-fifties and deeply tanned. He wore a tropical-weight suit of a light pearl gray with large, dark brown buttons on the jacket.

"You must be Mills," the brother said. "I'm Harry Claunch. I want you to return my sister's rental car this afternoon. You may borrow mine when you pick my brother-in-law up this evening."

"Yes, sir," Mills said.

"Did you rest, Judith?"

"I feel fine, Harry. Button your blouse please, Mary."

"What's in the bag?" Mary said.

"Oh," George Mills said, "I'm sorry, that's mine."

"Pi-uuu, it stinks," Mary said. "What *is* it anyway? Oh, it's *shrimp*. Mommy, look, did you ever *see* so many shrimp?" She took one of the boiled, cleaned shrimps and bit into it as though it were a chocolate.

"You're eating Mills's lunch, Mary," the brother said.

"There's so *many*. Oh, is this your lunch?"

"That's all right, Miss."

"He calls me Miss."

"There's good protein in shrimp," Father Merchant said.

Mary put the shrimp down and took up her mother's TV remote control panel. She flipped rapidly from station to station.

"Mary, *please,*" her mother said, "people are trying to have a conversation."

"Oh, it's 'Bugs Bunny' in Spanish!" She turned to Father Merchant. "Do you get 'The Flintstones' in Spanish?"

"Three o'clock. Channel 2."

"They get 'The Flintstones' in Spanish. Do you get Johnny Carson in Spanish? 'Laverne and Shirley'?"

"Turn that off. Button your blouse."

"Mom, it's so *hot.*"

"Would you like to go for a swim?" her uncle asked. "Do you want Mills to drive you back to the hotel?"

"Could I Mom? Could I?"

"Oh, Mary," Mrs. Glazer said mournfully, "you didn't bring a bathing suit, did you? Did you bring a bathing suit to Mexico? You did, didn't you?"

"You never opened my candy," Mary said.

"Your mother doesn't feel like any candy, honey," her uncle said. "But *you* open it. Pass it around."

"I'll take one, Mary," Mrs. Glazer said.

"Which? A caramel or a nut? Here's a chocolate-covered cherry. Which do you want?"

"Have the chocolate straw, *señora.* No no, the *dark* chocolate."

The child sat on the side of her mother's bed and kissed her. She put her arms about Mrs. Glazer and hugged her roughly.

"Mary," her Uncle Harry said, "let Mother rest for a bit."

"I want my hair brushed," Mary said. "I want Mom to brush my hair."

"Mary!" her uncle said.

"That's all right, Harry, I want to."

"I shouldn't have brought her," Harry told Father Merchant.

"If you want me to brush your hair I wish you'd button your blouse."

"Mommy thinks my boobs are too big."

"You have a lovely figure," Mrs. Glazer said.

"Milly's periods have started," Mary said. "She says they didn't but they did. I saw her underwear. She says she has an infection. That child."

"There," her mother said weakly.

"A hundred strokes," Mary said. "That wasn't even fifteen even."

"Mommy's so tired, sweetheart," Mrs. Glazer said.

"It didn't even feel good," Mary said.

"Mommy's weak, sweetheart," Mrs. Glazer said.

"It wasn't even fourteen, it wasn't even nine," she said, and started to cry.

"Take her swimming," Father Merchant said.

Mills looked at Mrs. Glazer's brother.

"I don't know," Mrs. Glazer said. "Why don't you?"

"You think I don't know what's going on," Mary said.

"Of course you do, darling," Mrs. Glazer said. "Of course you do, sweetheart."

"I know what's going on," Mary said. "I read your chart, I know your temperature."

The rule at Harry Claunch's hotel was that guests were not allowed in the pool area unless they were in suitable bathing attire. Mills told them he was not a guest, only Harry Claunch's servant, only Mary's babysitter, but they would not waive their rule for him, so he had to buy a suit in one of the hotel shops. At Mary's insistence he even agreed to let her pick it out for him. A yellow bikini.

"I can't wear that."

"Sure you can," Mary said, "it's the style."

"I can't," Mills said. "I won't."

"Please, Mills," she said. *"Please.* It's *such* a pretty color. *Please."*

"I'm over fifty years old," he said.

"I want to go back to the hospital," Mary said.

"Mrs. Glazer is tired. She needs to rest."

"Take me back."

"I can't do that."

"Now. Take me back now."

"Don't be like that."

"I'll go in a taxi."

"Come on, Mary. Don't be like that."

"You call me Miss."

"Don't be like that, Miss."

"Will you buy the yellow bathing suit?"

"Yeah, sure thing, Miss," Mills said.

He changed in a stall in the men's room. He loaded his genitals into the suit's small pouch, crushed them against his crotch. They seemed more sizable than in street clothes, and he felt like a man in a codpiece, curiously badged, an agreeable power. He had felt this way before, in the locker rooms of plants, naked on his bed. Stripped on examining tables or dressed at close quarters on couches, his erection

284

courting the girls, his shyness suddenly reversed, subsumed in waves, jolts of inexplicable swank.

He carried his underwear rolled in his pants and crossed the lobby. He still wore his shirt. White socks came up his shins and out of his black, unlaced shoes.

Mary treaded water at the deep end of the pool. She ducked her head down and squirted water at him through her braces, wetting his legs. "Ha ha, Miss," George Mills said.

"I'll race you," she said.

"I'm not much of a racer," Mills said. "I wouldn't stand a chance against someone who takes lessons from a swim coach or who's been to summer camp."

"How do you know I have a coach? How do you know I go to camp?"

"Your mother told me."

"Does she talk about me a lot?"

"All the time, Miss."

"As much as my sister Milly?"

"She's mentioned your sister."

"Only mentioned her? Let's race. *Come* on."

"I don't know if I could even swim in a pool. I probably wouldn't stay in the lane."

"I'll spot you. You can have a head start. Come on, get wet." She splashed him.

"Ooh. Oh."

"Then get in the water. Get in or I'll splash you."

"It's cold."

"It's lovely once you're in."

"It's too cold."

"Once you get used to it."

"Well," Mills said uncertainly.

"I'll count to ten."

"I'll take my shoes and socks off."

And George Mills, on a patio chair, crossed his legs, the gesture broad, difficult. He tugged at his unlaced shoes. He rolled his socks down his legs. Spreading his thighs, he leaned over and stuffed his socks into the front of his shoes. He felt a flap of testicle against his thigh and looked up. Mary was watching him.

"I've seen balls before," she said.

"Have you?"

"Sure, lots of times. My daddy's and uncle's. I'm on the swim

285

team. I've seen my coach's. I think they're ridiculous. Big old hairy prunes. Anyway, I go steady. Don't they hurt when you sit on them?"

"That doesn't happen."

"No?"

"Mother Nature keeps them out of the way, Miss."

"Boobs don't hurt either. Well sometimes they do. Before my period they can get pretty sore."

"Hmn," George Mills said.

"Are you coming in or aren't you? What did you mean you don't know if you can swim in a pool?"

"The poor don't know much about swimming pools. The schools didn't have them when I was a boy."

"Where did you swim?"

"Off piers. In ponds. In bodies of water where bait shops are found."

"Didn't you ever go to the beach?"

"We went there on Sundays, on Fourths of July. We sat on a blanket, we drank beer from a keg. We swam always in waters that were bad for our strokes."

"Come in," she said, "we don't have to race."

"I've a stroke like a nigger. I flounder, I thrash."

"That's mean, Mills. That's wicked to say."

"Black people are afraid of the water," George Mills said. "Poor people are."

"Wait," she said, "I'll come out." She swam to the side of the pool where George Mills was sitting and placed her hands on the coping. Using only her arms, she hoisted herself out of the water easily. "Brr," she said, "it *is* chilly. The air's cooler than the water. Where's my towel? Oh, there it is. Dry me off, Mills."

"Here," George said, "I'll hand it to you."

"*You* dry me," the girl said. She laughed. "A hundred strokes."

"I think you'd better do it yourself, Miss," Mills said.

"I'll let you call me Mary."

"I don't mind calling you Miss." It was true. He didn't.

"You're just scared Uncle Harry will see."

"See what, Miss?"

"Go in, get wet. I'll dry *you* off."

"I'm in a state of grace, Miss," George Mills said so gently that the girl might have thought she was being scolded. But Mills felt no anger. Even the mild, queer authority of maleness he'd felt, the odd thrust of his exhibitionist swagger, had somehow resolved itself, declined, his horsepower manhood gone off. I'm her servant, thought Mills. It's proper she should tease me. There was a compact between them, the ancient, below-stairs displacements and goings on of history's and the world's only two real classes. She was there for his character as, in a way, he was there for hers. And her mother didn't want to die until this child was ready. He knew that if he didn't do something with his loyalty he was lost. So he told her.

"Because," he said, "women always fooled me. Because whatever I thought about women was never what I should have thought.

"I mean their natures. I had this idea about their natures, that there was such a thing as a virgin heart. To this day I'm astonished young ladies let fellows. I'm not talking the sense of the thing. I mean if it makes sense, or even if it's right or wrong. I mean it seemed to me it couldn't happen, not shouldn't, couldn't. That the body itself wouldn't let it. That that's what a body was, being's buffer, a place to hide. Lord, Miss, the things I thought. That marriage wasn't so much a way of two people finding each other as something they did to keep others from finding them, from ever having to do again with anyone else what their bodies weren't strong enough to keep them from doing with each other. To give back sovereignty, you see, even if it was devalued now, like bad dollars or a fixed income. That courtship was impossible, that a fellow's lies and urgencies had to get past the hymen first, that they listen in their cherry, see Miss?"

The child, wrapped in towels now from head to toe, watched from where she lay in the deck furniture. Mills had a vagrant image of her mother in her sheets in the hospital bed.

He tells about the Delgado Ballroom. He tells about bringing Louise and her friends back to his apartment.

"This is swell," Louise says. "Isn't this swell?"

"Have you got television?" Bernadette asks.

"What's in the fridge?"

"I don't, no. Just some eggs. Some stuff for breakfast."

"Who wants cocoa? Raise your hand."

"I don't think there's cocoa," George says. "There may be some chocolate syrup in the cabinet where I keep the soap powder."

"Where's your phone?" Charles says. "Never mind, I see it. This directory looks like it's never been used."

"If you had the fixings I could make chocolate chip cookies. If you had the chocolate chips."

"There's Saltines," George says.

"At least there's a radio," Herb says. "I'll get some music."

"Somebody get the lights."

"Man, are you corny!"

"Who's horny?"

"Sometimes Ray acts very immature," Bernadette says.

"Got a church key?"

"In the drawer with my tableware."

"Okay, I've got it. Look at this, he's got service for one."

"Maybe he isn't registered."

"Hey you guys, be still a minute. . . . Is this Mr. Stuart Melbart of 2706 North Grand Boulevard? . . . It is? Congratulations, Mr. Melbart, this is Hy Nichols of KSD radio. If you can answer the following question you and Mrs. Melbart will be the lucky winners of an all-expense-paid vacation in Hot Sulphur Springs, Arkansas, as KSD's guests at the luxurious Park Palace Hotel. Are you ready for your question? . . . Good. All right, sir, name two members in President Eisenhower's cabinet. . . . Sherman Adams is correct. You're halfway there. . . . I can't hear you. John Foster who? Speak up, please. . . . Yes, yes, John Foster. We have to have that last name, sir. Can you speak up? . . . No sir, I can't. . . . Yes sir, I can now. Go ahead, sir, take one more try. . . . John, yes. . . . Foster, yes. . . . What's that? . . . It *must* be a bad connection, yes."

"Charles, that's cruel. The poor guy must be fit to bust."

"Did you hear him? Did you hear him shouting? What a goon!"

"Beer, everybody. Have a beer, George?"

"That sounds funny. Can't you get a different station?"

"This is the only one that works. George must be some Browns fan. They left town two years ago."

"Haven't you even got a *phonograph?*"

"No."

"How big are your breasts? . . . I said how big are your breasts? . . . No, ma'am, I'm not being fresh. Isn't this the take-out chicken place?"

"I'm expecting a call," George says.

"Bern?"

"What?"

"Want to take a shower?"

"Oh, Ray. You're the limit."

"What the hell, Bern. We're married."

"I don't have clean towels."

"Why don't you sit by me?"

"There, that's better. Isn't that better?"

"Hey, I can't see to dial."

"Why don't you sit by me?"

"Where are they going? That's my bedroom. Why'd they close the door?"

"George, they're engaged."

"Dibs on the couch."

"Shove over you guys."

"Okay. Quit your pushing."

"All the good spots are taken," Louise says.

"Did they just go into my bathroom together?"

"Maybe Bernadette had to go."

"They're running the shower."

"I know, you don't have clean towels. Maybe they could . . ." Louise giggles.

"What did you say?"

"Shh. Ruth and Charles."

"We heard you, Lulu."

"Well, mind your business then. You weren't *supposed* to hear me. I was talking to George."

"Don't, Charles, you could hurt the baby!"

"Do you like that?" she whispers. "Does that feel good?"

"Yes," George Mills says.

"Charlie, it could."

"Hmnn. *Hmmnn.*"

"You're shy, aren't you? You don't open your mouth when you kiss. Didn't you ever french a girl, George?"

"I french."

"Kch, kch. Take it easy, you want to cut off my air?"

Ruth, beside him on the sofa, touches his arm.

"What?"

"Shh. Listen."

Louise giggles. "Ruth, that's mean. They're in love."

"He's not going to sit next to *me* in those sticky pants."

"They've only been in there two minutes," Charles says. "Boy, was *he* hot to trot!"

"He couldn't help it," Ruth says. "She's been teasing him all evening."

"Well he's calmed down now all right, all right."

"I swear," Louise says, "wham bam. You men have no staying power."

"I don't know."

289

"Why don't we have a contest?"

"A *control* contest," Charles says.

"Everybody?" Louise asks.

"Sure. Tell those guys in there. Herb's already out of it. Herb's already lost."

"Hey, you can't go *in* there."

"Bet?"

Charles gets up and walks to the bathroom door. He opens it. "We're having a control contest. Herb's out of it. On your mark, get set, go." He leans his mouth against the bedroom door. "We're having a control contest."

"I thought Herb's out of it. That he already lost."

"Is Ellen Rose out of it?"

"Oh sure," Ruth says. "With her fella already come? That'll be the day, won't it, Louise?"

"You should have seen it, George. She's all lathered up. What a pair of tits on that Bernadette."

"Charlie!"

"Well it's true."

"Nicer than mine?"

"No, not nicer than yours. Not nicer than yours at all. Just bigger," Charles tells his wife.

"Only because she's four months' pregnant. It's all milk."

"You're pregnant too. She doesn't even show yet."

"She shows in her titties."

"Are we really having a control contest?" Ray shouts from the bathroom.

"Is it all right, George?"

"Why not? There's no TV, I'm out of cocoa, I haven't got a phonograph, and only one station on the radio works."

"Sure," Charles shouts back, laughing. "Come, I say *come*, as you are." He turns to George. "Count ten to yourself and start moaning."

"Charlie, that's cheating."

"No it's not, it's a joke. We'll make monkeys out of them." He moans, he purls. *"Everybody,"* he hisses.

"The water's running. They can't even hear us."

"No fair you guys," Charles calls. "Either turn off the shower or open the door. Hey," he calls, "you guys in this or not? ——Okay," he whispers, "go." In seconds he begins to moan again. He growls, he coos. He's the very troubadour of sexual melody.

"How come you never sound this way in real life?" Ruth Oliver asks.

"Come on, come *on,*" Charles tells his wife. "Oh. Oh *yeah,*" he says less quietly. "*I* lose," he cries. "I *lose.*"

"I guess we ought to humor him," Ruth says. "Mnn," she purrs, "mnn."

Mary looked at him wide-eyed. "Is this true? Did this happen?"

"I'm in a state of grace," George Mills said. "I don't have to lie."

Now Louise is chirping. Grace notes, diapasons, the aroused tropes of all dilate rapture.

"Louise?" the child said.

"All of them," George Mills said. "Doting love solos, Miss. Arias of concupiscence. Choirs of asyncopatic, amatory, affricative, low-woodwind drone."

"What a racket!" Mary said.

"Yelps, cries, askew pitch. All the strobic gutturals of heat."

It's quiet for a moment. Then, "This one's finished," Bernadette calls from the bathroom.

"Oh God," Ellen Rose shrieks in George Mills's bed, "*me,* me *tooooo!*"

"Go for it," Charles urges.

And, in the dark, George Mills can just make out his leer, his wife Ruth's. Louise is actually touching him now. His flies are in her fist. George's left hand is under her dress, his fingers snagged in her garter belt, his palm hefting flesh, the hard little button at the top of the strap. "Don't, you'll tear it," she says in his ear wetly. He introduces his fingers beneath the tough edges of her girdle. Where they are baffled by other textures. Elastic, the metal of fasteners, silk, hair, damp, curled as pica *c*'s. She squirms from his hand.

"Easy," she says, "take it easy. Don't *hurt* me."

"It's all this *stuff,*" he says, and tries to raise her dress, to pull it out from under her behind.

"No," she says, "don't," and moves away from him. This is when he tries to pull her down, when his head falls into Ruth Oliver's lap, thighs closed prim as pie. He feels a man's hand at his ear. It's Charles'. Mr. and Mrs. Oliver are holding hands across his face.

"Aw, he's suffering," Louise's friend Ruth says. "Put him out of his misery, Lu." And when Ruth's friend Louise moves her body against him. When his nerves shiver, spasm, when he whimpers his release. Not trumpets, not brazen blares. No boomy bray of barking majesty, but whimper, whine, fret. An orgasm like a small complaint.

The door to Mills's bathroom opens and Ray and Bernadette come into the living room. They are dressed. When Ray turns the light on in the hall George Mills can see that their hair isn't even wet.

"Maybe we ought to go," Charles says.

"What about the lovebirds?" Ray asks, indicating the closed door to Mills's bedroom.

"Knock on it. Tell them maybe we ought to go."

"Hey, break it up you guys," Ray says into the woodwork. "Give it a rest."

"How about that?" Herb says as he leads Ellen Rose into the living room. "It's not even midnight. Want to play some strip poker? Where's your cards, George?"

"Weren't you mad?" Mary asked.

"What for? To be proved right? She was a virgin. She was only protecting herself. She was a virgin. She wasn't in nature yet. None of them were."

"Two of those girls were married. They were pregnant."

"Yes," George Mills said, "they were protecting the unborn. It was hygiene is all. Marriage like a sleepover, like a pajama party. If it helped the husbands for the wives to talk dirty, if it helped to be together, to make crank calls, if it helped to excite each other until they didn't need excitement or protection either anymore, what harm did it do?"

"Ellen Rose wasn't married. Ellen Rose was whoosis's, Herb's, fiancée."

"His pants were stained."

"What?"

"Herb. His pants were stained too."

"You tell me the darndest things."

"Intimacy."

"Pardon?"

"Intimacy. Because that's the real eye-opener. The knockabout slapstick of the heart. Open secret, public knowledge. Those thighs on the sofa, those folks in the bed. Intimacy. Even friendship. Even association. Jesus, Miss, I'd thought my ass was a secret, my pecker hush-hush."

"I'm going to tell my mother how you talk."

"Your mother is dying. She's gorging herself on all the shrimp she can eat."

"Don't you say that."

"You can't evangelize grace. You can only talk about it. Ballpark figures."

"You're crazy. You're a crazy man."

"Because I was right. In a way I was right. You *can't* seduce virgins. Louise and I were practically engaged from the moment she found out I didn't have cocoa."

"You shut up," Mary said. "Take it back about my mother."

"Your mother is dying," Mills said calmly.

"Stop that," Mary said. "I'm just a little girl."

"Then behave like one. Practice the piano, be nice to your sister, bring up your math."

"Leave me alone," Mary cried. "Mind your business. Leave me alone." She was crying uncontrollably now, her sobs like hiccups, her nose and chin smeared with thin icicles of snot.

"Wipe your eyes," George Mills said. "Blow your nose. Use your beach towel."

8

Later George Mills would tell Messenger that he had known, that he'd been certain, that either his experience in Cassadaga as a child or the state of grace, which he'd be the first to admit he'd had no hand in, which he'd caught like a cold, or maybe something in each of us but compounded in Mills, who had a thousand years of history at his command, or anyway disposal, a millennium of what Messenger would call racial memory, hunch all the while increasingly fine-tuned in his stock until by the time it came down to George it was no longer hunch or even conviction so much as pure biological adaptation, real as the equipment of birds or bears.

"You're a fucking mutation? That it, Mills?" Messenger would ask. "The new man?"

"No no," Mills would say, "your people are the new men. With your kids and clans, your distaff and branches, all your in-laws and country cousins and poor relations. In me boiled down, don't you know? What do you call it? Distilled. Spit and polished back to immaculate, what do you call it, mass."

"Who do you like in the fifth race, George?" Messenger would ask. "What's to become of us?"

"No no," Mills would say, realizing it had been a mistake to tell. But he *had* known. Even as he sped the kid back to the hospital, risking the ticket in the foreign country, the cops' dangerous Mexican banditry, telling her not to waste time dressing but to bring her clothes with her as they rushed to the deathbed in their bikinis. Even, really, as he'd known that the child could shower, take her time, all the time in the world, eat a leisurely lunch, that that might even be preferable in fact, keeping the kid out of the way while her uncle made all the complicated arrangements with the hospital and government officials. (Which was why, in a way, he'd been glad to see him that morning, felt relieved to have at least *that* bothersome responsibility taken away from him. If her brother hadn't come, Father Merchant would have been all over him. And George would have listened, capitulating with genuine relief, grateful for the old tout's tips and counsel. [He was no hand at red tape. Forms and documents scared him.] If Merchant had proposed, as ultimately he actually would to Harry, that the hospital be permitted to perform an autopsy on Mrs. Glazer's body, Mills would almost certainly have agreed. She would have been returned to St. Louis without organs, all the metastasized Mexican cancer of her body cut away, scraped from her, koshered as a chicken in her casket —which Father Merchant would have picked out—like a Spanish treasure chest. The corpse would wait, the gruesome negotiations between Mary's uncle and the staff taking up the better part of the afternoon, going on, quite literally, over Mrs. Glazer's dead body, Father Merchant the go-between and arbiter to the peso's very fraction of the exact amount of the *pourboire,* the tip—— what went to the nurses to wash the body before it could be released to the undertakers, what to the doctor to make the appropriate—and true—remarks on the death certificate in order to forestall the routine investigation demanded by the municipal statutes in the instance of the death of a foreign national, what went by way of pure courtesy and ritual obligation to the company priest who was required by law to administer last rites, whether requested or not, to everyone who happened to die in the hospital, whether Catholic or not, what went to charity, what to the hospital bursar before the deceased could be discharged, what to the death teamsters who would cart the body away, what to the mortician's assistants who would treat it either gently and respectfully or, as Father Merchant would warn, with secret, invisible desecrations if the family did not take care of them. Officiating impediment too, guiding them through all the intricate bureaucracy of death, advising them which licenses were essential and, of these, which had to be notarized—Merchant was a notary—which merely witnessed.)

Knowing. Knowing in advance. (But not, it turned out, as far in advance as Father Merchant had known. At least a day and a half behind Merchant, maybe more. Perhaps from the time Merchant had first laid eyes on her, on Mills's ill charge, when they'd left the nightclub together—they'd gone after all—after the show, those terrible mixed doubles, and been tipped, that terrible time he'd seen first the ex-madwoman's face, then her pocketbook, the sheaves of bank notes, the unsigned traveler's checks.) (So maybe what he was going to tell Cornell was a boast, not prescience at all but ordinary induction and observed causality.) So that when he whisked the kid to the hospital and risked the speeding ticket it was not because he wanted to get her there in time, but because he knew that Mrs. Glazer was already dead, beyond embarrassment and concern forever, and would not see the brazen, floozy, bimbo kid in her gaudy bikini strips. Or Mills in the street clothes he had thrown on over his bathing suit when they had stopped for a light, the shirt and pants that still looked rolled, grass stains and the juices of crushed flowers about the knees and pockets where his shoe soles had touched them. Their rude parade a ruse, not deliberate at all, finally, but hidden, actually circumspect, broken out like hoard, trove, like the good champagne after the guest has gone, the best cigars and special chocolates.

Speeding not to the deathbed—that's what Sam would be doing —but to Father Merchant, the usurper retainer himself, and hoping he might yet make it—because Merchant could be wrong for once, because Laglichio might *not* need him, because if he made it he might not need Laglichio—that he could come like the cavalry (after all the hard work had been done, the legal stuff, the quasi-customary bribes dispensed, the extraconventional tips), not too late to play some part in the scene. (Haste hard on a man in grace, unaccustomed to pressure, who hadn't felt necessity more than two or three times in his entire life, whose family hadn't felt it eighty or so in a thousand years. Who'd resisted it in his courtship and during all those years of his oddly tame wild oats when he'd shoved dimes in jukeboxes and quietly popped for beers, when he'd neutrally revealed their feelings and explained their climaxes to those distracted women in whose automobiles and bedrooms he'd neither to his wonder nor dismay found himself naked. [Feeling, to the extent that he felt at all, only the mildest curiosity when it came to these women, as he might have been curious about the taste of certain dishes which no one had ever prepared for him.] Who—women—had not much played a role in the Mills history. Sisters rare as birth defects, widows and stepmothers uncommon as distinction. Something to do, perhaps, with that sense of default adaptation which he would speak of to Cornell Messenger, maybe even the random prescience some spilled remnant of neglected intuition. But, whatever, the whole business of having to rush, of there being something at last at stake, disagreeable to someone whose pride it was—and who meant by grace—that nothing could ever happen to him, that he was past it—— anticipation and interest and concern and disappointment and injury, and glory too.)

So what he found was what he should have expected to find—— a Tuesday afternoon like a lesson in the usual, a child by the Coke machine, nurses on pay phones, a distant relation bored in the waiting room on a worn leather cushion, his behind on the smooth front cover of a newsmagazine, someone sucking on a cigarette he hardly knew was in his mouth, patting his pockets for a match for a stranger, getting the time in return.

Yet the woman was dead. Her uncle stepped from the room and came into the corridor to embrace Mary, his gravity and the soured aromatics of his cologne and wrinkled linen giving it away, the distant early warning signs of worry and death. (This is how the rich attend their dead, Mills thought. Trailing some spoor of the bedside. Come from a deathbed as from a battle in a boardroom. But how had his clothes been mussed? How had his beard grown so fast?) All over her with apologies and explanations, including Mills even.

"Oh," Harry said, "good. You got my message. I thought I'd missed you. I had you paged, but when you didn't come to the phone I thought perhaps you'd taken Mary sightseeing. This is her first time in Mexico and she's an alert little girl. We even checked with the rental car people to see if you'd returned the car. It crossed my mind that you'd gone to the pictures. I was going to go out looking for you myself, but Señor Merchant advised me to wait another half-hour. It's fortunate he did. It would have been awful if you'd come back to the hospital and found Mother's room empty."

"A small precaution," Father Merchant said.

"They never paged us," Mills said. "There was no message. We were by the pool a couple of hours."

"Two hours? The child could have been badly burned. This is the tropics. Don't you know what our sun can do?" Father Merchant turned to the girl. "You expose yourself the first day fifteen minutes tops."

"I was covered up with towels," Mary said.

"Towels. Oh, that's all right then. Towels. You showed good sense. I hope they were white towels. White towels reflect the sun."

"Mama's dead?"

"Well you knew Mother's convictions, sweetheart. She was a very spiritual woman. I guess in a sense you could say she's dead, but she'll always be with us. She was tired, sweetheart. She was all worn out, dear. She was so glad she'd seen you. It's all she was waiting for. You remember that, darling. You made it easier for her. Didn't she, Father Merchant?"

"She was a tonic. That's my opinion," said the tout.

"See?" said her uncle. "Even he thinks so."

"She didn't see Milly," Mary said. "She didn't see Daddy."

"That would have been too hard, honey. That would have been so hard. Seeing all the people she loved would have upset her too much. Would you have wanted her to pass away while she was so sad? She left messages for everyone. She was at peace when she left us."

"I want to see my mother."

"Well, sweetheart, that wouldn't be best just now. The doctors have to do certain things, the nurses do. And we've got to get ready to meet that plane. It was a darn good idea for Father Merchant to make arrangements to keep the room an extra few hours. You can change in there. You can use Mother's shower."

The old man nodded. "The *c*'s for *caliente. Caliente* means hot. Just turn it lightly. You don't want to scald."

"Scald?"

"Mexico is an oil-rich country. Its hot water is its pride."

"Have I got time to freshen up?" the uncle asked.

"It isn't a question of time," Father Merchant said. "Flight 272 doesn't arrive till six. It will still be rush hour. I'd give you a special map I've drawn up, I'd tell you directions, shortcuts, which lane to be in when you're stopped at the border. You could leave at five-thirty and still meet the plane. But it isn't a question of time. It's a question of signs, what you look like to Sam when he gets off the plane, the signals he picks up. Go as you are. That's my advice."

Which, of course, he followed, looking, George thought, more the traveler than Sam, sending soiled semaphore, bereavement in the hang of his suit, the limp, creased cotton, got up like an actor in his tropical grief, his etched stubble. Merchant was right. Harry didn't have to say a word to Sam or the little girl, Mrs. Glazer's fate perfectly legible to them in Harry's solemn, lingering handshake, his wordless hugs. It was Mary who spoke.

"I haven't taken it all in, Daddy. I may be in shock. Feel my head. You think I have temperature? I was out in the sun. Maybe I burned. It *could* be a fever. It could be shock fever. They made me shower in Mommy's bathroom 'cause I was still in my bathing suit and we had to meet your plane. It was creepy, Daddy. I don't think I'll ever be able to shower again. I'll take baths and I'll douche but I won't ever shower."

There was no need to return to the hospital and on the way back to Harry's hotel Mills heard the brother-in-law tell Sam that they would all be flying back again in the morning, that Father Merchant, who'd been very useful, had made the arrangements, first class for Harry, Sam and the two girls, Mills in tourist. The old man had even returned Harry's rental car, since they were getting a rate, Merchant explained, on Mrs. Glazer's. He'd given the Mexican, Harry said, a hundred dollars. They probably wouldn't be needing the car that night but he didn't think they ought to be stuck in a third world country without one. The girls were tired, Milly had had a long day. They all had. Would George mind getting back to his motel on his own? Harry'd be happy to pay for the taxi.

Father Merchant was waiting for Mills outside his motel room.

"I could have been mugged waiting for that cab," George Mills said.

"No no," Father Merchant said, "everyone knows you're under my protection. Nothin' could have happen to you." Mills opened the door and Merchant followed him inside. "Did anythin' happened to you when you was flashin' the lady's money an' she was tryin' to get you both killed?"

"Was that you?" Mills asked without interest.

"I put in a word," Father Merchant said modestly.

George started to undress. "Aren't you tired?" George asked Merchant who was seated in the room's single chair. "All that running around you did today?"

"Yellow," Merchant said, *"yellow?* Yellow is for fairies. A man like you wants a dark blue bathing costume. Why should I be tired? I'm used to it. Anyway, I pace myself."

"He gave you a hundred dollars," Mills said.

"I left it up to him. Usually, when they come down, they come with family. It's rare to see a servant. What could I do? You were already here. I left a lot of it up to you. I let you assist me. We didn't get in each other's way. It should have been more, I suppose, but he, that Harry, only came down last night. He didn't know what to give.

My other clients are more generous, but maybe Harry isn't cheap. Maybe he don't really know."

"How come you didn't tell him?"

The old man shrugged. "A tout's pride," he said.

"Listen," George said, "I'm pretty tired. I'm supposed to be over at their hotel tomorrow morning at seven o'clock to get their bags and check out for them."

"Of course," Merchant said. "I'm gone in a minute. There's some things I want to tell you. Go on, get in bed. I'll let myself out."

"Could you get the light?" George said sleepily.

"Sure," Father Merchant said, and turned off the overhead light. He drew the night curtains and spoke to Mills in the dark.

"Maria is courted by all the eligible ranchers in that country," he said. "But she loves only one, the *patrone*, who is her father. She don' know he is her father, but *he* knows. He suspects. It makes no difference, by this time he can' help himself. She reminds him of her *madre*. Only this one is even *more* beautiful, *more* desirable. He tries to seduce her but she has too great honor. If he mean to sleep wit' her he mus' marry her. He arrange a fake pries', a young fellow from the south to do it. The real pries' is killed. *He* does this, the *patrone*. He knows he is damn to murder a *padre* but his passion has made him *loco*. The fake pries' is brought in an' they are married. They go away. He is a wonderful lover. Maria is sick with love, with sex. She has never experience nothin' like this. All he has to do is touch her, she is on fire. She can' get enough. But he's a old man, the *patrone*. All this love is killin' him, an' now she is pregnan'. She is no longer so beautiful to him. She knows this but makes demands. To stop her he tell her all about the fake pries', about himself. Now she is like her father, insane with passion. She don' care she is pregnan', she don' care she's his daughter. Maria is depraved. The old man is fearful about what he have done. He make a confession, first to a pries', then to officials. The pries' tell him God have forgive him if he is truly peniten'. He go to Maria. He fear for her soul. He tell her to confess. 'Why?' she says. 'I am sorry for nothing. Only that you love God more than your daughter. That, *that* is the filth.' They come for him, for the *patrone*. They take him away. They don' know she knows, her father don' tell them. He is hanged. For killin' the pries'. No one know. Only the pries' who hear his confession. He *can't* tell. He is waitin' for Maria to seek absolution. That how it end. We wait for the worse woman in the worl' to ask for forgiveness. That how it end.

"You're going back. These programs haven't been broadcast yet.

No one knows this in Mexico. Only the planners of the program. Only me. Only you."

"Why are you tell—— "

"I told Mrs. Glazer," Father Merchant said. "I whispered in her ear before she died."

"What are you talk—— "

"A hundred dollars," Merchant said contemptuously. "I just *see* that rich *gringo* bastard and *know* I won't get more."

"What do you—— "

"A hundred dollars," Merchant repeated. "I saved him *seventy* on the rate of exchange, on red tape even more. A hundred dollars!"

"*What do you want?*" Mills shouted. "*What do you want?*" He snapped on the bed lamp.

"How much would *you* say?" Father Merchant whispered. "You were here for a mont'. I kep' you *both* alive that first week. I didn't know there'd be a servant. There's not usual a servant."

"Do you want me to give you money? Is that what you want?"

"You? *You?* A go-between's go-between?"

"What do you want?"

"How could I know there would be someone to do the errands? Someone so indifferent he could bathe her, wipe her nose, her ass, take her for treatments, out for a ride? Death is what I do, the errands of cancer. The tips, the advice, all that's just sideline."

"What do you *want?*" Mills demanded.

"To give you *your* half," Father Merchant said, "these fifty dollars," and threw the money down on the bed.

9

In St. Louis, Louise still counted her breasts when she went to bed, taking inventory, too, since her husband's employer had died, of her glands, pressing her stomach and kidneys, examining her cervix and rectum, obtaining skintight latex gloves which George frequently found on the rug when he stepped out of bed. She was purchasing as well home urinalysis kits, checking for diabetes, excessive leukocytes, early warning signs of a dozen diseases. She had bought a thermometer which registered temperature electronically, a gadget which noted blood pressure, a full-size doctor's scale.

"Are we refurnishing?" George asked.

"Do you begrudge me a little security? It didn't cost you a penny. All the money for this stuff came from what was left over from my father's insurance policy. He even paid for the dress I bought for Mrs. Glazer's funeral."

They were going to the funeral, George as one of the pallbearers, Louise because she was a fan and because she had not forgotten the dying woman's condolence phone call on the occasion of her father's death.

Indeed, there was to be a small contingent from South St. Louis. Before she had left for Mexico, Mrs. Glazer had written to invite all the people on her Meals-on-Wheels route and had organized two limousines to pick up all those who were strong enough to attend and take them to the Church of St. Michael and St. George in west county and then on to Bellefontaine Cemetery. The limousines would return them to their homes in the city after a stop for lunch at Stouffer's Riverfront Inn. All this had been detailed in Judith Glazer's letters to the guests themselves, as well as to Crane, the funeral director.

Only George and Louise had not been invited, George learning he had been asked to be a pallbearer when Harry approached from behind the curtains of first class on the flight to St. Louis. "My sister," he said, "wanted you to serve as one of the pallbearers. She asked me to give you this." He handed him a sheet of folded hospital stationery. All it said was *"Please,* Mills," and had been written and signed with great effort. He examined the note closely. The signature would have been illegible had George not recognized it from some of the last traveler's checks she had signed.

"Yes, well I know it probably wouldn't stand up in court," the brother said, "but you have my word it's what she wanted. What do you say? They don't like passengers to stand in the aisles."

Mills's mood ring blazed.

The funeral had been much on her mind. George himself had written down the names of specific ushers she wanted, nephews and nieces and the children of friends who she had determined would replace the regular lay functionaries of the church. It seemed she wanted as many people involved as possible. Even after she had been taken to the hospital she had had George place a call to the organist at St. Michael and St. George. When he handed her the telephone, she burst into tears.

"Oh, Matthew," she said, "I don't know what's happening to me. I can't remember how Bach's 'St. Anne Fugue' goes. It keeps getting mixed up in my head with Mozart's 'Ave Verum.' " She had him hum them.

"Yes. Oh yes," she said. "I remember." And had gone on to discuss and approve the names of various trumpeters they could get for the Purcell anthem she had decided on only the night before.

"Do you really think so, Matthew? Ferd Turner? Do you trust his embouchure? Ask Willy Emerson for me, would you? And call me back. Mills will give you the number."

In the hospital, even in the motel, she barely glanced at the dozens of letters and get well cards sent by her friends, but had Mills read the acceptance letters of her designated pallbearers over and over to her, listening for tone, searching out reluctancies. She would take them from Mills and make him listen as if for sour notes in music. When she was satisfied that they meant what they said she dictated formal acknowledgments of their receipt, as if she had formed some binding legal accommodation with them.

She had spoken to Bishop McKelvey long distance. She knew, she said, there could be no eulogy as such, only the authorized prayers, but since they'd already agreed that certain special friends and relatives would be permitted to read the responses, she thought, *wondered* really, if she mightn't be granted one teeny dispensation. It was *awfully* important to her. Though it was the bishop's decision. *She* would submit no matter *what* he decided. Well then, she said, could they set aside some time toward the end of the service, for Breel, her psychiatrist, to address the mourners? No, not a eulogy. Nothing *like* a *eul*ogy. A clinical report on the state of her head, her symptomatology when she had been mad.

George had seen RSVP's from all six pallbearers.

One was flying in from Europe, another had postponed his trip till after the funeral. "Friends," she'd told George, "loyal friends."

Had she indicated, Mills had asked the brother, which one was to be bumped? "Come on, Mills, she was dying. These were practically her last words, just before she called that Merchant chap to the bedside. Did you expect her to think of everything? I suppose we can do some things for ourselves."

"She thought of everything," George muttered.

"How's that? Speak up. I can't hear you over the jets."

This was on Tuesday. The funeral was Thursday. It was too late for Mills to shop for a new suit, too late even to get the suit he had cleaned and pressed. But everyone, he thought, no matter his station, had a decent suit. She thought of everything. She even thought of that. She knew me, knew even I'd have one. She probably knew where it would be, anticipating the very closet, the yellowing plastic garment bag in which it would hang, protected from dust, moths, the wear and tear of poor men's air. She thought of everything. How could he be her brother and not know that?

So he looked for their white gloves. (Knowing they would not come from the cut-down carton in the church vestibule, just as he knew that the Bibles and hymnals they brought would be their own, as he knew that some of them would somehow have managed before-hand to obtain printed copies of the order of the service—just as he knew they'd be printed rather than mimeographed—as he knew they would have anticipated, and in perfect accord with Mrs. Glazer's wishes, the precise order of the seating arrangements, only himself and the contingent from the south side guided by the otherwise strictly ceremonial ushers.

(And how *did* he know, this George Mills in rare and tandem connection to privilege, his alliance occasional and metered as astronomy? Where did he even get off knowing? How had he known of the tuxedos and jodhpurs, spats and top hats that would be in their wardrobes? How had he intuited their pallbearer's customized gloves, the mother-of-pearl buttons like milk gems? What gave him his outsider's inside information?)

So he looked for the white gloves—— his own pair taken from the very carton he knew they would neither avoid nor wave off but were simply unaware of.

Then he was helpless. Having turned himself and Louise over to an usher, having followed the young fellow to a pew neither conspicuously close to nor far removed from the principal mourners, he relinquished himself to some principle of sheer minstrelsy, searching the laps of the men for white-gloved hands, looking over his shoulder, rubbernecking occasion and the congregation like some complacent proprietor of worship. He saw nothing. (Blinders on his intuition here, totally without knowledge of the tailor's contrivances, the special spaces that could be built into space, the secret concealing depths of bespoke pockets, ignorant of the reinforced material that could clothe a wallet or hide car keys without revealing a bulge or wrinkle.)

Someone came up. It was Messenger, the Meals-on-Wheels man, and George turned to him. "Excuse me," he said, "do you think you could point out the pallbearers?"

"Nice tan," Messenger said, "*ni-ii-ce* tan." He was stoned.

"The pallbearers," George said again.

But Messenger was enjoying himself. He indicated women, kids, some of his clients from Meals-on-Wheels, several with canes, walkers. "She loved her mischief," he said.

George mentioned names he recalled from the correspondence he'd seen in Mexico. "My God, man," Messenger said, "one owns the damned newspaper, and another introduced branch banking into this state. What'shisname just bought a franchise in the NFL, though he's probably never been to a game or even watched 'Monday Night Football.' Those other names *I* don't even recognize. You're here for the autographs, am I right? You want them to sign the psalms in your program."

"George is a pallbearer," Louise said.

"We all got our pall to bear," Messenger said.

So he looked for their tans, the special signals they radiated of wealth and leadership, all the lights of influence and pulled-string, procurate agency. But he had forgotten the decent suit in everyone's closet, appearance got up like a made bed, hospital corners. Why, even the Meals-on-Wheels group looked distinguished, their walking aids and wheelchairs lending them the look of pampered cranks. One old man in a lap robe might have been their line's coddled, consanguinitic first cause.

So he looked for the stalwart, for stamina, recalling the beefy first and second mates and ordinary seamen who had been sent by the Barge and Shipper's Union to carry his father-in-law's casket. He looked for the powerhouse honor guard of the rich.

Sam approached him. He leaned across Louise and whispered in his ear. "Professor Messenger said you were uncertain about the other pallbearers, that you weren't sure where to go."

"Nobody told me. Nobody told whoever I'm supposed to replace I'm supposed to replace him. I didn't know anything about any of this, Mr. Glazer. Mr. Harry sprung it on me on the plane."

"If you're uncomfortable," Sam said quietly. "If you're the least bit uncomfortable . . ."

"Well," George said, "Mr. Harry said it was what Mrs. Glazer wanted."

"All right," he said softly, "talk to the gentlemen in this row. This is the pallbearers' bench."

He looked down the aisle. "Gee," he said, "I never even gave my name. I wonder how the ushers knew." (Thinking even as he said it that the nieces and nephews had his number, that Mr. Claunch—Harry—had given it to them. Like a psychological profile of hijackers and bombers which even the girls at the airport metal detectors knew, the maintenance men in the public toilets.)

"Well," Sam whispered, "if you're all squared away." He started to leave, looking at the men and women on the aisles as he walked to the front of the church, accepting their handshakes, bending to receive the women's hugs. He was at once solemn and oddly hospitable, a flexibly expansive man.

Mills excused himself to the lady on his right—they were seated boy-girl, boy-girl, as if it were a formal dinner party—and asked if he might say something to the gentleman. The man smiled at him. "Pardon, sir," Mills said, producing his white gloves, "I took care of Mrs. Glazer down there in Mexico for a while and it seems she asked for me to replace one of the real pallbearers, but she didn't specify which real pallbearer I was supposed to stand in for. If you're . . ."

"Sure," the man said, "Judy was the coach. The coach calls the shots."

My God, Mills thought, it's what'shisname, the guy with the franchise.

(Because he knew nothing about obsequy, understanding well enough from his yokel's back bench condition the ins and outs of grief and loss—hadn't Mr. Mead, his father-in-law, a man he both respected and liked, died within the season? hadn't Mrs. Glazer?—reassured by the hang of his gut, the small, packed, sorrowful nausea there like a darning egg or some discrete, comfortable orthodoxy which fondled his sentiment and vouchsafed his heart. But nothing at all, not even curiosity, about the stately weights and measures of public ceremony—which may have explained the muddy color of the mood ring plugged to his mild, even-tempered boredom—the organ solos and responsive readings, the bishop's ringing exhortation of Heaven, his official encouragement of the immediate family, and his feeling denial of death, Mills in a way not even present, a time server, a clock watcher, waiting for whatever signal he knew must come when his pallbearing colleagues would rise and arrange themselves at the big, silver-handled box—and in what order? would the funeral director line them up, drill-sergeanting precedence, their disparate seniorities? or had Mrs. Glazer, who, Mills knew, called the shots here, called this one too, choreographing the last detail of all, the procession to and from the back door of her hearse, Mills's presence sheer habit by this time, as if the dead woman had become accustomed to his assisting her in and out of rental cars?—George ready to go it alone if there should be a hitch, prepared to throw his studied leverages into one final, mighty eviction.

(Listening again only when a chubby, acne'd, middle-aged man rose from where he had been sitting behind Sam and the two girls and took a position in the empty pulpit.)

The man waited for the anthem that had accompanied him (or that, rather, he had accompanied, his bearing gradually enhanced by the music) to finish. Then, glancing first at McKelvey and then at the

Glazers, he started to speak in a voice that was almost conversational, almost offhand.

"Well," he began, "the patient insisted that everything have meaning. That's familiar enough, I guess. Once they're into it I don't suppose there's been a dozen analysands in the history of analysis who haven't brought their dreams and even the least encounters of their day to their analysts for examination. Believe me, I've seen them come like cats with birds in their jaws, like kids with swell report cards. That's not what I'm talking about. Lots of people are like that. You don't have to be neurotic. I guess not.

"I mean the patient demanded that *everything* have meaning. She had no tolerance for things that didn't. 'Tom and Jerry' cartoons drove her up the wall and she couldn't understand why ice cream came in so many flavors. Let's see . . . Symptoms. She could be phobic about fillers in newspapers. As a matter of fact, during her worst years, she wouldn't even read a paper. She couldn't take in why the stories weren't connected, and it terrified her that an article about a fire could appear next to a piece on the mayor. She was the same about television. She couldn't follow a story once it was interrupted by a commercial. Variety shows, the connection between the acts. So that was one of her symptoms.

"Let's see . . .

"For a while she was nervous about bedspreads. They gave her the creeps. So did tablecloths, folded napkins. She thought they might be hiding something that wasn't supposed to be there. That whole business about bedspreads and tablecloths, though, that was a new one on me. Of course they're *all* new ones. I mean there's really no such thing as a classic symptom. If there were, madness would be easier to treat than it is. It's hard to treat. Actually, in a way, the patient's got to get tired of her disease. Well, that's *my* theory anyway. A lot of psychiatrists disagree.

"The patient was institutionalized eleven years. That's a long time. The saddest thing was this terrible fear. She was very intelligent, but because agoraphobia was another of her symptoms, she refused to go out and never quite grasped what was going on outside her window. She was afraid of weather. Autumn nearly killed her. When the leaves turned color. When they dropped off the trees, that gave her the heebie-jeebies altogether. Snow and rain, lightning and ice. You can imagine what spring did to her with its buds and green shoots and all the furry signals trees put out before they go to leaf.

"She couldn't understand temperature swings, why her windows were open sometimes and shut at others. What am I saying? She couldn't understand nighttime and daytime. So those were other symptoms.

"Look," he said, "this is difficult for me. I'm not sure this is even ethical. Strictly speaking, it's all privileged information. She *asked* me to tell these things. She arranged it with Bishop McKelvey. Well, they're open secrets anyway. Most of you were her loved ones. You know this stuff. But it's cat-out-of-the-bag, and it makes me nervous. Probably I seem ridiculous. Under the circumstances, even if I'd just been her orthopedist telling you about her broken leg or bad back, I'd still seem silly. It's all time and place. She's put me in a bad situation. I don't know what she thought she was up to. I suppose that sounds dopey too. I mean I was her psychiatrist, I charted her head like the New World. I'm supposed to know. Anyway, I don't.

"Maybe I shouldn't be so surprised.

"A lot of you know I was retained by the family. That I was her very own bought-and-paid-for personal psychiatrist. Like some high-priced music coach or the princess's astrologer. I lived in.

"I guess you know I wrote a book about her case. Or manuscript. It was never published. Well, that whole business was the patient's idea. She saw herself as material, subject matter for a book. Maybe you could put that down as another symptom, but if it is, God knows it's one the patient shared with nine out of ten people alive. I didn't *have* to write it, I suppose. I was on retainer and the family paid top dollar. (This was just after I'd completed my residency. I couldn't realistically have expected to make that much money for another five or six years at the inside.) The Claunches made it clear from the outset that I was, well, that I was the doctor. So I didn't *have* to write it. I guess I went along because I didn't have much else to do. Madness is a full-time occupation, but only for the madman. (That's really how the cure works. My notion of it anyway, though most don't agree with me. If the patient doesn't do herself an injury and just lives long enough she'll probably wear herself out.) Anyway, the patient was all the data I had. So I started to write her up about the middle of the third year.

"If you're interested, I guess I'd have to say that the transference dates from just about this time frame.

"I had my notes. And all those tape recordings of our sessions that I'd play over and over, wearing them out practically. As if they were favorite tunes, the top of the charts, say. Or like those half-dozen old movies in the ship's library they used to rotate and show us in the

Pacific during the war. She really was all the data I had. Never mind my two lousy years' residency at Cook County Hospital. Those folks were in a clinic, mad on the arm. (Which was how the family got me in the first place. Sure, if a psychiatrist already had a practice he couldn't just pick up and leave people who were dependent on him. It *had* to be a kid.)

"My notes and hers. The tapes that we made. Her madwoman's homework —— the journals she kept, the bad dreams she wrote down.

"And access, too, to those letters she wrote other patients. Witty —wit was a symptom—funny and malicious, reminding people whose own bad dreams had just been burned out of them by shock therapy of everything they had forgotten, rubbing their noses in their past, bringing them down from the thin, comfortable air of their electric amnesia. Not making it up but piling it on, some 'Hasty Pudding' rendition of their loony doings. Which she never showed me, but which their psychiatrists did, outraged as schoolteachers intercepting passed notes. Of course I spoke to her about it. I asked why she wrote them. 'Six years,' she said, 'I've been here six years. A bunch of these crazies are my best pals. I've made love to some of the men and a few of the women and spoken with the rest like Francis of Assisi making small talk with birds. What happens if they get well?' 'Don't you want them to get well?' 'No.' 'Do you want to get well?' 'Craziness ain't much of a birthright.' 'I have to give back the letters.' 'Their shrinks will destroy them. Or lock them up in the poor bastards' files.' 'I have to return them.' 'Make copies,' she said. 'They're poison pen letters,' she said, 'as much a record of my nuttiness as theirs. Make copies. Put them in that manuscript you're writing about me.'

"Because she said 'manuscript' now, not 'book.' Knowing that if the letters went in, it could never in either of our lifetimes be any published book, that even if I changed their names the facts would be there, that we'd be hung up in lawsuits the rest of our lives.

"But I did what she asked. The letters became part of the record too. I copied them into what only one of us still thought of even as the manuscript. Though the patient had never even seen it. Now she asked about it every day. 'You're some doctor,' she'd say. 'Eight years in private practice and you've yet to cure anyone. What's with the manuscript? How's that going at least?' 'There's a lot of material,' I'd tell her, 'I'm up half the night transcribing tapes. Copying those letters you write. I'm losing sleep. When I finally get to bed I toss and turn for an hour.' 'What's with the big deal opus manuscript? Do I get to see it soon or do you plan to take another seven years?' I think this obsession with the manuscript was probably one of her last symptoms.

"So I started to show her pieces of it. The character of our sessions changed. Each morning I'd read the patient part of a chapter. She was fascinated. When the hour was up she was reluctant to leave. I would read her the rest of the chapter during our afternoon session. This went on for about a year. She was very calm, calmer than I'd ever seen her. Those earlier symptoms didn't seem to obtain any longer. The fears, I mean. She was reading newspapers now, watching TV and switching from channel to channel in the middle of shows and going on to the next show and following it to the end even if she hadn't seen the beginning. She was getting tolerant about meaninglessness. And put bright bedspreads on her bed, flowery prints, complicated patterns. We'd been taking walks around the grounds together since the middle of winter.

"When spring came she even wanted me to drive her to town. We were with each other constantly now, though the manuscript, which was finished now, was always along. And though we'd long since finished putting it together, I started to read to her from the worst parts of her life. In canoes I would read to her from her childhood. Her symptoms and traumas. We'd go to the park and while she was setting the tablecloth out on the picnic table I'd have her listen to those cruel letters she had written the other patients.

" 'Hey, come on,' she said one day when we were driving back from a weekend visit to her home. She was driving. I had just taken the manuscript out of my suitcase. 'Give us a break,' she said. 'I'm getting awfully tired of hearing about that lady. That was some bad news, sad-ass lady. Why don't you do us both a favor and tear the damn thing up? Just throw it out the car window or deep-six it in the litter barrel when we stop to pee. I don't want to hear about that crappy lady anymore.'

" 'You shouldn't be so hard on yourself, Judith.'
" 'Why not? I was a jerk.'
" 'You were an interesting woman.'
" 'I was a sickaroony.'
" 'You're well now.'
" 'Eleven years. Hardly the nick of time, wouldn't you say?'
" 'Eleven years. That's how long we were together, Judith.'
" 'Should auld acquaintance,' she said.
" 'You're getting discharged next week. Then I guess you'll get

together with that graduate student who's been visiting you. I don't know what I'm going to do.'

" 'You? Eleven years at seventy thousand dollars a year? That's more than three quarters of a million dollars. Why, you're almost a rich man, Doc.'

" 'It's the transference,' I said.

" 'Yeah, I know,' Judy said. 'It was a hell of a transference. Thanks, Doc.'

"She thanked me. For the transference. I think it's what cured her. That I was the only man the patient knew who had loved the patient all those years."

The recessional! Trumpets and organ music! A bright bang of reverberant bliss! Out of the psychiatrist's, Breel's, gawky silence, his bumpkin shuffle. The big breakthrough as foolish grin, lopside heart. While the Meals-on-Wheelers, no longer charity cases so much as a special-interest group, invited observers, say, from some neutral but not indifferent commission, took, under cover of the music, collective liberties with the doings of their hosts, disputing intent and motive and all the ways of doing business that were not their ways, feeling had, the more religious among them, deprived of some final settlement and solace, who had ceremoniously come to grieve for the strange woman who for years now, rain or shine, had fed them lunch. Chatty in her way too, of course, but like some cheery columnist of the wide world whose tales of the fabulous had been, or so they'd thought, mere bedtime stories, meant to entertain or distract, told neither to enlist nor support sympathies, but out of the goodness of an enraged and generous heart, and not, or so they'd thought, to be taken seriously. Postcard information and detail. That there might have been a picture of the death camps on the face of the card had not struck them as unusual since they never expected to see such places themselves.

Now they stood in their pews, their faces turned toward the center aisle as first the thurifer and then the crucifer went by, followed by the acolytes and clergy. It was only when the immediate family passed that they struggled to put names to faces, placing individuals in the context of Judith Glazer's now heartfelt, retroactive gossip.

Dr. Breel had long since climbed down from the pulpit. Where he had seemed at once both faltering and certain. Now he was again hesitant, trying to decide whether to wait for those peripheral members of the family—cousins (he recognized them easily enough; he'd read the book), pals from childhood, the coaches, cooks, servants and tutors of Cornell Messenger's speculations—or to plunge himself into mourning's mainstream. He seemed ready to plunge, determined, deferential only to some graduated kinship principle of his own ordering. Wavering, he thrust himself behind Sam's sister from California and in front of the dead woman's first lover.

Last came the casket supported by the six pallbearers in paced and stately lockstep behind the ragged, difficult parade of the Meals-on-Wheels people.

Only Cornell Messenger still lingered in a row of pews. He waited for George Mills, whose right hand grasped and forearm supported half a yard of Judith Glazer's casket handle, and who was concentrating all his will on the task. When Mills was almost abreast of him Messenger winked and leaned forward. "The horror, the horror, hey Mills?" he said.

[Later it was Louise who called Harry to apologize for the bill that the Meals-on-Wheels people had run up at Stouffer's. "It was their idea of a wake," she told him. "They didn't mean harm," she said. "They were a little upset by what that doctor said. They knew your sister for years. Maybe they thought he dishonored her memory."

[Harry, who was not quite certain who Louise was but who had a vague memory of her having come back to the house after the burial, attempted to reassure her. "That was my sister's favorite charity. I'm sure Judith would have been pleased that they enjoyed themselves." She did not tell him that, from what she gathered, from what George had told her of what Cornell Messenger had told him, it had not been an entirely joyous occasion.

[Stouffer's round, glassed-in restaurant, "The Top of the Towers," offered a view of the city from twenty-eight floors up, its outer perimeter of tables revolving almost imperceptibly, 360 degrees in just under an hour. Those of Judith Glazer's guests who had to excuse themselves to go the toilet could not find their tables when they returned. They were a little drunk. Some stumbled trying to cross from the restaurant's fixed, stationary center to its revolving rim. Scenes were made. They reported purses missing, hats, entire complements of the handicapped. One old woman turned herself in to the hostess. "I'm lost," she moaned. "Everything's mixed up. There's tall buildings where the river was and a river where there used to be a stadium. You're the usher that seated me. Get me back." And a tipsy lady who had filched a bouquet of flowers from among the floral decorations at St. Michael and St. George reported to the manager that her friends were missing. "They was a dead person's flowers. I took them from the church because I was a good friend of the corpse. If they should fall into the wrong hands, if the wrong noses should smell them, that person could die, and no one could ever prove whether it was the flowers or your fancy food that took them off." Two or three, feeling themselves genuinely abandoned, had wept. At the last minute one man refused to let the driver pay for his lunch and insisted on settling with the cashier himself. ("The decent clothes," George had said. "What?" Messenger asked. "Those decent clothes," Mills said. "He looked presentable even to himself. Of course he wasn't going to let some chauffeur pay for his lunch in front of a woman who took cash at a register. These were your men-of-the-world poor. They didn't grow *up* in beds with hospital sides. They hadn't *always* pushed themselves around behind walkers." "So?" "So she knew," Mills said, who was a little tipsy himself. "Who? What did she know?" "She knew everything." "The mischief maker? Judy?" "Call her however you like," Mills said, "she knew everything." "Sure," Messenger said. "What?" Mills asked. "Sure," Messenger said. "The revolving restaurant. It was her last giveaway, the ultimate Meals-on-Wheels lunch.") "Almost three hundred dollars," Louise said, "and I can almost hear their backbiting." "Mnh," George said. "They must have said plenty," Louise said. "They don't know anything, Louise."]

Messenger drove with them to the Claunch home after the burial.

Invited to return to west county with the family afterward, Mills and Louise had hesitated. A delegation of women had come to them. Sisters-in-law, an aunt. Mills knew they had been put up to it by men, that Judith Glazer had been the only one of her sex to have any real power in the family, that someday—he didn't know how he knew this; it wasn't anything her mother had spoken of—Mary might have the same sort of authority.

"No, really," a widowed sister-in-law had said. "You were with Judith all that terrible time in Mexico. It would be a comfort to know certain things."

"Well," Mills said.

"It would make Mary feel so much better," the other sister-in-law said softly, almost whispering. "It would make *all* of us feel better."

"Gee," Mills said, "I don't . . ."

"Perhaps Mr. Mills would have to miss work," the aunt said. "It could cost him a day's wages to come with us."

"Oh that's awful," the first sister-in-law said. "Of course the family would . . ."

"No no," Mills said, "I'm not, I wouldn't be . . ."

"Oh splendid," she said, "it's settled then."

Cornell rode with the Millses in the Buick Special. "No guts," he told Louise. "Those folks are real moguls. The elect hoity-toity of earth. I recognized a couple of university trustees. The chancellor was there. That guy Sam was squiring around. God, he never let him out of his sight . . . If they saw me light up," he said, taking a joint from a package of low tar cigarettes. "You do pot, Louise?" He offered the pack. "Thanks but no thanks, eh? Ri-ight. I do it to enhance the ride. It already enhanced the funeral. But no kidding, Louise. There are some great houses out here. The stately homes of Missouri. Keep your eyes open, kiddo. Enjoy, enjoy."

But to Mills, who had never been in this part of the county, it had already begun to look familiar. It was not déjà vu. It was history. The hundred tales he'd heard. Their marked Marco Polo life. He seemed to recognize hedges, birds, the iron verticals of their rich men's fencing, their curving driveways like the packed, treated surfaces of tennis courts, the trees that lined them, their rare rich wood. He sensed porters' lodges, cunning, low-ceilinged space within thick stone gateways, and smelled, far off, stocked ponds, game, posted woods and sculpted rivers.

Magically, he seemed even to know the way. Instinct working in him now, not grace. His own instinct merged with that calculating one of whatever inceptive, raw, original Claunch it had been who had seen not just the tract's possibilities but its already in-place, on-stream, on-line de facto advantages.

"My goodness but it's a way," Louise said.

"Maybe we ought to get back to a main drag and stop over at a motel," Messenger said. "Would you like that, Louise?"

"We're almost there," Mills said. Who had noticed, miles back, that they had passed the last of the prettified Lanes, Drives, Roads, Courts and Places with their scrolled, artisan'd address. Squire country, he had thought dismissively over Cornell's easy admiration.

As they were past address itself now, on privatest property, still located of course, but in some geography of extraordinary jurisdiction where armed gillies and deputized gamekeepers enforced not law but custom, usage, tradition, folklore. Here they could be murdered for poaching, trespass. And not even instinct now but—his mood ring glows like ember, it sizzles his finger like a paper cut—his goofy, loyal, Mills-primed imagination: slain for a plucked wildflower or wrongly chosen bait. And suspects that what is operative here cuts deeper than statute, goes beyond compact and the legislative, scraping some raw nerve of the established ecological, their presence intrusive, pushing against a nature as fitfully balanced as a zoo, within striking distance, as Millses always were, of their oppressors' murderous pet peeves. And is somehow gloomily proud that such power, chipped at and chipped at, nickel-and-dimed by revolution and reform, still manages to hold on, hold out, continues to exist in such culs-de-sac as the one he drives past now at twenty and twenty-two miles an hour, watching for deer crossing, bridle paths, grazing stock. And is as certain that the Buick Special is observed, its position called out from walkie-talkie to walkie-talkie, as he is of the existence of the power itself. Who knows that he is this snob of history, this anachronistic partisan? Lancaster's man, York's? (He himself has forgotten which.) Louise, who has had his cock in her mouth, doesn't. She thinks, if she thinks about it at all, that he is Laglichio's man, or the late Mrs. Glazer's, or her own.

"Another couple miles," George said.

"Jesus!" Cornell Messenger said when they had entered the main gate and turned into the driveway. "There ought to be a drawbridge. It's a fucking goddamn castle!"

"They're not checking plates today," George explained. "There's often open house when someone dies."

"I never expected anything like this," Cornell said. "I'll tell you something. I bet Sam himself ain't ever been here."

Messenger could have been right. It was the girls, Mary and Milly, who took them on a tour of the house—though George felt, so familiar was he with its Platonic floor plan that he might have been able to do it himself—Sam and a few others following them about like visitors shy at the White House say, told it's their home, but knowing better of course, hanging well back of their minds' velvet ropes, not smoking and taking no pictures, their normal speaking voices lowered decibels.

"Hey," Messenger said, whose enjoyment of the house had been enhanced one last time before climbing out of Mills's car, "you think there's a gift shop?"

"Here's where I take ballet and fencing," Mary said. "Grandpa had the mirrors and warm-up bar put in when Mother was a little girl.

It's special wood. You can't get splinters." She ran to the practice bar, turned to them, and carelessly raised her leg. They could see over the tops of her stockings.

"I don't think someone should dance after a funeral," Milly said.

"Your sister's right, sweetheart," Sam said.

"Oh, Daddy," Mary said.

"I have to speak to you," Cornell whispered in George's ear.

"You have a lovely home," Louise was telling the two girls. "Really lovely. You must be so proud. I suppose in a house as big as this one each of you probably has her own room."

"We have our own lady's maids, too," Mary said. "We have separate cooks and our own private gardeners. We even have our own special milkman. And a postman who does nothing but just deliver our mail. Isn't that right, Milly?"

"Mary is teasing," Milly said. "We don't even live here. We come out sometimes on weekends."

"The really amazing, astonishing, wonderful thing is that Milly isn't even spoiled. I am, but old Milly is just like everyone else even if she does have just hundreds and hundreds of thousands of dollars in her own private savings account."

"It's in trust," Milly said. "I can't touch it till I'm twenty-one."

"Mary," Sam said more forcefully, "Milly. That's enough now."

"It's pretty urgent," Cornell Messenger said.

The psychiatrist, down from the catharsis in which he had taken refuge, frowned. "I'm crashing," he said. "I'm actually crashing. I'm sorry. I had no idea I was going to say all that stuff. I made a damn fool of myself, a stupid ass."

"Hey," Cornell said, "hey come *on.* It's what she would have wanted."

"You shut up," Sam said, "you just shut up."

"We ought to start back now, Louise," George said.

"You got it, Sammy," Cornell said. "My lips are sealed, Dean."

"Thank you, young ladies," Louise said. "It was awful nice meeting you, Doctor. I'm sorry about your wife, Mr. Glazer. She was very kind to my father when he was alive." Louise turned to go.

"I've got to speak to you, Mills," Cornell said, following him.

"I'm not in this," George said sweetly. "I'm not in any of this."

They were descending three abreast on a widely winding staircase that circumscribed a lavish keyhole of space. George had seen nothing like this house. Greatest Grandfather Mills hadn't, nor had most Millses in between. "Listen," he would have told his son, "I've

317

been to Architecture the way some have been to France. In rooms measured as philosophy. The furniture like pieces settled in nature, unremarkably there as trees. And the fabrics, George, the fabrics! Fabric like foliage or high husbandry's bumper crops. And woodwork like the sounding boards on stringed instruments. Paneling from panel mines, the oldest forests, all wilderness's concentric rings like the tracery of nerves in vitals."

Cornell saying "I've got to speak to you. I've really got to speak to you."

And so, it turned out, did others. The aunt, the sisters-in-law, had been emissaries, actual agents. In the manor's great drawing room with its brackets of wing and armchair and parentheses of sofa, its Oriental carpet deep and wide as infield tarpaulin, its armoires and marquetried escritoires checkered as gameboard, they were waiting for him.

"Did you enjoy your tour, Mrs. Mills?" the aunt asked. She sat in a large, curving wing chair of upholstered silk, her long, thin forearms and mottled, arthritic hands arranged over twin tracks of tight gold fringe, her large purse open and settled beside her like a queen's. Her fine, crossed legs were clear, firm as a dancer's, and her expression as she waited for Louise's answer, layered, a cool palimpsest of serenity, indifference and concern. Like several of the senior members of the family George had noticed at the funeral, she did not wear mourning. Indeed, her light woolen coat dress, exactly the color of fleshtone in a black and white photograph, seemed more the clothing of the owner of an odds-on Derby favorite in her special box than it did of someone who had just buried a niece. Mills noticed her long, misshapen, ringless fingers and wondered whether she had ever been married or if she had had her jewelry cut from her painful, blistered joints.

"Oh yes," Louise said, "oh yes, indeed. It may not be proper etiquette to say so, but this has been a very special and exciting day for us. I never expected to be invited to a house like this. Goodness, it's like something in picture books. Or what I imagine palaces in the old country must look like. George knows more about these things but I can tell he's as thrilled as I am. Aren't you, George?"

He sweltered for Louise in her black mourning dress, for himself in his dark suit. "Yes," he said.

"I know," his wife said. "And we want to thank you for having us. And the children are darling. I only hope that it had to be on such a sad occasion. I mean . . ."

"Of course," the aunt said, smiling. "But surely you needn't go yet, Mrs. Mills. My nieces-in-law want to show you the miniature railroad that Judith's father built for her to ride in when she was a child."

"You mean like the little train that takes you around the zoo?"

"Quite like that, yes. I'll tell Grant to organize a ride for you. My nieces will go with you."

"Oh, George, did you hear? We're going for a ride on a little train."

"Well, Mrs. Mills, I thought you and the girls might make do on your own. This might be a good time for Mr. Mills to speak with Mr. Claunch."

"Oh," Louise said.

"I go with Lulu on the choo-choo?" Cornell said.

The aunt—George was not sure of her name, though he knew that the rich did not always give their names, that they lived unlisted lives—glared at Cornell. "Yes," said the aunt, "of course. I should have thought to ask."

Mr. Claunch, as it turned out, was not Harry, but Harry's father.

The builder of the miniature railroad and the splinter-free ballet studio was waiting for him in a kind of trophy room. Plaques the shape of arrowheads hung next to framed oval photos of horses and riders, of dogs and handlers. There were mounted blue ribbons that fell away from inscribed rosettes big and round as clocks in schoolrooms, like pressed pants. Leather straps with tiny bronze horseshoes dangled from them, the sculpted heads of horses snugged into their curves. Silver bowls rested on bric-à-brac shelves next to porcelain animals, and everywhere, no larger than pocket watches, bas-relief medallions were pressed onto the walls like an equine coinage. Along another wall, high up, were prep school banners large as pillowcases, college pennants, the guidons of military academies like a felt heraldry. Beneath these were columns of framed team photographs— football, baseball, hockey, swimming, soccer, track—oddly like the Won and Lost listings in newspapers. Mary and Milly, in ice skating costumes, their arms spread, dipped toward the camera in clumsy arabesques. There were pictures of golfers and tennis players, and slalomers on skis kicking their bodies past gates like conga dancers. There were queer, high-altitude photographs of people on the summits of mountains. They seemed shy as foot shufflers, scuffers of shoes.

Claunch was seated beside a writing table with his legs crossed and his left hand resting lightly on the surface of the table. He wore a dark blazer and bright plaid trousers lustered as kilt. He had a large face, and thick black horn rims—dated as Mills's mood ring—hung on his eyes like shiners. Though he was smoking, Mills saw no ashtray in the room. Here and there thin columns of smoke rose from the silver trophy bowls into which Claunch Sr. dropped unextinguished cigarettes.

"You're here," he said glumly. "All right, come in. Beat it please, Aunt." Was she *his* aunt? George wondered. "I look," he said gloomily when the woman had gone, "like a past president of an International Olympic Games Committee."

"I'm Mills," Mills said meekly, "and I just want to say how sorry I am about Mrs. Glazer."

"All torn up, are you?"

"She was very nice," George said. "She went through a lot."

"I know what she went through," Mrs. Glazer's father said. "She went through all of us. She went through all of us like a high wind. Trailer courts arse over tip, dozens left homeless. I *know* what she went through." He leaned suddenly forward, like Milly and Mary in their ice skating costumes. "Was I missed? At my daughter's funeral, was I missed? What was the dark, black-ass buzz?"

"I didn't hear anything, sir."

Claunch closed his palms rapidly over his eyes, ears and mouth, and Mills shifted uneasily. "Oh come on, Mills," Claunch said, "she called me from Mexico. She called collect like some kid off at college. The things she said to me." He shook his head. "I tell you, George," he went on, "at first I thought that pancreatic cancer was a blessing. Not a blessing in disguise, but the outright, up-front, stand-tall stuff itself. Some no-strings cancer, three to four months at the outside and the patient so stuffed with pain, medication and final things she wouldn't have time for her dotty trouble campaigns. Even after she decided on her last-ditch stand, her hundred percent final effort, and went off for fruit therapy in old Mexico, I *still* thought blessing! Blessing, godsend, favorable balance of payments!

"It didn't occur to me until after I stopped accepting her calls and began to hear from two or three of her hot-lunch clients that even if there's no God the devil sure exists. And something else became clear, too. That the weight of those charges she continued to press even in extremis took on something of a deathbed power, that even a poor old bunch of poor old bastards in their own extremis would hear her out and make vows, pledges. Deathbed calling to deathbed in perseverant, unfaltering howl. The nerve of that woman! Intruding on their desuetude, enlisting the worn-out in her worn-out life."

"Meals-on-Wheels people phoned? I never heard this. She must have called them when I wasn't in the room."

"She gave away all my unpublished numbers. She put it out on the highest authority—her word as somebody terminal—that I was their absentee landlord, the s.o.b. who wouldn't pay for their crumbled plumbing or fix their faulty wiring, that I darkened their hallways and stairs and put governing devices on their water and electric. She told them that she became involved with Meals-on-Wheels when she discovered who owned those rat traps. She said it was to make moral restitution."

"They called you up?"

"They're poor, Mills. Do you know what poverty is? Real poverty? It's not having any conception of how rich the rich really are. They don't know doodly squat about us. Sure they called. I set them straight of course. Judith wasn't crazy enough to believe her campaign would fly. But she did her damage. She got what she wanted."

"What did she want?"

"What did she want? I'm an old man. It was those goddamn unpublished numbers. There must have been fifteen of them. It was to annoy me. All that trouble just to annoy me. Think! If I replaced them, tell me, how in hell could a man my age learn the new ones?"

Mills watched the old man, a rich old man who had the sturdy look of one who had had his children late in life, whose spiffy, offhand rich man's style, his blazers and rakish, researched plaids (and dozens more just like them in hotel suites along prime beach front properties on selected coasts) would be familiar in boardrooms and the cockpits of private jets, at golf classics and aboard presidential yachts, to popes come calling and heads of state dropped in on, to mistresses (they would not be beautiful or even all that much younger than he), to society and the horsy and doggy sets in the capital cities (because surely he liked to get out once in a while, down to Brasilia to see the generals, off to Brussels for cabal and conspiracy with the good old boys of the Trilateral Commission), which were clothes and climate too, serviceable as an Arab's burnoose. It was just possible, Mills thought, that Claunch alone had no decent suit, and he wondered how he came by his fervid imagination and privy fantasies. And just how rich the rich really are. Poor Mills, Mills thought. For all his serving-man's history and butler's genes, there had been no rich men in his life. These little litanies were a sort of crazy faith, the only one the saved, grace-stated man possessed. And was weary of his star-struck inventories which pulled against his nature in ways he did not even begin to understand.

He did not want to hear Claunch out, was suddenly ashamed of the services he'd already rendered. He told himself he listened out of courtesy, as a guest. For Lulu in the choo-choo for whom this day had been an outing. (And Messenger still to be heard out!)

"This," Claunch said, waving his cigarette about the room, "was my daughter's dollhouse."

"Sir?"

"Well she made it up," he said. "The team photographs were clipped out of yearbooks. The ribbons and trophies came from pawnshops, garage sales. Even the loving cups, the silver bowls."

"But they're inscribed," George said.

"To strangers. 'To Whom It May Concern.' "

"What for?"

Claunch shrugged. "She was nuts."

Mills wasn't interested. Not in Claunch's money and power nor in his abrupt, summary ways. There was nothing for him here. He did not need to know anything or have anything. It was astonishing to him that he had ever gone to Mexico, that he had supervised death-beds so unreluctantly. That his passions had been up. He was tired of all of them—of Breel, the Claunches, the Meals-on-Wheelers, Messenger, the Glazer girls, himself. Amazed he'd consented to be a pallbearer or given a moment's thought to the character of his suit. Dumbstruck he'd taken any part at all. He had let everyone bully him, everyone. Father Merchant, all his lockstep, aspic'd ancestors. Now he would turn to go and Claunch Sr. would embrace him with one more confidence, one last devastating request. He knew what it might be, knew he would decline. That whatever the disparity in their wealth or power, it was Claunch who was subject to temptation, snarled in gravity and desire, Mills who was free.

So he turned to go. Disengaged as the dead, indifferent as wood.

"What did she tell you?"

"Nothing," Mills said.

"She wasn't a quiet woman. She wasn't shy, she wasn't modest. Anything on her mind burned holes in her pockets. She spent confidence like a drunken sailor."

"Nothing was on her mind."

"You were with her for weeks. You saw her die, you watched her dress size come down."

322

"Yes."

"What did she tell you?"

"Your unpublished numbers."

"Don't tangle with me, Mills. *What did she tell you?*"

"Everything."

"Horseshit."

(And thought of Greatest Grandfather Mills.)

"Wait," Claunch said, "don't go. Please, Mills. Please, George."

"Tell me what you want," George Mills said. (Thinking: You can't have it, there's nothing left.) And didn't wait for Claunch to reply, telling him instead what any of them—his forebears—would have told him, mollycoddling grief and concern, handling his anxiety like something armed, primed, talking him in off all his rich man's window ledges—because much had been lost in the retelling, blurred in the father-to-son translations, distinction smudged as a ruin—seeing a thousand pairs of boots radiant in the hall, hearing even as he spoke them the rote and passionless lies, his ancient tribe's ancient there-theres and now-nows, the primitive consolations—for bread, a nickel for a cup of coffee, a coin for a candy, a place to hide from the wind—worn-out as a witchdoctor's gibberish. (And seeing for perhaps the first time in a thousand years something even more radiant and splendid than the cumulative shine on the cumulative boots. Glittering spectra beyond trust. Bright as belief. And thinking: Why, we could have *destroyed* them!)

"Was the pain ever more than she could handle?"

"Sometimes she'd take an extra aspirin."

"Aspirin? Only aspirin?"

"Her belief comforted her."

"Yes," Claunch said, "there was that. She believed."

(And Cornell to be mollified. Was something between them? Not his business. Nothing his business.)

"Tell me," Claunch said softly, "did she curse me?"

"There was a kind of message."

"Oh?" he said. "A message?"

"She didn't want there to be hard feelings."

"She told you she forgave me?" Claunch asked hopefully.

"No," Mills said, and looked directly at the ambassadorlike man. "She told me she apologized."

He passed a row of garages with their antique and classic automobiles. (He had noticed one or two at the church, three more at the cemetery. In the narrow roadway it had looked more like a rally than a burial.) And crossed past a middle-aged couple examining a restored 1933 Plymouth which Mills recognized as being exactly like Wickland's old car in Florida, the one his father had driven to De Land on his errands. The man smiled and waved, and George nodded at him.

He did not have to be told where to go. Not instinct this time either, and certainly not grace and down from déjà vu and history. Not even imagination so much as a blueprint knowledge of its location, certain, sure as a housekeeper where things went. Knowing there'd be a toy station, population, elevation signs, a town's given name high on the station nostalgic as a stand of trees or the iron horse itself. (It would bear the name of wood or game: Elmville. Deerfield.) Flowers would be planted around its platform, along its borders.

And started to climb a low knoll. And heard the train before he saw it. Not its comical whistle—certain of *this,* too: the outsize locomotive wail that would be hung about its neck like some apocalyptic joke—but its tinny chuff chuff as it pulled them along the banks and straightaways of its miniature routes. (Imagining Mrs. Glazer as a child, laughing hysterically, pissing her drawers, unable to help herself, seduced, ravished by motion.) Seeing it before he actually saw it (because despite reservation, protestation, all his low-grade weariness of their complicated, graceless lives, he had his Mills-given gift for the inventory of the rich, as intimate a knowledge of their safes, attics and basements as he had of his own clothes closet—— precious treasure's second sight).

At the top of the rise he spotted them in their luscious, bulldozed valley. Grant—who forebore to wear the engineer's cap Mills saw stuffed in his pocket—sat behind a long locomotive on a sloping tender which served as a seat, his hands on controls which poked out of the rear of the engine like levers in a tavern game. Four topless passenger cars the dimensions of desks were pulled along at about fifteen miles an hour. The coaches' only slightly scaled-down seats were plush, reversible, wide as rumble seat. George saw the heavy brass handles, tickets fluttering from them like bright feathers. Frames had been painted onto the wide safety glass that wrapped each car to give the illusion of windows. Milly sat primly alone in the last coach, his wife and Cornell facing each other in the second, their knees touching in the crowded quarters. Louise was the one who rode backward. Mary sat on a bench outside the station and glanced impatiently at her wrist watch and then up the line just as if she were waiting for a real train.

He started down the slope, his eyes on the single and sometimes double set of tracks which merged and seemed to cover each other like stripes on a barber pole. When he was halfway down the hill Louise spotted him and waved. She called to the engineer and Grant sounded the whistle, bass as a boat's, and rang the bell, his face obscured in the plume of steam which feathered back from the stack.

George came to a siding next to some signals and switches and waited for the train to pass. He smiled—instinct again, or reflex—at Milly. Messenger grinned and shouted something to him which he couldn't make out, and when the train had gone by he crossed the tracks and passed through the thin verisimilitude of tiny trees which masked the passengers' vision from their toy environment, and walked directly across the carefully landscaped oval to the station.

He sat next to Mary, who seemed subdued now, all interest lost, if she'd ever had any, in the elaborate rig.

"That train ain't going in your direction?"

"I never ride the day my mother is buried."

"Oh," Mills said.

"I bet they don't stop," she said. "Your wife and that Cornell character have been going round and round just forever. Not a thought for poor old Grant who has to catch all that steam in his face."

"The steam is hot?"

"Well no, it isn't hot exactly but it's not very pleasant. It's just especially horrible when you've just had your hair done, even if you're sitting well back in the cars like Milly."

"I see."

She shifted about to face him. "But it's all right at night if there's interesting guests and we all get inside and Grant puts the roofs on the coaches. Then one can have air conditioning in summer or electric heaters in winter. Then it's *very* cozy. Very especially if it's a boy-girl party. There's lots more track that runs through those woods yonder. Then it can be better than a sleigh or hayride. Then it's just like the tunnel of love."

The train came by without slowing and an enhanced Messenger stood up in the coach, his hands braced on top of the glass. "The horror, the horror, hey Mills?" He was laughing.

"If you want a ride you have to flag the train," Mary said.

"That's all right," Mills said.

"There's a toilet inside the station if you have to go. There's a potbelly stove."

"I know," Mills said. "There's a map of the line behind glass. There's travel posters and old waiting room benches."

Mary looked at him curiously. "Did Grandfather tell you?"

"No."

"My mom?"

"Is Grant nice?"

"Very nice. He's worked for the family years. We're all very polite to Grant."

"Is Grant his first name or his last name?"

"You'd have to ask Milly."

"Where's the flag?"

"Over there," she said, "but you can use your handkerchief or raise your hand as if you were hailing a cab."

"You do it," Mills said.

"No," she said, "it's stupid."

"Does Grant ever get to go for a ride?"

"He's riding now."

"I mean in the cars. I mean in the coaches."

Messenger, grinning, helped Louise down from the train when it pulled in. It's her big day, Mills thought.

"Can my husband have a ride?" Louise asked.

"I'm all right," George said.

"Just once or twice around," she said. "You can't tell from here but there's a tiny model city where the train makes its first turn. It's very unique."

"I've got to talk to you," Cornell Messenger whispered.

"Miss Claunch said that maybe we could bring Daddy's Meals-on-Wheels friends out for a ride someday," Louise said. "It's really amazing. You ought to try it, George."

"There's not much water in the boiler," Grant said. "I'd have to fill it and fire it up again."

"Oh yeah?" George said. "You'd have to go to all that trouble? For me? Oh yeah?"

And suddenly—Mills didn't know how—the two of them were bristling about each other, hackled as rivals dithered and suspicious over pawed ground, cautious, their glands giving off signal, tooth-and-claw stuff.

Mills asked if Grant were Grant's first name or last.

Grant wondered if George was the same George who'd taken Mrs. Glazer to Mexico to die.

"That's right," Mills said. "She asked for me."

"Specifically asked for you?"

"Specifically. That's right."

"She was very ill."

"Bereft," Mills shot back. "Bereft of folks to count on."

"Hey," Messenger said. "Hey, come on."

"Leave me alone," George said.

Milly was crying. Mary, sedate on the bench, looked from her sister to the others. Louise announced that if they were driving back to the city she had better stop in at the station first. Grant walked to his tender and started to climb aboard. Mills followed him.

"It's hot," he said. "Those cars are air-conditioned. You didn't turn it on for my wife."

"I'd have had to put the roofs up."

"You should have! She just had her hair done. Now it's all unkempt from the steam."

"It was unkempt when she got on board."

"Don't you talk about my wife that way." But Grant had already started the train up. George backed away from the steam shooting out from the pistons. "I'm talking to you. Where are you going? Someone is talking to you!"

Grant turned around and smiled. "Who?"

"I've got to talk to you," Messenger said behind him.

"What? What do you want?"

"Let's go down a ways. I don't want anyone to overhear."

"I've got to get back to the city."

"Hey fellow, come on, will you? I lit up again in the station. I'm so stoned you could make a citizen's arrest. Why do I do this? Do I do this for fun? It's the griefs, Mills. I owe it to my problems. It's medicine for the griefs."

"I don't care about your problems."

"Sure, if you did you'd get stoned too."

"Yeah, well, I've got my own troubles," George said, turning away.

"What, a saved, tucked-in guy like you? All snuggy snug and living the lap robe, deck chair life?"

"Louise told you that on the train."

"Who? Oh. Lulu? Nah. The mischief maker told me."

"Mrs. Glazer?"

"Long distance. She was dying. She reached out and touched someone. Cancerous bitch."

"Come if you're coming. I'm going back."

"Wait," Cornell said, and his voice was unenhanced. "Does *Mahesvaram* mean anything to you?"

When George turned back to look at him Cornell was standing on the tracks, all the fingers of his left hand stuffed into his mouth. "It's that word she gave you," he said quietly, "it was her mantra."

Messenger seemed as if he were going to collapse, and Mills rushed to support him.

"Watch out!" Grant shouted. "You're standing on the third rail!"

The two men leaped away from each other, tripping over the outside track. Grant roared. "Geez, that's the oldest one in the book," the engineer wheezed. "I used to get Judith with that one. Same as I got her kids. A third rail on a *steam* engine?"

"What else?" Cornell hissed, recovering, grasping the sleeve of Mills's suit coat. "Did she tell you about my kid?"

"Not now," George said, and pulled away. "You go on. I have to talk to that guy." He turned toward the engineer, already addressing him while he was still several yards away. "What's your problem, Grant?"

"Oh, *my* problem."

"This morning I was your dead mistress's pallbearer. The family knows the use I've been to them. I mean the girls, I mean the sisters-in-law, I mean the aunt. I mean Mr. Glazer and the Claunches, Jr. and Sr. both. If I were to mention your rudeness to me, or the people in my party . . ."

Grant was laughing, applauding his speech. "Hear hear," he said. "Har har."

"You're drunk."

"Do you play cards?" Grant asked suddenly.

"What?"

"Cards. Card games. Do you know how to play card games?"

"Yes," Mills said, "sure."

"How many games?"

"What are you talking about?"

"How many card games do you know how to play? Gin? Do you know gin?"

"I play gin."

"Call rummy? Michigan rummy?"

328

"Michigan rummy."

"Pinochle? Bridge?"

"I never learned bridge."

"You never learned."

"So?"

"You never learned. You don't know call rummy. Or a dozen games I could mention you've never heard of. The poker variations. Sure, *you* play cards. You never learned. You know who taught me bridge? Judith. Judith did. I was her bridge partner."

"You're crazy," Mills said.

"What do you think my father did? For a living? How did he support us?"

"How would I know?"

"Guess."

"I don't know. He worked for the Claunches. He was in service. I don't know. You're the gardener's boy."

They were at the station.

"My father was a pharmacist. He owned a drugstore."

"Guess what?" Louise said, coming out of the train station. She was laughing.

"My daughter programs computers and my son has three shoe-stores in Kansas City," the servant said.

"That john's no bigger than a child's potty," Louise said. "The toilet paper's no wider than a reel of tape. It's scale. Everything's scale."

He opened the door of his Buick Special and was about to get in —Louise was already in the back, Cornell in front—when someone called to him. "Hold on a moment would you?" It was the man who had waved to him, the one who'd been admiring the classic cars when Mills had passed the garages on his way to find Louise.

"Yes?" Mills said. "What?"

"Don't mean to hold you up," the man said, approaching the car. "Your Special?"

"Yes," Mills said.

"Sixty-three?"

"Yes."

"Thought so," the man said. "Spotted it when you drove up to St. Michael and St. George this morning. Recognized the grille straight off. Dead giveaway. Had that lovely grille on her the year she

329

was introduced and then they went to a different design the following year. Why'd they do that? Any idea?"

"No," Mills said.

"Could be birds. Scooped in birds. Some aerodynamic thing. You think?"

"I don't know."

"That's mine. Over there. The Studebaker."

"Very nice."

"Thank you," the man said. "Felt a *bit* odd about driving it to her funeral but if that's what old Judy wanted, why, hell, what the hell, eh?"

"What the hell," George said.

"Look," the man said, "take my card, will you? I know it's a long shot, but if you ever *do* want to sell, give me a call. If I'm not at the office call me at home. The number's unlisted but I've jotted it down on the back."

Mills told him he wasn't thinking of selling his car.

"I know," the man said. "I'd feel the same way if I were you. But call anyway. We'll do lunch at the club." He looked in the car window and tipped an imaginary hat.

"Sir," he said. "Madam."

PART FOUR

1

It wasn't religious this time, it was political and historical.

And maybe if I wasn't the thinking man's George Mills was the vocal one's one. A witness, in a dynasty of witnesses, one more chump who crewed history, whose destiny it was to hang out with the field hands, just *there,* you see, in range and hard by, but a little out of focus in the group photographs, rounded up when the marauders came, feeding the flames, one more wisp of smoke at the Inquisitions, doing all the obligatory forced marches, boat folks from the word go, but nothing personal on anybody's part. Not the government's, not the rebels'. Certainly not our own.

My own taling meant for more than just the story hour, that kid's garden of lullaby and closed circle of our family tradition. Your father-to-son disclosures I mean, all archived confidence and my spooked clan's secret recipes. And if I was different it's because I seemed to clamor for audience as well as style. Because we Millses have always had the latter. The former, too, if you come right down to it. Maybe *particularly* the former, even if it always turns out to be, as it always does turn out to be, some knee-jounced, lap-settled, thumb-sucking babe child who can't get over any of it, who takes it all in, who takes it, terrified and relieved too that nothing, nothing whatsoever, is all that will ever be expected of him. That the only thing he has to do is remember that primal incident in the Polish forest when Guillalume fixed forever the Millsian parameters and gave us—never mind revolution, never mind reform bills, modern times or the inchworm creep of hope—our Constitution. And one thing other of course: to be ready to spill it all out when the babe child was on the other knee as it were, meanwhile perfecting *his* style—which we Millses have always had—rendering the story to his own inner ear if he were still without issue, perfecting his nuance as another might perfect his French for a trip abroad, and taking care to get the magic parts pat.

Because we're not even a joke. After all these years, all these centuries. Not fabled in song and story, not even a joke. Our name, till I came along, never even in the papers. Our eyewitness unrecorded, our testimony not so much ignored as never even overheard, the generations sworn to secrecy, or if not actually sworn at least inclined that way. Content enough with our secret handshakes and coded bearing, our underground railway ways.

Which is just as well could be. Or so the story goes. Our version of it anyway, the way I heard it, how it came down to me, our baton-passed history apostolically successioned. Tag, and you're it.

Maybe we should have tried America, put in some time in the New World. Or maybe not. It's all new world for our kind anyway, ain't it? See why I began by implying I was the thinking man's George Mills? Not because I was any smarter than those other guys, God knows, but because I was capable of all this alternative, but-on-the-other-hand understood like some spiffy grammatical usage. My lot calls that thinking. Your lot too probably. (There I go again.) And if I had this Millsian perspective that lends detachment and magnanimous neutrality, perhaps it's really because . . . This isn't what I wanted to talk about.

It wasn't religious this time, it was political, historical. Perhaps the King himself opened the door.

I don't say answered. Opened. Perhaps he was on his way out as I was already knocking. Anyway, now I think of it, I must have startled him (despite his size, which was immense, he was big around as a kiosk) a good deal more than he startled me. I had the advantage, you see, of not knowing he was the King. (What advantage did he have? The man about to step out, nothing on his mind, to judge from his whistling, but his mood, calling, as was *his* destiny, all the shots of his daily round, and submissive at details as a tool, the arrangements already delegated, assigned, giving over his entire person like a horseman a heel for a hoist. And there I was, blocking *his* way, stuck in the doorway like an insurrectionist, a man, to look at me, to judge from my seedy clothes and peasant's seamy appurtenances, the countryman's straw helmet still on my head, the loose smock that could have concealed weapons, the rude boots like someone's who might have been in his mutiny suit, for rebellion dressed, a far-flung Jacobin say, some Luddite-come-lately uniformed for sedition and putsch.) Advantage to the hick. (Because what really alarmed him, I learned later, too late, was not my crummy clothes or savage bearing—he was King of Great Britain and Ireland, King of Hanover; he knew our homespun, had closets of the stuff made to order for the bumpkin balls and bogtrots, the hayseed hoedowns and rustic masquerades of his youth—but my simple failure to bow and scrape, to make a leg or flat out kneel. What did *I* know? My fourth day in town. To me he looked like any other fat, well-groomed London gentleman of breeding. Where were his crown and sceptre? His sash and ribbons? His sword? The feather in his cap no higher than any other man's. [Indeed, he was bareheaded.] And where, for that matter, were all the King's men? Some of them? Any? One? His appearance less regal finally than a footman's. Less regal than the livery of the men who drove the carriages in the streets. [Which was what I'd thought *I'd* do, why I'd come to London, with no weapons but only my letter of introduction greasy and rumpled under my smock that explained my presence at that particular door—it was not even the front door—at the very time when the man I did not yet know was my sovereign was about to emerge from it.] Dressed in long trousers, the plain style that had just come in, vestless, his neck unadorned save for a wide black circle of cloth that served as cravat.)

So we did this mutual side shuffle, feinting and parrying like swordsmen, like men before mirrors. I *would* have bowed if he'd given me a chance, displayed nape like a white flag, bobbed and bowed, ducked and dithered. Why not? It costs nothing to give way to squires, even when they're coming out servants' entrances, and it pleases them so.

"Stand still, damn ye," the old fellow said.

And I did, recovering my balance like a tumbler. He looked me over, asked my name.

"It's George," I said.

"George," he mocked.

"Aye," I said. Then, haughtily, as he'd been scornful: "George, son of George. Son of George, son of George, son of George. George, son of George to the forty-second or forty-third power if it comes to that."

"And *does* it come to that?"

"It sure does."

"British?"

"As the day is long."

"Bow to the King," hissed the aging dandy.

"What? *Where? Here?*" Startled, reflexive, bent as in cramp. Taking, before him, a kind of cover, as if shells had gone off, rockets, explosives, sunbursts of majesty. (A Mills first, an historical highlight, whose eight and a half centuries had been a kind of preparation for just such a moment. The subject is subjects. *The subject is subjects!* Who'd lived always in monarchical climes the low-liege life. Assured of kings as a Christian of God but who'd yet to see one. Never mind been in one's presence, had actual audience. Glimpsed his coach I mean, spotted retainers. Living centuries on a small island since practically the *invention* of kings, ringed by their circumstance and circumscribed by their ordinance, hemmed by decree, paying the rates and loyal at the levy, doing the death duties and making good on the ransoms, prizing the special commemorative coins and celebratory postage like heirloom, and coming up with the surtaxes and VAT's, the excise and octroi, all tolls all told and the taxes on war and peace and all the royal expeditions. Excused from nothing yet and exacting from ourselves what they'd tax collectors to exact. Among the poorest of their subjects and withal over the years and down through the reigns and dynasties—how we told time—contributing to their collective, cumulative well-being at least one gold spoke on at least one golden wheel that turned the coach we had yet to see.) I grabbed the sleeve of the old guy's coat and yanked.

"Get down, Guv! Get *down* for the sovereign!"

And, groveled as spider, did this dance of good citizenship. Palace farce. For the handkerchief that came off in my hand when I'd grabbed his wrist was embroidered with a silken seal of majesty, his royal monogram in king's tailored cursive, HMGIV like Roman numerals of state. By this time, too, recognizing elements of the declined, devalued handsomeness in the aging face from the mint, intact perfection of his image on my coins. (Thinking: Not merely a man, not merely even an important man, but actual animate money.)

We aren't stupid. It was so unexpected. Indeed, I got the picture before the King did, and made my adjustments, all my Kentucky windage reassignments of perception, the King himself still preoccupied with a king's terrors—— mutiny, red menace, rout and regicide. It was my *duty* to calm him.

Practically prostrate, I called soothingly to him. "Sire," I crooned. Calling him autarch, calling him dynast, calling him King, my mind all over him with all the stored-up honorifics of a captive race.

"Guv?" he said. *"Guv?"*

"A figure of speech, Father."

"To the forty-third power?"

"Or forty-second. More likely forty-second. Almost assuredly forty-second."

"Gee," he said wistfully, "we're only George the Fourth. Great Great Grandfather wasn't born till 1660."

No. It was my *duty* to comfort him. And still obeisant, my body language spelling Kick Me, I proceeded to betray a couple dozen generations just like that, appropriating his figures, confiscating for my low use his own long, lazy, highborn inherited primogenitive courtship patterns—their kings' prerogatives of annulment and divorce, eschewing girl children, all the extended foreplay and monkeyshine monarchics that come with reign, their fiat history and command performance arrangements—thereby appending years to, and actually doubling, our own regulation Mills-size generations. But for all my extemporized mathematics I could only squeeze us to the twenty-second or so power, a figure unacceptable to the parvenu Hanoverian. (Do I sound too larky? Wait. Have patience. I get mine.)

"You're some upstart pretender, ain't you?" His Majesty said.

"No, sir. I swear it."

"Yes you are. You're one of those wicked, wretched claimants."

"Me? In *these* rags?"

"A clever disguise."

"I'm your loyalest subject."

"My closest follower?" the King asked slyly.

"Sir?"

"Come come, you're not stupid. You're a spy."

"I never am," I told him forcefully. But you don't disagree with a king, and added, "Your Royal Highness."

"Oh yes," he said disconsolately. "Our Royal Highness indeed. Our Real Whoreness. Our Rogue Whoness."

"I may not listen to treason, sire."

"Treason," the King said miserably.

"Who disparages my king treasons my country."

Then, changing his mood once again: "How did you find the safe house?"

"The safe—— ?"

"Whom did you bribe? The neighbors, was it?"

"Sir, I don't even know the neighbors." And I looked around. We were standing in the kitchen. Or what would have been the kitchen if there'd been a stove, cooking implements, even a kitchen table. It was without furnishings. Through the open door at the back of the room I could glimpse other vacant rooms. "Would this be your castle then?" I asked, trying to keep the misgivings and nervousness out of my voice, for the place I'd seen from the outside was barely larger than the croft cottages at home, and I'd begun to suspicion that the gentleman was some mad imposter. George IV, or whoever he was, studied me a moment.

"Restored," he said. "What do you think? Not too busy?"

"Sir, *I* don't think so."

"We're so pleased."

Well we're *not* stupid. And of course I knew that it wasn't Buckingham House and that the King—if he was the King, for by this time I had more than doubts—was bantering with me, but how do you banter with royalty, or with madmen either, if that's what it came to? I haven't the gift of humoring people. (Or of hiding motives either, wearing my interiority on my sleeve like kings their handkerchiefs. I had actually taken a penny out of my purse and was glancing from it to the "king" as a man might check a map against the very landscape he stands in.) And now the man who claimed to be George IV had drawn a pistol and was pointing it at me. I could see that the handle was encrusted with jewels that formed the same same seal I'd seen on his kerchief.

"Who gave us away?" he asked sadly.

"But no one did," I said, and tried to explain what I was doing there and told him of my desire to drive carriages. "I'm here to guide coaches, sir. To handle traps and landaus, phaetons and broughams and tilburies. To make my profession in curricles, cabriolets, all the gigs and all the buggies. All the buckboards and berlins. I mean to follow my star in whitechapels, in shays and clarences, in shandrydans and charabancs. I would take my place behind the horses." The man watched me carefully. "I'm into traffic," I said shyly. And told him nothing of my having no destination of my own, just my vague wish to go where other men went. And breathed no word about my hackman's heart. But mentioned Squire's letter in my behalf which I carried under my blouse, offering to show it to him, already beginning to raise the loose garment when he extended the pistol, thrusting it forward in the close quarters, aiming as if it were his turn in a duel.

I closed my eyes. "Oh, I hope you *are* the King, Your Highness," I told him. "I hope you outrank everyone on this island. All the islands, all the continents, all the world. I hope this murder is sanctioned by divine right and ain't just the heatless, heartless, whimwham of just some anybody brokeheart bedlamite."

"You don't acknowledge the Hanoverian legitimacy! You, you——"

Of course it was possible that he was George IV and crazy too. There was plenty of precedent on the books. The rumors about his father, for example.

"I'm a Mills. If you're George Hanover I'm your subject. None loyaler. I've pledged allegiances. I've sworn oaths."

"Commoners don't swear oaths."

"Millses do."

"They're not required."

"Millses require them."

And that's when I told him some of our history, the long story I'd been memorizing and then rehearsing all my life. Since I'd first heard it. Bringing in details about my life I hadn't memorized only because no one had ever related them to me, and hadn't known I'd been rehearsing only because I thought of nothing else. Who was only eighteen years old and without a son and so had no one to tell it to but a king in his sixties. Not the whole story of course, only an overview, the themes and highlights, the way my father had introduced it to me.

"Oh, oaths," he said dismissively when I'd finished. "All fealty's faked submission holds. I know all about that. Why God limbered the neck and hinged the knee. You think kings care for your crawled compliance and cross-my-hearts? Or put much stock in dubious duty's danced obedience?

"We were Prince of Wales," he said. "Then Prince Regent. Ceremonially sworn ourselves, hands on Bibles, hands on hearts. On state occasions to Father cried 'God save the King!' when all we meant was 'Happy birthday.' Zeal just informed politics lying low. Lying.

"Come come, George the Forty-third——"

"Twenty-second."

"Indeed," he said shrewdly, "Twenty-second. Using our king's packed calibrations, statecraft's Celsius metrics. Come come, George. (See? I speak to you as George to George and put away my pistol. I couldn't use it anyway.) Come come then. What is it you want? Why do you lie in wait for me at my safe house?" Then his face darkened and I knew he was the King. Not his resemblance to the face on my penny nor his expensive accessories, nor even his strange manner of speech, but the suffusion itself, the royal blood heavy as sap with mood. "You've come from Brighton! You're a reveler! Something's happened to Maria!"

"Maria?"

"Mrs. Fitzherbert," he said.

"Mrs. Fitzherb—— "

And suddenly his hands were at his throat as if he meant to do himself an injury. Pulling clumsily at his neck scarf—he was King all right, valet-tended, no more familiar with the loops and intricacies of his complicated adornments than a babe in a nursery—unwinding, it seemed, bolts of the stuff, twirling it away from him like noose, like lariat, a dark silk spiral that rose over his face and head like black smoke. A huge diamond fastener rolled on the floor against his shoe. He kicked it furiously away from him. And now his hands were at his collar tearing at the precious cloth, murderously ripping it, and I thought: Why, he's choking, the King of Great Britain, Hanover and Ireland is choking, and rushed to his side, though I didn't know what to do, or no, knew well enough what to do but was reluctant to do it, too timid to pound the back of a king—even a king in extremis— as if he were just some pal in a tavern. So I stood there gawking, gawky, close up as some morbid witness, and could only moan over and over like an idiot, "God save the King, *God* save the King!"

And now, having stripped himself of cravat and torn his shirt, his hands tightened about folds of actual skin, working his neck as if he meant to strangle himself, me still incapable of interfering with him and able only to mutter my mad "God save the King's," and then, in crazy desperation, suddenly recalling *his* words. Leaning even further forward, my lips almost in his ear. "Happy birthday," I prompted, "happy birthday, George IV."

"Help," he gasped. "Help us for God's sake. We can't *get* the damned thing." It was that "us" and "we" that got me. A king bent on wringing his own neck and still mindful of the royal grammar, his brain still locked on the King's English, his sovereign's syntax. That was when the loyalest subject in the land raised his hands against his king, the two of us co-conspirators in his regicide. I placed my strong young hands over his fat old weak ones, as yet adding no additional pressure of my own, intending only to encourage him in his efforts, a new form, a sort of King's touch in reverse. Touching the King. He stared up at me with a wild eye and squawked through the muffling medium of our two pairs of hands, our twenty tight-knit fingers. "Are you—— are you trying to kill us? Take your hands *off* me—*us*—you —— you *Stuart!*"

My hands dropped to my sides and His Majesty rubbed his neck, which by this time was quite red. Then he asked if I would get the clasp. He was referring to a fine gold chain which hung around his neck and from which a locket was suspended. I raised my hands but when he saw them he seemed to change his mind again and, waiting till he was calmer, managed to undo it himself. Before he handed it over to me he pressed a button at its top and the locket sprang open.

"There," he said. "That's Maria—— Mrs. Fitzherbert."

The locket contained a miniature of a beautiful young girl. "This child is married?" I asked.

"What? Oh. Well. She was younger when the portrait was made. She's close to seventy now," he said. "Then you *don't* know her, do you?" I shrugged and returned the King's necklace. "You're not come from Brighton. You're not in costume. You're not from the revels," he said, disappointed.

"These are my clothes, Majesty," I said, and was reminded of the tapestry condition that Greatest Grandfather Mills had spoken of to Mills's horse centuries before in the salt mine.

"Yes," he said. "Of course they are."

"We dress this way."

"Yes."

"For the mowing."

"Oh yes."

"For the tilling and toiling."

"Yes, yes."

"For the tubers and turnips."

"Yes," he said, "we know."

"For the cabbage and kale."

"Naturally."

"For the beans and the beetroots." (Because I couldn't stop.)

"Certainly."

"For reaching the fruits, their ripe rife rums and boozy brandies."

"All right," the King said.

"Never for revels."

"No," he said.

Because I couldn't stop, you see. Or not couldn't, wouldn't. Who had never had audience. Not in forty-two or forty-three generations. Say forty-three. (Almost certainly forty-three. Forty-three absolutely.) Who've these passive, heirloom hearts you see, handed down father-to-son, father-to-son, father-to-son *ad infinitum,* who not only had sat out each riot, rebellion and revolt, every mutiny and coup d' état from Wat Tyler's defeated heroics to the fizzled Gunpowder Plot, but who'd never even signed a neighbor's petition or written a letter to the editor. Who *couldn't* stop, you see. Who might have in a palace or stately home, but not here in this unfurnished croft cottage of a "safe house"—who still didn't understand the term but took it to mean something gay, something spoofy and nostalgic, with carefully blended choruses of pretend peasants holding flower baskets and singing opera—with its rude, spic-and-span meagerness.

"Never for fêtes, never for galas."

"No, of course not."

"Not for affairs, not for occasions."

"I see."

"We dress *up.*"

"We understand," he said. "We do."

"We break out the cambric, we let loose the lace."

"If you're finished?" the King said.

"What picks up stains."

"Quite."

"What blemishes easy, what soils in the air." And stopped now. Not because I had gone too far, or even far enough, but because grievance made me breathless, took my wind away I mean. Seeing how easy it was, how even someone like myself, who'd seen no kings but only heard of them, gone all logy with my ancient, sluggish heritage and languid beefs, had only to wait—whether he wanted to or not, whether he was interested or not—to float in his patience, treading it like shallow water, and one day not opportunity but accident itself would knock. Not chance, not even time laying about and lining things up—— accident, bad odds, the potluck of doom and fate. And what made me breathless was that I perceived that all that differentiated me from the king killers and historical tuckpointers was inclination.

King George IV did not perceive this.

340

King George IV wanted me calmer, to talk me down from my resentment.

"I suppose you're pious?" he said.

"Pious?"

"Religious."

"No, not really."

"Civic-minded then."

"I don't think so. I don't think I'm civic-minded."

"French things? Social contracts, the Rights of Man?"

"I'm English. I don't take with wog ways."

"No," the Hanoverian said suspiciously. And explained to his subject what a safe house was.

I wasn't far off.

What King George IV told George XLIII:

"Kings aren't born. They're made. In the sense that contingency heirs thrones. The first-born could be an idiot; an inopportune girl; someone too sickly for the times; at odds with the ministers, current events, the Cabinet—— All manner of things can come between an apparency and a crown.

"But consider a prince. Assume what he assumes. That all will go well. That one day the King will die and, in the nature of things, he will be King.

"Now. There are only two sorts of kings. The battlers and the good time Charlies. You could look it up, but we assure you that history bears us out. (Shall we sit on the floor? Standing winds us. —There. Thank you, George. Oh, that's much better. Much.)

"Of course the battlers have practically disappeared from the thrones they used to sit on like so many saddles. I mean the warrior kings, the conquerors—Bonaparte, of course, but he was no proper king; more to the point he was never a prince—the horseback heroes, all that pup tent royalty with their iron-assed, cavalry sensibilities and real estate hearts. I don't mock them. I don't. They made the world, its true cartographers, and did all this not from Heaven but from ambush. On maneuvers, campaigns, sieges, blockades. On scorched earth in the dead of winter. With billets for palace and trenches for fort. With rations for banquets and their kingdom front lines. So I don't mock them. I don't. But if they made the world, they broke it too. Surely the Fifth Horseman of the Apocalypse was a king.

"Well—battlers are chiefly dead now. The chiefly dead. And they fell not necessarily in the wars they lost but rather in the wars

341

they won. Dead of politics and delegation and the piecemeal amelioration of the world. The battlers are dead, long live the good time Charlies!

"Princes I mean. Those ritual babes, those ceremonial children. In their toy tailoring, their plaything regalia. Up on their ponies, pulled in their dog carts. Taking trays in their bedrooms, their lunches from hampers on summer's golden bivouacs. Outranking their music and dancing masters. Calling the tune. Outranking *all* their masters. Outranking, for that matter, the King himself who, for all his now ornamental power, his own now baubled governance and ascendancy, owed no greater obligation to his so-called kingdom than simple, subservient fatherhood. Who could chastise and even discipline—my father once shot the dog who pulled my cart—but could never repudiate, never disown. (Who could in effect, Mills, write no will, all that having been done for him by the very principles of succession that the battlers had battled for. Who would die, as it were, intestate as the lowest pauper in the land. And incidentally, George XLIII, did you enter this into your equations when you so rapidly calculated the twenty-year differential between a king's generation and a commoner's? It was because kings knew—they'd been princes themselves, remember—how much harder it would go with them once their children were born, how their already depleted authority would be even further adulterated by their coddled kin. It could have been some vaguely flickering memory of the look on a prince's father's face—I can still recall the foiled temper on my own father's face when he shot the dog that pulled me about the royal park—his watered anger, his niggled rage. We battle passion, we good time Charlies, by fathering bastards.)

"We had it made. Princes, princes did. And lived with impunity like favored pets. It was sybaritic but don't say no good ever came of it. There are always spin-offs, Mills. They trickle down. Sooner or later they do, they trickle down. Why, education, *education* was invented for us! Toys, lad, toys and gewgaws! Cakes and cookies, chocolates and collections! The most important artisans and cooks and engravers doing their best to keep us entertained. Great inventors pressed us to accept their original working models. (The first candle, the first candle was made for a seven-year-old Italian prince because he was afraid of the wall torches that flared in his nursery!) Those were the glory days, Mills. Those were the glory days, kid. We had this privately engraved stamp collection. (I would have been fourteen or fifteen by then.) Young Bill Blake was awarded the commission.

(Hogarth was dead, and anyway I'd never really liked the wallpaper he sketched for my nursery.) He did this absolutely top-hole job, wizard work, wizard. A personalized postage on which our head was represented as the Crown Prince of three or four dozen imaginary kingdoms. Will I ever forget the New Jerusalem ha'penny? Coins were similarly minted for us and with them I purchased great pleasure of some of the most beautiful women in England and the Continent. Will I ever forget those ladies, most of them courtesans, cousins, dowager princesses—— all of them older?

"Because even at nine and eleven and thirteen I was still wet-nursing. I couldn't give up the tit. I've *never* given it up. (Enemies whisper it's why I'm so fat and that could be the case. Science may side with their slanders. I've too well known the nipple's weighty nourishment, the breast's milky syrups, its rich creams and thick butters. All its queer cheeses, its chest junkets and bust custards. We're addicted to tit. We love the *taste* we mean.) Though we'd never drawn Charlotte Sophia's, our mother's, milk. But this ain't a mother thing, we think, only obsessive thirst annihilating itself at the very wellhead of lixiviate, suffocate whelm.

"It was how I met Maria.

"This would have been forty-one years ago. I would have been twenty-two, Maria six years older. And it would have been at a ball, and I would have been strolling down the formal presentation line, barely glancing at the men's bowed kowtows and carefully observing the revealing curtsies of the women. *Examining,* I mean. Holding their hands and by a subtle pressure of my own keeping them down, availing myself of stunning vistas of bosom, controlling honor's duration and causing those ladies to heat and blush as surely as if I had kindled their dry white flesh with the oxygens of my gloves. Although some never took color at all, their breasts pale as lime, fixed as paint or whitewash. (Or as if, I thought when I detected among them some recent mother, all the blood in the world could neither stain nor stanch the tide of such milk. I was neither prospecting for virgins nor inspecting for trollops, these little litmus tests of mine not so much science as interested, evenhanded, even innocent forays into Nature, as a man might engage to witness sunsets, say.)

"Maria was the most charmingly endowed woman I had ever seen. But she was no flusher.

"If she had been I might not have ventured—though I may have, covered as a bed by my prince's privilege and anything-goes protocol and all my good time Charlie dispensations—to have offered my proposal.

" 'Would you,' I whispered, still on that inverted receiving line which was my style and preference and down which I ambled as if I were the only invited guest in some stuffed tenement of princes and princesses, 'be my wet nurse? I will give you Tom Gainsborough's; *Blue Boy.*'

" 'Sir, I have no milk.'

" 'My mistress then. I will give you a house in Brighton and five thousand a year.'

" 'Sir, I have a husband.'

" 'Two thousand for the husband. Could even a king say fairer?'

" 'Sir, I cannot.'

" 'Madam, I'm a generous prince.'

" 'Sir, I'm a virtuous woman.'

" 'You did not redden.'

" 'Redden?'

" 'When I leered your breasts, when I squinnied your nipples. When I leisurely look-see'd and gave them the once-over and the glad eye. You did not redden, madam! You did not plum or peach! I might for rise have well as ogled the stitch of your frock!'

" 'Then, sir, might I have glowed indeed for it is the very principle of propriety, if not of virtue itself, that the scrutiny of one's fashion in high company can betoken only the awry and amiss. I would, in such a circumstance, have warmed under the gaze of a tailor or the glance of a seamstress.'

" 'I am no *tailor,* madam. I am no *seamstress.* I'm Prince of Wales and I attentioned your tits. *You did not redden!*'

" 'Then, sir, I am no scarlet woman,' Mrs. Fitzherbert told me softly.

"This was still on the line, still ceremonial. That the others who had yet to be presented had entirely ceased the customary buzz they do even at Court, even in the presence of the King himself, let alone a mere Prince of Wales who wouldn't be Regent for another twenty-seven years or King for another thirty-six, ought perhaps to have given us pause or made one or the other of us a bit more cautious. Indeed, I suppose that at this point I should have smiled at Mrs. Fitzherbert's clever grace note, clicked what I had for heels, bowed, and gone on to the next person waiting to be presented. Or, rather, I suppose it's what you suppose. But the splendour of our arrangements, their true civility and grandeur, is actually quite opposite. Court must, simply *must,* have its gossip, its exclusionary spice. Well, do you understand, Mills, that gossip and rumor are always more or less horizontal, that, like certain species of fish, they swim only their customary strata and rarely attempt the antipathetical depths? Now, it ain't in Newton, but it's true as physics that in fixed societies like our own, nasty stories neither ascend nor descend but stay within their class of origin. It's why we have to spy on you people. It's why you're cordoned off on state occasions; it's why there's crowd control, squeeze play, spurs on horsemen; cosh, curb and roped-off street——all rule's royal leash law, all order's rerouted traffic, all rank's union shop. It ain't assassination we fear, the villain's and madman's bullet at close quarters; it's just hard by, at hand, stone's throw, simple spit distance earshot.

"So, if anything, we were not more circumspect but less, not less garrulous but more. Is the Prince a clam? Is he an oyster? He *brims* with prate! He *glibs* with gush! And this was audience indeed, *this* was! This primed, fervent, rubberneck, avid, all-ears bunch. My true subjects, Mills, and not *your* remote, long-range, arm's-length lot. The group. *Our* crowd. And I as much their subject this night as they mine. We were *soliloqual,* Mills!

" 'It is your breastplate, madam, those fleecy ramparts, that so astonish us. How may things which to our vision appear such soft and lenient stuff prove so intractable, so stony ground in the campaign of a prince? No no, don't answer. We would not hear prattle of husbands and virtue, or passion talked down as if 'twere only an obligation owed to pledge like the gambler a game debt or the poor student's circumstanced promise to redeem a watch from some pawnshop Jew. Is *this* your honor, madam? Is *this* your merciless, inconsequent, merely proscriptive character? I'll teach you *character,* ma'am, and it's nothing to do with promises, declarations, assurances, covenants or nitwit oath. Honor is simply not contractual, Fitzherbert! It does not blindly undertake action in a future it cannot yet understand at the sacrifice of the only tense in which it may reliably do anyone any good at all. Which is the present. Which is the *present,* Mrs. Madam Fitzherbert!

" 'Honor is ardor. It is dash and fire and thrill. It is the obligation skin owes blood, teeth appetite. My organ's duty to my mood. It is entirely obsessive and endures no third parties. It welcomes no middlemen.'

" 'The Prince of Wales is hot tonight,' said a guest.

" 'He is. He *is,* ' we acknowledged. 'We have our honor on us and we fly it like the colors.'

" 'And do you know, madam, in what my honor subsists? Why

345

in my peculiar, spangled lust. In the singularity of my ruling passion, my most feeling fetish. Which we neither hide nor hinder, watch nor ward. Why should we? Is the Prince custodian of his ruling passion or only the lowly drayman of his drives?'

" 'Hear hear!' said honored guests. And 'Three cheers!' And 'Give three times three!'

" 'I asked to milk you, madam. No husband but husbandman plain enough. Oh, plain. Plain, quite plainly. I've this sweet tooth for softs, this yen for your puddings. George the Famished, George the Parched. Georgie the pap prince. Feed us, ma'am. Slake the slake rake! Sow, *sew* this rip!'

"And 'Ahh,' mouthful'd the fellowship. And 'Ooh,' oratoried the witnesses.

"And still no more crimson than an eggshell. Why you, sir, are more raddled. Fitzherbert herself was glacial as pack ice. She said she'd pray for me.

"*Pray* for me, dun God with her demon orthodoxy! (Did I mention, Mills, that she was Catholic? She was Catholic, churched as a pope.)

" 'Do it then, madam,' I told her coolly. 'You know our prayers. You may say them *for* us!'

"And turned away politely to make the rest of my devoirs, saying my 'So glads' and 'How pleaseds,' aloof and indifferent as an already king.

"I learned she lived at Richmond and sent with my compliments my private yacht to fetch her. It came back empty. I sent it out again a week later, laden with gifts. The Gainsborough I'd promised, precious jewels, rare ivories. It came back empty, my gifts unopened. In a month I sent the ship out once more, this time with specific instructions to proffer my prince's compliments to *Lord* Fitzherbert and to invite him and his amiable wife to stay at Buckingham House with my family and myself. There was no 'Lord' Fitzherbert of course, and what I offered was not so much a bribe as the promise of a bribe. Titled Catholics were practically unheard of in the country at this time. I knew my man and what I was doing. The appeal was not so much to his ambition as to his churchianity. The bark returned empty.

"And empty again when I dispatched it to Pangbourne, where I'd learned the Fitzherberts summered with a colony of their co-religionists.

"The King had of course heard of my efforts and their failures. How could he not? All society knew what I was up to. All it had to do was glance out its window whenever it heard a ship go by. The chances were excellent it would be the royal bark plying its unsuccessful trade route, hauling its unwanted merchandise about its watery itinerary like some failed merchantman. My mad king father was not yet mad. He was only angry. The truth, George, is that he missed his princedom, his own long-gone good time Charlie days when he had all the honors of a king but none of his dubious duties. They had been pushing him in the colonies. They were pushing him in France. The truth is, Mills, I pissed him. All he had for amusement in those days was my lust's blunting against Mrs. Fitzherbert's obdurate recalcitrance.

"He summoned me and offered a father's advice in the throne room at Buckingham. He even removed the crown from his head before he spoke.

" 'Son,' he said, 'it disheartens us to see you so sobersides at a time in life when you should be all waggish and sportive. It tarnishes our comfort to perceive in you the mopes and melancholies of a distrait heart. We would have you cock-a-hoop, all frisk and frolic, and miss the horse laugh whoopee which was your once wont. Give us a chortle, love. Cackle a snigger for us. Titter—no offense, old son —titter your smirk. What? No? Not in we? Then send again to Richmond. I know what you demand of Mrs. Fitzherbert, and what you offer—— paintings and pretties, jewelry and gewgaw. The woman is pious, mavourneen. She's serious, treasure apple. You don't go up in public to a pious, serious, high-minded woman like this and order her to put her titties in your mouth. What, in public? A sensitive, religious, married lady? It isn't the way, it's not how it's done. You must be gentle, you must be discreet. You must offer reassurances. You must say: "Madam, I shall have my teeth pulled. The grinders and incisors, the molars and canines. All—— all shall come out. I vow you, ma'am, then only will I chew and nibble, suck and gum!" Send to Richmond, lad; send to Richmond, son. We'll make a picnic Thames-side and wait and wait till the cows come home.' And laughed like a loon.

"I did send to Richmond, had already sent for her when my father had sent for me. When the yacht returned Mrs. Fitzherbert was on it, standing near the bowsprit and, with her generous, billowy, partially exposed bosoms, looking for all the world like the very figurehead on the ship's very prow.

"I clambered aboard and took her in my arms.

" 'My darling,' I said. 'My dearest, you've come.'

" 'Fitzherbert's dead,' she whispered. 'Tomorrow we'll be married secretly by the priest. Then, suckling, shall you enjoy your little milkmaid to her bright twin pails' sweetest residuals!'

"We dress up," the King said. "We dress up, too. And lead free will these dumb show lives, our tastes a step behind our palates and our very existence revue, vaudeville, cabaret. And even our highest behaviors only simple 'turns,' studied as set piece, blocked as tableau. Sequenced as music hall and timed as spectacle. We don't want walls and floors, ceilings and rooms but back cloths, stages, flats and scrim. Not property but props. Not bad luck but tragedy, not even happiness, only comedy. So *we* dress up. Good time Charlie, the merry-andrew. The milkmaid. The milkmaid milkmade man.

"Yes. Well. We were married. Secretly. You spoke of oaths. *We* swore oaths. As heavily pledged as debtors. Proclaiming and promising, vowing, professing. All intention's by-all-that's-holy's.

"We honeymooned at Pangbourne while the royal yacht stood by. We boarded the ship and sailed to Scotland. We sailed to Ireland, where we anchored off a lovely blue bay. You could see palm trees.

"The marriage was secret, known only to the priest and to one or two of Maria's friends. I like to think that those of our class who lived along those shores must have seen the ship and guessed it on some romantic errand, engaged in some pretty myth—— all spurned love's Flying Dutchman. *We* dress up. Oh yes.

"Well. Even someone as apparently arbitrary as a prince or king with his edicts and decrees and his *ipse dixit* say-so style lives a life proviso'd and ordinanced as any tavern keeper's. And if there's more loophole than loop to my bonds—I could, for example, have shot you before without bringing any more trouble upon myself than if I had sent my meat back to my chef—there is a special pandect of law for royalty.

"The Settlement Act forbids any of the King's issue under the age of twenty-five to marry without first obtaining the consent of the King. This would have been forty years ago. I would have been twenty-three. The consent of the *King?* I knew better than even to ask for it. My only hope was to present my father with a *fait accompli,* thinking he'd think that the scandal which surrounded our relationship, and whatever embarrassment it may have caused him, might best be smoothed over by a royal announcement that we were now married.

"They had pushed him out of the colonies, they were pushing him in France. They were pushing him in his own Parliament. Now my father was now not only angry, he was actually mad."

"Please, sir," George Mills interrupted, "that was a rumor. Even our sort heard it. His political enemies . . ."

"Third was a lunatic, Forty-third. George was crazy, George," George IV said quietly.

"More loophole than loop, the laws bleeding into their crimes like loose and leaking bandages. French leave law. Because it was out of his hands now. Out of his hands and out of his head. And he *wasn't* embarrassed. And they didn't—I mean his ministers, I mean his council—even have to *use* the Settlement Act. More loophole than loop.

"There was a sort of conference to which I was invited. There weren't even barristers there, only a sort of solicitor from the Customs Office whom they'd rounded up at the last minute.

"The solicitor asked if I had reached my twenty-fifth birthday when I had been secretly married. He asked if I had obtained my father's consent. Then Mrs. Fitzherbert—he called her Mrs. Fitzherbert—was not my wife, was she? It was 'is opinion, the solicitor said, that the hact of 1701 was not even happlicable. *The act did not have to be enforced because under the very provisions of the rule the marriage was regarded as invalid!* Law squalid and stinky as secret passageway. Dodge and diddle law, gull and bubble precedent.

" 'They call you Mrs. Fitzherbert,' I told her.

" 'Do they?' Maria said. 'How very odd. It's divorce Catholics don't recognize, not death.'

"I built the safe house in Putney one year after the year they did not even bother to dissolve our marriage. It's an out-of-the-way sort of place, and the house itself is not much different from its neighbors. As you see it backs on the river. We came ashore in rowboats now, dugouts. We were probably seen. But ordinary people don't much gossip about the great. They don't know anything to say. As for the rest, the ruling classes, they know it all but are discreet. They talk behind our backs but only amongst themselves.

"We lived on and off here several years. We were very happy.

"A prince's credit is long, but it is not infinite. There were debts. There are always debts. It's empty now, but once this house was furnished like a palace. I did not buy, I commissioned. The greatest cabinetmakers worked for us, the greatest sculptors, the finest painters. One room was floored and walled and ceilinged entirely in delft. Josiah Wedgwood made our plates and pottery following Maria's sketches. Dick Sheridan wrote comedies using plots I myself suggested. I discovered a young woman in Bath, Jane Austen, and commissioned her to write novels for us. We gave her a general idea of the subject matter and the tone we were interested in and she fleshed out the rest. We sat on the finest furniture to be had in Europe and read aloud to each other. Delightful, delightful.

"Only our bedroom would have seemed eccentric. It was fitted out, as you may have guessed, like a dairy. The mattress and pillows were stuffed with ordinary hay, which we changed daily. I even had lovely little Chippendale milking stools made for us. Well. It was *all* delightful.

"And expensive. The bills mounted, though I was able to stall my creditors for a time on the basis of my great expectations. Then, suddenly, all together all at once it seemed, they began to hound me, coming not to Buckingham House but directly to Putney. Even Miss Austen, though I must say that of them all she was the shyest and seemed quite embarrassed to be here.

"I was not even sent for this time. I arranged for the meeting and went to the ministers myself.

" 'The King is not improved,' the Chancellor of the Exchequer said.

" 'Isn't it time you began to cast about for a suitable consort?' the Lord Chancellor asked.

" 'You're Prince Royal now. You may yet be Prince Regent before you're King,' the PM said.

" 'What is your view, counselor?' asked the Lord Privy Seal.

" 'Oh *my* view,' he said. 'Hi wouldn't 'ave no proper view now, would hi? My view's strickly the law. The law's what *hi* go by. It wants a hagreement.' This from the Custom's Office solicitor.

" 'What does?' the Prime Minister asked.

" 'Why the law does, your honor. It wants a hagreement. What we call a tort, a contrack.'

" 'But isn't a tort . . .' I started to ask.

" 'It's like this, i'n't it? Law's a hagreement entered into voluntarily by two parties. Hi except 'ighway robbery and murder and such because that hain't law so much has what we call *broken* law. Now the Prince 'ere comes to us game as you please hand wants us to push some bill through Parliament to pay off 'is debts. Now if we was to do hit hit might be what we call a *favor* but hit wouldn't be law. Not

350

proper law. Dere's no quo for the quid, if you gavver my meanin'. It wants a hagreement. Now, if 'e was to *marry* . . .'

"They did not get their agreement.

"The creditors came. They came with bailiffs and bum-bailiffs, with beadles and tipstaffs, with sheriffs and constabulary, process servers, catchpolls and Bow Street runners. I could see the Lord Chancellor and the solicitor off by themselves in a carriage parked behind a string of removal vans.

"To give them their due, the creditors seemed almost as shy as Miss Austen and, with the removal men, went quietly about their work. Silently the delft room was dismantled. Silently the Wedgwood was collected, the furniture. Sheridan was there and tried to make me a gift of the plays I'd commissioned. There was consultation among the constabulary and process servers who then sent one of the runners out to speak to the Lord Chancellor's carriage. When the man returned, he whispered something to a policeman who came over to Sheridan who then turned to me and shrugged helplessly.

" 'I'm sorry, sir,' Sheridan said.

" 'It's all right, Dick,' I told him, and handed over his manuscripts. 'We've read the plays. They're wonderful plays. We'll remember them always.'

" 'Oh we will, Richard. We will,' Maria said.

" 'As for the rest of you,' I called, 'one day I shall be King. I'll not forget what you've done to us this day. You, draper, and you, cabinetmaker, can forget all about your By Appointment to His Majesty crest. All of you can.'

"For reply they looked down listlessly at their feet and seemed to shuffle apologetically.

"For some reason they didn't enter the bedroom and left it intact.

" 'They've left us all we really need, sweetheart,' I told Maria.

" 'Oh yes,' she said and we went there and I sucked at her dry breasts and somehow they were moist now and what I sipped tasted like tears.

"Well," King George said. "It was the following year. This would have been thirty-three years ago. It was my birthday. I wouldn't be Regent for eighteen more years, King for another twenty-eight. It was my birthday. The house was furnished now with some of Maria's things from Pangbourne; the rest came from her house in Richmond. There were crosses on the walls. It was my birthday. We had always exchanged gifts. Though I was still in debt—princes and good time Charlies are never out of it it seems—I was not borrowing so much now since being humiliated by the creditors. I had given her some small thing, I don't even remember now what it was. She looked at me for a moment and went over to her writing desk, where she sat down and appeared to write something out. It couldn't have taken her more than a minute. When she had done she handed it to me. I looked at it and laughed.

" 'What's this then?' I said.

" 'A check.'

" 'Well I *see* it's a check. Is that the sort of gift you'd give me on my birthday? A *check?*'

" 'Did you read it?'

" 'No.'

" 'Read it.'

" 'It's for five hundred fifteen pounds, eight shillings.'

" 'Yes.'

" 'What an odd sum. Five hundred fifteen pounds, eight shillings. Maria, is this the amount you think will bring me out of debt? Darling, I owe thousands.'

" 'I know that.'

" 'Maria, I don't want your money for a gift.'

" 'It isn't a gift. I did not get you a gift.'

" 'What is it then?'

" 'The price you paid to have this house built.'

" 'You're giving me my own house? Oh, darling, that's very sweet but really I can't . . .'

" 'He said I'd have to ask you for the title. He said if you don't have it or it's not handy you could write something down on a paper making it over to me.'

" '*He* said? Who?'

" 'That solicitor,' she said, and began to cry.

"I went to him that afternoon. He was not at the offices in Parliament, where all our other meetings had taken place. The Lord Chancellor told me I might look for him at the Customs House.

"It was a dirty, dingy building smelling of brine and brackish water, of filthy contraband and sodden wood. I found him shirtsleeved in some petty clerk's office.

" 'What's this then?' I demanded, waving the check at him.

" 'Ahh,' he said, 'did you sign hover the deed then, my prince?'

" 'No I didn't sign over the deed. I'm trying to get some explana—'

" 'Well no matter,' he said. 'You've haccepted the money and in law that's a principle that shows your hintent to make a hagreement.'

" *'What are you talking about?'*

" 'Your own good, sir, your own good. You built that house in Putney in the year of our Lord 17 hand 86. This is 17 hand 92. That's six years, Prince George.'

" 'Say what you're talking about or I'll kill you.'

" 'That wouldn't be law, sir.'

"I went for his throat.

" 'Law, sir,' he gasped. 'Common law, sir. Common law marriage.'

"I took my hands from about his neck. 'Common law marriage?'

"Because there is no law finally, there are only arrangements. They had used the Settlement Act to arrange my bachelorhood, a sort of biding, buttoned spinstership of standby, wait-list eligibility. And repossessed our household goods to arrange, or so I thought at the time, simple, hobbled, clip-wing, rub-and-bottleneck let and hindrance.

" 'Oh no, sir,' the solicitor explained later, 'that would have been vitchious. The law his not vitchious. We done that for the presumption. The law wants a hagreement hand a presumption. What reasonable men might hinfer has to da troof of your and Mrs. Fitz's situation based on probable reasoning hin da absence huv, or prior to, hactual proof or disproof. If we'd let you 'ang on to the furniture, all them pricey, pretty penny harticles and hinventory what you'd put togevver, dere might be some reasonable man or huvver oo'd 'ave taken it into 'is 'ead that you'd hactually hintended to make ha 'ome togevver hafter the fashion of a 'usband and wife.'

" 'You left the bedchamber undisturbed.'

" 'We did, sir. Hafter the fashion of a man wif a maid.'

"Maria's check had been written to neutralize one more presumption. The solicitor explained that since I had paid for the house and lived with her in it I had seemed to imply that I regarded her as my wife. If they had not acted before the sabbatical year, our arrangement, under English common law, might have been considered a bona fide marriage. By getting her to pay for the house . . .

" 'I'll tear up the check,' I said, and did so, in a dozen dozen bits and pieces before the solicitor's eyes.

" 'Oh, sir,' he said sadly, 'Hi'm afraid dat were not wise. You see, sir, you're a debtor, and, hunder law, debtors are wiffout certain rights. Dey may not muterlate monies due deir creditors. "Hif a penny come deir way dat penny must be paid." Dat his de law, sir, so noble has your action was, befitting a sweet and noble prince like yourself, may I say, sir, it was not wise? Dough Hi 'ope an' pray dat if Hi 'ad de honor, sir, to be hin your position Hi would 'ave done de same—— if Hi was has hig'orant of de law as you are, Prince.'

"So we were undivorced and unannulled for the third time.

"We continued to meet for a time, but both of us could see that what all official England had contrived to turn into an affair was finally and effectively doomed. For one thing, now that Maria owned the house she wanted to redecorate the bedroom.

"Are you too uncomfortable on that bare floor? The remainder is quickly told.

"Now I had reason to borrow again. I had not realized how much money I had *not* been spending while Maria had been taking up so much of my time. Unattached, I began to resume some of my old pursuits. I was gambling again. There were fine new race horses to buy for my neglected stables. My appetites became again as grand as they'd been in my fledgling good time Charlie days. My wardrobe once more took on its old princely significance. And there was Brighton. There'd always been Brighton of course, but now I had begun once again to host the magnificent feasts and balls that had so distracted me when I was younger, affairs which for the most part Maria and I had attended as guests during the period of our closest alliance. So there were debts. And reason enough to seek out assistance.

" 'There's that girl in Italy,' the Chancellor of the Exchequer said.

" 'His cousin?' the Lord Privy Seal said.

" 'Caroline,' said the solicitor.

"This would have been thirty years ago. The marriage was contracted and I got my money.

" 'They're forcing me to marry a woman I cannot care for.'

" 'It doesn't matter,' Maria said. 'It's death Catholics recognize, not divorce.'

" 'Don't you see?' I told the ministers. 'You've made me a bigamist.'

" 'You're Prince huv Wales, sir,' the solicitor said. 'Take has many mistresses has pleases you.'

" 'Caroline's the mistress,' I muttered.

" 'Queen Caroline his your consort, sir,' the solicitor said. 'When she comes to term England will 'ave han heir.'

"Heiress he should have said. Princess Charlotte was born the following year. I asked the queen to taste her milk, which otherwise would have just gone begging anyway. She quite refused. It couldn't have been very good milk.

"'One thing,' I asked Maria when Caroline returned to Rome the year the Princess was born. 'What pressures did they apply? Did they threaten the Catholics? How did they get you to do it?'

"'Write the check?'

"'Yes.'

"'That solicitor explained it. It had been a prince's house. The home of the man who would be King of England. He pointed out what a good investment it was.'

"'Oh Maria,' I cried.

"'Oh George,' she said, 'it's divorce Catholics don't recognize, not reality.'

"This would have been almost twenty-nine years ago. The Young Pretender would have been dead eight years by this time. Did you say something, Mills? No? I thought you said something. Stuart eight years gone. Still, she would not have been entirely lonely in Italy, would she? Would she, Mills?

"Now what's all this about some damned squire's letter you claim to carry about with you under your blouse?!"

Which was when the man who could claim—for himself and for everyone in his family who had come before—never to have signed a neighbor's petition or written a letter to the editor or raised the mildest embarrassing question in public, let alone seen his name in the papers or done anything at all to make anyone nervous, produced from his very person, as the King of Great Britain, Ireland and Hanover warily watched, a document, character reference, personality sketch, which at once testified to his, Mills's, rude ambitions and to his squire's ("squire" because the man was merely a modestly prosperous small freeholder in Mills's district, some younger son of some younger family) cheerful disdain of, and sniffy scorn for, George Mills and George Mills's curious goals. The letter was not a hoax. (The man to whom it was addressed was actually known to the writer, and had actually lived in London, though now, three years dead, was no longer in a position to do anything for the young aspirant. And anyway, the directions he had given Mills, though careful and precise, were quite inaccurate, based both upon a lightly liquored memory and a flaw peculiar to the writer which caused him, whenever he was in the capital—occasions rare enough to strike him *as* occasions—not only to become overly excited but to lose, if not *all* sense of direction, at least that part of it which oriented him as to the side of the river he actually stood on at any given moment. Here was the fluky fortuity: that he had somehow managed to describe to Mills, even providing him with a hand-drawn map, which not only replicated the area to which George had come—with the exception of the house itself which was considerably smaller and in a different style than the one he'd described, a discrepancy George, who understood him, put down to the squire's sense of his own importance—but which was correct in all particulars save this: that the place George wanted was on the other side of the river in Fulham and not on this side in Putney.)

So the letter was no hoax. George Mills, fearing one, had even tampered the crude seal and read it, understanding well enough its heavy sarcasm and the dubious light in which he was portrayed, but putting it in *this* light, figuring it *this* way:

His sort don't mean my sort harm. They're afraid. As they might be afraid of Vandals or Visigoths. As they might be afraid of trained bears doing comic turns on the high street. They've heard things. Stuff about rough ways, muck about manners. They fear for their game, for their gardens and daughters. They misdoubt our religion, and put it about our condition is our character. They think we drink too much and dance makes us crazy.

His jokes are just nervous. All to the good in the end. Serving my purpose. 'Cause he don't mean me harm, not real *harm. One toff to another.*

Now the King will read it. Who to the fellow what wrote it is like me to some dog dead in the road. He'll *know. And discount the jokes and mark down the leg pull, all that lively pokebanter, all that scoff-merry and scoldbutt.* He'll *know. He's a king.*

King George IV took the greasy letter his subject handed him and, when he saw to whom it was addressed, began to read the letter of introduction as if it were some document intercepted by agents and delivered by urgent and pressing couriers.

He read:

Forgive if you can my blatant impertinence in addressing you in this way about a matter of absolutely no importance and of no small irrelevance, it being the very rule of scientific displacement that that which is of no weight, which is no thing, *saving of course our souls, which at all events are, if not by the laws of God then,*

356

to our shame, to our shame, at the very indiscreet least by the practices of men, more than we are inconvenienced to believe is good for us, "matters" of substance delayed, due bills to which, through the best grace of that same Divine Agency, accrue no interest, compound or even simple, though admittedly such "small" matters being the exception—the exception, nota bene— while that to which I now direct your offhand attention still participates in that aforementioned phylum or category relating to the antichronistic, metachronous and just plain out of date, and distracts in almost inverse mathematical degree to the extraneous pressures it puts upon us and has, for weightiness, no more power to signal fish than a sinker of soap bubble.

The damned thing's in code, the King thought. And read on.

Thus the stone in our shoe. Thus idle, vagrant worries which turn us from all true and dutiful concerns to peripheral speculation, random and curious as sudden unexampled messages from the villagers, their puny command-performance performances, shoddy balls, recitals, bumpkin dramatic entertainments and mystery plays, all those abrupt summonses at which our attendance is owed more to custom than obligation. Thus, in brief, all subtly finessed attentions to the self. Welcome enough, and noble enough too, Laird knows, when such attentions are diverted to God and Country, but disconcerting as a fly on your face when all that's at stake are the caterwaulings of silly young boys whose voices have not yet changed. Thus then this.

Laird? the King thought. *Laird* knows?

Which I cannot continue without first making certain courteous and proper, albeit, I do assure you, good fellow, entirely sincere inquiries regarding the healths and happinesses of your lovely lady and your remarkable bairn. It has of course been some time since I have been in your wonderful city. After the current reignant first brought Johnny Nash up from Brighton to do his royal imperial his Regent Street for him, but not since it was completed. Completed not, I'm relieved to hear, in the hybrid rajah cum emir cum mehtar cum, I-don't-know, chinoiseried cacique so many of us had at first feared (after the expensive vulgarity of Brighton itself), but a toned-down and at least vaguely *European architecture. I'm*

357

even told by some who have actually seen it that it reminds them
of a sort of classical Greece, Athens say, if Time hadn't trashed
it. I've seen prints of course. Athens indeed! We've lost a toned-
down Oriental fantasy to a tarted-up Mediterranean one. At least
the street appears broad enough. Which must be welcome to one
in your profession.
    Thus then *this.*

Bairn? he thought. *Remarkable* bairn?

The piece of work you see before you calls itself George Mills.
I must tell you at the outset that while he is not entirely native to
our neighborhood, he has been in residence hereabouts four years,
since 1821 I believe, doing agriculture, the sowing, mowing, tilling,
gleaning, threshing, reaping and picking so peculiarly designated
to his race and class of stoopers and benders. Though he claims
in his more defensive moments family—or, rather more particu-
larly, genealogy. It is a long and sometimes tedious story and if
you would hear it you will have to hear it from him. If you regard
it as his command performance, recital or dramatic entertain-
ment, as, in short, your own capital call to custom, you will have
discharged something so close to obligation that only a talmudic
philosophe might tell you the difference.

Four years? 1821? The year Wife Cousin Caroline died, the year
after I received my crown and she popped back from Italy to claim
her "rights" as Queen Consort. Where was that solicitor now that
England needed him? Now that even *I* needed him? The bill to
dissolve the marriage and deny her claims actually introduced and
passed in Lords, though she died before it could be put to the vote
in Commons. In *Commons!* When did I grow old who never gave a
fart for scandal? Who asked perfect strangers to wet-nurse me and
tweaked the tits of titled grandmas? Tweaking before barristers and
retainers and the not-so-loyal opposition and even on her deathbed
even my wife cousin's milkless, bloodless old dugs. Our daughter
would have been dead four years. Caroline would have been sixty-
seven. Where was that damned solicitor? It would never have gotten
as far as Lords or Commons with him on the case. He wouldn't have
needed any bills and petitions to quitclaim. She'd be alive today. She'd
be alive and back in Italy and thankful to God that the laws he would
have told her she'd violated didn't apply there. Seventy-one and alive

and happy and cultivating her olive and lemon trees, taking their juices, at least their odors, at least some extract of them in her pores now so that if I ever saw her again and rubbed her breasts out of passion or even only its phantom, the skin on my hands would at least have come away with the remnant oils of the breathing, breeding earth. So where was that jurisdictional solicitor, that legislature and police force and magistracy of a man?

"Sowing, mowing, tilling, gleaning, thrashing, reaping and picking," he read.

Picking? *Picking?*
". . . his command performance," he read. ". . . your own capital call to . . . obligation."

He looked at Mills sadly.
When did I grow old? he wondered again. When did good time Charlie become the battler king?
But this was later, this was afterward, when George Mills, driven to understand his predicament, had gone over it a hundred times in his head, when he had ceased thinking of it in terms of the artifact he now knew it to be, a pretentious letter of introduction, and began to look at it as the one man in the world must have done who not only had never been intended to read it but who, now that Mills understood what he had done by showing it to him, was the single person it should at all costs have been kept from. Mills would never forgive himself. But this was a later construction. Now the King was reading about him, and Mills was beside himself in dizzy, crazy glee.
The King read. The damage was done and the King read.

I know him to be, for his sort, a hard enough worker in precisely those areas his sort, though qualified for by Nature and Nature's God, too often and too often too deliberately neglects when push comes to dig. It may even be a sort of unwitting decep-tion on my part, a benefit of the doubt too generously given (though we both know that if no doubt had its generous benefit, there wouldn't be a king left on his throne or a satrap on his elephant in all the world), but I actually believe the baggage to have some ambition and even a kind of quality. Though, admittedly, of a

359

*most irregular and not immediately recognizable, or recognized,
sort.*

*Mills was never regularly employed on my holdings. Like
many of the peasants hereabouts he found it more to his taste and,
quite frankly, to ours in this backwater, more rattleborough than
riding, to declare himself rather more the day laborer than the
tenant farmer, though my managers tell me that he always appeared whenever he was scheduled and went through the motions
of his motions with no complaint and some enthusiasm. One has
gone so far as to declare that if we had more like him we might
actually manage to bring in a crop now and again.*

But to the point.

*He first called my attention to himself one day when I was
driving past on the road in the quaint little cabriolet which I think
I may have spoken of, either to you or to Ann, when I last visited
your fair city—can five years have passed since that golden time?
While I was still some distance off I glimpsed this callow, raw-
boned gawk standing at the edge of a field. To speak truth I might
not have noticed him at all, would not have noticed him at all—
well you know the people, how they partake in their very aspect
of the landscape itself, seeming as much to belong there as the
scrawny trees against which they lounge for shade, as much a part
of it as the clayish soil which hides their boots (the pun intended
of course; what else has an exile like myself to do than make word
games?), dry and dusty as the leaves, more like a sort of crop than
a sort of man—if it had not been for the fact that he must have
heard me coming even before I spotted him and snapped to with
an alacrity which would have been alarming had it not been so
dextrous and, well, practiced. When he whipped off his cap and
bowed low as a serf in my direction. I swear, old friend, that even
if I had not noticed the gesture, I would have heard its whoosh and
snap two furlongs off. He startled me. He startled my horse, and
I was already reining in, on the verge of a decision to turn to go
back the way I had come lest he should prove a highwayman.
What checked me was the thought that I had probably passed his
confederates and, if I had, they would have done me, running me
to ground like some damned fox. Why, by the very act of so
suddenly reining in I had probably already lost the momentum I
needed. Using my whip, I pressed the horse on and in that moment
decided that if the murderous son of a bitch should take but one
step out into the road I would run him down.*

But damn me, old friend, if the worthy not only did not *take that step but held his bow and scrape like some foppish frozen commissionaire till I had passed. This was two furlongs, mind. In that field he looked at once like some sculpture of rural servility and a piece of organic camouflage. Well. He was there the next day, not in the same field of course—he was no shirker—but the next one over. When he bowed in that way and flourished his cap he might have been a border guard of some picturesque country famous for its wines say, not so much questioning credential as already recognizing it two furlongs off and—I cannot say waving one on; he never moved a muscle after that ridiculous show of moving them all at once—seemed to encourage me past some imaginary finish line that could have been his own bent being. And there the next. And the next. Always advancing, mind, daily breaching the front lines of his tasks. And now I was deliberately slowing the horse, bringing it down from the full-out gallop of that first startled day to a canter the second and then to a walk and finally to a sort of lazed limp. I wanted to see how long he would hold that servile pose. It was scientific. (I have to have more than puns and word games; I have to have human nature itself, in nothing like the abundance in which it thrives in London of course. That's understood. That's given. Oh, soon shall I have to quit this lumpen, oafish exile and return once again to civilization! I swear it to you, I positively envy the bearer of this letter!) Not could,* would. Could *he could have done forever. It was* would *I was interested in.*

We had left my fields long ago and for some time now had been on the land of tenant farmers working for the country's greatest landowner, a gross Dutchman whose family cannot have been in England over a hundred years. His holdings are, as I have indicated, immense. Armies of peasants work for him. As always, the strange boy preceded me, those two constant furlongs fixed as if they had been struck off by surveyors' sticks and levels, as if I were one end of the reading and he the other.

At this most lackadaisical pace the horse and I had assumed, I had some hope of catching the young man's eye. I seemed to see him staring at me, his eyes fixed on mine as if I led a procession, but whenever we came abreast he looked away, his face in my direction but the eyes off center, gazing elsewhere so that his features took on the marked, pinched ones on a blind man's face. One day I even tipped my hat to him. He blushed but made no more response than that involuntary one of his blood. *On another day I bid him hello. The blush went deeper but I got no answer. My God, I thought, he's mute.*

You have never had the pleasure of being in my country, though I know I have invited you—I invite you now—nor do I scold so much as condone your decision to stay put in town. That is where all proper gentlemen properly belong, but if you had *come here you would have seen that it is all a gerrymandered fiction of contiguity. Farmers, even real farmers like the dumb Dutchman I alluded to above, live miles from their holdings like absentee landlords, so as we moved deeper and deeper into the Dutchman's hectares we were coming closer and closer to my own home.*

Which is where on the last day of our strange courtship he was waiting for me.

I had not even got down from the cabriolet when the piece of goods straightened and approached me. I cannot say that his hat was in his hands, I cannot say where it was. These humble types have a way with their hats (and with their hands too I shouldn't wonder). Why I remark this at all is that for days now he had been playing the milepost for me as I rode by and now his deference seemed as absolute as an act of aggression. If he had stepped out into the road that first day to halt my progress I could not have been more alarmed. Yet apparently he meant no harm, for all he did once he approached was done with an appropriate respect and shyness.

"Sir," says he, and so awkward as positively to seem to be directing his remarks into the horse's behind. "Sir, er, ah, uh," he says as if trying out strange new vowels he'd learned. "Squire..."

"Yes," says I. "What is it?"

"I am a good worker," says the brute.

"You are certainly excellent at finding the edge of a field and planting yourself in it," says I.

"You may ask Mr. Smith or Mr. Jones or any of them. I am a good *worker."*

"Yes, well, I congratulate you," says I, and remind him, "yet it is only what God expects of all of us."

"But, sir, I am no farmer," he says with some warmth.

"No," says I, "you are a scarecrow."

"Sir?"

"Never mind. What is it you want?"

"To be your coachman. To drive your coach."

"What, this?" say I, indicating the topless, two-wheeled, one-horse carriage in which I sat.

"Yes, sir."

"You are a coachman?"

"I would be," says he, "oh, squire, I would be!"

"Then must you first study your trade and learn to recognize what a coach exactly is."

In brief, old friend, he had no more idea as to the various sorts of vehicles that abound in his profession than I had regarding the whereabouts of his hat.

I told him I was a busy man. I told him he must go to the blacksmith and there make inquiries about the kinds of conveyances there be. I told him he must go to the inns and taverns along the post roads and there observe them. I told him he must undertake to learn what he could of harness and tack. "Why it is as necessary that you brief yourself in these matters," I told him, "as for a sailor to learn about ropes and rigging, sails and stars." Then, bethinking myself of you, I thought to add that if he could successfully demonstrate to me that he had become possessed of at least the basics of his would-be profession, I had an acquaintance in London who ran the most important public hack and livery system in all of England to whom I might recommend him.

Naturally I thought never to see him again.

He was back within the week, his mouth stuffed with definition, speaking so blithely of barouche, phaeton and sociable, buckboard, calashe, brougham and droshky that one would have thought he was as accustomed to equipage as he was to the very straws he sucked on. We went to my stables, where he challenged me as to the wisdom of using a particular thickness of harness on an animal whose feet had been shod with a certain shape of nail.

We went for a ride in the cabriolet. He drove. Brilliantly.

Of course I am reluctant to foist upon you someone whom you may not absolutely require, yet I did give my word and as the fellow, on the evidence, at least seems teachable, I overreach myself to the point that, amateur though I may be as to the requirements of the London livery trade, I send you an aspirant I have every reason to believe is one upon whose loyalties you may absolutely rely and who may, at the very least, do you some good on the new broad avenues of Regent Street.

In the hope that we may all soon meet again in the shining

city, and in the further hope that such reunion prove propitious and
jubilant, I remain ever your servant and now procurer . . .

The country's greatest landowner?

A gross Dutchman whose family cannot have been in England over a hundred years?

The King read and reread the prolix letter.

The pun intended? What pun? What word games? What had he missed? Why had he grown so old?

Exile? *Exile?*

George Mills waited while the King read.

Waited patiently. No: humbly. No: proudly. No: all atwitter. No: all of them. All of them all at once. Not one time thinking, He's going to do something for me. Not one time.

While the King read and reread, while he examined the anomalies and ambiguities, while he pored over the double Dutch double entendre, the political acrostic he took the letter to be. But the man is dead, he thought. Discovered and assassinated they told me. The most important public hack and livery system in all of England and all its jarvey spies and post-boy plotters shut down, under new management. (The wonder of their plain arrangements! King George thought. They had simply to overhear my clerks and ministers as they drove them down Pall Mall or along the embankment. And spring and summer the best time for spying they told me, during the mild weather, the carriage windows open to the breezes, and our Stuart enemies all ears on a fine day. Secrets lost to the warm front, to balm and ease. Very Nature a co-conspirator.) Not even understanding all of it, confused by their complicated shenanigans, by all held historical grudge, devotees, faction, the partisan life and the boring obsession of blood. Blood, he thought. Blood and milk. He didn't care a damn really. It was simply inconvenient to abdicate. And he would miss a king's perks. He had to admit. The handsome expense account, the lovely tributes. But I *don't* understand my enemies! The pains they take, the troubles and lengths they go to. And why would they send me this, this *aspirant?* (Yet his mind nagged: It *could* be a mistake; I could be attributing to machination what perhaps ought to be put down to the simple disfigurement of style.) Still, he thought, I suppose I have to resist. Who's King here anyway?

And Mills not only not thinking: *He's taking too long, he's probably going to do something for me.* But not even thinking: *He's taking too long, he's probably going to do something to me.*

The King looked up from the letter Mills had shown him and, seeing the expression of sly puzzlement on the young man's face, mildly asked, "What?"

"Oh, sir," George said, reddening, evasively shrugging.

"What?" he repeated.

"Well it's just . . ."

"What? It's just what?"

"What you told me. *You* know. All those things. About yourself."

"Didn't I also say that our nasty stories neither ascend nor descend but stay within their class of origin?"

"Yes, sir. Yes, sir, you did."

"Well," the King said, "there you are. It would seem you're one of us then, George."

"Oh, sir. You're teasing me, ain't you, sir?"

George IV considered him. "Yes," he said finally, "I suppose I am." Then, "You're our loyal subject you said."

"Sir, I am," Mills said.

"Your family swears oaths you said."

"Millses are pledged to their kings."

"Yes," he said, "yes. Look," he said, striking the document he'd been reading, "your squire's misinformed. This fellow's dead."

"Oh?" he said. "Was it sudden, sir?"

"It was very sudden," the King said, "but it was over three years ago."

"Oh," George said, saddened, not for the dead gentleman, whom he'd never met, or even for himself, so much as for the squire with his frayed, retrograde connections and his sad, dated influence.

"There go your plans, eh?"

"Well . . ."

"I think *I* might put you in the way of something."

"You, Your Highness?"

"It would be chiefly ceremonial of course and not really in your line, but as you've just been disappointed and as you're close by . . . Would you, do you think you could undertake a mission for us?"

365

2

They know, I think, that they're exotic. They must know. Not as the Chinaman is exotic, or the Jew, or red Indian, or savage African. Because, though I've never been to the places where such reside, I've seen their travelers. Even in England. In parades and circuses, in tailor shops where the government bought my outfits. Coming out here, too. On shipboard a black man poured my tea. And maybe because they were among strangers—here I'm the stranger—they seemed, well, cautious, watchful as boxers. But that's not it. Unless it's that these people, in the Jew's place, the nigger's, wouldn't know enough or maybe even care enough to *be* cautious, though God knows they're suspicious enough, even among their own. No one trusts anyone. The men doubt the women, the women the men. When a child falls and bruises himself in the street he doesn't run to his mum for comfort. Sisters don't look to their brothers to protect them, sons won't enter a room if their father is in it.

And that's not it either.

Maybe it's God.

I'm Church of England but the fact is vicars make me uncomfortable. Whenever I go—which is rare—I go to see society, to hear the choir and watch the gentlemen and gawk as they hand their ladies into and out of the carriages. (It's where I first spotted Squire.) I mean I don't belong. (And maybe it's queer for a Mills to make this admission. It was Greatest Grandfather, after all, who was the indirect deputy of the King himself when he went on that First Crusade. And didn't I come here myself in the first place at George IV's request?) So I'm supposed to be Church of England, though I might be more at home as a chapel-meeting Methodist or even as a dissenter, one of the sects. But I've been in even fewer chapels than churches, for if vicars and services make me uncomfortable, ministers and everything low church embarrass me. I'm not religious or even much of a believer so much as this snob of God. If there *is* a God He's an aristocrat. He'd have gone to the best schools and He'd speak in low tones this absolutely correct accent. He'd sound like the vicar and never shout or even raise His voice like all those others with their full lungs and loud, harsh words prole as low company. So maybe it's God, their version of Him, makes them so wild, more exotic than gypsies. So maybe it's God, some pierced-eared, heterodox, heresiarchical, zealous, piratical avatar.

And that's not it either.

Nor their fierce, rumpus-raveled history, incoherent as rout, mob, high wind.

It's pride!

I came to Constantinople with a king's courier, a tall lad named Peterson, not much older than myself, and though we shared the same table on shipboard during the first seating, he was a subdued, taciturn fellow and didn't enter into conversation easily. I thought at first it was because he was queasy, for I often saw him with his head hanging over the stern rail and caught him throwing up as I returned to my cabin after dessert and coffee and perhaps a brandy. I was nauseous as the courier but had never tasted such fine rare food and was determined not to lose it.

He sometimes summoned me to his cabin or occasionally came to mine, never to chat but to rehearse me in the protocols, my small, silly performance that seemed hardly worthy, even to me, of such expense, so long a voyage. When I questioned him he cut me off and asked me to demonstrate yet again my polished, practiced salaam.

"You've seen me do the thing a hundred times."

"Show me."

"You *know* I've got it pat."

"Mahmud II runs a tight court. Show me."

"Oh very well." I began the gyrations with my hand, bowed low and ended the fruity salutation with my right palm pressed to my forehead. "There you have it, my sultan." I thought he was going to be sick.

"Your right palm? Your *right?*"

"I'm teasing."

"This is serious. No teasing. Show me."

I did it again, this time finishing as he'd instructed me.

"You pull something like that before Mahmud . . ."

"Whoosis, what'shisname, is five years old already. I don't get it."

"Abdulmecid. The boy's name is Abdulmecid."

"I don't get it. Abdulmecid's over five years old. He's almost gone on six. George IV's his godfather. Why'd the King wait so long to send him his gift?"

"How often do I have to explain?" the King's man said with some exasperation. "Islam's different. The godchild must thank the emissary personally. He has to be able to speak."

"It's queer."

"Excuse me," Peterson said and rushed from the cabin. Through my porthole I could see him being sick.

My own collywobbles, determined as I was not to lose the unaccustomed delicacies, I still managed to suppress, by an act of the will transforming nausea into a noxious diarrhea, the magnificent broths, gorgeous fowls, grand game and exquisite sweets and pastries metamorphosed into a yellowish, stenchy paste.

Now, when I saw Peterson, I tried to commiserate. "Rough trip," I'd say.

"It's not a rough trip," he'd shoot back. "The sea's gentle as a lap."

"It appears calm today," I'd say, "but there are swells."

"In your brains," he'd manage, and vomit violently into the Tyrrhenian Sea.

Often, after my salaams, there would be additional exercises, "the Walk of Prostration," a difficult, almost acrobatic negotiation in which the one approaching the throne has somehow to give off a full-blown ceremony of obsequious, barehead awe, an impression that he hats-in-hand for all mankind, for everything in fact, for whatever life there might be on other planets as well as all there is on this one, the whole while making his salutations and progressing a corridor the length, could be, of two or three good-sized tennis courts at angles of humility which defy gravity. (Not, at that, too difficult a maneuver for a Mills.)

But our cabins were too small and Peterson sometimes insisted that we go up on deck where I might better practice the movement, the suspirant motion of the ship making everything even more difficult, much to the amusement of the sailors and the other passengers. Peterson would stand fifteen or twenty feet in front of me, walking backward, drawing me on.

"Palace architecture was at least partially designed for just this purpose," he'd explain, "its long throne rooms, the slight pitch of its slippery marble floors. It fair delights a potentate to see men bellyflop."

"Why do you do these things?" a fellow passenger might ask.

And before I could respond Peterson would answer, "His Majesty's business." And rush to the rail, where he would be sick again.

We never took the goldfoil-wrapped gift out on deck with us for fear the wind would knock it from my hands and soil the handsome package with its golden cords. Indeed, when I made my salaams and practiced "the Walk of Prostration," I always used a box which replicated in size and weight the one that Peterson kept locked safe in his courier's diplomatic pouch.

He had shown me the splendid original once or twice and I was more than a little curious as to what it contained. His Royal Highness's descriptions of a prince's playthings had piqued my interest.

"What's in it, Peterson?"

"I don't know I'm sure."

"Well let's open it up then and see what the King got the little guy."

"We can't do that, Mills."

"Why can't we then? Ain't I one of Nature's true-born shipping clerks? I could pop that parcel open, toss its contents about and button it all up again as if the gift, box, foil, gold string and all were part of the same single piece of material, like a doll carved from driftwood say, or a bench from stone."

"His Majesty's business. Against all diplomatic procedure."

"You removed it from the pouch. Ain't that against all His Majesty's messenger boy diplomatic procedure too?"

His face was whiter than the canvas sails which drove the ship through the Aegean and toward the Dardanelles.

"Hey," I said, "not to worry. I'm no blurt tattle." But he had run to the rail to pitch his insides. "Hey," I tried to reassure him, "hey, do I look like some blab squeak? You think I'd peach on a pal? I ain't no snitchwhisper, what do you think?" But he was retching now something beyond the contents of his stomach, something beyond digestion itself. "We'll forget about what the King sent whoosis—Abdulmecid. It's none of my business. I shouldn't have asked. If even one person knows it can ruin the surprise."

They're called Janissaries.

They're called Janissaries and they're this elite corps, very famous, very feared.

For their cruelty.

They've existed as a fighting force since the second half of the fourteenth century and were originally recruited from among young Balkan Christians, often made over to the Ottoman Empire by the parents themselves according to a policy known as *devshirme,* a human payment collected in lieu of taxes. These "tribute children," as they were known, were dispersed among Muslim families, who instructed them in the ways of Islam. When the local mullahs were convinced they were ready, they were converted and formally sworn to repudiate their parents, a ceremony which involved a vow to take, if the state required it, the lives of everyone in their family, from a mother or father to a distant cousin. If they were considered fit enough for the rigorous life of a Janissary, they were sent to Constantinople and received into the Corps. This was not actually a formal induction. There *was* no formal induction; no loyalty oath was ever sworn to the Sultan or any representative of the Empire, only a pledge of celibacy. Then the recruit simply began his training. If he survived he was a Janissary. If he died, as many did, during the course of his preparations, his corpse was used to help train the others.

They were—we are—slaves.

Because the King knew his man, understood to his giblets and neckbones not just the proximate character and quality of each royal counterpart and political analogue throughout Europe and the Orient, but the taste and aroma of his very soul. Because he knew him as a cordon bleu chef knows vegetables, meat.

It wasn't the length finally, it was the height. Slender pillars, high as trees, vaulting into heavy blocks of shrewd color faceted as gem which supported a great fanned ceiling like some Persian rug in stone. The height, the weight of the height.

Peterson presented his letters to the Grand Vizier's secretary, who started to call for a translator. The courier shook his head vigorously. "No," he said. "They're in Turkic. In Turkic."

The secretary looked up. "Eh?"

"In Turkic," Peterson repeated, and made a great show of writing in the air. "Turkic."

The man smiled and duplicated Peterson's gesture. He held up the letters. "Turkic?"

Peterson nodded and I looked at His Majesty's courier.

We were told to return to the embassy and wait for instructions.

As Christians are distrusted and are discouraged from having official, long-term connections with the Ottoman government, the British ambassador to the Court of Mahmud II is a Jew.

"I am Moses Magaziner," the ambassador said, a shaggy-bearded, great hook-nosed old fellow with long curling earlocks and a shiny black skullcap that seemed cut from the same bolt of gabardine as his jacket and trousers. "Is His Majesty vell?"

"Quite well, thank you, Mr. Ambassador," Peterson said.

"Oy, tenks God," the ambassador said. "His veight, he's vatching his veight?"

Peterson frowned. "No one can know for certain, sir, but his intimates estimate he's above twenty-two stone by now."

"Tventy-two stone. A good eater. He vas alvays a good eater."

"Indeed," Peterson said.

"Vell," the ambassador said, rubbing his hands together, "you boys come a lung vay. You're ready a little lunch?"

"I know *I* am, Mr. Ambassador," I said.

"Dot's nice," Moses Magaziner said affably. He indicated Peterson. "Your mate, the *langer locksh,* the skinny merink, he's also ready a nibble grub?"

"At your convenience, sir," Peterson said.

The strange diplomat shrugged the large, fringed prayer shawl that fell like a scarf about his arms and shoulders and clapped his hands twice. "Mrs. Zemlick," he told the maternal-looking woman who appeared in the doorway, "tell Gelfer lunch for three. The state dining room." The woman smiled at us, nodded and left. "Very pleasant, very refined. A doll," Magaziner said when she'd gone, "a

371

regular *baleboste.* I vish only the best for Yetta Zemlick." He sighed. "Listen," he said, "a heppy steff is a busy steff."

"She seems quite cheery," I said.

His Highness's representative shrugged. "A vidow. A vidow voman *finf* years. I vould like to arrange maybe a *shiddech* vit her and the tchef. Don't be shy, hev a fig." Magaziner held a bowl out to us. I accepted but Peterson declined. "You don't like figs?" Magaziner said, "try a date. Sveet like sugar."

"I'm afraid I should ruin my appetite," Peterson said coolly and Magaziner looked as if he were surprised to discover that Peterson possessed one.

"He's had a rough time with his stomach, Mr. Ambassador," I said. "The voyage."

"Oh yes," he said, "the woyage." Mrs. Zemlick reappeared in the doorway and waited till she caught the ambassador's eye. "Lunch, Mrs. Zemlick?" He turned to us. "Vell gents," he said, rising, "soup's on."

In the state dining room Moses Magaziner recited Hebrew prayers over each course that the servant, Eli Nudel, set before us. Peterson and I looked down at our laps.

"You don't got an eppetite for brisket, Mr. Peterson? You hardly touched."

Peterson mumbled something that was difficult to hear.

"He says he filled up on soup," Eli Nudel said. "He says he's all *shtupt* from *cholleh.*"

"Eli," Magaziner said, "bring me vat Mr. Peterson don't finish, Gelfer Moonshine's feelings shouldn't be hurt." Then he turned to us as he sopped up gravy with his bread. "Don't feel bad, young man," he told Peterson. "If you ken't you ken't. Oy, everybody's a prima donna. I'm not referring to you, Mr. Peterson. I can tell, you are an angelface. It's Gelfer Moonshine, my tchef. He's a pick-of-the-litter, vorld-cless, A-number-vun tchef but he gets depressed if a person don't eat up everyting on his plate. I tell him, 'Gelfer, it's not you. Sometimes ve got a guest his stomach ain't accustomed to traditional cooking.' I tell him, 'Gelfer, cheer yourself, sometimes a fella's hed a woyage didn't agree mit him.'" Eli Nudel had been serving the coffee and was standing now beside Peterson, who seemed oblivious to the man.

Magaziner went on. "I tell him, 'Gelfer, all right, maybe she's too old to hev any more children, and all right, maybe she *ain't* a beauty, but nobody could deny Yetta got a smile on her *punim* could light up the *shabbes* candles. And what about you, Gelfer Moonshine? You got it in your head you're the Supreme Being's gift to the ladies? You're fifty-one years old, your bek aches, your feet get sore, you got a constipation could choke a horse. A nice person like Yetta could be a comfort to you. That time her son and son-in-law came to the embassy mit the grendbabies ven the *mumsers* ver making a pogrom, you saw for yourself. Like horses they ate, may the Lord, blessed be His name, make His countenance to shine upon them.' Two tiny little girls, Mr. Mills, Mr. Peterson, couldn't be seven years old, eight tops, and they ate for a regiment. Vat dey couldn't finish Gelfer made up to *shlep* in a beg. You'll take a cup coffee, Mr. Peterson?"

"What? Oh. Yes please. I don't seem to see the—— Would you have such a thing as cream?"

Moses Magaziner looked at him. "Dairy mit brisket, Peterson?" he asked sharply, then abruptly changed the subject. "Vell," he said softly, "how'd it go at the pelace? Dey taking good care you boys?"

"We had a preliminary interview this morning with the Grand Vizier's First Secretary. He told us to await further instructions."

"Ah," Moses Magaziner said, "further instructions. You speak the lingo, Mr. Peterson?"

"Sir?"

"Turkic. You hev Turkic?"

"Guidebook Turkic. Nothing more. Nothing as fine as I'm certain yours is, Mr. Ambassador."

"Me? I talk Yiddish to them."

Peterson raised his napkin to his lips. For some time now he had been looking quite ill. "I say, would you excuse me, sir? It seems . . ."

He never finished his sentence. Eli Nudel hurried him away and Magaziner and I were left alone.

"So," Magaziner said. "So so so."

Mills grinned at him shyly.

"Yes?" Magaziner said.

"It was delicious," Mills said.

"My pleasure."

"I particularly liked the pudding. What did you call it, 'lucksh and cook'?"

"*Kugel. Lockshen kugel.*"

"That's it," Mills said. "*Lockshen kugel.* It was delicious. It was *all* delicious. It was my first state lunch. My friend's been off his feed."

"Your friend?"

"Peterson. Mr. Peterson."

"Oh yes," Moses Magaziner said, "Mr. Peterson."

"The *halvah* was wonderful too. With the coffee. I loved the *halvah*. Is that right, *halvah?* I'm very ignorant. I don't know the names of these aristocrat dishes."

"*Halvah,* yes," the ambassador said. "Tell me again, Mr. Mills. King George sent you as his personal emissary with Abdulmecid's gift? The letter the courier showed me vas a little unclear."

"Yes, sir. Queer, ain't it? Me a boob and all."

The ambassador waved off George's self-deprecation and questioned him further. He seemed particularly interested in the circumstances surrounding their meeting, and when Mills began to repeat what the King had told him of his relationship with Maria he stopped him at once. "Skip all that," he said. George assumed it was because it was gossip with which the man was already familiar and was at a loss as to what else to tell him. "Vat did *you* say? Vat did you told *him?*" Mills recounted his reasons for coming to London, mentioned the useless letter of recommendation his squire had sent with him but did not go into detail because he was still ashamed for the proud man he had so conscientiously pursued with respect, waiting each day for the cabriolet (which he still thought of as the squire's carriage) to pass, planting himself beside the road those two furlongs before it not because he was afraid he'd miss it but because he enjoyed watching it, seeing it come. Not telling Magaziner any of this either, burdened by his queer guilt for the squire's failed liaisons and associations.

So he told him what he had told the King, blocking out for him a general idea of Millsness, what he had been rehearsing not since he'd first heard it, since what he'd first heard he had no need to rehearse, had remembered, would always remember, but what had happened since, describing the circle, his ring of the wood, the tree, going over it—Magaziner was impatient, waving him quickly through certain passages, slowing him down at others, actually leading Mills's story like a conductor, directing it like traffic—as even now, speaking to the ambassador, he was at once telling the tale and living some new part of it, the telling, living, remembering and rehearsing additional increments he knew it would have made him dizzy to contemplate if he had dared. (He didn't need to dare. The strange pressures and weathers of his life had already acclimatized him to conditions and practices that were no longer even second nature but something actually biologically autonomous.) Magaziner stopped him. "Forty-third? He called you Forty-third?" Mills nodded. "Go on." George backed and filled, telling the story randomly, stumbling a little, not permitted to do it as he'd rehearsed it in his head but forced by Magaziner to improvise, by Magaziner who interrupted him, conducted him, taking him forward to the voyage, the practice sessions in the cabin, Peterson's silence at table, the courier calmly taking food into his stomach that moments later he would give up to the sea. Redirecting Mills another time to what George had said to the King, what the King to George, but always refusing the gossip, not as much shocked by it as bothered that it should have come up at all, asking George what *he'd* said, whether he'd encouraged it, Mills swearing he hadn't, insisting his own embarrassment to Magaziner. "Yes?" Mills nodded. "Go on." George related some more details. Magaziner raised a finger to his lip. Mills stopped. " 'There you are,' he said? 'It would seem you're one of us? *It would seem you're one of us then, George?'*

"Ah, Mr. Peterson," the British ambassador to the Ottoman Empire said, "fillink better?"

"Yes, thank you, sir."

"Dot's nice. Dot's terrific."

In the morning he accompanied George and the courier to the government carriage that had been sent for them. Peterson climbed in first and George handed the golden package in to him to hold for a moment before he got in beside him.

Just as he was about to do so, as he was raising one foot onto the carriage's metal stirrup, the ambassador briefly embraced him and almost imperceptibly slipped something into his jacket pockets. It was *halvah* wrapped in two of the fine linen napkins from the embassy service.

So it was the height even more than the length.

"Well, old buns, it was more than eiver acherly. Dere I was den, weren't I? A great green nineteen-year-old gawm what never got no closer to de movers an' shakers 'n a trooper's widow to de mighty King of Spine. What never till dat day in Putney"—Mills telling a small circle of his intimates in a corner of the kitchen, near the tripe barrels and offal buckets, speaking their language, the broken brogue of barracks and parade ground, a sort of Ottoman-Persian-Yiddish he'd picked up from his mates in the year to year and a half he'd been there, a dialect (and *of course* it would be low, bits and pieces of what the locals had brought with them from Tripoli and the Crimea, from Hungary and Mesopotamia, from Crete and the Balkans, from Thrace

—— places, some of them, Mills would not have been able to locate on a map, not because he was such a poor geographer but because, except for his thoroughgoing knowledge of his own antecedents, he was such a rotten historian, the nations and kingdoms having changed hands and names since the great days of the Ottoman Empire, the Empire itself having rearranged if not the lands themselves then their borders, so that what he spoke, had learned to speak, was a lingo of the disinherited and misbegotten, a patois which finally proved tougher than those old arbitrary state lines of demarcation themselves, the nations and kingdoms having been reabsorbed elsewhere, restaked, changed like partners in a dance, taken like trumps in bridge) which still retained neologisms centuries after the countries that originally contributed them were no longer required (some of the more gung-ho among them would have said "permitted") to serve. He couldn't have held up his end of a conversation either in Turkic (the official language of the Court) or in Farsi (the language spoken by most of the people). What he spoke, if poorly, was an elitist tongue: Janissary. A language (which he would actually attempt to render, if a sworn celibate like himself ever got the chance to get them, to his progeny in a chipped pidgin, some bent bloopered, crooked Cockney) the now greatly reduced but still fierce force shared (perhaps five thousand men could speak it), no matter their mother tongue, only among themselves—— a grammar like a password, a syntax like a signal—" 'ad never e'er even seen a king much less haddressed one. Who now 'ad saw not only 'is first king but a certificated courier too, as well as a hambassador in a hembassy and most of 'is hoficial 'ouse'old staff an' not only dat but a first secretary to a grand vizier (an' you may throw in too, if you'd haccount for my toney turnout, a Savile fooking Row tailor). An' caught a glimpse in de far off, an' just as I was bending to my Prostration Walk, of de Hemporer of de Hottoman Hempire an', by 'is side, Abdulmecid, de godkid, de Hemporer in Whiting. It was ever so much more den a poor boy could bear.

"De courier 'ad goon to stan' next old Maḥmud 'imself—may Halla 'crease 'is camels an' rise de horanges in 'is hoāses—an' on an preharranged sidgnal, winkies me for'd oo, 'igh church dat was, on'y now begins to take hin wot *'igh* church 'mounts to, in dis wool. Usin' de goldern packadge for balance, sendin' it hout hinches afore me as a man down de mine might send de rays huv 'is lampern. Like some bloke on an 'igh wire I was. Feelin' me way an' doin' dis piecemeal shuffle. Blooody ridiclus. Me eyes on de groun', on de runner, de

376

Horiental carpet wif its dizzy spaghetti an' red rose geometrics till I were sick at stomk an' might 'ave thrown up my own self if I thunk it wouldink show. Acherly thinkink: Yar. Dat's wot dese flower arrandgements is——— vomit, tummy rosettes, barf bouquets. An' navigatink by de acheral pull a gravity oo 'ad wanted to guide carriages, to 'ave the tug of bits, an' make my 'ands felt in an 'orse's mouf. The gravities loose, flowink like wind thoo a draughty house. Feelink it. Hin my nauseated stomk, hup my 'eavy leggings, hon my 'ands wot 'eld de goldern packadge. Hall at once. Goin' thoo me like ha dose a salts. Oo 'ad wanted de control of reins an' 'ad dem now, but transformed, see? Redistribted like. Oo pulled 'isself alorng dat runner of decorated rug by reaction, resistance to the hints of heaving, falling, dropping. So dat I was like some long, deep, earthboundried hanimal, er snake say, hor a worm, dealink with space by constankly making dese adjustments of muscle, forever 'itching me pants so to speak. Wot all der time felt de high weight of de complicated ceilink threaten my neck like a guillotine.

"An' knew I was close when I could ear 'em whisperink. De Hottoman Hemperor. De Hottoman Hemporer hin Whiting.

"Peterson 'eld my packadge whilst I did my salaam.

"Startink at me belly an' brinkink it hever 'igher, I spun me left hand habout an' brung it to rest wit me palm on me fore'ead.

"The two potentates, 'im wot was in power an' 'im wot was in whiting suddenly silent. Wartching me close now oo before 'ad barely give me de odd ogle. I haccepted de box from Peterson wot we'd brought all de way from Blighty an' shoved it toward Abdulmecid, oo proved to be a strapping tall spotty-faced lad, much holder in happearance dan de five years 'e was reported to be. An' me thinkin' to meself, If 'is gardfather was on'y whiting for 'im to get big ernough to be tanked for 'is gift in Hinglish instead oov Islam 'e might 'ave sent it years ago. 'e's big ernough now, God bless 'im, to say 'Thank you so very very much' in Hinglish, German, or Chinese eiver.

"When 'e'd taken it from me I repeated me salaam as Peterson 'ad hinstructed me ter do, an' now de Hemperor was growling in Hottoman Hempirese.

"Peterson spoke up in wot must 'ave been the same language an' turns to me.

" '*You,*' 'e shouts, 'what are you on about then, you great scummy gonad? You press your *left* hand to your forehead? Your *left? You salute His Majesty with the same hand with which you wipe your arse?!*'

"By dis time Abdulmecid has got 'is packadge hopen an' is lookin' at me wif murther in 'is 'eart, an I don' 'ave to see no Court records to know 'e ain't been five years old for nine or ten years now, do I?

" 'What?' says Peterson. 'What?'

" 'It's nappies,' Abdulmecid says, standin' arn de goldfoil wrappings. "It's bloody fucking nappies,' says Abdulmecid hin 'is perfect Hinglish.

" 'Seize him!' roars 'is dad hin 'is. 'Seize him and send him for a Janissary!'

"I look to Peterson for an hexplanation, but all 'e can do is shake 'is 'ead real sad like. 'e's got dat same look on 'is dial wot I've seen when 'e's about to come down wif the sicks.

" 'Wot?' I arsk all confused like, 'wot?'

"But I can see de guards comink. It's just the job, i'n't it? Dey grab me an' start ter 'ustle me orf ter de flowery dell.

"Peterson wot 'as run orf quick as dammit 'oldink 'is sweet linen snotrag in front of 'is mouf turns an' lifts 'is duster long ernough ter sing out ' *'is Majesty's bidness! 'is Majesty's bidness!*' an' 'e's doin' twenny in a ten-mile zone ergain. But de Hemperor's lads ain't exactually takin' their time eiver, are they, an' pretty soon we've caught up wif 'im, an' I think uh oh, e's for it too, is Peterson, but dey don' evern *try* ter stop 'im. 'Wot?' I arsk again as they're bum's rushin' me past 'im. *'Wot,* for Gard's sake?'

" 'Rosencrantz and Guildenstern are all dead, kid,' Peterson says in a white whisper an' goes all sick on the carpet."

3

"You, *Mills!*" cries the Meat Cut.

"Mills? Who shouted Mills?" calls the Latrine Scrub.

"Sir, I did," the Meat Cut admits.

The Soup Man watched his junior officers.

Mills was reluctant to approach the Meat Cut with the Soup Man so visible, but Paradise Dispatchers were all about the yard and had heard what amounted to a direct order. If he did not respond, one of the more eager among them might well have taken it into his head to do something about it. They resented him for a Christian, and though Mills had formally repudiated his religion over a year before and had become, if not for all the world then for all his comrades to see, a practicing Muslim, he could not, however hard he tried, keep the disgust from his face whenever he and his brothers-in-arms—an odd term, since it was the boast of the special service into which he'd been impressed by Mahmud II that they never used anything as effete as weapons, that their killing scrimmages were conducted with nothing more elaborate in the way of tools than might be found on the ordinary strangler or murderer—— garotte collars and neckwrings, daggers and slingstones, brass knucks and brickbats, throwsticks and coshes, matches, fuel, the rocks in one's tunic, the hangman's fat hemps—prostrated themselves for sunrise, morning, midday, after-

379

noon and evening prayers. The fecal stench that came through the soiled, thin clothing in the tightly formed ranks of worshippers was terrific, and, if his expression was hidden by his earth-pressed face, he could never suppress the sound of his gagging.

Bufesqueu, a not unsympathetic Balkanese of approximately his own age and tenure in the Corps, had chided him for it.

"We're most of us converts, Mills. I myself was a very devout Greek Orthodox. You know what I miss most?"

"No," Mills said.

"The incense."

"I miss everything," Mills said gloomily.

"It's a good thing we're buddies, Mills. Talk like that could be construed as treasonous. Anyway it would be better for you if you got into the spirit of things. When we're stretched out nose to arsehole on the prayer rugs, pretend it's incense."

"Incense," Mills said.

"Sure incense. Certainly incense. Of a sort. Of a kind. Raging candlesticks of bowel. The guts' aromatics. Fart fragrance. The piss perfumes and come colognes, all the body's musks and effluents. It makes it easier."

"Easier."

"The celibacy. Sometimes I whiff the great poisoned cloud of dirt and intimacy we make and I imagine myself among women, entire overwhelming harems of them, hordes, their menstrual smell, their stinky mystery. It's deep I am, deep and lost down salty holes. Down and dirty. I bite the ground I lie upon and chew the earth until it turns to mud in my mouth. And they put me down for a religious zealot because the others have risen and I'm still praying. Oh yes. Not to lose my hard-on till I've come."

"Bufesqueu!"

"Why, Trooper, you're blushing! You're actually blushing."

"You're bloody outrageous you are."

"Oh, am I?" said his friend. "You'd best brush up on those vows you took, mate. You know what they mean in this outfit by celibacy? They mean the pure, true pukka gen. Pope, Patriarch, Ayatollah and Lord Swami Guru Indian Chief. Not only can't you get it off with a woman, you can't get it off with a man or animal either. You can't pull pud or touch yourself downtown or even *think* dirty jokes much less tell them. They hang for wet dreams here, and all that's left for a lad is to make them think he gets off on God. That's why I'm sopping when I rise from the rug. Incense, think incense, and make a wish, Mills."

And the odd thing, Mills thought, was that despite everything—George IV's tricks and the courier's treachery, Abdulmecid's and the Emperor's misplaced rage, his forced conscription with all its concomitant hardships—he *had* got into the spirit of things. That he understood the source of his fierce loyalties, could trace them back forty-two or so generations to a strange curse delivered by a pampered young nobleman in a Polish wood who, for the authority to deliver it, had only a fair approximation of his greatest grandfather's number and none at all, really, of the old man's descendants (and who, at the time, did not really believe that either of them would live long enough to get out of their scrape in time even to *get* descendants), mitigated not at all his dumb cheer or caused him a moment's pang. Cursed were the meek. He knew that. So be it. The last would never be first. He knew *that*. He knew everything, his low-born essence, his unswerving blue obedience and commissionaire's style—— everything. He could not help himself, would not. He was proud to be a Janissary. Proud of hardship, humiliation, his hardcore elite corps humility. So he *had* got into the spirit of things. And if he was no model soldier —I'm not, he thought, I'm not even good at it—he understood esprit de corps. None better. And valued most what he'd been forced to put up with. What few men living had had to endure, what most would have rebelled against out of hand, turning them tattles, turning them traitors. But not Mills. A hero of hardship, a big shot of bane and outrage.

There were the free-for-alls, the battles royal construed as preparation, training. The Soup Man's cynical dictum: "Janissaries are brothers. A true Janissary will lay down his life for his brother as casually as he would stand him a beer or buy him his breakfast. If an enemy slays his colleague, even in the act of self defense, even protecting his family, deflecting a torch, say, from the thatched lean-to where his babes lie sleeping; or wrenching the firebrand from a corpsman's hands with which he'd have ignited a wife's pubic hair simply to take the chill out of the air, then the surviving Janissary is obligated by the laws of God and the traditions of his company not only to avenge his fallen comrade but to read that comrade's original intent and to atrocify and consummate even to the nth degree his chum's lewd scheme. He must perfect death and touch the bottom of punishment. He must annihilate all the friends of the family and, years later, should

381

he meet someone in a peaceful street who, in a certain cast of light, merely resembles his cohort's killer or perhaps, by a word or gesture, so much as *reminds* him of his former teammate, or even only of the incident, then must the veteran Janissary dispatch him at once and with the same concentrate rage and fury at his disposal as had been available to him on the initial occasion of his wrath. If the wrath is not there he must pray for it. If his prayers are unanswered then he must make indifference do, and call on reserves of insouciance and apathy to hone his cruelty and generate out of neutral nonchalance the worst usages of his imagination. We are Janissaries, on the fence, middle of the road in every cause, and patriots only to each other."

And dropped his handkerchief, the signal on the day of their practical, for the recruits to attack each other. Mills, watching for the handkerchief to fall, touch the actual ground, was distracted for that fraction of a piece of a second it took Khoraghisinian, a friend, a young lad from his own barracks with whom he spoke on fire guard and after lights-out in his newly acquired makeshift Janissary diction of deep things, lost things, of home and absences, loved ones, of plans (mere desires now, simple idle longings, yearnings) and the high mysteries of the starry sky and the pungent, sacred memories of kitchen smells, the breads and sweets and savories of childhood, to drop on his neck from a tree's low limb and scratch at his eyes with its brittle, leafless, wintry sticks. Before Mills could recover, Khoraghisinian had shoved handfuls of steaming, acidic horse dung into his eyes and nostrils and smeared it across Mills's astonished mouth and tongue. Blinding George, choking him, leaving him breathless, gagging, gasping. Felling him, turning him over and, still in those split seconds it took Mills to recognize the source of the attack (permitting him to think Khoraghisinian—— Khory), driving the twigs up his nose, hammering them home with his fists and frozen turds.

It was his sneezes that saved him. Sudden, furious, reflexive and unwilled. His entire body was behind them, some good immunological angel so repudiate to the foreign matter trapped in his face that the sneezes brought his neck and head up like the solidest of uppercuts, roundhouses and haymakers, brutally butting Khoraghisinian and catching him, who was already leaning over to receive them, smack in the center of his nose, between his eyes, on each temple and, stretching to evade Mills's repetitive jackhammer blasts, full in the throat. Khoraghisinian's neck was broken, the bridge of his nose. His eyes had been pounded deep beneath their sockets and smashed like egg yolks, spread like jelly. Khoraghisinian had been killed instantly.

"Excellent. Good recovery, excellent," the Soup Man called from his horse. "Fine alertness, Muslim."

Now, still dazed, Mills used his good friend as a kind of fort—Fort Khoraghisinian, Camp Khory—arranging his old friend's body about him like a rampart and flattening himself behind it. The melee continued about and above him, a strange, pointless and issueless battle which Mills dreamily contemplated from the shieldy security of his pal's corpse. He had not bothered—or thought: he was still stunned, still bound by the low conscientiousness of shock—to rub the dung from his eyes and his steaming, teary vision was distorted, not blurred or dulled so much as squeezed and biased with a queer, buckled clarity, like someone's behind strong new prescription lenses. He perceived the incredible sharpness of blunt objects and instruments, so that rocks seemed thorny to him, cudgels torn from trees serrated, ordinary belts and bits of clothing—buttons, shoelace—sawtoothed. All about him he perceived the cusp of detail. The faces of his companions assumed a sort of tooled devastation. Their awled eyes and axey chins and spiky noses. Their scalpeled teeth and the hair on their heads brambly as barbed wire. Their nettled flesh, the fierce briery and cutting edge of their expressions. Even the sky—it was a bright day—seemed capable of stinging. Only the fighting had no point.

The combatants engaged and disengaged tempestuously, almost restlessly. They flung themselves upon and away from each other as if impatiently seeking something specific and valuable in one another. They were. Their opponent's weakness like buried treasure. If an adversary seemed capable of absorbing a body blow, his challenger quickly withdrew it, administered instead sharp kicks to the shins, the groin. If he withstood these his assailant abandoned him, changed tactics, sought a more vulnerable victim, great fistfuls of whose hair he might pull at almost as if he were riding bareback at full gallop and clinging to the mane to keep from falling. (Mills wondering how he, the assailant, could bear the pain, the sword edge sharpness of the hairy, glassy shards. He looked for stigmata, bloody palms.)

Meanwhile the Soup Man barked out commands, abuse, encouragements.

"Are you blind? Don't you see Suleiman has fallen? That he's rolled to the sidelines? Go after him. Put him out of the picture.

"You, Taurus Konia, you foul mistress of a mildewed eunuch, you sleazeball, you slimy slop jar of an excuse for a man, *bite* the scuzzy son of a bitch!

383

"That's it, that's the way, Mills, that's the way to do it. Khoragh-isinian's dead. Use him, *use* him! Hide in your buddy, use him, live off the land! Did you rob him yet? What? No? What are you waiting for?

"What are the rest of you Muslims waiting for? A comrade has fallen. Have you forgotten the bribegold he carries in case he's taken prisoner? And what about the rations that must still be on him? It's not yet lunchtime, the muezzin hasn't yet called us to midday prayer. His cinch is still good and would make a glorious noose. Are you just going to stand there and let Mills gobble up all the spoils? Rush him. *Rush him, you pussies!*"

Which brought him out of his daze. Which refocused his eyes. Which detranced him and canceled his lassitude, his tourist's glum stun, his protective shock like a blast of first aid.

The Janissaries were coming for him and, still behind the fallen Khoraghisinian, he brought himself up on his hands and knees and began to lunge and lurch about like an animal—— not like a dog or anything even remotely domestic, nor, for that matter, even like an animal in the wild. Rather he seemed to them, must have seemed to them, like someone stricken with a dazzling terror. But terror would not have stopped them, not even if it had been accompanied—as it *was* accompanied—by anything so spectacular as the noises now issuing from George Mills's mouth, if an instrument ordinary as a human mouth could be said to be capable of producing such sounds. Surely, they thought as they pulled up short of the galvanically com-pelled man loose and lurching now as live wire, he produces those noises in his vitals, his organs, his liver and lungs, his spleen and kidneys and guts and glands.

"After him," the Soup Man bellows. "Do you think he's haunted?" But even the commander's horse shies.

The Janissaries do not think he's haunted. They recognize the animal analog they had previously perceived. Mills is not terrified. He is outraged. His brutality now is the brutality of bereavement, his bestiality somehow, well, *maternal.* As though Khoraghisinian were his cub, Khoraghisinian's corpse something to be defended to the death, all affined biological kindred's interdictive, no-trespass taboo.

"The bribegold, the bribegold!" the Soup Man calls out. "He carries it too. Fan out, surround him. Smother the bastard."

And a few of the Janissaries begin to drift away from the main body. Slowly.

They sweep so widely about the flanks of Khoraghisinian's tautly

384

drawn bow of a form that they seem almost to disperse. Silently, and so very gradually, they sneak-shuffle past him so Mills, glaring round at them, seems to freeze their motion with a glance as if they were subjects in a boy's game. As soon as he looks elsewhere they are on tiptoe again. Even the Soup Man is silent. Even his horse does not stir. Someone snickers and Mills darts a look behind him, but this time the troopers don't even bother to suspend their motion. He sees that he is encircled. Taurus Konia holds a dagger in his hand. Suleiman grins from the sidelines where somehow he has managed to survive his tormentors. The Soup Man watches impassively. And sees——

Mills not so much standing, regaining his feet, as actually rearing, rampant as a furious figure in heraldry. He seems suddenly so fierce he might be mortally wounded perhaps, or seized by a peremptory madness. The dung he has not even bothered to remove has dried on his face, assumes some tribal quality of ultimate warpaint. A few bare twigs hang from his nose like an extra row of teeth.

This is the *Christian,* his fellow recruits think, the fastidious Englishman. *How he is transformed!*

But he does not apprehend his effect. If Mills is posturing he does not know it. For all the redeemed clarity of his vision, he is unaware of how he must appear to them, is not so much furious or fierce or outraged or maddened or even exalted by his terror as simply alarmed. That they are suddenly so wary—he sees this—he attributes to the complexity of their situation. He has observed their fitful skirmishes, the way they have sought quick advantage, their trial-and-error, upperhand experiments, their sudden disengagements, the violent storms and subsidences of their almost tropical hostility. Their to's and fro's like compass work. If they are wary now, he thinks, it is of each other, not of him. He they could dispose of in minutes, seconds. What threat could one Englishman—and that one a Mills, a forty-second or so generated, underwilled survivor on the strength not of strength but of loyalty, good behavior, all the quiet citizen virtues—possibly pose to these elite Paradise Dispatchers?

So their wariness—and this bothers George, seems to proviso and moderate still further this already mitigated man—is only a sort of extemporized battle plan. First they *will* kill him. Easy work. No sooner said than done. What are the odds? Twenty against one? Twenty-five? He is momentarily outraged—more Englishness; perhaps his fellow recruits have his number after all—by the sheer unfairness of his situation. Even the Soup Man, who has complimented him, who has given him high marks for his alertness (though to tell the truth he had not quite taken in at the time what his commander had meant), has sanctioned his slaughter. (And this English too, his complacent pride not so much in distinguishing himself as in pleasing a superior.) So. They will kill him. Steal his bribegold, Khoraghisinian's. Harvest their corpses for anything of value—— matches, a heel of bread, rope, the oranges both carry. What holds them back is what comes next. The free-for-all, that winner-take-all frenzy of their terrible tontine arrangements. Surely, Mills thinks, this is why they stare at him, glance furtively at one another. They are sizing each other up, remembering the power in that one's fingers, this one's arms. Dead reckoning will, viciousness. Savages, Mills thinks. They're savages.

The Soup Man sees Mills squat over Khoraghisinian's body, the dead man momentarily disappearing beneath the flowing cape George Mills wears. He sees Mills's quick movements but they're obscured by his robe and he cannot make them out. Quite suddenly there is blood, but it seems almost of a different color and viscidity than that which flows from the wounds of punctured men. He can't tell, but it seems cooler.

Mills is standing. He turns in what seems to the troopers a magic circle. Khoraghisinian's entrails lie gleaming in his left hand. The shit-encrusted bribegold shines in his right. He holds out both.

"We were friends," he intones. He speaks extra slowly in his new, barely mastered tongue so that he may be understood. He turns so that all might hear him. He means to mollify them with guts and gold and stench. He means to curry favor, to bribe them with atrocity. "We were friends," he says again of the man whose body he has just mutilated. "At the last minute, at the last minute I remembered something he told me once when we were on fire guard. 'Bribegold must be well hidden.' We were friends. He was wily. I frisked his shift and groped his robes. I did his duds like a dowser. *'Well* hidden,' he said. And it came to me he must have swallowed it. "See," Mills says and he raises his arms still higher, bringing his palms together in which Khoraghisinian's bowels slosh, collision and shift like so much damp, dark, swollen seaweed beneath his offering, the surgical, amputate bribegold steaming like carrots in soup.

It is just then that the muezzin calls from his tower and the Janissaries sink to their bellies as if shot. Only Mills, the pagan, gentile infidel, fails to prostrate himself at once. Then he too lowers himself, but he cannot remember the prayers. All that rings in his head is a nursery rhyme from childhood. He recites, first to himself and then aloud, "Little Jack Horner."

It was meaningless as the violence in Punch-and-Judy shows. One man had fallen that day. Hardly anyone had escaped injury. There were no doctors. They didn't take prisoners and they didn't have doctors.

"*Sir!*" Mills says smartly as he reports to the Meat Cut.

The Soup Man and Latrine Scrub drift over. Seeing that it is Mills who has been singled out, other officers join the group. The Superior and Inferior Scullions, two Water Carriers, a Cook and Pastry Cook, the Salad Man and three Steam Table Men. There are a handful of noncommissioned officers as well—— Waiters and Dining Room Orderlies, Dishwashers and Busboys.

Mills waits for the Meat Cut's instructions, and though he does not know what the man will say to him he knows it won't be pleasant. Perhaps he will be ordered to dredge latrines. Or work the potato gardens. Or clean prayer rugs. Or groom the mascot. Or stuff the mattresses. Or bathe officers.

Neither the officers nor the troopers have forgotten—or for that matter understood—his actions on the day of the practical when first he sneezed Khoraghisinian to death and then prospected his friend's body, as he himself doesn't understand much of the hocus-pocus of his position or the official status of the Corps. As he barely understands the parodic kitchen or menial nomenclatures of the officers' titles. Steam Table Men, Meat Cuts, Pastry Cooks, Inferior Scullions, Latrine Scrubs, Butcher Boys and all the rest. As he barely understands the reasons for eschewing ordnance, guns, bows and arrows, weapons even the most modest armies have at their disposal, savage tribes do. Or comprehends even the mission of the Janissaries. There has not been a major engagement in years, and although there have been "incidents," most of these have been political, demonstrative in nature, militant, bloody and editorial, often in support of the Sultan's policies but just as frequently in opposition. (He knows now that Mahmud II is not an emperor at all but a sultan and somehow this knowledge has altered something important in his life. He had been the loyal subject of a king. The King had had his reasons—which Mills not only retrospectively understands but actually respects—to question his loyalty and had tricked him into what George thought of—Ottoman Empire had sounded grand to him, Ottoman Emperor

387

had—as a lateral subordination, a sort of transfer of allegiance, collateral and fixed as the equivalency of currencies or the official provisions for exchanging prisoners, diplomats. But the subject of a sultan? For all that he has seen Yildiz Palace, George feels somehow desertized, sand-abandoned, wrapped in Persian rug, the lavish and decadent wall hangings of a tent. And though, except for patrols, bivouacs and marches, he can't have been away from the fort for ten weeks altogether, he feels oddly nomadic. It is because he works for a sultan, sheiks and pashas, and thinks of the solid fortress, the brick barracks in which he sleeps, as an oasis, of the water he drinks, though it's sweet and plentiful as water from any English lake, as collected, trapped, sluiced toward his mouth and throat and belly by gates and gravity, by a sort of clever and desperately engineered husbandry. Somehow, since the Emperor became a sultan, he is always parched now.) Nor is their function ceremonial. They rarely parade and when they do it is chiefly before the reviewing stands of other Janissaries. Never do they make a contingent in the pomp and pageantry of the Court. Their officers (for all the queer deference of their official designations) do not much talk to them or offer explanations, so they have no very clear idea either of short- or long-term goals. Newspapers and periodicals are not permitted inside the fort, and all they really know about what is expected of them relates to style, history. Whenever the Soup Man addresses the Janissaries (since the day of their bloody practical the one-time recruits are full-fledged Janissaries, integrated with troops who have spent years in the Corps), it is to remind them of their odd traditions, the queer pantheon of their heroic bullies.

"Remember," he says, "Godukuksbabis who slaughtered all the cows in the village of Szarzt. Pray for Tchambourb, of blessed memory, who villained the women of Urfa and drove their goats twelve miles through dangerous country to drown them in the Euphrates. Recall Abl Erzuz who captured the children of Tiflis, stripped them of their clothing, and led them on a forced march up the icy, precipitate slopes of Mount Ararat, where they fell thousands of feet to their deaths in nameless crevasses and lost, lonely fissures. Celebrate Van and all his glorious brother Janissaries who stole everything of value in the city of Plovdiv and bequeathed a life of poverty to all its inhabitants."

On one occasion even Mills has been singled out.

"Think," the Soup Man had said in what passed among them for public occasions, the boring convocations of garrison life, "of George Mills, who sniffled a man to death and then ransacked his guts for booty, who plundered a pal's bowels as a highwayman might go through his pockets. Think of Mills, whose blows were *blows* and for whom another man's flesh was of no more consequence than a handkerchief. Think of Mills's ingenuity and cough your enemies into submission. Drown them in your blood, smart their wounds with your tears. Disease and contagion them. Give them your colds and your cancers and, when you fall, fall on *them.* Rupture them with your weight. Recall George Mills, my treasures, and remember that cruelty is as real a legacy as the family silver."

Fearing reprisal, he'd shuddered. But there was no reprisal, is none. True enough, he gets the shit details, but since when has a Mills been without shit details? So, to answer Bufesqueu once more, he *was* in the spirit of things and, if he couldn't claim actually to *enjoy* the jobs that fell to him—he loathed them, they insulted his nostrils as much as the prayer cycles in which he found himself—there was that ancient business of the family curse, his old hereditary hardships like recipes in his keeping. Perhaps what he prayed for down on that rug was for them to keep it coming, to keep the pressure on, to keep it up. Perhaps all he wanted out of life was to do his duty. (He was not yet twenty-one years old.) It was, he understood, what most men wanted, the difference between himself and others being that he left it to others to define that duty. Demanded they define it. As if, like any truly despairing man, he would do anything, anything at all, just to get the chance to thunder his smug, contemptuous *There, you see?* at them. He was, that is, at home only in his outrage. And he almost hoped aloud as he awaited the Meat Cut's orders that it would be an officer this time, that it would be the Meat Cut himself whom he'd have to follow, soap in hand, to the huge soup kettles in the barracks square.

Imagining the conversation:

"Tonight is the eve of the Rabaran, Mills."

"Sir! The eve of the Rabaran, *sir!"*

"In my village, when I was a boy, husbands would bathe their wives, wives their husbands, parents children, children pets. Even the old, even the poor, had their bath partners. It was a community scour, Mills. I was still Christian then of course and had no more understanding of this ceremony than the Muslims had of our saints and martyrs. Indeed, I was a sneaky, oafish sort of boy, not even a very good Christian, and I took the occasion to satisfy my lustful curiosity. Together with other gentiles of my age and sort, I snuck off to the river, where many Muslim families went for their ritual cleansing.

There we would deploy ourselves behind boulders and trees and spy on the women as they unpinned their *chadors,* the young girls who rubbed handfuls of lather into their clefts. I didn't understand then that even if we'd been discovered they'd never have driven us off, that we'd have been invited to find our own bath partners and join them That on the eve of the Rabaran the cleanliness that must not be hidden from God need not be hidden from men, even from foolish, curious children. Do you understand what I'm telling you, Mills?"

"*Sir!* I understand what you're telling me, *sir!*"

"That there's nothing shameful in a holy scour. That the cleanser is blessed as the cleansed. That it's a privilege to brisk and shine another's affairs, to polish his business as one would one's own "

"*Sir!* I understand, *sir!*"

"Of course you do. Others mightn't, but *you* do."

"*Sir! I* do, *sir!*"

"Who stuck his hands past the wrists into a colleague's intestines. Now there's no need to blush. There's no reason to go all girly on me, George."

"*Sir!* No reason, *sir!*"

"Of course not. You were doing your duty. You were doing your duty in *his* duty. Do I have it? Is that about it?"

"*Sir!* You have it. That's about it, *sir!*"

"Well of course. And we understand that if it weren't the eve of the Rabaran I wouldn't be asking *you* to bathe me?"

"*Sir!* We understand, *sir!*"

"And that even if it is Rabaran eve we still wouldn't ask if these were places we could comfortably reach ourselves?"

"*Sir!* We understand, *sir!*"

"*And that I choose you only because you've been there before?*"

Requiring that he—the Meat Cut—speak to him in ways that even the King George IV himself would never speak to him. And requiring that Mills answer in ways that King George wouldn't, indeed couldn't, ever permit himself to demand. Already aggrieved. Hoping if it weren't the Meat Cut then some lesser officer, or noncommissioned officer perhaps—a Waiter or Busboy—or even someone from the ranks, a Paradise Dispatcher like himself. Or something to do with the mascot—maybe the mascot was his best bet—Mills commanded to entertain it, to throw sticks for the old blind dog and fetch them himself when the arthritic animal wouldn't move. (And could imagine *that* conversation too, not conversation, really, just plain boorish ragging: "Would you look at the bloody-minded beast? Do

390

you see him frolic? Did you e'er see such pep? When Shep goes we won't even have to replace him. What do you think, Konia? Mills for mascot when old Shep gets demobbed?" "There's advantages and disadvantages." "Well I *see* the advantage. Shep could fetch good as any when he was healthy, but he never did get the hang of throwing. What disadvantage could there be?" "Well, there's his age." "His age?" "A human's lifespan is seven to one compared with a dog's. Shep's ninety right now in human terms. Suppose Mills *is* made mascot, suppose he enjoys it, suppose he takes it in his head he's only *technically* human, that only some rare vagary of Nature put him in pants in the first place? My God, don't you see? He could will himself beast. He's already five sixths of the way there. On a dog's diet he could live to be three hundred and fifty!" "There's that," Konia's collaborator admits. "There's more." "More, Konia?" "This one don't have Shep's temperament. He's vicious." Because he's a living legend by now, so accredited ever since the day the Soup Man chose to single him out for his deeds—of yes, *deeds,* lifted forever beyond anything as normal as actions or reactions—which is all they were finally: reactions, hard, simple, knee-jerk—and into rhetoric, semiofficial shoptalk, regulation Lister bag company scuttlebutt whenever men stopped by for a cool drink of water—along with Van and Abl Erzuz and Tchambourb and Godukuksbabis and all the rest of that Star Chamber lot of cutthroat bullies.)

A living legend? A living joke.

Okay, he thinks. Swell. Why not? So be it. I'm your man. Fine. I'm your dogsbody. Of course. You want me to bath down the whole naked, goddamn garrison? Every last mutt and horse on campus and all the slops in all the tripe barrels and offal buckets, too, by running them bit by fucking bit through the blue collar saliva in my poor man's mouth? *Sir!* If that's what you want, *sir!*

And is as close at this moment to harboring a pure revolutionary thought as anyone in the entire history of the world.

And is still waiting on the Meat Cut for the man's command, which he still hopes will be as devastating as the officer can make it, and prays that he still has whatever it takes neither to blench nor blink when he finally hears it.

He finally hears it.

He blenches. He blinks.

"Mills," says the Meat Cut. "I say, George, why don't you take the rest of the day off and go into town for a bit? Take your friend with you."

"Sir? Into town, sir? *Town?*"

"Dress uniforms. To show the flag. Take your pal, you know, the one that survived. Bufesqueu. Take Bufesqueu."

It didn't need newspapers, it didn't need periodicals, it didn't need chalk talks or elaborate background briefings by the officers. It didn't even need the barracks wisdom and tittle-tattle of a Bufesqueu for Mills to understand that they had just been condemned to death. There were no provisions in the military code for Janissaries to be discharged. (There were Paradise Dispatchers in Mills's own company in their seventies and eighties.) The reasons were obvious and, in an odd way, peculiarly compassionate.

It was not just that a veteran Janissary, celibate, old, failing and without family, ill equipped to do business in the outside world, would be lost as a civilian. He would be torn to shreds. This much came through the crazy pep talks of the Soup Man. They were despised as much as they were feared. This was their glory, their elitism.

And Mills well enough understood their ultimate mission. They all did. It was not so much to protect the state as to suppress the people. Indeed—those frequent demonstrations against the government—it was to suppress the state as well. (Though Mills had never seen it, there was something that terrified people and government both: the symbolic moment of Janissary rage when the troopers hauled the tremendous cauldrons in which they boiled soup out of the mess and into the square and upended them.) At the height of their strength two centuries earlier there had been upward of a hundred and thirty thousand troops in the Corps. Now there were barely five thousand, all of them concentrated in the huge and possibly impenetrable fortress where Mills had trained and until now lived as a prisoner. But this was the point. Not that their ranks had been diminished by a hundred and twenty-five thousand men, but that with two hundred years to work it out, a hostile government had been unable to abolish an organization of just five thousand that it openly feared and had little use for—— except on those occasions when it meant to punish the people.

So they would be killed. Certainly Mills would be. He was the living legend after all. At least so far. Bufesqueu himself had said as much.

"How do they know?" Mills asked.

"How do we get hashish? How do we get *halvah?* Where do the fashions come from the fellows like to wear at parties? How do we get the forbidden boozes? Where do the rifles come from?"

"We don't have rifles."

"We don't, no. The officers do. To use against us if we make trouble." And when George looked at him in disbelief, Bufesqueu went on. "Kiddo, kiddo, it's a Byzantine world. There's plots and intrigues under every fez. There's bucks to be made and merchants to make them. You want to know the real reason our outfit still exists?"

"We're the greatest fighting force in the world."

"The *real* reason."

"That *is* the real reason. Man for man and hand to hand no one can touch us."

"Listen to this bird," Bufesqueu said. "He's marching off to a town where the first guy to spot him will already be thinking not how to kill him but how best to dispose of his body after he's dead, and his heart's in his head and his head's up his ass. What, you're a snowman? You got coals for eyes? Open them up, you're melting. *Kickbacks!*"

"Kickbacks?"

"Sure kickbacks, of course kickbacks! Kickback kickbucks! The fix is in. The fix has always been in. The two-hundred-year-old fix. The peddlers vigorish the Busboy, the Busboy kicks back to the Steam Table Man, the Steam Table gives to the Meat Cut, the Meat Cut slices off a piece for the Soup Man, the Soup Man ladles it out to the Grand Vizier, the Grand Vizier sees to the Sultan and the Sultan gave at the office. And that's why we continue to exist! You know what's the best business there is?"

"I don't know anything," George Mills said.

"The best business there is is a deprived, captive population. A prison's a good business. A garrison like ours is. Mom and Pop stores on desert islands."

"If you're so smart why ain't you rich?"

"I am rich. They say they let you keep Khoraghisinian's bribe-gold."

"They say I captured it in a fair fight," Mills said gloomily.

"More snowmen."

"But me? How would they know about me?"

"In town you mean? The good people who want to kill you, who want to hide your face?"

"Yes."

"George, George, those walls only *look* impenetrable."

"Money talks."

"Talks? It sings soprano. But it didn't need any money to make you famous. Penny dreadfuls tell your story. There's broadsides and chapbooks and solos for cello. The ruthless, Christian Janissary from Blighty Limey Land. The folks hate you, Mills!"

"I'm done for."

"Nah, I have a plan."

They were caparisoned, their formal uniforms more like frock than battle dress. In their flaring knee-length skirts and high bodices they seemed rather like warriors on vases, urns. Percale as sheet or pillowslip, even their fabrics felt sumptuary, voluptuous. Though he had the reputation, Mills did not feel vicious. And if he'd had no knowledge of what Bufesqueu had described as the Janissary's Byzantine arrangements—indeed, he'd only first heard of them moments before—he felt, in his Attic, high-stepper uniform, more raiment than clothing, more gown than garment, oddly venal, sharp and shady. (Already memorizing it, figuring ways it could be rendered.) But then, recalling his jeopardy—Bufesqueu he figured was there for the ride, along as a witness, no more (suspicion reinforcing his new Tammany heart)—chiefly he felt foolish, vulnerable as a traffic cop. "Oh yes?" Mills said. "A plan?"

They were on the open plain that ringed their fort—men watched from the ramparts and parapets—land that had once been valuable and held some of the city's most venerable buildings. As recently as Mills's induction the year before, a sort of grandstand and playing field had stood there, but over the years, as the original defilement became a parade ground, the parade ground an entrenchment, the entrenchment a breastworks, the breastworks a camp, the camp a fortification and the fortification the fortress that the Janissaries now permanently occupied, there had been a sort of piecemeal retreat, gradual as balding, of the old residences and public buildings. Now, however, they left the open area and entered the city proper, slicing into it through a failing neighborhood. Here, Mills guessed, the vendors and profiteers lived whom Bufesqueu said supplied his colleagues with their black market contraband. (I didn't know, he thought. Sitting aloof and ignorant on my double bribegold. Starving for *halvah* and they didn't even tell me, wouldn't, not even Bufesqueu. Sent to *halvah* Coventry.)

A few women and old men returning from market spotted them

and were already whispering among themselves, gesturing and, so far at least, only vaguely pointing in their direction. Boys saw them, watched silently, their faces expressionless. Dogs barked. "It better be good," Mills said into his hand as if he were coughing.

"Trust me," Bufesqueu said.

"Sure," Mills said, out of sight now of the Janissaries on the battlements but still closely scrutinized by Bufesqueu.

"When I give the word," Bufesqueu said.

"Sure," Mills said, "the word." (And thought: The word will be Mills. Hey, everybody, here's George Mills that you heard so much about. Come and get it!)

"Just watch me," Bufesqueu said. "When I give the signal."

"When you drop the handkerchief?" Mills said.

Bufesqueu glanced at him out of the corner of his eye. "Just watch me," he said.

They might have been strolling in the park, Bufesqueu slowing his pace and Mills slackening his own in order not to get out in front of him, when Bufesqueu suddenly began to run full out, shouting as he came. *"Blitzpounce!"* he shouted. *"Thrustrush! Raidgrapple!"* They were Janissary commands for attack and Bufesqueu was yelling them at the top of his lungs. *"Flakshoot!"* he screamed. *"Swipeslam! Flailshove! Harrywaste!"*

The people divided before them and Mills fell in beside his friend, matching him stride for stride. Bufesqueu continued to shout. *"Sallystorm! Knockstrike!"* he shouted.

"Chargepelt!" Mills joined in. *"Lungehavoc! Siegescorch!"*

Now the crowd was taking actual flight, disappearing into passageways, alleyways, niches, hiding in the bays and cubbyholes of architecture like matadors behind the barriers in bullrings.

Leaving Bufesqueu the final word. *"Charge, men!"* he roared so passionately even Mills looked around to see if they were not the vanguard of a full-fledged invasion.

The trouble was it was a city, that as they cleared one street their sheer noise attracted new groups in the next. The good part was the new groups saw the old ones disperse, and, when the pair was close enough for their war cries to be distinguished, they'd already gotten the message and begun to scatter. There wasn't a soul in the streets who hadn't himself either been beaten by a Janissary or known or heard about someone who had. Beaten or killed, beaten and killed. So what worked in their favor was history, time's and memory's bad press.

And they looked as they advanced like engines of destruction, like some great avenging avalanche of trouble and death, some spilled Vesuvius of molten bad news and worse intentions. Guzo Sanbanna himself was a witness that day and later admitted that it seemed to him that nothing, no one, could have stopped them. "I ran myself," Guzo would say, "with one thought for my life and another for my profits!"

The trouble was they were only human first and Janissaries second. That the spirit was willing but the flesh was an old story. That charges like theirs, even with the adrenalin flowing like a chemical bonanza, could not be maintained. Already Mills was winded, already Bufesqueu was. The good part was traffic was already beginning to back up, that, seeing the townspeople scatter, lunging recklessly in front of the rearing nags, drivers and passengers alike called from their carriages to the fleeing crowds. Mills could hear them. And the isolated replies of brave men: "An attack," they called back over their shoulders as they fled. "Janissaries," they shouted, "the entire force." "Janissaries, including that legion recalled from Africa." *"Janissaries!"* they cried. *"Janissaries on a rampage! They've overturned their soup kettles in the square!" "I heard someone say that Mills himself is leading the charge!"*

So what they had going for them was rumor, rumor and panic and the prepped fear which greased them, which perspired imaginations all round—so alarmed were the Constantinopolans that out of some inspired sense of emergency the news was passed instantly from neighbor to neighbor, leaping neighborhoods, entire arrondissements and administrative quadrants of the city, flashed across the Bosporus from Europe to Asia so that they already knew at Yildiz Palace—and caused what had only been a traffic jam to become a sort of evacuation.

The trouble was they were exhausted. For two blocks now they had ceased their war cries altogether and for once they had seemed, had anyone troubled to look, more the pursued than the pursuers. For half a block—Mills had pulled up first—they had stopped running entirely. Winded, they leaned up against a shop window and vomited. The clerks and people who'd run inside to escape might have captured and killed them easily but their sudden appearance on the other side of the glass had only served to startle and frighten them further. Perhaps they thought that the vomit and spew which issued so violently from their stomachs and throats was only a sort of Janissary way of spitting. At any rate, no one thought to investigate when Mills and Bufesqueu pulled away from the window and staggered on a few steps. "What—— what," Mills panted through the foul, bile that burned his throat, "do we—— do we do now?" And Bufesqueu, who did not have the strength to reply, pointed vaguely toward the road.

Where doors hung ajar on abandoned carriages and the driverless horses that pulled them backed and filled or turned halfway round in the street to stare into the faces of other horses, milling about, or frozen in maneuvers—they seemed more burdened now that their drivers and passengers had quit them, hobbled by their loose reins like so many leathery trip wires and the dead weight of their vehicles— which gave them the actual appearance of loiterers.

Mills understood at once. Thinking: Here's something I can do. Here's something I can do if I can still do it. "All right," he told Bufesqueu, indicating the Overland, "go on, get in."

But Bufesqueu pulled the shades and slammed the carriage doors shut and climbed up to sit beside Mills on the driver's bench.

"Great," George said. "*Two* Janissaries. Now we make twice as big a target."

"Someone who knows the city has to tell you where to go. I pulled the shades."

"Fine," George Mills said. "Now the sun won't fade the upholstery."

"I pulled the shades," he repeated. "They'll think we're carrying God knows who. The Soup Man himself probably. Turn left," Bufesqueu said. "Make a right at that mosque."

No one stopped them. No one interfered. Everyone had heard of the invasion and thought that the two Janissaries topside the Overland with its tightly drawn shades drove God knew who, the Soup Man himself probably.

Bufesqueu directed Mills past the logjam of vehicles and into the broader avenues. He told him which turn-off to take in traffic circles, guided him into narrow lanes that widened into grand boulevards. Mills was actually beginning to enjoy the ride when Bufesqueu instructed him to pull up before a thick wrought-iron gate surrounded on all sides by a high stone wall. "All right," he said. "You can stop now. We're there."

Mills did not yet know that it was the harem of Yildiz Palace.

Guards were there to challenge them. They stared at the Janissaries' uniforms.

"You girls want something?" one said, leveling his rifle at them.

"Hey you," Bufesqueu said, "watch your language. All *we* ever did was swear off. We never took no low shave like the rest of you capons." Mills poked Bufesqueu with his elbow.

"I'll measure my dick against both you young ladies. I'll put one of my balls on the ball scale and bet you double or nil it's heavier than all four of yours put together."

"Big deal," Bufesqueu said, "you got fat balls." The second guard laughed and Bufesqueu put a finger to his lip to silence him and jumped down from the driver's bench. *"Sir!"* Bufesqueu snapped suddenly. "Yes, *sir!"*

Mills supposed his friend would be shot before his feet touched the ground, but all that happened was that the Balkanese ran about to the blind side of the carriage, opened the door and stuck his head in. Mills grinned sheepishly at the two guards but both stared quizzically at the drawn black shade on their side of the locked Overland. They appeared to be straining to overhear. Mills strained too and was just able to make out brisk guttural murmurs, and then, seconds later, Bufesqueu's crisp, military *"Sir!* Yes, *sir!"* and the door slam smartly.

When Bufesqueu reappeared the two guards had already lowered their rifles. The Balkanese climbed back beside Mills and turned to the first guard, the man who had challenged them. Bufesqueu glared at him. "Himself wants to know what's causing the delay. Unlock the gate," he said.

"Where's your authorization?"

"Why don't you stick your face in that carriage and find out yourself where's my authorization? Then, if we can anybody find the stub of a prick or two whole entire balls between us, we can have that little weigh-in you were so anxious about. Open the gate!"

The first guard glanced anxiously at the carriage's drawn shade and turned to the second guard. "Go on," he said. "Better unlock it."

Mills shook his head when they were safely inside the extensive grounds. "That was a close one. How'd you have the nerve to talk to those fellows like that?"

"Not close."

"No? Even the horses were getting nervous."

"Service rivalry," Bufesqueu said. "Not close."

"Oh," Mills said.

"Look, Snowman," Bufesqueu said sharply, "how long am I going to have to carry you? We've been in this chickenshit outfit practically the same time but I've got all the answers and you've got all the questions. It's simple. Soldiers and sailors are *supposed* to hate

398

each other. Every branch of the services is supposed to hold the other branches in contempt. It's sanctioned. It's how the mother fuckers induce pride."

"I don't hold sailors in contempt."

"No," Bufesqueu said. "You don't hold *anyone* in contempt. How you ever got to be the *cruel* Janissary is beyond me."

"I told you about that," Mills said softly.

"Yeah," Bufesqueu said.

He wanted to ask Bufesqueu where they were but he was ashamed. Instead he tried to concentrate on the directions the guard had given Bufesqueu at the gate when he'd asked him how to find the Kislar Agha.

It was like fairyland. Where their own grounds had been barren —except for the tiny patches of cultivated forests and jungles and special terrains used for their training exercises—these were universally lush. Everywhere there were formal gardens with plashing fountains that made an almost sensible music as the water dropped from varying heights back into their basins. There were fabulous mosaic forms, intricate spires and minarets, round arches like giant keyholes, great domes that might have been dull and massive but refracted light in such a way that they seemed more like precious stones than bits of functioning architecture. Domes like crown jewels. Emerald domes, diamond domes, ruby.

Here and there Persian rugs were spread about on the grass. They could have been flying carpets.

Everywhere he looked there were Negro gardeners to tend the arranged landscapes, dark-colored technicians to adjust the fountains, men who might have seemed fat if they had not been so obviously powerful. He saw other blacks, dressed in strange colors, in rich, queer fabrics he'd never seen before. They hurried along pine needle pathways and carried fine silver trays covered with damask cloths toward low-roofed, beautifully tiled buildings. With their pitchy skins against the deep green background of the clipped, splendid lawns they looked almost like the exotic, carved and painted barks of some of the elaborate, topiary trees.

I'll say one thing, Mills thought, these sailors live well!

"This is it," Mills said with forced cheer. "Where they said that Kislar Agha is we're looking for." He pulled into a long, curved driveway, eased the horses to a gentle stop and brake-locked the Overland, hoping that Bufesqueu had noticed his skill. Bufesqueu said nothing, of course, and Mills leaped down from the bench first. He did not ask his friend what a Kislar Agha was, or where they were, or what they were doing there in the first place.

He was determined to change his friend's ideas about him and, though he had no notion yet of why they'd come, to beat Bufesqueu and get to the Kislar Agha guy first. He hadn't a clue what he would tell him, could only imagine his poses, his folded arms and knowing smirk. Perhaps, while waiting for the lightning to strike, he would kibitz the black boys, let the Kislar Agha bloke, and Bufesqueu too, see who they were dealing with.

(Because he'd already forgotten the danger, because this was an adventure, because it had been an adventure since he'd first started out for London to make his way in the world, before: since he'd accepted that letter of introduction which had been obsolete before it was written. Because it was *all* adventure: his meeting with King George, his—he understood this now—expulsion from England, his journey with the spy, Peterson, and his meeting with the Jew ambassador and the complicated betrayal at Mahmud's Court; all, all of it adventure; being given over to the mullahs, to the Janissaries, killing Khoraghisinian and becoming a living legend, all of it—— being sent down with Bufesqueu to take Constantinople with no more weapons between them than their two full-dress Janissary suits; the confiscation of the Overland and the grand ride they'd had, vulnerable and open-air'd as a Roman triumph; the business with the guards at the gates, even the peaceful drive through this voluptuary candyland. Because it was *all* adventure and he was an adventurer and an adventurer did not so much forget danger as acknowledge and then ignore it, that only then could he be vouchsafed immunity. Because it was *all* adventure and he lived now within some rhythm of action and respite which were as much the physical laws of adventure as ebb and flood tides were the governing physics of the seas. And because his feelings had been hurt, and there was no room or way to accommodate fear and sulk in the same place at the same time.)

Mills entered the building.

"The Kislar Agha," George demanded of a huge fat black fellow in sheer, billowing trousers that tapered tightly at the ankles. He was shirtless and his full, hairless chest was barely covered by a light vest. He glanced at the man's shoes, smooth and soft and slightly curling at the toes like a jester's slippers. George lightly touched the Negro's turban. "Hair not dry yet, darling?" And leaned toward him. "Let the air out of your pants, why don't you?" he whispered. "Get your toes fixed. You look like some pansy-assed Nancy boy."

The black man lifted Mills off the floor by the neck and quietly choked him. "Is this the way you address the assistant Chief Eunuch in the Sultan's harem?" he asked mildly.

Mills's frightened, high-pitched squeals brought another black man, even larger, into the room.

"Let him go, Suliem. I said let him *go!*"

Reluctantly the giant withdrew his strangler's hands from Mills's neck and George dropped a good half foot to the floor.

"What's this all about?" the Kislar Agha demanded.

And before George Mills could say "Service rivalry," Bufesqueu had come up behind him and flung him aside.

"I'm Bufesqueu and he's Mills," he said, "and we're deserters from the Janissaries seeking sanctuary."

4

Which was how George Mills and Bufesqueu, his protector and bene-
factor, came to live as the only unimpaired males in the largest full-
service harem in the world.

What he couldn't get over were the scents.

As if they lived in a basket of fruit or box of wondrous candy.
As if they lived in a great garden or amongst the savory headwinds
of the juiced seasons. As if they lived in a kitchen or spicery, in a
bakery, or within some balmy climate of luxurious merchandise pliant
as trousseau. He sniffed the cloves, civets and gums of carpentry, the
jeweler's musky metals, the pomander of gemstone. In the groves and
greenery of the planet. All cosmetics' pervasive attars.

But there was more that he couldn't get over:

King, he thought. King and Courier, Ambassador, Soup Man
and Sultan and Sultan-in-Waiting. Chief Eunuch too, he thought. It
was getting to be quite a list.

Or the fact, though he had forgotten the danger, that they were
alive at all. His throat was still sore from Suliem's attempt to choke
him. But at last he was beginning to get his voice back. For days he
had been silent as a giraffe. So silent that when Fatima, one of the
slaves who attended the harem women, came into the laundry where

he and Bufesqueu had been assigned to work, he had been unable to answer the woman's questions regarding a particular satin sheet her mistress had inquired after. Mills had seen the sheet in question and had gone to fetch it, handing it to her wordlessly.

"Oh dear," she said, "it's been starched, hasn't it? Lady Givnora specifically asked that it be laundered in rose water with no starch but only a touch of unscented olive balm to take the roughness off." She held an edge of the sheet to her nostrils. "Why, this is lemon curd. Smell for yourself." Mills pressed the sheet to his nose. "Well?" Fatima said. Mills shook his head. "Can you tell me why my mistress's orders weren't followed?" Mills shook his head. Fatima glowered at the new man and ordered the sheet to be rewashed. "Do you think you people can get it right this time?" Mills nodded and with a pen carefully noted her requirements as Fatima looked on, a gradual sympathy reflected on her thin face. "Oh my," she said, "*you* can't talk at all, can you?" Mills shook his head. "Poor guy," Fatima said. "They really did a job on you, didn't they?" Mills nodded. "Yes," she said, "I know. It must have been one of the deepest bits of barbering in the entire history of this plantation." Mills looked at the thin slave. "Clipped ballocks, jolly roger, bush, asshole and all, did they? They couldn't have left you with enough strings, snails and puppy dog's tails to make a noise when you fall downstairs." Mills shook his head vigorously and tried to talk but his throat was still too raw. "Don't go on about it, luv," Fatima said. "*I* can't hear you. I doubt anyone can, even your co-boy sopranos in these wildwoods. Maybe you sing your own song now, like those dogs whose screaks can't be heard by other folks, only by a few fellow doggies who pick up the frequency on clear, cold nights when reception is good. See to the sheet, will you, luv?" Mills nodded.

He salved his throat with honey and licorice, coated it with sweet oils and unguents. When the week was up he sought out Bufesqueu.

"They think I'm a eunuch," he rasped.

"Lord bless you, boy, why wouldn't they? What's the good of plumbing if it's always leaking? No sooner do I rise in the morning than I rise in the morning. I remember where I am and start spilling my seed like some hungover farmer. I come into the laundry here and see their frillies and unmentionables and my piece starts to melt like a burning candle. Jeez, George, will you just look at this trim? The bedgear and belly dance togs and all the sweet else? I tell you, kid, even their soiled veils give my glands something to think about. I'm losing weight. Pounds and inches. I was better off down on that prayer rug."

"Maybe you should have thought of that," Mills said hoarsely.

"Because you can never get enough," Bufesqueu said, not hearing him, not listening. "Because you can never get enough. Not if you lived till the end of the world. No one can. Not if you were Sultan Mahmud II himself and all his helpers. Not if you were not only irresistible to quiff but positively necessary to their welfare, like air or money. Because you can never get enough. Not if you were dying and the priest was already giving you last rites. Hell," Bufesqueu said, "you'd already be in bed anyway, wouldn't you? What would be the point of wasting perfectly wonderful machines like a bed and pillows, sheets and covers, on anything drab and ordinary as death? Maybe that's why they administer last rites—— because you're in that damn bed all alone, and even if you know you can't ever get enough it's a sin not to try."

"It'd be worth your life to try in this place," Mills scraped.

Bufesqueu looked at him. "Listen to him," he said. "His voice is cracking on him all over again. Well, why not? He's in this harem a week and it's a new puberty. I shouldn't wonder if my own voice didn't start to do duets with itself. Not to worry," he said abruptly, heartily. "We'll get it all straightened out. Weren't we grand? Weren't we grand though?"

He meant their two-man invasion of Constantinople, the pair of them taking the city by storm. Mills smiled. They *were* grand. No Mills since the first George Mills had been grander, and even if his own had only been a sidekick's grandeur—briefly he wondered if it were enough to lift the curse—a crony henchman's auxiliary one, Bufesqueu couldn't have done it by himself. It had been his name, the living legend's, that had been passed in the street. George was satisfied. They had taken Constantinople together.

They'd done more, and this was something else he couldn't get over.

The Janissaries no longer existed. When Mills and Bufesqueu had been ordered to town, when Bufesqueu's defiant war cries had first rung in the streets and panicked the Ottomans, there'd been a fire storm of alarm. Rumors had flashed from street to street like signal fires. Before Mills and Bufesqueu even spotted the abandoned Overland, the Sultan had heard of the incursion at Yildiz Palace. Mahmud's information had been no sounder than anyone else's of course, and when he'd been informed that the Janissaries had overturned their soup kettles the Sultan convened the chiefs of staff of the entire military. What he was thinking was how best to save Yildiz. But by this time the story had taken on additional detail, an oblique verisimilitude. It was rumored that the soup had actually been at the boil, that most of an entire phalanx of Janissaries had been scalded along their shins and calves in the effort. In the hasty consultation that followed, the outraged Sultan advised his advisers he now concluded that because the soup had been still hot when it had been spilled, the action had to have been a precipitate one, an angry gesture of the moment. He was heartened, too, by news of the scaldings, and was supposed to have said: "They haven't thought this one out. Some incendiary must have roused them. We must counterattack now. While their passion prevails over their strategy. Before their third-degree burns heal. Send in the cannon. Reduce the fort to rubble!"

So they were feeling pretty good, Mills and Bufesqueu. Splendid, in fact. Two reluctant recruits who not only had conquered a major world capital but in the act of conquering it had turned round and conquered by way of ricochet the very force in whose name they had done it. And if five thousand men had died in the Sultan's surprise bombardment—if, indeed, a week after the event, perhaps a couple of hundred of their former comrades were still smoldering—it was nothing either of the condemned men cared to take on his conscience. Bufesqueu because he genuinely believed the other Janissaries had repudiated women, Mills because he had not once chosen in all the time he had lived.

Fatima came in for towels and looked, in passing, in the direction of Mills's crotch. She shook her head sadly. "Please stop that," Mills said, and Fatima stared at him, clapping her hands to her mouth in astonishment.

"It's grown *back?*" asked the superstitious woman.

"Sure," George said, "you think they can keep a good man down?"

So, though he didn't know it, among certain of the staff at least, he continued to be a living legend.

Bufesqueu, of course, was in seventh heaven. "In the country of the blind," he liked to say, patting his pants and winking, "the one-eyed man is king."

But so far neither Bufesqueu nor George had come within even hailing distance of the Sultan's harem girls, let alone seen one. If this was a torment to the former, to the latter it was something of a comfort. George had not so far forgotten his danger as to lose respect for it entirely. He complimented himself on his Millsian ability to appreciate and honor a taboo. If he had swallowed whole whatever guidelines his Janissary superiors had laid down for him, if his credulity had kept him down range of the black marketeers who Bufesqueu said visited their fort almost daily to take orders for the cold comforts they dispensed for bribegold and a portion of a Janissary's small pay, he had at least managed, if innocently, if ignorantly, to abide by the rules, to live within the letter, to the last crossed *t*, to the last dotted *i*, of the laws of appearance. This, Mills thought, was what preserved them. To view things otherwise was subversive not only to those who held power over them, and not only to their own sort, but more importantly to themselves, to one another, to every Mills who'd ever lived under the curse of kind. He understood what was permitted and behaved himself.

Now a sultan's harem, Mills thought, a sultan's harem was just the last place on earth one should think about running amok. And if that sultan also happens to be one of your emperor sultans, as this one is, with sway not only over entire countries and populations but over entire climates as well, from deserty Africa to the frozen Kush, then that sultan is one hell of an important man; and if, without batting an eyelash, he can cannonade a complete elite corps off the face of the world simply because it was rumored that they might have spilled some soup, and if he's gone to the trouble of becoming a sultan emperor in the first place with all the expense of men and matériel *that* takes just so he can have dibs on two or three hundred of the prettiest girls in all those respective countries, populations and climates, and if he's taken the additional pains to house them all in one place where he can keep his eye on them, and in a style like this where the girls themselves don't do a thing, not wash a bowl, dry a dish, make a bed, fix a meal, rinse something out in the sink of an evening or even just pick out their own clothes, what they think suits them best, shows off their color or makes them less hippy; and if he's gone to the further bother of training up specialist surgeons who have nothing better to do than cut the nuts off fellows who themselves have nothing better to do than see to it that the two or three hundred girls don't either, then that sultan is not only one hell of an important man but one hell of a jealous one, too. And I for one, Mills thought, who changed my life and sealed the fates of maybe five thousand others because I happened to throw him a salute with the wrong hand, I for one, who already have, don't want any part of him. I already took those vows to stay on the wagon. What harm will it do me to keep them? No sir. It don't bother me that I may be losing Bufesqueu's respect, or that old Fatima used to think of me as just one more steer around this place. I don't want no part of *him,* and I don't want no part of *them.*

What he didn't know was that he was more a living legend than ever.

Alib Hakali asked to see them, and he and Bufesqueu left the laundry where for almost a month now their official assignment had been to fold sheets for the harem. "Maybe he wants to put us to work doing something else. After all we're trained Janissaries. We're wasted in that laundry. Maybe he wants to try us out guarding the ladies. Wouldn't that be something?" Bufesqueu said, patting his pants and nudging him. "I mean there's nothing wrong with the nig-nog slave broads, but those harem women must be wondrous. I tell you, George, in the country of the blind the one-eyed man is king."

Mills forbore to answer. He said nothing in response to Bufesqueu's rhapsodies as his friend went on about their possible new duties.

A eunuch stepped stolidly in front of them, barring their way.

"Bufesqueu and Mills to see the Kislar Agha as ordered," Bufesqueu told him and the man moved aside.

It was the first time either of them had seen the Chief Eunuch since Bufesqueu had asked for sanctuary. Even reclining, fat and sassy as some Sumo Santa Claus, his black bulk spilling over the pillows he pressed against on his heavily reinforced litter, he was as large as Mills remembered him. He sucked on a hookah and watched benignly as first Bufesqueu and then Mills offered their deferential salaams. Without bothering to remove his water pipe he absently returned their greeting, a huge hand briefly flickering from black to pink like flash cards turned in a stadium.

"If you're worried about the guards," he said, setting the hookah back on its stand and exhaling a thick steam of sweet smoke, "they're gone. The Overland has been burned. I took care of the guards."

"The guards, Kislar Agha?" Bufesqueu said.

"Chief Eunuch. We won't mince words. Call me Chief Eunuch. At the gate, the guards at the gate. I pulled the tongues out of their necks personally. I broke their bones in my torture chambers. I tore their equipment off with my hands."

Mills flinched.

"Why do you pale? They were bad guards. You'd never have gotten past good ones."

"Torture chambers, Chief Eunuch?" Bufesqueu said.

"This is the best-equipped seraglio in the world," he said. "We have fourteen mosques on the grounds. We have two hospitals and an arsenal with the latest weapons. We've kitchens and bakeries and the finest schools. We've sports fields and stables, conference rooms and hospitality suites. We're centrally located and close to a major body of water. Why shouldn't we have torture chambers too?" He sat up abruptly, effortlessly, showing none of the strain heavy people reveal when they move in furniture. He leaned forward conspiratorially. "The torture chambers bother you? Relax please. You think I'd send two incompetent guards to a torture chamber? Of course not. That's for the big fish." He held out his right hand. *"This,"* he said, and extended the left, "and *this.* These are my torture chambers."

Bufesqueu nodded and Mills stared. The Chief Eunuch laughed merrily. "No," he said, "you don't understand. You think I'm trying to intimidate you, to threaten obliquely like some fat Mex bandit with silver teeth. I didn't call you here to threaten you. I called you here to *comfort* you. That about the guards should have taken a load off. They'd have talked. Your whereabouts would have gotten back to the Sultan. Oh, Lawd, dis nigger be misunderstood sho 'nuff.

"Because I'll tell you why you're here and it's got nothing to do with sanctuary.

"I was fourteen years old when the slavers captured me. Fourteen! Do you know what that means? Do you?"

Mills shook his head.

"You don't? What were you like when *you* were fourteen? Did you have a girl? A crush on the teacher?"

Mills shook his head.

"No? Then I bet you wrung it out. What about it? Did you wring it out?"

Mills blushed.

"Sure you did. You *still* wring it out."

Mills shook his head fiercely.

"No? Why'd God give you hands? Why'd God give you hands you don't wring it out?"

"I wring it out," Mills said shyly.

"I *never* wrung it out," the Chief Eunuch said. "I was fourteen. In my tribe, among my people—the beasts in the jungles, the parasites in the turds, the great apes and lions, the slavers and mortality tables

—you were a man when you were eleven. I never wrung it out because I already had a wife. The real thing, you know? The genuine article. Absolute pussy.

"So I already had a wife when the slavers got me. Listen, am I breaking your heart? You think this is some love story I'm feeding you? That I pine for lost love, our burr-headed kid? Or maybe you think you're way ahead of me. That they took her too, that she's here now perhaps, the Sultan's favorite with her jackknife fucks. Why would I tell you? Why would I tell white boys? You Christers! What, you're going to deny your faith? Jesus, you Christers! It's all a little barbaric, ain't it? The idea of a harem. Or maybe you don't think it's barbaric, only wasteful. You Christers. To tell you the truth, if you want the opinion of one fatted, sufflated, darky gelding, it isn't. It isn't barbaric. If you're the Sultan himself it ain't even wasteful.

"I was fourteen years old. I'm talking about full-blown puberty. I'm talking about interest and appetite and lust and prurience, all the successive sexual steps like the diatonic scale. Because there ain't any blade long enough or keen enough either to cut *that* out of a man. They buried me up to my chest in the sand for three days to let my wounds heal. But desire don't flag. It swarms like the hair on the *kopf* of a corpse. And I *still* want to wave it around like an amputated hand, or lean my weight on it like a missing leg. So I walk around with this hard-on of the head. Alib Hakali," Alib Hakali said. "Alib Hakali, the spayed spade.

"All right. You can go now. Watch your step."

"What was that all about then?" Mills asked his reality master when they were alone.

"I'm not sure," Bufesqueu said. "I think he was trying to tell us that he understands."

"I don't know."

"Those guys at the gate," Bufesqueu said, shuddering.

"I know."

"I mean why'd he have to do that? He must want us around."

"Why?"

Bufesqueu shrugged. "You know," he said speculatively, "all the rest of those freemartins, they must be the same way he is."

"Horny? You think?"

"Why not? If those slavers picked them after they was already ripe. Why not? If he's telling the truth. If he ain't one in a million like some bloke in a textbook. That'd be awful."

"Hey," George said, "I bet that *was* what he was trying to tell us."

"There must be some way," Bufesqueu said. "There must be some way Nature has of getting to a eunuch."

"He was warning us," Mills said.

"Warning us, hell. He was teasing us."

This was the table of organization:

At the bottom of the chain were the female slaves, women like Fatima who served not only the harem women but their eunuch overseers as well. Above them were the novices, females new to the seraglio who may or may not have slept with the Sultan. Above these were the officially decreed favored ladies, and above the favored ladies were women who had already mothered one or more of the Sultan's children, called royal prince or princess but of no more real rank than the female slaves. At the top of the chain was the Valide Sultan, the Sultan's mother, a figurehead who maintained a residence in the seraglio, which she rarely visited except for those two or three times a year when she presided as hostess at teas. Officially she was also headmistress of the harem schools, but in actuality had even less to do with these—they were for the royal princes, and the curriculum dealt entirely with court protocol and was administered by women who had never been presented there: the female slaves, the novices— than she had with any of the other functions of the seraglio.

It was the Chief Eunuch's show. With his private army—the guards had been part of it—he ran the seraglio like a small country, supervising everything from deciding the menu to choosing which woman would be sent that night to the Sultan, and for all that they had a table of organization, for all that they were centrally located and had schools and riding stables—by tradition the Chief Eunuch was awarded three hundred or so horses for his personal use, one for each woman in the harem proper—there was little for any of them—the women, the eunuchs and slave girls—to do. Mills would learn this.

One day a woman came into the laundry where Mills was folding sheets. His arms raised, extended, he held a piece of sheet in his teeth, leveraging it with his upraised chin to fold down the middle. He was arched backward to keep the bottom of the sheet from touching the floor. He was watching the sheet's edges, trying to align them, when she spoke.

"My," she said, "it's grand you're so tall, that you've such long arms and strong jaws. It must be ever so sublime to have such balance."

"It's bloody marvelous," Mills said, still not looking at her. "If I wasn't so lovely endowed, the goddamn sheet could go all untidy from dragging along the ground and some bimbo might get bedsores from calf to ass. Bufesqueu's on break. He's in back watching the laundresses."

"What a manly voice," she said. "If I had such a voice I'd boom out work songs while I toiled. Would you know any sheet-folding work songs you could sing for me?"

Mills turned to look at her and thought she was smiling at him behind her veil. She was a large woman, older than the slaves he had seen, and it occurred to him that she might be one of the women from the harem. Not a novice certainly, since novices were usually in their teens and, to judge from her looks, what was visible to him above the veil that covered the lower half of her face, probably not one of the favored ladies. It was possible she was the mother of some royal prince or princess. "Was there something I could help you with, ma'am?" he asked, looking over her shoulder for the eunuch who would be sure to accompany her.

"And so gallant!" she exclaimed.

"There are some extra sheets and pillowcases in the back. If I asked someone I'm sure I could . . ."

"Blankets!" she said. "A dozen of those special thick woolly blankets."

"A dozen," George said. It was high summer.

"I'll wait," she said.

"I could only find one," he said when he returned. "The rest are in storage."

"Aren't you kind to take all that trouble," she said. "You know," she said, "I *could* use some sheets. Eight might just do it. And some pillowslips too. Sometimes it gets so warm of an evening I'll wake in my bed and it's soaked so with perspiration it's just impossible to fall back to sleep. If I had extra linens . . ."

"Oh sure," George said. "Sheets is no problem."

"Lovely," she said.

"Eight sheets," George said, taking them from a pile he'd already folded. "And eight pillowcases."

"Super," she said. "There *is* just one problem."

"There is?"

"This pile. It's so heavy. I don't think I could carry it back by myself." Mills had seen slave girls half the size of this woman lift baskets of wet wash that had to weigh over a hundred pounds. "Your eunuch?" he suggested.

"I'm a daughter of the harem," she said.

"A daughter . . ."

"One of the Sultan's daughters," she said shyly.

A royal princess, Mills thought, adding to his list.

"I have no status," she said. "Eunuchs don't even bother to guard us." She actually closed an eye and winked at him. Mills thought of Bufesqueu's country of the blind.

"Well," he said, "I have no status either. I can't leave my post."

"I meant with the others," she said. "I'm certain I have status over *you.*"

"Oh me," Mills said, picking up the blanket and pillowslips, picking up the sheets. "Me," he said, "sure."

She led him across soft lawns, she led him across paths of crushed pine cones. Eunuchs saw her and waved familiarly. They went by a schoolhouse where the royal princes were learning their lessons in court protocol. The windows were open and Mills could hear one of the younger children reciting. "One may walk in the palace with his head covered if my father, the Sultan, is away on state business." George glanced into the open windows over the stack of laundry he carried. Nine royal princes, he thought. "Evrevour?" the teacher said. Evrevour rose to stand beside his desk. "One has no right to chew his food after my father, the Sultan, has already swallowed," Evrevour was saying as they walked on.

It was odd. He had a sense of shortcut, a feeling not that he had been here before (though quite possibly he'd viewed the same buildings and grounds when he'd driven through the seraglio in the Overland; he and Bufesqueu had never felt comfortable enough in their surroundings to stroll through them freely and, except for the laundry and tiny apartment near it in the eunuchs' dormitory where they ate and slept, they had not yet established landmarks), but that he'd had this experience. Then he remembered. It must have been the way George Mills and Guillalume had felt when, leaving it to the horses, they had ambled, drifting toward Poland. Mills had no more reserves. It wasn't adventure anymore since adventure depended upon the adventurer's sense of goals, some spunky checklist of arrangements and priorities—— some "There, that's done" notion of progress. Mills had nothing left. When the woman reminded him that he had no status there, he had acknowledged the truth of the statement and come along. He knew she was up to something. He didn't much care. And the sense of shortcut he felt was as much a sense of falling downhill as it was of greasing distance. He had a fate and was rushing toward it. It was just that he was so indifferent to what it might be.

So indifferent that when the woman said, "In here will be fine. Watch yourself, there are steps. Oh good, wasn't it clever of you not to trip," he already knew where she had taken him—to the harem— and might almost have said what was about to happen. It made no difference anymore. When she said, "Oh, just leave those there. Llwanda will bring them up later," he put the blanket and sheets and pillowcases down on the table she indicated and straightened up to listen to what she would say next.

"That was hard work," she said, "you must be all overheated from carrying such a load. If you'll just step through those doors, Mally will fetch you cold water."

"Sure," Mills said.

Though his eyes weren't shut he felt like asking if he could open them when he entered the room. Except that he didn't really feel anything. Then he did.

They were in a sort of lounge. Though he'd never seen any—he'd been excluded, Bufesqueu had told him, by the traffickers themselves —the room corresponded to some notion of pornography lining his head like bone. Behind the room's appearance, governing its design and appurtenances, dictating its appointments and vaguely tiered arrangements, was the manifestation of some blue will, some peep-hole, parlor car resolution. If earlier he'd had a sense of shortcut, now he had a conviction of threshholds forever sealed behind him, of borders crossed and compromised. He was like an accidental traveler in dream and had just exactly that mixture of dread and joy the dreamer sometimes feels, fearful of discovery, but pleased he has been lured where he is.

The room was spacious, its size incremented by treillage and light, the openwork lattice of a wall through which he could see blue water lavished by swans and geese like a pond flower garden. There were gorgeous, opulent couches, their plush backs and arms curved as alphabet. There were frames of unfinished embroidery and fat pillows on the marble floor like a soft sausage of lion and leopard. Here and there folding screens were covered with starkly realistic paintings that made a sort of intimate, high-minded documentary— — lone figures of women soaping themselves, pinning their hair, stepping tentatively into water, holding fans and examining them-

413

selves in mirrors. Mills had the feeling sperm might be boiling in the lamps that glittered in the wall sconces.

What added to his sense that he had stepped into a brothel, and contributed to his idea of some carefully controlled sexual climate, was the presence in the lounge of so many women of different races. Orientals were there and Negresses, white women and women pink as pork. And a feel of laze, of timeless tea party.

He was the only man there, and, though he was certain he was expected, no one spoke to him or even looked at him directly. Indeed, they seemed deliberately to ignore him and even the woman who had brought him dropped the pretext of getting him water. Briefly it occurred to him that he was as much on display as the women, and though he had not been with so many females (if ever) in more than a year, and though there were no eunuchs about, he knew these were the Sultan's women and were as reluctant to stare at him as he was at them.

He knew Bufesqueu would chide him if he learned he'd entered the harem and never even looked at the girls, so despite his restraint he glanced at them nervously, quickly registering an impression of bulk, of clothing too tight, of arms dripping with weight.

"Well," he said, clearing his throat and making ready to leave, the word vaguely aimed at the Royal Princess.

"See?" a familiar voice said. "Did I lie? Did I exaggerate?" It was the slave woman, Fatima, and she stepped from behind a screen. "Now you must give Fatima what you promised, my mistresses."

"Oh no, not yet," one of the pork pink women said. "Eunuchs speak. Mine pipes like a magpie on all manner of subjects. Sometimes I have to kiss him on the lips just to get him to stop." The rest of the women giggled and Mills flushed thickly.

"In a voice deep as this one's?" Fatima challenged. "Why there's no comparison."

"He was singing work songs when I found him in the laundry," the Royal Princess said. "I heard his deep bass voice. Go on, Mills, show them." They were playing him, George knew. He was going to be seduced. Seduced and killed. When the eunuchs found his body he would already be dead. The Royal Princess would testify against him as blithely as she had lied about his singing. She would say that he had charged into the harem and attacked them. They'd never dare not to accept her version of the proceedings and, despite himself, a part of Mills was outraged on behalf of the deceived Sultan.

But then he thought how to save himself. The eunuchs! he

414

thought. They would have to be about. And began, even as they coaxed and teased him, to sing in a voice loud and deep as he could muster, crazed, desperately improvising:

"Fold the sheet, fold the sheet.
See how neat I fold the sheet!"

He looked about to see which of the eunuchs would respond to his cries. Perhaps he'd be familiar, one of the fellows from his dorm. The women stared at him.

"Fold the sheet, fold the sheet.
I want to eat, I fold the sheet!"

"What did I tell you," Fatima asked triumphantly, "would you find a voice like *that* on a eunuch?"

"Can't find nothin' on no eunuch," a hefty black woman said.

"What a lovely low voice," Fatima marveled.

"All right," a large Oriental woman said listlessly, "he's no countertenor, but all I'm hearing is volume."

"Sure," someone else said, "nobody ever put no one in trouble with just noise."

The women seemed skeptical, ready to leave, when Fatima thrust herself forward again. "Ladies, ladies," she said. "And aren't I as far from home as any of you? And don't I know from experience the difference between coiled rope and taut? Just because I'm a slave and not some fine lady-in-waiting like the rest, do you think I've lost memory, senses and all the kit and caboodle of my normal nature and ain't able to distinguish between capons and roosters? And haven't I been around these castratos long enough to know what I'm talking about? Ain't they just about all I got to look at on this damn desert island? Can't I recognize from one sight-see of their crotch when they sit, no more shape down there than a cloudless sky, that nobody's home, that their wounds, if they even *are* wounds anymore, are all sealed like empty envelopes, shiny and slippery as scars, hairless as gemstone, smooth as fat? And ain't I even been flashed by a few of these sports, their limp machinery dangling like busted thumb and no more flexed than buds in snow, just all broke, shriveled retrograde flesh like old folks' skin?

"Didn't I *tell* you? Didn't you *hear* him? When has a eunuch commanded such growl? Or are your ears accommodate only to the higher registers, the piggy squeals and sharp shrills of all noise's unballed din? But didn't you feel these very marble floors vibrate? And if your ears don't tell you, what about your eyes? Look, just look." She stepped beside Mills and touched the planes of his face, raised his shirt and pointed out his ribs. "See? See how sleek? Look at his sharpish elbows, feel his pointy knees. There are angles to this one, some hard geometry of maleness." She touched the front of his pants and, pinching an imaginary inch between her fingers, made as if to trace the length of his cock. Terrified, Mills was not unstirred as she drew her hand slowly up the inside of his thigh. "There's lust and longitude to him," she said, and, cupping his testicles, started to squeeze. "Bags and bones."

Mills winced and tried to pull away. The women, impressed, watching closely, gasped at his pain. They spoke aloud, shocked by his distress into their original tongues. (Because he knew two languages now. No, three. English, Janissary. and Harem.) Fatima released him and stood by his side, showing him off like an accomplishment, flourishing for him like a lesser acrobat. Suddenly she went into a sort of incantation, sounding nothing at all like the clownish woman who had spoken to him in the laundry. "Because there are some men like paradigms," she intoned, "their manhood burned into them like brands in cattle. Concupiscent, prurient, bawdy boys with heated hearts never cooled to room temperature." And was speaking to him now, her voice low, almost a whisper. "Flirts," she said, "philanderers, rakes and rips. Randy as pirates, ruttish as goats. Skittish as scarlet and wicked as wanton, filthy as folly and scabrous as smut. Lawless libidos, loose and licentious. Gross and coarse. Dissolute. Dirt. Salacious seducers, carnal as meat. Naughty as nasty and vulgar as vile." She reached out to touch him and shook her head, signaling him not to cry out or back away.

Fatima begins to stroke him. "Filth and defilement, lickerish lust. Whoremonger, wencher, womaner, wolf. Satyr and ravisher, fucker and lech. Steam and steam the stews of the heart. Who keeps the knock shop and flaws the flesh. You rapist. You ruiner. You wrecker, you lewd. They pulled off your balls, but they grew back like hair. Like nails they grew back, healed as young skin or second-growth teeth." His trousers swell where she strokes him and the superstitious concubines look on in awe, silenced. Abruptly Fatima withdraws her hand, and Mills whines helplessly.

"Well," she said, "there you are, my mistresses. What do you say to old Fatima now?"

They said nothing and continued to stare at George, not so much fearful as fascinated, almost, he thinks, devout.

"Because some men," Fatima explained, "have itch and need so powerful they can't be scratched, even by the Sultan or the Sultan's surgeons, the Sultan's men. Cutting don't do no good. You'd have to kill them to drop their erection. They spoke of this back home but until Mills came I didn't believe it, had never seen it. I still don't understand how it works, but maybe the erection is *inside,* starting at the bellybutton, say, or the high erogenous zones, the skin at his nipples, the roof of his mouth. You can't burn it out or cut it out, because all that happens when you try is that the need grows downward, falling toward earth, closing on the very dirt and filth you tried to keep it from when you trimmed the hedge by clipping it in the first place.

"Anyhow, that's how some account for it, though maybe it's just pride and will and determination, and Mills here ain't no more manly than those other eunuchs, only more set in his ways. I don't know," she said, "I don't know. But I don't have to, do I? I told you about him and even worked out with Lady Givnora how best to get him here and prove my claims, and I think it's just mean and shameful if you don't give me my treat like you promised."

All the odd power Mills had sensed in the woman seemed suddenly to have deserted her and she was only Fatima again, a woman too old to have to do any of this, too old to have to hold his balls in her hand.

The Royal Princess who had brought him put a heavy arm around Fatima's shoulder. "Now, Fatima," she said, "of course you'll get your treat." And she put a hand inside her robe and brought something out which Mills thought he recognized. She instructed the other women to do the same.

"Oh, *thank* you, my lady!" Fatima said and hurriedly pressed pieces of the *halvah* they had given her into her mouth. "Oh *thank* you," she said again, her lips flecked with flaking candy. "Mnn," she said, "it's delicious." The overweight women seemed indifferent to her enjoyment.

The seraglio was overstaffed. There was little to do. When he finished his work in the laundry, usually in the early afternoon, he was through for the day. He could return to the dormitory, talk to the eunuchs or, like Bufesqueu, chat up the slave girls.

417

By his own admission Bufesqueu wasn't getting anything off them. They seemed, he said, frightened to have sex with him.

"They're scared of the eunuchs," he explained. "Listen," he said, "could I borrow some of your bribegold?"

"Why not," George said, "what's there to spend it on?"

"I'll be damned," Bufesqueu said when he returned it a few days later. "I never saw anything like it. The sons of bitches are incorruptible."

"Which sons of bitches?"

"The eunuch sons of bitches. I tried to pay them off, maybe they could get lost for an hour or two, but they weren't having it. Listen," he said, "could I have some of that back again? I ain't ever paid for it yet, but there's just so much a man can take."

He's the one, George thought, not me. He's the one whose hard-on starts up around his ears.

"Here," Bufesqueu said, returning the bribegold a second time. "I added this to my own but the sons of bitches are abso*lute*ly incorruptible."

"The eunuchs," George said.

"No, man, the slave girls."

"Hey," Bufesqueu said another time, "can I hit you up once more? I think I found a live one."

"Sure," George said, "why not? You always pay your debts."

Bufesqueu had a broad smile on his face when he returned that night to the dormitory. "It was terrific," Bufesqueu said. "I won't say it didn't hurt to put out the dough, but after all this time it was worth it."

"Eunuch or slave girl?" George asked.

"Slave *lady,* man. Slave woman, slave *grandma.* It was that old broad, Fatima."

Mills hadn't told Bufesqueu about his experience in the harem. He didn't want to be needled. In *his* place, Bufesqueu would have said, if he'd had *his* opportunities . . .

"Fatima?" George said. "Wasn't she surprised to find out that, you know, you still have your balls?"

"The way *I* went at her? I think she was surprised I only have two."

"She didn't want to show you off?"

"Show me off? Maybe. If the whore could charge money."

"Hey," Bufesqueu said a day or two later, "I may have to borrow more of that bribegold."

Which he was willing to let him have though Bufesqueu could not have said what use Fatima could have made of money.

They lived, all of them, in a closed shop. Only the Chief Eunuch was free to come and go as he pleased. Even the guards at the gate, though Bufesqueu and Mills were so preoccupied at the time neither had noticed, were shackled and attached by long chains to the gates they guarded. A harem girl might leave the grounds of the seraglio but only to go to the Sultan's bedroom and she had to be escorted there by a eunuch through a passageway that led from the Valide Sultan's house to Yildiz Palace.

So not only was it a closed shop, it was also a sealed one.

Though they had the run of the grounds now and could go almost anywhere they wished. Mills liked to hang about the extensive stables. With the Chief Eunuch's permission he was sometimes allowed to exercise the horses and, on occasion, even to hitch them up to the elaborate, exotic vehicles he had only read about until now.

But with no one actually to drive for, soon even this diversion lost its appeal. As everything did. He no longer dreamed his cabby dreams, no longer often thought about England. If he regretted anything it was that he might not live to get a son to whom, like the Millses before him, he could tell the story he continued to live and even, in private now, to rehearse. Bufesqueu he had told it to long ago, telling him all, telling him everything, bringing his tale up to the time their lives had begun to coalesce and willing to go over even that part of their history, if only for practice, had only Bufesqueu been willing to listen, Mills reserving to himself only that part of the story which dealt with his trip to the harem. He realized now it was not the fear of a scolding that caused him to withhold this incident from his friend—the man had taught him much, saved his life, George owed him; of *course* he could have his bribegold—but that if it ever got out, and too many people already knew—Mills dreaded another summons to the interdicted harem—he would be castrated. Then, even if he lived, there could be no son. His tale would go untold. And what a tale, he thought. Kings and sultans had shaken him down, royal princesses, slaves and high officers had. He had nothing to be ashamed of. Except his bachelorhood. Except his sonlessness.

For his part Bufesqueu continued to go to Fatima, returning one night and tossing the remains of George's double portion of bribegold down on the cot.

"What's the matter?" Mills asked.

"I'm saving you money," Bufesqueu said. "If I ask for more bribegold don't give it to me."

"What's the matter, what's wrong?"

"I didn't mind that she was old," Bufesqueu said bitterly. "I didn't even mind that I was paying for it. But I'll be damned if I'll pay out any more of your hard-earned blood money bribegold to some old whore who's too fat to fuck back."

"Fatima?"

"You could hitch her to one of those carriages you get such a kick out of. Though I don't think she'd move."

"Fatima?"

"You said it, Fatima. *Fat*-ima."

"Fatima?"

"What's wrong with you, Mills? They run out of nuts to cut on around here? They started on eardrums now too?"

"Fatima's not fat."

"No? You seen her lately? You could rupture yourself holding her hand."

"Where do you get it?" George demanded. "The harem girls?"

"Get what? Take your hands off me. What do you think this is?"

"Where do you get it, Fatima? Who sells you the *halvah?*"

When he threatened to report her activities to the Kislar Agha, she confessed. Her supplier, she said, was Guzo Sanbanna.

"We could borrow equipment," Mills told his friend. "We could go down to that field and play soccer."

"No thanks, George, I don't think so. But you go if you want to." He was biting a fingernail, examining it.

"Suffi ben Packka's in hospital again. Maybe we ought to pay him a visit." Suffi was a eunuch whose wound had never healed properly.

"Jeez," Bufesqueu said, "the mood I'm in, the way I feel, I don't think I could cheer anyone up, even a eunuch."

Bufesqueu had become melancholic since he'd stopped seeing Fatima. He was nervous and listless at once.

"I could teach you to drive a team," Mills offered. "Hey, why don't I do that?"

"Thanks, George. I appreciate what you're trying to do but I don't think I could concentrate. Really, George, thanks."

420

"It's just that, you know, you shouldn't wallow."

"I'll be all right," Bufesqueu said. "I'm sorry I'm such bad company. I've got time on my hands." He forced a thin smile.

"Listen," Mills said, "I've still got the rest of my bribegold left. Maybe you should take it and, well, you know."

"No," Bufesqueu said. "Out of the question."

"No, not with Fatima. Somebody else."

"Who, man? Don't you think I tried? It's absolutely no go." He pulled a hair from his head and, using it like floss, tried to run it through his teeth. He set it down and looked at George. "You know," he said, "when she began to blow up like that, I thought maybe I'd knocked her up."

George nodded solemnly.

"But she's too old," Bufesqueu said.

Mills held his chin sagely.

"I even asked if she'd missed her period."

And raised an eyebrow.

"You know what she said?"

He shook his head.

"She hasn't had a period in five years."

"Well," Mills said, "that lets you off."

"It was the fucking," Bufesqueu said. "I fucked her to fat."

"We could drop in on a class," Mills said. "You know, not take it for credit. I don't think they'd object to auditors."

"I have this high-caloric jism. Fatima must have told them. That's why they tell me I can shove my bribegold."

"All right," Mills said and watched his old pal, the flashy Janissary who had taken Constantinople and was eating his heart out, destroying himself. And he told him about the harem.

Bufesqueu was in seventh heaven again, happier than Mills had ever seen him. He raved about the girls and invited George along whenever he went for a visit.

"I can't," Mills said. "It's too dangerous."

"Listen," Bufesqueu said, "nothing *happens*. They're running some Arabian Nights scam over there. But like I always say, 'In the country of the blind.' You've just got to be patient is all. They'll come round. But they're really charming. A little heavy, but what the hell, right? They ask for you all the time, you know. You must really have charmed them. They still talk about that hard-on you had."

"He told us to watch our step. It's too dangerous."

"Yeah, well, you know what I think? This harem thing is an old business. I mean it's really an ancient institution. Who'd think that in a civilized world such things could go on? I mean, really George, *eunuchs?* Concubines? Novices? Favorite ladies? I mean *slaves,* for God's sake! Or even sultans for that matter. I'll tell you the truth, George, I honestly think it's had its day. It was all very well when everyone rode around on a flying carpet, but in the nineteenth century? It's all but finished. They're all gone soft. All right, individually, individually they're incorruptible and won't give me a tumble, but as a group? As a group they're flawed as old Rome. How much more time can it possibly have? Fifty years? Sixty? These are the final days, George, and more especially the last nights, if you know what I mean. Just like the Janissaries. The last nights of the final days and I don't want to miss a minute of the outrageousness. I don't want to miss a second. Come on, Georgie, what do you say?"

"I've got a class," Mills said.

He'd been taking lessons in Court protocol with the Sultan's bastard children. For aristocrats they seemed surprisingly docile. At first, as he had on the day Lady Givnora had brought him to the harem, Mills stood at the window and listened, but when their teacher saw him she motioned him in and asked his business.

"I have this interest in protocol," Mills said.

The children giggled. Even their teacher smiled.

"Yes," George said, "I suppose that's funny."

"Well it *is,*" a young man said. "I mean I'm going to be twenty and I've been coming to the schoolhouse all my life. You know why? I keep getting these crushes on my teachers. But I've never even *been* to Court. I've never seen my father."

"I have," Mills said quietly, "I've seen your father."

"What, you? You work in the laundry."

"I was even presented at Court once," he said.

"You never were," the young man said.

"Perhaps he'd like to tell us about it, class," the slave girl said. "Would you? Would you like to tell us about it?"

"So you see," George said when he'd finished, "if I'd known more protocol I wouldn't be in the fix I'm in today."

They listened carefully to everything he said and, when he'd done, even asked questions. They wanted to know what the throne room looked like. They were curious about the furniture. They asked him to describe their half brother, Abdulmecid, and to suggest, if he could, what sort of voice their father had. Was it deep? Was it breathy? Could Mills list any mannerisms for them he might have noticed?

At the end of the two hours—even their teacher was taking it all in—he was asked to return.

"Well," George said, agreeably conscious that he was giving stipulations to the highborn, "only if I get to listen next time."

He soaked up the protocol lessons.

"Did you know," he asked Bufesqueu, "that only someone who has been to France may inquire after the Sultan's health?"

"Oh," Bufesqueu said, "why's that?"

"I don't know," George admitted, "it's tradition and it goes back thirteen hundred years."

"You know more than any of them, Mills," Bufesqueu told him once. "You're the one who ought to teach that course."

George shrugged deprecatingly.

"No, you should."

"It's not my place," he said shyly.

Though it was probably true. The school he'd attended that first day was not the only one in the seraglio. He went to all of them. Some teachers were better than others but each had something to teach him. He absorbed it all.

He learned other things too. About the Sultan's strange, sluggish, unacknowledged children. Evrevour, the little boy he'd heard that first day he'd passed the schoolhouse, had become a sort of friend.

"I have seventy-four half brothers," Evrevour told him. "I have eighty-one half sisters. You think it'd be fun, so many children."

"It isn't?"

"We have to be very careful about the incest," Evrevour said.

"They're burned out on birthday cake," Mills told Bufesqueu.

"You ought to hang out with me in the harem, George," Bufesqueu said.

"Too dangerous."

"That's the thing. It really isn't."

"He told us himself."

"The Kislar Agha? He's a pussycat. You should get to know him. Sometimes he comes to the salons."

"The Kislar Agha does? Salons?"

"Salons, teas, open house. I don't know what you'd call them exactly, but sure, he's there. Lots of the eunuchs are. And I'll tell you something else, George. They're not bad fellows. They've got some great stories to tell. There's marvelous talk."

Mills thought his friend was under a spell, a kind of enchantment. He thought they all were. When he saw them in the harem—he agreed to go when a eunuch brought Ali Hakali's invitation to him personally in the laundry—they, the men as well as the women, seemed immensely sociable, hugely cheerful, terribly gay. He did not see the Kislar Agha.

"Oh, there you are, Mills," Bufesqueu said, rising up off his cushion like a host when he spotted George. "Perhaps you can settle a little argument for us."

"It isn't an *arg*ument, Tedor. We weren't *arg*uing," a eunuch Mills didn't recognize said.

"It's about the female slaves," Bufesqueu said. "Qum el Asel contends they're actually improved by servitude while I hold that whatever civilizing effects their condition provides, is motivated by the universal hope of getting on, being noticed by their mistresses, et cetera. It's merely public relations, a sort of show business, a means to an end rather than the end itself."

"Oh please, Tedor," Qum el Asel said. "Ends? Means? Mean you to end so meanly, man?" He looked at the harem women and George followed his glance. They batted their eyelashes, silently fluttering their gauzy veils with their tiny poutlike breaths. "I *mean,*" and he looked at them again before he continued, "toward what end should any discussion strive? Fact, *I* should say.

"All right, what *are* the facts? You take a girl out of the jungle —I know, I know, many of these girls are as white as you are, Tedor —out of her *village* then, whatever tiny patch of cultivated wide spot in the road—all right, I *know;* some of these ladies are from no farther off than downtown Constantinople—she's accustomed to distinguish by the name of 'home,' but anyway you *take* her, and, to this point, probably all she's learned of the observable world is how to prepare a *couscous* or, if she *is* from that jungle, the local mean sanitation practices for—please forgive me—wiping her behind.

"But what happens? You steal the girl or perhaps buy her from her parents or a surviving brother (and I've known of cases, girls right here at Yildiz incidentally, where the seller has actually been a bona fide husband), and introduce her into a totally alien milieu, *say* the Yildiz seraglio, though it could be anywhere really, the British Empire, suburban San Francisco, the Argentinian pampas, and all of a sudden, if she's assigned to the kitchen say, she's learning new recipes, preparing alien dishes in alien pots and pans and eating the alien leftovers with an alien cutlery. She's *learned,* you see, her experience broadened perforce by force itself.

"Multiply this. Compound it by all the techniques indigenous to whatever culture she's been entrusted to and you have a girl—enslaved she may be—who is indisputably more cultured and knowledgeable than her unsold sister in the sticks. You have more. You have a girl who's probably more knowledgeable than the woman in whose charge she finds herself if only because she knows—please, you *must* forgive me, Tedor, but it was you who introduced this business of ends—*two* ways of wiping her behind while the mistress knows only one."

Several of the women applauded, their left hands making a delicate brushing motion against their right. Others blew against the veils which covered their mouths, briefly exposing bits of naked jaw, chin, flashes of mouth, the mysterious flesh paler than the skin which covered their cheeks and the thin strand of brow just visible beneath their *chadors*.

"Qum gets that round, Tedor," a woman said. Bufesqueu nodded in pleasant agreement. "Have you anything to add, Mr. Mills?"

George shook his head.

"I can lift five of you at once," a big eunuch said.

"Five of us? At once? Oh, I don't think so. Your arms aren't long enough to fit around *five,"* said the Oriental woman whom Mills had seen there the last time.

"Yes," he said, "five." A dozen women volunteered and the eunuch who would be doing the lifting began to choose among them.

"Sodiri Sardo's picking only the lightest," a fat Negress whose name was Amhara objected.

"Oh no," the eunuch said and chose Amhara too. He led her to a chair and directed the others to sit on her lap, arranging them in the order of their size.

"See? He doesn't have to get his arms around all five of us," said the woman on top.

"I didn't know there was a trick to it," the Oriental said.

"It isn't a trick, it's strength," the eunuch said. "Is everyone ready? Don't squirm now."

The women, clumsily balanced, were stacked in a heap of diminishing laps. They couldn't stop giggling. The other eunuchs moved around them, professionally estimating Sodiri Sardo's task as they might a golf ball along a difficult lie.

The big eunuch squatted, one arm under the black woman's thighs, the other behind her back. "All right," he said, "I'm going to pick everyone up now. Stay still as possible."

He lifted them easily and crossed the room with them. He set them down carefully.

There were more brush strokes of applause, more veil blowing.

"Sodiri's strong," a eunuch admitted, "but let him try that stunt with *me* underneath and the girls in *my* lap."

"Are you saying I can't?" Sodiri challenged. "Go on then, sit in the chair."

They started to arrange themselves again, the eunuch on the bottom this time. "Amhara got to hold all of us last time," a woman said. "She's not that much heavier than I am. You rest, Amhara. The girls can sit on *my* lap."

"Horsey shit," Amhara said.

"Amhara sat on top of the woman who had displaced her and the others piled on top of her.

"You ready now?" Sodiri asked. "They ready, En Nahud?"

"Not quite," the eunuch said. "They've got the giggles. Let them calm down first."

"Go on," Amhara said, "see can you pick us up."

He picked them up.

"See can you carry us cross the room and back," Amhara said in the air.

He carried them across the room and back.

"See can you climb the stairs," En Nahud said.

Sodiri, climbed a few stairs at the rear of the lounge. He set everyone down. The women who had been carried professed astonishment. They shook their heads vehemently, their veils flaring like the ballooning skirts of dancers.

"Did you think he could do it?" they asked each other.

"No," they answered, shaking their heads wildly, raising the edges of their veils, "did you?"

"No! Did you ever see someone so strong?"

"No! Never! Not!" they answered, doing that thing with their heads again. "How about you?"

"Negative! No! Not me! Not one time! Eunuchs are the strongest!"

Which gave Bufesqueu his opening.

He discoursed on the proposition of whether it was possible for eunuchs to rupture.

Bufesqueu was brilliant, locating his argument scientifically but saving his great point till the end of his speech when he announced in a low, husky voice that if eunuchs *couldn't* rupture it had to be because they were without testicles. He drew the word out and mentioned it repeatedly. He need hardly point out, he said, that women, too, were without *tesss*ticles but had love holes where *tesss*ticles would go if they were men, and everyone knew that women with love holes —he called them love holes—could rupture. He said "love holes" repeatedly also.

There was additional applause, tunes genteelly whistled into veils, astonishment registered by a forceful constriction of the brows, a general female giggling and swooning, heads vigorously thrown back till veils were hiked midnose.

They loved, they said, metaphysical discourse.

Someone raised the metaphysical question of whether or not eunuchs could expose themselves. Debate raged angrily on both sides of the question. Mills thought the eunuchs might come to blows.

Yoyu, the Oriental woman, interceded shyly.

Theory, she said, was all well and good when one had recourse only to theory, but might she point out that here they were with an entire roomful of eunuchs. It was rather like arguing, whether rain were falling outside when all one had to do was look out the window, she said.

The eunuchs ceased their quarrel and looked from one to the other.

"Yoyu is right," En Nahud said. "The only thing left to decide is which of . . ."

"Let Mills!" said Bani Suwayf, the young woman who had exchanged places with Amhara.

He could almost do it, Mills thought. He was so terrified by the strange goings on in the lounge that his testicles were completely retracted, his penis no more surfaced than the scab on the peel of an orange.

But Sodiri Sardo had already dropped his trousers.

"Aaaiieee," said the girls, and Sodiri adjusted his pants.

"He is built like a soccer ball," Yoyu said, modestly averting her eyes.

The women laughed.

"He's seamed like one too."

"*He* sure wasn't flashing."

"More like mooning."

Mills could see the big eunuch was getting angry. Even muscles seemed to flush.

The women laughed so hard their veils were askew again, dangling from one ear, or hanging beneath their chins like bibs.

"Hsst," Mills said, poking Sodiri Sardo's hard belly with his elbow. The strongman turned to him fiercely. "No no, *look,*" he whispered. The eunuch glared impatiently in the direction Mills pointed. "Nostrils," George whispered. "And look there. Those are *lips,* man! Male *lips!* Huh? Huh?" The big fellow nodded. "Huh?" George said. "Huh?" Sodiri squinted. "How about those *teeth?* Would you look at the gums on that one? Is she built? Huh? Huh?"

"Were you staring at our mouths?" one of the women asked. They had arranged their masks again. "I asked if you were staring at our mouths," she repeated coolly.

"Nothing human is alien to me," Mills mumbled lamely.

It was time to go, George knew, but Bufesqueu was in no hurry. And neither, evidently, were the eunuchs. Nor, for that matter, the ladies themselves.

So the salon continued its philosophic investigations, what Bufesqueu had called their "marvelous talk." The men and the women. The men and the women and the eunuchs.

They discussed whether what a sultan felt toward his favored ladies might not actually be a form of love.

They discussed whether what the concubines felt toward their round-the-clock, day-cared-for children was.

Bufesqueu laid down a premise: that a woman in a harem necessarily entered a sultan's bed, particularly a sultan who was also the head of a vast empire, with a certain amount of fear. In such circumstances, he speculated, was it possible to achieve orgasm?

"Define your terms," Bani Suwayf said.

Was fate a question of bone structure, an individual geometry that made one woman a concubine and the other a slave?

Were all human skills acrobatic, Sodiri Sardo's strength acrobatic and the girls' jackknife fucks too?

"Horsey shit," Amhara said.

"We've got to get out of here," Mills told Bufesqueu. They were back in their dorm.

"You worry too much, George. It's very simpatico."

"We've got to get out of here."

"No way, pal. That private army the Kislar's always talking about? They're deployed *out*side the walls. They're over them like graffiti."

"We've got to get out of here."

"Look here, Mills. Look here, George. Don't you think I know what you're up to? Your problem's written all over your face. You want a kid so bad, knock up one of the harem girls. Take her aside and rape the cunt. They catch you, they take your balls off. Big deal, it makes you strong."

"A son. It's got to be a son."

"Yeah," Bufesqueu said, "I see what you mean. You get one shot. If it's a girl or it don't take, then—— pffftt."

"We've got to get out of here."

"Maybe you could adopt."

"We've got to get out of here, Bufesqueu."

"Yeah, well, I know it. Don't you think it's all I think about morning, noon and night? In the laundry or out? Don't you think it's all I think about?"

He didn't, no. Because he understood now what the Chief Eunuch had warned them of on the occasion of their interview.

Complacency, lassitude, getting used to things. The piecemeal slide of the heart. All submissive will's evolutionary easement. Seventh heaven was seven heavens too high. They were having, Mills knew, the time of their lives. (Even the smells, he thought. Balmed, luxurious as jungle, sweet and fruity as tropic, as florid, shrubby produce. He'd had a cold a week—— fever, runny eyes, headache, stuffy nose. The pampered, lovely smells had still insinuated themselves onto his very breath, caught on his tongue, snagged on his teeth, so that what he tasted, its flavors overriding the very food he chewed or liquids he drank, was like some perfumed, sexual manna, the gynecological liqueurs. A sort of climate raged in him, headwinds, the fragrance in his head, mingling sweetly with the ache in his bones, swooning his soupy sleep like delicious ether. And he'd experienced, as he experienced now, as he'd experienced that first time in the harem —why did he have the impression that he had come not among women but into some vast and sensual female wardrobe?—a useless and cozy semitumescence, idle and abstracted.) And they could live there comfortably, whatever the mysterious authority for their dispensation, in their strange sanctuary forever, for as long as their lives, immune as diplomats, tenured in tease and tea party, servicing some ideal of fairy tale pornography, as, when they'd been Janissaries, they serviced some ideal of epic viciousness.

Complacency. Acceptance. Bufesqueu was used up. Had probably been used up on those Janissary prayer rugs. "Incense" he'd said to a Mills too dumb to scoff.

Mills had his first conviction and suddenly seemed dangerous, even to himself.

He sought out Fatima.

"All right," he said, "his name is Sanbanna. I want to see him. I want to find out what's going on."

And Fatima mollifying him, all over him with her slave's flattery as earlier she'd been all over him with her hands. "He's only a tradesman, Master. A niggling peddler. Foolish women dicker in the millets with him over *kurus*. A street Arab. Common as straw. It isn't drama, Lord. It's barely negotiation. He's a cheat, Honesty. A rascal, Righteousness. Let Fatima do for you."

"I want to see him, Fatima."

And changed her tack. "What, you think only the males in this place get operations? The women too. The royal princesses have their wombs cut out. They lose breasts. Or their faces are so disfigured beneath their veils that not even a eunuch will look at them."

"The royal princesses?"

"And offending slaves, offending slaves do. There are harem women, some of them once highly regarded concubines, some of them once favored ladies, who insulted the Sultan, who didn't writhe enough to suit His Majesty, or who entered his bed by the side rather than raise the coverlet at the foot and hold it to their faces to crawl the bed's length like some veiled reptile, who've been carved into fright masks and sent out into the world again. Think, Boss, if they cut off a hungry man's hands for picking up lost coins in the gutter, what would they do to a woman's lips for speaking out of turn or returning unlawful kisses?"

"What did they do to you, Fatima, when you lay with Bufesqueu?"

"I disfigured myself," the now grotesque fat woman said. "Shameless, shameless," she said. "Oh," she said, "I'm such a greedy greedy girl. I'm so *hungry*. Oh, I have such a sweet tooth. Bribegold. Will you give me bribegold?"

He gave her the last of his bribegold. In a week or so, she said, when Guzo Sanbanna might next be expected, though he made no regular rounds, she said, she would introduce him, she promised.

Three weeks went by and still no Sanbanna.

"You've put on a few pounds," Mills said. "Where is he, Fatima?"

"I hoard," she said. "He's old, he could die, so I hoard."

She came into the laundry. Bufesqueu spotted her and went into the back.

"The Kislar Agha wants to see you," she said.

"Hey, Bufesqueu," Mills called.

"Not Bufesqueu. He didn't ask to see Bufesqueu."

Four months earlier a summons from the Kislar would have terrified him, but Bufesqueu was right, the man wasn't a bad fellow. At the salons—he was no regular, and neither was Mills, but he came to their affairs perhaps once every three weeks, always on the afternoon preceding an evening when a virgin was scheduled to attend the Sultan—the Chief Eunuch was often the most amusing man there, outdoing Bufesqueu and Qum el Asel himself on the thorny philosophical points they so loved to raise. Nor was the sexual horseplay, though not proscribed, so much in evidence when the Kislar was there. Although the sexuality of these afternoons was even more forthright than any Mills had witnessed when the great eunuch was absent.

Ostensibly the love lessons—everything they did could be perceived as instruction; Mills was fascinated (when he wasn't terrified), as he was by all protocols—were for the benefit of the young virgins among them. It fell to the women to tell these girls which things seemed most to please the Sultan, which parts of his body she was forbidden to kiss or to touch, which she was encouraged to, what obeisance she was required to make after he climaxed, what she must do to protect the Sultan's skin from the blood or, if there were danger of spilled semen contacting his body, which remedial actions were permissible, which taboo. It seemed there were dozens of things for a virgin to remember, not the least of which was the virgin's "tribute." This was some new technique or position she was required to bring to his bed should the Sultan require it, some clever trick he'd never seen or heard of before. (Comprehensive lists, updated each time a new virgin paid a visit to the Sultan, were posted in all the dormitories in the harem, and it was an offense punishable by death if a virgin attempted to contribute something which another virgin had already offered. It did a girl no good to rely on the man's faulty memory, since duplicates of all lists kept by the women were kept by the potentate.

"He old, honey," Amhara might say. "He an *old* man. Likely he won't do more than ask can you tell him your moves."

"I'm not here," the Chief Eunuch would explain, "to embarrass anyone. I'm here to choose one of you and I'm here to protect you.

431

I don't believe that women by nature are either more or less duplicitous than men. We're only human, alas, and if I'm privy to these discussions it's not, in this instance at least, prurience which draws me. Rather it's my conviction, one or two steps up from belief, that the nature of any organization is built on the principle of self-interest. In a harem the natural enemy of a woman is another woman. The mothers are jealous of the favored ladies, the favored ladies are jealous of the novices, and *everyone* is jealous of the virgins. Only in sexual organizations like our own, you see, does the jealousy leak downward.

"I'm fairly certain you've already been briefed but suspicious enough to believe that it's only because I was expected. If I didn't show up on these occasions it wouldn't be outside the realm of possibility that these ladies could fail to tutor you in what's expected. You could fault tonight, you could die. In any event I trust a review can do no harm, and I enjoy our chalk talks. —Yoyu?"

"Sir?"

"Would you be kind enough to recite for Shariz the Prayer of Virgin Gratitude?"

So he followed Fatima.

In his office the Kislar Agha was speaking to a short man in a striped gown just long enough to trip over should he step rather than shuffle. He wore a small fez—it could have been cut for a child—from which the tassel had come loose. "Oh, Mills," the eunuch interrupted himself, "come here a moment, would you?" And then to the man: "Show Mills, won't you? Fatima's right, he's the one with whom you should be taking up this point. Thanks, Fatima, it was a good idea, your bringing Laundry into the discussion."

"Laundry," the man said, "you've seen one of these?" He produced a strange, toylike object from inside his caftan. "Now this is only what we call a 'mock-up.' It's scale, however, and should give you a pretty good idea. In real life this particular item goes forty-five by sixty. You've seen this?"

Mills shook his head.

"No? See, Kislar Agha? Even Laundry ain't seen nothing like it. It's brand new but I'm not offering you no novelty item. I don't take nothing away from novelty goods, but in Yildiz? They don't look right in a palace, novelty goods. They're a masses thing—— kickshaw, straws and pins."

"Get on with it, Guzo."

Guzo? This? This was Guzo Sanbanna?

"I'm piquing his interest, Kislar. In my line you don't get no-where you don't pique their interest. All right, Laundry, you want to take a guess what this mock-up is a mock-up of?" He handed Mills the model, which, now it was in his hands, he saw was actually two components, one on top of the other, the first a sort of cloth-covered frame, the second a thick rectangular pad which fit on it. "Can you guess? Remember, it's only a model."

Mills shook his head.

"I'll give you a hint, Laundry. What's the dimensions of your sheets?"

George shrugged.

"It's a box spring and mattress!" Sanbanna said as if delivering a punchline.

"A box spring and mattress," Mills repeated dully.

"You've never heard of mattresses?"

"Sure," George said. "I've heard of mattresses."

"Well the box spring fits *under* them! On a *bed* frame! It gives *back* support! You know, before the Industrial Revolution none of this would have been possible. Look—here, give me, I'll show you, this cloth part snaps off—rows of coil springs! Just imagine what one of these could do for the backs of all those favored ladies you got around here. Or the novices. Or anyone else for that matter whose back takes a beating from time to time. Why, sleeping on one of these is like sleeping on a cloud! For the rest of your life you wake up refreshed!

"And I'll tell you something else. With these new firm support mattresses there's never any sag. You're healthier, more cheerful. They put a spring in your step. They help keep you regular."

Sanbanna lowered his voice. "The whores of Amsterdam, where this product was researched and developed under the supervision of the world's most distinguished orthopedic scientists, the biggest men in the field, the whores of Amsterdam have been using these box spring and mattress sets on an experimental basis for months now. The incidence of pox has never been lower and some of the girls claim literally to have doubled their business. I can't vouch for that part of course, but I saw the biggest smiles on those Dutchmen's faces when I was up there last time. Ear-to-ear. I thought their damn faces were cracking. Here, you can look at my passport you don't believe I was up there." He shoved an Empire passport under Mills's nose and snatched it back quickly. His lowered voice was laced with confiden-

433

tiality. "Listen, *I* know the Sultan is no ordinary john. What, are you kidding? A *carte blanche* guy with the pick of the litter? I'll let you in on something, Laundry. This is strictly a company store in a strictly company town and what makes its owner happy can't help but trickle down and make some of its clerks happy too. Am I talking out of turn here, Kislar? Am I out of line on this?"

Mills looked at the Chief Eunuch.

"Guzo's enthusiastic," the Kislar Agha said, "but we've been doing business with him for years now."

"Did I steer you wrong on the baby doll nighties? Did I steer you wrong on the filmy lingerie? Tell him, Kislar."

"He's not the purchasing agent, Guzo. He folds sheets in the laundry."

"Yeah," he said, "and don't know their size. I can't help it," Sanbanna said, "I *believe* in my products. I'm this progress ambassador."

A king, Mills thought, a sultan. Princes and princesses. A progress ambassador.

"He folds *sheets,* Guzo."

"Well the *question* is sheets. Sheets are what's under discussion. Look, I'll lay my cards on the table. What are we talking about? Two or three hundred box springs and mattresses? My foot we are! We're talking revolution! A *sleep* revolution! *Sure,* I want to sell you the box springs and mattresses. And of *course* it would be a feather in my cap to bring two hundred sets on line in Yildiz Palace Seraglio. But the *real* feather in the cap would be to get my box spring and mattress under the Sultan's ass!

"*Think!* Who does the fucking? Those two hundred or so girls? The *Sultan* does the fucking. Those favored ladies are lucky if they see him three or four times a year. The mothers of those kids got stretch marks on them like lines on rulers. Maybe *they* have relations twice a year. As for the novices . . . Well, I don't have to tell you. So it's the Sultan. This is the man with the smile on his face! *That's* the direction of my thinking. The box spring and mattress under *his* back! If I could tell the world its greatest lover only trusts his body to one of these babies—— well, I *don't* have to tell you! *That's* where the plumage in the millinery is!"

"Guzo," the Chief Eunuch said, "our seraglio is not a test kitchen."

"So I asked myself, I asked myself, 'Sanbanna, you got a problem. How does a person like yourself, less than a commoner, get next

434

to the sultan of the Ottoman Empire? How do you advise such a person?' 'Good will. Word of mouth, Guzo,' I told myself. 'That's the way to handle it. Let the broads do the job.' " He was staring directly into Mills's eyes.

"He folds sheets, Guzo," the Kislar said.

"Forgive me, Kislar, haven't we been talking about sheets? Didn't I ask him sheet dimensions? Ain't that what our whole deal hinges on? Ain't that why we called Laundry in for consultations?"

"But, Guzo, he doesn't *know.*"

"Maybe because it never came up. Maybe because Laundry's too conscientious for idle speculations. Maybe because he was never bored enough to say to some co-worker, 'Hey, pal, for the hell of it, why don't we get a tape and *measure* the goddamn things?' "

"They won't fit," George Mills said. "They're only forty by sixty."

"You shouldn't listen to crap, George," Sanbanna said.

"They won't fit your whatchamacallits. They're five inches too narrow in the width."

"Why did you want to see me?"

George looked at him closely. "It's not important," he said.

"Sure it's important," Sanbanna said.

"No," Mills said. Suddenly he was very tired. "I thought maybe I ought to talk to the man who's making these women so fat."

"Sure," Sanbanna said.

George studied him a moment. He went on, keeping his voice flat, draining all curiosity from it. "They, you know, nibble."

"They gorge."

"Probably when, you know, the eunuchs aren't around."

"They cram it down."

"Not that, you know, I've ever actually seen them."

"They pack it away," Sanbanna said. "They wolf the stuff."

"Even Fatima. Even Fatima's, you know, put on a few pounds since I've been here."

"She's a guzzle gut. She's a gourmand glut gobble."

"She lives high," Mills said.

"Not because it's contraband," Sanbanna said, "not even because it's cheap or plentiful."

"It's strange," Mills said, almost to himself. "He's a sultan. Any race you can think of."

"Yes," Sanbanna said.

"Every body type. Women with bones under their faces like fine welts, women with bone structures like log cabins."

"Yes."

"And their *hair,*" Mills said. "My God, their hair soft as down or rough as the stuffing in bad furniture."

"That's right."

"He's the fucking *Sultan.* He wants girls, he invades countries with armies, for Christ's sake. He sends generals out with glass slippers. He has an entire empire to choose from. There's pageants and beauty contests. Miss African Village, Miss Sand Dunes. Miss Off-Shore Islands."

"Yes," Sanbanna said.

"They're all *fat!*"

"Not even to get out of it," Sanbanna said, "not even to make themselves unattractive or too heavy to handle."

"No," Mills said.

"Not even because they're bored," Sanbanna said. "But because *halvah* and the delicatessen I'm able to bring in are the only things still available to them that tickle their palates. Who knows? Maybe the palate is the only organ they have that's still alive. Maybe that's what burns out last. Everything mortified but the nerves of the mouth, the sweet and sour synapses."

Suddenly Mills shuddered with questions. "Cheap?" he said. "Plentiful?"

Sanbanna looked at him. "Fatima shook you down?"

"I gave her my bribegold," he said and could have bitten his tongue in half. The man didn't seem to have heard. "Listen," Mills said, "I've seen them giggling, I've watched them carry on."

"Eunuchs," Sanbanna said contemptuously.

"Not the eunuchs, the women."

"I'm talking about the women," Sanbanna said.

"The women?"

"Didn't I already tell you it's a company town?"

"All right," Mills said, "good will, word of mouth. You get on their bright side. They talk up the merchandise to the Kislar Agha. They say swell things about the dry goods. Then what?"

"Come on, Mills," Sanbanna snapped, "you said it yourself. Forty by sixty. They don't even fit. What do you suppose just a contract for new sheets would be worth in this place? Wouldn't I be jumping up and down if I was who you think I am? Or are you some eunuch too? Big time Paradise Dispatcher!"

436

"Hey," Mills said.

"Hey yourself. Why not? Why wouldn't you be? Everyone else around here is. The prickless princes and parched princesses. The favorites and novices and slaves. Who *ain't* a eunuch? Your pal Bufesqueu? Come on, he's spoony as the rest of them. They're a loony, loopy, lovelorn lot, Mills. All the screw-loose steers, all the hindered heifers. What a picture!"

"Eunuchs in love," Mills said.

"Who said anything about love? Love*sick*ness! Sentiment. Rapture and craziness. Doting. Dottiness. Fan mail and fantasy. Coquetry, swoon, languish and yearning. Ogle. Intrigue and eye contact. The heart's round robin. Who mentioned love? There ain't enough love in this place to wet a dream."

And Mills thinking maybe it was a part of adventure when perfect strangers told you things, when they took trouble with you. Or perhaps straight talk was only a kind of condescension. Sanbanna would never have spoken this way to the Kislar.

"Well?" said the *halvah* trader.

"Gee, Guzo," Mills said, "you know the part I don't get?"

"You? You don't get any of it."

"Who made you candy man?"

"George Fourth," Sanbanna said.

Mills stared at him. Moses Magaziner returned his gaze. "Oh no," Mills said, "no no. This isn't the way a world works. No no. You can't get *me* with that stuff. What, there's magic in the moonlight? No no. Look," Mills said earnestly, almost severely, "sometimes things happen and you'd have to give long odds. Sure, and throw in a point spread just to get someone into position where he can't afford not to take your bet. Freaky things. Not just coincidence but coincidence called. *In*expectation! Jolts and starts and thunderclaps, percentage and probability not just caught unaware or caught napping but caught napping unaware with its pants down. I mean out-of-the-blue-you-could-have-knocked-me-down-with-a-feather stuff, things so improbable as to be imponderable. Junk, you know? A fire at the ball game or an earthquake in the park. So farfetched and implausible it would be like spitting in God's eye. One chance in a million would be a dead cert, foolproof, sure thing, safe bet, lead pipe cinch next to what I'm talking about. Or *not* talking about. Because what I *am* talking about you *can't* talk about. Because if you could," and he was weeping now, "because if you could, you could talk about everything, think about anything. Lovely things would happen, spec-

437

tacular things. Friends like women who love you. Like lawyers who can save you or doctors that can heal. Everything would work out. The world would come true. I don't mean God or saying your prayers. I don't even mean hope. Hell, you could make a wish over a lousy birthday candle and it wouldn't even have to be *your* birthday and the candle wouldn't even have to be stuck in a cake. Shit, it wouldn't even have to be *lit!*"

"All right," Moses Magaziner said, "you wanted to see me, see me."

"All right? Yes? All right? Didn't you hear anything I said?"

"All right," Magaziner said.

"Why?" he asked. "Why *you?*"

"You're the believer," the Jewish British ambassador dressed like a street Arab said. "You're the hopeful one. What do you believe? What do you hope?"

"That you're a spy, that you work for our king. I don't know, that your eye is on the sparrow."

"All right," he said, "I'm a spy, I work for my king. Sure, sometime. Sometime my eye is on the sparrow."

"I get it," Mills said. "Good will. Word of mouth. The harem's best-kept secrets traded for candy."

"*Schmuck,*" Magaziner said, "have you never measured any despair but your own? Why *not* candy?"

"Why not? Because they don't *have* secrets."

"They sleep with the Sultan. What's the matter with you? You never heard of pillow talk? Look, I'm busy. I'm a man of affairs. It's already midafternoon. I've got a courier waiting and I still haven't looked at the diplomatic pouch. Tonight Yetta Zemlick and I are entertaining the Spanish embassy, and if I don't get back soon to approve the arrangements Gelfer Moonshine is going to have conniptions. So don't hock *me* about likelihoods and probabilities. What do you want?"

"What do you *think* I want, Moses?" Mills cried. "I want to get out of here! I want you to part those eunuchs like the Red Sea!"

"Nah," he said, "too risky. I'm a foreign national. We ain't allowed to interfere in the domestic affairs of other empires. Here, have some *halvah*. No, go ahead, there's plenty more where that came from."

Mills stared after him as the old man walked off. At the door to the laundry Magaziner turned. "Listen," he said, "it's a long shot, longer than you think, not the sure thing, shoe in, when-you-wish-upon-a-star crap you were talking about. His Majesty don't want you. He wouldn't authorize air from petty cash to get you back. He still thinks you're some Pretender or other. Maybe he's right. He don't need subjects like you. So it's a long shot. So long it ain't even mathematics. But if you ever do manage to escape, drop by the embassy, why don't you? Maybe I can get you on a ship."

"I figured it out," he told Bufesqueu an hour later. "We can make our break. Be ready after dinner."

"What, tonight? I was going to see Yoyu tonight. Everybody's going to be there. They say even the Valide Sultan may put in an appearance. They're expecting me. Why don't you come too, George? The women are going to play cards. The girl with the lowest score has to take her veil off for ten minutes."

"I think we can make it. Watch me. Do what I do."

"Gee, George, it sounds like a nifty plan. It really does. I wish you'd spoken up sooner. The eunuchs have been telling me about this game. It's supposed to be really something to see."

"We can get out of here," Mills said. "The odds are a little tight, but I think we can make it. We just have to be careful not to panic."

"Hey," Bufesqueu said, "you didn't say anything about odds."

"Forget the odds, Tedor. What were the odds when you took Constantinople? Why do I say Constantinople? You took the whole entire Ottoman Empire that day. What were the odds against that?"

"You know that novice, Debba Bayuda? You know——— the tall one. The one they say is this far away from becoming a favorite lady. Well the morning line on old Debba is that she's almost as gorgeous as she is rotten at cards."

"How long do you think they'll leave us alone? Sooner or later they've got to castrate us."

"Yeah," Bufesqueu said. "In a way you can't blame them."

"Are you coming with me?"

"Hey," Bufesqueu said, "I really wish I could."

Mills looked at his friend. "If I make it," he said, "they'll cut your balls off."

Bufesqueu, embarrassed, looked down at his shoes. "Yeah, well," he said shyly, "it's like part of their dress code."

Inside the Valide Sultan's residence Mills squared his shoulders and knocked on the big door in the rear hallway. Beyond it was the short passageway that led to Yildiz Palace. He knocked on it five times rapidly, paused for as long as it took to recite the invocation to Allah that began the evening prayers, then rapped again, slowly, eight more times. Straining, he was just able to make out voices, then, moments later, footsteps. He adjusted his regimentals, the full-dress Janissary uniform laundered now and clean as it had been on the day it was issued.

A large man dressed in a fantastical costume was standing on the other side of the big oak door. The Palace Invigilator. Two armed guards stood behind him, their rifles pointed at George's chest.

Mills held up his empty hands and turned in a slow circle.

"You're a Janissary," the Invigilator said.

"These are my campaigns," Mills said. "Khash, Bejestan, Krym and Inebolu. Victories at Khash and Krym, wounded in Bejestan, taken prisoner at Inebolu."

"Where are your ribbons?" the Invigilator demanded.

He looked at the citations stitched on the guards' uniforms, the medals and chains of entitlement that hung from the Invigilator's neck.

"Burned 'em," Mills said. "Burned the ribbons and buried the medals when I disgraced myself at Inebolu by being captured instead of outright killed."

"Escaped or ransomed?" the Invigilator said.

"Exchanged," Mills said, "for thirty-seven lads from the enemy side."

The guards murmured to each other. The Invigilator hushed them and turned back to face Mills. "You came through the doorway of our Sultan's mother," he said harshly.

" 'As did my father, so does his son,' " Mills said, quoting the proverb.

The Invigilator nodded. "State your business," he said with some kindness.

"Mind yours!" Mills shot back.

"Put up your rifles," the Invigilator commanded the guards. "I'd better get the Imperial Chatelain," he told Mills.

The guards came to attention as Mills and the Invigilator brushed past them, Mills slightly in the lead, the Invigilator studying him from behind to see, in a final test, if he could thread his way through the complicated building to the office of the Imperial Chatelain.

Near the grand staircase—he was trading on instinct now, not only what he remembered of the palace on his single brief visit there

440

almost two years before, and not even only what he had pieced together from the hours and hours of protocol lessons he'd attended
("I'm told that if one is observant," an instructor had mentioned in
class, "he can read the rugs as savage Indians might follow trails in
a forest." Fringe, it had to do with fringe, fringe and color, Mills
thought, but couldn't remember *what* it had to do with fringe and
color, and then, where the fringe seemed thickest and whitest, actually
inspired, thinking: Of *course!* It would be lushest where it was least
traveled), but some felt tickle in the guts and blood, his way suffused
with actual magnetic essences, some lodestar ceremony of the atmosphere that pulled at the hairs on his legs and guided and tugged his
bowels—he could no longer hear them behind him.

Mills turned round. The Invigilator, halted with the guards at a
crossroads of corridors, had drawn his scimitar. One guard's rifle was
aimed at his head, the other's trained dead center on his belly.

"Kill him," the Invigilator said, "he doesn't know the way."

Mills closed his eyes.

(" 'Corze Oy 'uz prayn," Mills would say later " 'Corze Oy 'uz
prayn 'n' didn' evern know who I erz prayn *at!* Jeezers er Arler er
de Jew Gard eiver. 'Corze Oy 'uz prayn 'n yer natchrul instink when
yer makin' yer praise is ter shut yer eyes 'corze yer don' wan' ter be
lookern hat de Lord's own face when yer aksin' 'im ter save yer arse!
'Corze dat's protcool, 'corze dat's protcool, too. Yer nose in de dirty
'n der arse what wants savin' up hin de hair like soom fooking flame
held up in de sky like han off'rin'. 'Corze dere ain't nought han athist
'n Vauxhall. Nill nought none, I don' care whatcher say. 'N it's on'y
just Mum Nature's own natchrul protcool yer shoot fram yer eyes
whan yer prayn yer praise. Ye loook away joost like yerd loook way
from sun. 'N de protcool oov Christers de same. Kneelern, 'ead
bowed, er beatin' yer titties. *All* of it protcool. Protcool ev'y time.
Why Gard deigned, I guess, ter gimme 'is Sign.")

"Hold!" Mills hollered before they could fire. "I've stripped her
bed!" he told them in protocol.

"Hold your fire!" the Invigilator said, countermanding his earlier
order. "Go," he told one of the guards, "check." Which was protocol
too.

The guard was back in minutes. He carried his rifle, barrel pointing toward the floor. Behind him a trail of undischarged shells lay
scattered on the runner. He had unbuttoned the flap of his ammuni-
tion pocket and was disposing of the last of his shells when the other
guard saw him and began to do the same. The guard who had gone

to check nodded gravely, and the Invigilator lay his scimitar across the strip of Oriental carpet where he stood. Which was also protocol.

Because it was *all* protocol. The thirteen knocks on the door, the Invigilator's protocol questions and Mills's protocol claims—his burning the ribbons and burying the medals—the fantastical man's protocol harshness when Mills said he'd been exchanged for thirty-seven of the Empire's enemies and his protocol kindness in response to the Janissary's protocol proverb. Because it was *all* protocol. Mills's protocol rudeness, the protocol moment of protocol truth when they'd let Mills precede them (because an honest subject would know the way without being told), all of it, all protocol. Because you couldn't draw two unprotocol'd breaths in a row in this, or, for Mills's money, any other empire either, which was why he'd granted to God what everybody agreed belonged to God—— the Sign, the providential deign-given Sign, which was only careful planning, knowing one's onions, the known onions of protocol, knowing it was tradition, going back centuries, thirteen could be, maybe more, and that the first to learn of a royal's death had the right to strip the bed, signifying not only grief but continuity too, and not only grief and continuity, but the grief part absolutely of the highest, purest order, pure because often as not removed from all consanguineous ties and arrangements, the shrill, pure grief of subjects, bystanders, citizens—— good clean taxpayer grief!

Because it was *all* protocol, and why *wouldn't* Mills know about it? Since it was for people like him that protocol was invented, back doors and servants' entrances, folks on whom the protocol was piled sky high, who walked around stooped over from its weight, the burden of so much precedence and protocol turning their stances into the very image of a protocol'd people, like men and women carrying each other miles piggyback. Why *shouldn't* he know? Learn? Be on a perpetual lookout for dead royals? (Hadn't Moses Magaziner himself quoted odds so long they would be outside the realm of what wouldn't even be mathematics?) Strip their beds and tell the first one he saw higher than he but still low enough in the order for it not to matter much to, someone with anything really at stake—and this was where the continuity part came in—the bad news?

So they changed places. Mills and the Invigilator, Mills and the guards. Not physically of course, though the shoe was sure enough on the other foot, but psychologically, Mills no longer responsible by law and protocol to the guards and Invigilator—in theory the grief getting precedence now, the upper hand—just four guys, two pairs of bereaved working stiffs too shocked, again in theory, to know what they were doing, even though what they were doing was their duty. Because grief was the ultimate duty sanctioned, even ordained, by protocol.

"You'll want to let the Grand Vizier know," a guard said solemnly. (Because it was *all* protocol.)

"What?" Mills said. "Oh. Yeah. Right."

"He's left for the night," the Invigilator told him sadly.

"I can't still catch him?"

"He was going to the country," the other guard said. "To his residence there."

"I hate to have to be the one . . ."

The guards nodded. The Invigilator put his hand on Mills's arm.

So he protocol'd his way out the front door of Yildiz Palace and was protocol'd into an Imperial coach standing in the spectacular driveway and told the driver to take him to the British embassy, where he asked for and was granted a political sanctuary which was never violated the whole two months it took Moses Magaziner to get him aboard a French ship which was bound (since Magaziner had said "my" and not "our" king, and evidently Mills really was no longer a British citizen) for America.

Which was also protocol.

PART FIVE

1

Laglichio sued the black furniture removal company and obtained a restraining order. His lawyer argued that Laglichio's civil rights had been violated, that he was being prevented from doing business in the projects and black neighborhoods strictly on the basis of race. The judge agreed and, in addition to issuing the restraining order, awarded Laglichio damages.

"Landmark decision, Prince," Laglichio remarked to Bob, the dashiki'd warrior who had tried to bust his truck. "What do you say, George? The system works."

So Mills was once again employed full time, though he found that, having been away from it so long he was no longer in shape. His back troubled him, his breath was short.

"You wouldn't think," he told Louise, "such shabby stakes and sticks could weigh so much."

"Get out of it, George," Louise said. "Why don't you talk to some of your new contacts? You could ask Mr. Claunch if he's got anything for you. Even Cornell could probably put you in the way of something. And Sam, Mr. Glazer, is settled as dean now at the university. He probably has lots of influence. I'm sure he could get you a position with maintenance or housekeeping."

"Buildings and grounds. He already offered."

"Buildings and grounds," Louise said. "He offered?"

"He said I could work indoors in winter and keep warm, and outdoors in summer and get my fresh air."

"He knows all you did. It's nice when people appreciate."

"I'd push the clocks forward an hour in spring and turn them back again in fall," Mills said. "There were strings, Louise. I told him no deal."

All this during the first phase after George Mills returned from Mexico.

When he'd been their whatdoyoucallit, Father Confessor. They were spilling their beans, dumping their crap in his lap. Gossiping, tattling on themselves, one another.

As if he gave good advice. As if he even believed in it.

He gave no advice, put his faith in the insolubility of problems. You never laid a glove on the serious stuff. Disease played for keeps, and though he was no expert on world affairs, he knew that if things as inanimate and impersonal and off to the side of real life as nations could get into difficulties they couldn't slip, people had no chance at all. Things gone off like butter would never be sweet again. His back would fail him, the shortness of breath he now felt hustling furniture for Laglichio would show up again while he was sitting on the toilet one day, while he was watching TV, when he slept.

In the months following Judith Glazer's death Messenger continued to keep in touch. Sometimes he phoned, more often he just popped in. He was still driving Judith's Meals-on-Wheels route. (Rust along the wounds of his notched car like a sort of jam.) "The Judith Glazer Memorial Meals-on-Wheels Luncheon Rounds," he called it. He brought the Millses news of Mrs. Carey and Mr. Reece and the others on his itinerary and sometimes—you could smell the pot on his breath, his clothes, pungent, sweet as campfire, burning leaves—came to them with covered styrofoam trays of leftovers.

"What am I going to do about my kid, George?" Messenger would ask between mouthfuls of cooling chili-mac. "What do you say, Lulu?"

The Claunches, too, were into him, or their lawyers were. Judith's sanity was in question. She'd made no eleventh-hour revisions of what they regarded as her cogent, ordinary enough wishes, but her wild, middle-of-the-night calls to her friends, even to some of the Meals-on-Wheels contingent, had prompted some of them to believe that she'd intended to make provision for them. She'd hinted at, and evidently actually promised, small gifts, semiprecious jewelry, shoes, dresses, coats—— relics.

No codicils had been formulated, no substantiating notes found. The claimants, though even the lawyers acknowledged that "claimants" was too strong a term—no one had actually made or even threatened a legal claim against the estate—had all rather shyly indicated their limited expectations in condolence letters—— to Sam, to Harry Claunch, to Judith's father on his now public private phone numbers. One or two had appealed directly to Mrs. Glazer's daughters. The Claunch lawyers were inclined to honor what they called these "nuisance claims" on the dead woman's estate. (Louise herself, though they'd never met, only spoken to each other once on the phone, had been the recipient of one such gift—— a tiny pillbox, purchased during their first days in Mexico, in which Mrs. Glazer had kept her Laetrile. Like the others to whom such tokens had been granted, she'd had to sign a notarized quitclaim.)

But something was up.

One night the senior partner—he was the man who'd indicated an interest in Mills's car the day of the funeral—in the law firm that was handling things for the Claunches, called George at home.

"Still got that car, old man?"

"What car?"

"That snazzy Special of course."

"Oh yeah," Mills said, "sure."

"You'll come round. You will."

"Make me an offer."

The lawyer chuckled. "You make me one."

"Four thousand dollars," George said, not knowing what it might be worth but certain he'd asked too little.

The lawyer laughed into the phone. "Oh that's a good one," he said heartily. "It really is. Never mind. I'm a patient man, you'll come round. Actually I guess I deserved that," the lawyer said, "trying to mix business with pleasure."

"Business?"

"Well, it's just that we'd like you to drop by the firm. At your own convenience of course. We'd like to take an affidavit from you."

"What for?" Mills asked nervously.

"No real reason," the lawyer said, "we'd just like to have it on file in case anything comes up. We'd like your statement that Judith was in unexceptionable health when you were caring for her in Mexico."

447

"She was sick as a dog."

"No no." The lawyer laughed. "I mean her mental health."

"I can't give any affidavit," George said. "I can't come down at my convenience. My boss would dock me."

Then Sam Glazer called.

"I understand they're trying to pressure you," he said. "Listen, you hung in there. I'm grateful for that." Mills didn't know what he was talking about. "No kidding, George—may I call you George?—I really am. I'd just like your assurance that you'll continue to resist them when they start turning the screws on you."

"No one's going to turn the screws on me."

"That's the way," Sam said, "that's the way to handle it."

When he called again he sounded as distraught as Messenger.

"She must have been crazy, George. She must have been out of her head. I blame myself. I'm at fault. Partially. Partially I am. Poor Judith. Poor, poor Judith. God knows what she must have suffered. All that pain and anger, all that mental anguish."

"No, no," George said, trying to reassure him. "Her spirits were *good.*"

"How can you say that?" Glazer demanded furiously. "Is that what you said? Is *that* what you told them? Her spirits were *good?*"

"Hey," George said.

"What about the pesos? What about all those pesos she gave away? What about the time she tried to get herself murdered? What about that funeral service? Her psychiatrist's ruined. You know *that,* don't you? Being made to say that stuff in public. Judith washed *him* up with her crazy arrogance. You call that cheerful, you call that good spirits?"

"Listen, Mr. Glazer . . ."

"Listen? *Listen?* No I won't listen. *You* listen! What about heredity? What about our daughter Mary? You call *her* sane? She's crazy as hell. All she thinks about is sex. She doodles genitalia in her geometry book. She doodles fellatio. The men have embouchures like symphony musicians. She draws gleaming wet pussy in her Latin text. The labia are tattooed with boys' names. She does tits, stiff, ugly little hairs coming up out of the nipples. She says she's engaged to be married. Some squirt at school she says she's been sleeping with since fifth grade. She *tells* me this! She says 'He can't come yet, Daddy. I got my orgasm even before my periods started, but Stevie still can't come. I tell him to be patient,' she says, 'that he'll probably be in puberty by the time we're married and it'll all work out.'

"This is *sane?* What a*bout* heredity? These are good spirits? The kid's a nympho. That stuff has to come from somewhere. It comes from her mother."

"Why are you telling me this?" George said.

"It comes from her mother, the madwoman! How'd they get to you, Mills? Just tell me what they promised."

"Nobody promised anything. Nobody got to me."

"You swear you didn't give them your affidavit?"

"I didn't," George said.

"Jesus," Sam Glazer said, "you scared me there, George. You really had me going for a time."

It was crazy, George thought. As if by saying his wife had been in good spirits he had somehow slandered her. Glazer was calm now. He was calm when he spoke to George about the possibility of something opening up in buildings and grounds, calm when with practically no transition *he* asked Mills for his affidavit, calm when George turned him down, calm, even smooth, when he told him that all he really wanted was for George to keep an open mind, not to say anything to the Claunches until he'd had another chance to speak with him.

"You're in the catbird seat, you know," Sam Glazer said pleasantly before ringing off. "You're the only eyewitness."

The senior partner called again.

"You know," he said, "I've given more thought to what you asked for your Special. You did say it's the original grille, didn't you?"

Even Laglichio. He was impressed, he said, with Mills's apparent ability to deal with blacks. He wanted, he said, his input on some schemes he'd been developing.

Then there was Coule. The minister wanted to know when Mills was going to make good on that sermon he'd promised.

"What sermon I promised?"

"Testimony then."

"Oh yeah," George said, "sure thing."

"You're *not* saved, are you?" Coule demanded. "You made all that up about grace. Boasting."

"Who'd brag anything small potatoes as salvation?"

"You're outrageous."

"Yeah? Am I? You're this man of the cloth, this cloth man. It rumples your tail feathers, don't it, Reverend, I got grace, you got

449

shit? Sure. I'll fill in for you. I'll give you my affidavit on holiness. Name the day. Easter? Christmas?"

As if they were waiting for him to pounce, as if he were some blackmailer. As if all they ever thought about was that whatever he'd learned in Mexico would be used against them. Or not a blackmailer at all—— a sort of cop. George Mills, the arresting officer, their prosecutor, the law, the state. Their rights read at them like charges, boredom and cynicism built into their inner ear, hearing fair warning, the rattler's obligatory sizzle—— then sock! pow! blammo! and all bets off.

Mills unable to reassure them, unable to convince them they had nothing to worry about.

"Why did you let me take her to Mexico?" he asked Harry Claunch.

"She was inoperable," Harry said. "Even the oncologist said the chemotherapy was tearing her guts out. Under the circumstances, could we deny her her long shot?"

"But why me?"

"Why not you? She would have laid it all out for the woman who brought her bedpan."

So he had his legacy too. Their secrets like so many pieces of costume jewelry, like so many hand-me-downs. The repository now not only of Mills history but everyone's. And he'd told Coule he was saved.

But mostly Messenger. Messenger's hang-ups, Messenger's circle, Messenger's kid.

"Yeah," Cornell, high, told him one day over a ham and ravioli sandwich, "I take the cake. Here I sit, enhanced and laid back as some California surfer—want a drag? no? it's sensamilla, two hundred fifty bucks a lid—and . . . What was I on about then? Oh yeah, the cake. It's Chocolate Mint Heart today, Lulu. I'm going to tell you something, George. You think it's because I'm enhanced I say this. But I was telling whoosis, my paraplegic lady, Gert. She thinks so too." He fell silent. The rusts from his ham and ravioli sandwich smeared the corners of his mouth and lips, turning them down like the sad-face expression on a clown. "It's the applesauce. Meals-on-Wheels puts out a great applesauce, maybe the best in the world." And he tore into the applesauce, shoveling it into his mouth with his plastic spoon. "You got a slice of bread, Lulu, I can soak up the juice? Hey," he said

450

giggling, "don't bother. I'll use a Kleenex. The horror, the horror, hey Mills?" He grinned at them. "I'm bold," he said. "What the hell, what's there to hide? Judy G. told you all about me. She gave you my mantra. Well, *her* mantra. I can't get the goddamn thing to work. Did you know they were her last words? Big-deal holy lady, big-deal saint. Pain up to here and her brother bending down over her bed for, for God *knows* what—— instructions probably. 'Do thus and so with the kids. Give Sammy my love. Tell the Mex to leave the room and smother me with the fucking pillow.' God *knows* what! 'Christ's a redhead. He wears designer jeans.' And what does he hear? '*Mahesvaram, mahesvaram, mahesvaram.*' The born-again son of a bitch off to Heaven on a wave of transcendental meditation, at one with her cancer, the lint on her pesos. That lady could have been buried out of the Ethical Society, the Automobile Association. I tell you, George, she left me a haunted mantra. She squeezed the blood out of it, Lulu. I can't even levitate. The horror, the horror."

"You can't levitate? You're high as a kite."

"Because I'm in pain, George and Lulu. Because I'm in pain. Because the griefs ain't leaking no more, they're *whelming*. There's flash-flood griefs, man overboard. Let me just tell you a few of the things that have been happening in my neighborhood. Oh, look at Lulu, she likes it when I talk Despair. Despair's her turn-on."

Louise did enjoy Messenger's visits. The man was a crybaby and blabbermouth, and Mills saw that Louise took the same comfort from him that Mrs. Glazer had taken from Maria's sad adventures on Mexican television. Because she knew most of the people involved— the Claunches had invited her to return to the estate and bring some of the Meals-on-Wheels people with her; Sam Glazer had called and asked them to dinner; she'd met his girls; she'd met Messenger's dyslexic son when Cornell brought Harve to the house one day; she had even spoken to Losey, Messenger's surgeon friend, about George's bad back, had met Nora, his wife, when the failing student of architecture had come to South St. Louis with a classmate on an assignment to study the city's "vernacular architecture" (Cornell had given Nora Losey Mills's name; neither Louise nor Nora knew at the time that the classmate was the girl with whom the surgeon was having an affair, George didn't)—they'd taken on an immediacy and importance in her life which George Mills resisted but could do little to discourage.

Meanwhile Louise was thrilled with other people's bad news,

tried to catch Mills's eye and nod at him knowingly each time Cornell delivered himself of some new heartache in the portfolio.

"We don't have it so bad," Louise told her husband one night.

"No sir," George said. "We've got it made."

"When are you going to play your China card, George?"

This was Messenger's phrase. George had told him about the calls—— the dean's job offer, Claunch's lawyer's bid on the Buick Special. He thought Mills beyond bribery and did not know that the only reason George had mentioned the calls was to get some idea of what his affidavit was actually worth to them. Either side could have it for top dollar. He had liked Judith but Judith had died, convinced of her salvation as he was of his. Nothing he said about her now could alter either of their conditions.

She was absolutely sane, solid as a rock. I swear it by all that's holy!

I was with her day and night for more than a month and had plenty of opportunity to observe her. She tried to get us killed. She was bats, nutty as a fruitcake. So help me God. Amen.

But he was no good as an examiner, was without subtlety, could not lead his witness, could not trap him—it's the blood, Mills thought, it's my thousand-year-old blue collar blood—could, in the end, only ask outright his cruel, crucial question.

Messenger, surprised, looked at him.

"These are my friends," Messenger said. "You understand that, don't you?"

"Sure," Mills said.

"I mean both sides."

"Sure."

"Sam's a colleague."

"Yes."

"However difficult Judith may have been, I always respected her."

"Yes."

"She was nobody's fool."

"No."

"Why are you doing this?"

"There's a buck to be made."

"Come on."

"Operation Bootstrap."

"You're too late, George," Messenger said sympathetically.

"Maybe not."

452

To stall him he told him something else.

"Victor couldn't take it anymore," Messenger said softly. "He had Audrey committed. They took her belts away. He had to sign for her shoestrings. Restraints, the whole *schtick*. She won't swallow pills, so they have to force-feed her. When they put her on an IV she tried to chew through the tube and jimmy an air bubble into her vein. They can't use an IV. They're afraid she'll try to turn on it and impale herself. A male nurse who used to be her student gives her shots in her arms, in her ass. Two men hold her down. She's black-and-blue from these euphorics, so dry from drugs her tongue is chafed, the roof of her mouth. She can't close her mouth for the pain. She cries even when she's sleeping and the salt tears run into her mouth. There are lesions inside her cheeks, all the soft tissue. They slake her from eyedroppers like you'd feed a sick bird. When he visited her last time she signaled him over to the side of the bed. She could barely talk. He had to lean down. Even then he could hardly understand her. She was smiling. The first time he'd seen her smile in almost a year.

" 'Yes?' he said. 'The shore? What about the shore? You want to go to the shore? Get better, sweetheart. When you get well. I promise. When you get well we'll go to the shore.' They have this place on Cape May. He patted her forehead and promised to take her.

"He says you'd have thought he'd given her a jolt of—— "

"This is—— " Mills said.

"——electricity," Messenger said. "That's how fast she jumped away from his touch. Her loathing was that clear. 'Well, what *about* the shore?' he said he said angrily. 'You don't want me to come? Swell,' he said he said hurt, 'get well. Go by yourself. I won't stop you.'

"She shook her head and now he said he could see that it wasn't loathing at all. He said it was a different thing entirely, and while she wasn't smiling the expression on her face was almost a sane one and some—— "

"This is all—— " Mills said.

"——thing else he hadn't seen in almost a year. It was just sane, ordinary, angry, outraged human frustration, and he realized he'd misunderstood her. He apologized and leaned down again over her pillows. 'What?' he asked. 'What?'

" 'Not shore,' she said. 'Bedshore. *Bed*shore.'

" 'What?'

" '*Bed*shore!'

"She was telling him about her bedsores, that she meant to kill

453

herself by poisoning her bedsores, by peeing on her bedsores and infecting them, by rolling her sores in shit. He told her doctor he wanted her catheterized. He demanded she be rigged to her bedpan.

"All right," Messenger said, "what is it?"

"The public record, the sunshine laws. They write this stuff down on her chart," Mills said coolly. "They say things like this at the nurses' station. They'd tell me this crap if I called the front desk."

He thought Messenger was going to hit him.

"It's gossip, Cornell. A king told my ancestor that gossip's horizontal, that nasty stories neither ascend nor descend but stay within their class of origin."

"What am I, a traitor to my class? I ain't even high. This is my best stuff."

"I don't want gossip," Mills said.

"What, what do you want?"

"The goods. *I want the goddamn goods on them!*" George Mills exploded.

Which he was not to have for a while, Messenger feeding him as he might have fed the Meals-on-Wheelers, in installment, moiety, some awful, teasing incrementality, telling him what Mills did not care to hear not because he enjoyed, as Judith Glazer might, the damage of the thing, the tightening, dangerous coil of consequence he could not keep his hands off and wound and wound like the stem of a watch, but because of the flashy, reflexive, ricochet'd attention and glory, perhaps his melodramatist's or bad gambler's hole-card hope —— the same thing that kept him glued to the telethon, that drew him to "20/20," "Sixty Minutes," the news, that made the Watergate years—how he envied Deep Throat!—the best of his life.

"He can't stand what he's done. I think Victor's gone nuts. Losey says so too. The man's a surgeon but he sees plenty of this emergency room guilt. Sure. When they sign the papers. To lop off a leg, to hacksaw crushed fingers or take away tits.

"He thinks he should have sent the kid off instead. He could have sent his son to aunts in Pittsburgh, to a brother-in-law in Maine."

"What happened?" Mills asked. (Because he was asking questions now. Because he knew that Messenger would tell him what he needed to know but that first he would have to hear all of it, Messenger's scandals like the devised sequences and routines of the Cassadagans. Because he was something of the straight man now too, the old

Florida Follies Kid. Thinking: You don't ever grow up. Nothing changes, nothing. Certainly not your character.) "What happened?"

"She wasn't suicidal. Even the psychiatrist said so. She wasn't suicidal. She just wanted to die.

"That's what she kept telling the boy. That she wanted to die. Can you imagine? How old can he be? Eleven? Twelve? The kid home from school and making chocolate milk, Horlick's, his Ovaltine. Slopping sardine sandwiches together and nibbling Fritos off some cleared portion of the dining room table. (Because the kitchen table's overflowing. Not from breakfast, understand. Or anyway not from that morning's breakfast, or even yesterday's, but the cumulate dishes, spoons, knives and egg-tined forks of maybe three days' meals. And more in the sink. Sure. There's three in the family. Say they've got two sets of dishes, for dinner parties, for everyday. Service for twelve, say. The cleaning lady comes once a week. That's four days of meals on the everyday. Another two or three on what they'd serve to their guests. But be fair. Audrey's not eating. But *be* fair. They fill up her plate. Even she *don't* eat they got to dirty a dish. And suppose the girl calls in sick? I mean she's *seen* that mess. She hired on as a cleaning lady, not a pearl diver. Suppose she calls in sick. In eight days they have to take their meals on the coffee table in the living room. In two more they're taking them separately. On the back porch, the stairs. The kid's fixing his snack on the ironing board in the basement.)

"So there's, what'shisname, Danny, trying to make a simple sardine or peanut-butter-and-jelly sandwich and drinking now out of the jelly and *yahrtzeit* glasses and actual Corky the Clown mugs from the old highchair days, wolfing it down because though he's not athletic and is normally a housebound child content to stay home and read, do homework, it breaks his heart to hear his mom cry and he can't stand absolutely to hear her complain how if there was a God she'd be a goner by now, and he's got to get out of there, back to the playground to get in a game which he knows he's not only bad at but hasn't even learned the rules of yet, even the goddamn object. Not go for a walk, kick leaves, ride bikes with a pal, read books on a bench, but back to the playground, where he doesn't like to be even at recess, back to the actual goddamn playground where he knows damn well they'll choose him, even choose him early, before the better players, the ones who've got it together, whose reflexes hum like gears in fine machinery, whose timing and power and speed and concentration make them good up at bat, who wear their fielders' mitts as naturally and comfortably as Dan wears scarves, coats; who'll choose him early for the simple good fun of just making them laugh, giving them by simple dint of picking him for their side the right—the *right*—to denounce his errors, mock his play, him. To call him bad names and nudge him with elbows and push him around.

"Not, Victor says, as you'd suspect, to take his mind off things but to get it back on them. To see just what his mother meant when she told him each morning when he went to school that she hoped noon would find her stricken and when school let out dead.

" 'I'm destroying it, Danny. I'm ruining your life, sweetheart,' Victor says she'd tell him, re*mind* him, in her soiled robe, over the greasy dishes and scummed silverware and smeared cups and glasses which by this time served as their everyday, almost unrecognizable now, almost, under the three- or four-day growth of mold, indistinguishable from the good stuff, the sterling and Aynsley china, the dirty novelty mugs and glasses, six-of-one, half-a-dozen-of-the-other, with the cups and crystals of sanity. Because that's why Victor, who'd prepare the meals but wouldn't do the dishes, who'd put fresh sheets on Danny's bed every five days—the girl came every week but couldn't get out of the damn kitchen—but wouldn't change the ones he'd been sleeping on with Audrey for almost eleven, allowed the house to get in such a state in the first place.

"Not, Victor says, out of narrow principle say, you-made-your-bed, lie-in-it say, not out of *that* principle at least. (He's ridden with guilt, George. *He* tells me this, not the front desk.) As an object lesson, a lesson in objects.

" 'I was trying to show her how easily the world is reclaimed by jungle. How simple it is to go mad. I thought I could shame her back into her senses. See? "See," I'd have had that house scream, "see?" What's makes *you* so special? I've gone bats too, the furniture has, the dishes and linen. Look at Dan, look at Danny. His clothes have gone nuts. It's 80 degrees, he's dressed for the winter!'

"She must, Victor says, have thought he *was* crazy. She didn't know where she was. There was soup in her bowl. She hadn't made it. If she'd been paying attention to what he was saying she might have thought he'd lost his mind in some swell restaurant.

"But then Victor came home one day from the office and the house was clean. Spotless. The living room had been cleared, the dining room, everything had been picked up, all the carpets vacuumed. There wasn't a dish in the sink. This was a Monday. The cleaning lady wasn't due till Wednesday. Victor says his heart turned over. He raced upstairs. Audrey was in bed, asleep on clean sheets.

" 'I didn't wake her. How could I? She must have been exhausted. Anyone would have been exhausted.

" 'So I didn't wake her. I just sat by the bed and cheered on her sleep. I sat there two hours. When she finally woke up she gave one of those great yawning stretches you imagine Rip Van Winkle must have given, or Sleeping Beauty, or someone recovered from coma. She blinked a few times to get her bearings and looked at me.

" ' "Oh," she said, "hi. You home from work? God, it's almost dark out. I'm sorry. I lay down for a nap. I must have fallen asleep."

" ' "Who wouldn't?" I said. "You worked like a horse. Are you feeling better?"

" ' "No," she said.

" ' "You tried to do too much. You should have saved a little for tomorrow. Then Dorothy comes on Wednesday."

" ' "Oh God," she said, "what are you talking about now? Leave me alone, will you? Or kill me. I just want to die." ' "

"Because *he'd* done the dishes. Danny. The boy. He'd cleaned the place up. Victor knew it as soon as he heard him and turned, and saw him standing there, in the doorway, whimpering, sucking his thumb.

"He made the arrangements that night and packed her off to the asylum the next day.

" 'Now,' Victor says, 'we're just another broken family in July, me and the kid, driving back from Burger Chef in a blue K Car.' "

"Poor kid," George Mills said.

"Who?" Messenger said. "Danny? The hell. He's in the ninety-ninth percentile. The little fag reads six years above his grade level."

"That doctor's wife was over, that student, Mrs. Losey?"

"Nora," Messenger said. "Yes?"

"She was over to the house. Some sort of homework for her school. She took pictures."

"There's this rehab project."

"She the one flunking out?"

"On academic probation, right."

"Whose husband's having the affair?"

"With Jenny Greener, yes."

"A girl was with her. That was her name I think."

"They're classmates," Messenger said. "Nora introduced them."

"Then what happened?"

Because he was listening now. Because there were only reruns on television anyway and he was listening now. Salvation or no salvation. Listening despite himself. Because they could almost have been more Millses.

"He goes out of town," Messenger said. "He's much in demand. Symposiums. Universities. He's an expert in the new microsurgical stuff. Sutures finer than spider web. Instruments no bigger than computer chips. He can sew on your fingerprints, he can take out your germs. Like the little cobbler in fairy tale. He's much in demand. Sun Valley and Aspen, Fiji, the Alps. All the pricey climes of the medical —— Palm Springs Memorial, the Grosse Point Clinic, Monaco Mercy, Grand Cayman General.

"He goes out of town. He lectures his colleagues. He screws their wives. Never the nurses, never the help.

"He says 'I won't touch a student. And my patients—— forget it. If I touch a patient I've already scrubbed. I'm not talking what's ethical, what's professional or ain't. None of this has fuck-all to do with my Hippocratic oath. It's just I still think it's kicky I'm invited places. Maybe I'm spoiled. I won't cross a street if it's not on the arm. I won't *take* a vacation. I've this thing for doctors' wives.

" 'Country club country. I love being made over, wined and dined, fussed. I *never* get used to it. I don't think I will.

" 'Lunch turns me on. Tennis-togged women, ladies in tank tops. I like to take off their sweat bands. I love those little bracelets of the untan, the wrist hair where it's been pressed down under the elastic. I love the way it smells, sweat running with perfume and the better soaps. I like their jewelry, their diamond rings and great gold chains. I love the way their *jewelry* smells. You know what, Cornell? I can make out the karats, the troy grains in pearls. You believe me? It's true. The expensive like a whiff of sachet. I can smell money in a purse, coins, even checkbooks, the stamps in their passports, plastic on charge cards, a Neiman-Marcus, a Saks.

" 'Christ I'm a bastard. I cheat on my wife. If I had a dollar . . .' he tells me. (And I listen to this stuff, who got lucky maybe a dozen or so years ago, and that with a drunk, a woman under the influence, who may have been a little crazy *behind* the alcohol. But who celebrates the occasion—March 19—like some dear anniversary.) He tells me this shit. *Me.* So I tell you. You can't cheat on your wife, you cheat on your friends.

" 'We'll have left early,' he says, 'gone separate ways to the parking lot. She gets in my rental car or I get in hers, but I love when *they* drive, when they take me 'cross bridges and she grabs the toll. When she picks the place, where we can go. Listen, it's Cairo, what do *I* know? It's Cairo, it's Russia, it's somewhere South Seas. It isn't the money, you know that, Cornell. I'm the one being fussed. I've published the paper, made the keynote address.

" 'And maybe they *are* nurses, or were before they married their husbands and became doctors' wives. Hell, I suppose lots of them *were* nurses, most of them maybe. But up from the nursery and doctors' wives now. So it's all right, it's okay.

" 'Because I'm this snob of betrayal, this rat of swank. Your fop of collusion, your paste asshole. And nothing against their husbands. On the contrary. They're pals, I like them. Every professional courtesy. I second their opinions. We wave on the slopes.' "

So Messenger told Mills of Losey's code.

"Code?" George said. "He's got fuckall to do with the Hippocratic oath, he's got a *code?*"

"Didn't I tell you?" Messenger said. "He goes out of town. He makes love on the beaches, on cruises, off shore. Everything handled, you know, discreet. Shit, Mills, *I* don't know. Maybe there are gentlemen's agreements. Maybe they don't go to each other's papers. I don't know how it's done. A guy tells me he's been with a groupie I don't ask to see the matchbook from the restaurant. I'm an old-fashioned guy. People get laid it's a wonder to me you don't read about it in the paper. It's amazing there's no extra or the programs ain't interrupted. Someone makes love . . . But that's just the point. *That's* Losey's code. You can wing it like birdies, do anything, everything. Just don't fall in love. Though that's the part I don't understand. I'd wonder who's kissing them now.

" 'The family,' Losey says. 'The family comes first. The home.'

"It's the long view, you see. The long view he takes. Marriage like principal. Not to be disturbed. He's a doctor, a surgeon. He hates a complication. Side effects spook him, they give him the willies. Sure, that's *got* to be it. The principles of science carried over into life. Well, why not? What the hell? I'm glad we had this chat, George. It's clearer to me now."

But not to Mills.

"Well," Messenger said, "he has trucks."

"Trucks."

"And an interest in freight cars."

"I don't—— "

"That he bought with some guys, that he leases back to the railroad."

"I don't—— "

"Because a lot of this shit must have been in her name, joint tenancy, something sufficiently complicated so that even if he's audited and they find against him it's probably a judgment call. And, oh yes, meanwhile he gets the use on the money, the interest compounding against the penalty even if there is one. A divorce could . . . Well, you can see for yourself. And maybe that's what he means by 'home.' Maybe it's only his pet name for tax shelter. The horror, the horror, hey Mills?"

Who wanted names and dates, the places of these horrors, whose own interest was compounding now too, but in a different direction, so that when he again asked "Then what happened?" Messenger only looked at him. "What happened?" he repeated.

"What do you think happened?"

"I don't know, that it got out of hand."

"It was his idea that Nora become a graduate student."

"I see," Mills said, but didn't.

"He even picked the discipline. And picked it mercilessly, pitilessly. Architecture. She'd need math, she'd need mechanics. She'd need drawing skills. She'd need calculus and physics, statics and dynamics, and a knowledge of mechanical systems. She'd need to know stresses. She'd need acoustics and drafting, axonometrics and isometric projections. She'd need to know project financing. She'd need a knowledge of real estate and whose palm you greased to get round the zoning codes. So she'd need political science, and a little law too. You see?"

"But—— "

"Medical school would have been a breeze, compared."

"But why did—— "

"Because he really *is* your paste asshole, your rat of swank. Only I didn't know he was so clever. Christ, he must have studied the catalogue like a doting daddy. He must have *pored* over that fucker. He must have laughed his ass off when he had to look a term up.

"But I don't know. I don't *know* why he did it. Maybe it was only that same hierarchical predilection for profession that put nurses off limits but drove him into their arms once they were doctors' wives. Maybe that's why he married her in the first place, maybe it's why he loved her. Maybe he was just showing off. Because once he got his license to practice he could, by the simple act of marrying her, take any girl off the street and turn her into a doctor's wife. *Any* girl. A typist, a beautician, someone in trade school.

"Maybe excitement quits on you. Maybe it pales. Maybe pride is the least complacent of the qualities, and it's true what the songs say—— the thrill is gone, the blush off the rose. Passion like the seasons, like land that gives out."

"Maybe he didn't want her around at those doctor conventions," George said.

"Symposiums, conferences," Messenger said. "Maybe. But I don't think so. I think he's better than that. I take him at his word. I believe he really is this rat of swank, that he has this toney, back-of-the-book vision. The couple—she's a brain surgeon, he sits on the Supreme Court; she skydives for relaxation, he's into archeology; they swig tiptop scotch and lie around listening to old 78's—that has it made. The best condo at the fanciest address, who weave great salads and whip up Jap foods which they eat off the carpet before great open fires. (He gets closed-circuit TV, pulls big Vegas bouts from his dish in the yard.) Because he really thinks like that. And what *I* think, what *I* think, is that he was honestly trying to make her over. Take this perfectly nice, ordinary girl whom he'd already turned into a doctor's wife pretty as any he screws in Europe, well dressed as any, tricky as any in bed, well heeled and knowing as any, and go for it. That's why he chose architecture to be her fate. Out of love and an honest pleasure and pride in just more gracious living. And that could explain Jenny Greener, too." Mills looked at him. "Think about it." Mills shrugged. "They're classmates. They're classmates, George. She came to your house. What did you think?"

"I didn't think anything. Why? What should *I* think?"

"Did you notice anything special about Jenny?"

"Jenny?"

"Jenny Greener, yes."

"I'm trying to remember."

"That's right. Do you?"

Mills tried to recall the polite, somewhat nervous young woman who'd come with the doctor's wife that day. She was, he'd thought, ill at ease, and had given him the impression—stiff, unmoving, perched on the edge of their sofa, holding herself carefully, almost tenderly, as if she were sore, as if she held a saucer and teacup in her lap, a napkin, invisible cakes—of restrained fidgets. She hadn't talked much. He couldn't remember that she'd said anything. She hadn't asked questions, as Nora had, about the house, the neighborhood. Louise had said afterward that Nora had taken Polaroids of the house, flashes, three or four rolls. That she'd gone around shooting one picture after another, of the cellar steps, the ceiling, the basement, their closets and doorways, their small backyard. "I tell you, George, she could have been from the insurance," Louise said, "taking pictures of water damage, busted pipes." He couldn't remember Jenny Greener having a camera.

"I think she was embarrassed," George told Cornell. "I don't recall what she looked like."

"Plain?"

"I don't remember."

"Nora Pat. Mrs. Losey. What did Mrs. Losey look like?"

"Oh, she was beautiful. Very well dressed. She had on this linen suit. Boots. She had beautiful boots. Sort of a blonde. I don't know. I can't describe people's looks. She was very pretty. I remember she was very pretty."

"A smasher?" Messenger said. "A knockout?"

"Yes," George Mills said. "She was very beautiful." He remembered that when they were introduced she'd taken his hand and held it in both her own.

"You were with Judy," she said. "You're the man with the back." And she'd touched Mills there, where his back ached, and her touch had radiated comfort through his shirt, warming him.

"I suppose if you thought about it you could remember the boots, how they laced up the side, the way they were tooled, the particular purchase they gave to her stance?"

"She stood," George Mills said, "like someone poised on a diving board. Jenny Greener was plain."

"Nora wouldn't let her alone once she found out how smart she was. She kept inviting her over to the house. (She introduced them.) After a while Jenny couldn't figure out how to turn her down anymore. She had this way of explaining things. Formulas, principles. Better than the professors. So that for as long as she could keep Jenny talking even Nora believed she'd get the stuff. She could even give it back, work out the problems, solve them, get round the doglegs and sand traps of architecture, cracking all the difficult ciphers of the discipline Losey had chosen for her. That's what they talked about. This was their dinner table conversation. Housing, the redevelopment of downtown, the drawbacks of solar.

"And her husband beaming, beaming, ready to bust his buttons.

Proud as a pop with a kid on the dean's list—— on the arm at the ball park, management's, the home team's straight-A'd, honor-roll'd guest. (Listen, listen, I know how he'd feel! I don't blame him, I don't even apologize for him. This isn't sublimation, reflected glory, suspect, vicarious motive. I'm not talking about pride of ownership, I'm not even talking about pride. Love. I'm talking about love, all simple honor's good will and best wishes. So I *know* how he'd feel!)

"Losey may have been having second thoughts. He must have had them. Thinking—I don't know—thinking, Gee, maybe I made a mistake, maybe there's something harder than architecture, higher. (Not better paid, because, be fair, he didn't give a damn whether his wife ever earned back from the profession even half what it had cost him to get her into it in the first place. What could he do with more money? Figure new ways to hide it? He was still busting his hump on the old ways, which, face it, be fair, were only his accountant's ideas anyway, only the tried and true evasive actions of sheltering dough. Because he's right. When he says 'You know me, Cornell, it isn't the money.' He's right, it isn't. It's just another way of having and doing what others in those brackets have and do.) Thinking: Gee, maybe I should have pushed her into astronomy, aeronautical engineering. Maybe I should have run her for governor.

"Till that damned letter came. It was addressed to Losey. It could have been an honest mistake. It could have been the chairman's joke; I hope it was Nora's. But it was actually very nice, very sympathetic and concerned. Like those letters company commanders write next of kin when the news is bad.

"It said that while Nora gave every indication she was trying, *really* trying, and was extremely cooperative and obviously bright, and, oh yes, especially gifted as a draftsman and quite clearly imaginative, there was this problem with her math, this basic flaw on the scientific side. He was sorry, he said, but he was afraid that if she couldn't bring that part of it up, Dr. Losey, his daughter was in danger of going on academic probation.

"Losey was furious. 'Does that son of a bitch actually think I'm old enough to be your father?'

"But be fair, give him credit. He would get her a tutor. She could bring up her statics and dynamics, she could bring up her knowledge of mechanical systems. She was extremely cooperative and obviously bright. Even that pompous prick of a chairman thought so. He'd get a licensed architect to help her, maybe a partner in one of the big firms downtown. He'd pay his fee, whatever those highway robbers charged when a house was commissioned. She wasn't to worry. All she had to concentrate on was bringing up her axonometrics and isometric projections.

" 'I had no idea,' he said. 'If you'd told me earlier maybe we wouldn't be in this mess.'

"I'm not her confidant. I'm not even his. I mean he won't talk about this stuff. I had no idea either. If I asked how Nora was doing in architecture school he'd mumble something vague and tell me all about some doctor's wife he'd screwed in the islands.

"She told Judy. Judy told the Meals-on-Wheelers. The Meals-on-Wheelers told me. I tell you.

" 'Well,' he said, 'spilled milk. I'll ask around. Don't worry, I'll be discreet. I'll speak to the head of the architectural firm that's doing our hospital annex.'

" 'Jenny Greener,' she said.

" 'Jenny Greener?'

" 'Only she's already working for you.'

" 'Working for me?'

" 'I pay her to explain the stuff. I pay her to eat supper with us.'

" 'Jenny Greener? The mutt?'

" 'She's the head of our class. She's the one with the grade point average. She's the one you want.'

"She was right of course. But he didn't trust her now. How could he? She'd kept everything to herself. All he knew was what he'd heard at the dinner table, and now he thought all the bright chatter was just some scam.

"So he checked up on her. On Jenny Greener. He called the chairman and told him he was Dr. Losey.

" 'Who's top of that class?'

" 'Our students' records are confidential, Dr. Losey. I'm sure you can understand that.'

" 'Sure,' he said. 'It's just that I'm so concerned about Nora. I thought maybe if I talked to him he could give her some tips. Maybe not. I guess you're right. Maybe women just don't have it in the thinking department, maybe they're just not cut out to be architects. I guess you have to accept them. Some affirmative action thing.'

" 'We don't have to accept anyone,' the chairman said. 'Women do quite as well as men.'

" 'Sure,' Losey said. 'I guess you were only kidding when you wrote that letter about Nora. I'll tell her you said she's a shoe-in. That you don't put girls on academic probation.'

" 'As a matter of fact, Doctor,' the chairman said, steamed, 'it's a "girl," as you put it, who's head of that class.'

"But he wouldn't say which girl so Losey still didn't know.

"He got the names of her teachers and saw them during their office hours. He'd mention Jenny Greener and their eyes would light up. 'Jenny Greener,' one prof said, 'Jenny Greener's a genius.'

" 'A genius? Really? A genius?'

"And another told him she was the most promising student he'd ever had. And one showed him sketches. They were plans for the hospital annex. Even Losey could see how beautiful they were.

" 'Beautiful?' the man said. 'This is an actual project you know. Many of the problems we set for our students are. This is being built. Oh, I don't mean *this*, I don't mean *Jenny's,* but the building, the building's already under construction.' The professor laughed softly. 'Though they would have done better to use Jenny's plans. I told McTelligent.' McTelligent was the name of the head of the firm of architects, the one Losey was going to speak to. 'Not only more beautiful but more cost-effective too. Do you know anything about materials?'

" 'I'm a surgeon,' Losey said.

" 'Then perhaps you'd be interested in these,' and showed him sketches of the new operating theaters. 'What's your professional opinion?

" 'I'm sorry,' the professor of architecture said, 'I didn't quite hear you.'

"Because he was swallowing so hard. Because his pulses were pounding. Because his heart rate had taken away his voice.

" 'I said they're revolutionary,' he said.

"He showed Jenny the chairman's letter. And even made his proposal in front of Nora. Because he knew they were friends, and because he *certainly* knew a thing or two about the strategy of seduction and that's what he was up to now. So he asked in front of Nora.

" 'You can see how it is,' he told her. 'My wife's flunking out.'

" 'I understand, Mr. Losey. Some of these things are awfully difficult. I guess I didn't pay enough attention to the basics. I should never have agreed to be her tutor. I'd like to return the money.'

" 'Are you saying Nora's too stupid to learn? I thought you were friends.'

" 'We *are* friends,' Jenny said. 'We *are* friends. Nora knows that. She's my best friend,' she said. 'I love Nora. I feel terrible about this.'

"Which was what he'd counted on of course.

"And slapped the side of his head. 'Do you think I showed you that letter because we want to *fire* you? On the contrary, Miss Greener. What you say makes perfect sense. She *does* need more preparation in the basics. That's what the fellow says in his letter. That's what we're asking of you. We don't want to fire you. We want to hire you full time. It was silly of Nora to think you could do the job on an hourly basis.'

" 'Full time?' she said. 'I'm going to school myself.'

"She was a scholarship student, from Cape Girardeau, Missouri. He'd learned that at the university. But all he really had to do was look at her. Her frumpy clothes and hick hairdo. Her country girl's astonishment in his gorgeous house.

" 'Of course you are,' he said. 'I'm gone much of the time. Nora gets lonely. She doesn't complain much, but she does.'

" 'I know,' Jenny said.

" 'Then you know she'd like you to move in with us. You're the architect. You can see for yourself we've plenty of room. We'd still pay you, of course. I couldn't think of it otherwise.' He'd been prepared to name an outrageous sum, almost as much as the fee he said he'd pay that now not-so-hypothetical architect to design a house, but something in Jenny's face told him she'd turn that down flat and walk out. So he actually lowered the hourly rate she'd already been getting. 'And your own work comes first. That goes without saying. But if you could see Nora through . . .'

"Nora didn't speak out because she figured it was her only chance. Thinking—I don't know—thinking, The *bastard,* the *bastard!* Maybe he could make me a hairdresser, a hostess in restaurants, a girl at the checkout, a clerk in a store. Thinking, Maybe she *can* see me through. Maybe she's the only one who will.

"He never so much as kissed her. (The family, the family comes first.) He never said anything out of the way. If he ever tried to get fresh I don't think she knew it. At the time knew it.

"One night, after dinner, Nora was in the kitchen. Jenny was clearing the dessert dishes. She had leaned down to take Losey's and he put his hand on her arm. Not even his hand. Some fingers. 'I've seen your sketches of the operating rooms,' he said in a low voice so his wife wouldn't hear. 'I think you may have some respect for my judgment as a surgeon. They're wonderful. The best I've ever seen,' he told her passionately.

"So that's where it stands.

"She's still on probation but her grades have improved. She'll never make Dean's List but she's still hanging on. But she isn't a dummy. She can read the handwriting on the wall. Both of them can. All three of them. She may even get her degree, but that's not what it says.

"He's in greater demand than ever but he doesn't travel so much as he used to. He turns down invitations. He stays home more. He's writing, publishing papers. He likes to sit in his study while the women are off in theirs. (He's converted one of their six bedrooms into a study for Jenny.) He likes to sit there, thinking about the future, thinking about the time she graduates next spring and the divorce has gone through.

"Thinking, They can do wonders with hair. With exercise and cosmetics. With diet, *haute couture*. Under their tans, behind their high fashions and starved, high-relief cheekbones, those broads in Barbados I went down on and vice versa might have been frumpy as Jenny once. As inexperienced as she probably is in bed.

"Because he really *is* a surgeon. Anything can be excised. Anything put back. He can sew on your fingerprints, he can take out your germs. Everything is remediable. It better be. Everything is remediable or your patient dies. She'll just need some coaching.

"It's a griefhouse, George. It's a goddamn griefhouse. I can almost hear them, make out the tripled, separated weepings of the house's tripartite griefs. Grieving for status, grieving for lifestyle. Grieving for bastards, for fops of collusion, for paste assholes. Mourning best friends and all fall guys."

Messenger paused. Then said what George expected him to say. "The horror, the horror, hey Mills?"

"Yes," George Mills said. "Yes!"

Messenger, enhanced, was sitting in Mills's living room weeping when George came in.

"Hey," George Mills said, "hey now. Hey don't."

Cornell looked up, surprised. He wiped his eyes with his fingers, licked them. "You know that's delicious?" he said.

"I know," Mills said.

"You lick your tears, George?"

"I chew my nails. I nibble the hair on my arms."

"Really?"

"Millses have always had pica." (Because he was interested now. Because Messenger had him. As he'd had Louise the first time he opened his mouth. And whatever might become of his

467

own battered case, he was interested in theirs. Enough to talk, to tell him of his.)

"In me under control, arrested, marked down. But, you know, still there. I still have a piece of this sweet tooth in my mouth."

"This sweet tooth, George?"

"A loose appetite sort of."

"Clay? You eat chalk?"

"The flavor's okay. I don't care for the texture."

"You're a connoisseur."

"Certain flowers, the stems on fruit. Newsprint. Erasers."

"I chewed erasers," Cornell said.

"No no, from the blackboards. I'd lick dust from their fur."

"Better than a connoisseur. You're a gourmet."

"I sucked on stones. When I could get it I put sand in my mouth."

"When you could get it?"

"You know, still wet. After the tide had gone out. A sand bouillabaisse. When I was a kid. Most all of this when I was a kid. Not now not so much."

"You don't do this stuff now?"

"I watch what I eat. Sometimes I binge. You know, fall off the wagon."

"You're not kidding me now?"

"No. I'm not kidding."

"Well, what do you eat?"

"I eat cigarette ash. I like to get the juice out of cotton."

"Are you kidding me, George?"

"No," he said, "I already said. Not now not so much."

"A meat-and-potatoes man," Messenger said.

"Only the gristle, only the peels."

Messenger watched him through his still red, still puffy eyes.

"Rust," George said wistfully, "I used to like the taste of rust. And rotten, discolored wood from trees fallen in forests."

"That's good?"

"Brown water in puddles. Autumn leaves like a breakfast cereal. Sweat like a summer drink."

"Insects? Dead birds?"

George Mills made a face. "No, of course not," he said. "Things only declined from the ordinary sweets and seasonings, things gone off, the collapsed cheeses, sour as laundry."

"You're pulling my leg," Messenger said.

468

"This is how I used to be. It's mostly all changed. I like stale bread. I don't really mind it when the milk turns, the butter. A hint of the rancid like a touch of hors d'œuvre." And then, already missing his own old straight man's circumstances, "You were crying."

"Me?" Messenger said, his nose and eyes still a little swollen. "Hell no."

"You were. You were crying."

"I was making lunch."

"Is it Harve?" George Mills asked. "Were you crying about Harve?"

"Harve's my kid," Messenger said. "I don't talk about my kid."

"All right," George Mills said.

"Fourteen his last birthday," Messenger said.

"Yes," George Mills said, and sat back.

"He doesn't get the point of knock-knock jokes."

"No," George Mills said, and felt stirrings of appetite, his pica curiosity making soft growls in his head.

"I'm no woodsman," he said. "I can't tie a fly, I don't know my bait."

"No," George Mills said.

"I can't build a fire or assemble a toy. I haven't much, you know, lore. I was never much good at the father-son sports. We don't go out camping. I don't take him to circuses or watch the parades. We don't tan shirtless in bleachers or root for the teams. He doesn't sip from my beer. I can't name the stars, I don't show him the sky. We didn't play catch. I never taught him to ride. We didn't do float trips or go to the zoo.

"I like to wrestle, show him the Dutch rub, Indian burns, but the kid thinks I'm angry. His eyes fill with tears.

"I don't, you know, I don't set an example. I don't teach him, well, morals. Whatever it is they say has to start in the home—respect, I don't know, good manners, how you have to appreciate the value of a dollar, that sort of thing—never started in ours."

Uncle Joe, Mills thought, he means Uncle Joe.

"Fourteen years old and he doesn't get the point of damned knock-knock jokes!

"I thought we'd go on a trip. This was a couple of years ago. I thought I'd take him on a trip. Just the two of us. We'd just load up the old bus . . . I mean the car, we'd drive in the car. We'd stay in motels. We'd order from room service. I had to promise we'd stay in a place with a Holidome."

Mills looked at him.

"You know. One of those places, they're enclosed, like a penny arcade. It has a swimming pool, it has a whirlpool and sauna, it has indoor-outdoor carpeting, it has swings and seesaws, computer games."

Mills nodded.

"I had to promise. Otherwise he wouldn't come. I had to promise to give him money for the machines. I had to promise he could choose what we'd watch on TV.

"We wouldn't wait for a weekend. We'd make it special, go during school.

"I woke him at six. 'We'll catch breakfast on the highway,' I told him. He was very cranky. He went to sleep in the back.

" 'Harve,' I said, 'we're crossing the river, you're missing the sunrise. Wake up, sleepyhead.'

" 'Why'd you wake me? I'm nauseous, I may have to throw up.'

" 'Anything you want, scout,' I told him in the restaurant when the waitress came over. 'What do you want?'

"He was angry as hell. He can't read a menu. His mother says, 'You want a hamburger, Harve? You want french fries and Coke, son?' Me, I don't do that. I want him to sound it out. He gets so impatient.

" 'What'll it be?' the waitress said, and I gave her my order. 'What'll it be?' she said to the boy.

" 'Can you come back? I'm not ready.' He glared at me.

" 'Anything you want, Harve. What do you want?'

"When she brought me my breakfast she turned to the kid. 'Have you made up your mind yet?' and stood poised with her pad.

" 'Yeah, I'm not hungry. I can't eat a thing.'

"When I paid at the counter he pointed to candy, he pointed to gum.

" 'Why don't you come up in front, Harve? Why don't you put that airplane down and sit here with Dad? Goddamn it, Harve, I'm not your chauffeur.' But we drove on in silence, the both of us sore.

"We'd gone a hundred miles maybe, Harve back there sulking, me sulking in front. He'd make sound-effect noises. With his planes, with his cars. A mimic of engines, impressions of speed. He'd imitate crashes, do disasters, explosions, ships lost at sea.

" 'Knock knock,' I said when we'd driven another hour. 'Knock knock, Harve.'

"And stopped for lunch. Harve not glaring at me over his menu this time, Harve equable, placid, almost benign. Don't I know that kid? Because I'd figured it out in the car, knew what he'd do, knew he'd figured it out too—don't I know him? don't I?—knew it wasn't even me he was mad at anymore. No, angry at himself for not thinking of it at breakfast. So I *knew* what he'd do. When the waitress came over I was ready for him.

" 'Have you decided?'

" 'Well, no,' I said, 'actually I haven't. Why don't you ask the boy?'

"And, triumphant, looked at him, saw the smile leave his face. No, not leave it, but hanging there crooked, like make-up mismanaged, like cosmetics deranged. But I had to hand it to him. I did. I had to take off my hat. I could have kissed him.

" 'Two eggs,' he said slowly, remembering, getting it perfect, 'scrambled. Orange juice. Toast. Coffee,' he said.

" 'Wouldn't you rather have milk, Harve?'

" 'Sure.' He grinned. 'Milk.'

" 'Sounds good,' I told her. 'Bring me the same.'

"We stopped off for ice cream, stopped off for Coke. When we filled up in Kentucky I gave Harve three bucks. He offered me candy when he came out with the bag. I told him, 'No thanks, Harve.' You know what kids eat. Crap from the space age—— sugar fuels, fizz. Candy with noises, a licorice that whistles, a licorice that whips. Panes of sugar so brittle like cracked glass in your mouth. Pop drops and doodads, candy like toys. 'Your mother would kill me, she saw what you got.' I made him promise to save some, not to fill himself up.

"He was sitting up front now. More like it, you know? We got into Nashville just after five.

" 'This is Nashville,' I told him, 'where they make all the country-and-western records. Nashville is famous.'

" 'Sure,' Harve said, 'Motown.'

" 'No, Motown's in Michigan, Motown's Detroit.'

" 'Where they got all the niggers.'

" 'Christ, where do you get that stuff? Your mother doesn't talk like that, I certainly don't. Black people are just like everybody else.'

" 'They're poor,' Harve said.

" 'Yes,' I said, 'many of them, many of them are.'

" 'Chicken George, Kunte Kinte. Slavery's bad.'

" 'That's right, Harve.'

" 'That's why they kill us. That's why they steal. That's why they

471

set fires and rape old white ladies and take our bicycles. That's why they're lazy and cheat on welfare.'

" 'Harve, that's bullshit. You're a bigot, you know that?'

"We were downtown now, stopped at a light. Some people were waiting on line for a bus.

" 'Your *mama!*' Harve called from the car.

" 'Roll up that window! *Goddamn it, Harve!*' " George Mills was giggling. "We could have been *killed,*" Messenger said. "We could have been jabbed in the eyes with their hatpins, we could have been slashed in the guts with their shivs." Enhanced, he began to laugh. "They could have pulled us out of the car and OD'd our asses with bad skag. They could've done us an injury with their Saturday Night Specials. Oh Jesus!" He wiped his eyes, licked his fingers. "Delicious," he said. "Weeping delicious and laughter delicious too. All, all of it delicious."

"Did you find the place?" Mills asked.

"The Holidome?"

George nodded.

"Oh sure," Cornell said. "But we didn't order from room service. Harve decided he'd rather eat in the restaurant.

"I was ready for him. I mean things had gone better. He'd been sitting up front with me, and cooled it on the sound track. Things had gone better, but I was ready for him. Before she even came over I laid down the ground rules.

" 'All right, Harve,' I told him, 'that was a cute one you pulled at lunch. I give you that one. Anything you want, anything.'

" 'Anything?' he said. He had this sly, shit-eating grin on his face.

" 'Absolutely,' I said, and dropped the big one. *'But you can't have eggs!* You can't have toast or juice. You can't wait for me to order and tell her "Same here." What I did this afternoon was a gesture. Ordering eggs, ordering juice. Do you understand me, Harve? It was a little salute from me to you because you used your head and you tricked me. That was smart, Harve, but it's not helping you read. Sound it out. When the girl comes over and gives us the menus we'll just tell her we need more time. Sound it out. I don't care how long you take, Harve.'

" 'Not out loud,' he said. 'I'm ashamed.'

" 'Not out loud,' I agreed. 'To yourself. Whatever you want.'

"So when the waitress came over and left us the menus he knew where he stood. I have to admit. He certainly studied the thing. He touched each letter with his finger as if the menu were printed in a kind of Braille.

"She asked if we were ready.

" 'How about it, Harve? Are you?'

" 'You go first,' he said.

" 'All right,' I said, 'sure.' I drew it out, chose, changed my mind, talked it over with the waitress, asking in Opryland, 'Is your swordfish fresh, your poached salmon?' Not wanting it even if it was, you understand, just giving Harve time, not wanting to embarrass him in public. Just giving him time, letting him rehearse whatever it was he'd so painfully sounded out. Harve finally looked up. I smiled at the waitress.

" 'Shrimp cocktail to start, please. Bring lime, not a lemon. You can get a wedge from the bartender,' I told her decisively. 'Kansas City strip. Medium rare. Baked potato. Have the chef remove the aluminum foil in the kitchen. You have a house dressing?' She nodded. 'House dressing. Coffee. We'll see about dessert later.' I looked over at my son. 'The ball's in your court, Harve,' I told him.

" 'Milk,' he said. 'I'll have milk.'

"I was staring at him, but sure enough there it was, his finger under the beverages at 'Milk,' pressing his finger down on the page, holding on to the word as if, if he let go, it would take him forever to find it again.

" 'Anything for starters? What for a main course?' the waitress asked. Harve looked over at me.

" 'The lady wants to know if you feel up to an appetizer, Harve. She's waiting for your decision vis-à-vis the entree.'

" 'Milk,' he said, 'just milk.'

"The waitress looked at him sympathetically. 'Too much Opryland, sweetie?' she asked. 'You swallow too much chlorine in the Holidome?'

"Harve shrugged.

" 'Where you from, darlin'?'

" 'St. Louis,' Harve said.

" 'You drive all that distance with your daddy today?'

"Harve nodded.

" 'That's a long drive,' she said. 'No wonder your tummy's all sour. How about two nice soft-boiled eggs and some unbuttered toast? The chef don't like to do that this time of night, but maybe if I tell him it's for you he'll make an exception. Tell you what, if he puts up a stink I'll do it myself.'

473

"Now I really have to give him credit. He could have made me the hard guy, I might have had to take this fall. I mean all he had to do was look over at me for permission, for God's sake. Because I wouldn't have given it to him. He knew that. I *wouldn't* have given it to him. I'd have looked like a shit in that nice waitress's eyes with her damned Southern hospitality. There I am, George. Practically praying to God that the kid wouldn't do it, that he'd start making his F-15 noises again instead, that he'd dive-bomb, strafe the fucking civilians, drop the big one on the niggers, anything. But I have to hand it to him. I *do*. He never took his eyes off that waitress's face. He never even blinked them. And when he spoke, which was at once, he was as southernly hospitable as the waitress herself, as gracious and charming, giving it back to her in spades who couldn't read a menu but who'd picked up in five minutes at the registration desk the actual idioms and inflections, perfect pitch not just for machinery but for the United States of America, maybe for the whole world.

" 'No, ma'am, no thank you. I don't really crave eggs this evening. I'll just have that milk if it's all the same to you and that chef don't mind pouring it.'

" 'Sure, sugar,' she said, and smiled at him and scrambled his hair with her hand. 'Why do they ever have to grow up?' she asked when I gave back her menu.

"And me thinking the same, Mills. Why do they? Why do they have to grow up? Why do they have to learn to read? And had already relented, and wanted to thank him, say, 'That was nice, Harve.' But thinking, No, talk is too cheap, I won't spoil it by saying anything. Thinking, The kid must be starving. After the food comes, after the food comes and she's left us alone I'll take a bite and sigh and tell him I'm not as hungry as I thought I was, and push my plate across the table at him. Thinking, Yes. That's *just* what I'll do.

"I couldn't even look at him yet, Mills. I couldn't even look at him I loved him so much. I didn't want to see his fine hair, his slight body, his soft, perfect skin.

"She brought my shrimp cocktail. She brought Harve his milk.

"I arranged the napkin in my lap and lifted my shrimp fork. I didn't squirt lime on the shrimp because I didn't know if Harve would like it. Most people don't. I still couldn't look at him. I heard a kind of noise, Harve's ventriloquized conversation, but low, almost under his breath, sounds no one could spell. Which even I realized was perhaps why he made them. I didn't recognize this one. It wasn't, well, mechanical. It didn't have that special gift of speed and divided,

474

juggernauted air he was so good at. It didn't rumble like avalanche or crackle like fire. I couldn't recognize it at all. It had none of the crisp rasp and bristle of Harve's natural disasters, forests coming down, the earth quaking like a stutterer. They weren't the nasal trills of siren and emergency. It wasn't the rapid fire of war. It was a kind of long-drawn-out sliding, a soft rubbing noise like something being slipped out of a package.

" 'Here, Harve,' I said, 'these are good, but you eat the rest. I'm not nearly as hun—'

"It was the paper bag. It was the paper bag with the candy I'd made him promise not to eat all at once. It was the paper bag he was sliding out of his pocket, that he overturned on the table letting the bars and confections rain down on the cloth like bombs from a bomb bay and then covered with his napkin so the waitress wouldn't see it when she came by with my steak.

" 'You put that—'

" 'You said I could eat anything I want. I even asked you. I said "Anything?" and you said I couldn't have eggs.'

"Because he was waiting, setting me up. Because he knew, you see. Knew in Kentucky when he spent his three bucks. Because he was ready for me before I was ever even close to being ready for him. Because he's hawk through and through. Because that megaton noise, those sounds that he makes, are war games, maneuvers, some worst-case scenario he has by heart in his head.

" 'If you're so smart,' I taunted, 'if you're so smart why can't you read? Knock knock. Hey, knock knock, Harve.' "

Messenger's hands were shaking. "Do you get this? Do you see what I mean?" he asked George. "Big deal I don't take him hunting, big deal I never taught him to fish.

"His suits," Messenger said suddenly, leaning toward Mills, fervent. "The power of my father dressed! His suits. Their ample lapels, their double-breasted plenitude. The fabrics like a gabardine energy, their sharkskin suppleness, the silk like a spit-and-polish swank. His trousers riding his hips like holsters and giving off not an illusion of bagginess but some natty, rakish quality of excess, bolts, cloth to burn. Full at the calves, full at the shins, and spilling over his shiny shoetops, fabricrolling over him like water. He stood in his clothing like a man swaggering in the sea. His suits, my father's suits, the power of my father dressed. The fierce force of that middle-aged man!

"In shorts, George. In pajamas the same. His thighs spread in

475

swim trunks, on beach chairs, in hammocks, his long old balls hanging out. An old testicle prophet my pop!"

"I don't—— "

"Did he teach me engines? Did he teach me to drive? You pass
on what you can. He sold costume jewelry. He taught me a gross is
a dozen dozen. A hundred forty-four rhinestone necklaces, a hundred
forty-four pairs of earrings. Term insurance a better deal than straight
life. That you pay cash you lose the interest on your money. His
traveling salesman's weights and measures."

"I don't—— "

"Wait, wait. I gave Harve five dollars to play the video games.
He was back in an hour with a kid half his age.

" 'This is my friend, Dad. This is my dad.'

" 'Hi.' The kid giggled. 'Let's splash my sister, let's go run
around.'

" 'We found the secret tunnel,' Harve said, 'where they keep the
machinery. Where they keep all the chlorine, where they keep the
equipment that works the whole pool.'

" 'Mister, Harve turned off the lights. He shut off the games.'

" 'Could you step out for a minute? I want to speak to my son.'

" 'The janitor's after us, that guy who makes change.'

" 'Please,' I said, 'little boy.'

" 'I'll be in the tunnel,' the kid said to Harve. 'Unless I'm captured.'

" 'Don't get captured, Pete. Gas him. Unscrew the caps off the
chlorine.'

" 'You know how old that kid is?' I thundered. 'Christ, Harve,
he's *six!* There must be half a dozen boys out there your own age.
Why choose babies to play with?'

" 'He's eight.'

" 'He's a fucking baby. He's crazy as you are.'

" 'I'm not crazy,' Harve said. 'Don't call me crazy.'

" 'I don't understand you. Why can't you find someone closer to
your age?'

" 'They're boring.'

" '*You're* boring! All you do is run around and make trouble. All
you do is run around and act wild.' He started to leave. 'Forget it.
You're not going out. Where's my change from the machines? You're
not stuffing yourself with any more candy.' He threw down some
quarters. 'Pick those up! Pick them up!'

"He undressed in the bathroom. When he came out he switched

channels. A movie with airplanes, another with spies. He flipped back and forth during commercials. He bit off his nails. It wasn't even eight-thirty.

" 'Mom packed your suit, Harve. Want to go for a swim?'

"He wouldn't speak to me.

" 'Want to go for a ride, Harve? See what Nashville is like?'

"Paula says I overreact.

" 'Harve, are you hungry? They could send in fried chicken, a burger, some fries. What do you say, Harve? How does that sound? Harve, answer me, damn it, I'm talking to you! Harve? *Harve?*'

"I'm not his enemy, Mills. He thinks I'm his enemy. I love watching television with him. I love it when he falls asleep next to me.

" 'I'm watching a movie. You took back the quarters. I can't eat what I want or play with my friend.'

"I snapped off the TV.

" 'Sulk now I'll smack you, I'll break you in half!'

" 'I'm watching my program. I suppose I can't watch my program?'

"When I sat down on the edge of his bed he moved away. I pulled the chair over from the desk. 'All right,' I said, 'I'm going to tell you some jokes.'

"I told him the one about Johnny Fuckerfaster. I told him the one about the three kinds of turds—— mustard, custard and you, you dumb shit. I told him book-and-author jokes—— *The Panther's Revenge* by Claude Balls, *The Spot on the Mattress* by Mister Completely. I told him all the jokes I could remember from when I was Harve's age, the age of the kid Harve had brought to the room. I did maybe twenty minutes. He looked at me as if I was crazy.

"Then I told him the one about the whore and the rooster and I had him, really had him. He screamed, he howled, he doubled over with laughter. There were tears in his eyes, snot ran from his nose.

" 'Tell it again.'

" 'All right,' I said, 'what's the difference between a rooster and a whore?'

" 'I don't know, Daddy. What?' He was already laughing.

" 'The rooster says cock-a-doodle-doo. The whore says any cock'll do.'

" 'One more time. The last. Please, Dad, I promise.'

" 'I've already told it twice.'

" 'Go ahead. Ask me.'

" 'What's the difference, Harve, between a rooster and a whore?'

477

" 'I know, I know,' he said. He was waving his hand.

" 'Harve?' I called on him, Mills. I called on the kid.

" 'The whore says—— '

" 'The rooster says, Harve.'

" 'The rooster says—— '

"Mills, I was praying. I swear to you. *Praying.* I was holding my breath.

" '—cock-a-doodle-doo. The whore says—'

"My mouth, my lips were moving. The way they move when you're feeding a baby, the way you might breathe by the guy that they work on that they pull from the sea.

" '—*any* cock'll do!'

"I screamed, I howled, I doubled over with laughter. There were tears in my eyes, snot ran from my nose. The kid thought he was Bob Hope, the Three Stooges. I thought so myself. I praised his delivery. I made over his timing.

" 'Again,' he said, 'let me try it again.'

"I let him try it again. He was letter perfect.

" 'Letter perfect,' I told him.

("Because they've got to have confidence. Isn't that what they say? Because they've got to have confidence, believe in themselves? Because they must be encouraged, ain't that the drill?")

There were tears in Messenger's eyes now too. And now he was weeping openly. Snot ran from his nose.

" 'I want to tell a different one this time.'

" 'Go ahead, Harve.' "

George Mills could barely understand him.

" 'Once more?'

" 'Not that one again. Tell another.'

" 'Please, Dad, I promise.'

" 'All right, but this is the last time.'

" 'Can I tell it again?'

" 'Harve, you promised.'

" 'Claude Balls,' he snickered. 'Mister Completely,' he roared. 'Do I have to go to sleep now?'

" 'Of course not,' I said. But I got into bed. I turned off the bedlamp.

"I could hear him giggling. 'Will you tell me more jokes, Dad?' Harve asked in the dark. 'Please?'

" 'Wouldn't you rather watch television?'

" 'I'd rather tell jokes.'

478

" 'All right,' I told him, and waited till he'd calmed down. 'Knock knock,' I said.

" 'Who's there?' Harve asked me.

"Shit, George, you pass on what you can."

Again Mills had difficulty understanding him.

"I said it's the confidence," Messenger said. "I'm crying for the confidence, all that Special Olympics confidence, all that short-range, small-time, short-change, small-scale, short-lived, short-shrift, small-potato, small-beer fucking confidence. I'm weeping for the confidence."

"Hi, Lulu," Messenger said, pecking her cheek. He'd taken to kissing her when he greeted her, giving her hugs. Mills knew Cornell was attracted to his wife. He'd seen him negotiate proximity, caught him watch her do housework, wash windows, scrub the floors on her knees. He touched her arm when he spoke, he patted her shoulder. Mills knew he had some vagrant fix on her, that she popped into his head, that he speculated about her as he soaped himself in showers, as he jerked off in bed, as he came in his wife. The Louise of Messenger's imaginings who might finally actually have had a thing or two to do with the real Louise. She may have appealed to him as a woman of great sexual reserves, the farmer's grown daughter, the unsatisfied wife. There was much talk of needs. Women spoke openly on radio call-in shows of their sexuality, asking the experts, showing, even proclaiming, a side of their natures that had not been known. Mature women, ordinary women, the women you saw in supermarkets, the women you saw in discount department stores, the women you saw in the streets. Not theatrical beings, not movie stars, glamor girls, chippies in bars. Not great beauties whose beauty was only some cautionary flag of the genital—Mills had always had his theories—but housewives, mothers and matrons you'd have thought had calmed down. It was this sense of her energies, undepleted and compounding that attracted Cornell. He could probably have had her. She probably would have let him, though he doubted she had. He was glad of his grace.

"The horror, the horror, hey Mills?" Messenger greeted George cheerfully. And Mills had forgotten whose turn it was, who was up for today. Because they might almost have been in *his* repertoire now, his bumper crop company, his cache of familiars. They could have been in the inventory, the muster, the record. Not forebears but precursors. Not that fat trousseau of antecedents, that thick portfolio

479

of kin, but a sort of harbinger. They *might* have been Millses, but cousins, say, in-laws this or that many times removed. Grateful for the information he could take in with no view of ever having to render it. And if he asked questions, how they were making out, what they were up to, he asked with an expansive detachment, a loose, uncommitted laze. As you might question a barber or talk on a train. He wasn't indifferent. He was just glad of his grace.

"Well," Messenger said, dropping down on the sofa, "it's gone, the car's gone. I was over there yesterday, I drove by today. It's gone. The little puddle of litter has been swept away. I think something's up."

"Max and Ruth," George said. "The ones who live in that car." They *might* have been Millses. He was that certain of whom Messenger was speaking.

"You know they take a paper?" Messenger said. "I don't know how they got the guy to agree to deliver it, but they take the paper. They keep up."

"Are you going to tell us about people who live in a car, Cornell?" Louise asked.

"Max and Ruth? I don't know a thing about Max and Ruth. No one does. Max and Ruth are a mystery. All I know is their car's gone. Something's happening. I'd bet on it. They keep up."

Two days later he was back. "He's in disgrace," Messenger said pleasantly from his unreachable enhancement, the fleeting grace that made him kin.

"Sam Glazer," George Mills said.

"Look," Cornell said, "I shouldn't be telling you this stuff. I know George has an interest, that's why I do it."

"I'm interested, Cornell," Louise said.

"No, I mean he has to make up his mind. Decide which way to go. It's only rumors anyway. No one's talking, least of all Sam. Even the Meals-on-Wheelers are in the dark about this one. It's very hush-hush. You'd need a fucking clearance to get to the bottom of this thing. Actually, I wasn't the first to notice the car was gone. Jenny Greener mentioned it last week. I was in the neighborhood so I checked it out. Hell, it's all neighborhood anyway, ain't it? Three or four blocks or the next county over. The way I figure it's *all* neighborhood."

Yes, Mills thought. Yes.

"Probably nothing will happen till the end of the term. But nobody's talking. This is just, you know, dispatches, news from the front. Buzz and scuttlebutt. You'll have to take it from there, George. You'd have to start from that premise."

"What does he mean, George?" Louise said.

George hadn't heard her. He was watching Cornell.

"What's known for certain is that the chancellor gave this party for the board of trustees. What's known for certain is the guest list. The trustees of course, the higher-ups in the administration—the provost and deans, a handful of chairmen from the important departments. All the wives and husbands. One or two coaches, even some students—— the editor of the campus newspaper, the president of the student council, kids like that."

"Harry Claunch Sr.," George Mills said.

"You heard this story, George?" Messenger said.

"Go on," Mills said, not just interested now but, as Messenger had said, with an interest.

"What's known for certain is the menu."

"The menu?"

"Melon and prosciutto," Messenger said. "Salmon mousse. Sorbet. Provimi veal with artichoke sauce. Fiddlehead fern as a veggie and cold fresh lingonberry soup for dessert. Piesporter Gold Tropchen was the white wine, a '70 Cheval Blanc was the red. They didn't sit down to dinner, you understand. This was buffet the servants brought round."

"How do you know all this?" George Mills asked.

"The editor of the student paper ran an editorial. He won't be asked back but what the hell, he's graduating."

"We used to serve fiddlehead," Louise said. "We used to do salmon mousse."

"In the school cafeteria?" Cornell said.

"Sure," Louise said, "at the end of the month. We did all sorts of gourmet meals. It's how we saved money. The dietician would spend thirty or forty dollars on this fancy food. She knew darn well the kids wouldn't touch it."

Messenger shook his head. "That's truly astonishing, Lulu."

"It was a trick of the trade," Louise said modestly.

"What happened? What's known for certain?" Mills asked impatiently.

"I've got Georgie's attention," Messenger said.

"You've got my attention too, Cornell," Louise said.

"I hope so, Lulu," Messenger said. "All right," he said. He

481

turned to George Mills. "Nothing's known for certain. I already told you."

"The car is gone. Where's it parked now?"

Messenger shrugged.

"Did you think to call the paper boy?"

"Hey," Messenger said, "that's an idea. No," he said, "he delivers to a license plate. We'd never be able to track them down."

"What's all this about?" Louise asked.

"Sam Glazer's been fired," George Mills said. "He's lost his job."

"Offered to resign," Messenger said.

"Asked to resign," Mills said.

"You could be right. His friends say offered."

Because they were bargaining now, haggling. Negotiating over fact like a rug in the bazaar.

"None of this came from that other paper boy," Mills said, "the one that edits the student paper?"

"He published the guest list, he published the menu."

"The kid sounds like a go-getter. Why do you suppose he'd stop there?"

"Shit, I don't know, George. That's not even important. They can come down pretty hard on these kids if they have to. What you have to understand is power, campus politics. Take my word for it, George. I'm the professor here."

"I'm the butler," Mills said. "No," he said, "all you have to understand is that guest list. He wasn't there."

"Who?"

"The paper boy."

"Of course he was there."

"For the meat and the fish. For the soup for dessert. He wasn't there *then.*"

"When?"

"When he was asked to resign. When he did whatever it was Claunch said he did and then nailed him for. Practically nobody was."

"Some butler," Messenger said. "No one may leave before the king. A lot *you* know."

"The king gave the party. It was the king's own house."

"Yes?" Messenger said.

"Because it works in reverse. Because that's protocol too. Ask, what'shisname, Grant."

"So the students would have left first? Is that what you're saying?"

"That's right," Mills said.

"Then the chairmen and coaches?"

"That's right."

"Then the lesser deans. The dean of the night school, the dean of the—"

"That's right."

"No," Messenger said. "The provost outranks him. According to your own protocols he'd have been on his way out before the provost, before the trustees and all those wives."

"That's right," George Mills said. And felt as Wickland must have felt when he'd shown him his sister in the square in Cassadaga during their seance forty years earlier. As he'd felt himself when he'd shown Wickland Jack Sunshine's father and the fourteen-year-old girl with the withered body of an old woman who'd given Jack Sunshine his height.

"But if he'd already gone home . . ."

"I didn't say that," George Mills said.

Messenger looked at him. "Been on his way out?"

"That's right," Mills said.

"All right," Messenger said impatiently, "been on his way out. What difference does . . ." He stared at Mills.

"That's right," George said.

"You know you've got a nasty mind?" his friend said. "You know you're one heavy-duty son of a bitch?"

"What?" Louise asked. "What? Are you following any of this, George?"

"Following? Shit, Lulu honey, he's leading the goddamn band." He put his arm around her shoulder. "Nothing like this is in the black buzz," Messenger said. "I mean this isn't the way they're talking on the Rialto. What they're saying up there is much milder. 'Offered to resign' is the worst of it."

"What are they saying?"

"Well, it's a joke really. It started when it got out that Max and Ruth had taken their car away from the front of his house."

"Yes," Mills said.

"Max and Ruth? You're crazy. You actually think they were invited?"

"No," George Mills said.

"They'd have been thrown out. They'd have called the cops on them if they dared crash that dinner party. And don't tell me they helped serve. They don't have uniforms. Even if they did, do you think

483

the chancellor would let them? Run a downer on his guests by having those two characters get close enough to pass out actual food? People who live in a fucking jalopy, a beat-up, stale-aired old clunker that probably looked used when it came off the goddamn assembly line? Who take baths in the rest room sinks of gas stations? Moochers with freeload cookie crumbs in their scalp and bits of old poetry-reading cheese stuck to the creases of their clothing? With Gallo like mouth-wash on their breath? Jesus, George, they'd be lucky if they got as far as the back door for a handout."

"That's right," George said.

Messenger was stunned. "Is that what you think? Jesus, is *that* what you think?"

"Is what what he thinks?" Louise said.

"Your husband just said they were in the kitchen eating above-their-station leftovers when it happened. He says the chancellor's residence is so huge that they had to have been shouting loud enough for Max and Ruth to hear every word all the way in the back of the house. He says that whatever it was they heard must have been so damning it scared even them off, that they just climbed into their house and drove it away and never returned."

"He said that?"

"That's right," Messenger said. "Yes," he said, and turned back to George, "but how would they even know about that dinner party?"

George Mills smiled at him.

"All right," Messenger said, "so he was dressed to kill, so he had on his best bib and tucker. All right, so it was the dinner party hour when they saw him come out of his front door and get into his car. All right, so they followed him. That still doesn't explain what he was supposed to have done."

"You never told me what they say he's done."

"Well they don't *know,*" Messenger said. "The usual stuff when a dean offers his resignation."

"Is told to resign."

"You said 'asked.' "

"You said 'disgrace.' "

"All right, all right. That he's made some mistakes, been high-handed with tenure, let good people get away, worked the buddy system, kept people on that he likes, allowed salary discrepancies between favored and unfavored departments to get out of hand, not been aggressive enough raiding other schools, made too many ene-mies."

x

484

"Has he done these things?"

"I don't know. Some. Any dean does some. It's not an easy job. Sam's record is as good as most. He's only been in the job a year. He wouldn't have had time to do all of them."

"He lost his wife," Mills said. "They're gentlemen. They wouldn't have been shouting if he had."

"They're princes of industry," Messenger said. "Soft-spoken guys."

"That's right," Messenger said. "They'd have had to be outraged."

"It was the last week of August for God's sake. A mild, beautiful night."

"That's right."

"He wouldn't have had a topcoat with him. He wouldn't have had a raincoat. So what did he put it in? Tell me that."

George Mills looked disgusted.

"I wish someone would tell me what's going on," Louise said.

"Damn it, Lulu," Messenger said, "haven't you heard a word he's been saying? Your husband thinks Sam is a thief."

"He likes souvenirs."

"What do you suppose it was?"

"I don't know. Houses like that," Mills said dreamily, "it could be almost anything. Something with the university's crest, I suppose. A slim gold lighter. A pen. A letter opener. A paperweight or ashtray. Sugar tongs. Stationery even. Anything."

"And Claunch fingered him?"

"He never took his eyes off him," George Mills said. "He counted his drinks. He toted up the hors d'œuvres he ate."

"That's right," Messenger said.

"He hates him."

"That's right."

"Tell me about the will, Cornell."

"Jesus, George," Messenger said, "I have some loyalties here. I—"

And *that's* when Mills chose to play his China card. He stormed out of the house.

Leaving Louise and Messenger staring after him on the couch next to each other.

Because it wasn't a will she signed in Mexico but an *inter vivos* trust. Because she'd left no will. Because if she had there'd have been an instrument for the widower to set aside, renounce, by simply filing a paper, a paper, not even anything fine-sounding as an instrument. He could have written it on a scratch pad, on the back of his marriage license, and been awarded his widower's aliquot third. It was that *inter vivos* trust. Because if she left no will and had had the grace or just simple good conjugal sportsmanship to die intestate he wouldn't even have had to trouble himself about the scratch pad. Half the hereditament would have come to him by sheer right of descent and succession. Half, not a third. It was the numbers, it was the arithmetic.

Cornell figured Sam figured it had to be enmity. She was essentially a lazy woman. Cornell figured Sam figured she was jealous of his health. Hadn't it been held up to him on more than one occasion not that he was free of cancer while she carried hers to term like some malignant pregnancy, but that he'd been sane the whole eleven years she'd been nuts? So it *had* to be enmity. She was lazy. Intestacy wouldn't have caused her to lift a finger. But there were those numbers to deal with, the difference between that half and that third she was screwing him out of by lifting the finger, by painfully crabbing all her suffering fingers around the uncongenial Mexican motel pen and laboriously writing out the *inter vivos* trust that either her father or brother—Cornell figured Sam figured—had dictated to her over the phone and that left everything to the girls with Harry as trustee, and that she had to be at pains just to get the handwriting right, probably working from actual memory to recall the once free-flowing cursive, the idiosyncratic flights and loops of her own signature.

"I feel sorry for the guy," Cornell told Mills on the telephone. (He hadn't seen him since the night George had walked out of his home leaving Messenger alone with his wife.)

"Yes?"

"She put him through hoops. The hoops were on fire. There were prenuptial agreements, did you know that?"

"Prenuptial agreements," George Mills said evenly.

"He didn't have a pot to piss in. What was he? Some poor graduate student. Maybe he had a typewriter and a ream of paper to do his assignments on. Maybe he had a few dollars' worth of dictionaries and a handful of those composition manuals and examination copies they hand out to TA's to look over.

"The poor bastard was marrying big bucks. I told you. There were prenuptial agreements. He had to sign to go the distance. If the marriage broke up before they got through the first fifteen years he wouldn't get a penny. He was on probation, for Christ's sake."

"Yes," George Mills said.

"They were married seventeen years," Messenger said. "She did him anyway."

"Yes," George Mills said. He sounded distant even to himself. "What does he have to do now?"

"What do you mean?"

"To fight it. To break the trust."

"I don't know, George. I'm no lawyer."

"Victor's a lawyer," George Mills said. "Find out. Call me back."

"He says he's got three ways to go," Messenger said when he called back the next day. "If he can prove fraud, undue influence or mental incapacity."

"There was no undue influence," George Mills said.

"No," Messenger said slyly, "but there may have been fraud."

"I don't see it," Mills said.

"The prenuptial agreement, the numbers. If she left everything to the girls in a will he could set aside, he'd have taken a third, half if she left no will at all. He thinks it could be fraud because she didn't leave him *anything* to set aside. Not a bad will or a nonwill either. There was malice and intent. He served more than his time, those fifteen-year articles of apprenticeship. Those fifteen-year articles of apprenticeship and then some. He was entitled to his expectations."

"Thank you for your trouble," he said. "She was crazy," George Mills said flatly.

"It's good I'm enhanced," Messenger said. "I don't owe you shit. I never fucked your wife."

"I know that," George Mills said. "All you ever did was want to."

Messenger called again instead of coming over.

"You might as well have all the facts," he said.

"Yes?" George Mills said.

"Grant's dead."

"Mr. Glazer?" Mills said.

"Who's this?"

"George Mills," George Mills said.

"What is it?"

487

"I've been thinking about what you said."

"Yes?"

"It's my back, sir. I'm afraid what might happen to it this winter."

"Yes?"

"If that job in buildings and grounds is still open, I wouldn't be out in the weather."

"I'm not sure it's available," Sam Glazer said.

"That's too bad," Mills said. "Oh, Mr. Glazer?"

"What?"

"That senior partner called. After I spoke to you last? But I'm doing just what you said."

"Oh?"

"Yes sir."

"Good."

"I'm keeping an open mind."

"Look," Sam Glazer said, "I want to be frank."

"Sure," George Mills said, "me too. Absolutely."

"I'd be looking around for something else if I were you."

"I'm hanging in there," Mills said, hoarsely rushing the message into the mouthpiece. But at the other end the line had already gone dead.

He decided he would go in person. He wore his suit, the one he had worn to the funeral. He was going to take a hat he could hold in his hands but decided that would be too much. A receptionist passed his name in and in five minutes a young man Mills had never seen came out to greet him. The young man walked briskly over to where George was seated on the edge of a deep leather couch and stuck out his hand. Mills started to rise, but by pushing his handshake at him the young man managed to keep George off balance and shoved him further back into the couch.

"Good to meet you, sir," the young man said. "What can I do for you?" George Mills realized that the kid meant for him to state his business there in the outer office. He hesitated and the young man's smile became even wider. He's going to sit down next to me, George Mills thought. That's what happened. The young lawyer leaned toward him and lowered his voice. "They've painted my office," he said. "It's a relief to get away from those fumes for a minute." Mills smelled cologne. The receptionist smiled.

488

"I asked to see your boss," George Mills said. "My business is with your boss."

"Hey, pal, give me a break," the kid said. "Harvard '8o, editor of the *Law Review,* two summers clerking at the Supreme Court. Why do you want to make me feel so bad? Don't you think I can handle it?" The receptionist was grinning.

"This isn't a law thing," George Mills said. "It's about a car."

The young man looked at the receptionist, who shook her head.

"This is the automobile department," the kid said.

"Give him a message," Mills said, speaking past the young man to the receptionist huskily. "Tell him the price of the Buick Special is negotiable."

"I'll let him know that, George," the receptionist said.

"Tell him," and now he was standing, "tell him I just heard about the terrible tragedy and . . ."

"The terrible tragedy, George?" the receptionist said.

"Grant's death," George Mills said.

The receptionist and the guy exchanged puzzled looks.

"Ask him to extend my condolences to the Claunches, and to tell Mr. Claunch Sr. that if there's anything I can do . . ." But he couldn't finish. He walked past the snotnose kid and the girl at the desk and out the suite into the hall.

It was a good building but not a new one. An operator was still required to drive the elevator. He wore a uniform like a doorman's but much more subtle. He called George "sir" and greeted many of the passengers personally as they got on at their floors. About George's age, his name was George too, and several passengers passed the time of day with him while they descended.

"How's it going, George?" a tall gentleman said. "Your wife's cold any better?"

"She's fine, Mr. Brooks."

"Get that yard work done this weekend?"

"No ma'am, Miss Livingston," the elevator operator said. "My brother-in-law never brought my mower back."

"How were those seats, George?"

"Considerably better than the Cardinals, Judge."

The judge chuckled. "I think I can get two more for you for the Dallas game."

"I'd appreciate it."

"George, if you see Mr. Reynolds would you hand him this for me? The mailman left it in our office by mistake."

"Sure thing, Mr. Kafken." They were at the lobby floor. "All you folks have a fine lunch now, hear?" the elevator operator said. "Anything wrong, sir?" he asked the sobbing George Mills.

"Allergies," Mills said, and blew his grief and envy into his handkerchief.

He called Claunch directly. He didn't beat around the bush. He asked if the lawyers had passed on his message.

"What message was that?"

Mills told him.

"Oh, that message." The old man laughed.

He was just wondering, Mills said, if Mr. Claunch was pressed for good, loyal help at the compound till he could find a suitable replacement for Grant.

"Someone to play with the trains?"

"To take over his duties," Mills said softly.

"Well," he said, "my sister normally hires the staff."

It was just that he'd gotten along so well with Mrs. Glazer, Mills said, had been so close to her that last month, had grown so fond of her and respected her so much. He said he felt he knew the family almost as well as he knew the daughter.

He tried to say the rest of it lightly as he could. He realized, he said, that it wasn't usually the place of the employee to furnish the employer with "character references," but his feelings about Mrs. Glazer were so strong that he'd be happy to testify to them.

"You mean swear an affidavit?"

"If that's what's required."

"Uh huh," Claunch said. "I already got seven hundred seventy thousand dollars in tax-deductible affidavits lying around the house signed by a psychiatrist. I don't think I need another one. Everyone knows what Judy was. Anything else I can do for you, Mr. Mills?"

Look, George Mills, he knew no one owed him anything, that he'd been paid well for his services, but his back was acting up, he was getting on, feeling his age. He didn't know how much longer he'd be able to horse furniture around. Would Claunch help him?

"You want me to move furniture?"

"I want you to get me a job as an elevator operator in one of your buildings."

"Why?"

"I think it might be interesting work. You get to know all those people. They give you tickets to the games. You get to exchange the time of day with them. There's probably pretty fair money in it. Tips, gifts at Christmas. I never thought about it before. It's not the loftiest goal in the world, but I think it's something I'd enjoy doing."

Claunch considered for a moment. "No," he said, "I don't think so. I don't want to help you. Tell you what though," he added amiably, "hold on to the job you got. Because if you lose it you won't be collecting any unemployment insurance. Not in this state you won't. You're still a few years away from Social Security, am I right?"

"Yes," George Mills said.

"That's good," Claunch said. "Because I'm making a note. I'm having you jerked off the Social Security rolls."

"Can you do that?" George Mills asked. "Why?"

"Sure I can do it. As to why, I don't know. You're a guy gets a kick out of other men's power. Maybe I'm doing you a favor by showing you mine. Now don't bother me again. Stop calling my lawyers. There's unsolved capital crimes. You bother me or my people I'll see to it you get convicted of some of them. Nice to hear from you."

Laglichio said he was just the man he wanted to see. He was starting a new service he said. Federal law required that trucks that hauled food be thoroughly scrubbed down before a new load could be placed in them.

"It's this nuisance, make-work, government-on-our-backs sort of thing, but shit, kid, the job's yours if you want it. I'd kind of like to see you in the crew."

"The crew," George Mills said.

"The bucket brigade in the trailer," Laglichio said.

"And the pay?"

"Every bit as good as you make right now."

"I see," George Mills said.

"Money isn't everything. There are other advantages," Laglichio said.

"Yes?"

"The niggers would see your white ass and think you're foreman. I wouldn't tell them otherwise, George," Laglichio said. "Look," he said, "it's up to you what you do with your life."

Messenger phoned. "It was this roll of fast color film they do in Japan," he said. "It was this roll of super fast film he brought back with him. It's not on the market here in the States. It retails for maybe three or four dollars," he said, something manic in the edge of his voice. "Talk about your mess of pottage, hey Mills? The horror, the horror, huh?"

"What are you talking about?"

"Well you were *wrong,*" Messenger said.

"What are you talking about?"

"Well it wasn't any gold goddamn lighter, it wasn't any pen-and-pencil set. He didn't touch the place settings. He never stole the silver."

"I don't—— "

"It was *film,*" he said. "It wasn't any damn souvenir. It didn't have any damn royal crest on it. That was just your idea. It was this roll of fast film with an ASA rating of several thousand. On a cloudy day you take sharp color pictures of the dark side of the moon or something."

"He stole the chancellor's film?"

"No," Messenger said. "That was your idea too. It was Claunch, Sr.'s film. He was passing it around. He saw Sam pocket it."

"That's why he was shouting!" Mills said, everything clear to him. "The son of a bitch set him up!"

"No," Messenger said, "that's your idea too. What is he, a mastermind? How could he know Sam would slip the roll of film into his pocket? You're one of these conspiracy suckers, Mills. Things happen, that's all. This was just simple, honest, innocent rich man's show and tell. And Sam, Sam was so mad at how they'd been treating him he pulled this dumb kid's trick. It wasn't even theft. It was vandalism."

"He was caught red-handed. They were shouting. They made him resign."

"Yeah, well," Messenger said, "they worked it out."

"The trust," George Mills said.

"The works," Messenger said gleefully. "The car is back."

"It's Harve," he said when he phoned again.

"What is it?" Mills asked. "Has something happened to your son?"

"Who is it?" Louise asked. "Is it Cornell?"

Mills nodded. "It's his kid," he told her.

"Oh my God," Louise said, "what happened?"

"No, no," Messenger said. "Tell her it's all right."

"What is it, George?" Louise asked.

"I don't know," George Mills said. "He says it's all right."

Messenger was laughing and talking at once. Mills could barely understand him.

"But he says he'll be all right?" Louise said.

Mills handed his wife the telephone. "You talk to him. I can't carry on two conversations at once."

"Cornell, it's Lulu," she said. "George tells me Harve's going to be all right. That's the important thing. Listen," she said, "kids that age have incredible powers of recovery. I saw it all the time in the lunchroom. They'd bang their heads open on the slippery floors, get into fights. A few days later they were completely— What? Oh," she said. "—Oh. —Oh."

"What?" George Mills said. "What?"

Louise looked at him crossly and shook her head. She put her finger to her lips. "What? What's that, Cornell? Oh," she said smiling, and began to nod. George Mills watched her nod and smile into the telephone. Messenger might have been courting her. She looked seductive, almost coy. "That's wonderful," she said at last. "I certainly will." She replaced the phone.

"What?" George Mills said. "What?"

"It was the alphabet," she said.

"The alphabet," Mills repeated. "The kid's learned the alphabet."

"That's just it," she said, "he never did."

"That's what's so wonderful?"

"Well yes," she said, "in a way. I mean they didn't know he *hadn't* learned it. He sang that song when he was a little kid."

"What song?"

"You know," she said. Louise started to sing. " 'ABCDEFG, HIJKLMNOP.' You know," she said.

"Oh yeah," George Mills said.

"I mean Cornell says that was practically his favorite song when he was a kid, so naturally they assumed . . . They didn't know he didn't understand the connection between the sounds and the letters. Now they think that when they taught it to the kids in preschool that must have been the month he had strep throat. And that when they reviewed it in kindergarten that was when he had his tonsils out." Mills stared at her. "They just caught it," she said. "After all those years. Can you imagine? They just caught it."

"Was he high?" Mills asked.

"Cornell? No. I can tell."

"You can?"

493

"A woman knows," his wife said.

"I see."

"He's been sight reading," Louise said. "All these years. He's been sight reading. Do you know how hard that is? Cornell says it's as if we were set down in Japan or Russia or anywhere else they have those peculiar alphabets, and could read only the words we'd had some experience with. Stop signs or the word for 'bakery' if we see cakes in the window."

George Mills nodded.

"Once they caught it they were able to do something about it. He learned it in a day and a half. You know Cornell says he's been through two readers this week? They're color-coded. He finished the orange, he finished the red. He starts on the blue one, *Let's Read* five, tomorrow. Cornell says it's confidence. Isn't it queer, George? Isn't it queer how things work out?"

Messenger dropped in again at the house. He had phoned first to make sure that George would be home. "You don't have to phone," Mills told him at the door. "Just come when you feel like. I acted a little crazy is all."

"No no," Messenger said. "That's all right. I want to see the both of you."

"You want something to eat? Lulu's fixing lunch."

"How's the back?"

George shrugged. "Comes and goes. Comes and comes, comes and stays. You know how it is. It acted up some today so I knocked off early."

Messenger nodded.

"Say, that's great news about the kid," Mills said. "I didn't get a chance to tell you."

"Thanks," Messenger said. He smiled.

Louise came into the living room carrying a tray. "Oh hi, Cornell."

"Louise," Cornell said.

"I thought it was you. It's good to see you again. I opened a large can of Spaghetti-O's."

"You'll love it," George Mills said.

"No, you two go ahead. I'm not much on Italian cuisine."

"Hey," George Mills said, "ain't you enhanced?"

"Me?" Messenger said. "No." He looked embarrassed.

"I'll fix you a sandwich," Louise said.

494

"No thanks, Louise. I'm not very hungry."

"What's new?" George asked. "Are Max and Ruth still parked in front of the dean's house?"

"Well, for the time being," Messenger said. "Jenny Greener told them they'll have to find someplace else."

"Jenny Greener?"

"When she moves in with Sam. When they're married next month."

"Jenny Greener and Sam?"

"It surprised all of us," Messenger said.

"Jesus," Mills said, "your friend must be devastated."

"Losey?"

"The doctor, the paste asshole. Yeah, Losey."

"No, he's taking it very well."

"He is?"

"Very well."

"I thought he loved her so much."

"He loved her grade point, he loved her blueprints."

"Well still," George Mills said.

"She dropped out," Messenger said.

"She dropped out of school? Nora?"

"Jenny Greener. Sam says she felt guilty."

"Guilty? About the love affair."

"Well, that too, I suppose. But mostly about Nora. Going to school, she couldn't devote enough time to Nora."

"Her own schoolwork came first. Even Losey said so."

"That's right. Losey said so. Jenny didn't feel right about that."

"This isn't clear."

"They're best friends. She wasn't satisfied just to get Nora off academic probation. Now she's able to spend more time with her. Losey doesn't mind. Already there's been incredible improvement. She's shown Nora certain tricks. Well, *she* says they're tricks. But you know? Nora has as much to do with it as anyone. She's making tremendous strides. Jenny's dropping out must really have motivated her."

"But what a sacrifice," George Mills said, shaking his head. "A brilliant career down the drain."

"Down the drain?" Messenger said. "No, I don't think so. She's, what, seven or eight years younger than Nora? When Nora graduates next semester Jenny can just pick up where she left off."

"She'll have been out of school a year."

"Sure. Getting a fresh slant on things. With the pressure off she's come up with all sorts of new ideas. Helping Nora, she's been able to rethink basic principles. Sam says her concepts are better than ever."

"I see," Mills said.

"She's never been happier," Messenger said.

"Jenny."

"Jenny of course. The business with Losey only confused her. She says Sam's the only man she's ever really loved. So Jenny, too, of course. And Sam. Sam's a new man. With the dean thing settled and Jenny in his life he looks fifteen years younger. But Nora. Nora too. She's quite proud of herself. You can guess how her husband must feel."

"Losing a genius?"

"I told you. The man's a surgeon. He fixed up his marriage. Jenny would only have been a transplant. But Nora, Nora's a whole new scientific reconstruction. Some from-scratch Galatea."

"It must be tough on the kids," George Mills said, "their daddy taking a new wife so soon after their mother died."

"Oh," he said, "Sam's kids. That's a whole other story. Gee," he said, glancing at his watch, "I've got to run. Nice to see you, Louise. George, I hope your back feels better."

"That's a kick in the ass about Ruth and Max!" Mills shouted after him. "Getting booted into traffic!"

George Mills was in bed. Again Messenger had phoned first. Louise had taken the call. "Is he high?" Louise shook her head. "Let me get dressed first," Mills said.

Messenger rapped lightly on the closed bedroom door.

"Jesus," Mills whispered.

"Come in, Cornell," Louise said.

"Hello," Cornell said. "Louise said you were indisposed. There were a couple of extra trays. I brought them over for your lunches."

"We've eaten our lunches," Mills said.

"Sure," Messenger said. "You can warm them for dinner."

"That's sweet, Cornell," Louise said.

Messenger pulled a chair up to the side of the bed. "You were right," he said. "They *were* upset. At least Milly was. Mary too, I suppose, but Milly made the rumpus. She called her grandfather. She's the one who caught them in bed together."

"Really?" George Mills said. "At her age that sort of thing can get to you for life."

496

"When Milly told him what happened, Claunch did some hard thinking."

"This is the part that gets me," Louise said. "Oh," she said, "I heard some of this on the phone."

"He'd been squeezing him pretty hard. Sam written off by his wife, by the family. Having to claim Judy was nuts, having to claim fraud because of those prenuptial agreements he'd lived up to to the letter of the law. The incident at the chancellor's dinner party, Claunch calling him out in front of all those people, screaming for his resignation over a three-dollar roll of film.

"When Milly told him she caught him screwing some schoolgirl —Jenny's textbooks were at the foot of the bed—Claunch figured Sam was determined to disgrace them, get back at him and the rest of the family by forcing them to step in and take the girls away from him too."

"Is *that* what he's up to?" Mills said, brightening.

"That's what Claunch thought he was up to. It was the last thing Claunch wanted. He's not a young man, after all. He hadn't had all that much luck with his own daughter. The idea of two adolescent girls around the place, one of them not the most stable kid in the world— Well, you can imagine. That's when he knew they'd have to sort things out. That's when he thought he had to buy him off. He tore up the resignation himself. He had his son reassign his trusteeship to Sam."

"Still," George Mills said, "stuck with a stepmother they never bargained for."

"This is the part that gets me," Louise said.

"But they *did* bargain for her," Messenger said. "At least Milly did."

"Milly?"

"Because Milly's the respectable one," Messenger said. "You saw her, Mills. The day of the funeral. You saw how she acted."

Mills recalled the little girl conducting them on the tour of Claunch's home, then later, alone, sitting well back in the trains, prim as a spinster.

"Because Milly's the respectable one," Messenger repeated. "She always has been. She couldn't abide her father's disgrace. She couldn't stand it that he'd taken a mistress. She couldn't stand it that he wasn't going to have money. She couldn't stand it he wasn't going to be dean. That he thought of challenging her mother's sanity in a court of law.

497

If Claunch did some hard thinking it was about ideas Milly herself had put in his head.

"Because once everything was restored to him it was all right again. She's the one who actually spoke to them."

"Spoke to them," George Mills said.

"Well questioned them."

"Questioned them."

"Well lectured them then. About their intentions. She told Jenny that what she was doing was wrong, her father that if he had to have a woman they'd all be better off if he married her. She's the one who set the date."

"Now her life's okey-dokey," George Mills said.

"Milly's happy as a clam, George," Messenger said pleasantly.

"Sure," Mills said.

"She's throwing the shower."

"I see."

"She's organized the wedding. She's worked out the arrangements, she's made out the guest list. She hasn't decided if the bride should wear white. She's leaning toward white but she hasn't decided."

"What about the other one?" George asked hopelessly. "What about Mary?"

"George, you wouldn't recognize her."

"She's a changed person," Mills said.

"You remember how oversexed she used to be?"

"Used to be," the straight man said.

"How she'd doodle all this really raunchy stuff in her schoolbooks, put it all around her separators like a kind of embroidery, work it into her biology papers so that even her teachers couldn't tell if she were a scientist or kinky?"

"This is the part that gets me," George Mills said.

"She started sketching the stuff on her bedroom walls."

"Fouled her own nest, did she?"

"Jenny saw it. Well she was *meant* to. Mary left her books all over the place. She never bothered to shut her bedroom door."

"It was a cry for help," George Mills said.

Messenger looked at him. "Well it was," he said. "I mean there's Milly and Sam yelling their heads off, shouting how sick she was, how a kid her age ought to get her head up out of the gutter. Then Jenny came along. Jenny has a trained eye, you know. You'll never guess what happened. Jenny thinks she's terrific, that she's this anatomical savant or something. I mean no one noticed how really good the kid was till Jenny saw what she was up to. You know what she did when she first saw the stuff?"

"What did she do?"

"Stripped for the kid. Right then and there. Took off her dress, pulled down her panties, ripped off her bra. 'Draw *me*,' she told her. 'Get all my details.'

"She tried to get her enrolled in a life class at the university but they've got this rule that no one under sixteen—"

"Get on with it," Mills said.

"She's having her own show. When she gets a few more drawings together she's having a show at this really important gallery. She draws her boyfriend, the kid she used to fuck. She poses him straining on the pot, she poses him whacking off. Sam shows them around, the sketches. The kid doesn't mind. Nora's agreed to pose for her, Jenny has. Even Sam."

"Her *father*? Her *father* poses for her?"

"Even her sister," Messenger said. "Even Milly. Even the respectable one."

"Isn't it queer, George?" Louise asked. "Isn't it queer how life works out?"

"My back is killing me," George Mills said. "Why are you telling me this stuff?"

"Because," Messenger said. "Because it *is* queer how life works out. And because," he said, *"because I'm the epilogue man, George!"* He rose to go, turned at the door to their bedroom. "Oh," he said, "I don't guess I'll be dropping by anymore. I won't be in the neighborhood much. I've given up my Meals-on-Wheels route."

"Oh," Louise said, "we'll miss you, Cornell."

"I turned it over to Max and Ruth. They've got a car. Meals-on-Wheels will pay for their gas. They qualify for free meals themselves. Meals-on-Wheels will provide them."

Mills sprang out of bed and raced toward Messenger. Louise had to hold him. She forced her husband back to his bed, his feet sliding backward on the bare floor. He waved his raised fist at Cornell, who stood his ground in the doorway.

"They jumped at the chance," Messenger said calmly. "It turns out they never really liked cheese. It turns out cookies were a stopgap. It turns out they don't care much for poetry. It turns out lectures bore them. It turns out they've tin ears and won't even miss the recitals."

It turned out it was not the last time he was to hear Messenger's news. He saw him again about a week later. Louise was in bed with a sore throat and George had stopped off at a supermarket to pick up some things for their dinner—— canned soup, a frozen pizza. It was not one of the places they usually shopped. Mills was in the express lane waiting to be checked out. The store had installed scanners to read the universal product code stamped on the labels and packages like cramped, alternating thicknesses of wood grain in cross section, or marks on rulers, or passages of spectography, or like boxes of pencils, like awning, like pin stripes on shirts. The lines and numbers could have been ciphers, hieroglyphs, but when the checkout girl brushed the mysterious little blocks of code across a glass plate, a vaguely digital readout appeared in a banner like a red headline above the customer's head. It registered the name of the item, the quantity, its cost. Mills had never seen the machine operate before. He had no idea how it worked and was so absorbed that at first he was unaware that someone was talking to him, saying his name. It was Messenger.

"I was going to call you," he said. "There's some loose ends to tie up."

"Sure," Mills said.

"The name Albert Reece mean anything to you?"

"Arthur Reece?" Mills said absently. He wasn't paying close attention. A woman he thought he recognized from the neighborhood had come into the supermarket. She wore a man's loose-fitting khaki trousers and a tan jacket. She wore a fedora and carried a big leather drawstring bag. A heavy key ring on a retractable steel cord hung from her belt loop.

"*Albert* Reece. One of the Meals-on-Wheelers. A sour-hearted old bastard. I told you about him."

The woman had taken the key ring and stretched it out as far as it would go. She slipped a key into a lock in the copy machine at the front of the store, turned the key and pulled out the cash drawer where the change collected. She dumped the money into the bag. When she replaced the drawer she took a rag and a bottle of Windex from her jacket pocket and proceeded to polish the glass facing plate where the customers set the originals they wanted copied.

"Sure, I told you about him," Messenger said.

"Probably," Mills said. "You told me about everyone else."

"He won a hundred thousand dollars," Messenger said. "He's going to be on the six o'clock news."

"A hundred thousand dollars?"

500

"In one of those contests. Some sweepstakes thing. *Reader's Digest,* Publishers' Clearing House—— something. He was so excited I couldn't get it straight."

The woman was cleaning the money out of the bubble gum machines, the dime and twenty-five and fifty-cent candy and toy vending machines with their miniature NFL helmets and tiny major league baseball caps folded like fetuses inside their clear globes. She took about twenty dollars from the plastic pony. She owns them, he thought. She *owns* them, they're hers. She makes a fortune. I'll be, he thought.

"He says he's going to buy a house with it," Messenger said, "that any Meals-on-Wheelers on his route who want to can move in and live with him."

"I'll be," Mills said.

"How do you like that?" Messenger said.

"I'll be." But he was staring at the woman from the neighborhood who owned the machines. She was talking to a man Mills guessed was the manager, who was checking the money with her from her drawstring bag and who accepted a percentage of the receipts from the machines and wrote out a check to her in exchange for the rest of the coins.

And that still wasn't the last time. The last time was a few days later. Messenger phoned.

"Did you see him?" Messenger asked. "On TV? Did you see him?"

"Yes."

"Did I lie?"

"No." He could barely speak.

"Well there's something else," Messenger said.

"Yes."

"Remember I told you about that story I wrote? The only one I ever published in *The New Yorker?* The one Amos Ropeblatt took out an option on? That he's been renewing every year for eleven or twelve years now for five hundred dollars a year?"

"Yes," Mills said.

"Well he *bought* it!" Messenger said. "The son of a bitch actually *bought* it. They're actually going to make the movie."

"That's fine," George Mills said. "Congratulations."

"How do you like that?" Messenger said. "How do you like the way things work out? How do you like this idyll vision, this epithalamion style? How do you like it the game ain't over till the last man is out? How do you like it you can dig for balm? That there's balm and joy mines, great fucking mother lodes of bower and elysian amenity? How do you like *deus ex machina?* How do you like it every cloud has a silver lining? What do you make of God's pastoral heart? How do you like it there's pots of gold at the end of rainbows and you can't keep a good man down? How do you like it ships come in, and life is just a bowl of cherries? How do you like it it isn't raining rain you know, it's raining violets? What do you make of it every time I hear a newborn baby cry or see the sky then I know why I believe?"

"Audrey," George Mills said.

"What's that?"

"Audrey," he said. "Audrey Binder. Victor's wife. In the hospital. With the kid who can't throw. Audrey. Whose shoelaces have to be signed for. Who cries in her sleep. Audrey. Who chews her IV. Audrey! *Audrey!*"

"Audrey?"

"That's right."

"Didn't I tell you?"

"What?"

"Audrey's fine. Audrey's all better."

"All better," Mills said.

"Sure," Messenger said. "She's out of the loony bin. Audrey's home."

"Just like that," George Mills said. "She's all better."

"Sure," Messenger said. "All the happy endings. All the good news. She snapped out of it. She just cheered right up when she heard," Messenger said. "Oh yeah," Messenger said, "the horror, the horror, hey Mills?"

2

About a year after he had become convinced of his salvation George Mills delivered his sermon to the hundred or so people in Coule's congregation at Virginia Avenue Baptist.

They had not consulted about a date. One Sunday morning in September Mills had simply appeared and, after Coule led them through the formal parts of the service—the opening prayer, some announcements, a hymn, the offering, another hymn, some prayers for the sick, and a scripture—the preacher seemed suddenly to spot Mills among the congregation and, probably without their knowing anything of the impromptu circumstances, so seamless was his conduct—this is how he must have done it on television, George Mills thought, told to hurry it along or to stretch by his director—introduced George, and invited him to come up to the pulpit.

Brother Mills—it was Coule's term—eased past his wife's knees and came down the aisle to where the big preacher stood behind his deconsecrated lectern. Coule shook Mills's hand and retired to an empty chair on the platform.

"I'm a little nervous," he began, surprised by the amplification of his voice when he spoke. It was the first time he had ever heard the vaguely metallic sound of his amplified voice, and for just a moment he thought that perhaps his voice was going out over the radio or was somehow being beamed to other churches.

"I'm here to testify," he said. And looked out over the congregation as if he might almost be searching for someone in particular, some latecomer yet to arrive. He recognized a handful of neighbors. They smiled their encouragement at him, as did others he did not recognize, raising some Sunday morning umbrella of benevolence and good will, inviting him to step in under it, kindhearted and tender, well meaning and fraternal as hippies. But he was not encouraged. Indeed, he had a sad sense of intricacy. He told them that. He told them he supposed that would be his text.

And started, for reasons that were also intricate and sad, to tell them a story about charity, "I used to watch the telethons," he said. "One of the first to call and make my pledge when the poster kid pled. One time—it was the Jerry Lewis, Muscular Dystrophy—I phoned in and got to speak to Ed McMahon. Someone told me to turn down my set, Big Ed wanted to speak to me on the air. I'd gone into the bedroom to phone. Our TV's in the living room. I couldn't hear it. Before I understood what was happening Ed McMahon was already talking to me. He asked my name and I told him. 'I want to pledge five dollars,' I said.

" 'Where are you calling from, Mr. Mills?'

" 'St. Louis. I called the number at the bottom of the screen. I thought it was a local call.'

" 'They patched you through to Vegas. Jerry and I want to find out what gets the average viewer involved enough to get off the dime. What was it with you, Mr. Mills? Can you tell us?'

"I told him it was the kid.

" 'Stu? Great kid, isn't he?'

" 'Yes,' I said.

" 'Yes.'

" 'I want to pledge five dollars. Do you take my name and address?'

" 'One of our lovely volunteers will do that.'

"Then, forgetting I was on the air, and because I had someone on the phone who probably knew, I asked what had happened to the little girl, how she was coming along, last year's poster child. Mr. McMahon was embarrassed. He told me she'd died.

"My wife was watching in the living room. She'd seen it all. Ed McMahon had been stunned, she told me. There were tears in his eyes. It was an affecting moment, she said.

504

"I never sent in my five dollars, I never watched another telethon."

It wasn't what he'd meant to say. It hadn't anything to do with the sad intricacy of things. I'm grandstanding, he thought. I'm not in the right place, he thought. He should be seated in the congregation. He shouldn't have come. He glanced at Louise, who remembered the story and seemed to nod in agreeable confirmation. He knew she was pleased to have made it into his anecdote. George wanted to cry.

Then he tried to tell them who he was, how there had been a George Mills since the time of the First Crusade. He told them about the curse they lived under, the thousand years of blue collar blood. He told about the Millses' odd orphanhood, their queer deprivation of relation.

"I mean Coule called me 'brother.' That's the last name we go by. We don't have brothers. We're brothered to fathers, brothered to sons."

He told them of their alliances, their long, strange allegiance to class.

He couldn't explain it, he said.

He knew he was failing, knew that if Coule were sitting where he could see him he would not see the God panic in his eyes he put so much stock in. And though he could not see the preacher either, he knew that if he could, he would see himself bathed in waves of tolerance, some queer smug tide of forgiveness. Not love, not even gloating, but a sort of neutral recognition of his, of all failure, a patience with it, good temper, composure, even acquiescence, even compliance.

And now he stood apart from his inability to deliver, cool as the preacher. Whatever of urgency or nervousness he'd felt had dissipated and he felt he could go on forever, like each Mills before him, filibustering his life. He could say anything to them, tell them anything.

"Years ago," he said, "I saw the double helix. I saw it thrashing around on the floor of the Delgado Ballroom refracted from the light of a chandelier. I didn't know what it was. I never followed through. I recognized it many years later in a photograph.

"I don't *know* anything. I mean I drank it for years but I can't tell you what Ovaltine is. What *is* Ovaltine? Why is it good for us?"

He listened for Coule to clear his throat, shift in his chair, offer some signal that enough was enough. Coule was silent. They all were.

From time to time his eyes swept the congregation. From time to time he searched the church. He did this covertly, like an agent,

505

like an actor peering out from behind a curtain examining the house. He couldn't himself have said what he was looking for. Not old Messenger Merlin, the epilogue man. He'd broken with Messenger, though it may have been Cornell's compulsions which served him now, which drove him to breach secrecy and decorum, which drove him, he realized, to stall. Then he didn't want to go on forever. He told them more or less what he'd promised Coule he would tell them. He told them he was saved. He told them he had grace. That nothing could happen to him, that he was stuck in his grace like a ship sunk in the sea.

"Amen," someone called, startling him. George looked up. All over the church people were calling out their amens, not patient now, neither considerate nor tolerant so much as dutiful, not even fervent, nothing so much as accustomed, almost like actors answering promptings. "Amen, amen," they called.

"Amen," a woman in Louise's aisle said in her print dress, in her hat, in her gloves and white shoes.

Which was why he hadn't recognized her, the woman from the supermarket. Because she'd been in men's clothing. Now his bowels ached, now his hands sweated, now his heart labored, now his tongue thickened and his mood ring ignited like the mirrored ball on the Delgado ceiling, running with color, bruised with light. Now his pulses leapt and things closed in, his ideas rushing him, swarming, his words issuing from, crowding from, rudely shoving from his head and throat and mouth and lips, jostling for priority as if head, throat, mouth and lips were on fire.

Now he felt shaken, blasted by the truth of his life. Which he found himself delivering in this public place in messages so Pentecostal and private they might have been the jumbled, contradictory tongues and bulletins of disaster.

She's dressed up! No wonder! He laughed.

"Because I never went home. Because I never went back to——" And held his tongue. Thinking: I can't say that. I mustn't say Cassadaga, I mustn't even say Florida. I can't even say that what I'd seen in that supermarket was not just a lady in men's pants but the actual sister I might by now actually have, and that what I saw in her, who might in that jacket and those trousers and that hat have been an honest-to-God brother, who *was* I thought then, and not just that masculine businesswoman got up in drag I see now she didn't mean and wasn't doing for fun but out of some necessity of the vending machine trade, protecting herself from the dark oils and thick greases much as I myself wear my eviction habit, the heavy furniture pads, not, as I'd once thought, out of deference to the furniture of the poor, but, as Laglichio says, the *illusion* of deference, keeping myself safe from splinters, blood poison, the rough, unvarnished and nail-studded underneaths of a black man's dining room suite.

"Because I never went home to see, to find out.

"And who may by then and certainly by now, as all Mills kids do, have already left home herself, quit the roost, split, gone off not to make their fortune but simply to repeat it.

"Hell, it's a long shot. Don't I know it's a long shot? I know that. Could it be any longer than a thousand years of George Millses?

"Hey," he said, "it isn't plausible. What long shot is? They're all sucker bets."

(And he *thought* of long shots, numbers so high they were beyond mathematics, beyond odds, outside hope. What Magaziner had told George XLIII just before that old campaigner had found the Valide Sultan's body on one of the two or three days out of all the year when she was in residence at the seraglio, and that had enabled him to say the words that turned the keys that moved the tumblers that released the bolts that sprung the locks that opened the doors of Yildiz. And not just her body, and not just on the two days—three at the outside—she came to pour tea, but rather on the one day—she was seventy-one years old—out of the twenty-five thousand, nine hundred and fifteen—at the inside, the *in*side; there would be eighteen leap year days, plus the days she had already lived beyond her seventy-first birthday—that body would be dead and available for him to find! So he wasn't even talking about long shots. He was talking about out-and-out *miracle!*)

"But no Mills made her up," he said. "She'd be——— " He couldn't say Wickland. "She'd be named something else. Not Mills. She'd never even have heard the name Mills. Our mother wouldn't have told her, and the man who would have been her stepfather would have been long gone once he saw she was a girl. Millses didn't make girls. His wife was unfaithful. So he'd have been long gone. Just a few months behind his son, just five or six months behind me.

"She's about the right age," he added quickly, but they were beginning to stir, to make what was not yet noise.

"We never had children. The line's played out, watered." Louise was crying into her handkerchief, the others merely shifting, easing themselves, seeing what he saw himself, that what he spoke in was not tongues but incoherencies. Coule would stop him, he would come up

507

beside him and take him by the elbow and lead him off gently. Coule would certainly stop him. Fuck him, Mills thought, if he wants me to shut up he'll just have to make me.

Because he knew what his testimony was now, and was prepared to make it.

"I was kidding you," he said. "I ain't saved. I spent my life like there was a hole in my pocket, and the meaning of life is to live long enough to find something out or to do something well. It ain't just to put up with it.

"I'll tell you something else," he said. "It wasn't a curse," he said, into his text now, "it was a spell, an enchantment, a thousand years of Sleeping Beauty, a thousand years of living on the dole.

"Hell, I ain't saved," he said, oddly cheered. "Being tired isn't saved, sucking up isn't grace."

Now he was certain he would hear it, the peremptory cough, the dangerous premonitory shuffle of feet, and he began to move away from the microphone, to start back to his seat. Coule had him before he could leave the platform. Mills flinched, but all the big preacher meant to do was shake his hand.

"Thank you," Coule said. "Thank you," he repeated, still pumping his hand. "That was very interesting."

Mills stared at him. "You're welcome," he said. He moved toward Louise.

"Amen, brother," his sister said, rising in the aisle to let him pass. She touched him on the shoulder.

So she wasn't his sister. Because she'd have had to have one. Born in Florida, raised there. Because she'd have *had* to have one. But there was no more trace of a Southern accent in her voice than in Laglichio's or Messenger's, than in Sam's or Judith Glazer's, or any of the rest of them.

Of course she's not my sister, he thought, but was convinced now that he had one, and that wherever she was she would be doing well. Of course she isn't, he thought, only some stand-in in red herring relation to the real one, who captured my attention for a while and led me by what grace I got to believe it was all over.

So he stood there, in what grace he had, relieved of history as an amnesiac.

"Amen," some of the others were still saying. "Amen, amen."

George Mills looked at them in wonder. "Brothers and sisters," he acknowledged lightly.